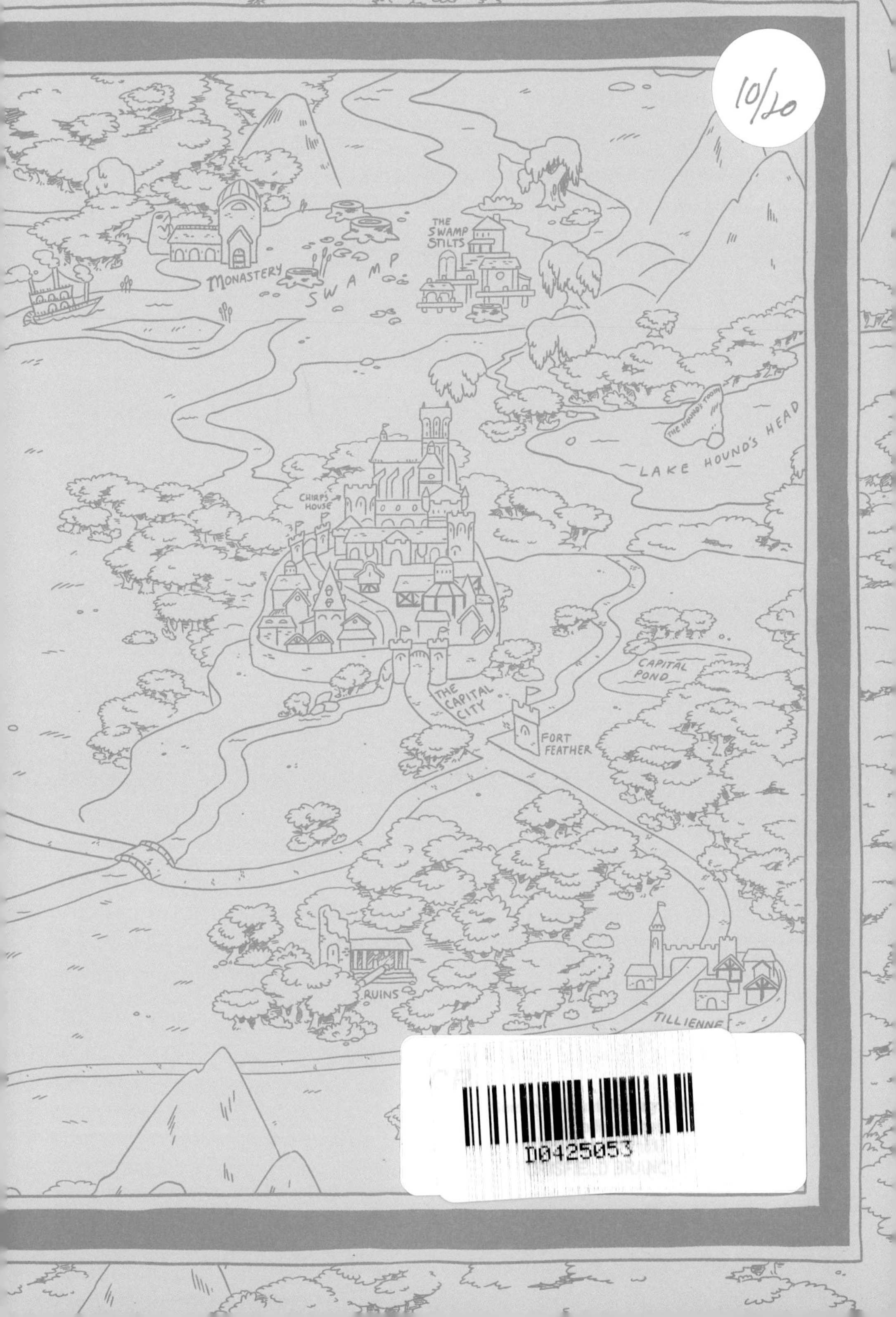
THE SWAMP STILTS
MONASTERY
SWAMP
THE HOUND'S TOOTH
LAKE HOUND'S HEAD
CHIRP'S HOUSE
CAPITAL POND
THE CAPITAL CITY
FORT FEATHER
RUINS
TILLIENNE

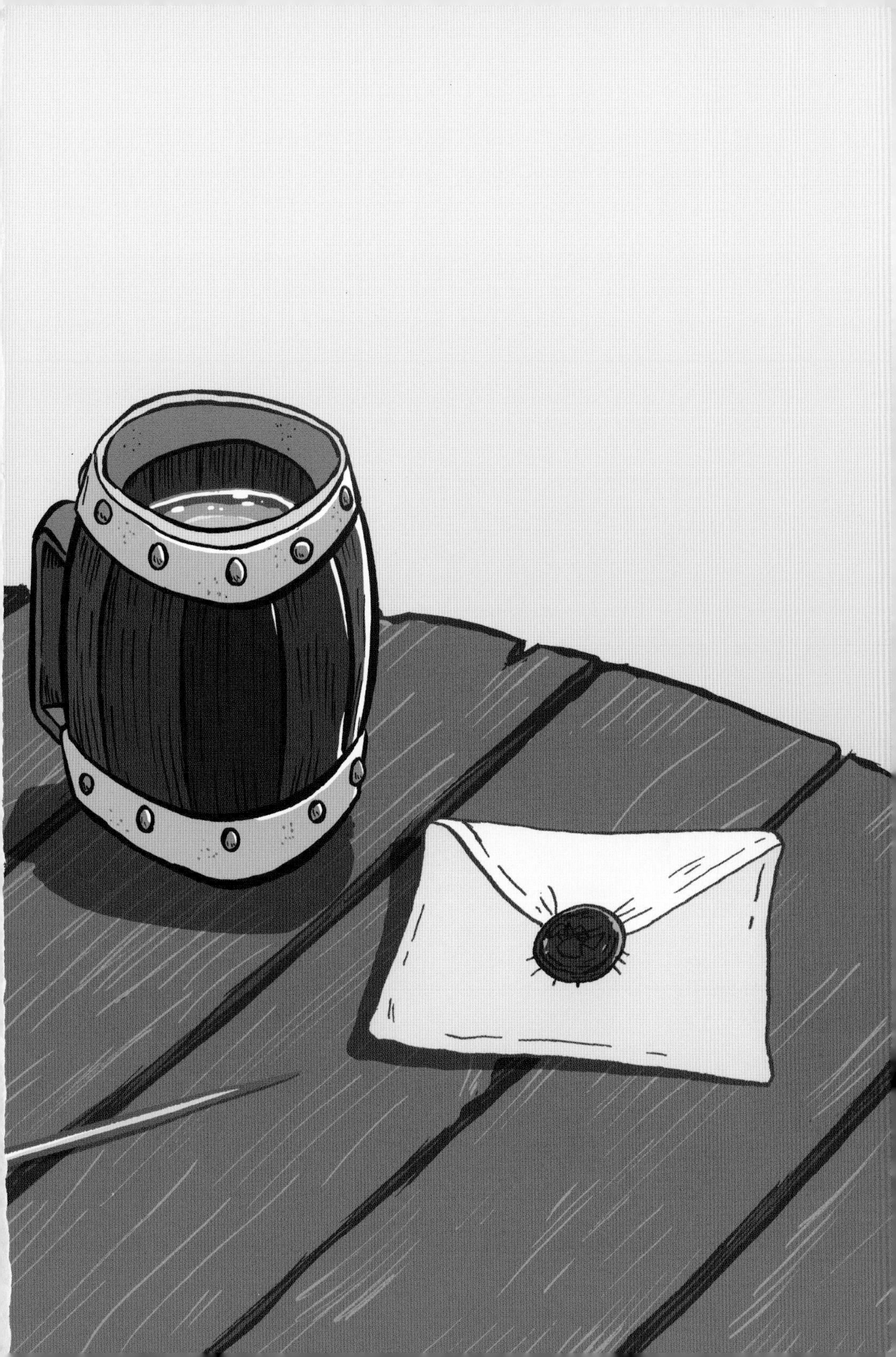

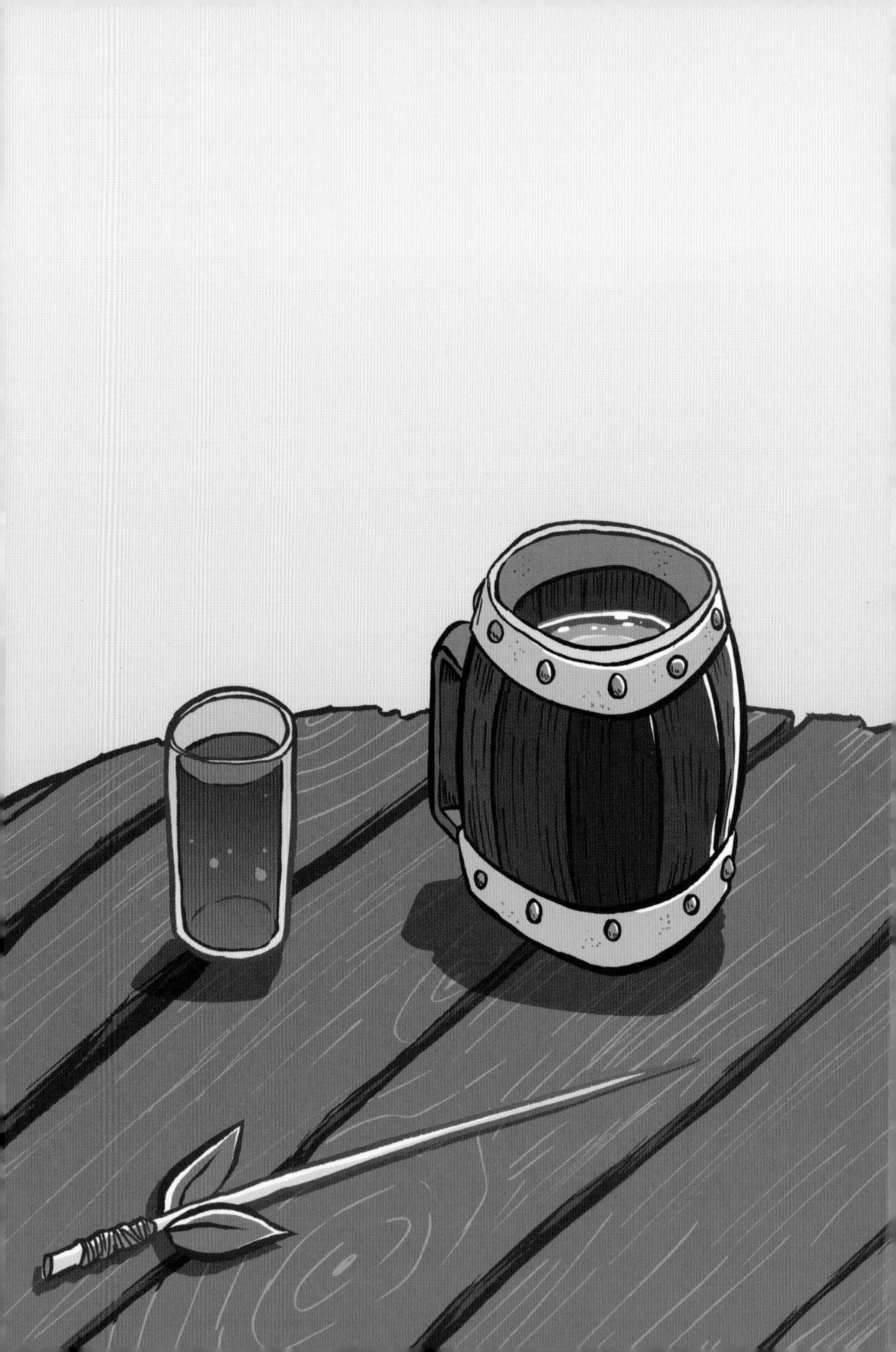

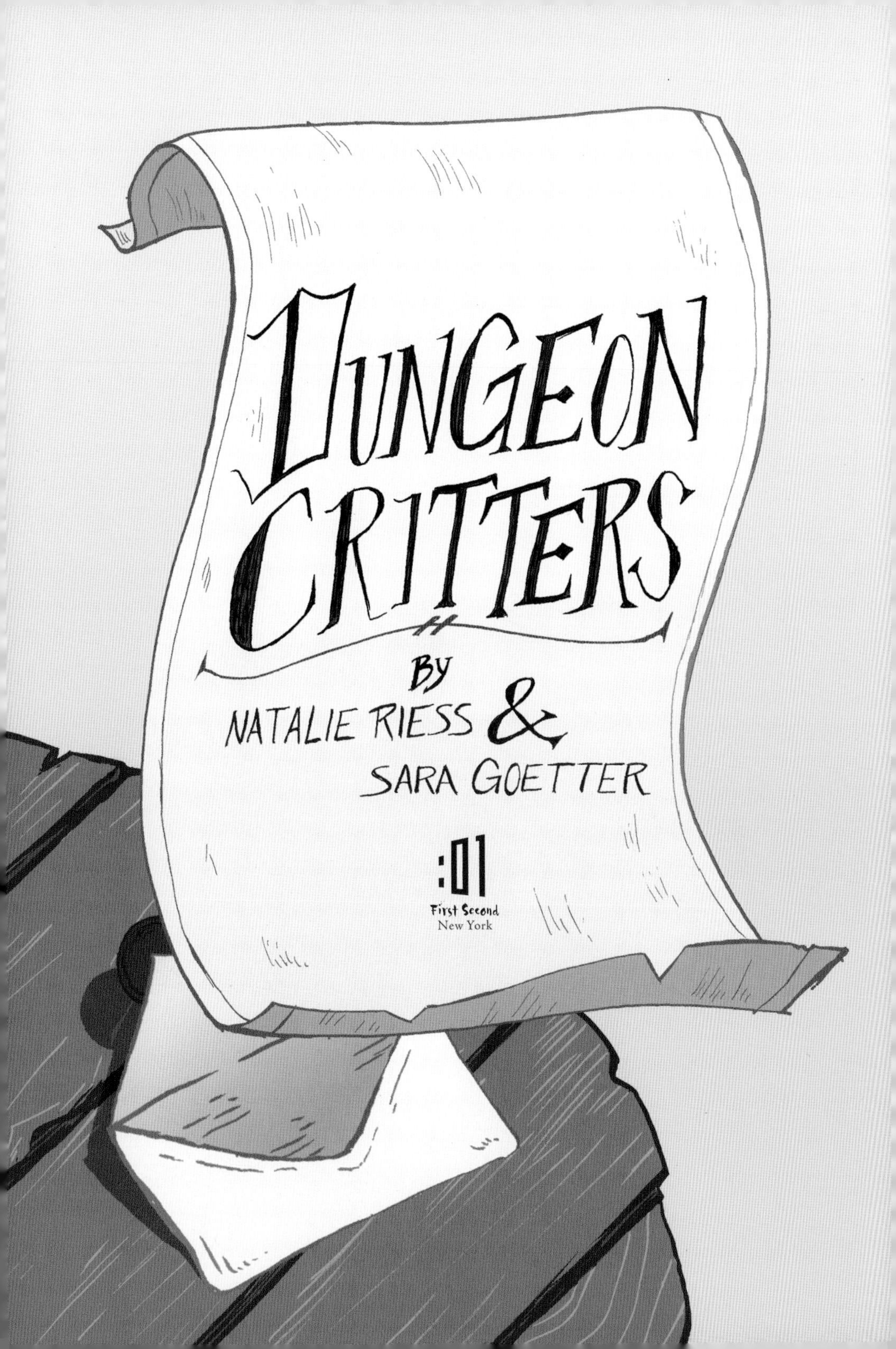
DUNGEON CRITTERS
BY
NATALIE RIESS &
SARA GOETTER
:01
First Second
New York

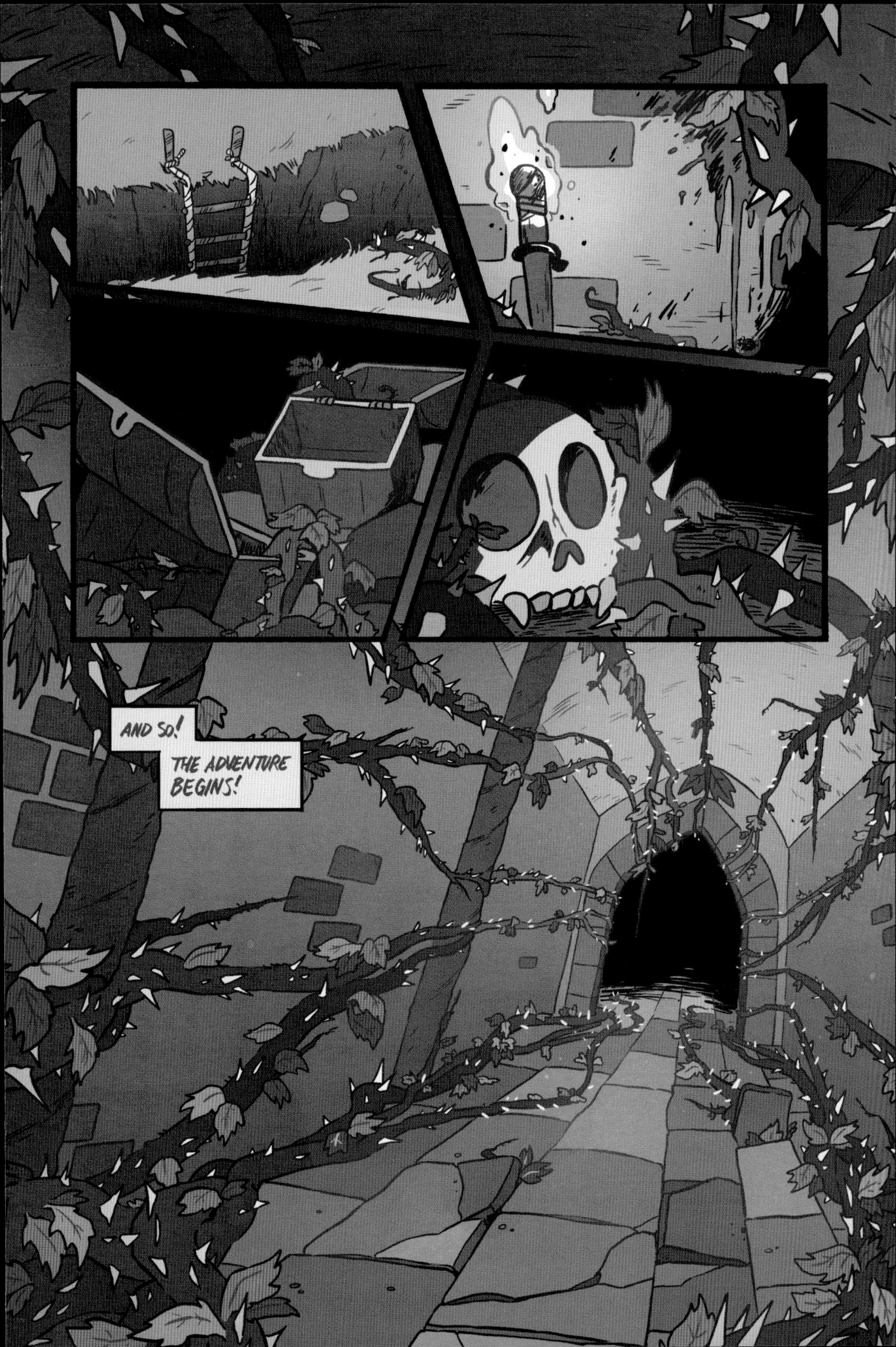
AND SO!
THE ADVENTURE BEGINS!

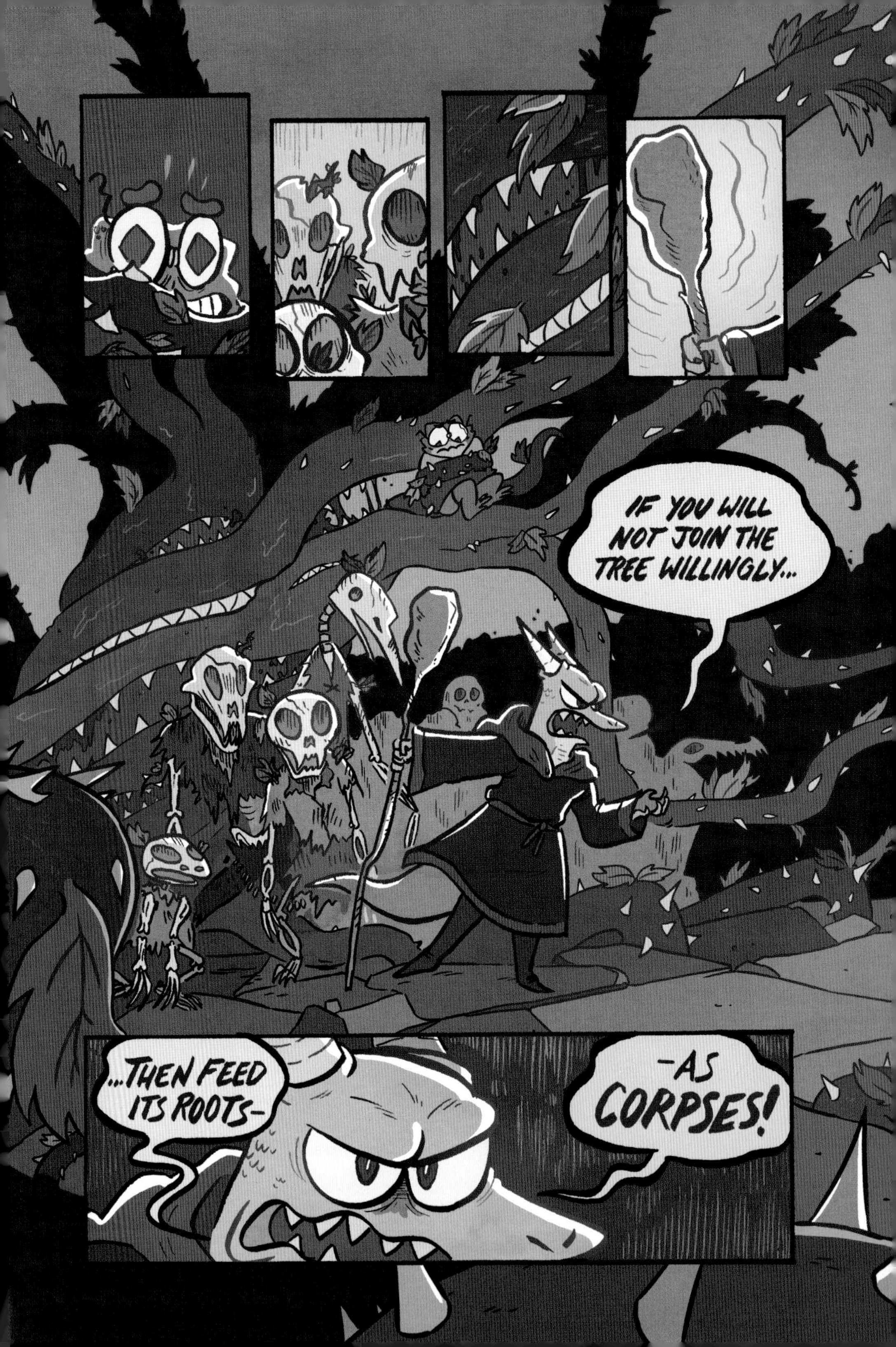
IF YOU WILL NOT JOIN THE TREE WILLINGLY...
...THEN FEED ITS ROOTS-
-AS CORPSES!

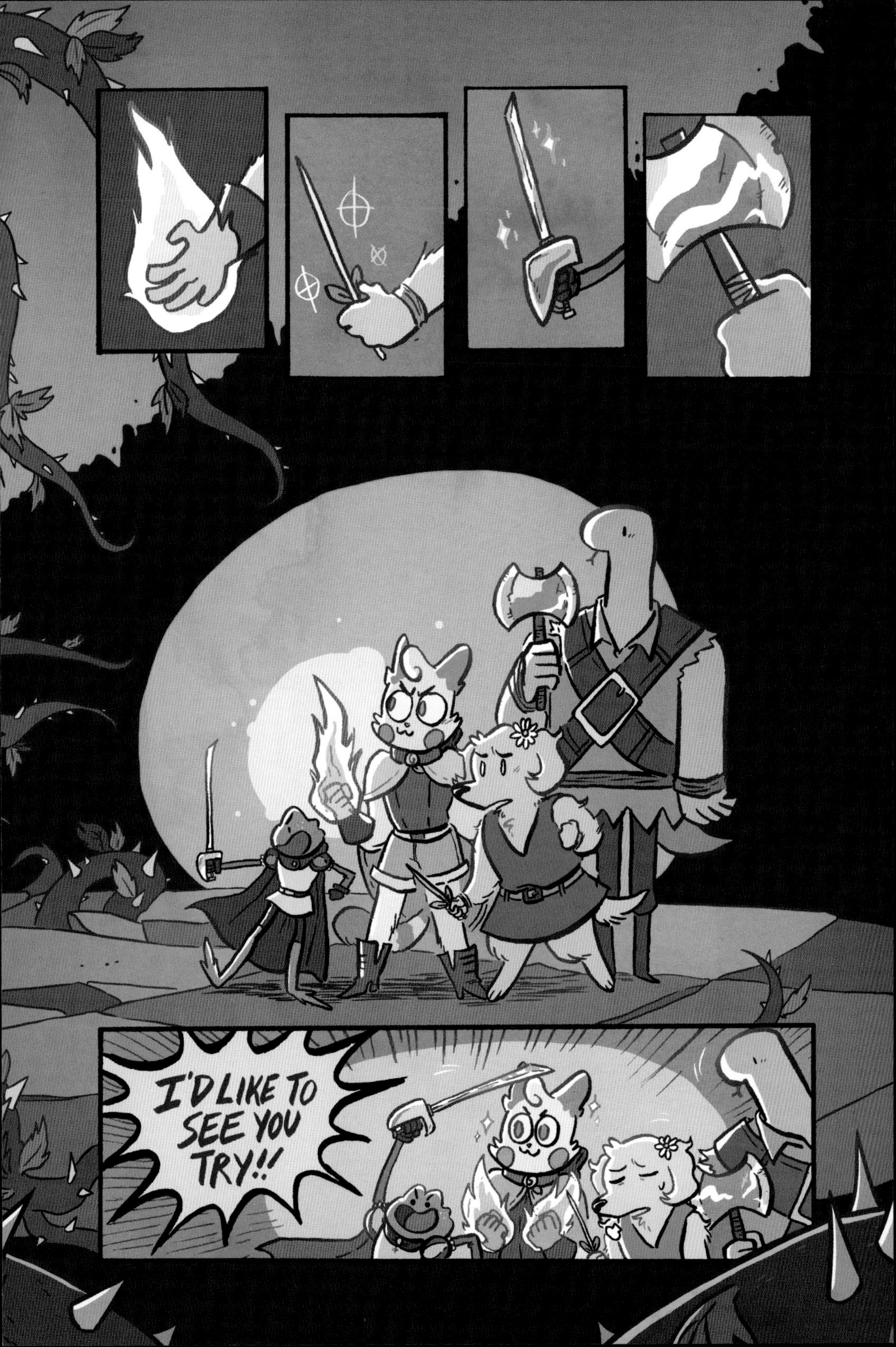
I'D LIKE TO SEE YOU TRY!!

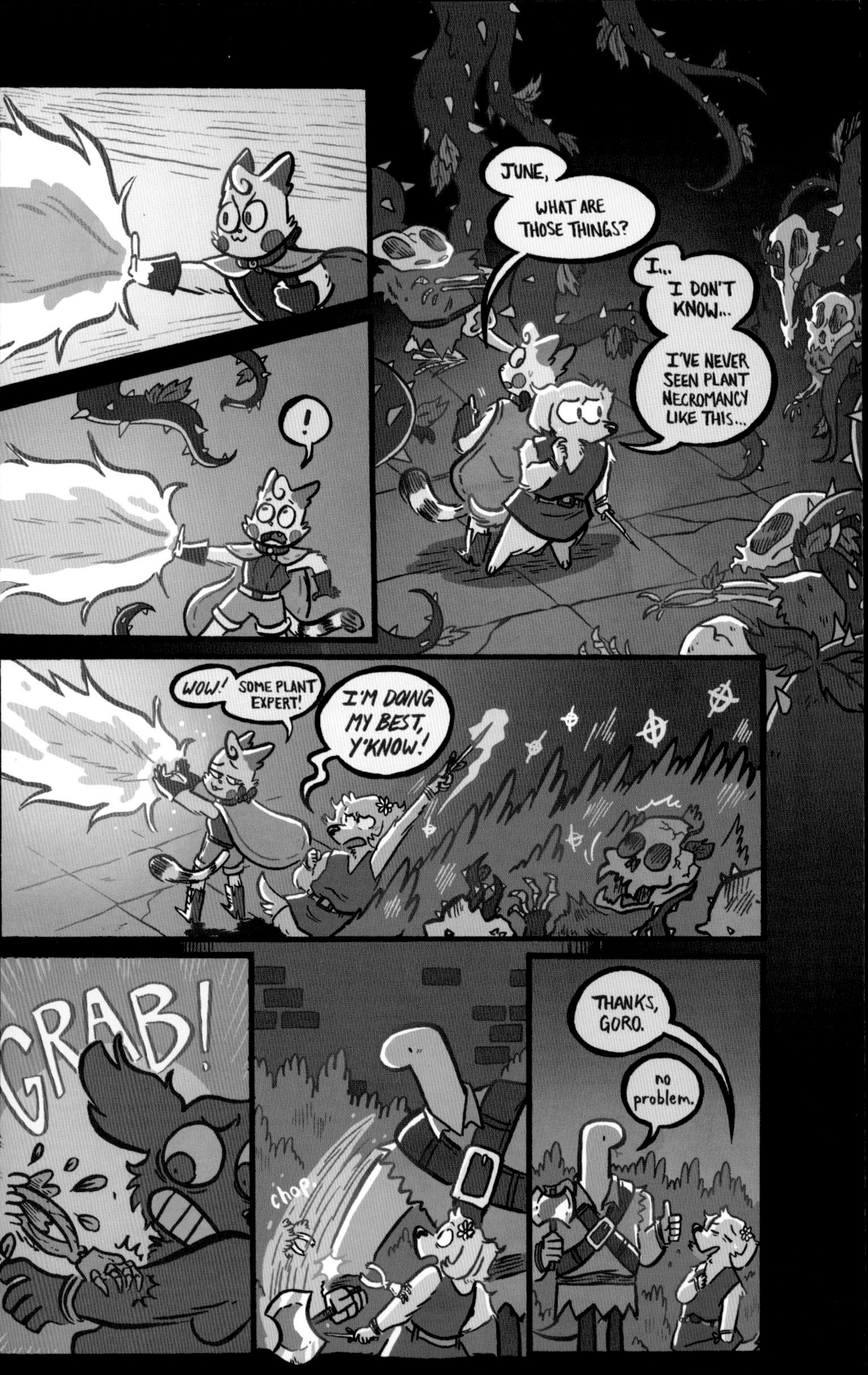

JUNE,
WHAT ARE THOSE THINGS?
I... I DON'T KNOW...
I'VE NEVER SEEN PLANT NECROMANCY LIKE THIS...
!
WOW!
SOME PLANT EXPERT!
I'M DOING MY BEST, Y'KNOW!
GRAB!
chop
THANKS, GORO.
no problem.

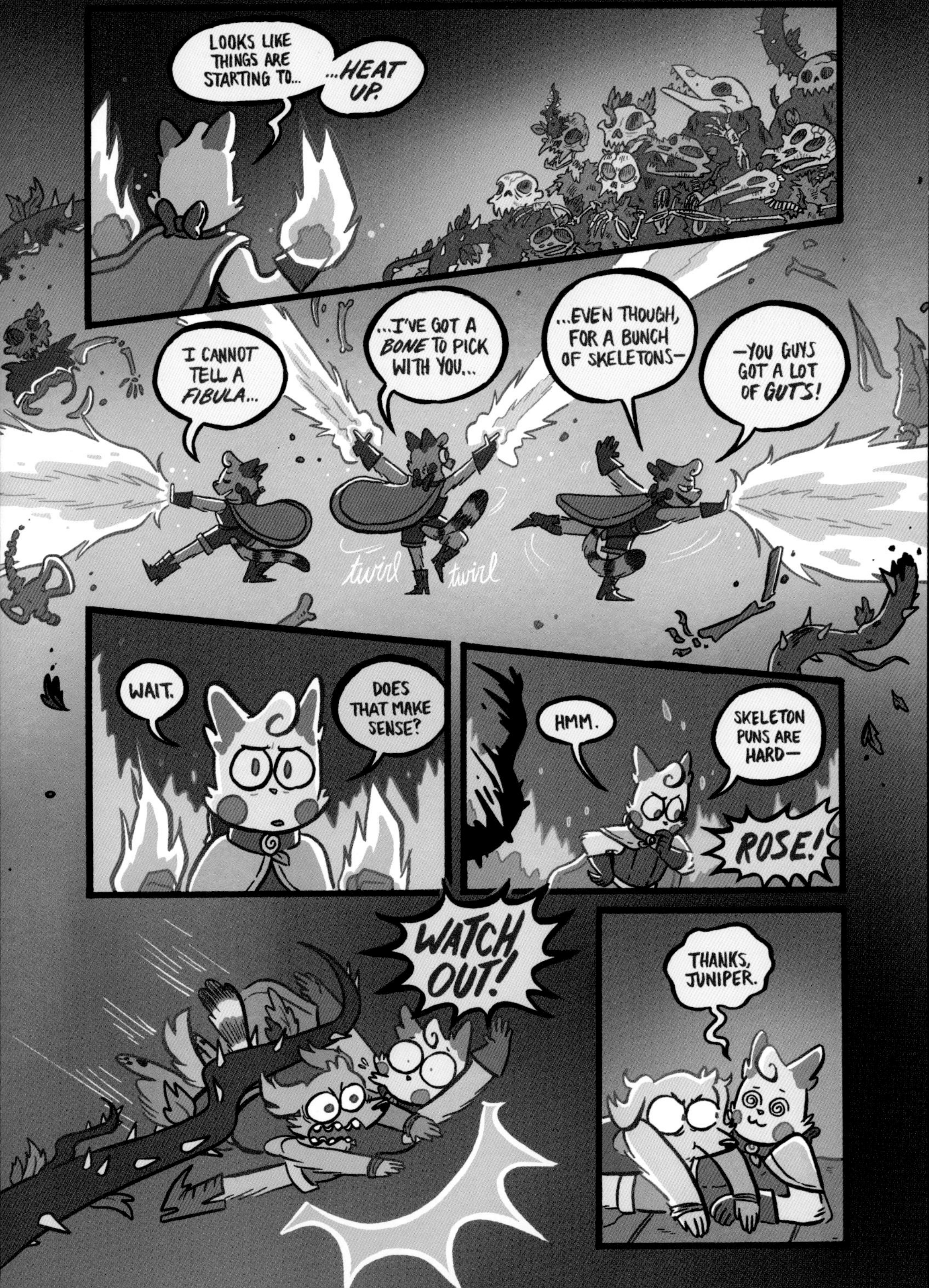
LOOKS LIKE THINGS ARE STARTING TO...
...HEAT UP.
I CANNOT TELL A FIBULA...
...I'VE GOT A BONE TO PICK WITH YOU...
...EVEN THOUGH, FOR A BUNCH OF SKELETONS—
—YOU GUYS GOT A LOT OF GUTS!
twirl
twirl
WAIT.
DOES THAT MAKE SENSE?
HMM.
SKELETON PUNS ARE HARD—
ROSE!
WATCH OUT!
THANKS, JUNIPER.

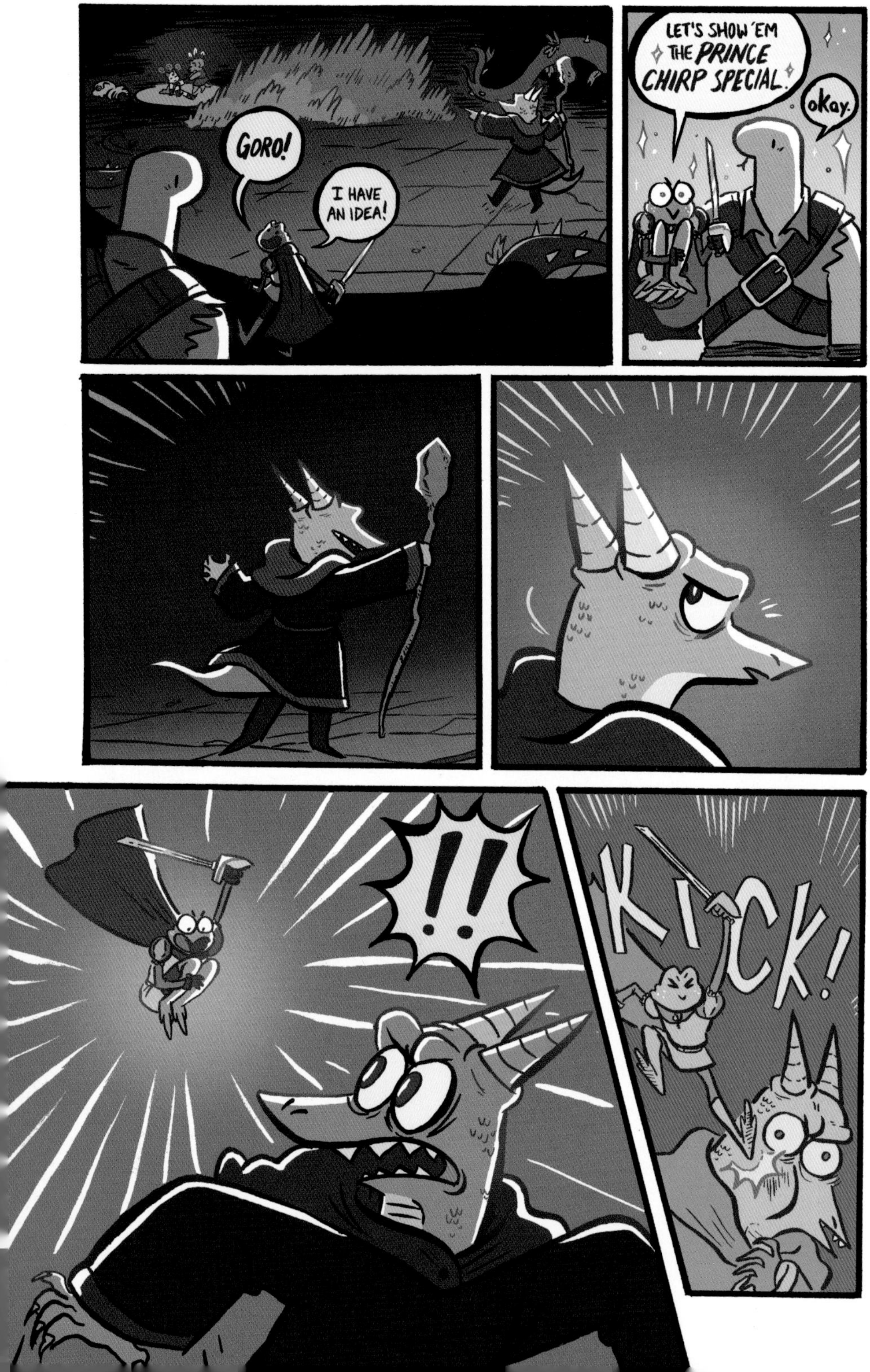
GORO!
I HAVE AN IDEA!
LET'S SHOW 'EM THE PRINCE CHIRP SPECIAL.
okay.
!!
KICK!

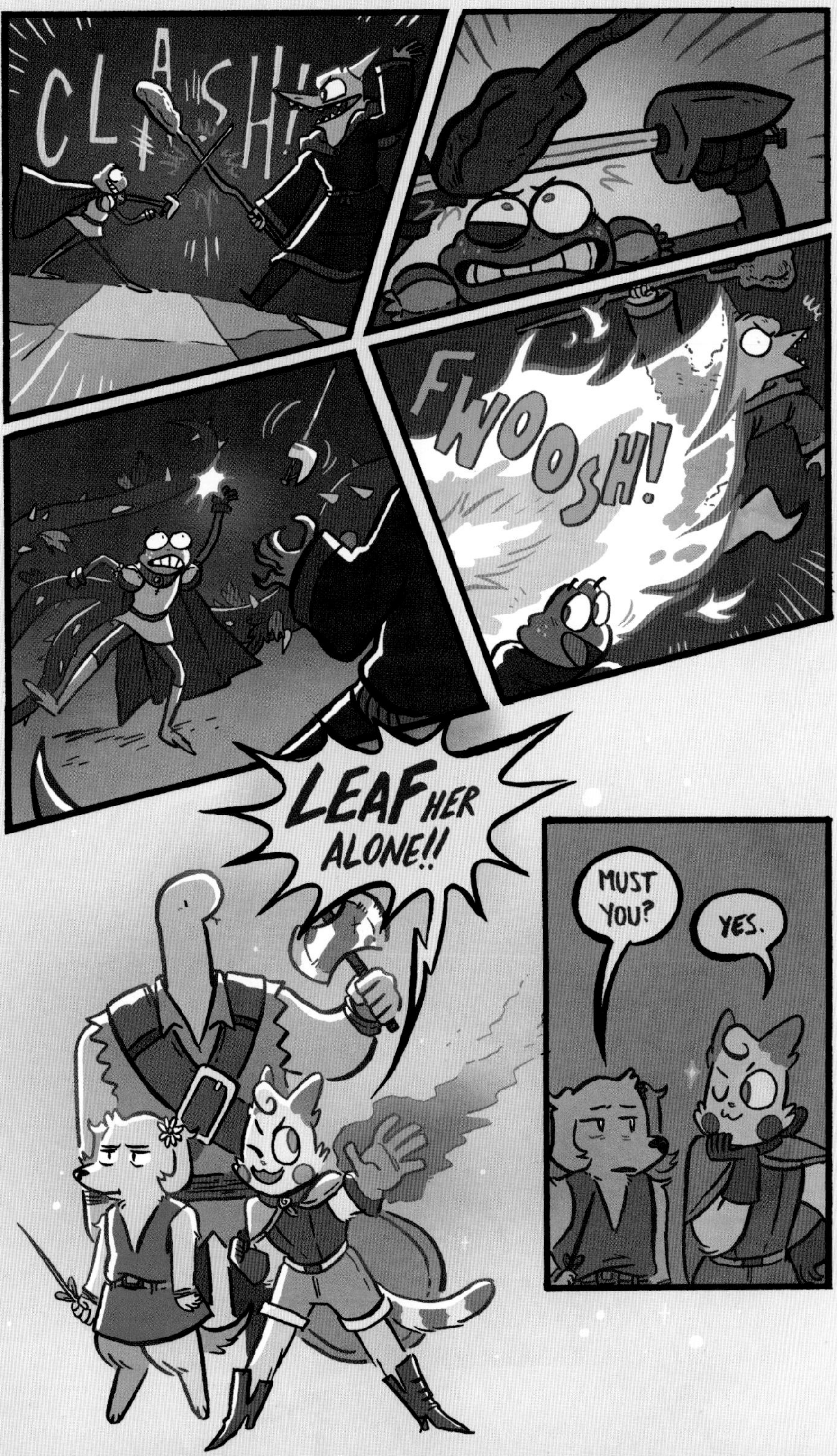
CLASH!
FWOOSH!
LEAF HER ALONE!!
MUST YOU?
YES.

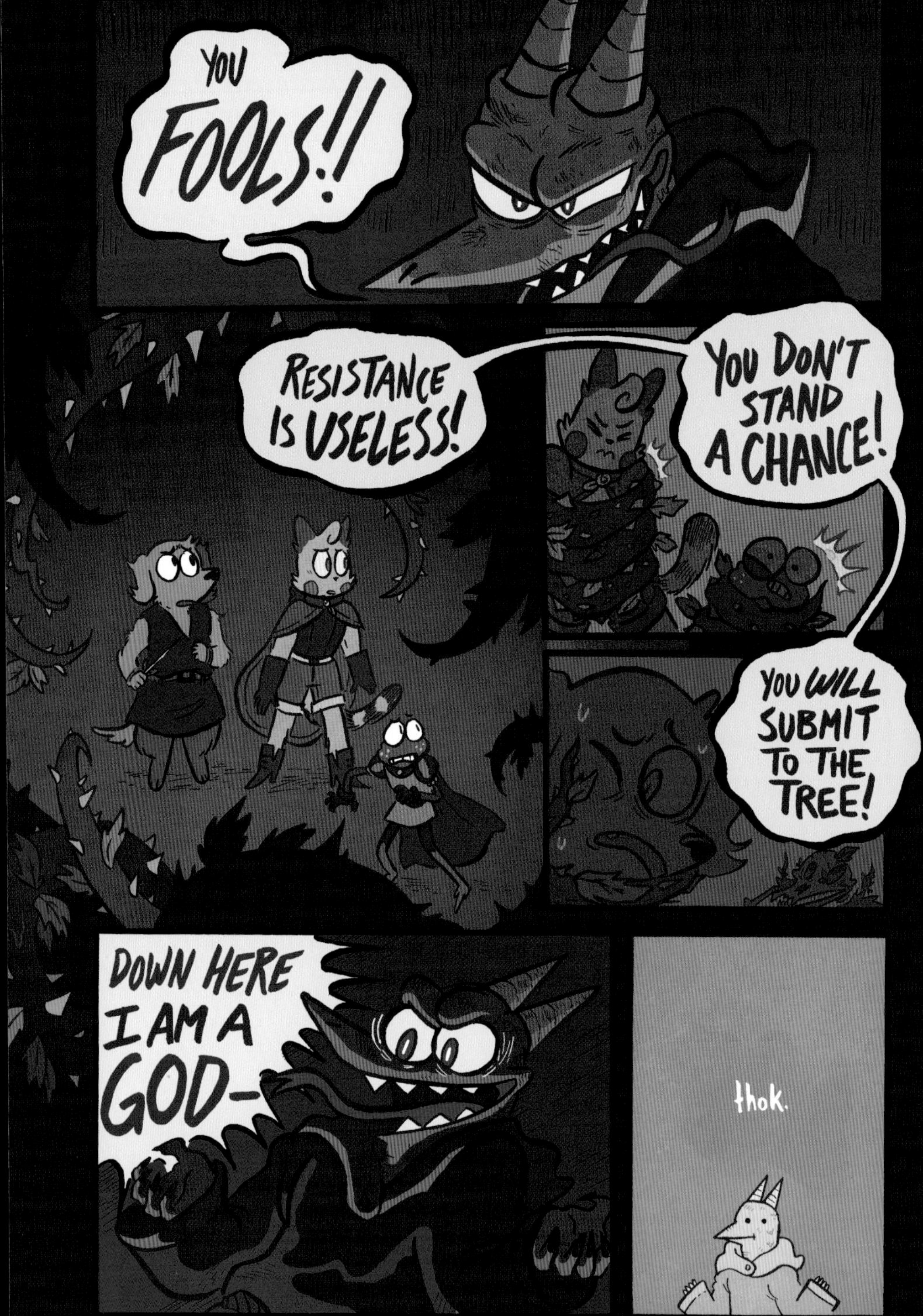
YOU FOOLS!!
RESISTANCE IS USELESS!
YOU DON'T STAND A CHANCE!
YOU WILL SUBMIT TO THE TREE!
DOWN HERE I AM A GOD-
thok.

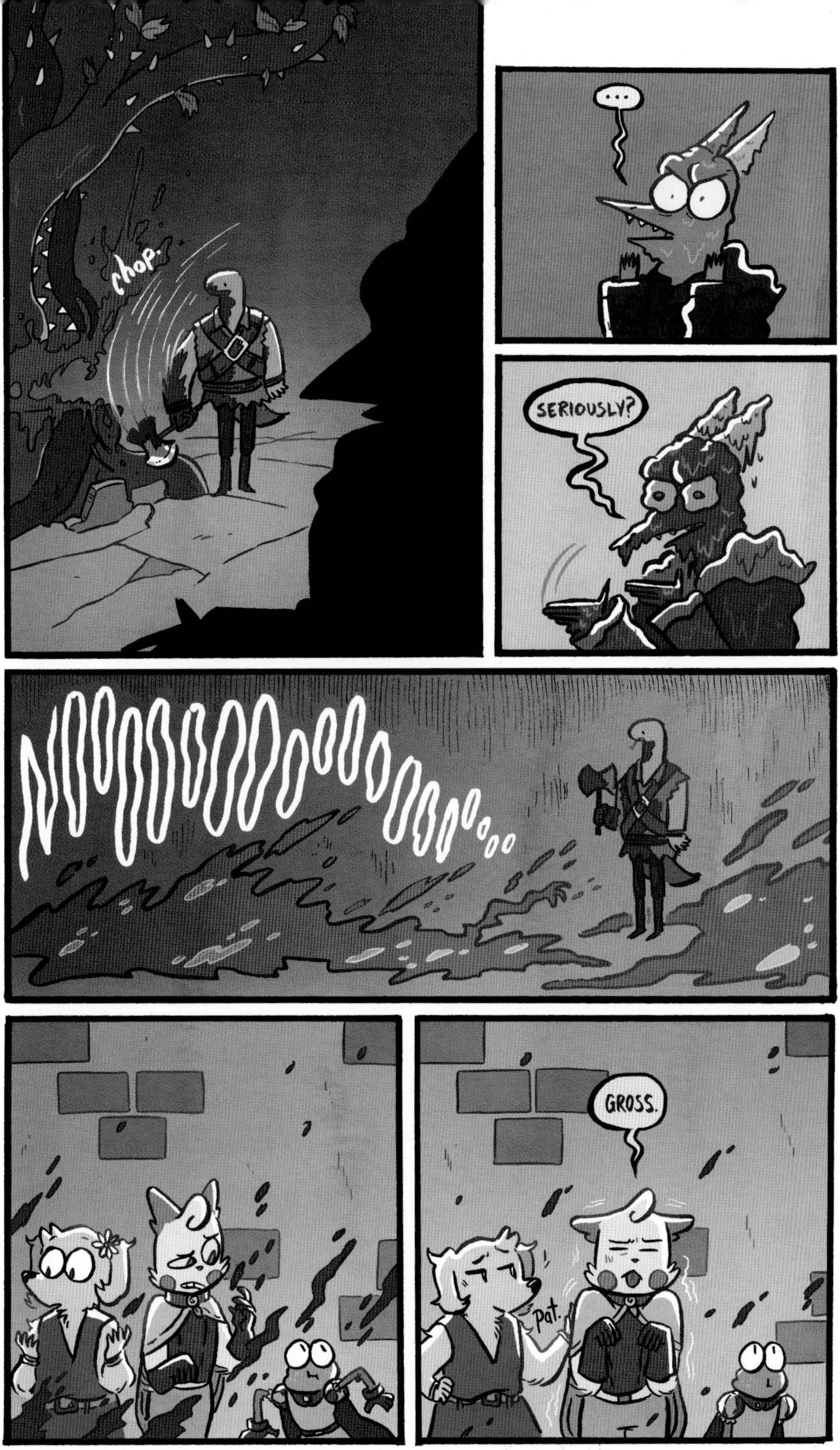

chop.
...
SERIOUSLY?
NOOOOOOOOooooooo...
pat.
GROSS.

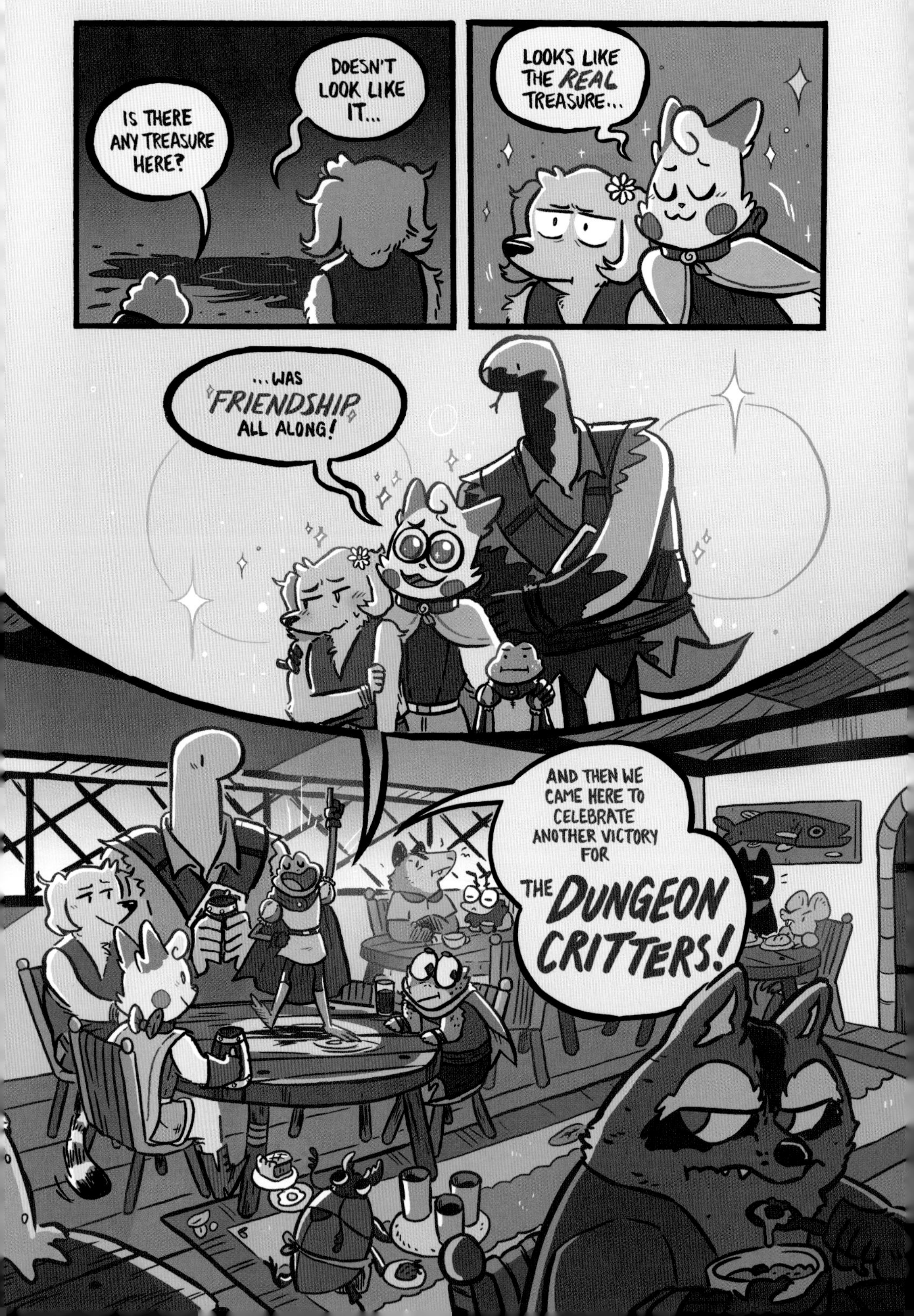
IS THERE ANY TREASURE HERE?
DOESN'T LOOK LIKE IT...
LOOKS LIKE THE REAL TREASURE...
...WAS FRIENDSHIP ALL ALONG!
AND THEN WE CAME HERE TO CELEBRATE ANOTHER VICTORY FOR
THE DUNGEON CRITTERS!

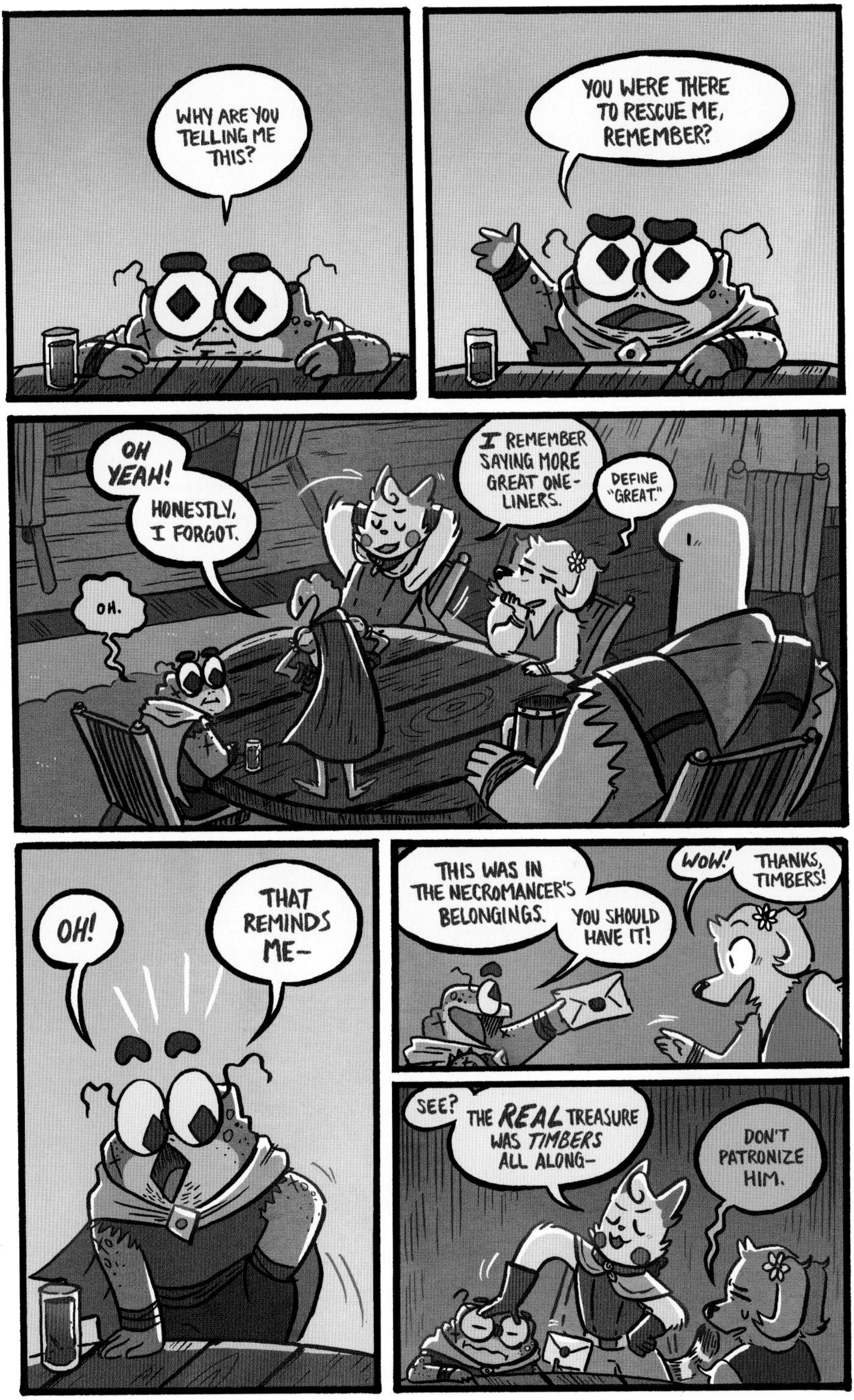
WHY ARE YOU TELLING ME THIS?
YOU WERE THERE TO RESCUE ME, REMEMBER?
OH YEAH!
HONESTLY, I FORGOT.
OH.
I REMEMBER SAYING MORE GREAT ONE-LINERS.
DEFINE "GREAT."
OH!
THAT REMINDS ME—
THIS WAS IN THE NECROMANCER'S BELONGINGS.
YOU SHOULD HAVE IT!
WOW!
THANKS, TIMBERS!
SEE?
THE REAL TREASURE WAS TIMBERS ALL ALONG—
DON'T PATRONIZE HIM.

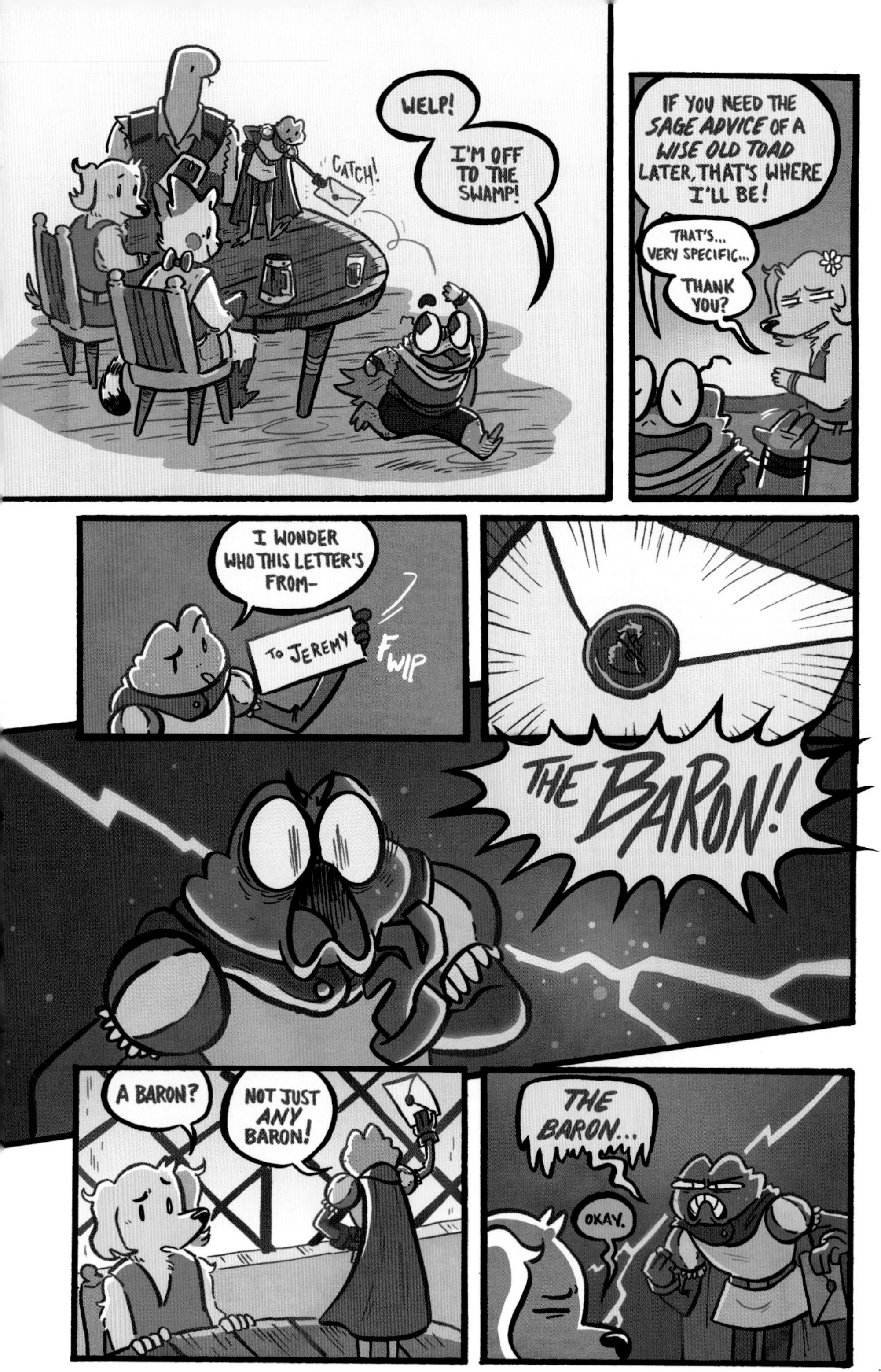
CATCH!
WELP!
I'M OFF TO THE SWAMP!
IF YOU NEED THE SAGE ADVICE OF A WISE OLD TOAD LATER, THAT'S WHERE I'LL BE!
THAT'S... VERY SPECIFIC...
THANK YOU?
I WONDER WHO THIS LETTER'S FROM-
TO JEREMY
FWIP
THE BARON!
A BARON?
NOT JUST ANY BARON!
THE BARON...
OKAY.

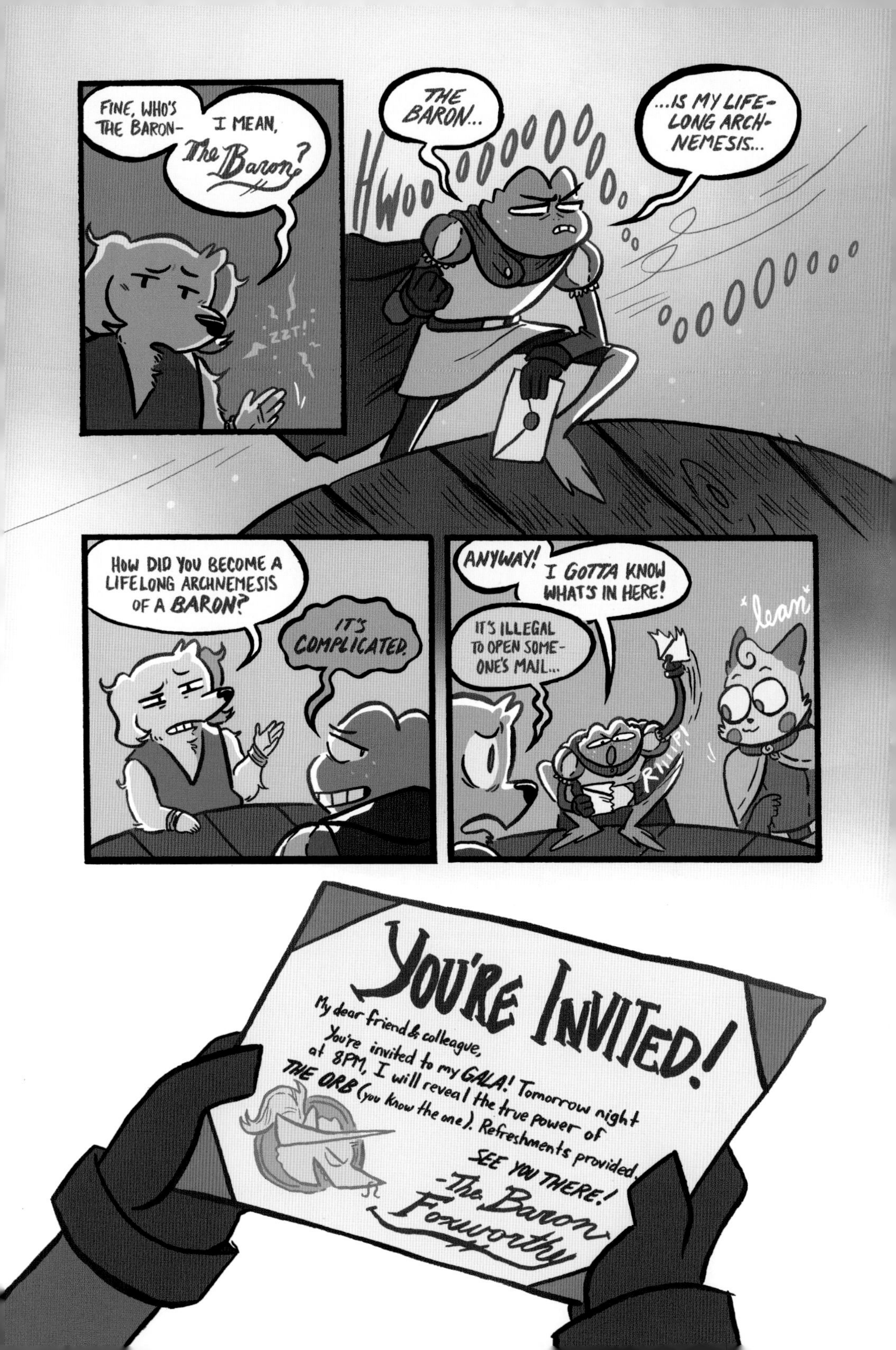
FINE, WHO'S THE BARON-
I MEAN, The Baron?
THE BARON...
HWOOOOOOOOOOOOOo
...IS MY LIFE-LONG ARCH-NEMESIS...
OOOOOOOOOOoo
ZZT!
HOW DID YOU BECOME A LIFELONG ARCHNEMESIS OF A BARON?
IT'S COMPLICATED.
ANYWAY!
I GOTTA KNOW WHAT'S IN HERE!
IT'S ILLEGAL TO OPEN SOME-ONE'S MAIL...
lean
RRIIP!
YOU'RE INVITED!
My dear friend & colleague,
You're invited to my GALA! Tomorrow night at 8PM, I will reveal the true power of THE ORB (you know the one). Refreshments provided.
SEE YOU THERE!
-The Baron Foxworthy

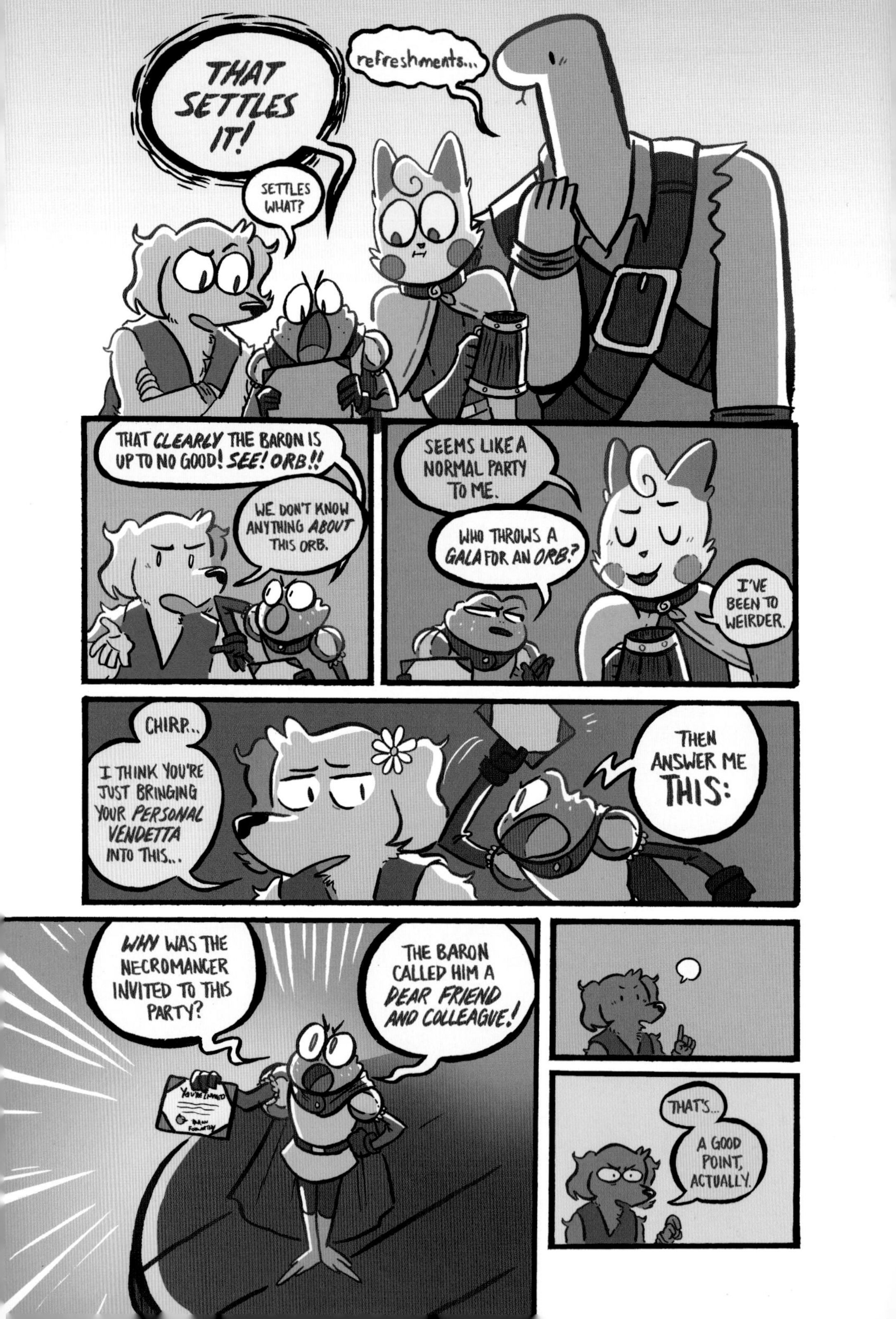
THAT SETTLES IT!
refreshments...
SETTLES WHAT?
THAT CLEARLY THE BARON IS UP TO NO GOOD! SEE! ORB!!
WE DON'T KNOW ANYTHING ABOUT THIS ORB.
SEEMS LIKE A NORMAL PARTY TO ME.
WHO THROWS A GALA FOR AN ORB?
I'VE BEEN TO WEIRDER.
CHIRP...
I THINK YOU'RE JUST BRINGING YOUR PERSONAL VENDETTA INTO THIS...
THEN ANSWER ME THIS:
WHY WAS THE NECROMANCER INVITED TO THIS PARTY?
THE BARON CALLED HIM A DEAR FRIEND AND COLLEAGUE!
THAT'S...
A GOOD POINT, ACTUALLY.

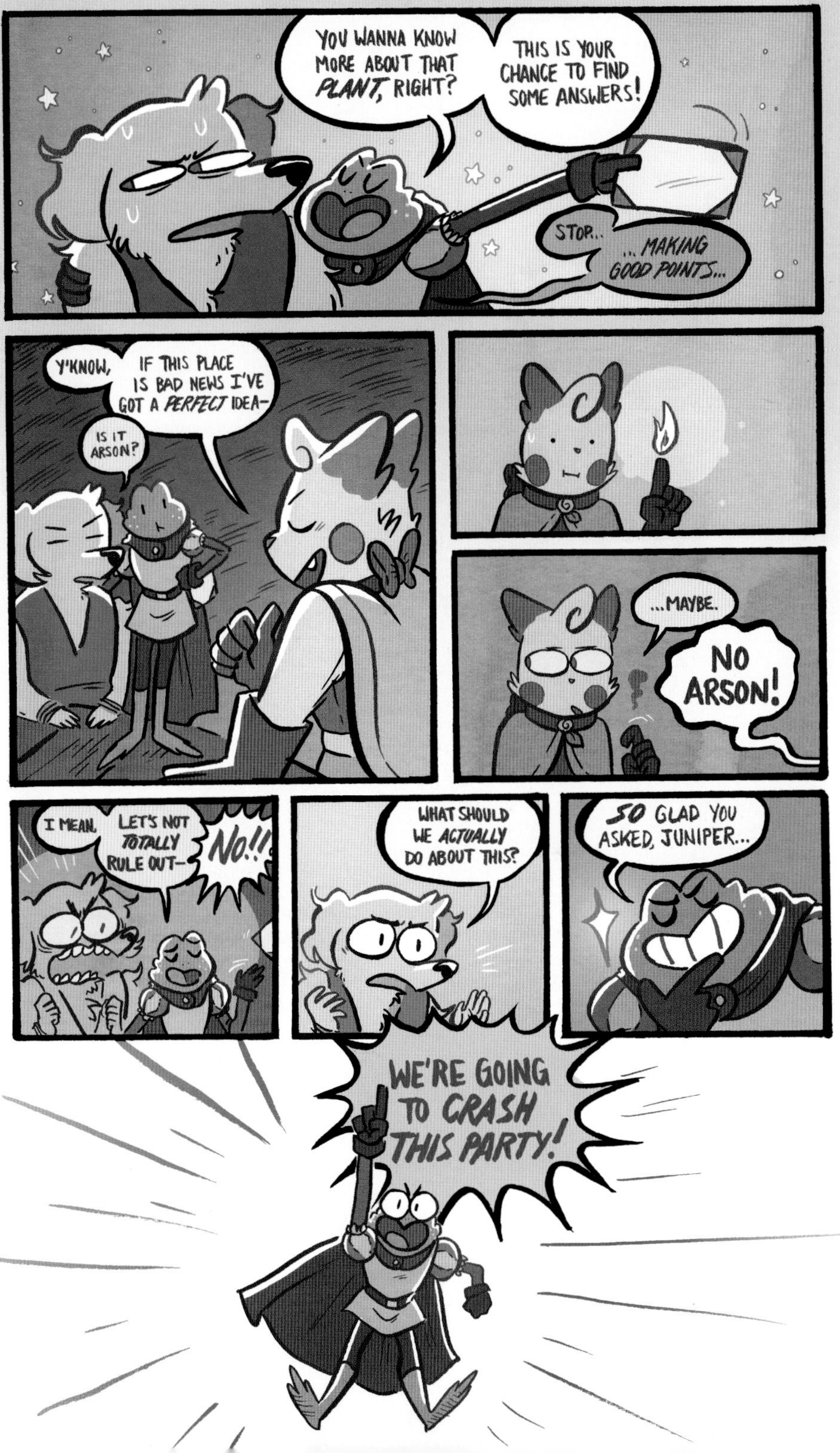
YOU WANNA KNOW MORE ABOUT THAT PLANT, RIGHT?
THIS IS YOUR CHANCE TO FIND SOME ANSWERS!
STOP...
...MAKING GOOD POINTS...
Y'KNOW,
IF THIS PLACE IS BAD NEWS I'VE GOT A PERFECT IDEA-
IS IT ARSON?
...MAYBE.
NO ARSON!
I MEAN,
LET'S NOT TOTALLY RULE OUT-
NO!!
WHAT SHOULD WE ACTUALLY DO ABOUT THIS?
SO GLAD YOU ASKED, JUNIPER...
WE'RE GOING TO CRASH THIS PARTY!

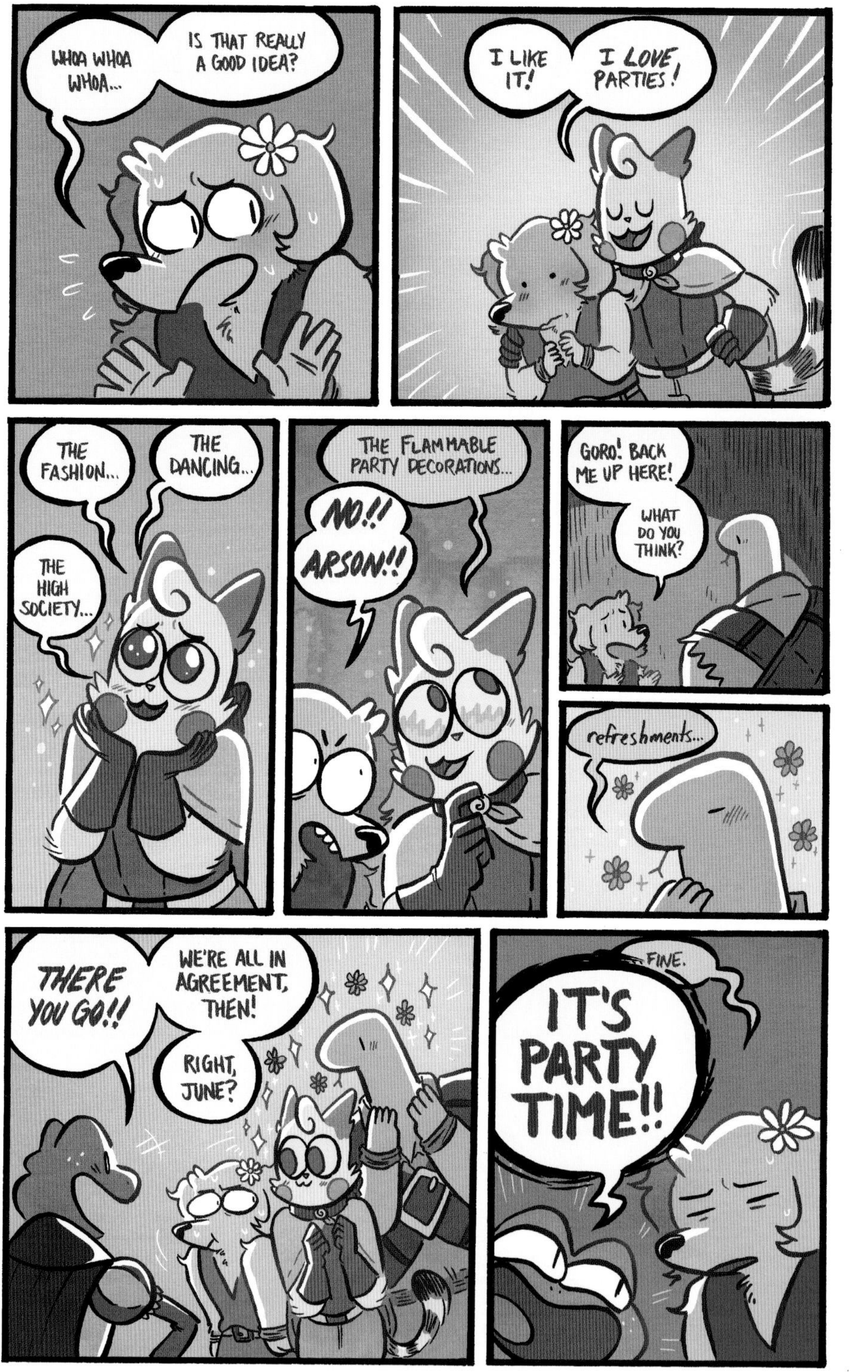
WHOA WHOA WHOA...
IS THAT REALLY A GOOD IDEA?
I LIKE IT!
I LOVE PARTIES!
THE FASHION...
THE DANCING...
THE HIGH SOCIETY...
THE FLAMMABLE PARTY DECORATIONS...
NO!! ARSON!!
GORO! BACK ME UP HERE!
WHAT DO YOU THINK?
refreshments...
THERE YOU GO!!
WE'RE ALL IN AGREEMENT, THEN!
RIGHT, JUNE?
FINE.
IT'S PARTY TIME!!

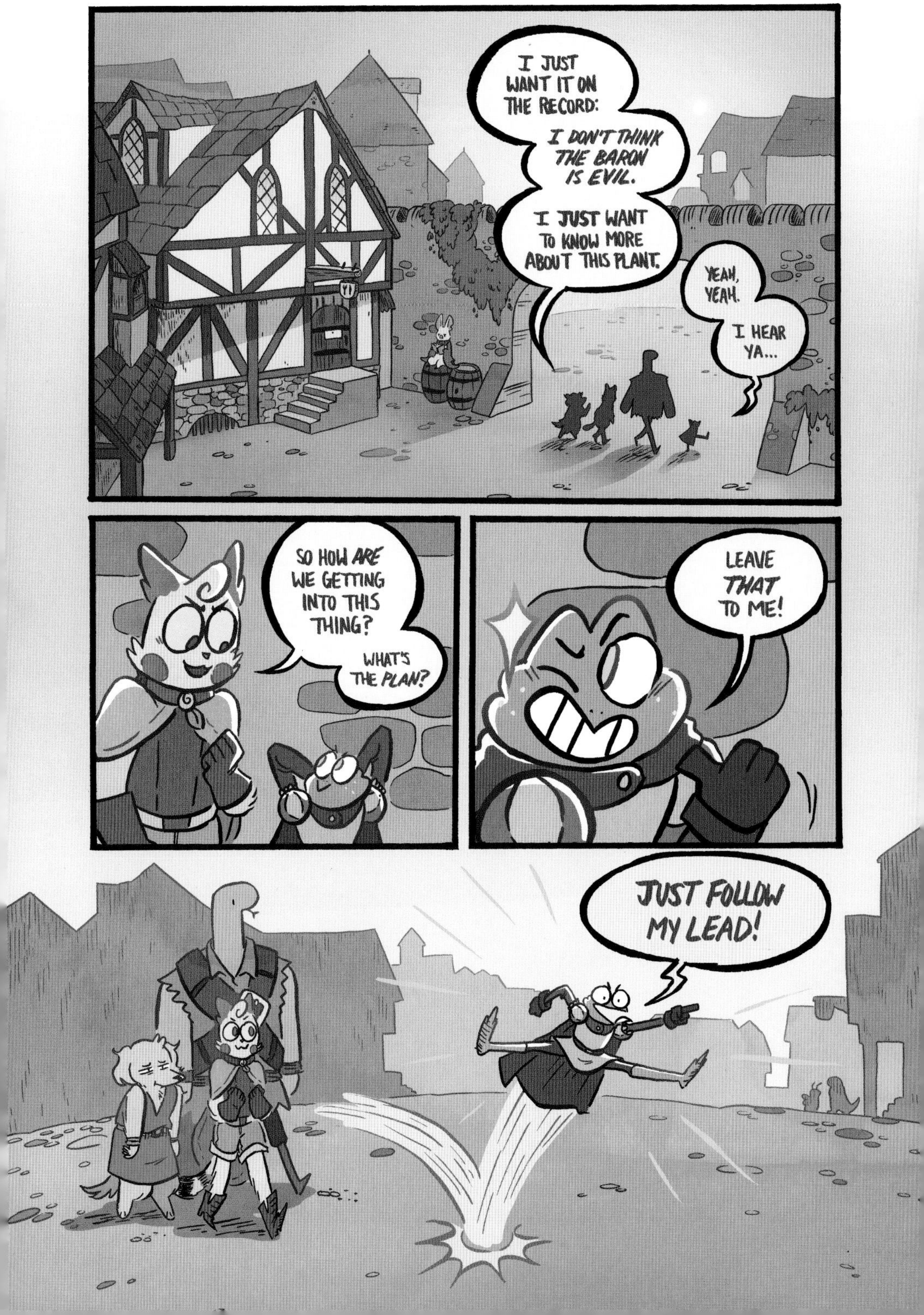
I JUST WANT IT ON THE RECORD:
I DON'T THINK THE BARON IS EVIL.
I JUST WANT TO KNOW MORE ABOUT THIS PLANT.
YEAH, YEAH.
I HEAR YA...
SO HOW ARE WE GETTING INTO THIS THING?
WHAT'S THE PLAN?
LEAVE THAT TO ME!
JUST FOLLOW MY LEAD!

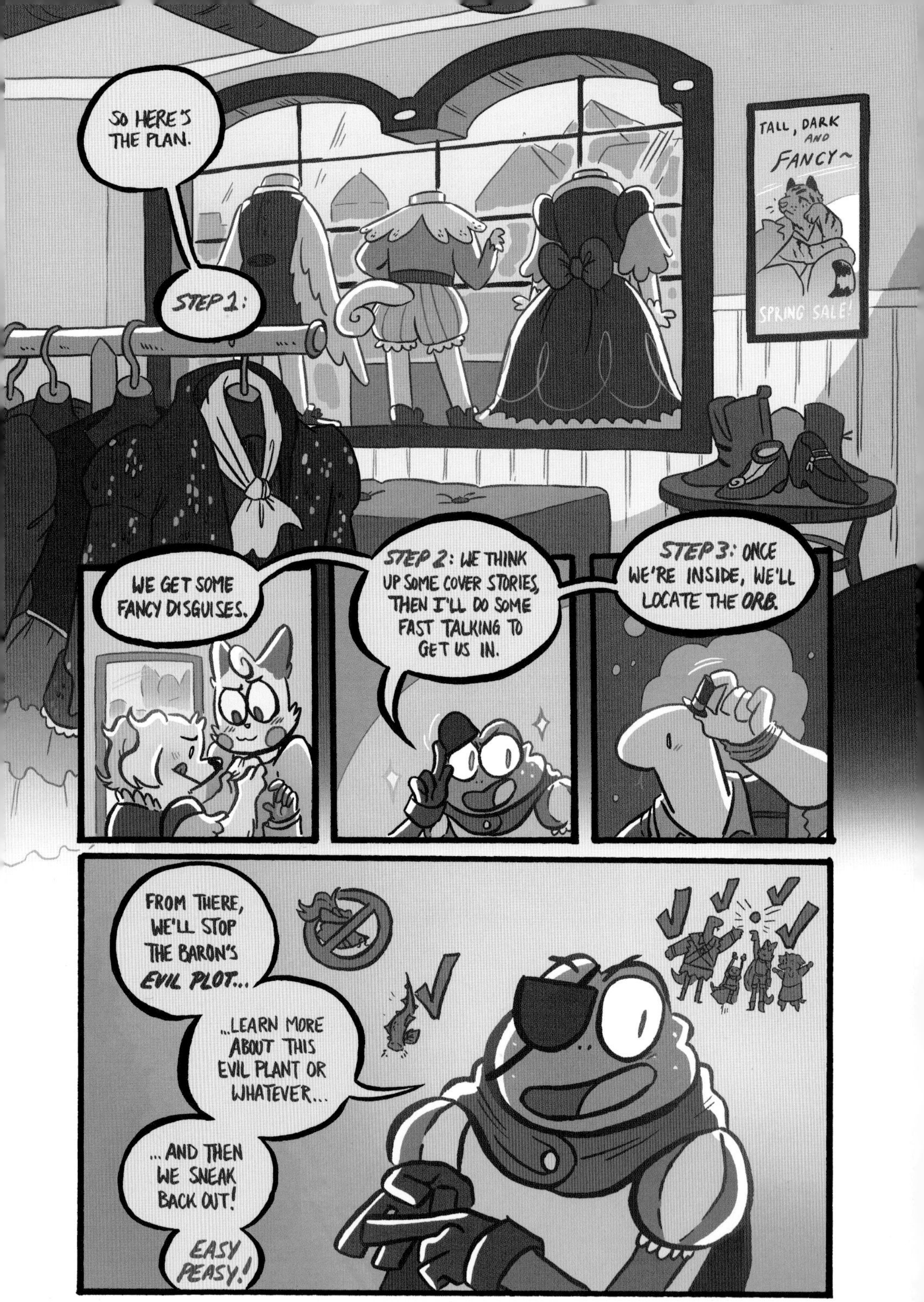
SO HERE'S THE PLAN.
STEP 1:
TALL, DARK AND FANCY~
SPRING SALE!
WE GET SOME FANCY DISGUISES.
STEP 2: WE THINK UP SOME COVER STORIES, THEN I'LL DO SOME FAST TALKING TO GET US IN.
STEP 3: ONCE WE'RE INSIDE, WE'LL LOCATE THE ORB.
FROM THERE, WE'LL STOP THE BARON'S EVIL PLOT...
...LEARN MORE ABOUT THIS EVIL PLANT OR WHATEVER...
... AND THEN WE SNEAK BACK OUT!
EASY PEASY!

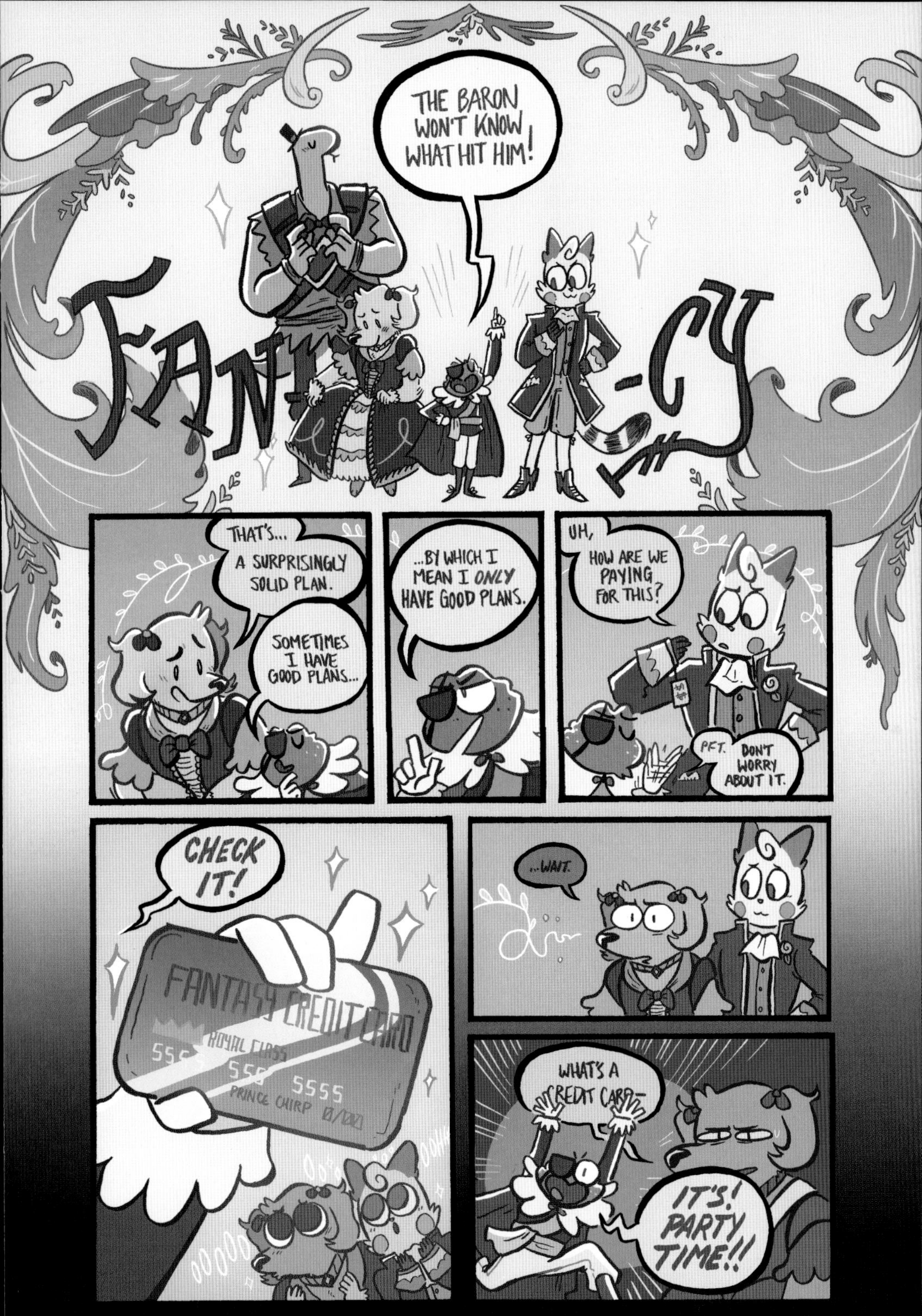
THE BARON WON'T KNOW WHAT HIT HIM!
FAN-CY
THAT'S... A SURPRISINGLY SOLID PLAN.
SOMETIMES I HAVE GOOD PLANS...
...BY WHICH I MEAN I ONLY HAVE GOOD PLANS.
UH, HOW ARE WE PAYING FOR THIS?
PFT. DON'T WORRY ABOUT IT.
CHECK IT!
FANTASY CREDIT CARD
ROYAL CLASS
5555 5555 5555
PRINCE CHIRP
...WAIT.
WHAT'S A CREDIT CARD-
IT'S! PARTY TIME!!

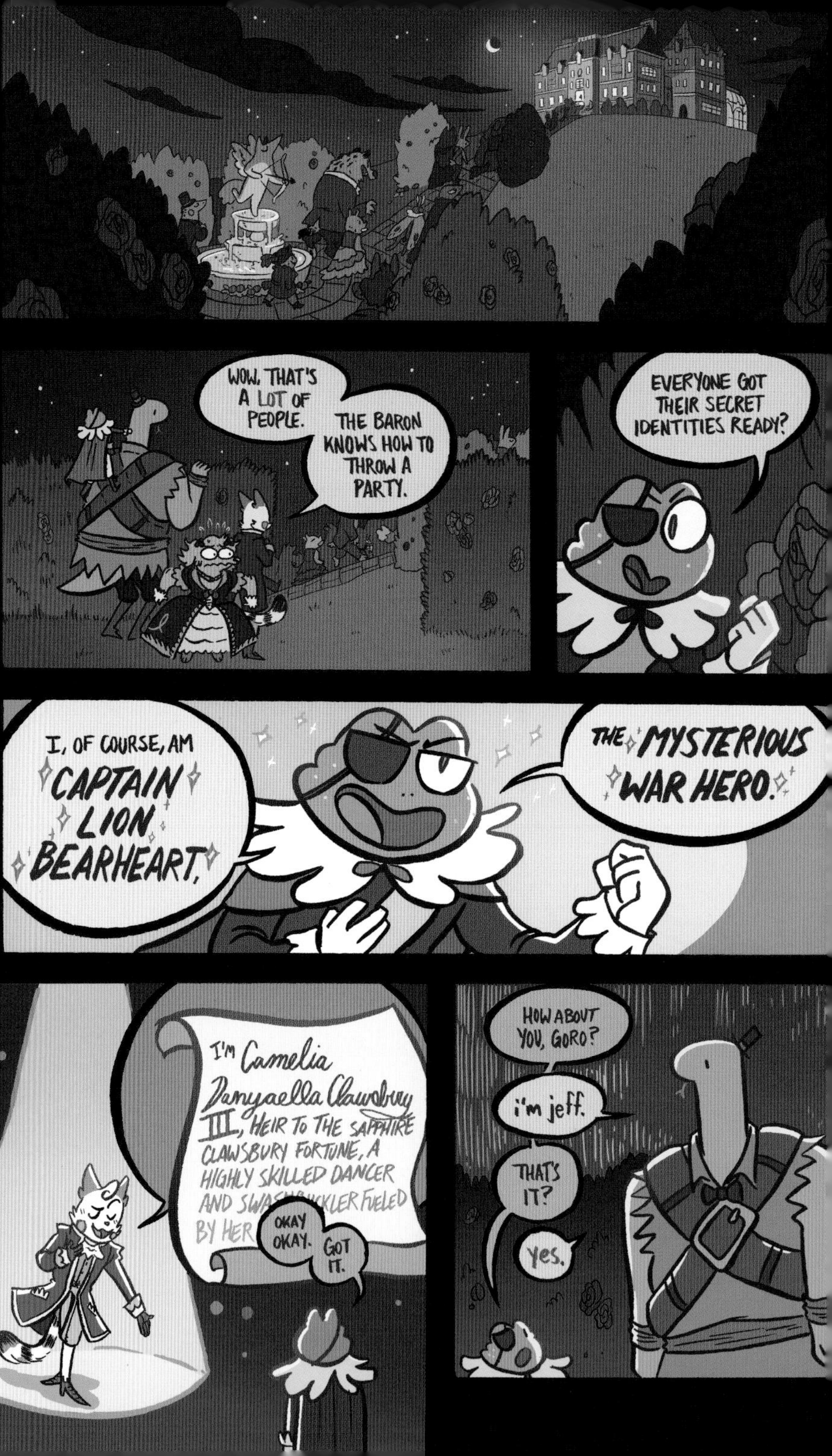
WOW. THAT'S A LOT OF PEOPLE.
THE BARON KNOWS HOW TO THROW A PARTY.
EVERYONE GOT THEIR SECRET IDENTITIES READY?
I, OF COURSE, AM CAPTAIN LION BEARHEART,
THE MYSTERIOUS WAR HERO.
I'M Camelia Danyaella Clawsbury III, HEIR TO THE SAPPHIRE CLAWSBURY FORTUNE, A HIGHLY SKILLED DANCER AND SWASHBUCKLER FUELED BY HER
OKAY OKAY.
GOT IT.
HOW ABOUT YOU, GORO?
i'm jeff.
THAT'S IT?
yes.

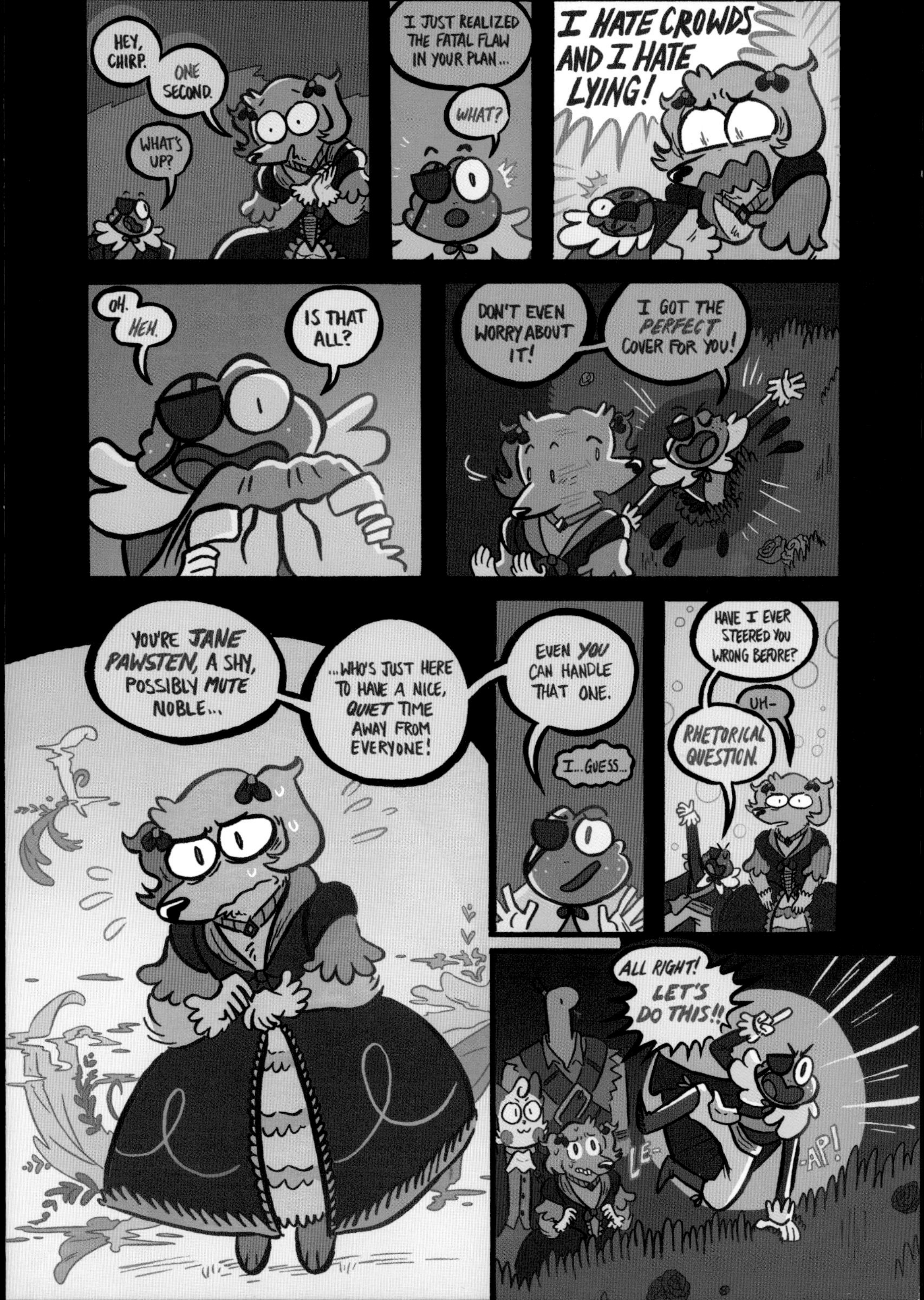
HEY, CHIRP.
ONE SECOND.
WHAT'S UP?
I JUST REALIZED THE FATAL FLAW IN YOUR PLAN...
WHAT?
I HATE CROWDS AND I HATE LYING!
OH. HEH.
IS THAT ALL?
DON'T EVEN WORRY ABOUT IT!
I GOT THE PERFECT COVER FOR YOU!
YOU'RE JANE PAWSTEN, A SHY, POSSIBLY MUTE NOBLE...
...WHO'S JUST HERE TO HAVE A NICE, QUIET TIME AWAY FROM EVERYONE!
EVEN YOU CAN HANDLE THAT ONE.
I...GUESS...
HAVE I EVER STEERED YOU WRONG BEFORE?
UH-
RHETORICAL QUESTION.
ALL RIGHT! LET'S DO THIS!!
LE-
-AP!

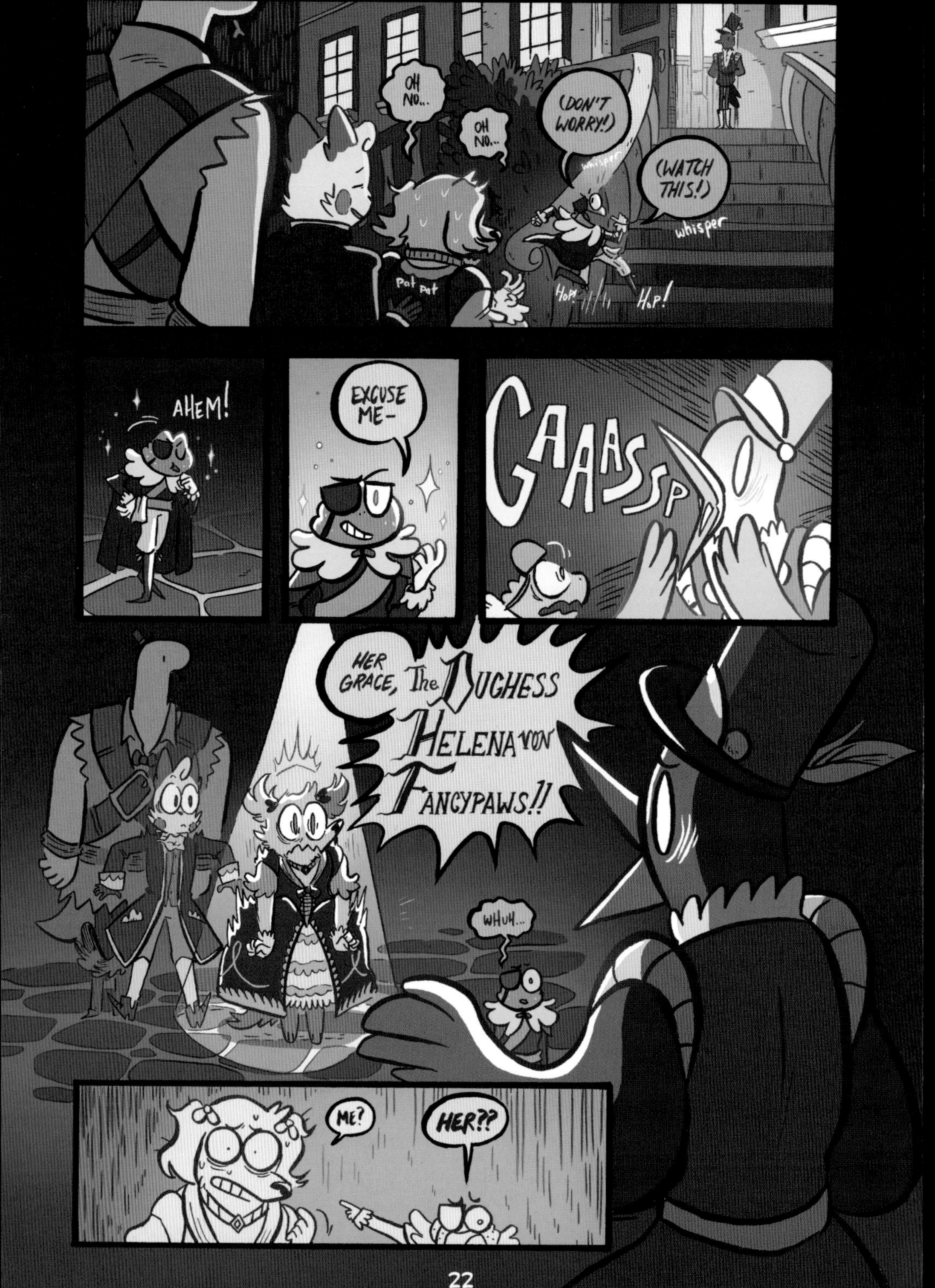
OH NO...
OH NO...
(DON'T WORRY!)
whisper
(WATCH THIS!)
whisper
pat pat
HOP!
HOP!
AHEM!
EXCUSE ME-
GAAASSP
HER GRACE, The DUCHESS HELENA VON FANCYPAWS!!
WHUH...
ME?
HER??

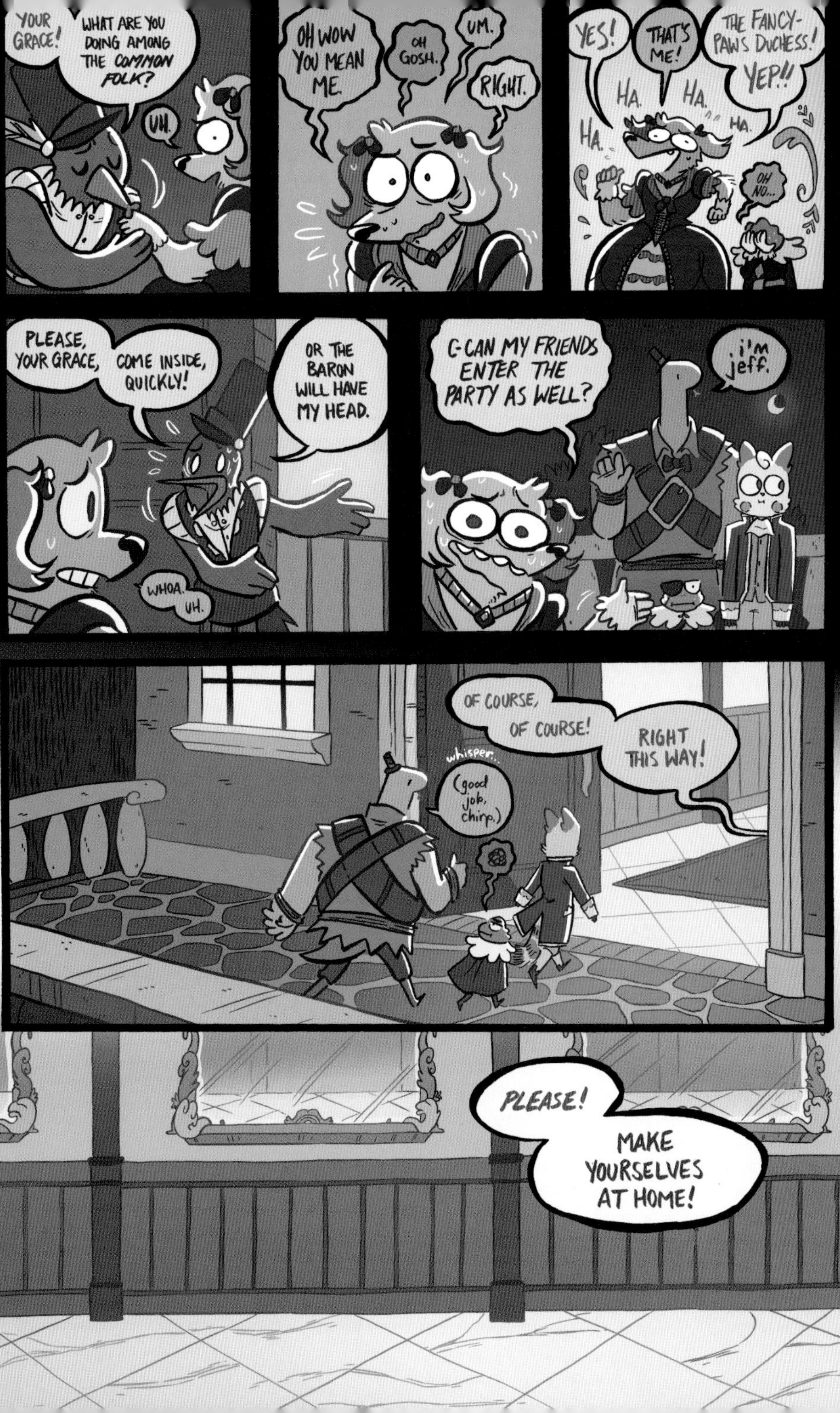
YOUR GRACE!
WHAT ARE YOU DOING AMONG THE COMMON FOLK?
UH.
OH WOW YOU MEAN ME.
OH GOSH.
UM.
RIGHT.
YES!
THAT'S ME!
THE FANCY-PAWS DUCHESS!
YEP!!
HA. HA. HA. HA.
OH NO...
PLEASE, YOUR GRACE,
COME INSIDE, QUICKLY!
OR THE BARON WILL HAVE MY HEAD.
WHOA. UH.
C-CAN MY FRIENDS ENTER THE PARTY AS WELL?
i'm jeff.
OF COURSE, OF COURSE!
RIGHT THIS WAY!
whisper...
(good job, chirp.)
PLEASE!
MAKE YOURSELVES AT HOME!

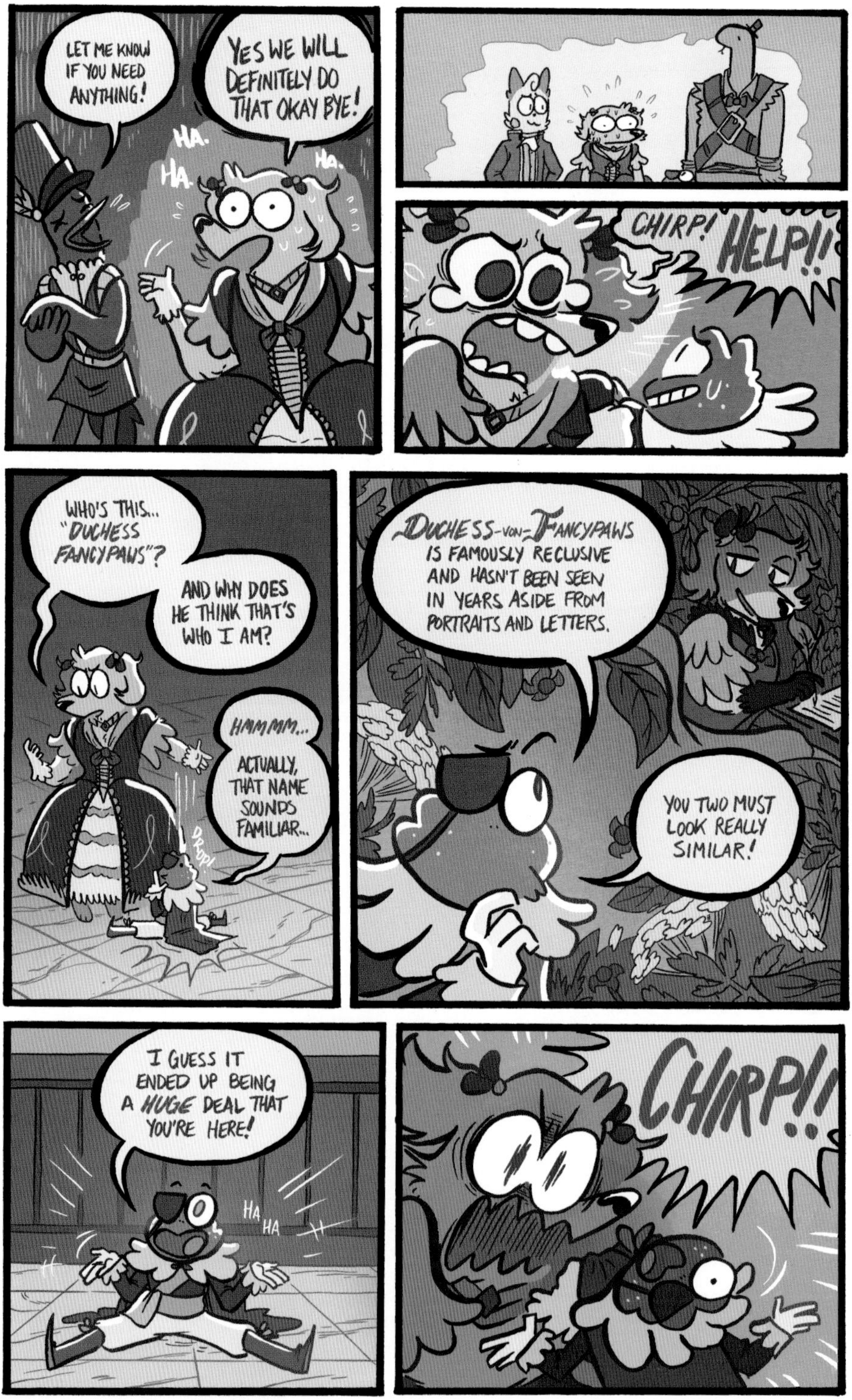
LET ME KNOW IF YOU NEED ANYTHING!
YES WE WILL DEFINITELY DO THAT OKAY BYE!
HA. HA. HA.
CHIRP! HELP!!
WHO'S THIS... "DUCHESS FANCYPAWS"?
AND WHY DOES HE THINK THAT'S WHO I AM?
DROP!
HMMMM...
ACTUALLY, THAT NAME SOUNDS FAMILIAR...
DUCHESS-VON-FANCYPAWS IS FAMOUSLY RECLUSIVE AND HASN'T BEEN SEEN IN YEARS ASIDE FROM PORTRAITS AND LETTERS.
YOU TWO MUST LOOK REALLY SIMILAR!
I GUESS IT ENDED UP BEING A HUGE DEAL THAT YOU'RE HERE!
HA HA
CHIRP!!

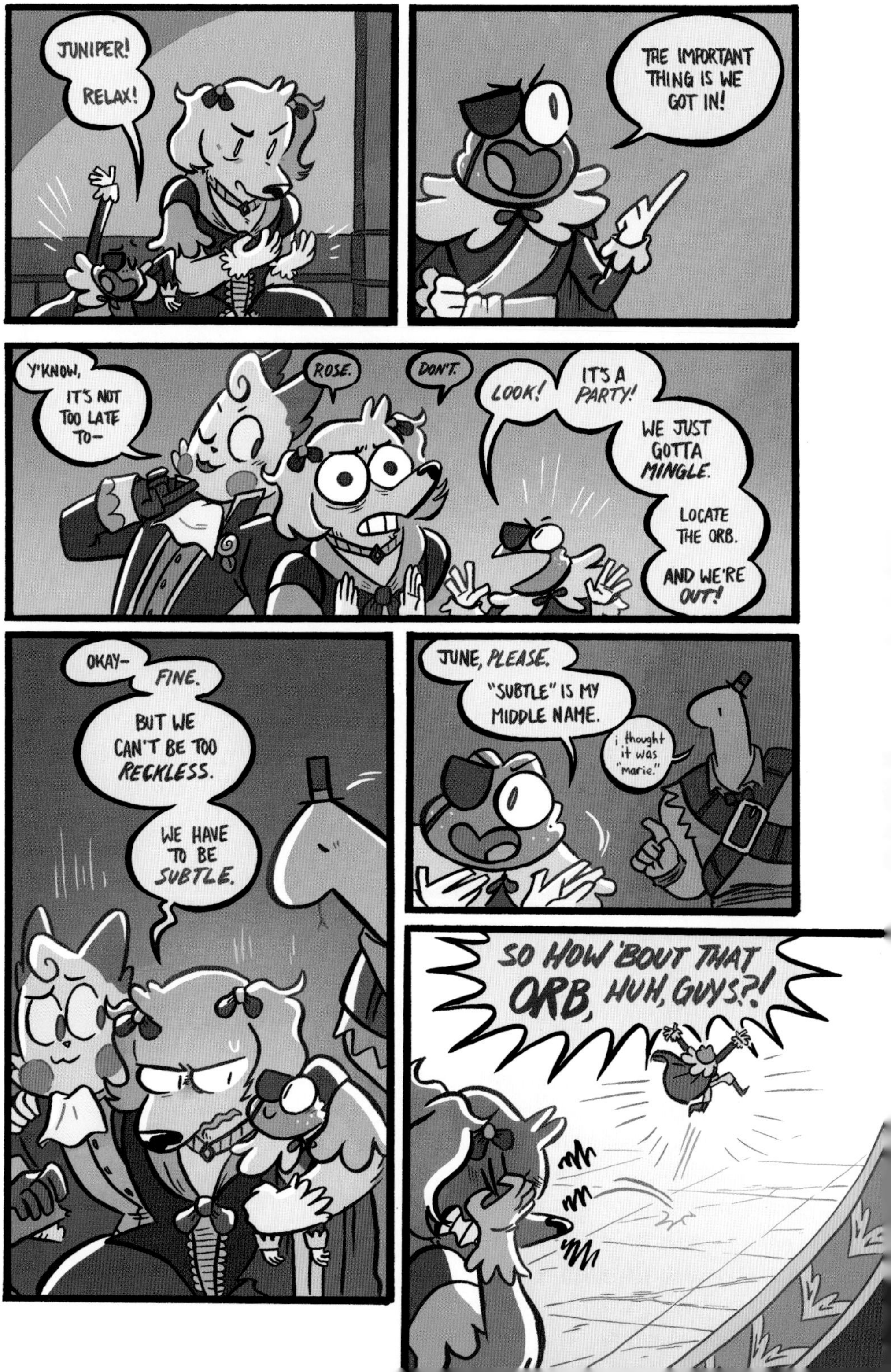
JUNIPER!
RELAX!
THE IMPORTANT THING IS WE GOT IN!
Y'KNOW, IT'S NOT TOO LATE TO—
ROSE.
DON'T.
LOOK!
IT'S A PARTY!
WE JUST GOTTA MINGLE.
LOCATE THE ORB.
AND WE'RE OUT!
OKAY—
FINE.
BUT WE CAN'T BE TOO RECKLESS.
WE HAVE TO BE SUBTLE.
JUNE, PLEASE.
"SUBTLE" IS MY MIDDLE NAME.
i thought it was "marie."
SO HOW 'BOUT THAT ORB, HUH, GUYS?!

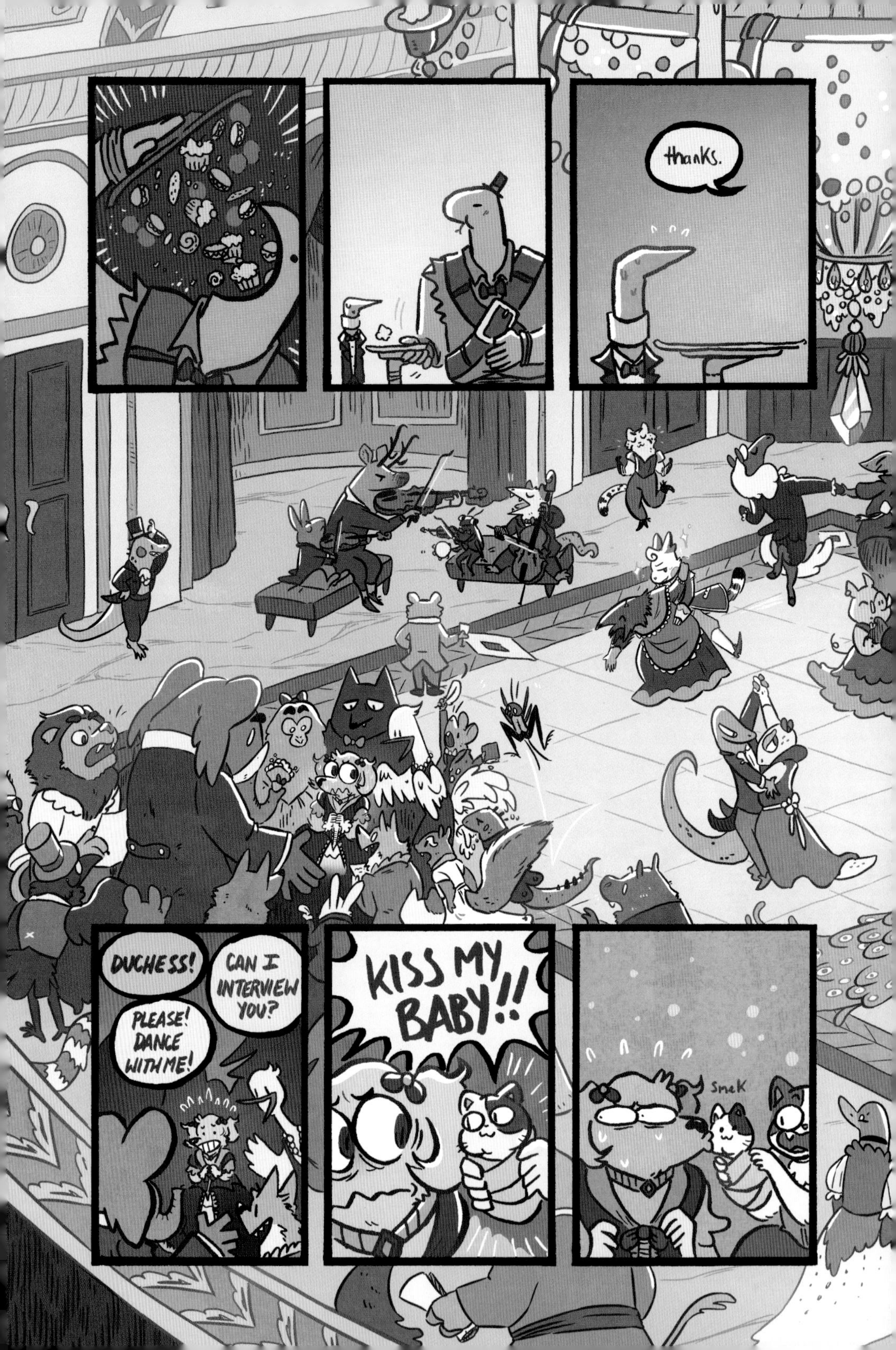
thanks.
DUCHESS!
CAN I INTERVIEW YOU?
PLEASE! DANCE WITH ME!
KISS MY BABY!!
SMCK

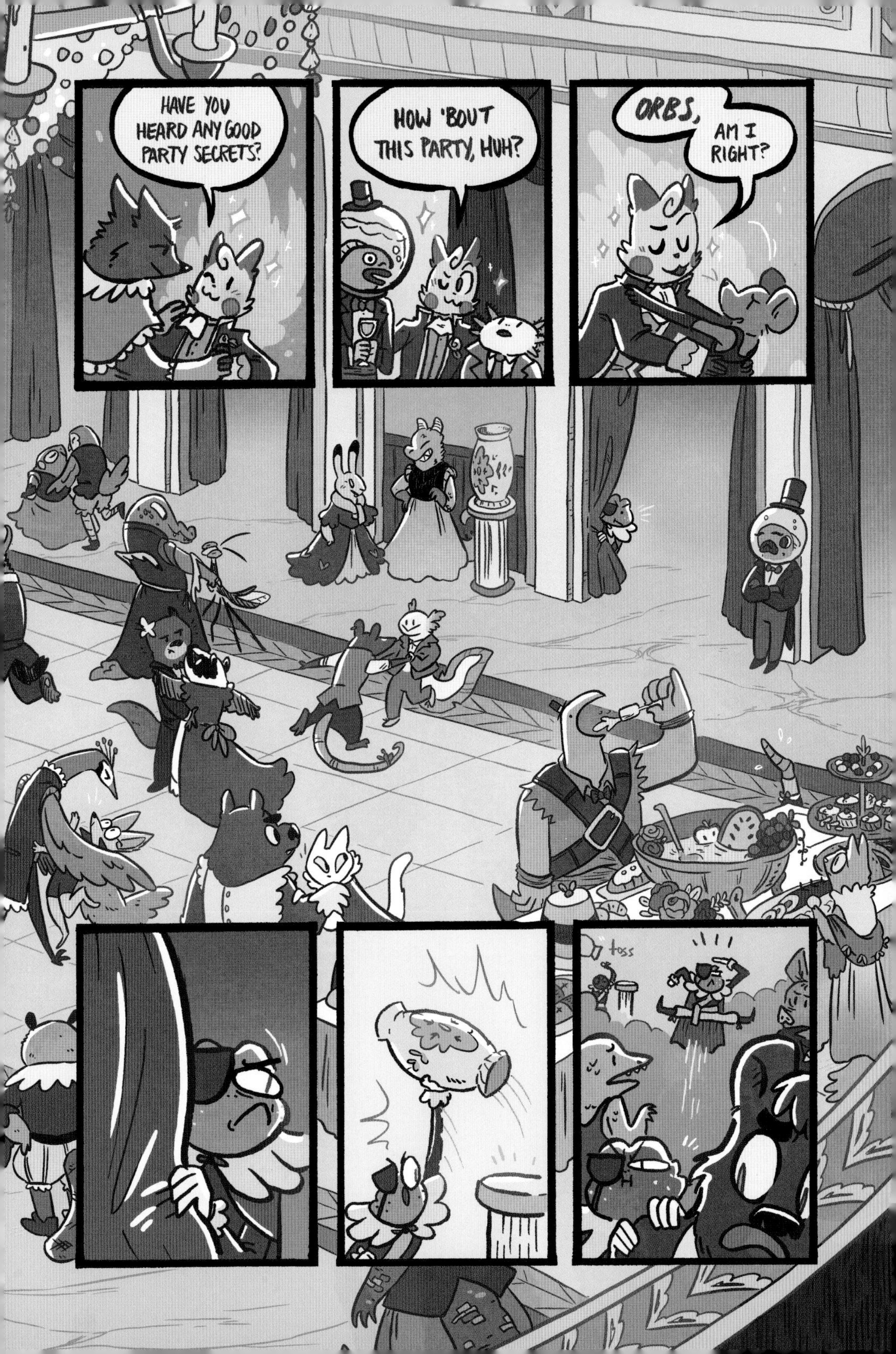
HAVE YOU HEARD ANY GOOD PARTY SECRETS?
HOW 'BOUT THIS PARTY, HUH?
ORBS,
AM I RIGHT?
toss

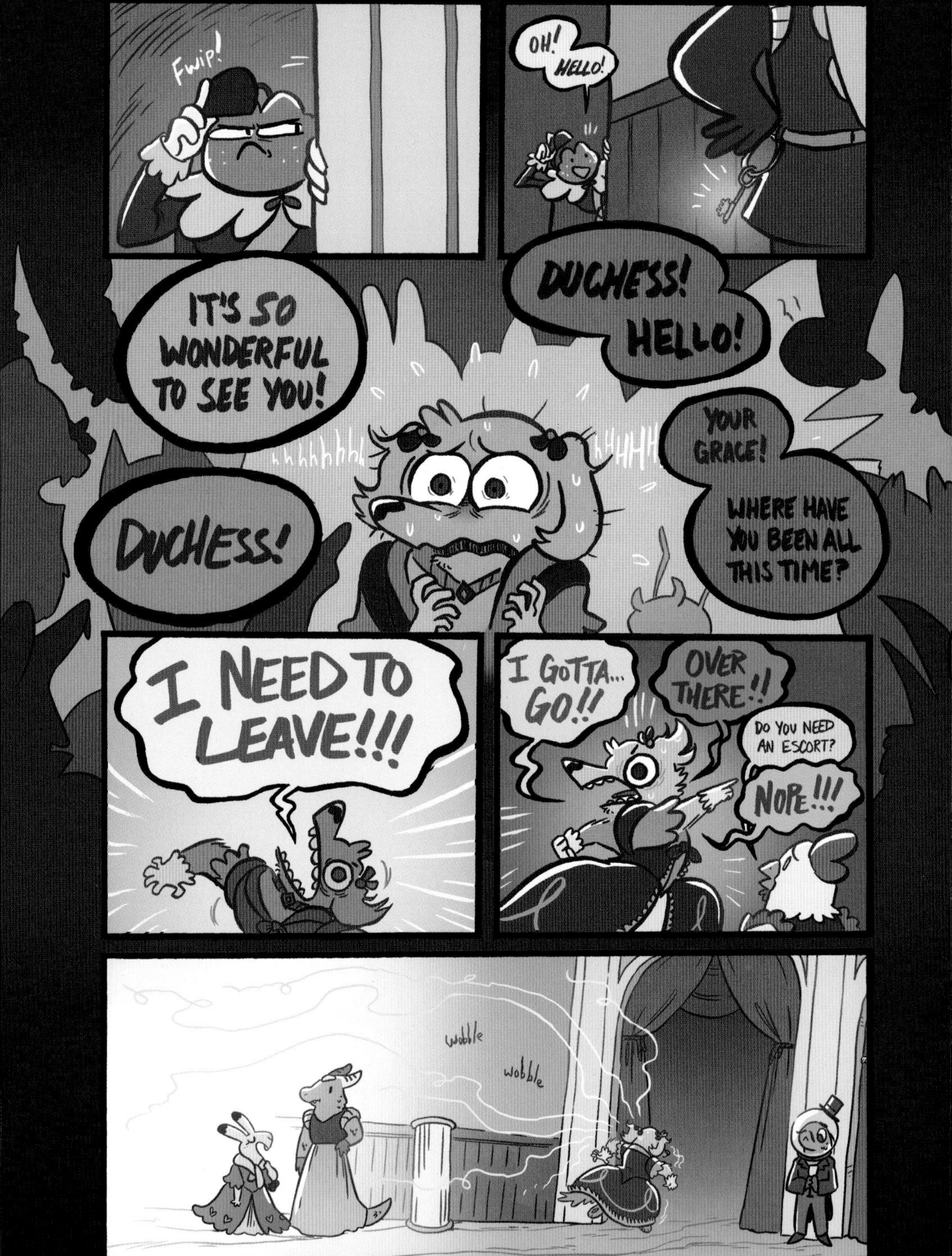

Fwip!
OH! HELLO!
IT'S SO WONDERFUL TO SEE YOU!
DUCHESS! HELLO!
hhhhhhhh
hHHHH
DUCHESS!
YOUR GRACE!
WHERE HAVE YOU BEEN ALL THIS TIME?
I NEED TO LEAVE!!!
I GOTTA... GO!!
OVER THERE!!
DO YOU NEED AN ESCORT?
NOPE!!!
wobble
wobble

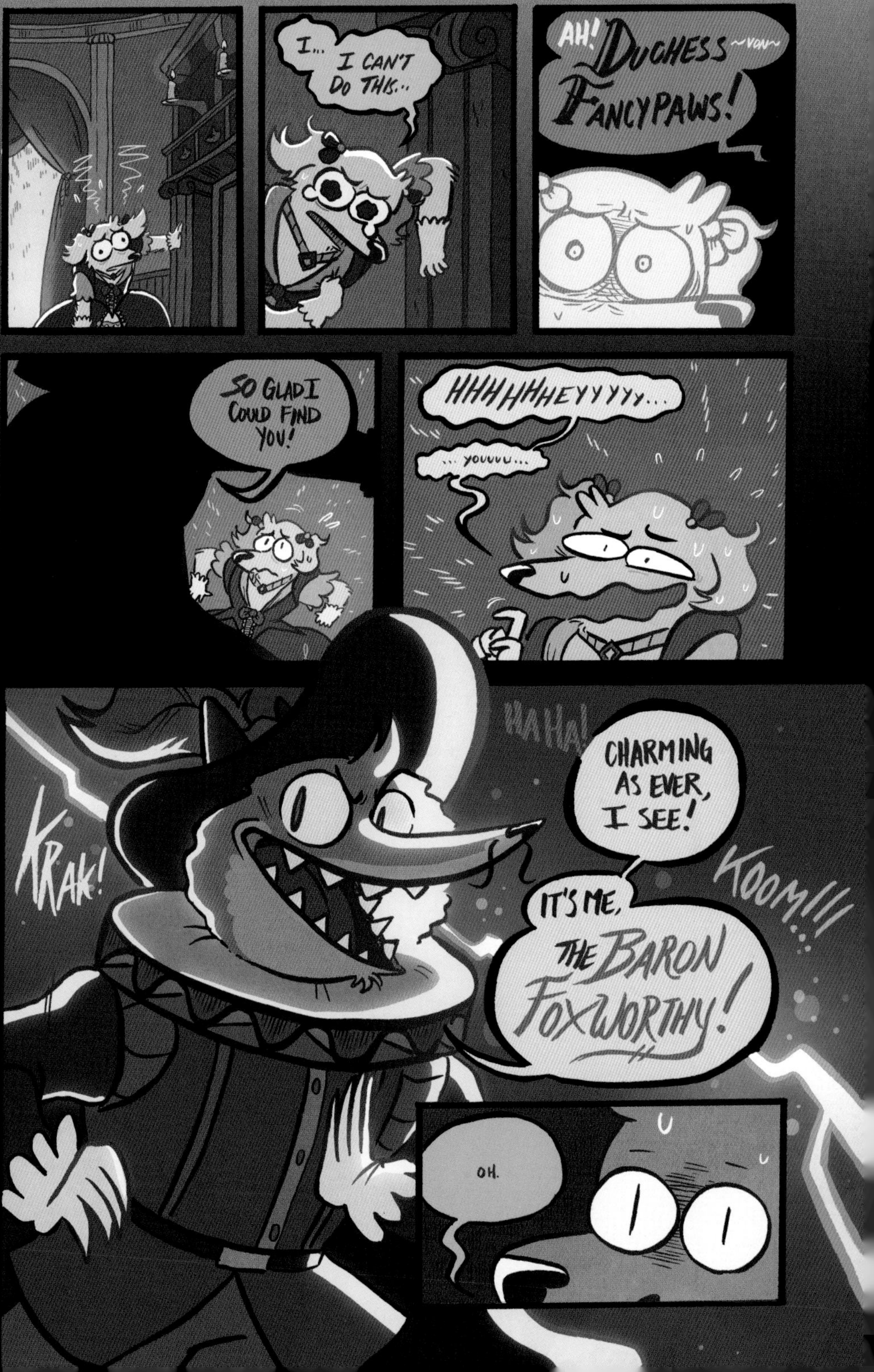
I... I CAN'T DO THIS...
AH! DUCHESS ~VON~ FANCYPAWS!
SO GLAD I COULD FIND YOU!
HHHHHHEYYYYY...
...YOUUUU...
HAHA!
KRAK!
CHARMING AS EVER, I SEE!
IT'S ME, THE BARON FOXWORTHY!
KOOM!!!
OH.

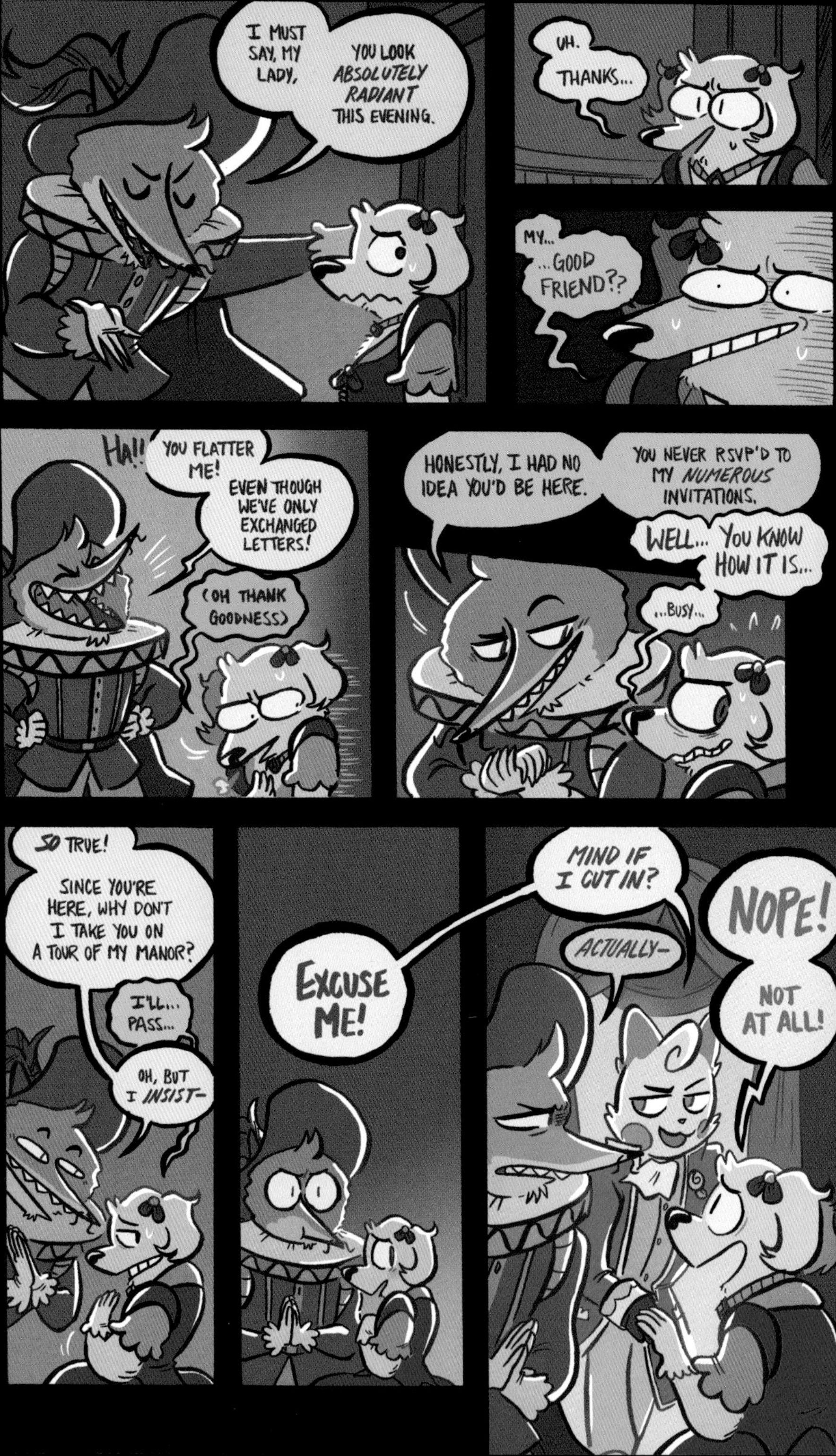
I MUST SAY, MY LADY,
YOU LOOK ABSOLUTELY RADIANT THIS EVENING.
UH.
THANKS...
MY...
...GOOD FRIEND??
HA!!
YOU FLATTER ME!
EVEN THOUGH WE'VE ONLY EXCHANGED LETTERS!
(OH THANK GOODNESS)
HONESTLY, I HAD NO IDEA YOU'D BE HERE.
YOU NEVER RSVP'D TO MY NUMEROUS INVITATIONS.
WELL... YOU KNOW HOW IT IS...
...BUSY...
SO TRUE!
SINCE YOU'RE HERE, WHY DON'T I TAKE YOU ON A TOUR OF MY MANOR?
I'LL... PASS...
OH, BUT I INSIST—
EXCUSE ME!
MIND IF I CUT IN?
ACTUALLY—
NOPE!
NOT AT ALL!

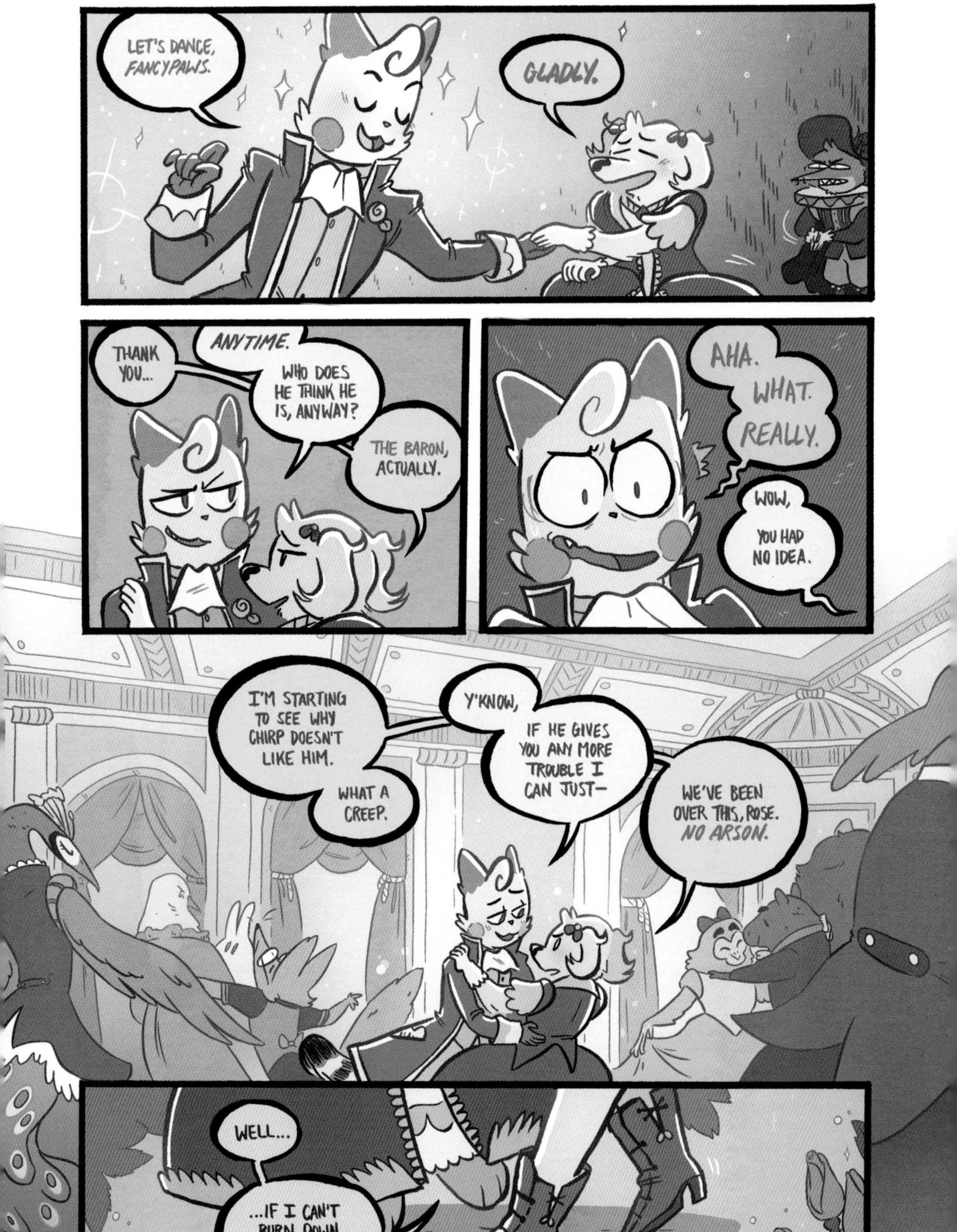
LET'S DANCE, FANCYPAWS.
GLADLY.
THANK YOU...
ANYTIME.
WHO DOES HE THINK HE IS, ANYWAY?
THE BARON, ACTUALLY.
AHA.
WHAT.
REALLY.
WOW,
YOU HAD NO IDEA.
I'M STARTING TO SEE WHY CHIRP DOESN'T LIKE HIM.
WHAT A CREEP.
Y'KNOW,
IF HE GIVES YOU ANY MORE TROUBLE I CAN JUST—
WE'VE BEEN OVER THIS, ROSE. NO ARSON.
WELL...
...IF I CAN'T BURN DOWN THE MANOR...

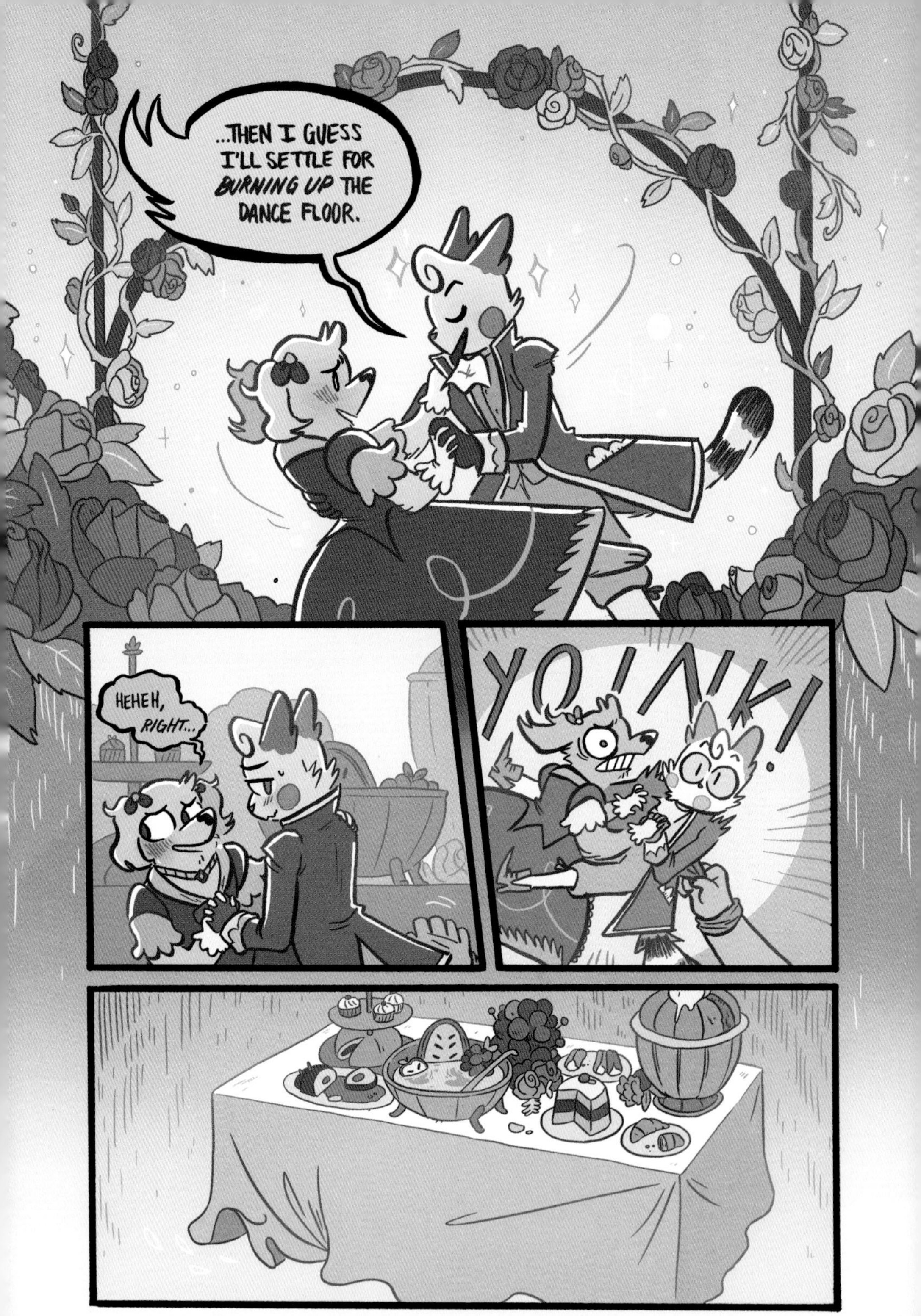
...THEN I GUESS I'LL SETTLE FOR *BURNING UP* THE DANCE FLOOR.
HEHEH, *RIGHT...*
YOINK!

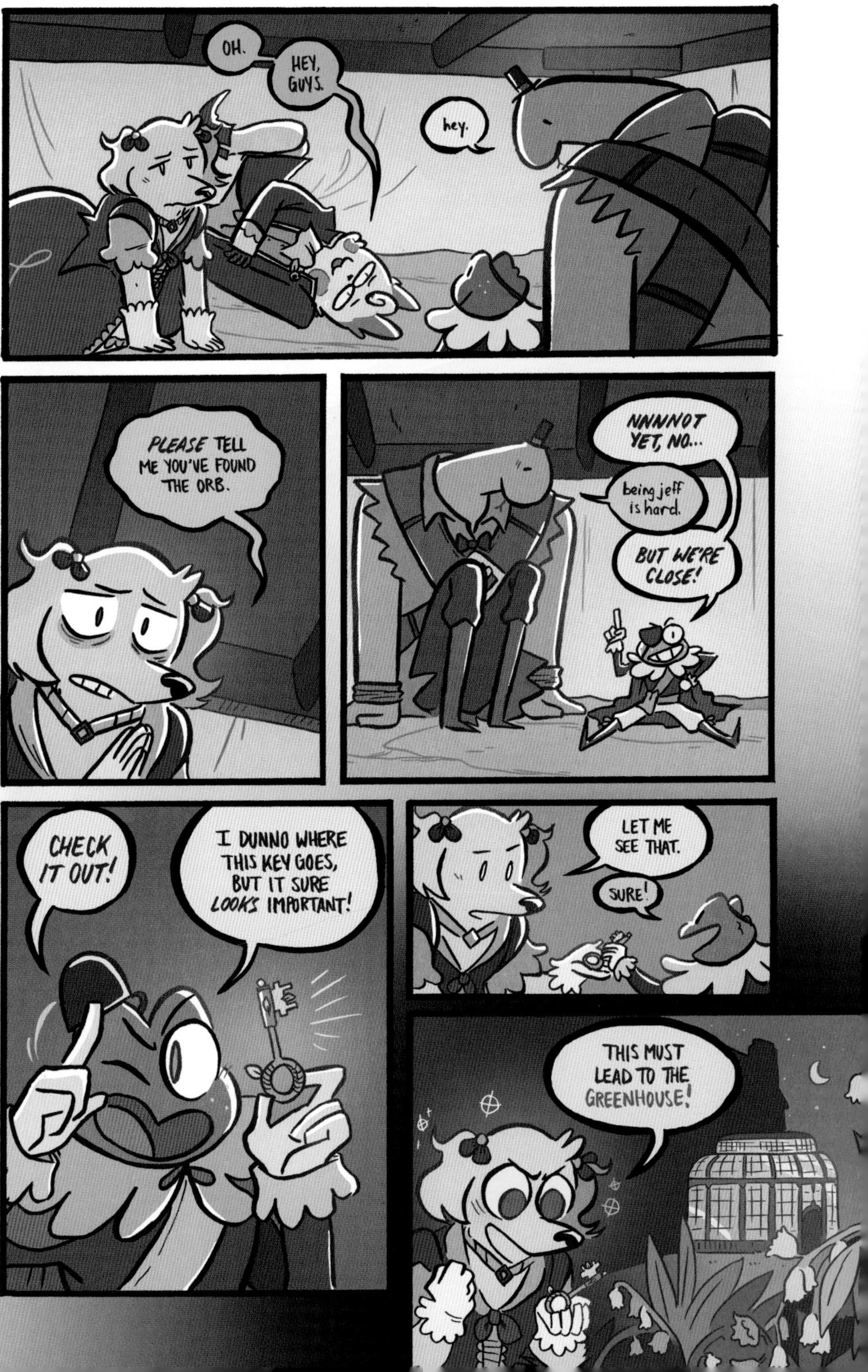
OH.
HEY, GUYS.
hey.
PLEASE TELL ME YOU'VE FOUND THE ORB.
NNNNOT YET, NO...
being jeff is hard.
BUT WE'RE CLOSE!
CHECK IT OUT!
I DUNNO WHERE THIS KEY GOES, BUT IT SURE LOOKS IMPORTANT!
LET ME SEE THAT.
SURE!
THIS MUST LEAD TO THE GREENHOUSE!

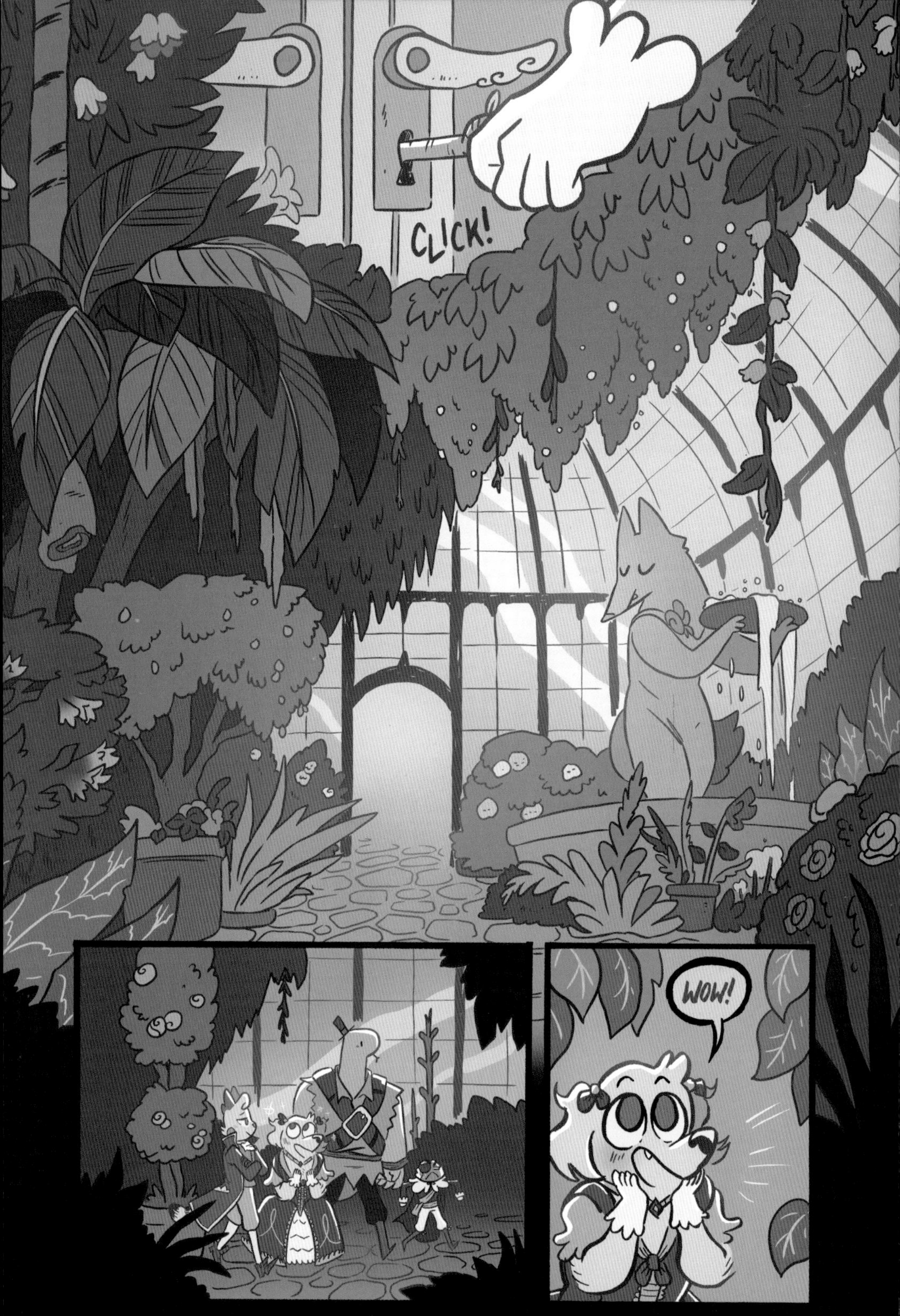
CLICK!
WOW!

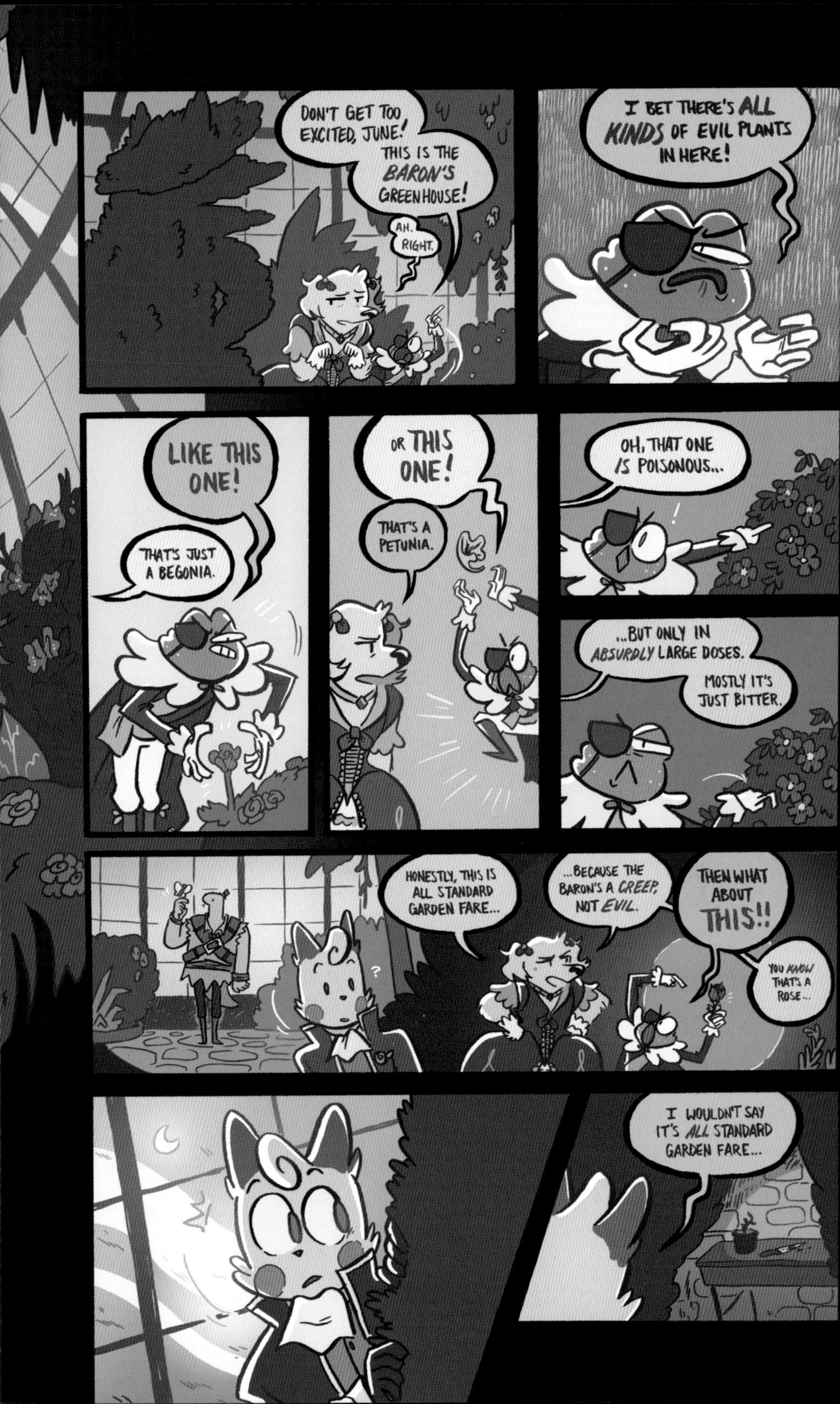

DON'T GET TOO EXCITED, JUNE!
THIS IS THE BARON'S GREENHOUSE!
AH. RIGHT.
I BET THERE'S ALL KINDS OF EVIL PLANTS IN HERE!
LIKE THIS ONE!
THAT'S JUST A BEGONIA.
OR THIS ONE!
THAT'S A PETUNIA.
OH, THAT ONE IS POISONOUS...
...BUT ONLY IN ABSURDLY LARGE DOSES.
MOSTLY IT'S JUST BITTER.
HONESTLY, THIS IS ALL STANDARD GARDEN FARE...
...BECAUSE THE BARON'S A CREEP, NOT EVIL.
THEN WHAT ABOUT THIS!!
YOU KNOW THAT'S A ROSE...
I WOULDN'T SAY IT'S ALL STANDARD GARDEN FARE...

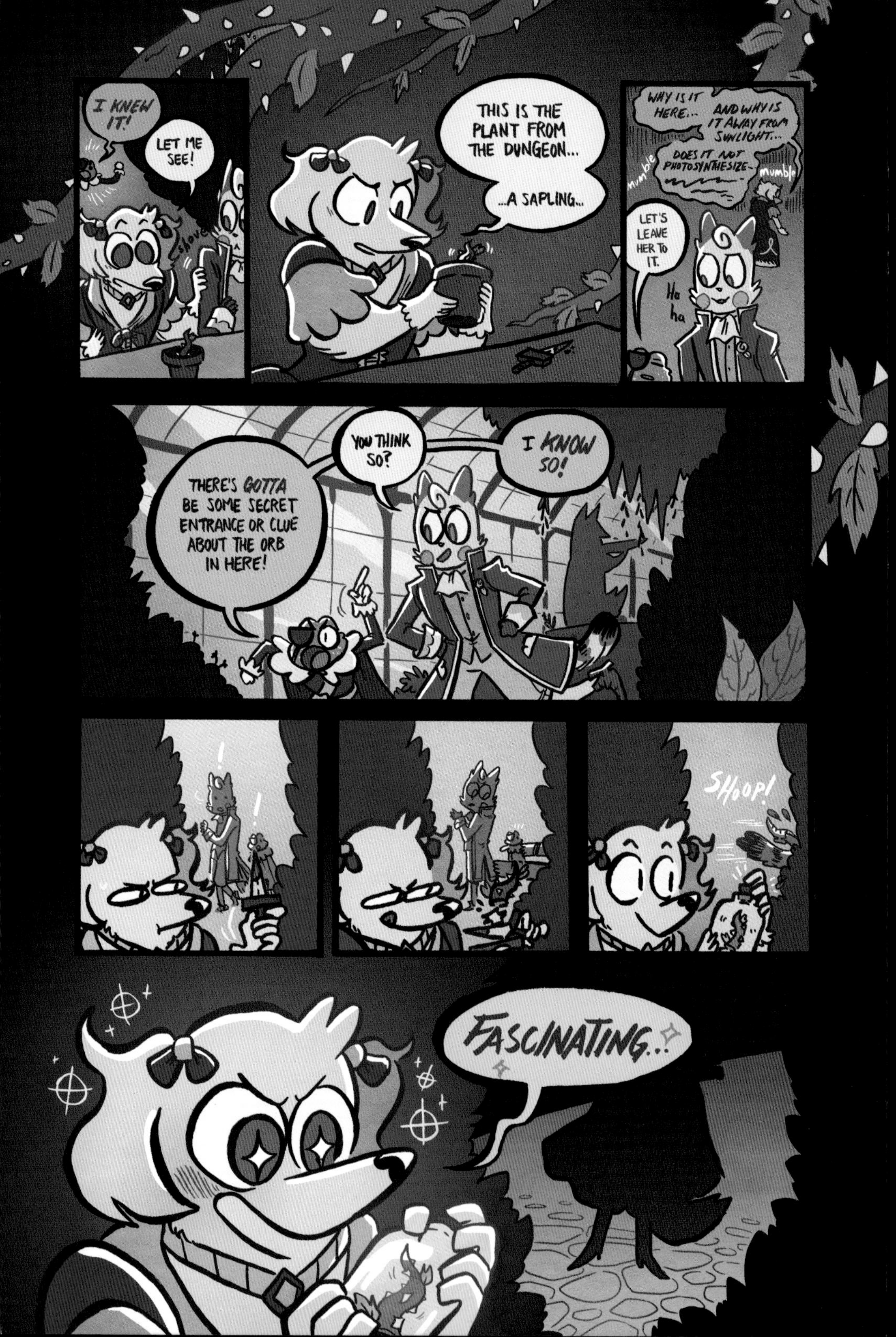
I KNEW IT!
LET ME SEE!
shove
THIS IS THE PLANT FROM THE DUNGEON...
...A SAPLING...
WHY IS IT HERE...
AND WHY IS IT AWAY FROM SUNLIGHT...
DOES IT NOT PHOTOSYNTHESIZE
mumble
mumble
LET'S LEAVE HER TO IT.
Ha ha
THERE'S GOTTA BE SOME SECRET ENTRANCE OR CLUE ABOUT THE ORB IN HERE!
YOU THINK SO?
I KNOW SO!
SHOOP!
FASCINATING..

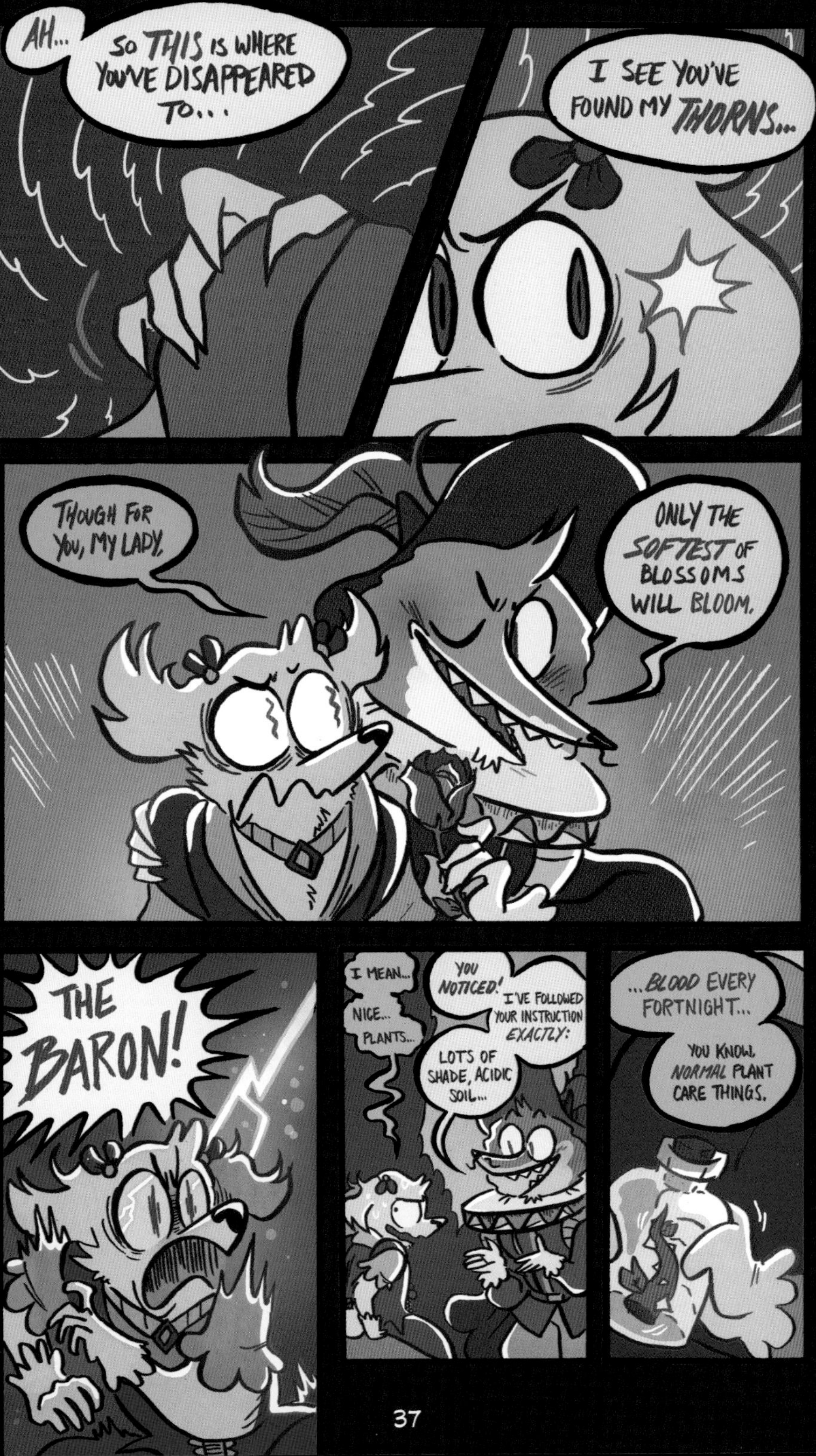
AH...
SO THIS IS WHERE YOU'VE DISAPPEARED TO...
I SEE YOU'VE FOUND MY THORNS...
THOUGH FOR YOU, MY LADY,
ONLY THE SOFTEST OF BLOSSOMS WILL BLOOM.
THE BARON!
I MEAN...
NICE...
PLANTS...
YOU NOTICED!
I'VE FOLLOWED YOUR INSTRUCTION EXACTLY:
LOTS OF SHADE, ACIDIC SOIL...
...BLOOD EVERY FORTNIGHT...
YOU KNOW, NORMAL PLANT CARE THINGS.

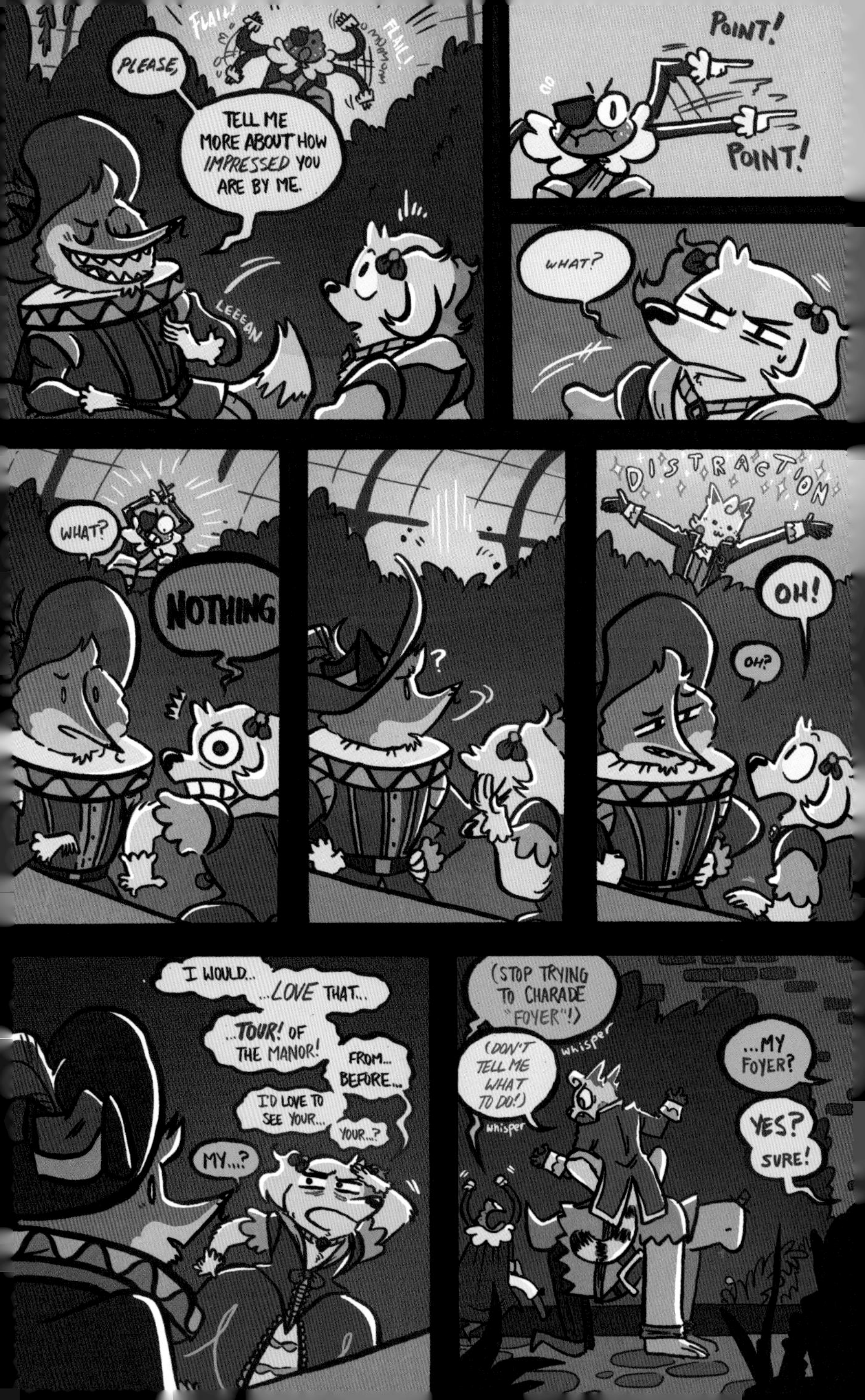
FLAIL!
FLAIL!
MMMPH
PLEASE,
TELL ME MORE ABOUT HOW IMPRESSED YOU ARE BY ME.
LEEEAN
POINT!
POINT!
WHAT?
WHAT?
NOTHING
?
DISTRACTION
OH!
OH?
I WOULD...
...LOVE THAT...
...TOUR! OF THE MANOR!
FROM... BEFORE...
I'D LOVE TO SEE YOUR...
YOUR...?
MY...?
(STOP TRYING TO CHARADE "FOYER"!)
whisper
(DON'T TELL ME WHAT TO DO!)
whisper
...MY FOYER?
YES?
SURE!

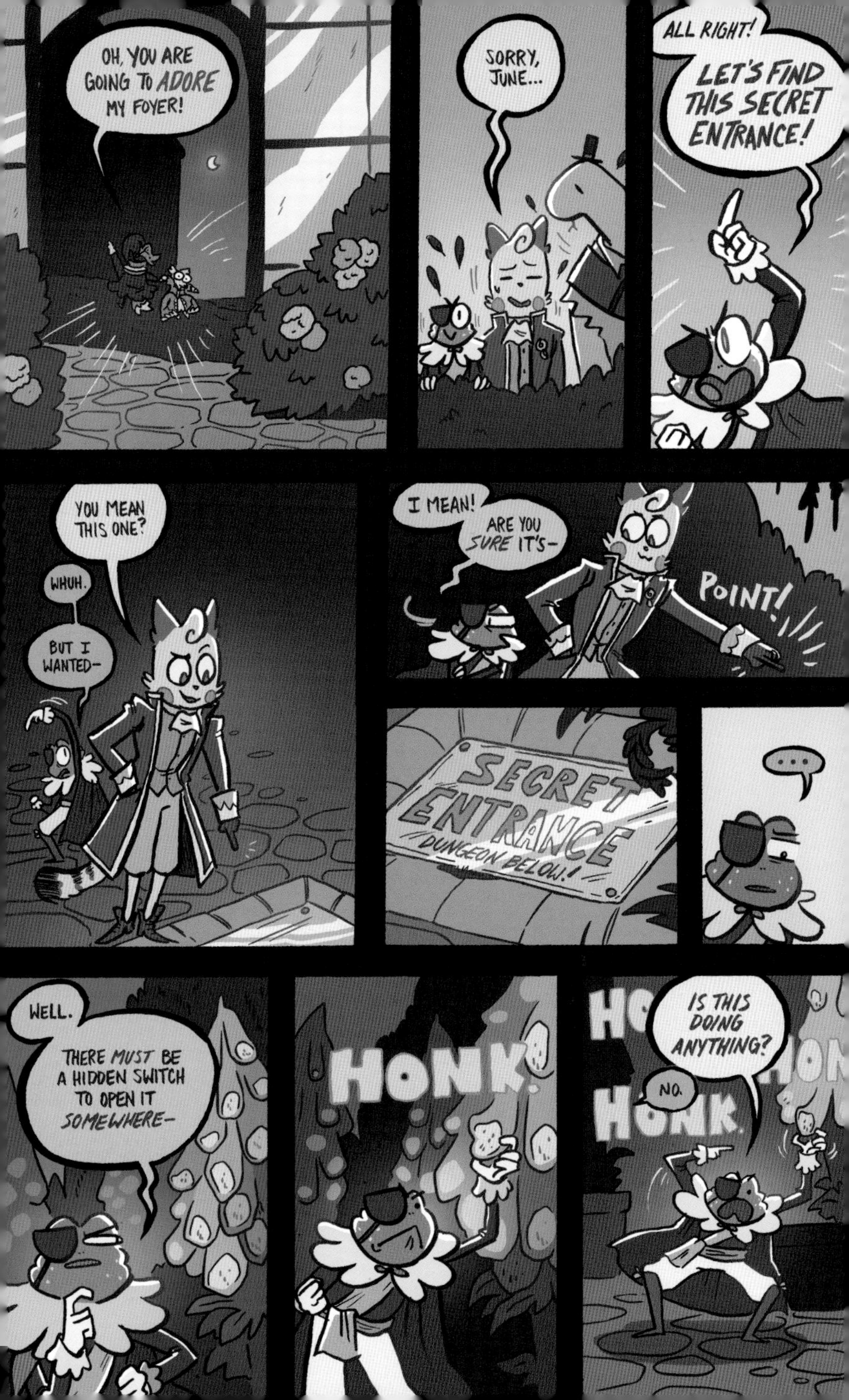
OH, YOU ARE GOING TO ADORE MY FOYER!
SORRY, JUNE...
ALL RIGHT!
LET'S FIND THIS SECRET ENTRANCE!
YOU MEAN THIS ONE?
WHUH.
BUT I WANTED-
I MEAN!
ARE YOU SURE IT'S-
POINT!
SECRET ENTRANCE
DUNGEON BELOW!
...
WELL.
THERE MUST BE A HIDDEN SWITCH TO OPEN IT SOMEWHERE-
HONK.
IS THIS DOING ANYTHING?
NO.
HONK.

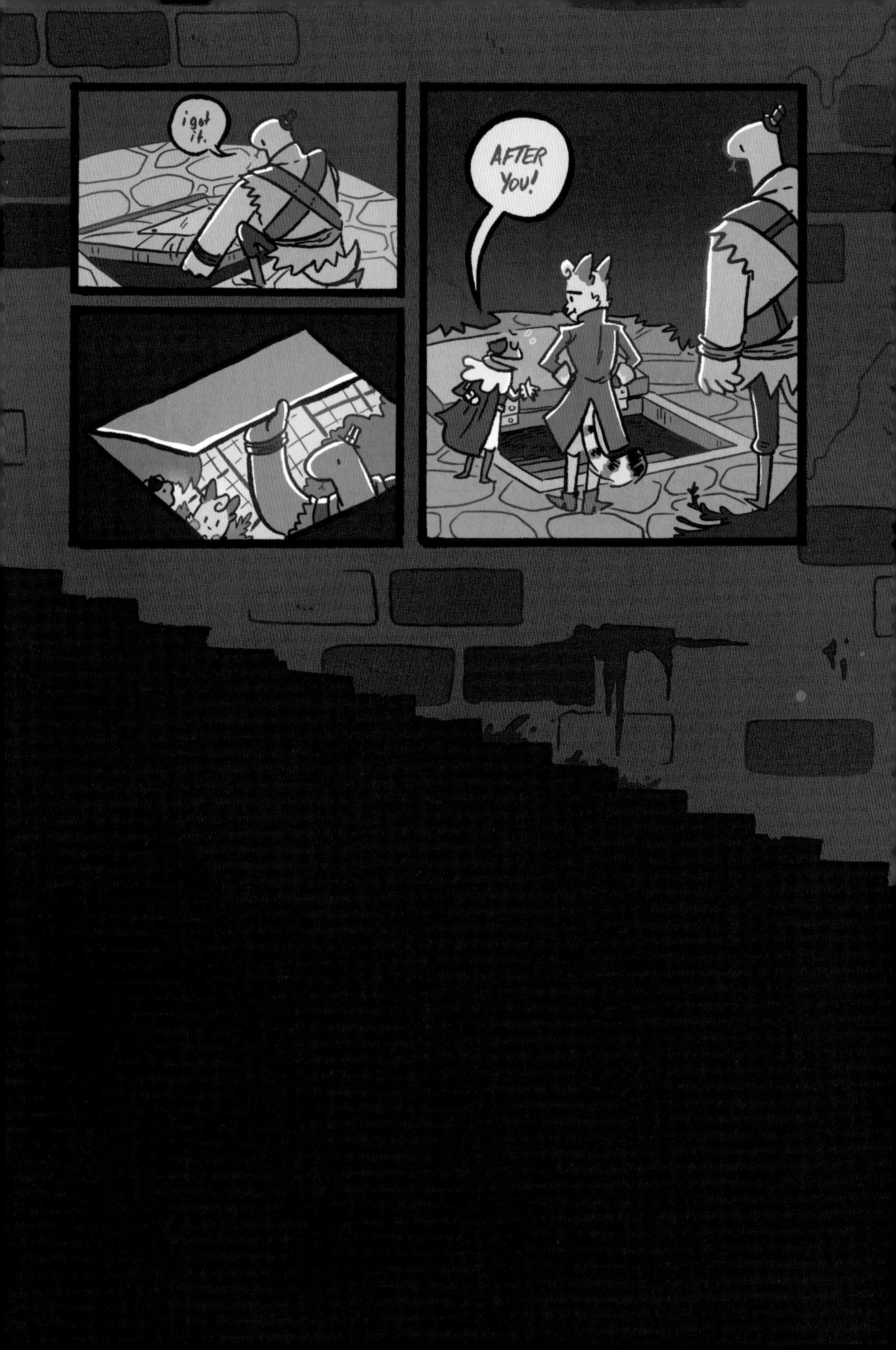
i got it.
AFTER YOU!

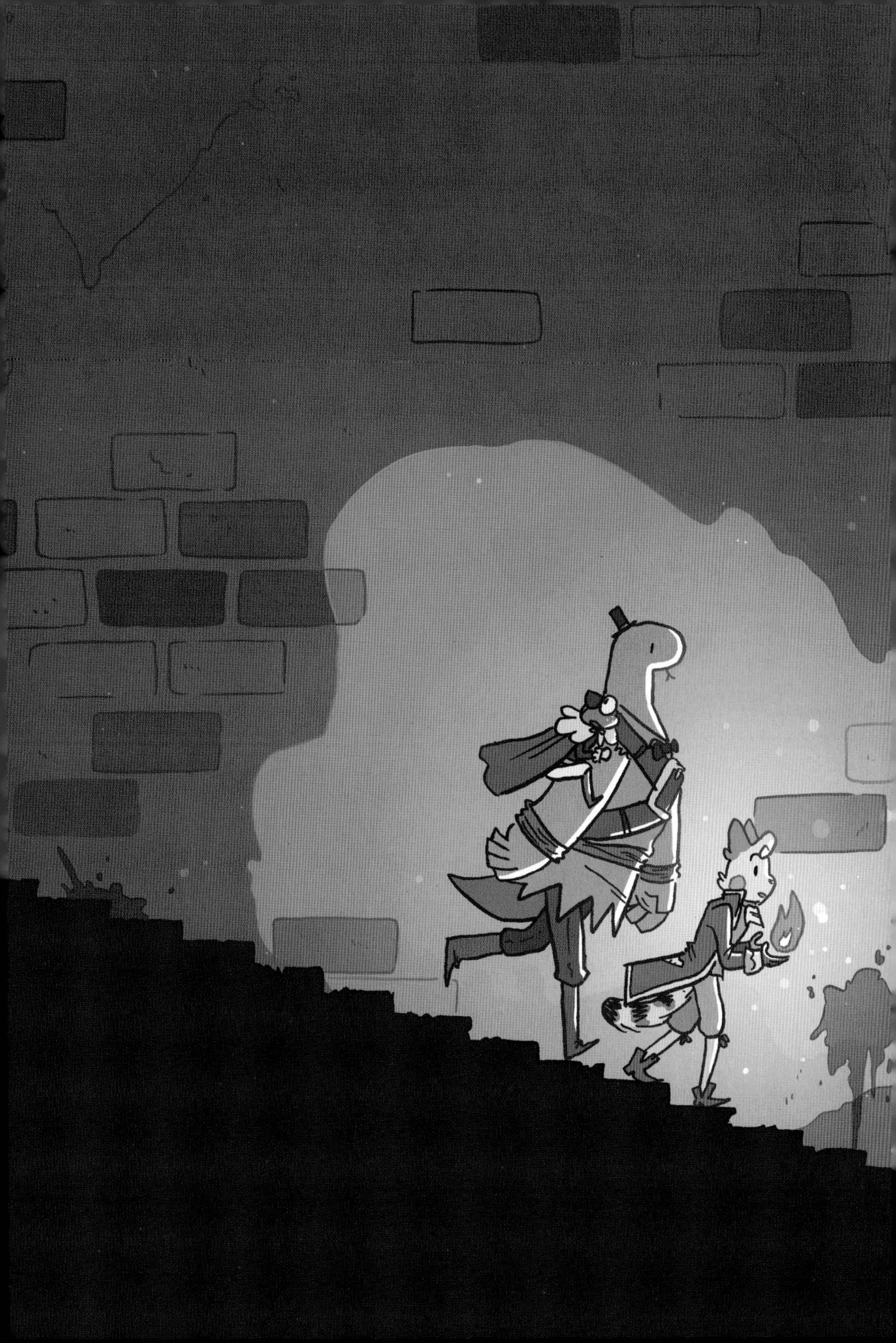

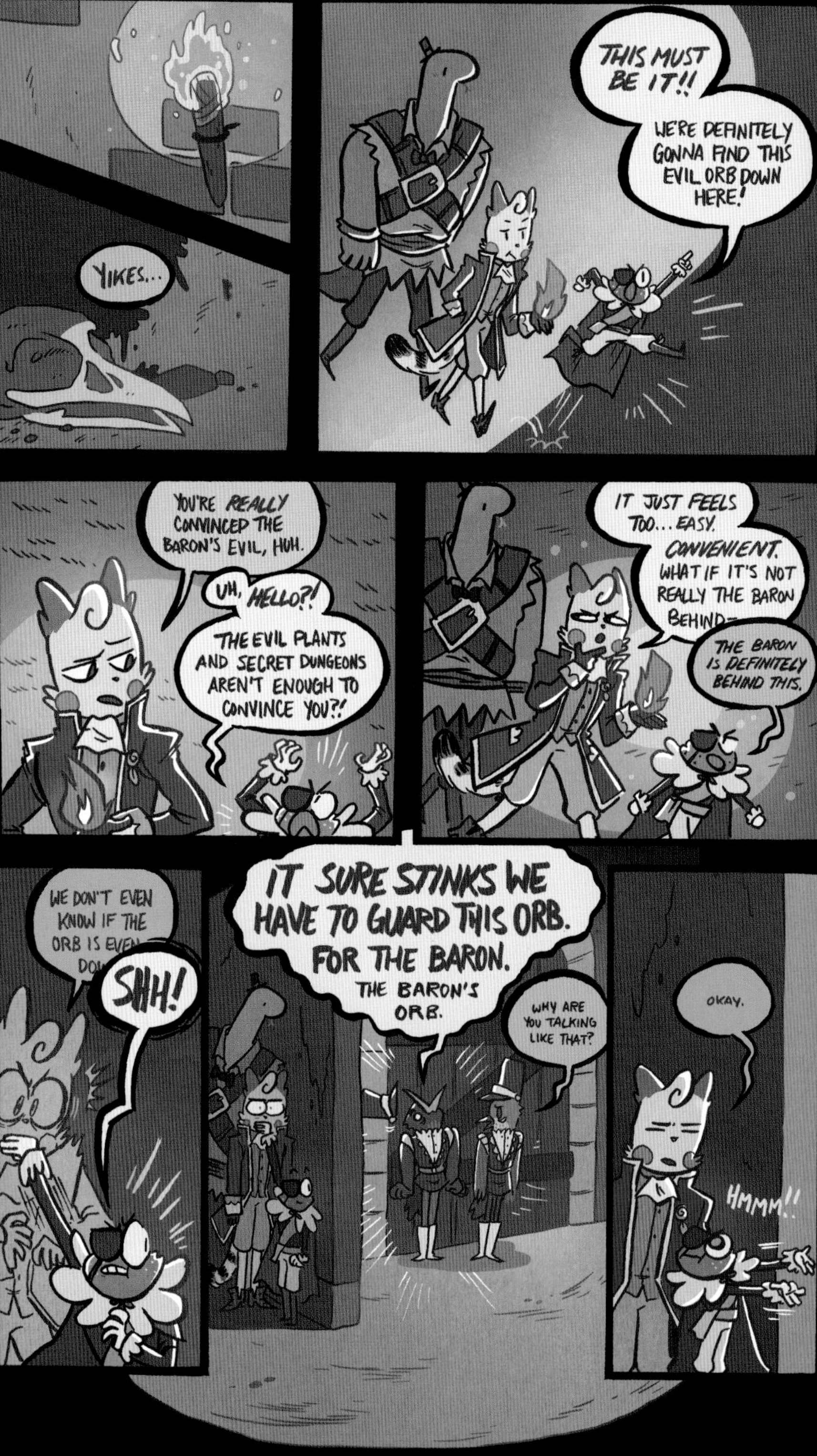
YIKES...
THIS MUST BE IT!!
WE'RE DEFINITELY GONNA FIND THIS EVIL ORB DOWN HERE!
YOU'RE REALLY CONVINCED THE BARON'S EVIL, HUH.
UH, HELLO?!
THE EVIL PLANTS AND SECRET DUNGEONS AREN'T ENOUGH TO CONVINCE YOU?!
IT JUST FEELS TOO... EASY.
CONVENIENT.
WHAT IF IT'S NOT REALLY THE BARON BEHIND—
THE BARON IS DEFINITELY BEHIND THIS.
WE DON'T EVEN KNOW IF THE ORB IS EVEN
SHH!
IT SURE STINKS WE HAVE TO GUARD THIS ORB.
FOR THE BARON.
THE BARON'S ORB.
WHY ARE YOU TALKING LIKE THAT?
OKAY.
HMMM!!

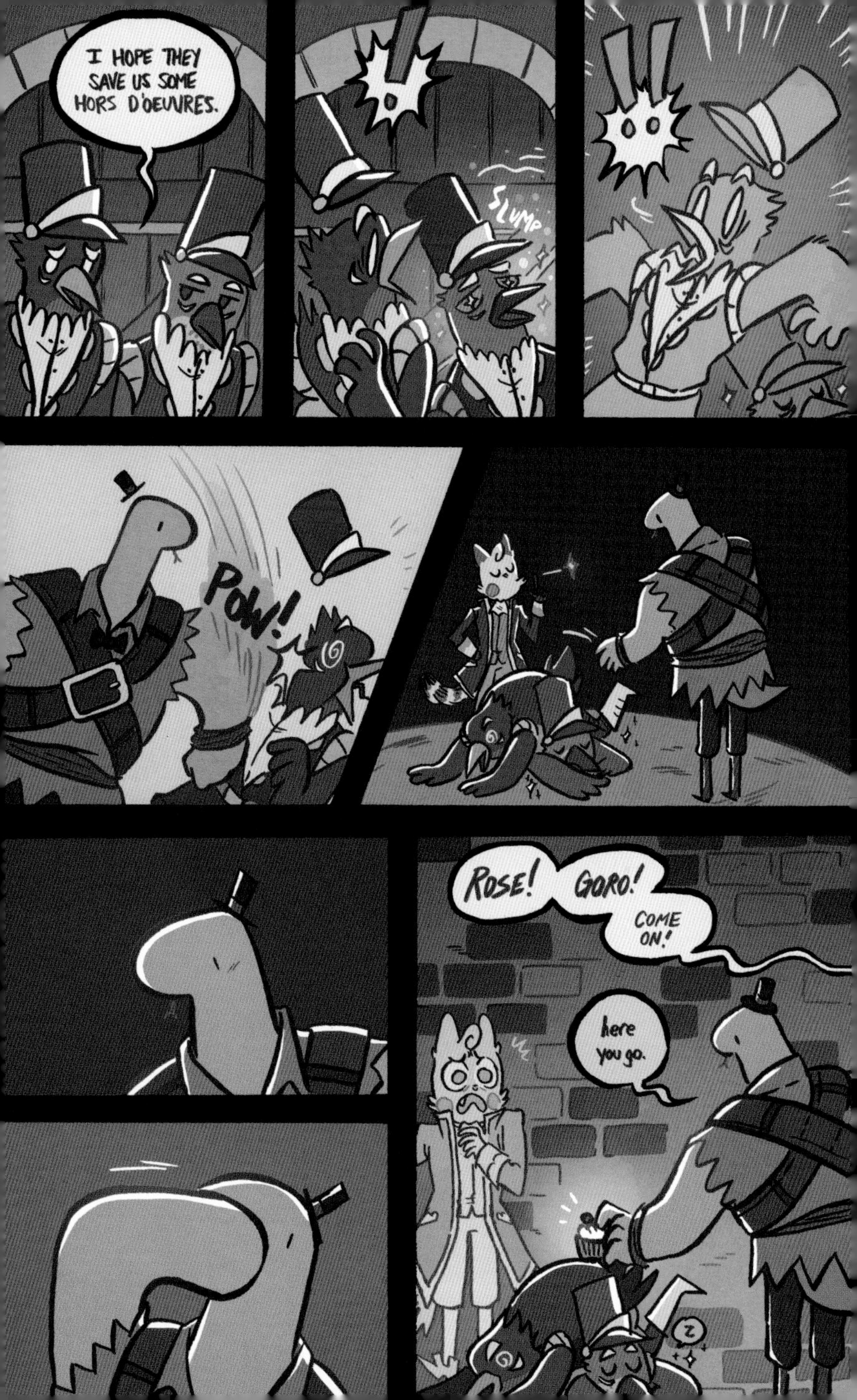
I HOPE THEY SAVE US SOME HORS D'OEUVRES.
SLUMP
POW!
ROSE!
GORO!
COME ON!
here you go.
Z

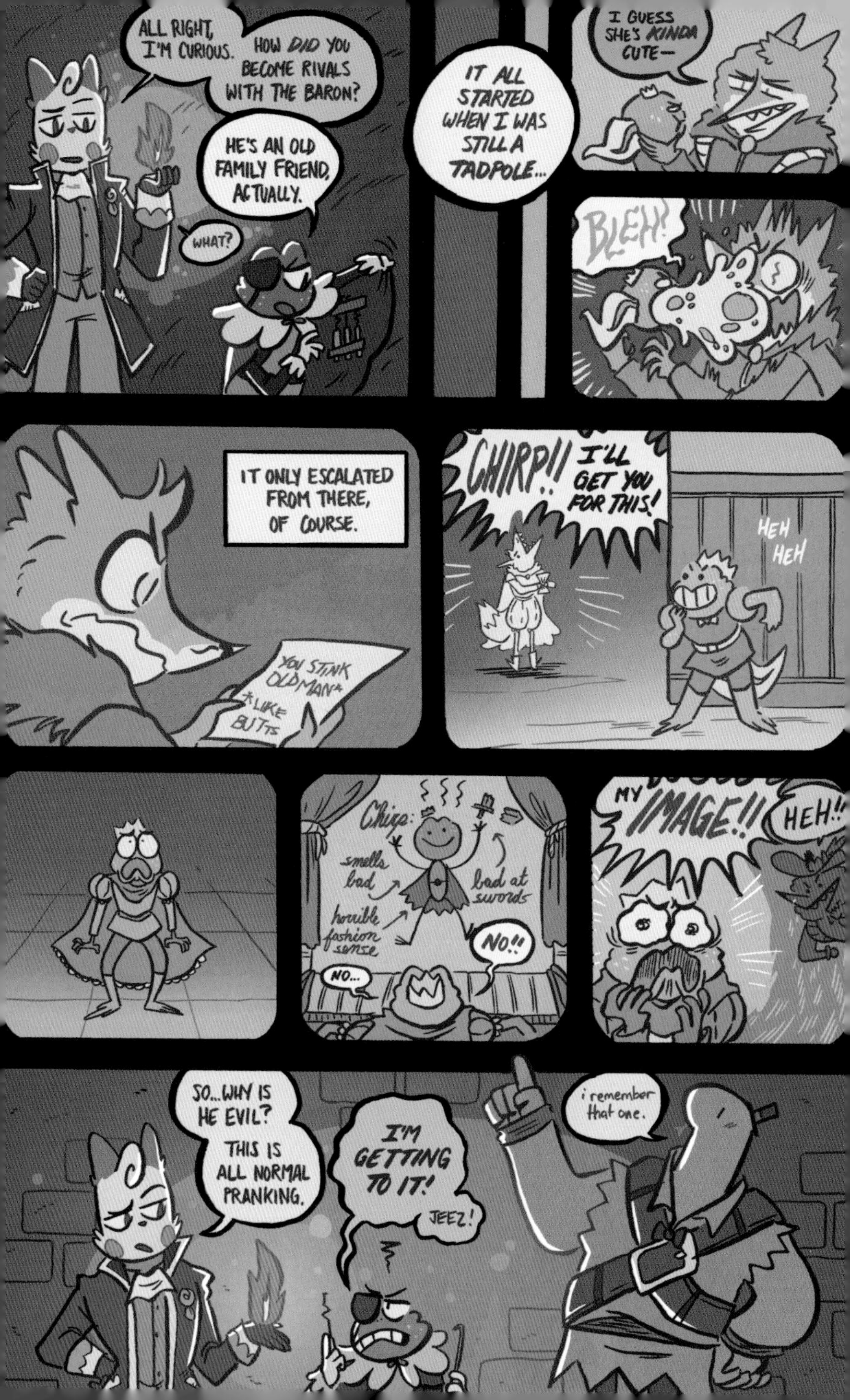
ALL RIGHT, I'M CURIOUS. HOW DID YOU BECOME RIVALS WITH THE BARON?
HE'S AN OLD FAMILY FRIEND, ACTUALLY.
WHAT?
IT ALL STARTED WHEN I WAS STILL A TADPOLE...
I GUESS SHE'S KINDA CUTE—
BLEH?
IT ONLY ESCALATED FROM THERE, OF COURSE.
YOU STINK OLD MAN*
*LIKE BUTTS
CHIRP!!
I'LL GET YOU FOR THIS!
HEH HEH
Chirp:
smells bad
horrible fashion sense
bad at swords
NO!!
NO...
MY IMAGE!!
HEH!!
SO...WHY IS HE EVIL?
THIS IS ALL NORMAL PRANKING.
I'M GETTING TO IT!
JEEZ!
i remember that one.

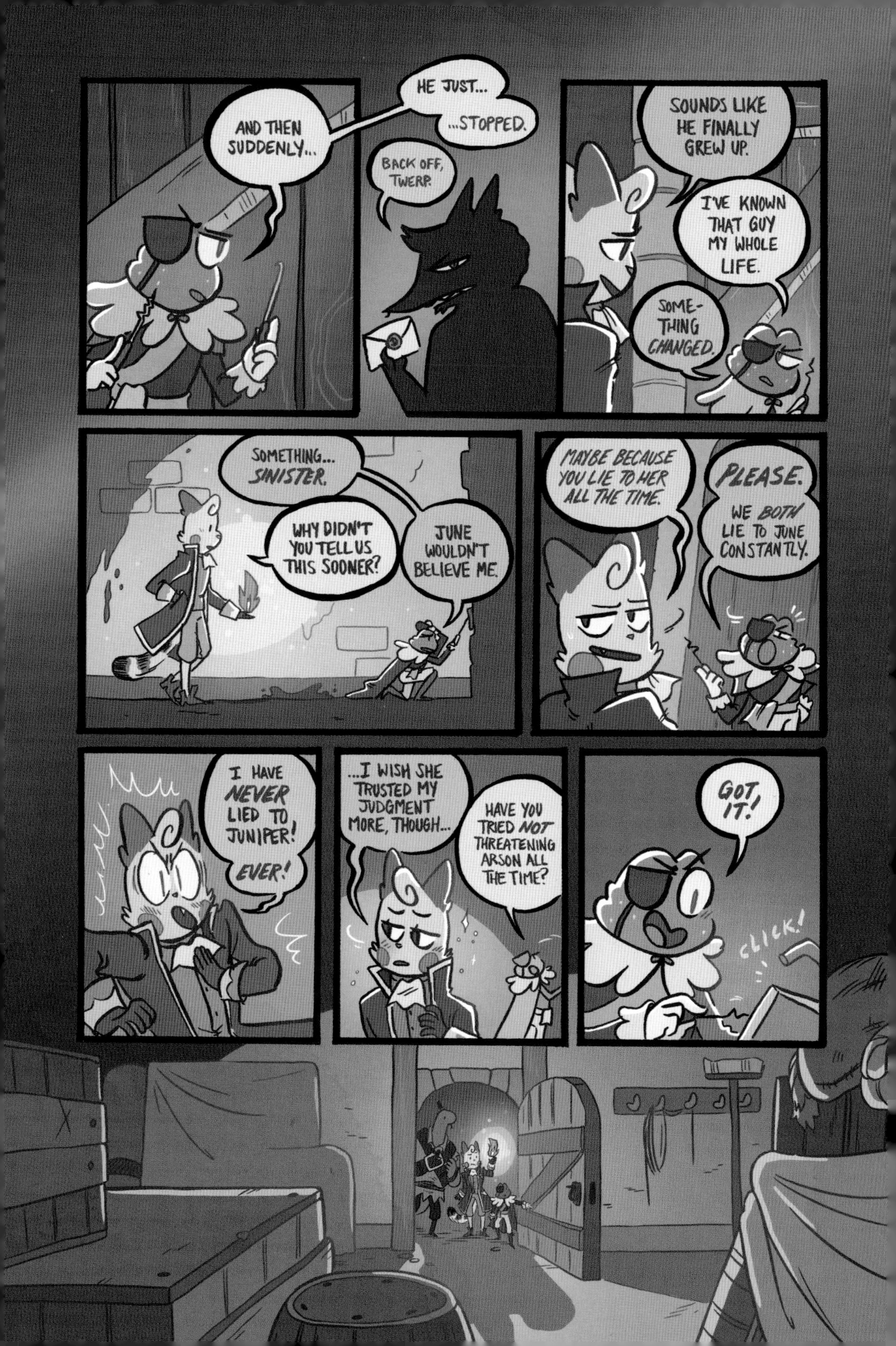
AND THEN SUDDENLY...
HE JUST...
...STOPPED.
BACK OFF, TWERP.
SOUNDS LIKE HE FINALLY GREW UP.
I'VE KNOWN THAT GUY MY WHOLE LIFE.
SOME-THING CHANGED.
SOMETHING... SINISTER.
WHY DIDN'T YOU TELL US THIS SOONER?
JUNE WOULDN'T BELIEVE ME.
MAYBE BECAUSE YOU LIE TO HER ALL THE TIME.
PLEASE.
WE BOTH LIE TO JUNE CONSTANTLY.
I HAVE NEVER LIED TO JUNIPER! EVER!
...I WISH SHE TRUSTED MY JUDGMENT MORE, THOUGH...
HAVE YOU TRIED NOT THREATENING ARSON ALL THE TIME?
GOT IT!
CLICK!

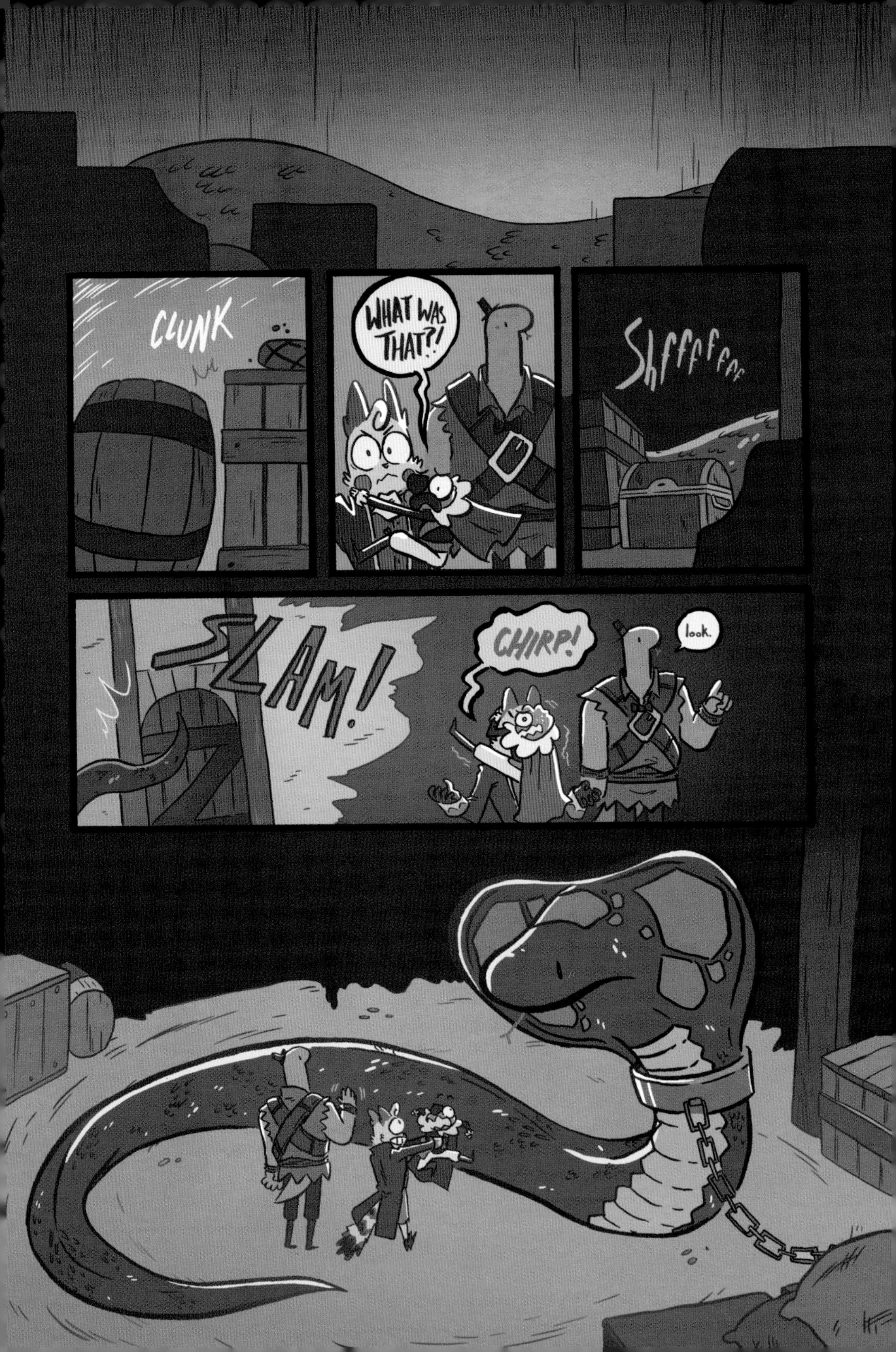
CLUNK
WHAT WAS THAT?!
Shffffff
SLAM!
CHIRP!
look.

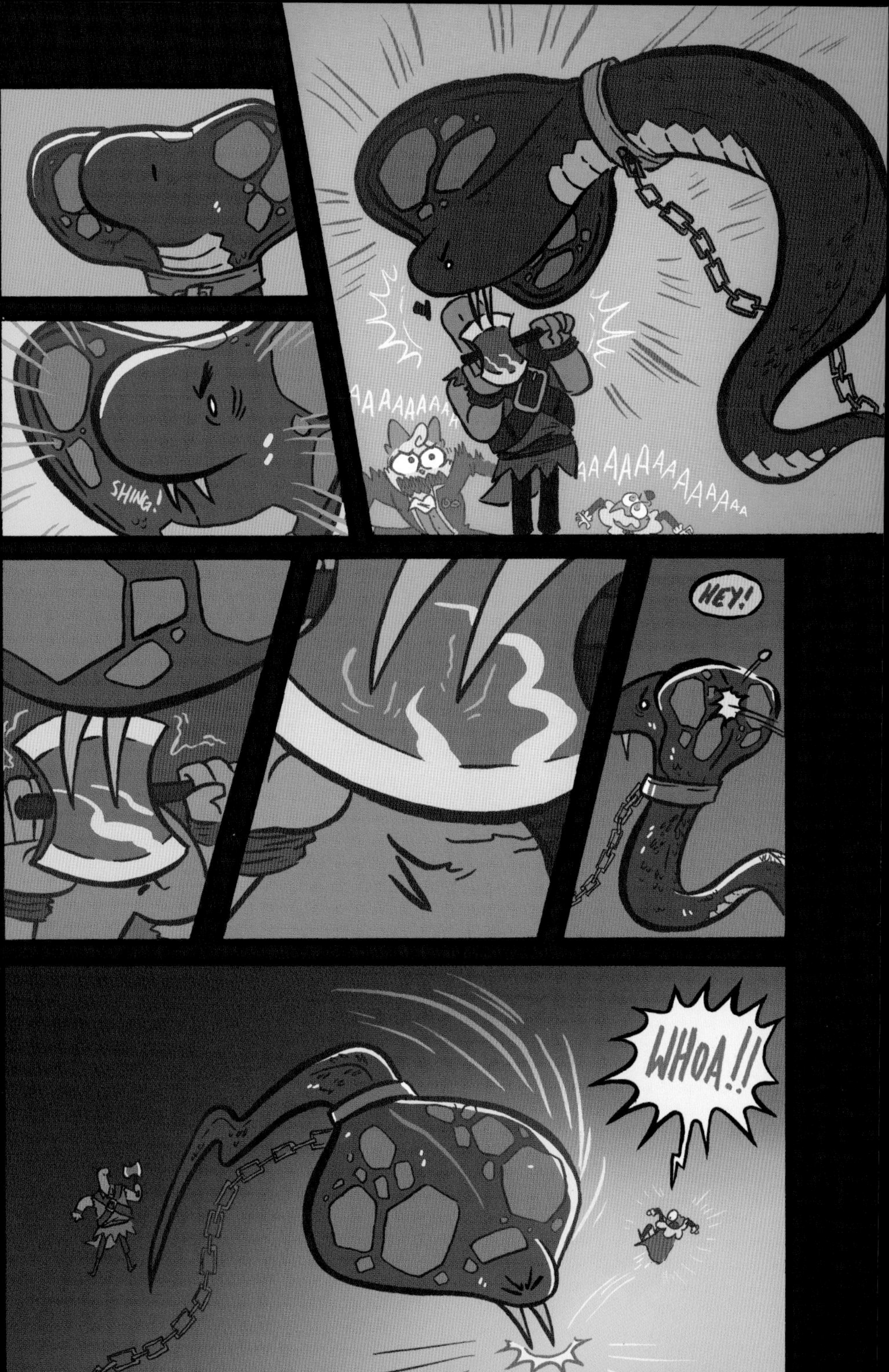
AAAAAAAAA
AAAAAAAAAAAAAAA
SHING!
HEY!
WHOA!!

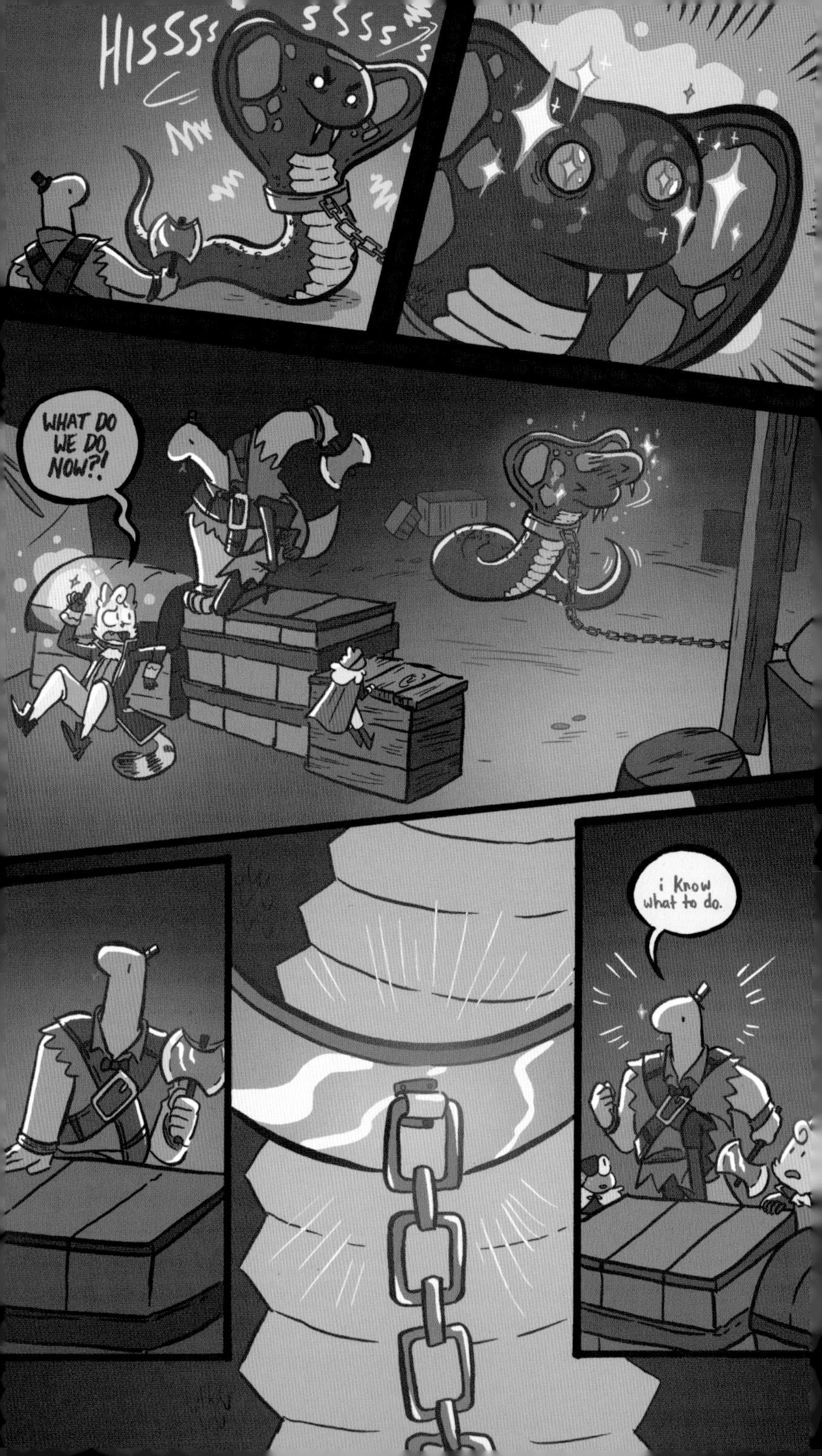
HISSSS SSSSS
WHAT DO WE DO NOW?!
i Know what to do.

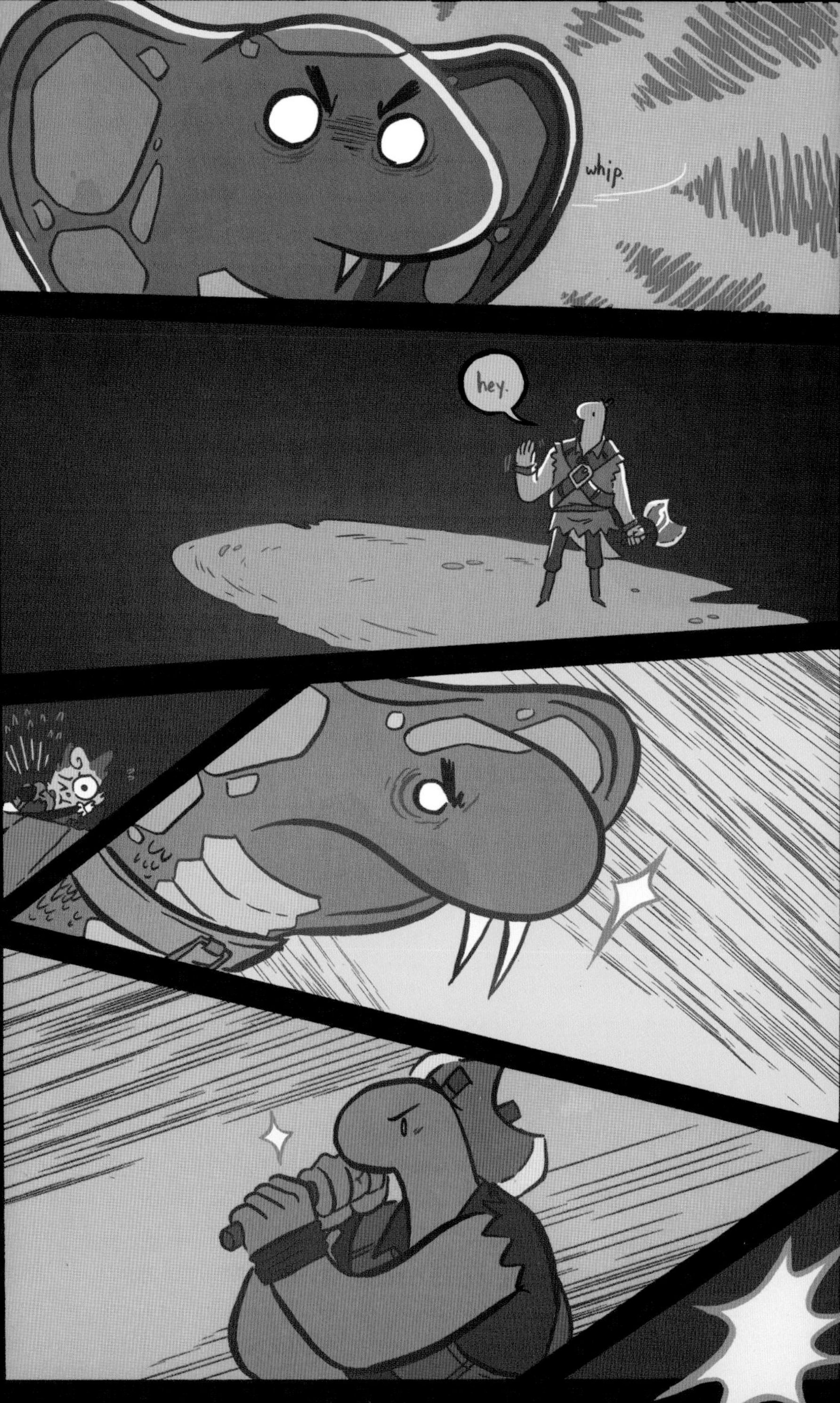
whip.
hey.

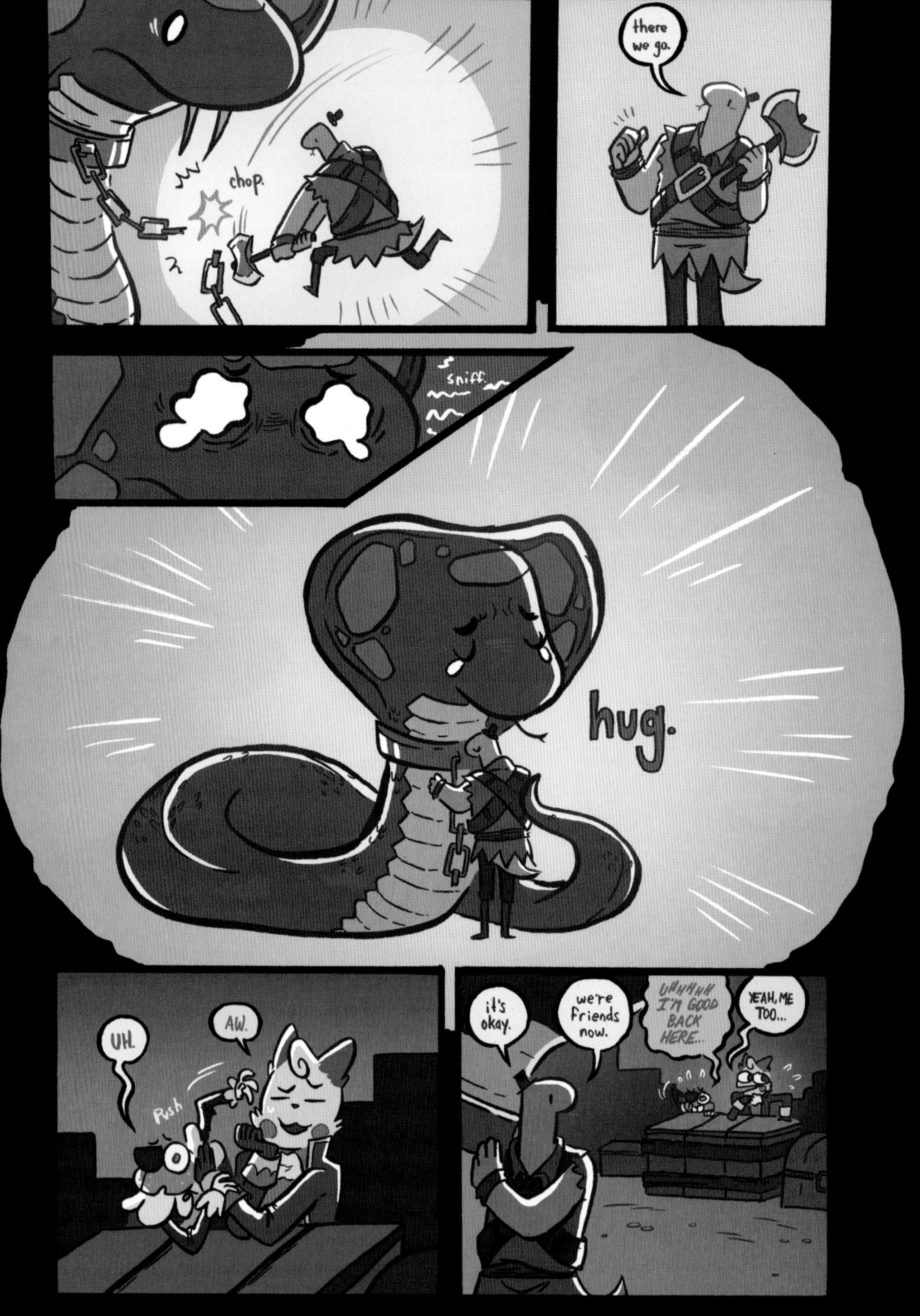
chop.
there we go.
sniff.
hug.
UH.
AW.
PUSH
it's okay.
we're friends now.
UHHHHH I'M GOOD BACK HERE...
YEAH, ME TOO...

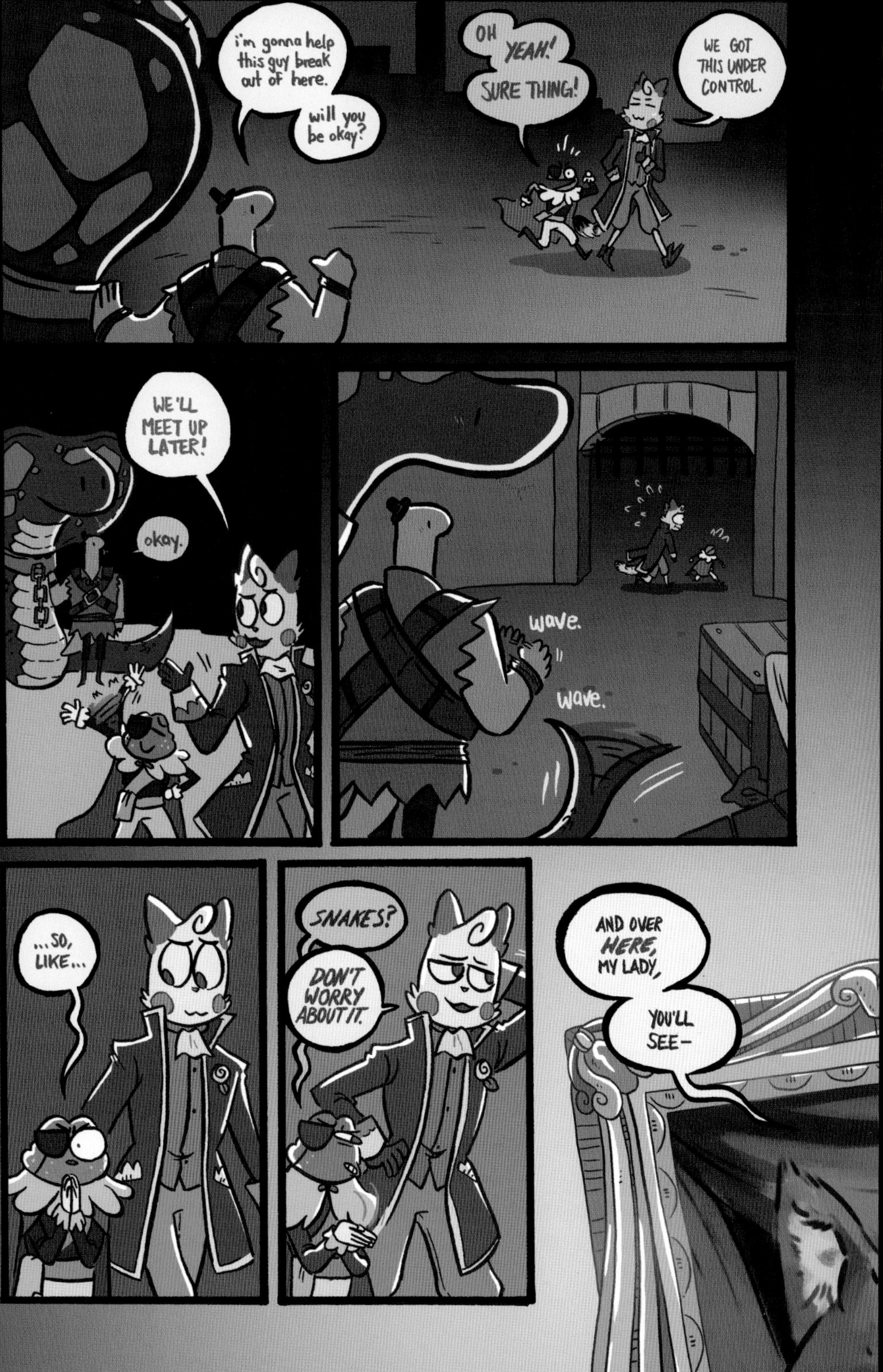
i'm gonna help this guy break out of here.
will you be okay?
OH YEAH! SURE THING!
WE GOT THIS UNDER CONTROL.
WE'LL MEET UP LATER!
okay.
wave.
wave.
...SO, LIKE...
SNAKES?
DON'T WORRY ABOUT IT.
AND OVER HERE, MY LADY,
YOU'LL SEE-

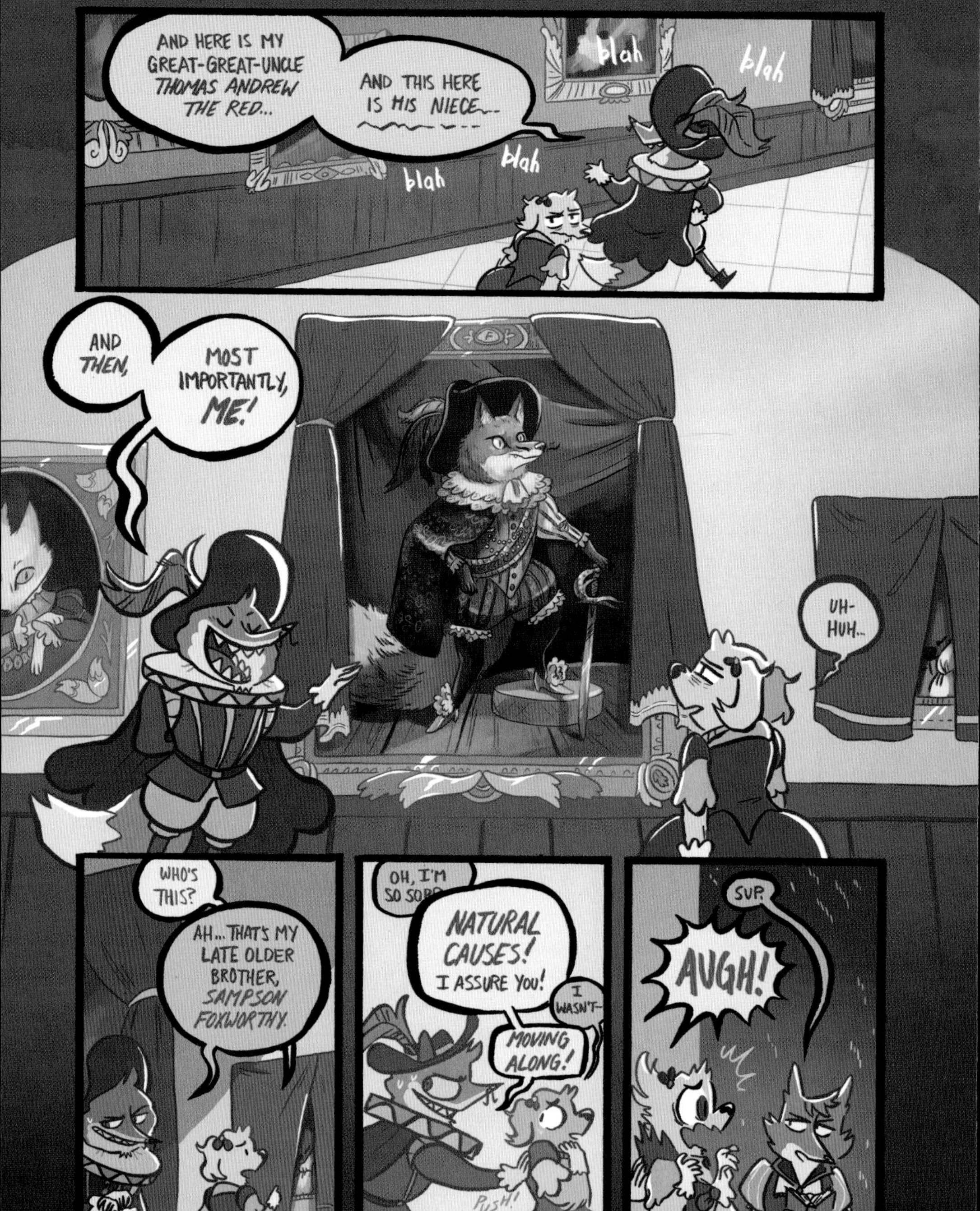

AND HERE IS MY GREAT-GREAT-UNCLE THOMAS ANDREW THE RED...
AND THIS HERE IS HIS NIECE~~
blah
blah
blah
blah
AND THEN,
MOST IMPORTANTLY, ME!
UH-HUH...
WHO'S THIS?
AH... THAT'S MY LATE OLDER BROTHER, SAMPSON FOXWORTHY.
OH, I'M SO SORR
NATURAL CAUSES! I ASSURE YOU!
I WASN'T-
MOVING ALONG!
PUSH!
SUP.
AUGH!

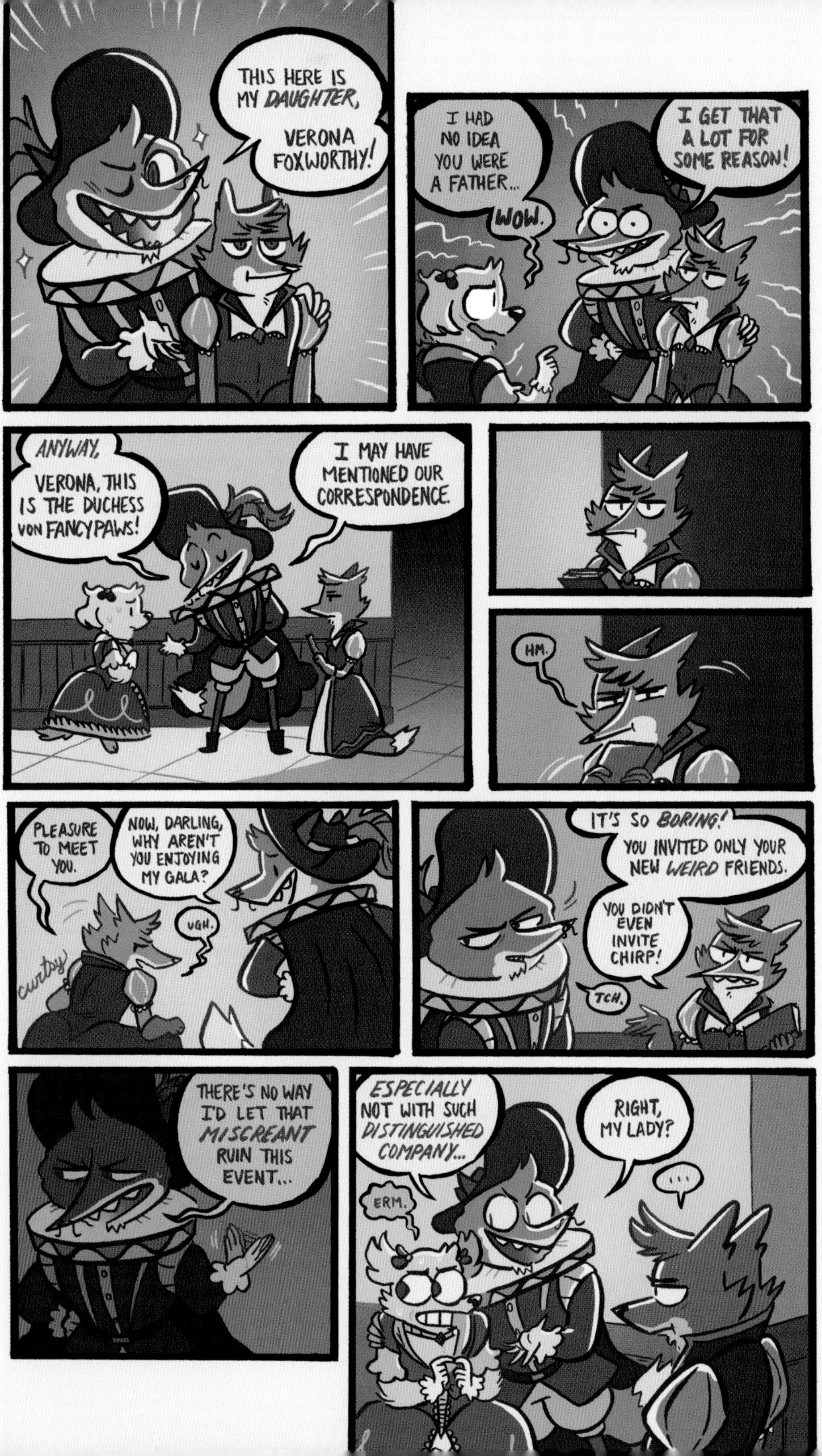

THIS HERE IS MY *DAUGHTER*, VERONA FOXWORTHY!
I HAD NO IDEA YOU WERE A FATHER...
WOW.
I GET THAT A LOT FOR SOME REASON!
ANYWAY, VERONA, THIS IS THE DUCHESS VON FANCYPAWS!
I MAY HAVE MENTIONED OUR CORRESPONDENCE.
HM.
PLEASURE TO MEET YOU.
curtsy
NOW, DARLING, WHY AREN'T YOU ENJOYING MY GALA?
UGH.
IT'S SO *BORING*!
YOU INVITED ONLY YOUR NEW *WEIRD* FRIENDS.
YOU DIDN'T EVEN INVITE CHIRP!
TCH.
THERE'S NO WAY I'D LET THAT *MISCREANT* RUIN THIS EVENT...
ESPECIALLY NOT WITH SUCH *DISTINGUISHED COMPANY*...
ERM.
RIGHT, MY LADY?
...

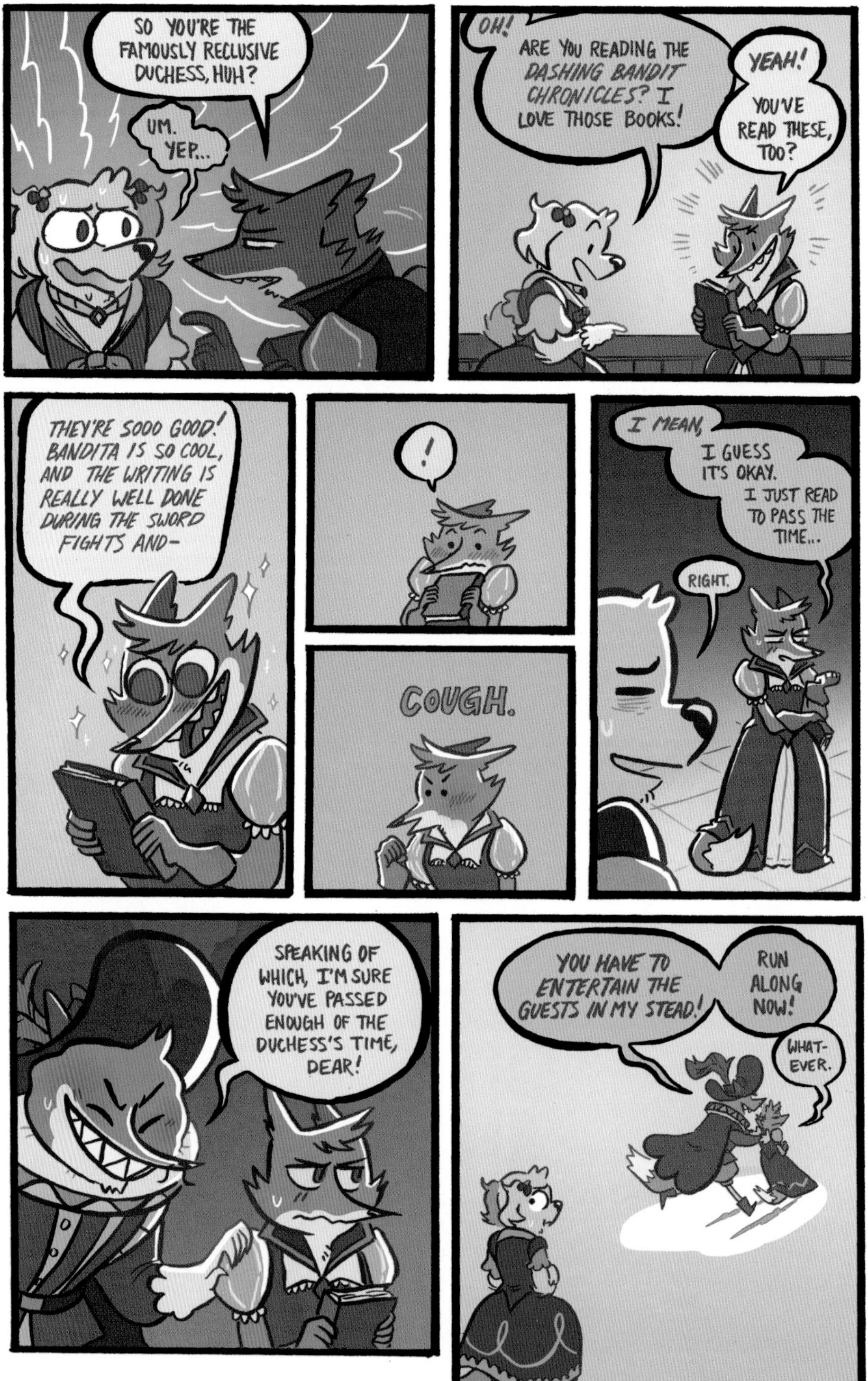
SO YOU'RE THE FAMOUSLY RECLUSIVE DUCHESS, HUH?
UM. YEP...
OH!
ARE YOU READING THE DASHING BANDIT CHRONICLES? I LOVE THOSE BOOKS!
YEAH!
YOU'VE READ THESE, TOO?
THEY'RE SOOO GOOD! BANDITA IS SO COOL, AND THE WRITING IS REALLY WELL DONE DURING THE SWORD FIGHTS AND-
!
COUGH.
I MEAN,
I GUESS IT'S OKAY.
I JUST READ TO PASS THE TIME...
RIGHT.
SPEAKING OF WHICH, I'M SURE YOU'VE PASSED ENOUGH OF THE DUCHESS'S TIME, DEAR!
YOU HAVE TO ENTERTAIN THE GUESTS IN MY STEAD!
RUN ALONG NOW!
WHAT-EVER.

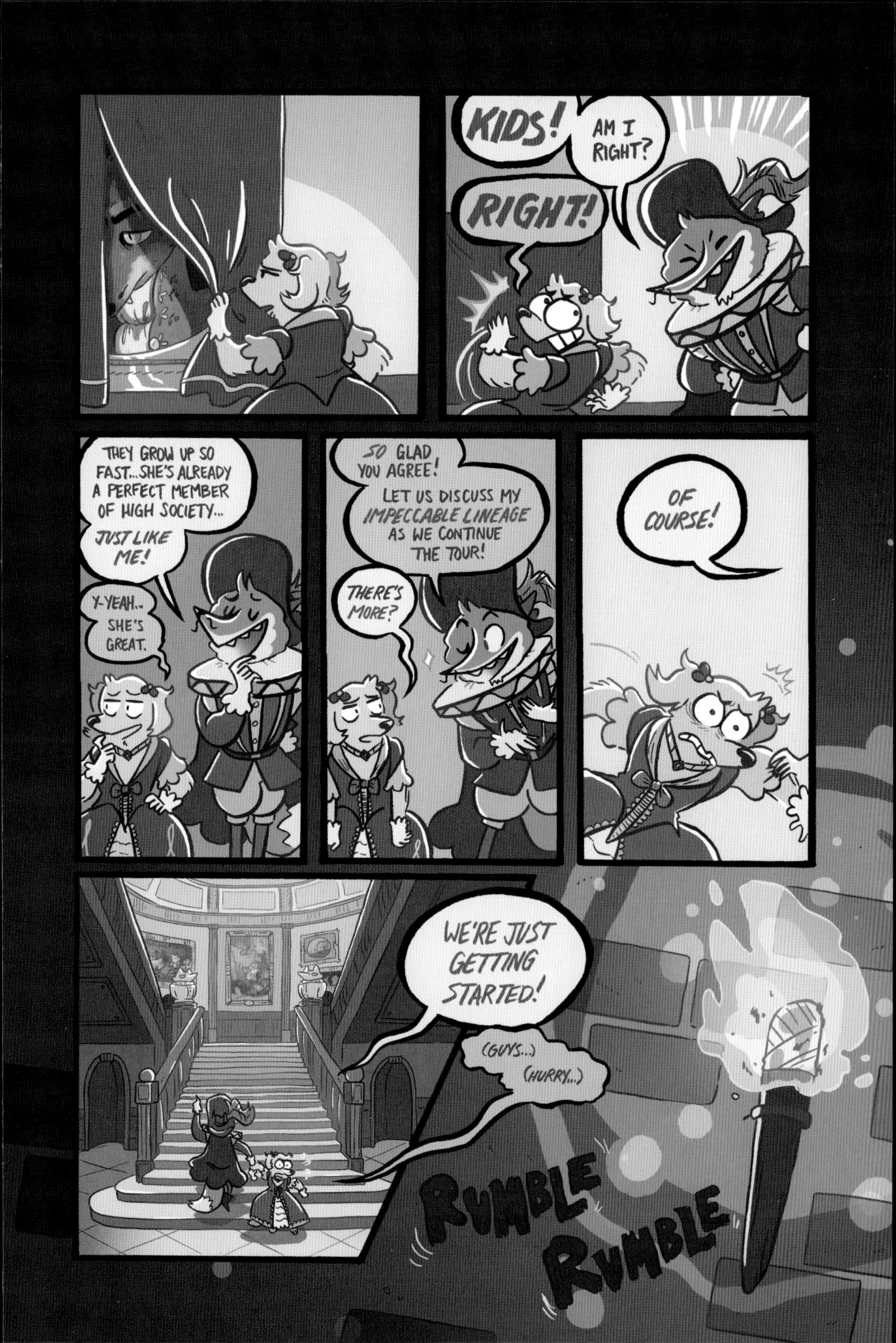
KIDS!
AM I RIGHT?
RIGHT!
THEY GROW UP SO FAST...SHE'S ALREADY A PERFECT MEMBER OF HIGH SOCIETY...
JUST LIKE ME!
Y-YEAH... SHE'S GREAT.
SO GLAD YOU AGREE!
LET US DISCUSS MY IMPECCABLE LINEAGE AS WE CONTINUE THE TOUR!
THERE'S MORE?
OF COURSE!
WE'RE JUST GETTING STARTED!
(GUYS...)
(HURRY...)
RUMBLE
RUMBLE

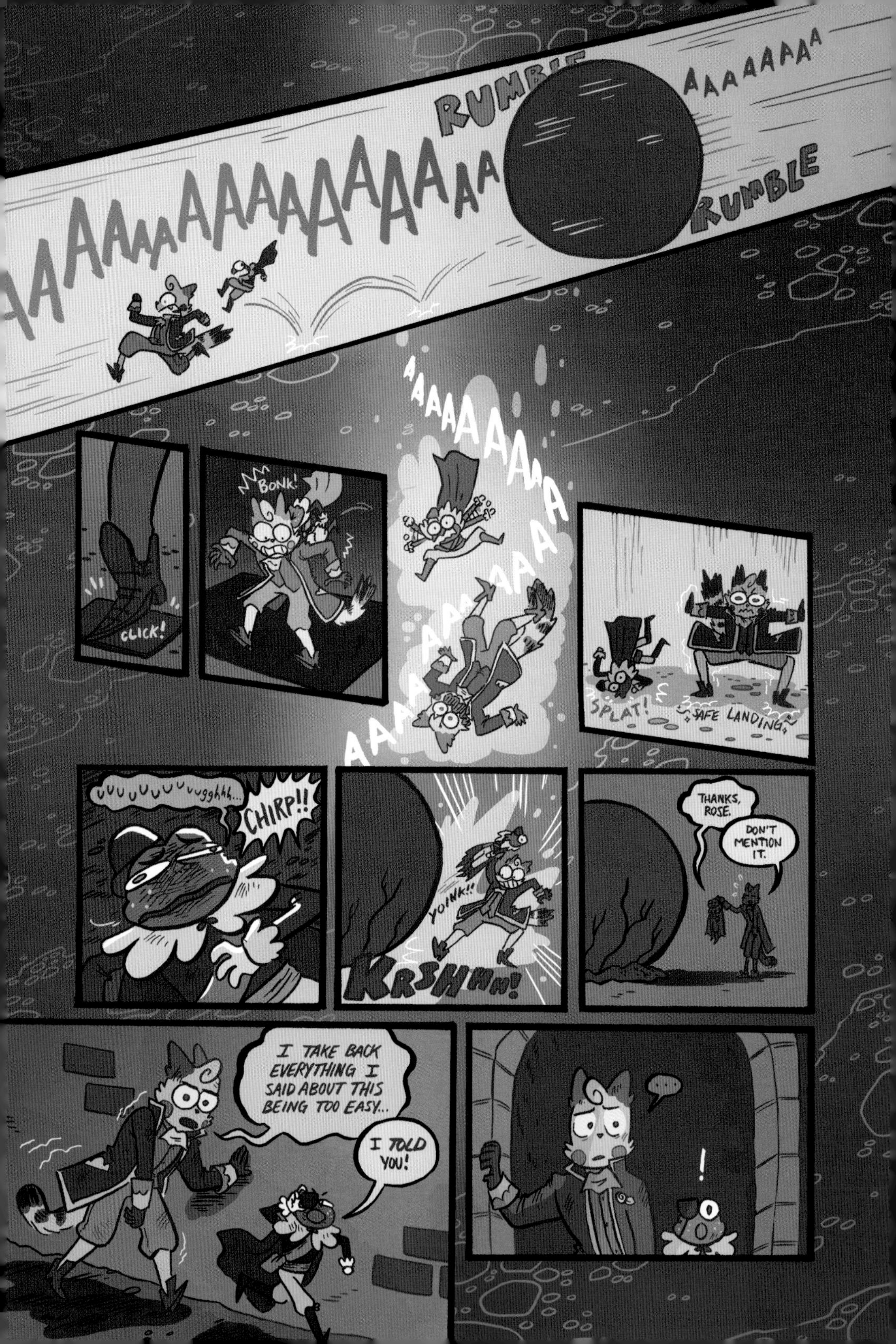
AAAAAAAAAAAAAAAAAA
RUMBLE
AAAAAAA
RUMBLE
CLICK!
BONK!
AAAAAAAAAAA
AAAAAAAAA
SPLAT!
SAFE LANDING
UUUUUUUuugghhh...
CHIRP!!
YOINK!!
KRSHHH!
THANKS, ROSE.
DON'T MENTION IT.
I TAKE BACK EVERYTHING I SAID ABOUT THIS BEING TOO EASY...
I TOLD YOU!
...
!

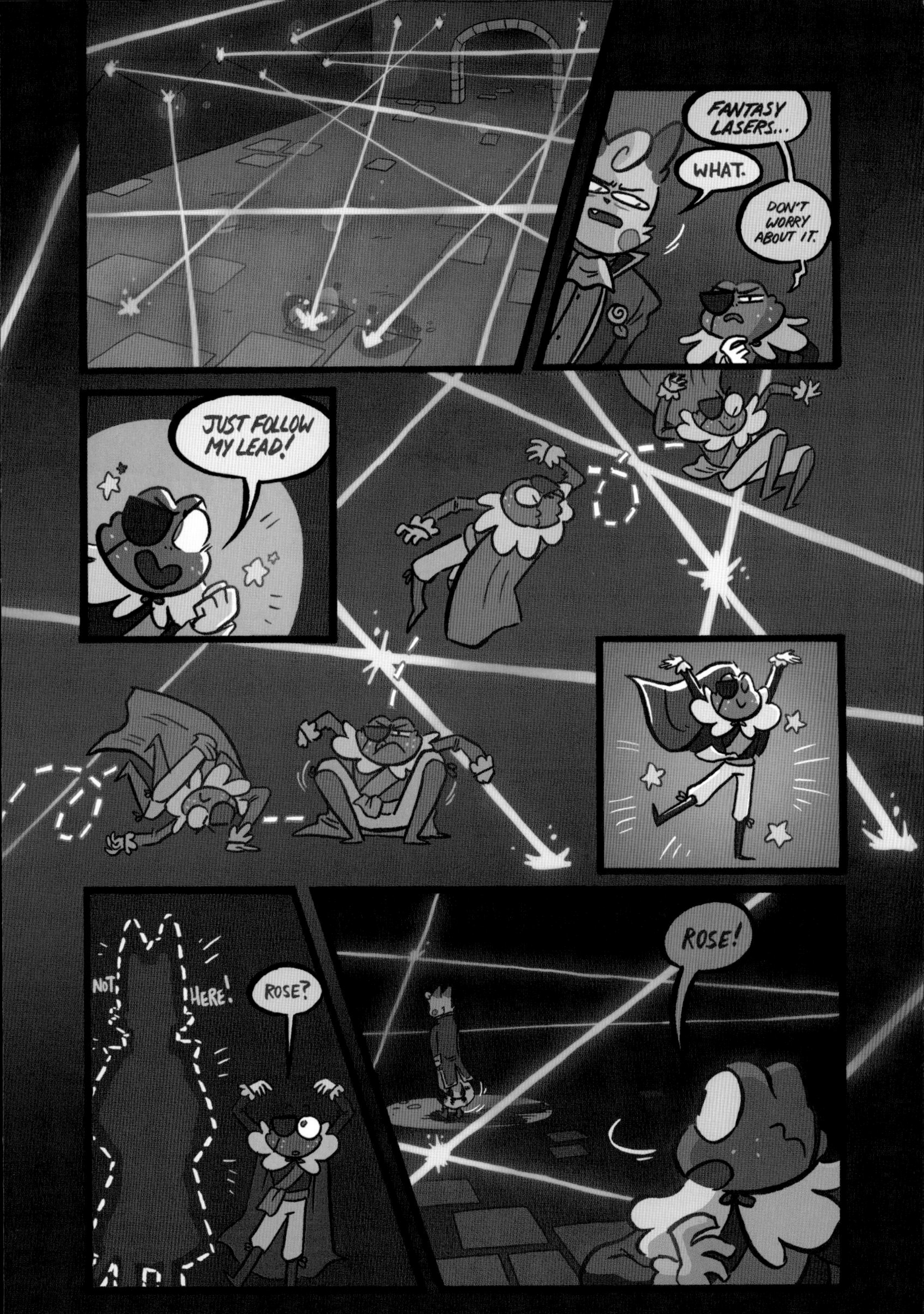
FANTASY LASERS...
WHAT.
DON'T WORRY ABOUT IT.
JUST FOLLOW MY LEAD!
NOT HERE!
ROSE?
ROSE!

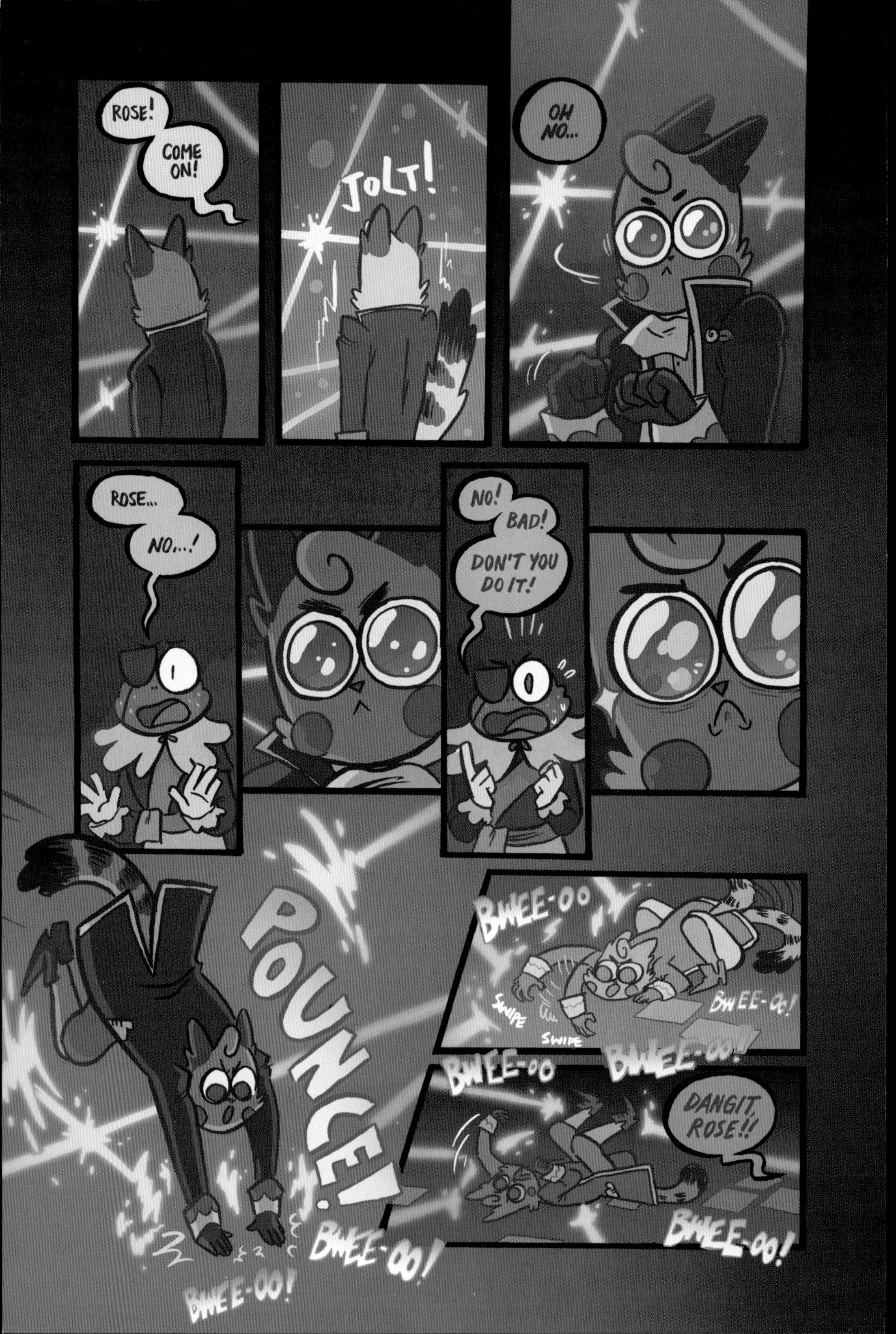
ROSE!
COME ON!
JOLT!
OH NO...
ROSE...
NO...!
NO!
BAD!
DON'T YOU DO IT!
POUNCE!
BWEE-OO!
BWEE-OO!
BWEE-OO
SWIPE
SWIPE
BWEE-OO!
BWEE-OO!
BWEE-OO
DANGIT, ROSE!!
BWEE-OO!

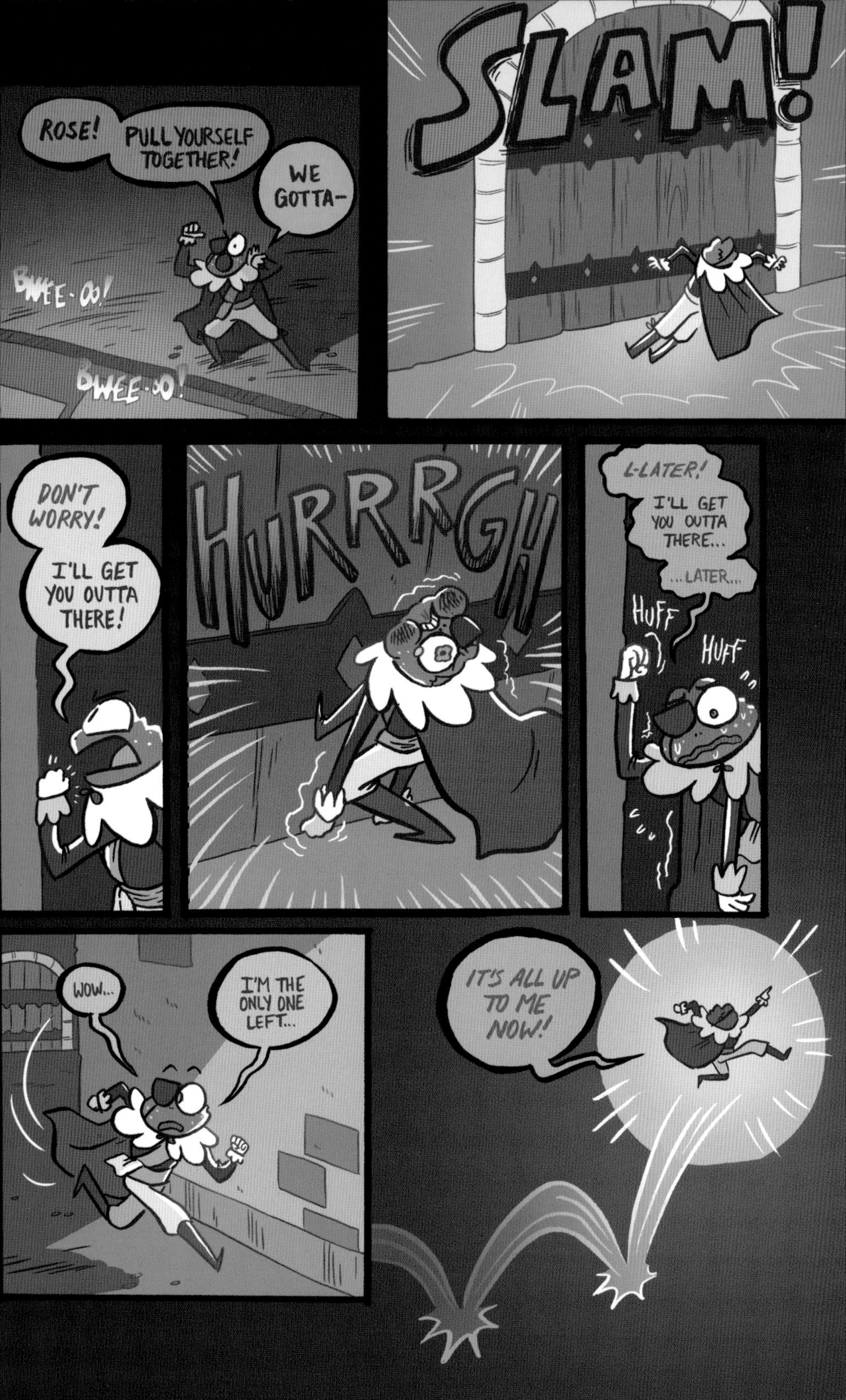

SLAM!
ROSE!
PULL YOURSELF TOGETHER!
WE GOTTA-
BWEE-OO!
BWEE-OO!
DON'T WORRY!
I'LL GET YOU OUTTA THERE!
HURRRGH
L-LATER!
I'LL GET YOU OUTTA THERE...
...LATER...
HUFF
HUFF
WOW...
I'M THE ONLY ONE LEFT...
IT'S ALL UP TO ME NOW!

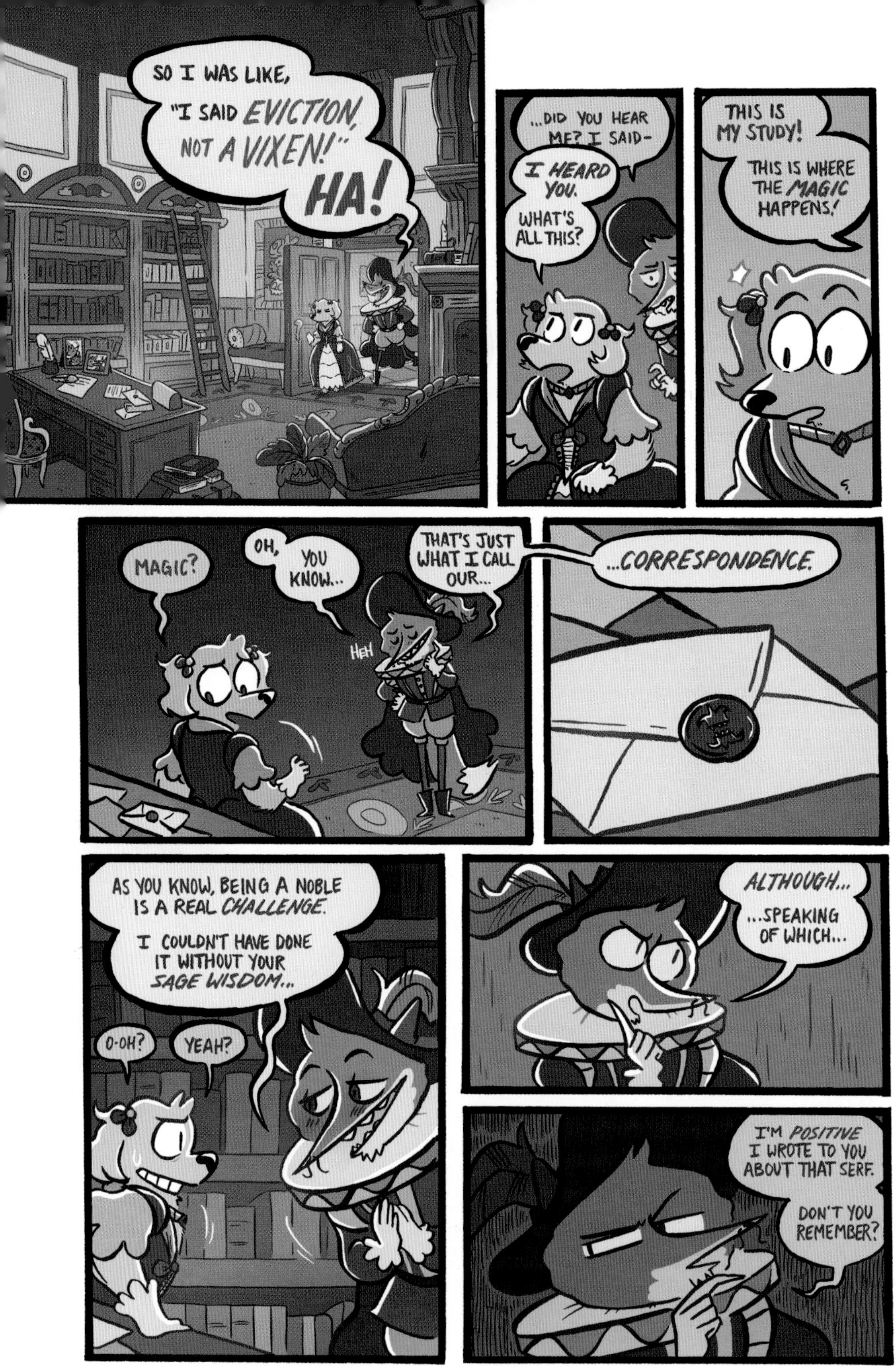
SO I WAS LIKE, "I SAID EVICTION, NOT A VIXEN!" HA!
...DID YOU HEAR ME? I SAID-
I HEARD YOU.
WHAT'S ALL THIS?
THIS IS MY STUDY!
THIS IS WHERE THE MAGIC HAPPENS!
MAGIC?
OH, YOU KNOW...
HEH
THAT'S JUST WHAT I CALL OUR...
...CORRESPONDENCE.
AS YOU KNOW, BEING A NOBLE IS A REAL CHALLENGE.
I COULDN'T HAVE DONE IT WITHOUT YOUR SAGE WISDOM...
O-OH?
YEAH?
ALTHOUGH...
...SPEAKING OF WHICH...
I'M POSITIVE I WROTE TO YOU ABOUT THAT SERF.
DON'T YOU REMEMBER?

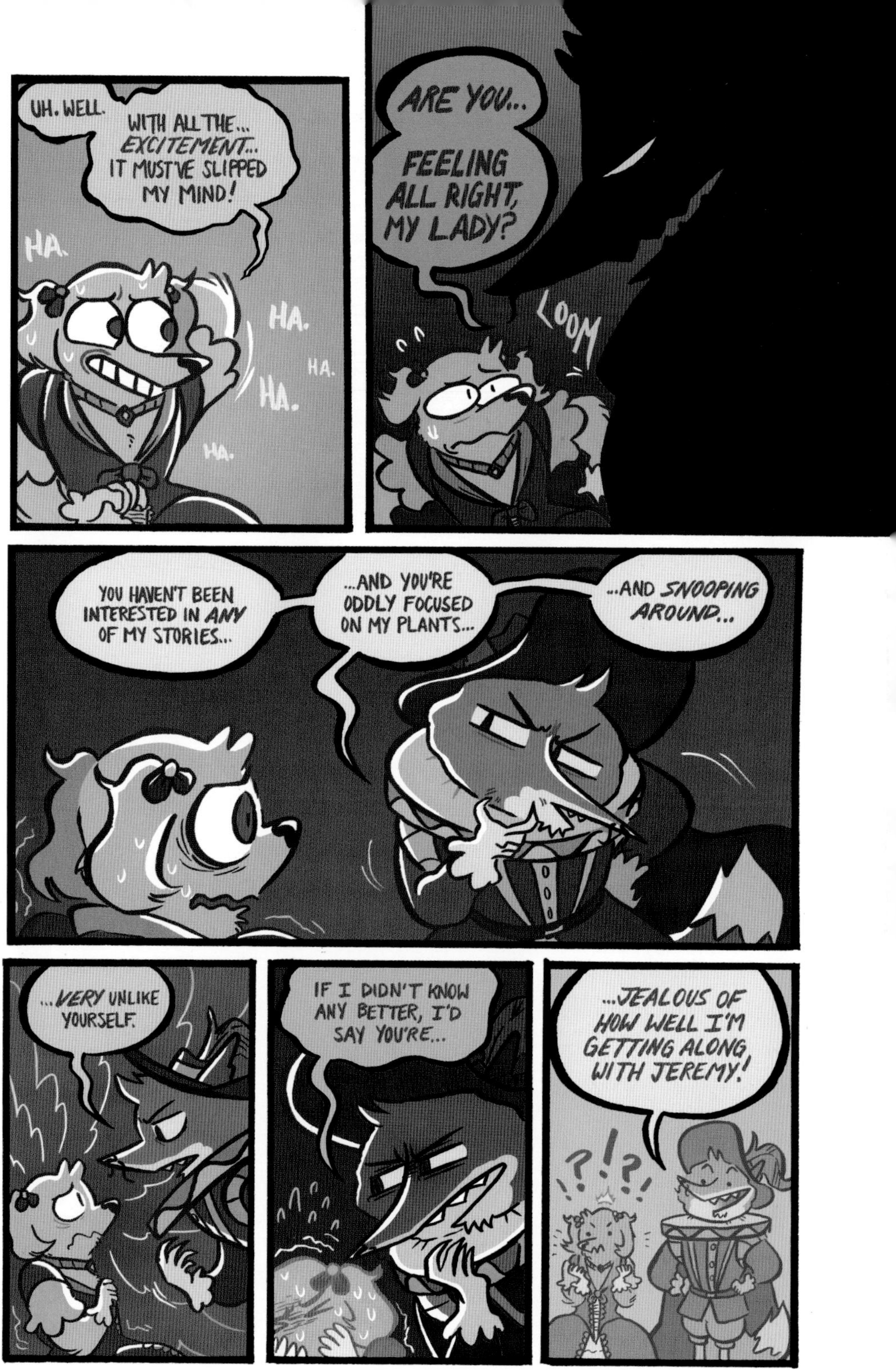
UH. WELL.
WITH ALL THE... EXCITEMENT... IT MUST'VE SLIPPED MY MIND!
HA.
HA.
HA.
HA.
HA.
ARE YOU...
FEELING ALL RIGHT, MY LADY?
LOOM
YOU HAVEN'T BEEN INTERESTED IN ANY OF MY STORIES...
...AND YOU'RE ODDLY FOCUSED ON MY PLANTS...
...AND SNOOPING AROUND...
...VERY UNLIKE YOURSELF.
IF I DIDN'T KNOW ANY BETTER, I'D SAY YOU'RE...
...JEALOUS OF HOW WELL I'M GETTING ALONG WITH JEREMY!
?!?!

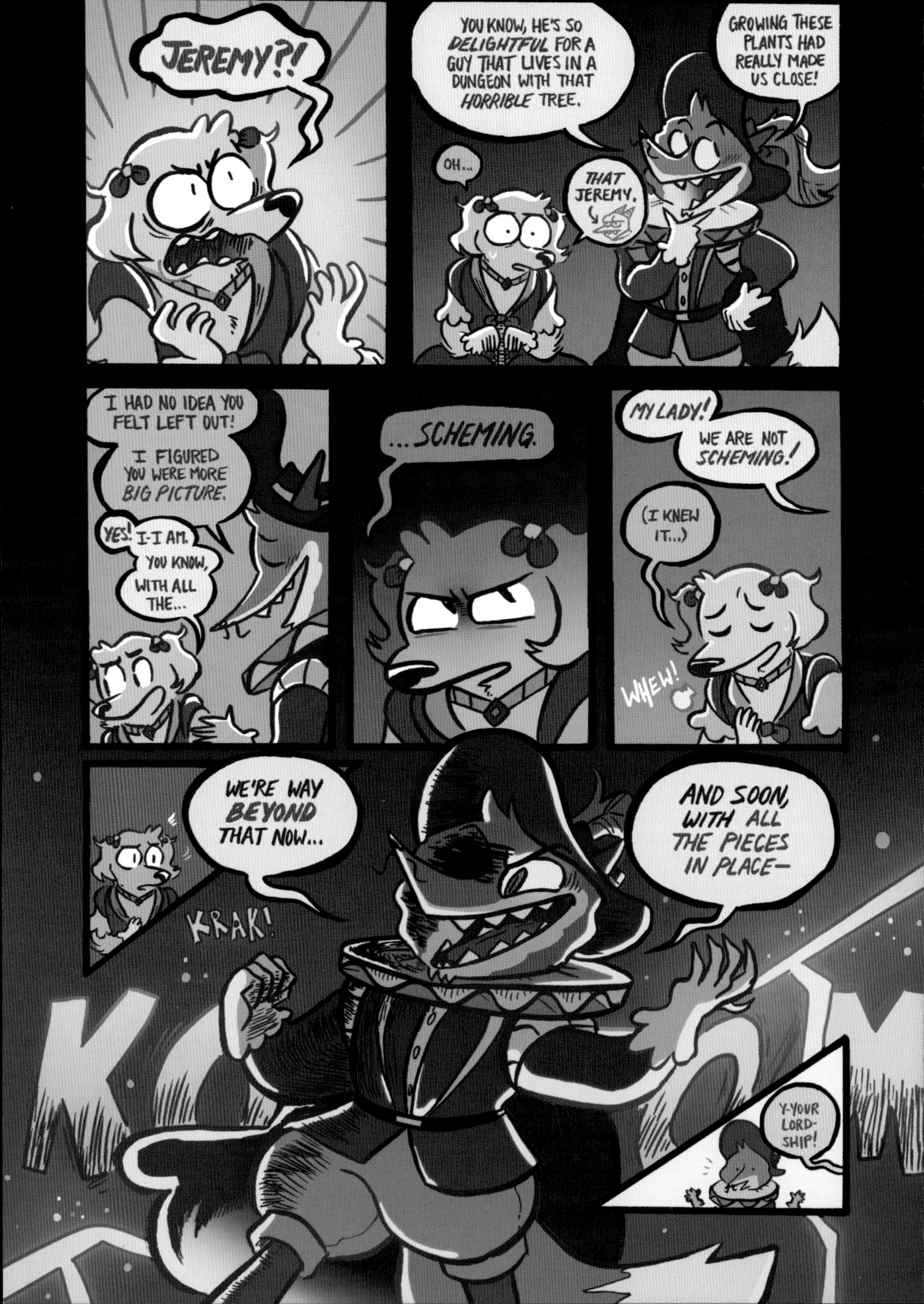
JEREMY?!
YOU KNOW, HE'S SO DELIGHTFUL FOR A GUY THAT LIVES IN A DUNGEON WITH THAT HORRIBLE TREE.
GROWING THESE PLANTS HAD REALLY MADE US CLOSE!
OH...
THAT JEREMY.
I HAD NO IDEA YOU FELT LEFT OUT!
I FIGURED YOU WERE MORE BIG PICTURE.
YES!
I-I AM. YOU KNOW, WITH ALL THE...
...SCHEMING.
MY LADY!
WE ARE NOT SCHEMING!
(I KNEW IT...)
WHEW!
WE'RE WAY BEYOND THAT NOW...
AND SOON, WITH ALL THE PIECES IN PLACE—
KRAK!
Y-YOUR LORD-SHIP!

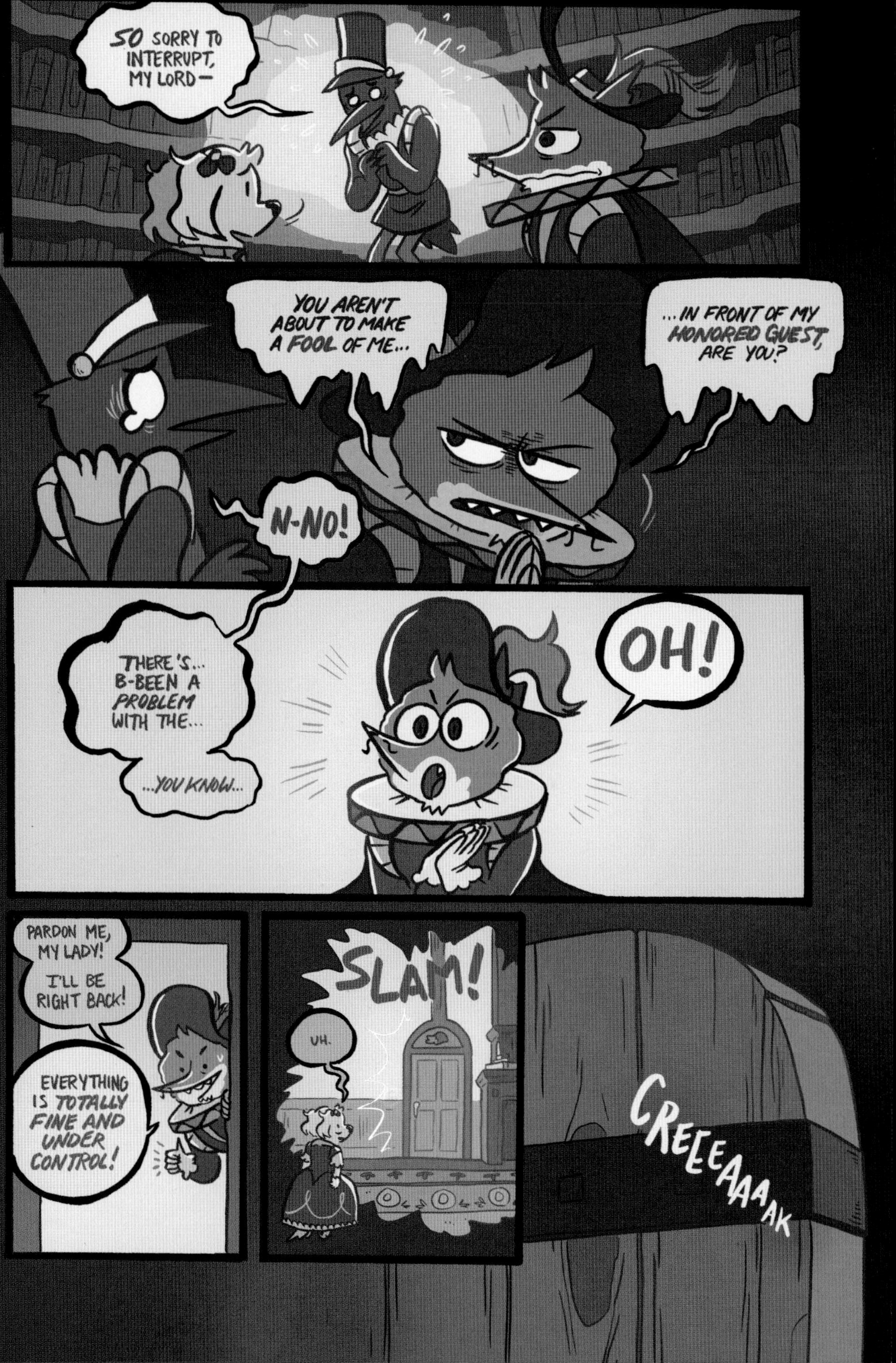
SO SORRY TO INTERRUPT, MY LORD—
YOU AREN'T ABOUT TO MAKE A FOOL OF ME...
...IN FRONT OF MY HONORED GUEST, ARE YOU?
N-NO!
THERE'S... B-BEEN A PROBLEM WITH THE...
...YOU KNOW...
OH!
PARDON ME, MY LADY!
I'LL BE RIGHT BACK!
EVERYTHING IS TOTALLY FINE AND UNDER CONTROL!
SLAM!
UH.
CREEEAAAAK

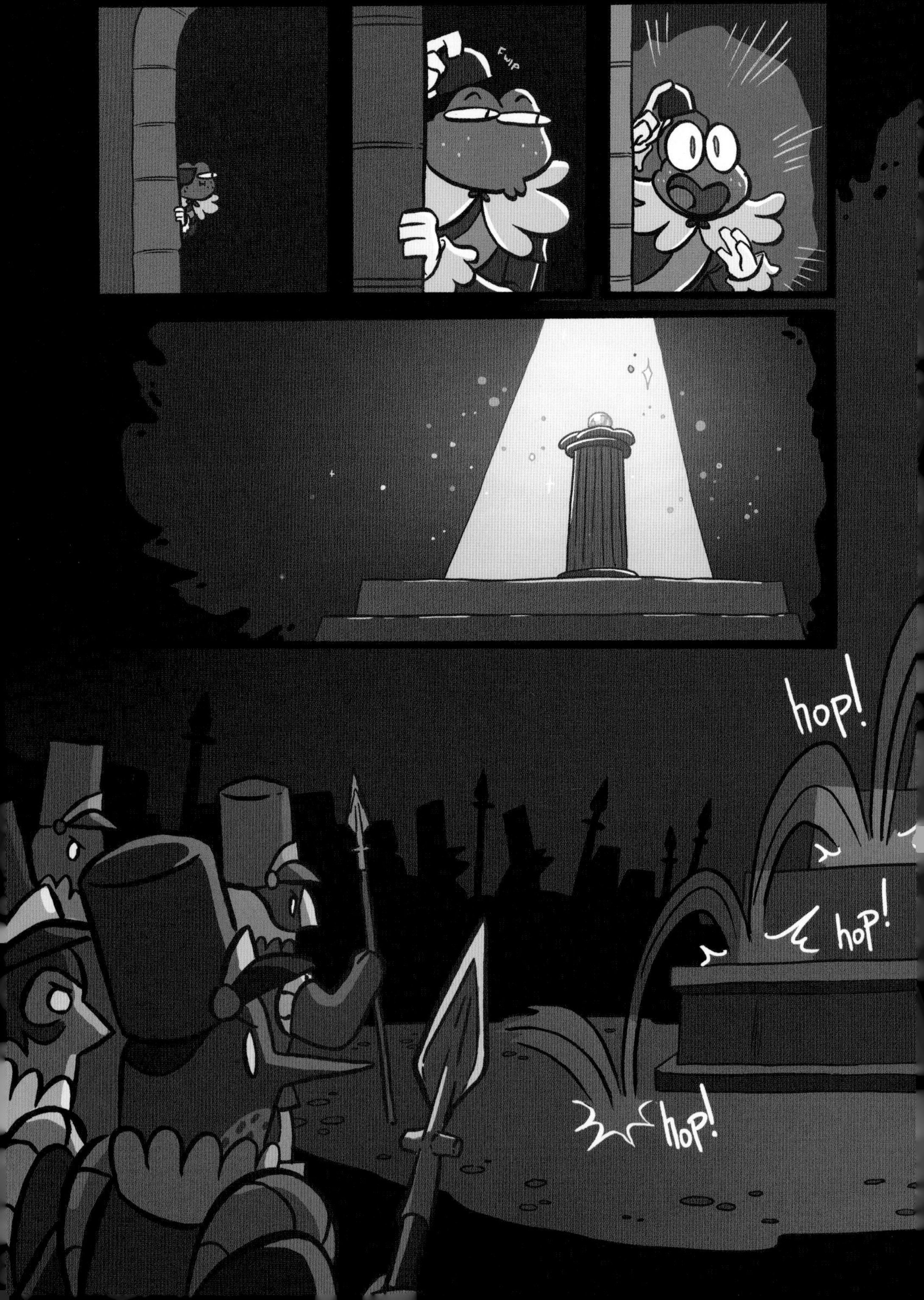
FWIP
hop!
hop!
hop!

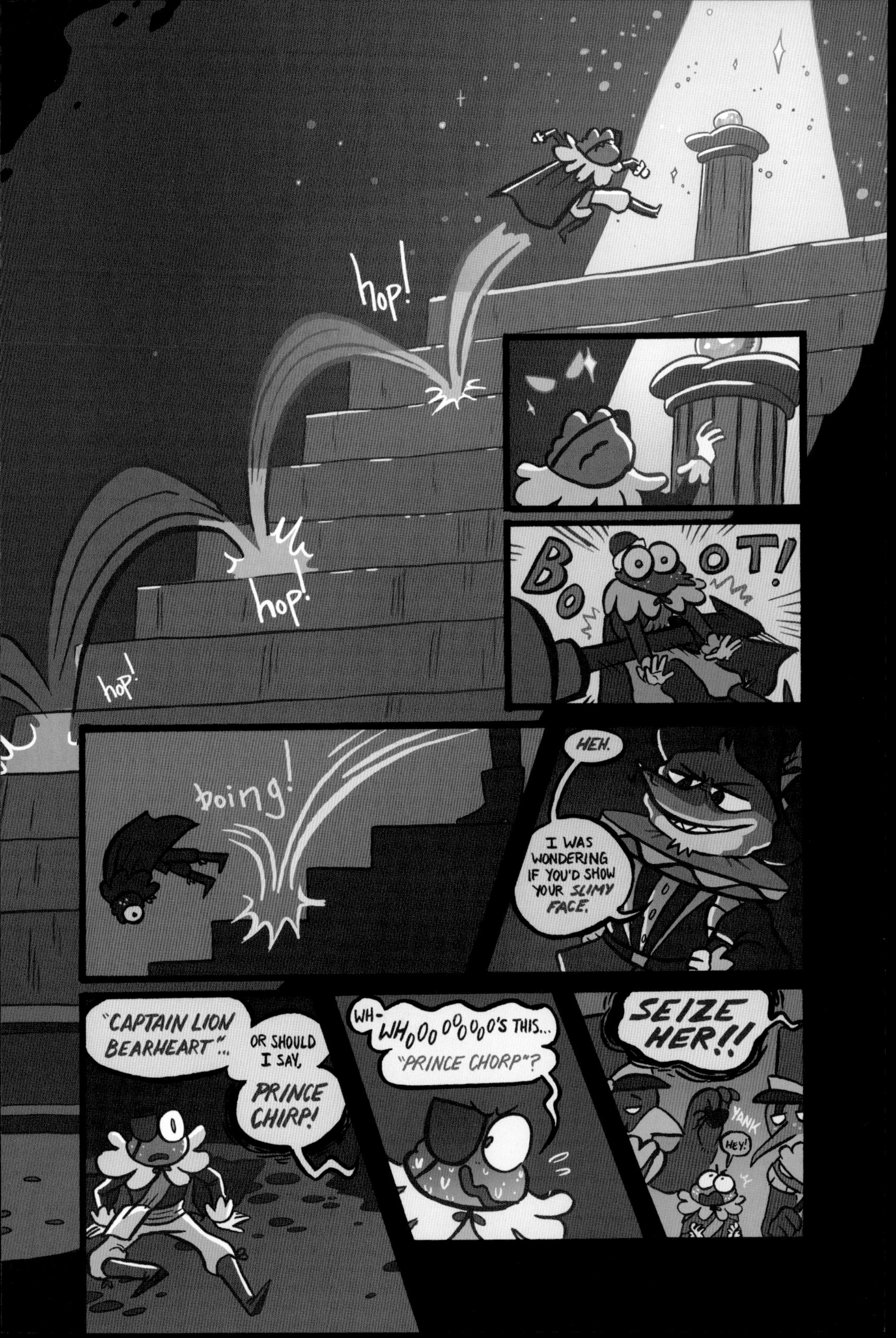
hop!
hop!
hop!
BOOOT!
boing!
HEH.
I WAS WONDERING IF YOU'D SHOW YOUR SLIMY FACE.
"CAPTAIN LION BEARHEART"...
OR SHOULD I SAY,
PRINCE CHIRP!
WH-WHOOOOOOOO'S THIS... "PRINCE CHORP"?
SEIZE HER!!
YANK
HEY!

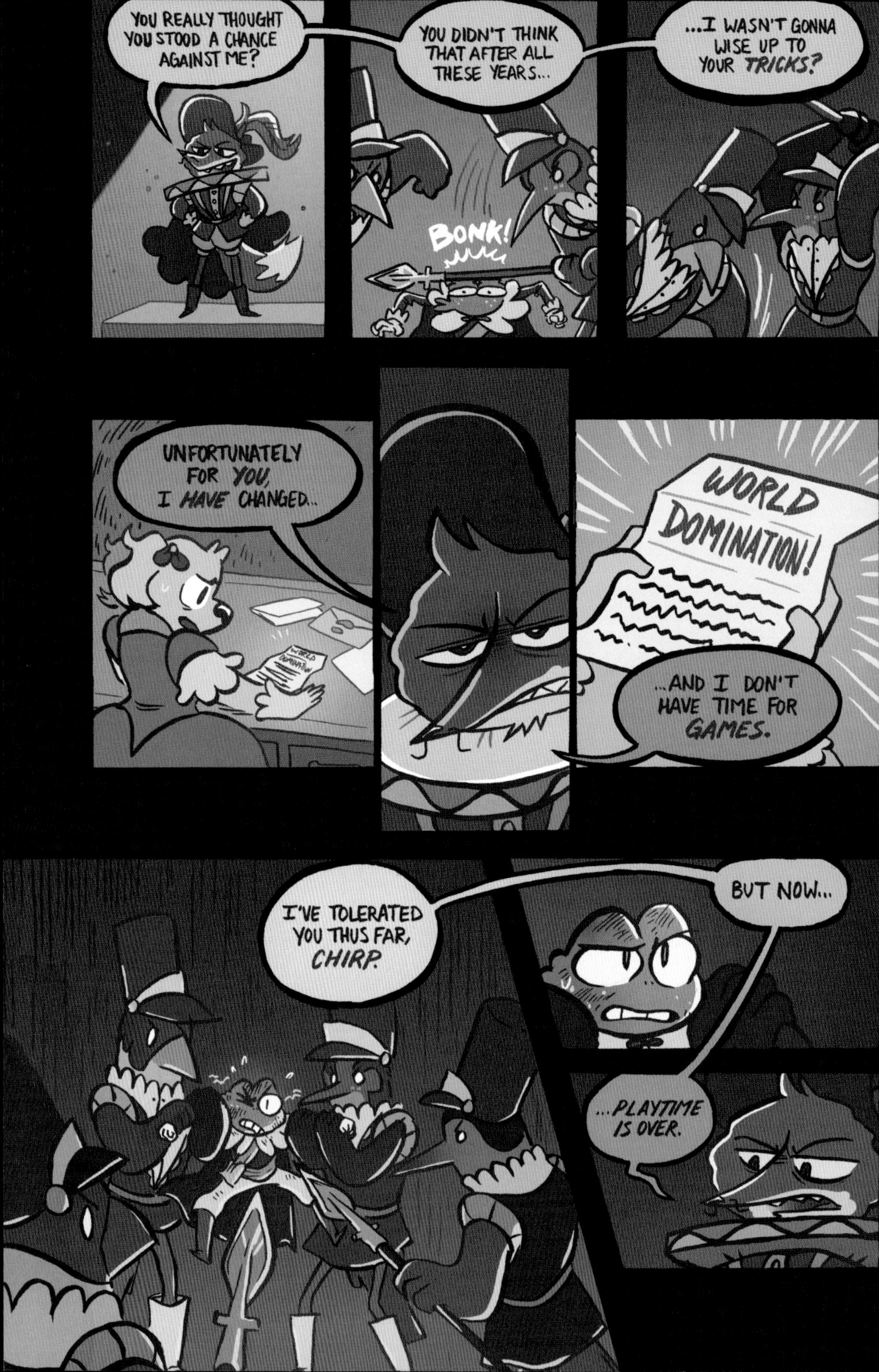
YOU REALLY THOUGHT YOU STOOD A CHANCE AGAINST ME?
YOU DIDN'T THINK THAT AFTER ALL THESE YEARS...
...I WASN'T GONNA WISE UP TO YOUR TRICKS?
BONK!
UNFORTUNATELY FOR YOU, I HAVE CHANGED...
WORLD DOMINATION
WORLD DOMINATION!
...AND I DON'T HAVE TIME FOR GAMES.
I'VE TOLERATED YOU THUS FAR, CHIRP.
BUT NOW...
...PLAYTIME IS OVER.

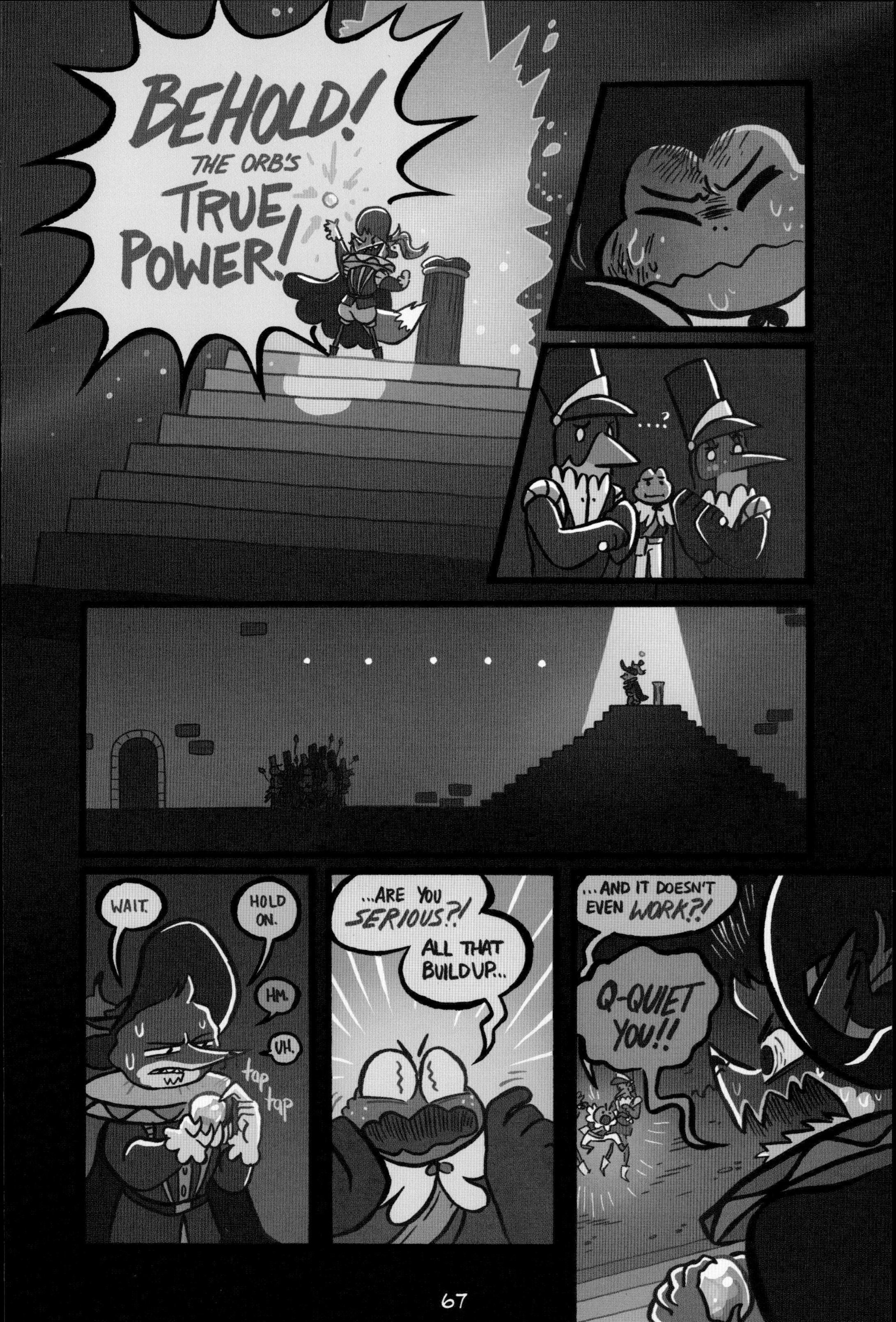
BEHOLD! THE ORB'S TRUE POWER!
...?
WAIT.
HOLD ON.
HM.
UH.
tap tap
...ARE YOU SERIOUS?!
ALL THAT BUILDUP...
...AND IT DOESN'T EVEN WORK?!
Q-QUIET YOU!!

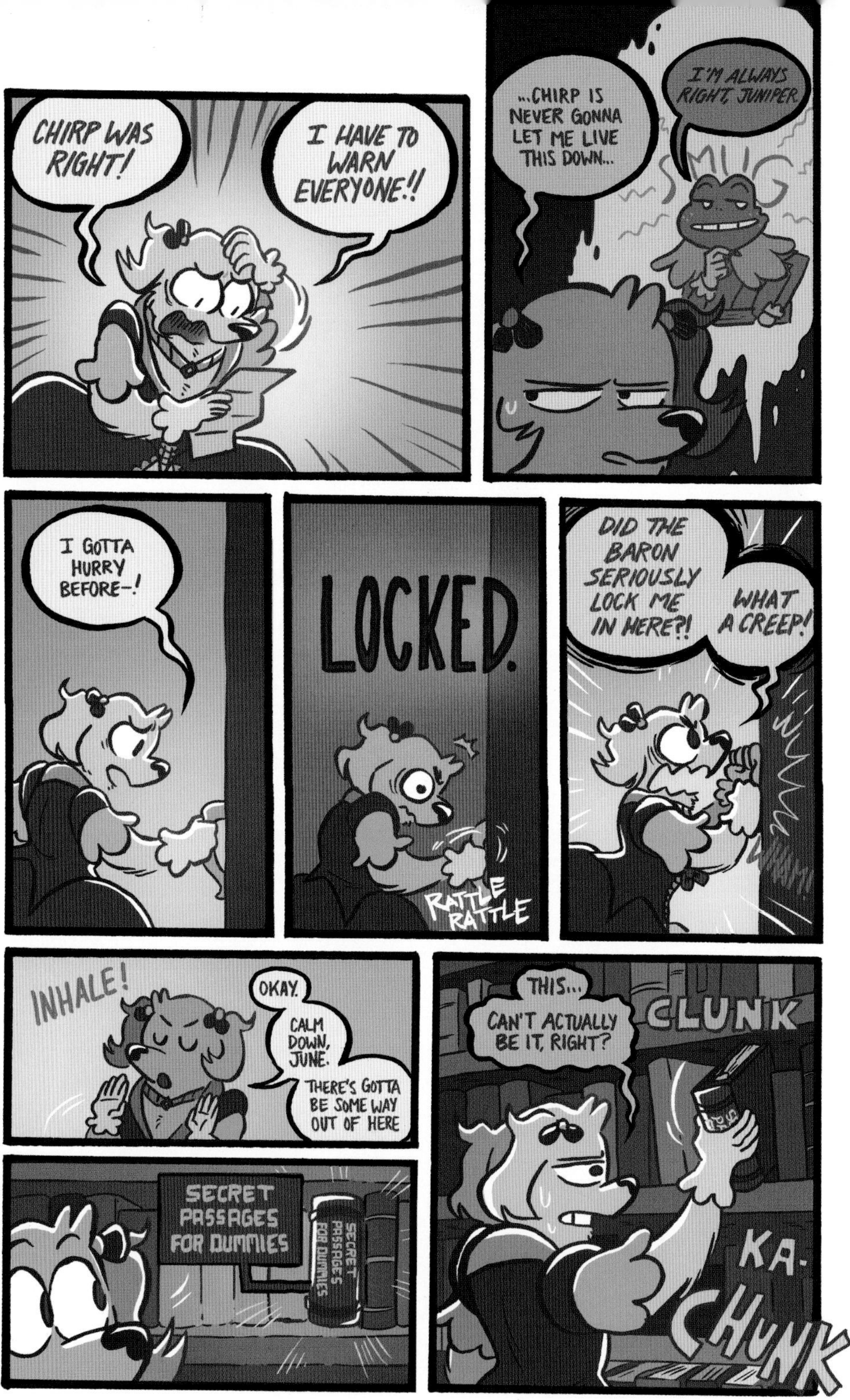

CHIRP WAS RIGHT!
I HAVE TO WARN EVERYONE!!
...CHIRP IS NEVER GONNA LET ME LIVE THIS DOWN...
I'M ALWAYS RIGHT, JUNIPER.
SMUG
I GOTTA HURRY BEFORE--!
LOCKED.
RATTLE RATTLE
DID THE BARON SERIOUSLY LOCK ME IN HERE?!
WHAT A CREEP!
INHALE!
OKAY.
CALM DOWN, JUNE.
THERE'S GOTTA BE SOME WAY OUT OF HERE
SECRET PASSAGES FOR DUMMIES
SECRET PASSAGES FOR DUMMIES
THIS...
CAN'T ACTUALLY BE IT, RIGHT?
CLUNK
KA-CHUNK

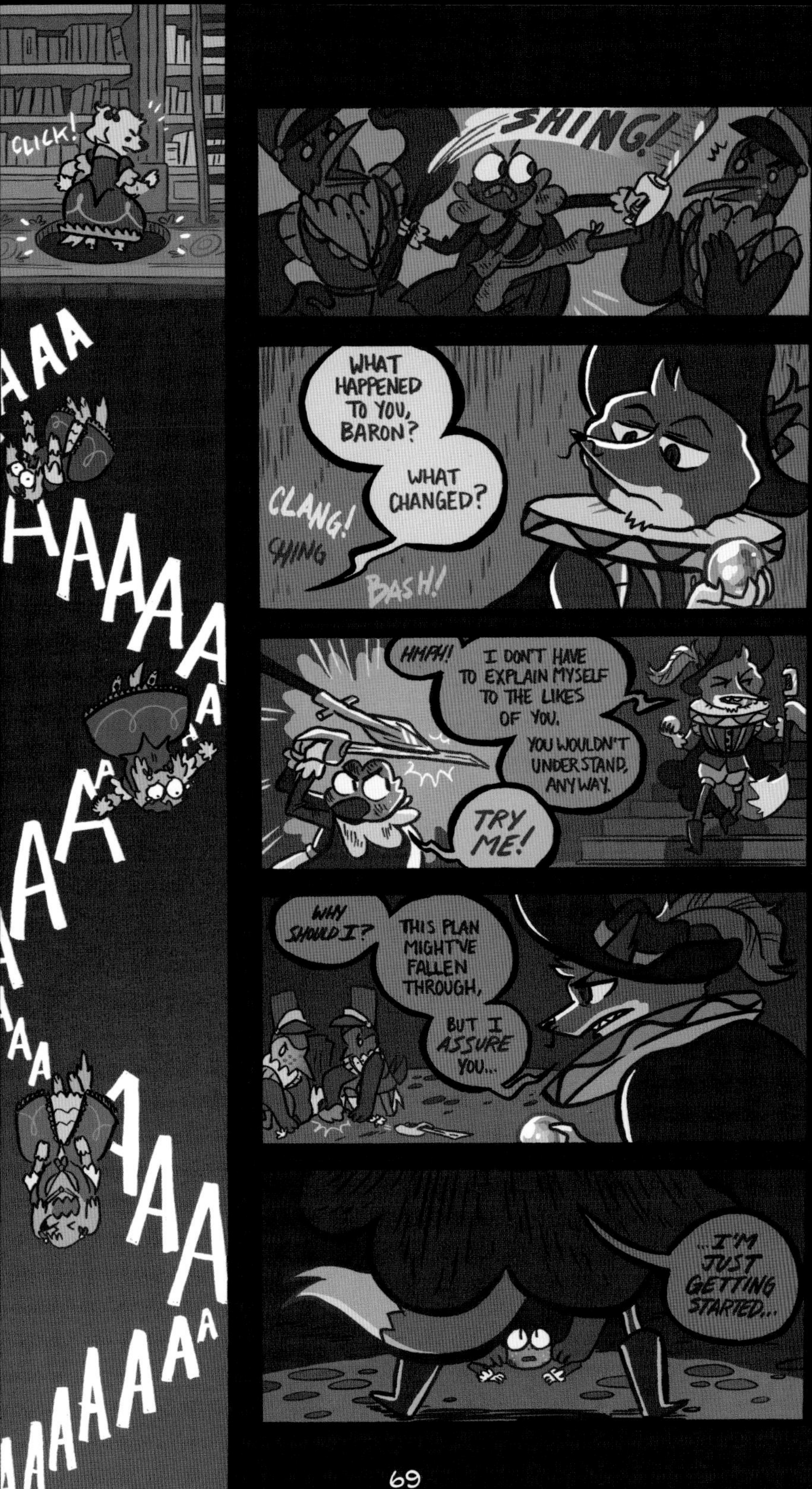
CLICK!
SHING!
AAAAAAAAAAAAAAAAAAAAAAAAAAAAAA
WHAT HAPPENED TO YOU, BARON?
WHAT CHANGED?
CLANG!
CHING
BASH!
HMPH!
I DON'T HAVE TO EXPLAIN MYSELF TO THE LIKES OF YOU.
YOU WOULDN'T UNDERSTAND, ANYWAY.
TRY ME!
WHY SHOULD I?
THIS PLAN MIGHT'VE FALLEN THROUGH,
BUT I ASSURE YOU...
...I'M JUST GETTING STARTED...

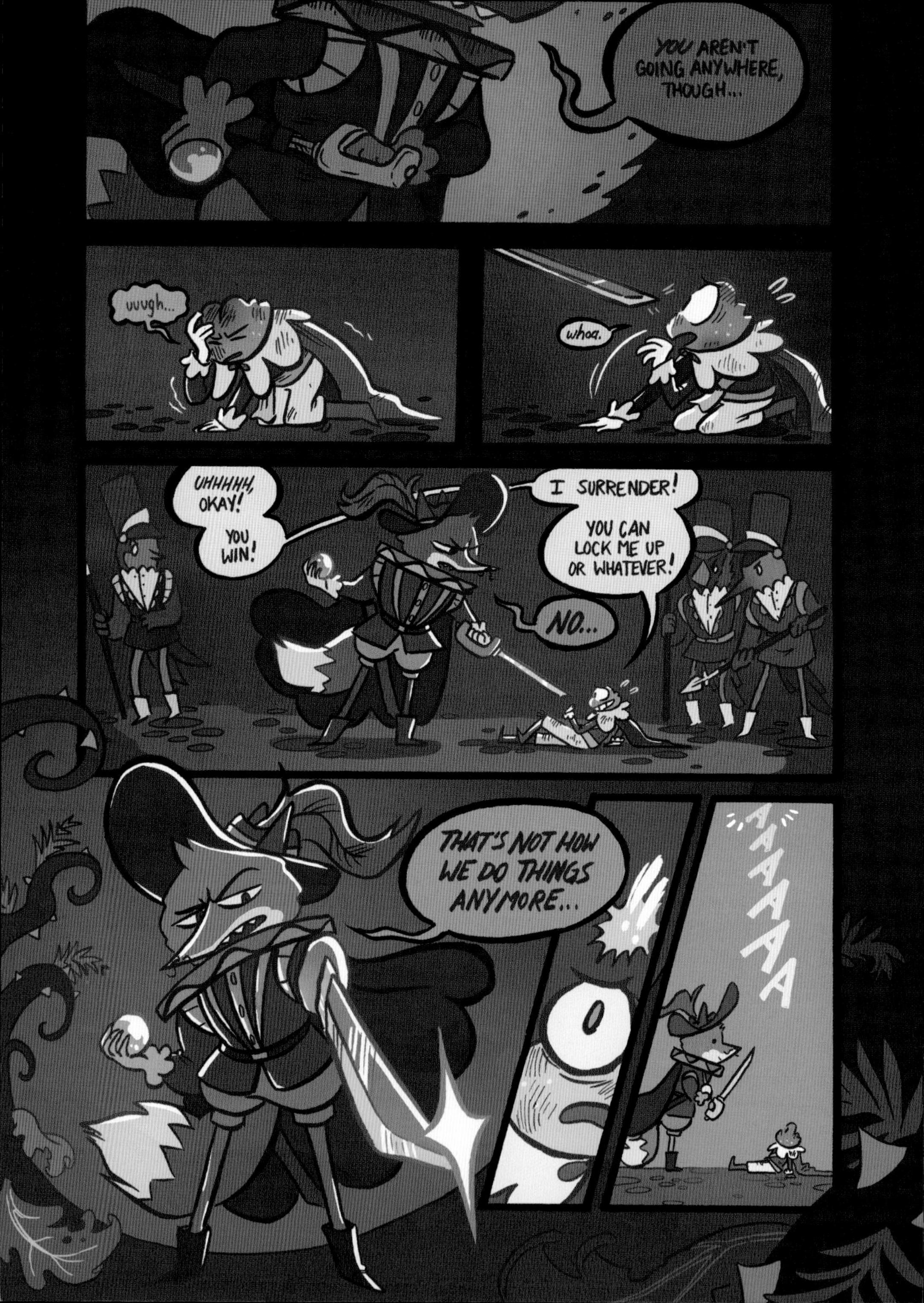

YOU AREN'T GOING ANYWHERE, THOUGH...
uuugh...
whoa.
UHHHHH, OKAY!
YOU WIN!
I SURRENDER!
YOU CAN LOCK ME UP OR WHATEVER!
NO...
THAT'S NOT HOW WE DO THINGS ANYMORE...
AAAAAAAA

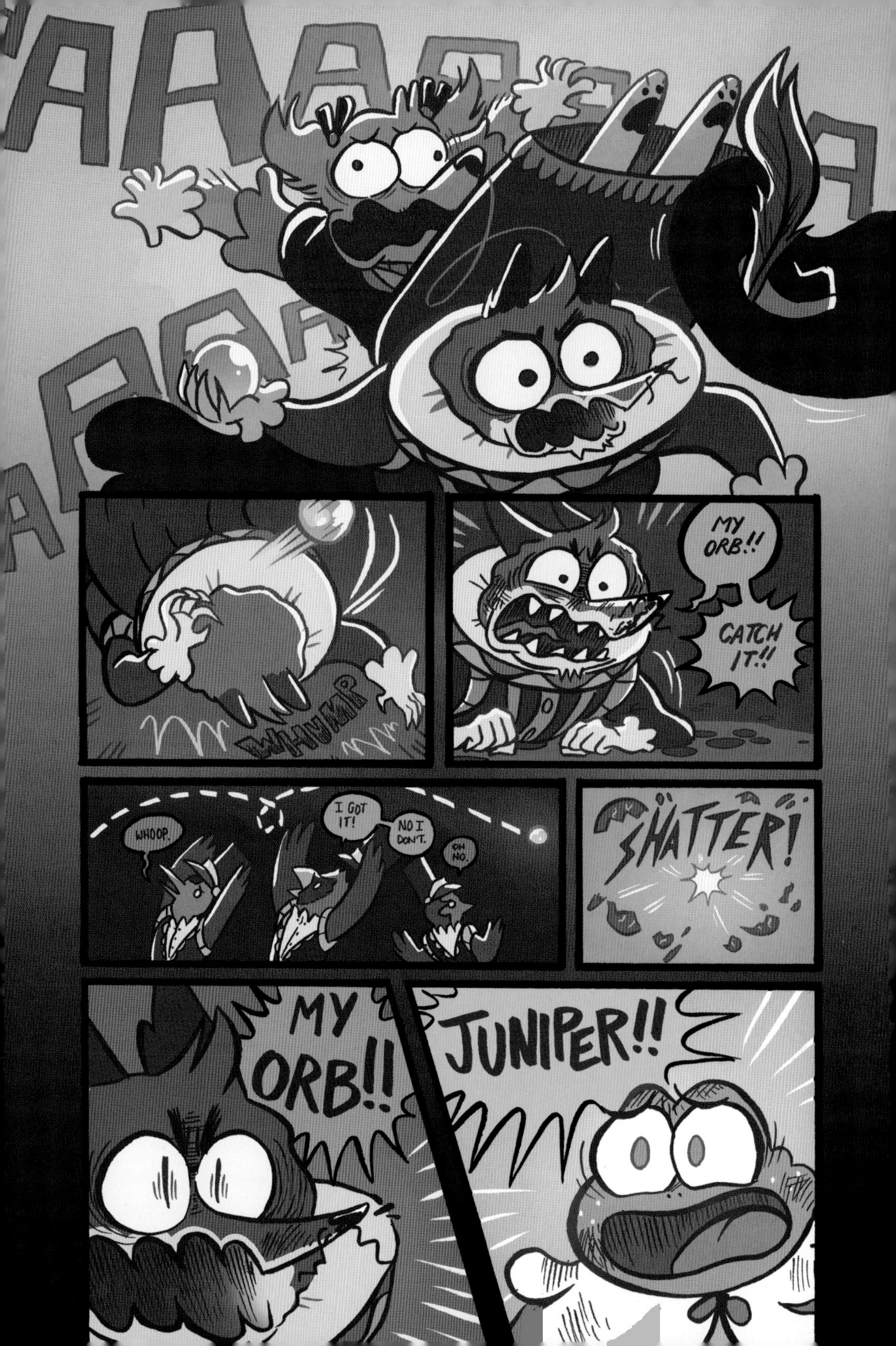
AAAAAAAAAAA
WHUMP
MY ORB!!
CATCH IT!!
WHOOP.
I GOT IT!
NO I DON'T.
OH NO.
SHATTER!
MY ORB!!
JUNIPER!!

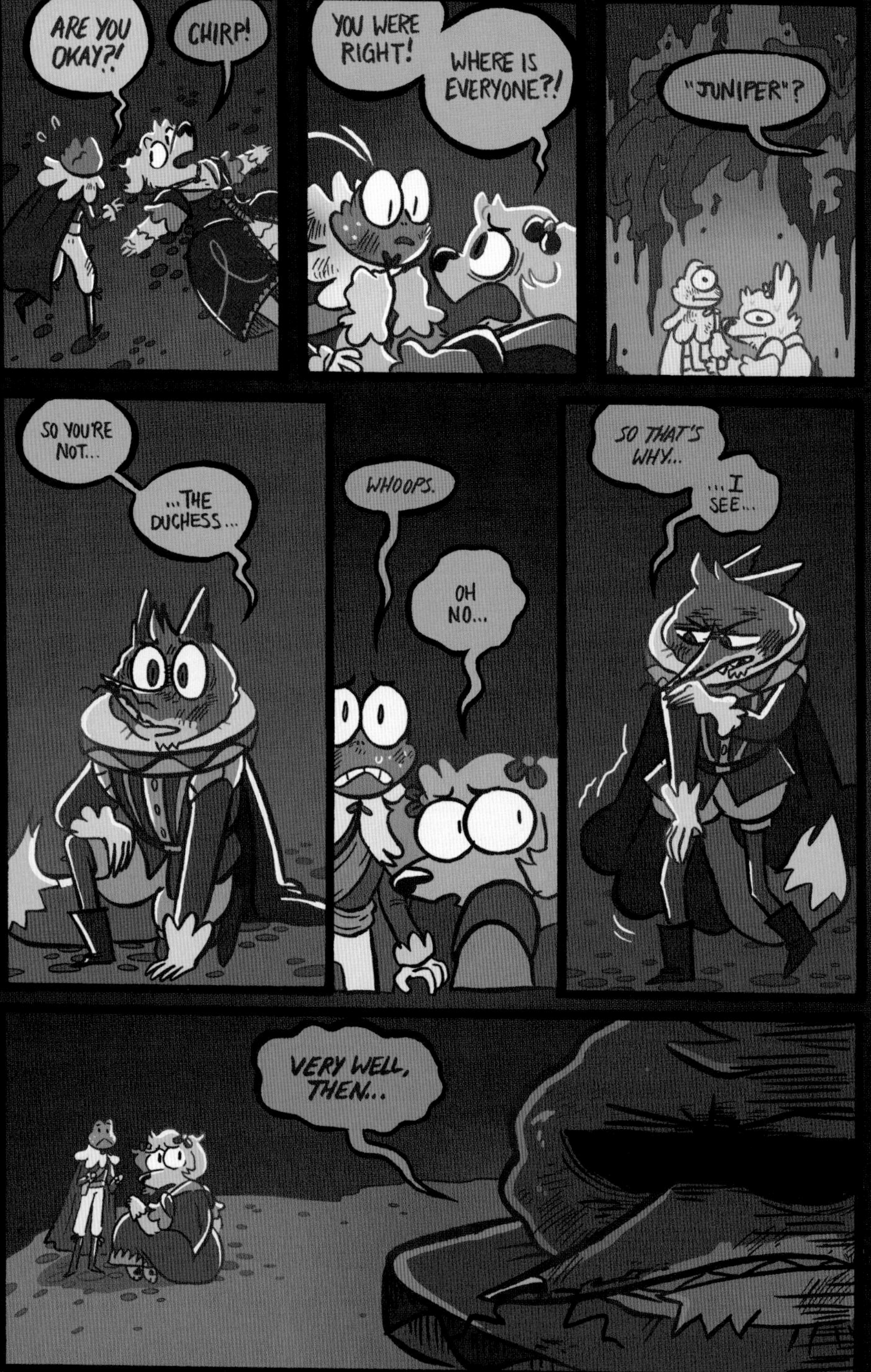
ARE YOU OKAY?!
CHIRP!
YOU WERE RIGHT!
WHERE IS EVERYONE?!
"JUNIPER"?
SO YOU'RE NOT...
...THE DUCHESS...
WHOOPS.
OH NO...
SO THAT'S WHY...
...I SEE...
VERY WELL, THEN...

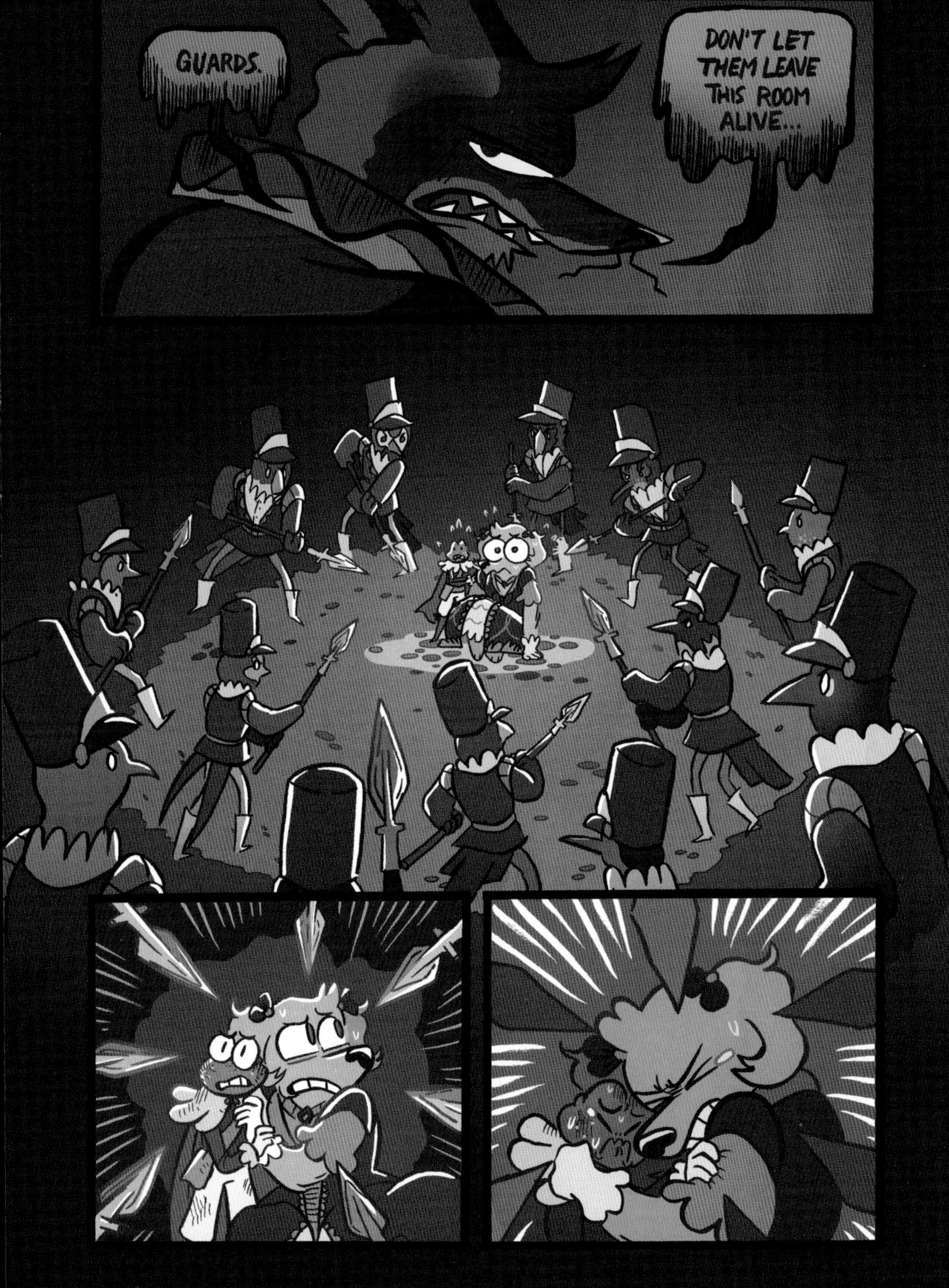
GUARDS.
DON'T LET THEM LEAVE THIS ROOM ALIVE...

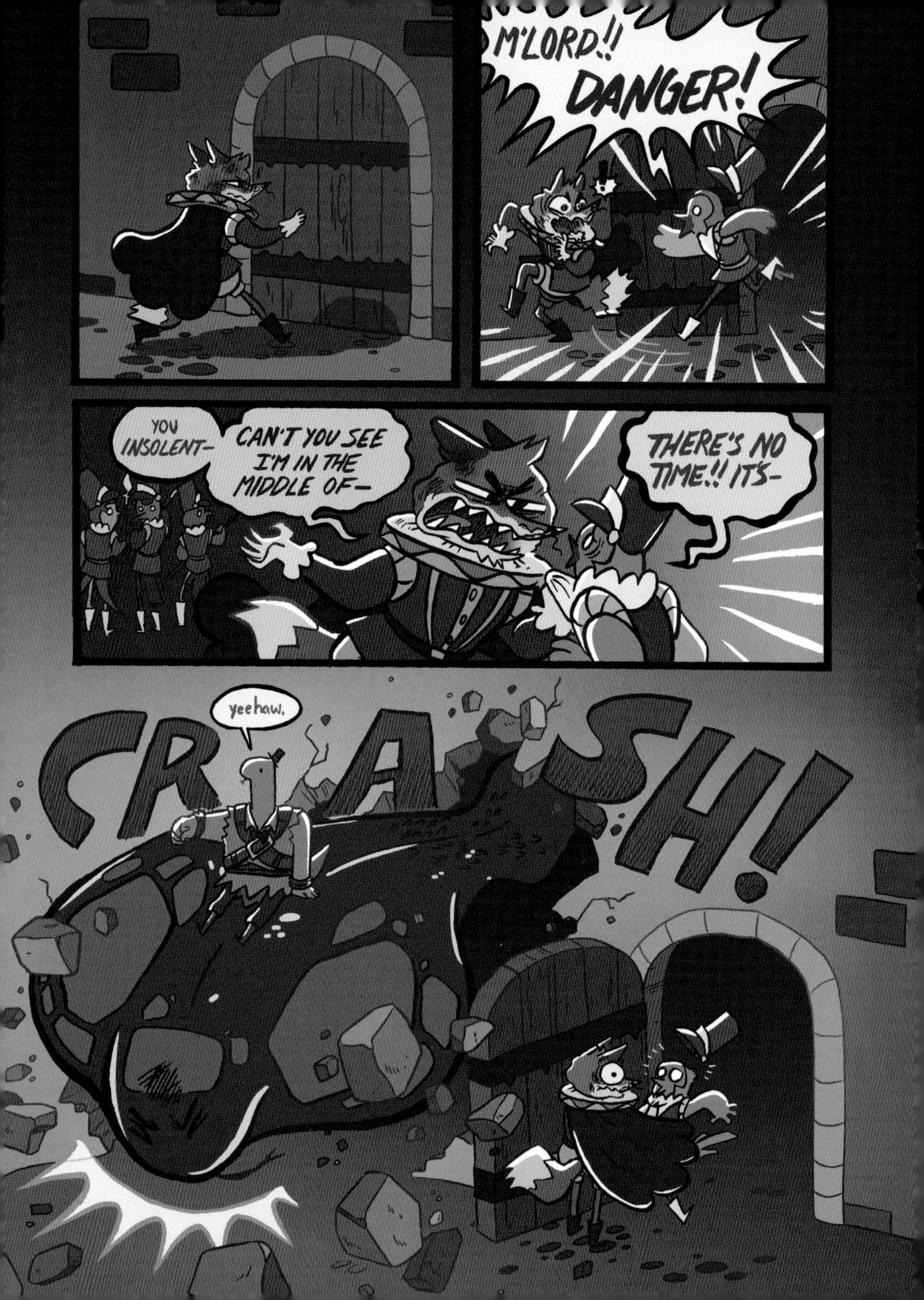
M'LORD!!
DANGER!
YOU INSOLENT-
CAN'T YOU SEE I'M IN THE MIDDLE OF-
THERE'S NO TIME!! IT'S-
yeehaw.
CRASH!

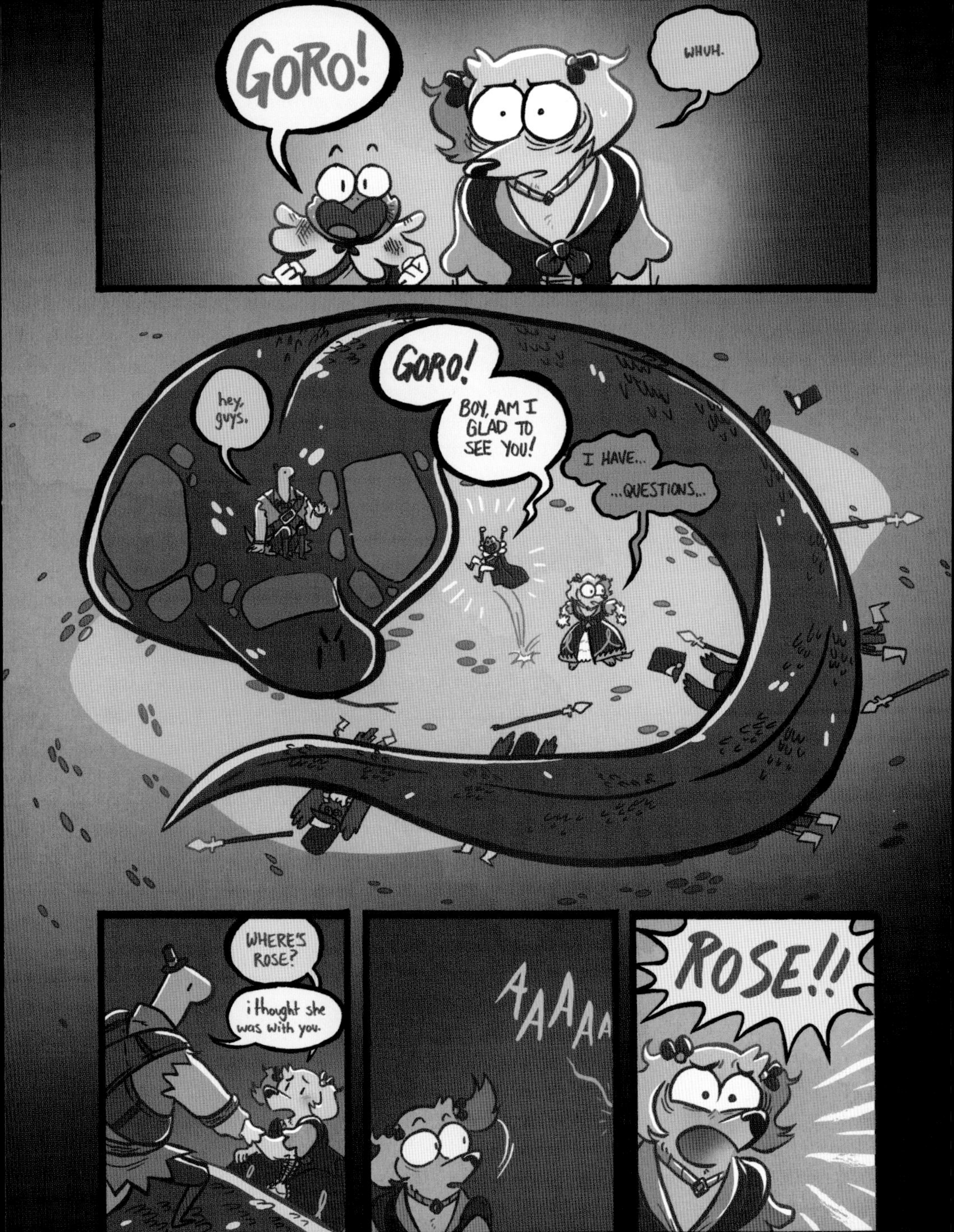
GORO!
WHUH.
hey, guys.
GORO!
BOY, AM I GLAD TO SEE YOU!
I HAVE...
...QUESTIONS...
WHERE'S ROSE?
i thought she was with you.
AAAAA
ROSE!!

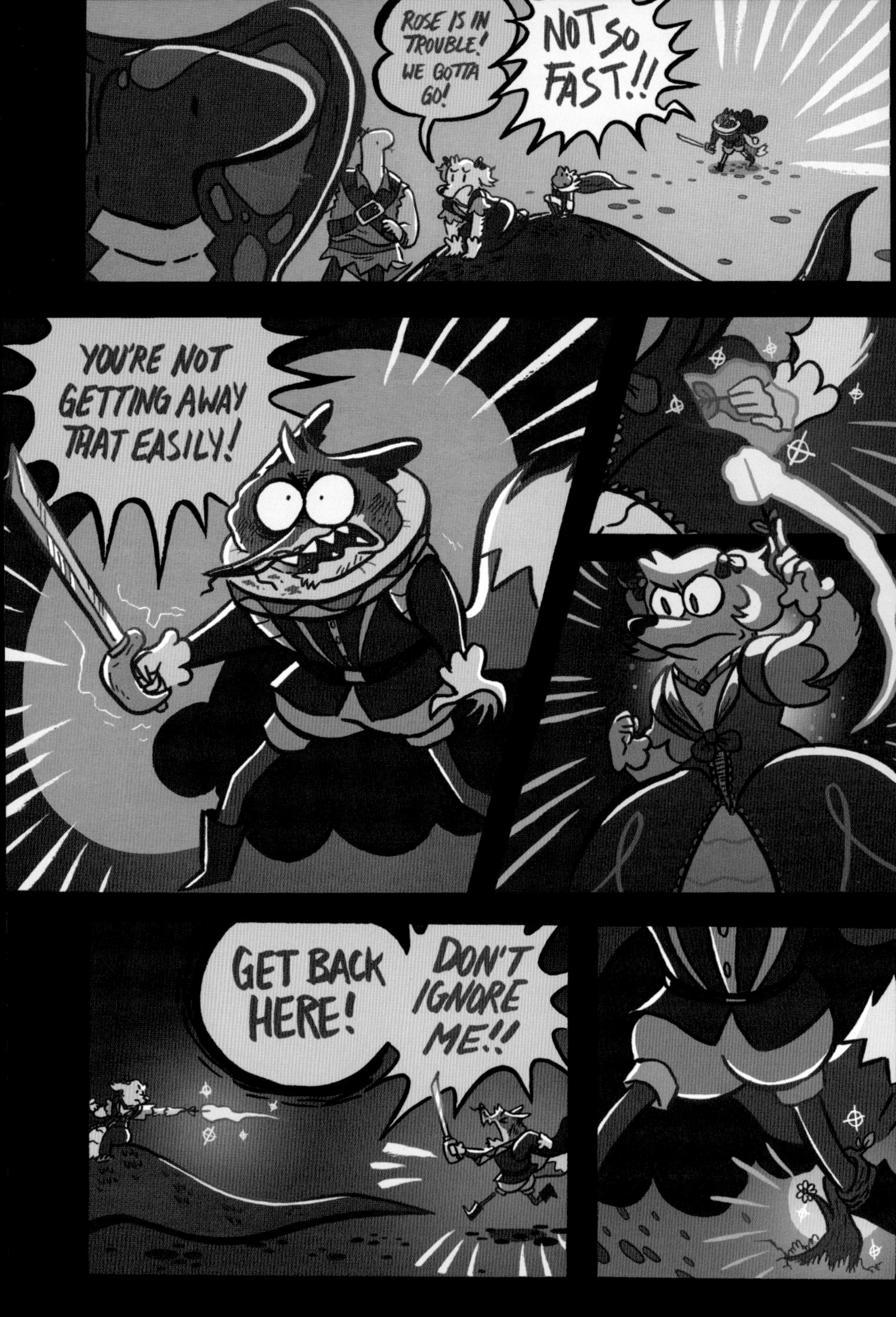

ROSE IS IN TROUBLE! WE GOTTA GO!
NOT SO FAST!!
YOU'RE NOT GETTING AWAY THAT EASILY!
GET BACK HERE!
DON'T IGNORE ME!!

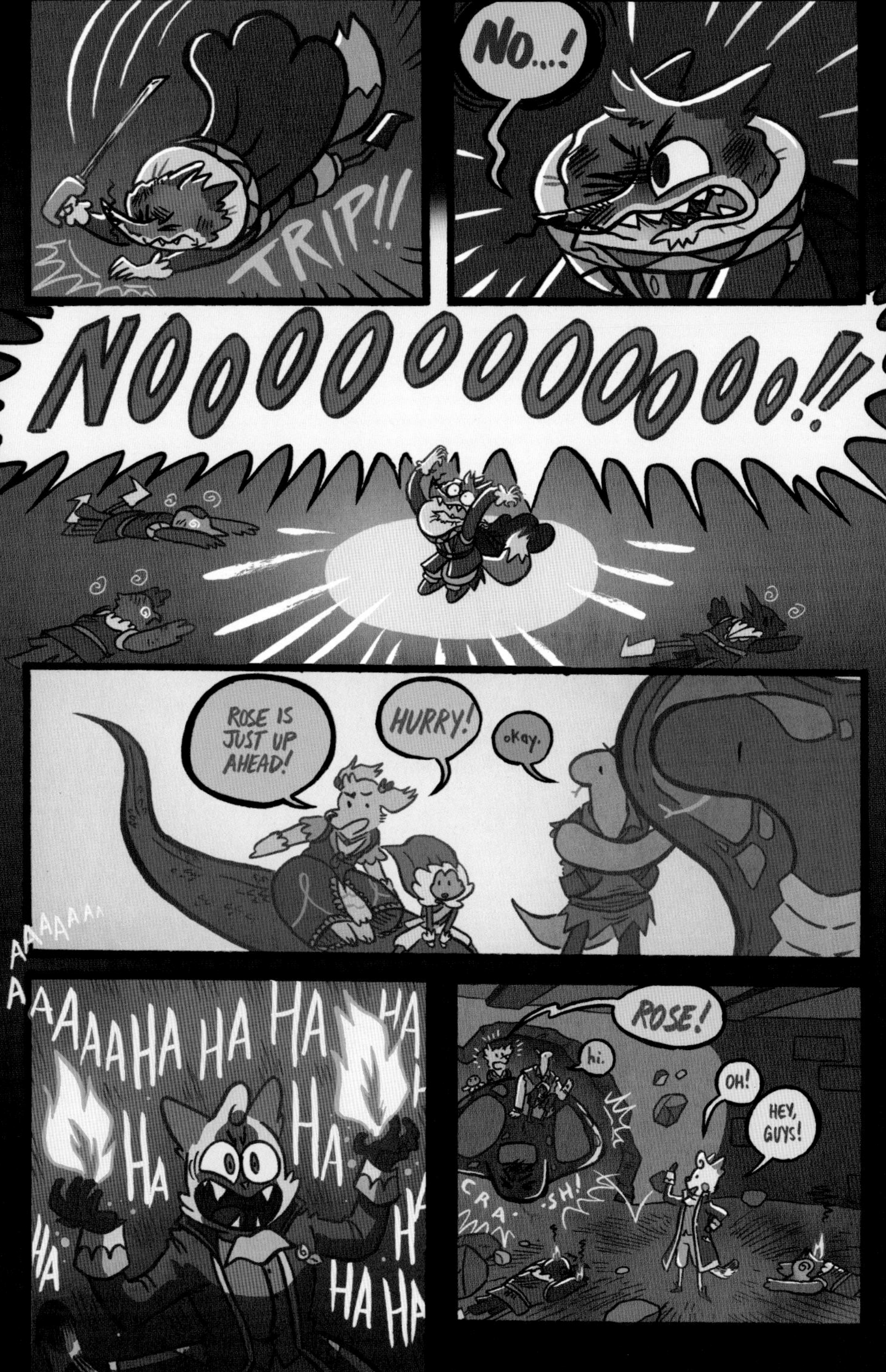
TRIP!!
NO...!
NOOOOOOOOOOOO!!
ROSE IS JUST UP AHEAD!
HURRY!
okay.
AAAAAAA AAAAAHA HA HA HA HA HA HA HA HA HA HA HA HA HA
ROSE!
hi.
OH!
HEY, GUYS!
CRA-SH!

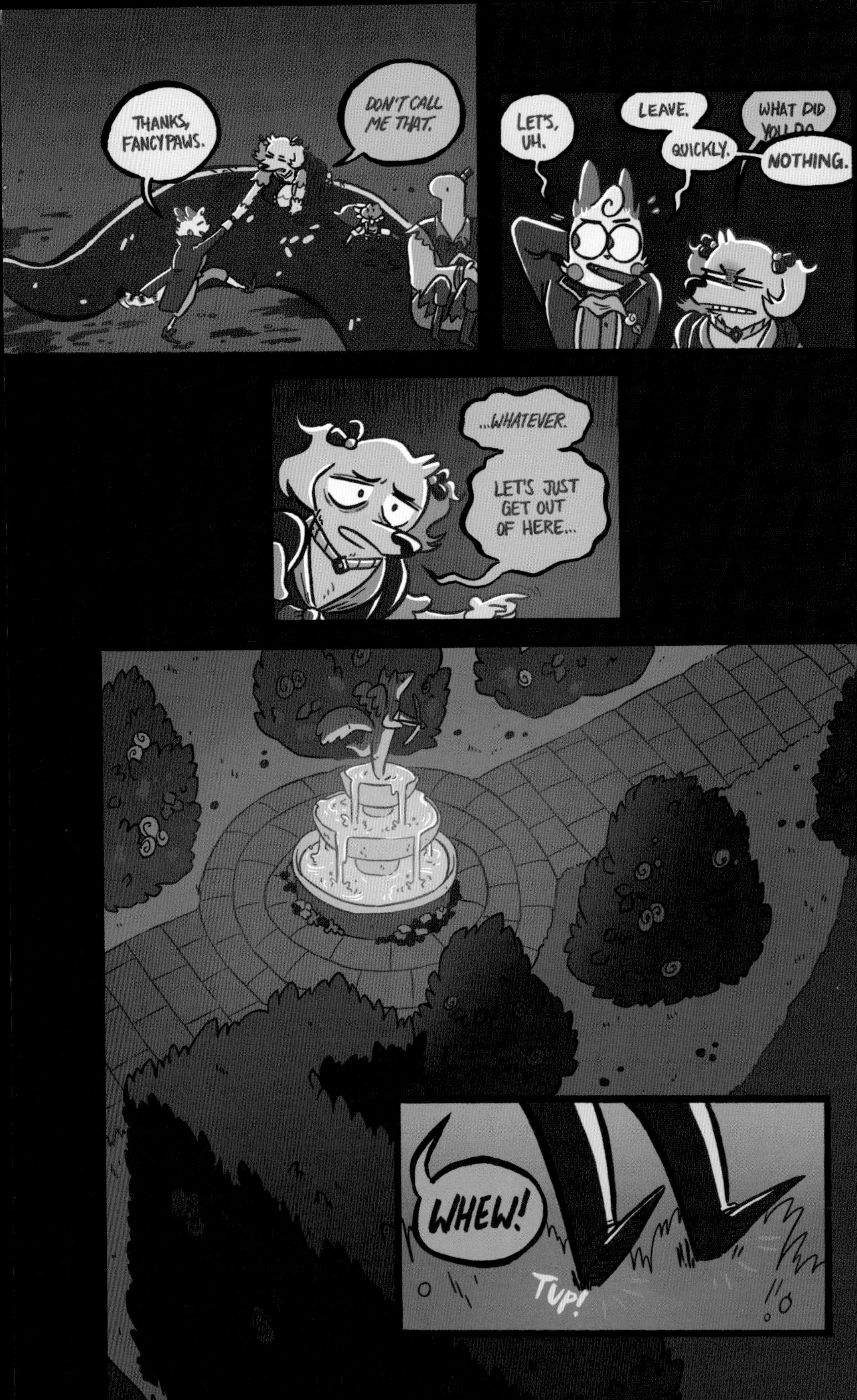
THANKS, FANCYPAWS.
DON'T CALL ME THAT.
LET'S, UH.
LEAVE.
QUICKLY.
WHAT DID YOU DO
NOTHING.
...WHATEVER.
LET'S JUST GET OUT OF HERE...
WHEW!
TUP!

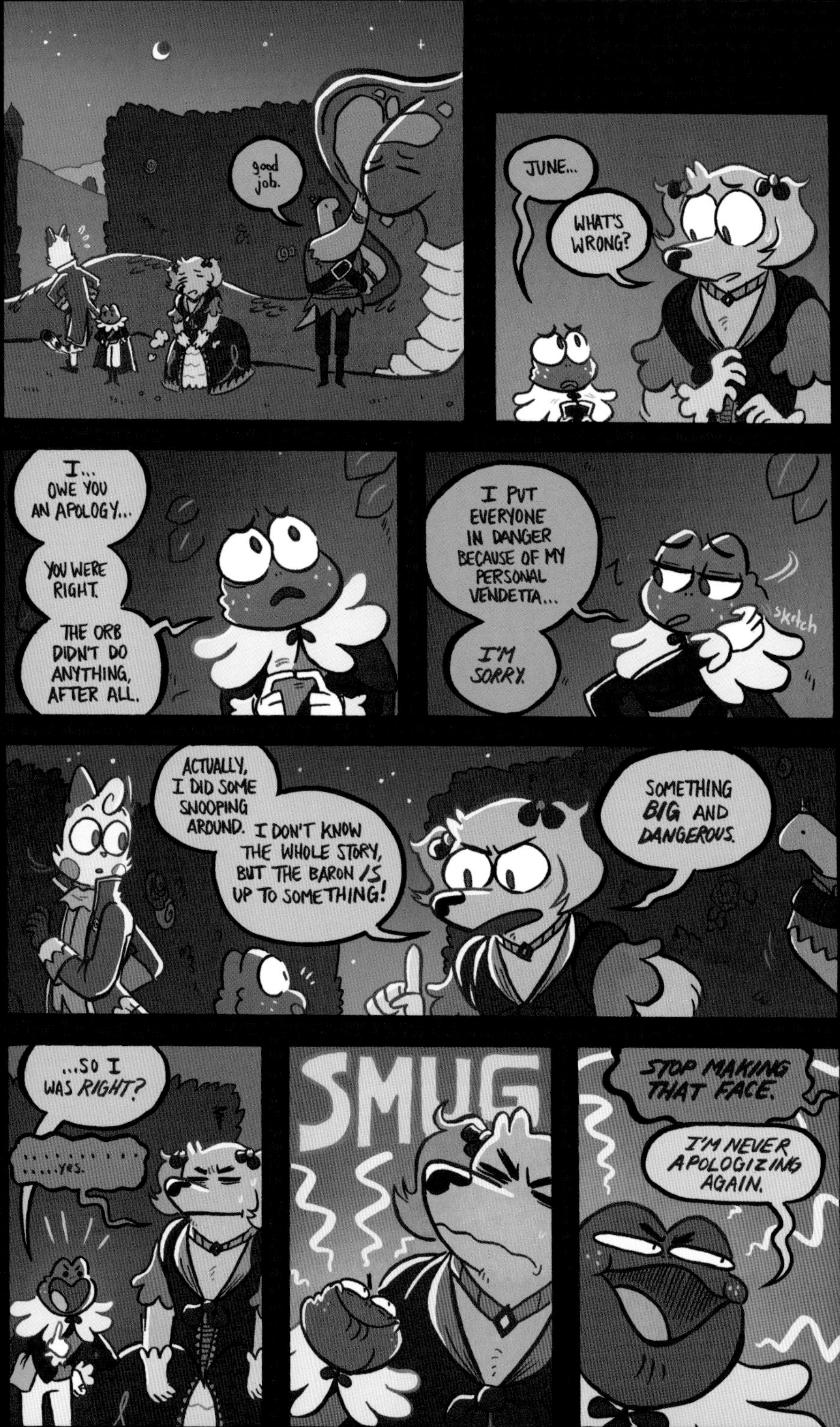
good job.
JUNE...
WHAT'S WRONG?
I... OWE YOU AN APOLOGY...
YOU WERE RIGHT.
THE ORB DIDN'T DO ANYTHING, AFTER ALL.
I PUT EVERYONE IN DANGER BECAUSE OF MY PERSONAL VENDETTA...
I'M SORRY.
sktch
ACTUALLY, I DID SOME SNOOPING AROUND.
I DON'T KNOW THE WHOLE STORY, BUT THE BARON IS UP TO SOMETHING!
SOMETHING BIG AND DANGEROUS.
...SO I WAS RIGHT?
....yes.
SMUG
STOP MAKING THAT FACE.
I'M NEVER APOLOGIZING AGAIN.

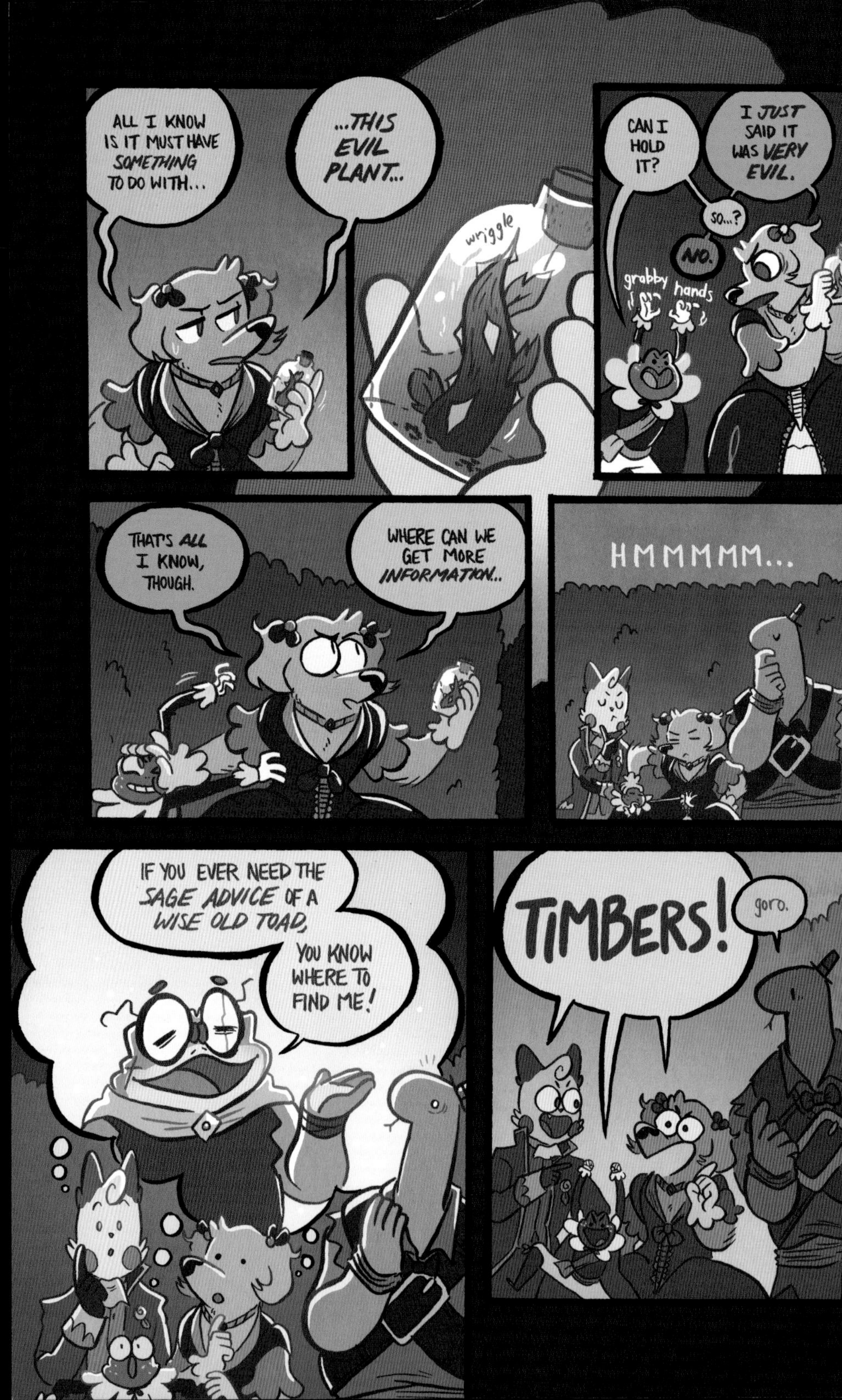

ALL I KNOW IS IT MUST HAVE SOMETHING TO DO WITH...
...THIS EVIL PLANT...
wriggle
CAN I HOLD IT?
I JUST SAID IT WAS VERY EVIL.
SO...?
NO.
grabby hands
THAT'S ALL I KNOW, THOUGH.
WHERE CAN WE GET MORE INFORMATION...
HMMMMM...
IF YOU EVER NEED THE SAGE ADVICE OF A WISE OLD TOAD,
YOU KNOW WHERE TO FIND ME!
TIMBERS!
goro.

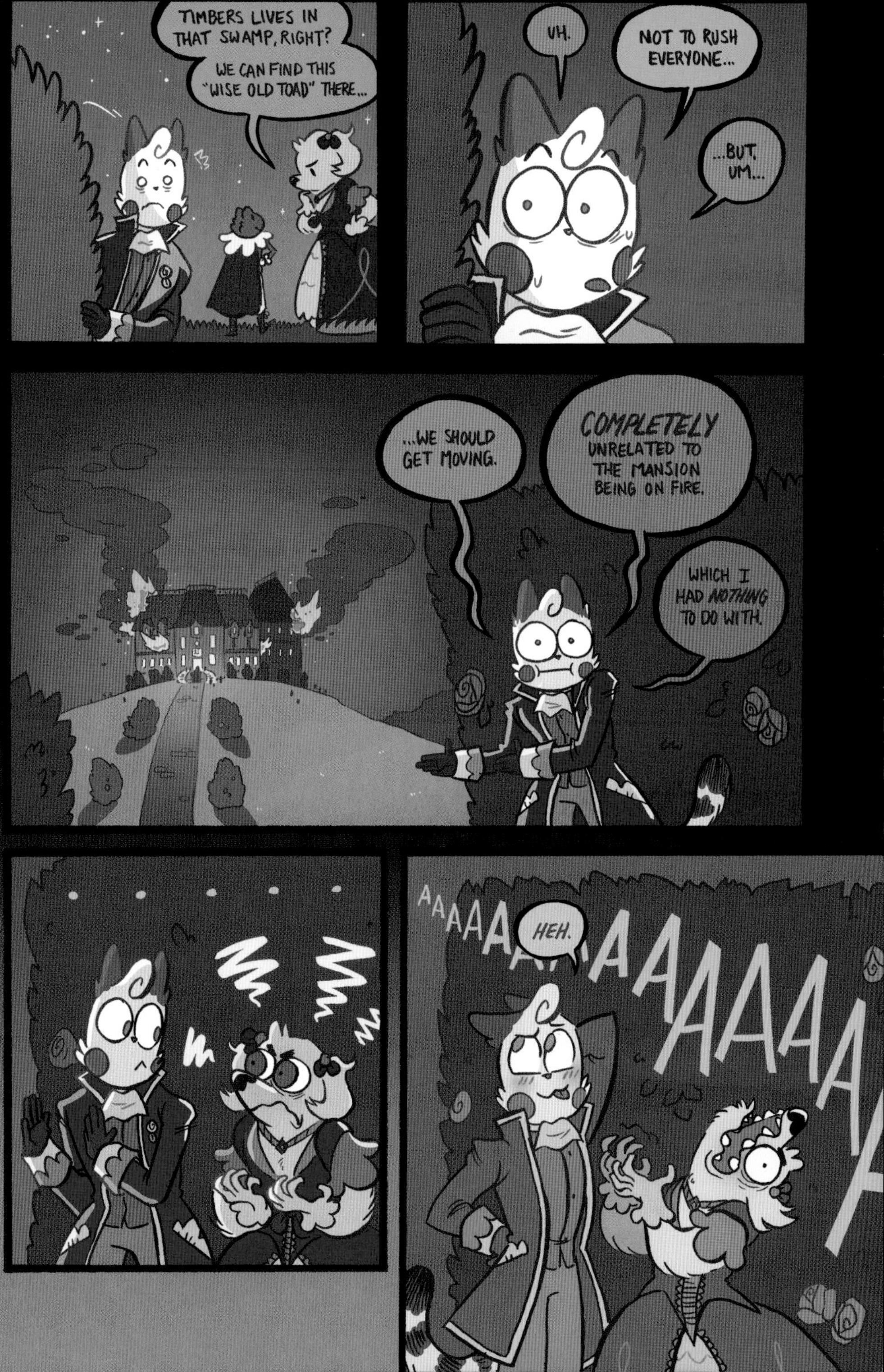
TIMBERS LIVES IN THAT SWAMP, RIGHT?
WE CAN FIND THIS "WISE OLD TOAD" THERE...
UH.
NOT TO RUSH EVERYONE...
...BUT, UM...
...WE SHOULD GET MOVING.
COMPLETELY UNRELATED TO THE MANSION BEING ON FIRE.
WHICH I HAD NOTHING TO DO WITH.
• • • • •
AAAAAAAAAAAAAAAA
HEH.

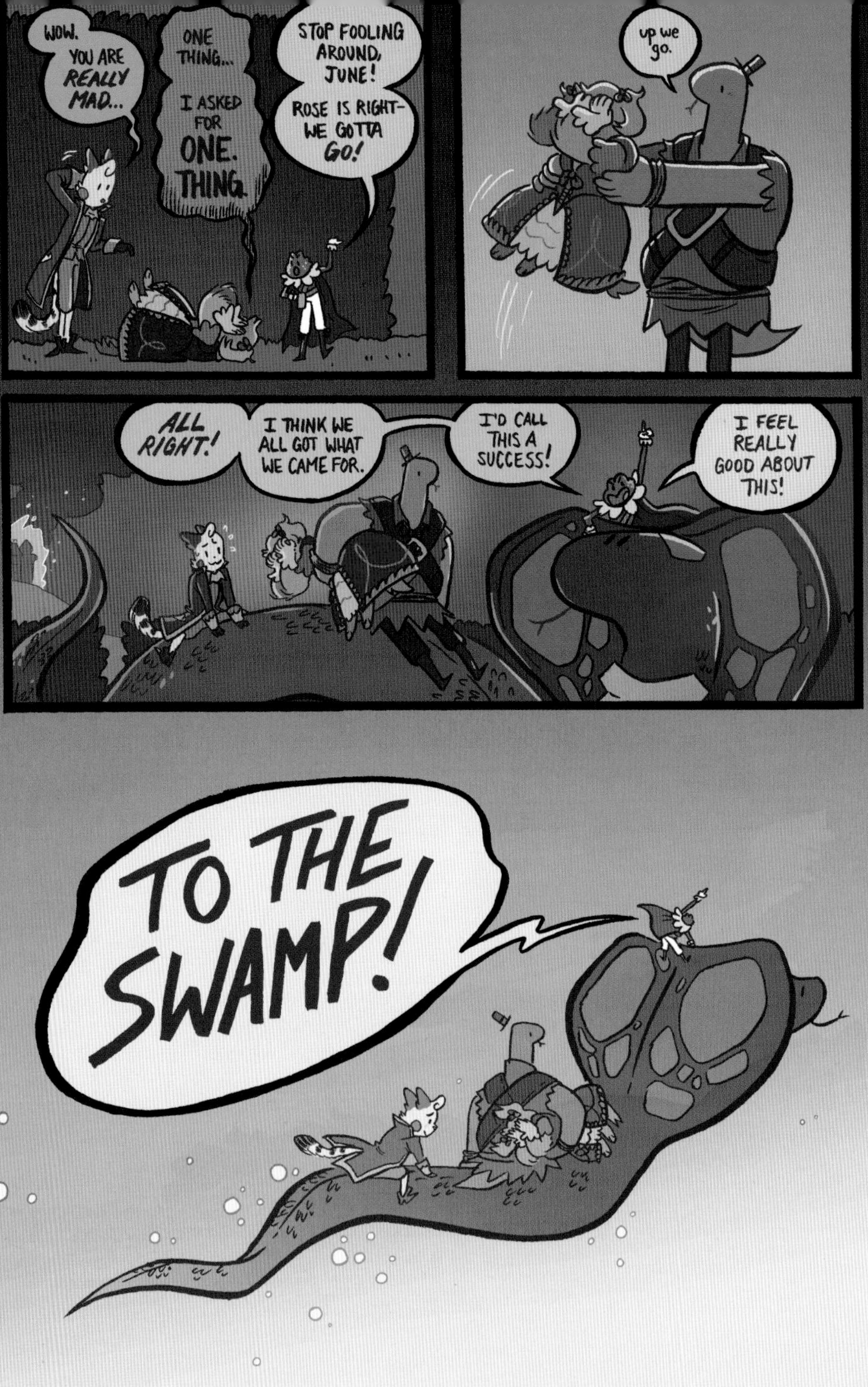
WOW. YOU ARE REALLY MAD...
ONE THING... I ASKED FOR ONE. THING.
STOP FOOLING AROUND, JUNE!
ROSE IS RIGHT- WE GOTTA GO!
up we go.
ALL RIGHT!
I THINK WE ALL GOT WHAT WE CAME FOR.
I'D CALL THIS A SUCCESS!
I FEEL REALLY GOOD ABOUT THIS!
TO THE SWAMP!

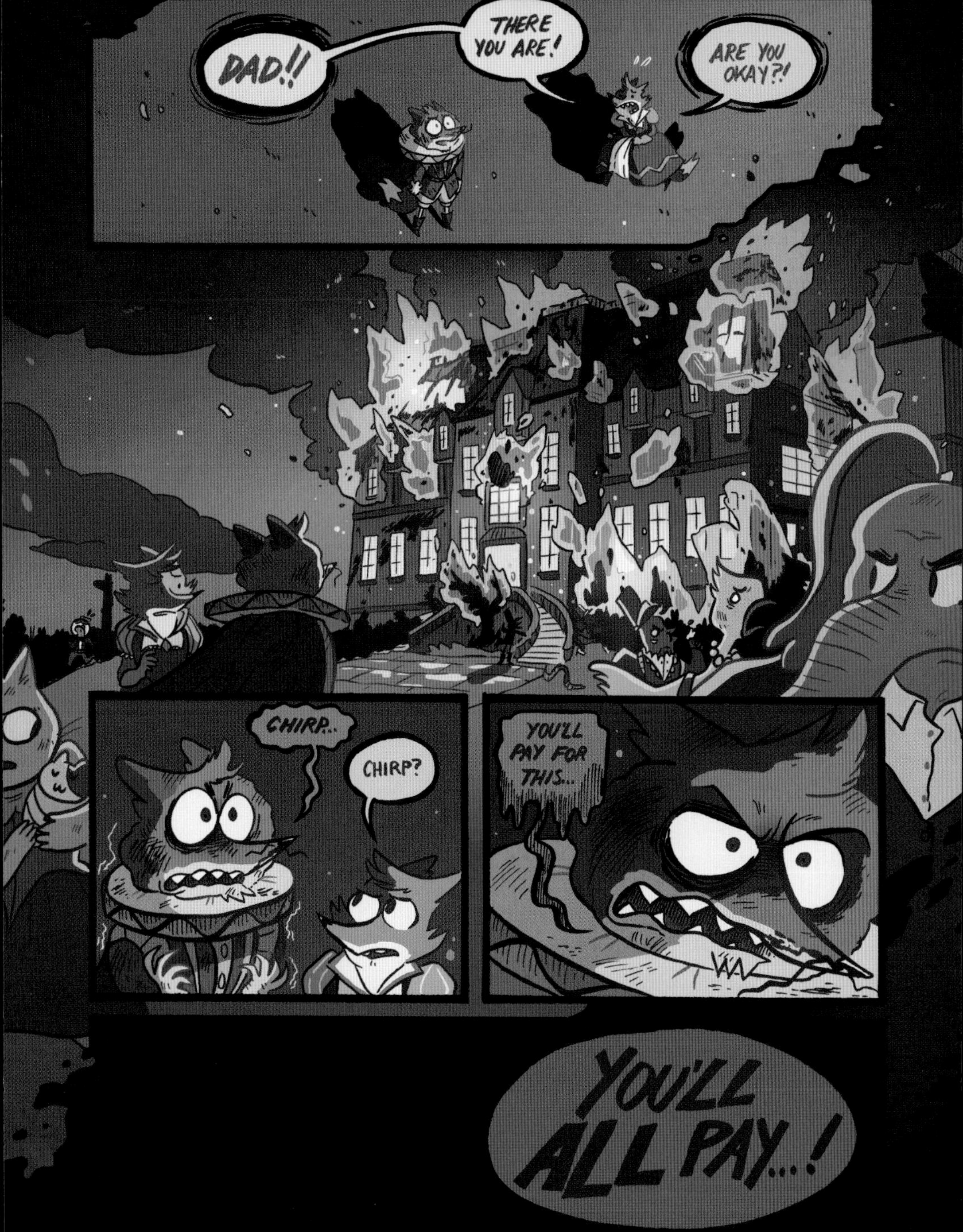
DAD!!
THERE YOU ARE!
ARE YOU OKAY?!
CHIRP..
CHIRP?
YOU'LL PAY FOR THIS...
YOU'LL ALL PAY...!

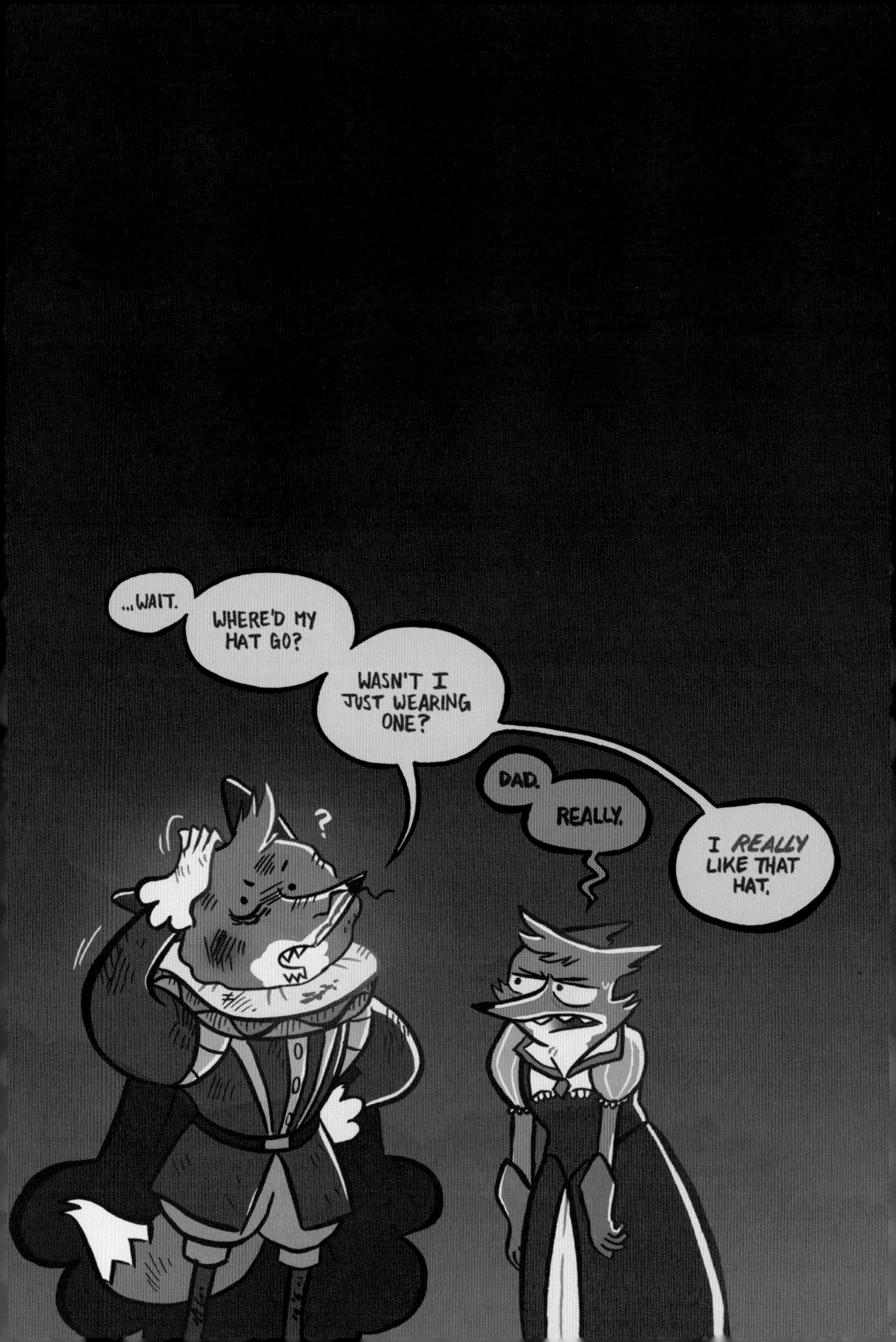
...WAIT.
WHERE'D MY HAT GO?
WASN'T I JUST WEARING ONE?
DAD.
REALLY.
I REALLY LIKE THAT HAT.

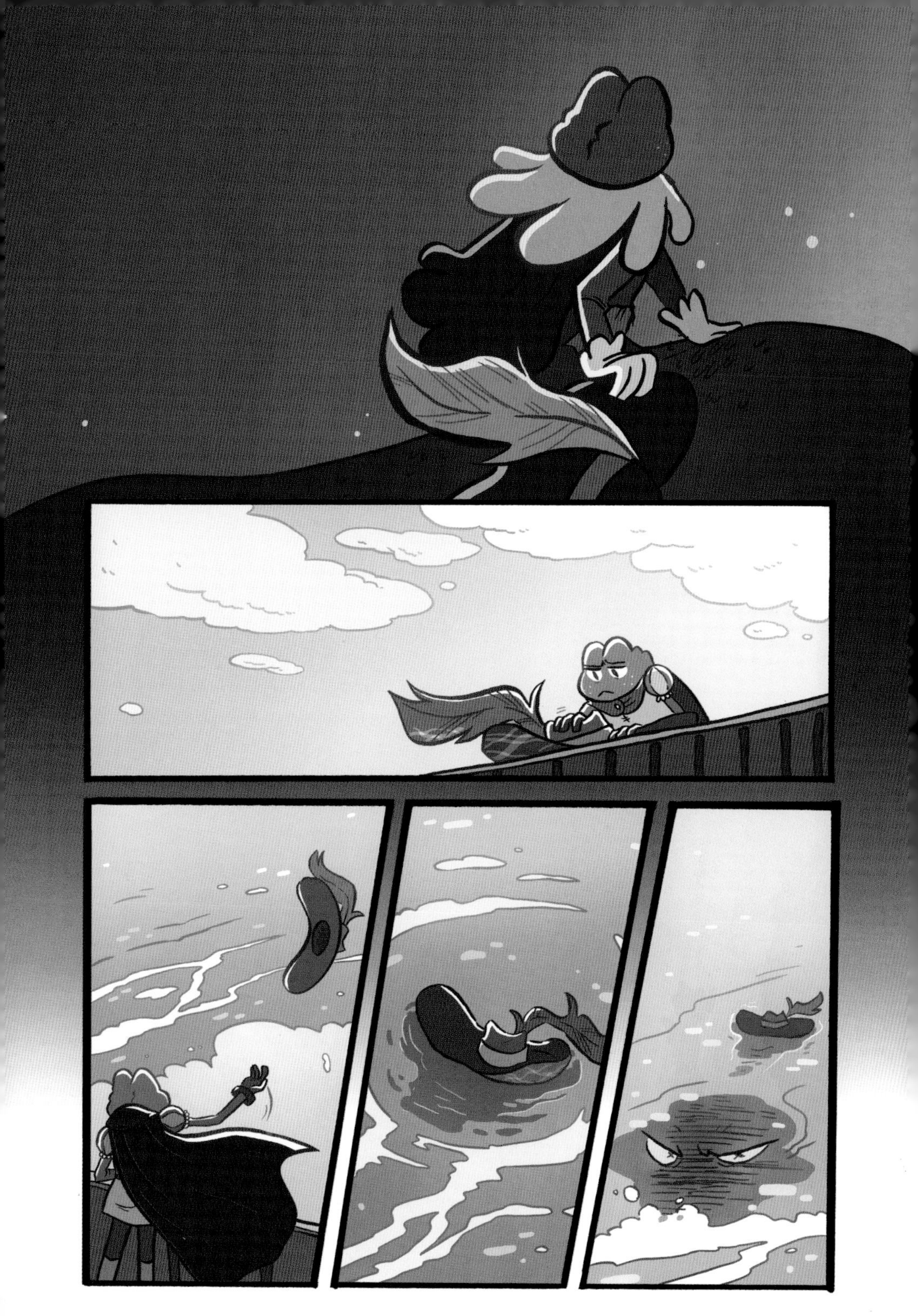

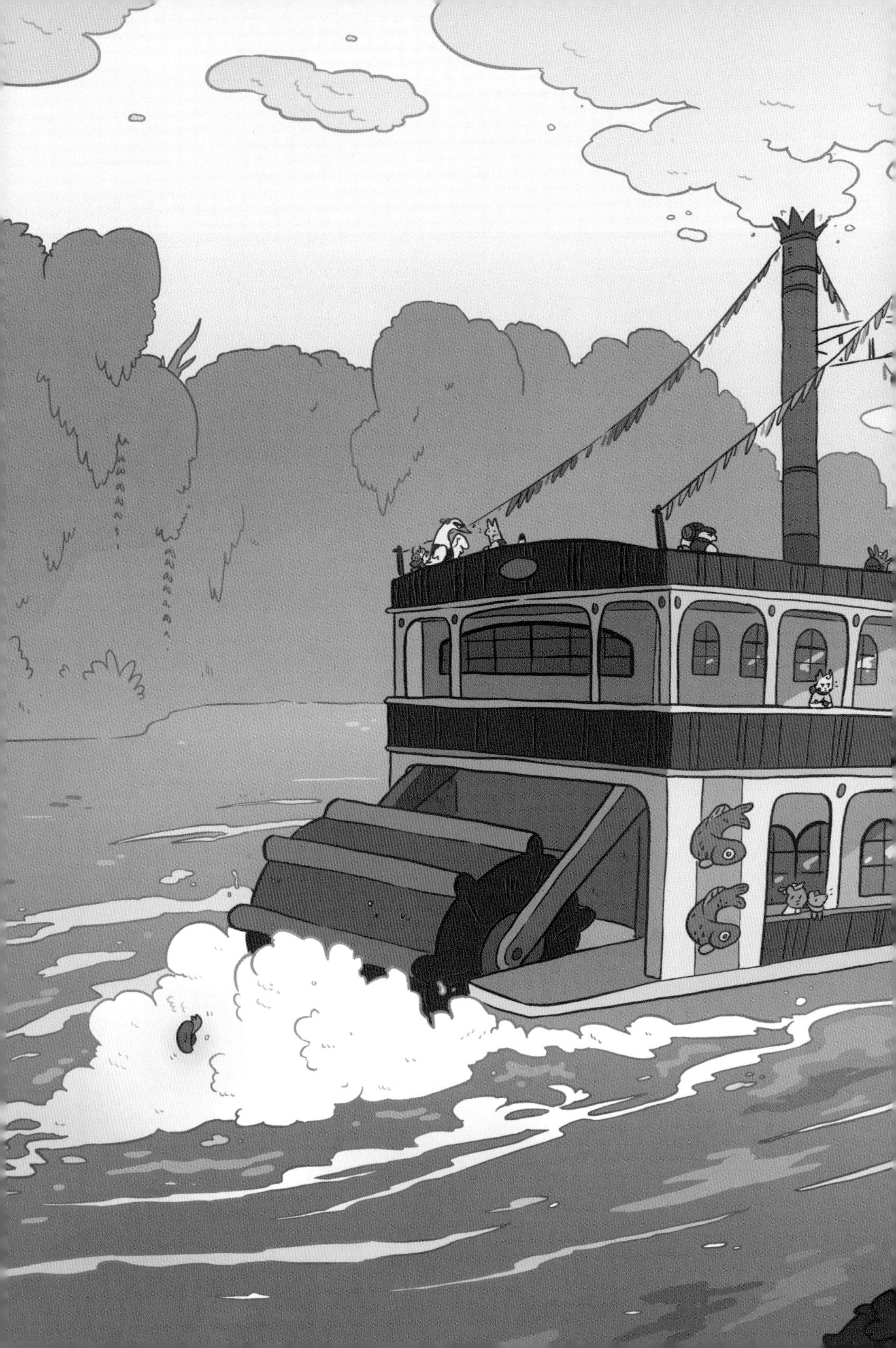

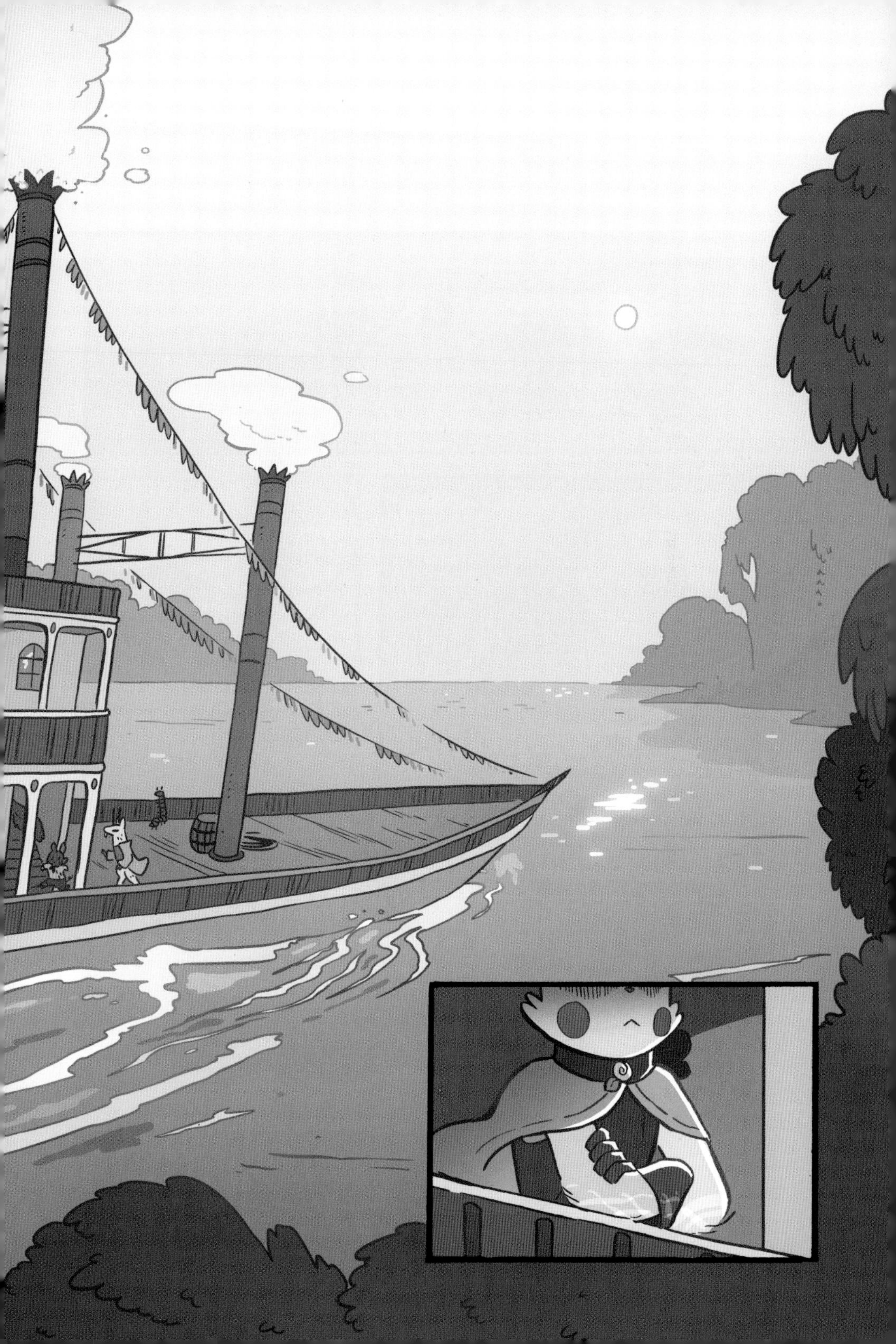

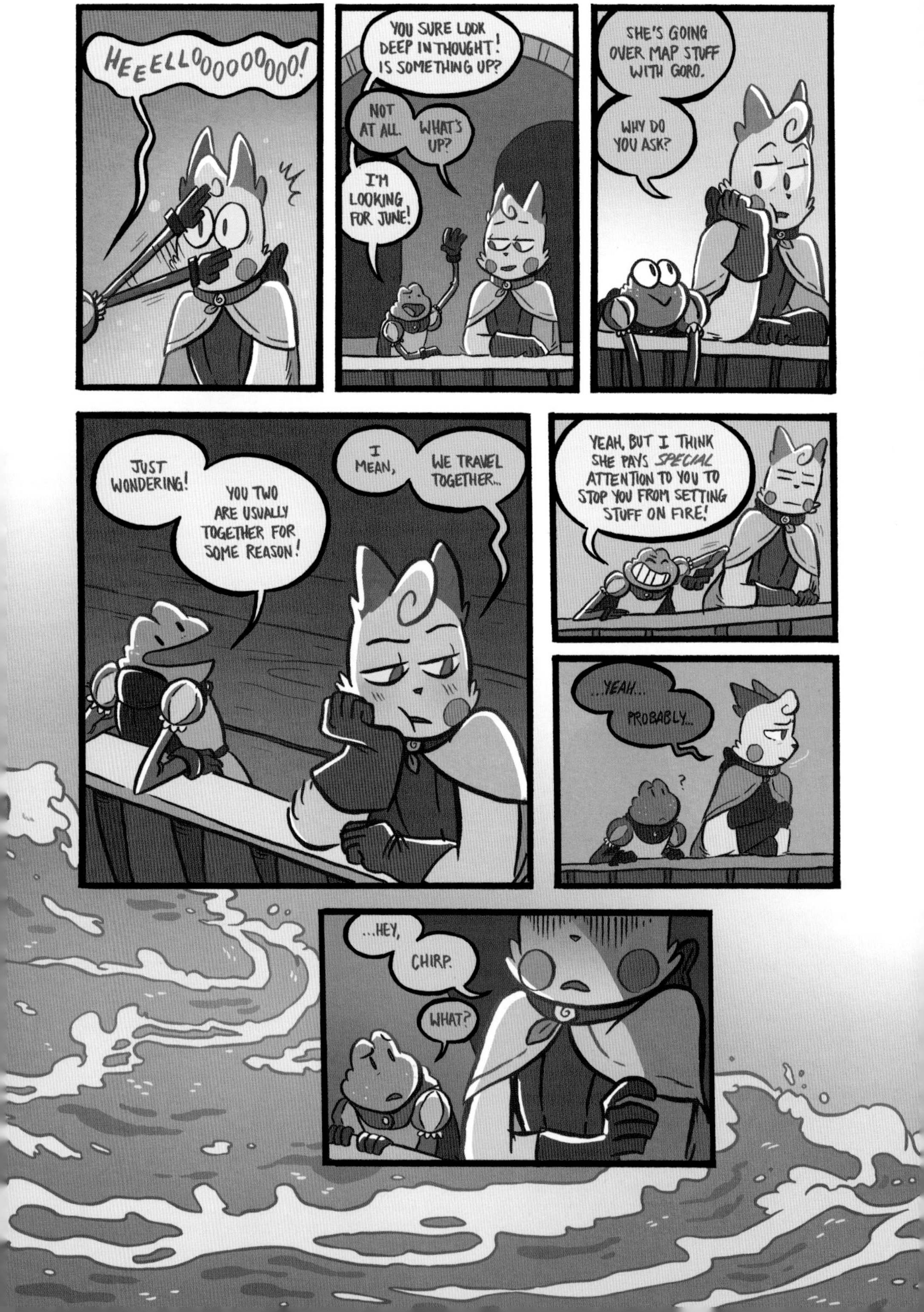
HEEELLOOOOOOOOO!
YOU SURE LOOK DEEP IN THOUGHT! IS SOMETHING UP?
NOT AT ALL.
WHAT'S UP?
I'M LOOKING FOR JUNE!
SHE'S GOING OVER MAP STUFF WITH GORO.
WHY DO YOU ASK?
JUST WONDERING!
YOU TWO ARE USUALLY TOGETHER FOR SOME REASON!
I MEAN,
WE TRAVEL TOGETHER...
YEAH, BUT I THINK SHE PAYS SPECIAL ATTENTION TO YOU TO STOP YOU FROM SETTING STUFF ON FIRE!
...YEAH...
PROBABLY...
?
...HEY,
CHIRP.
WHAT?

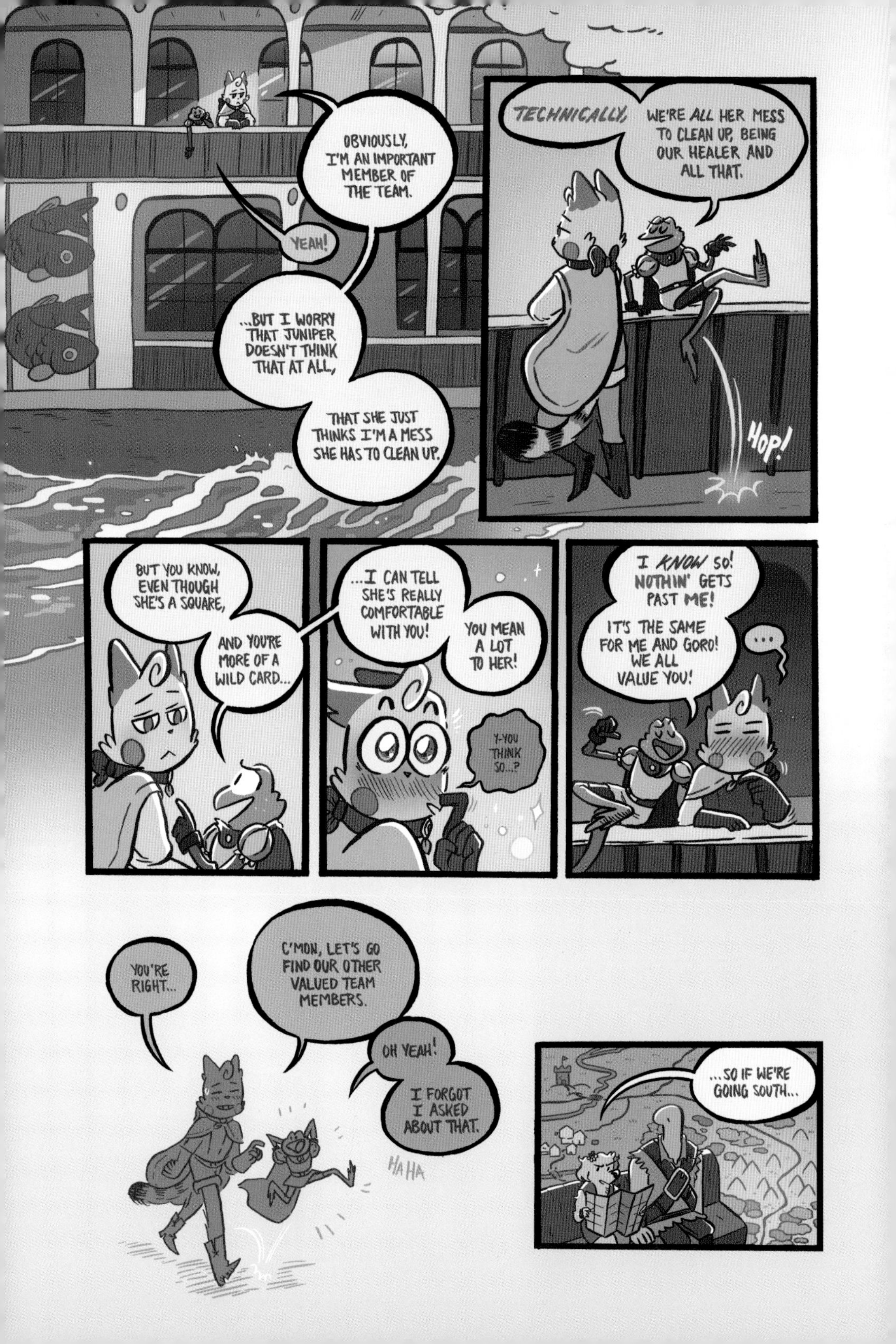

OBVIOUSLY, I'M AN IMPORTANT MEMBER OF THE TEAM.
YEAH!
...BUT I WORRY THAT JUNIPER DOESN'T THINK THAT AT ALL,
THAT SHE JUST THINKS I'M A MESS SHE HAS TO CLEAN UP.
TECHNICALLY,
WE'RE ALL HER MESS TO CLEAN UP, BEING OUR HEALER AND ALL THAT.
HOP!
BUT YOU KNOW, EVEN THOUGH SHE'S A SQUARE,
AND YOU'RE MORE OF A WILD CARD...
...I CAN TELL SHE'S REALLY COMFORTABLE WITH YOU!
YOU MEAN A LOT TO HER!
Y-YOU THINK SO...?
I KNOW SO! NOTHIN' GETS PAST ME!
IT'S THE SAME FOR ME AND GORO! WE ALL VALUE YOU!
...
YOU'RE RIGHT...
C'MON, LET'S GO FIND OUR OTHER VALUED TEAM MEMBERS.
OH YEAH!
I FORGOT I ASKED ABOUT THAT.
HA HA
...SO IF WE'RE GOING SOUTH...

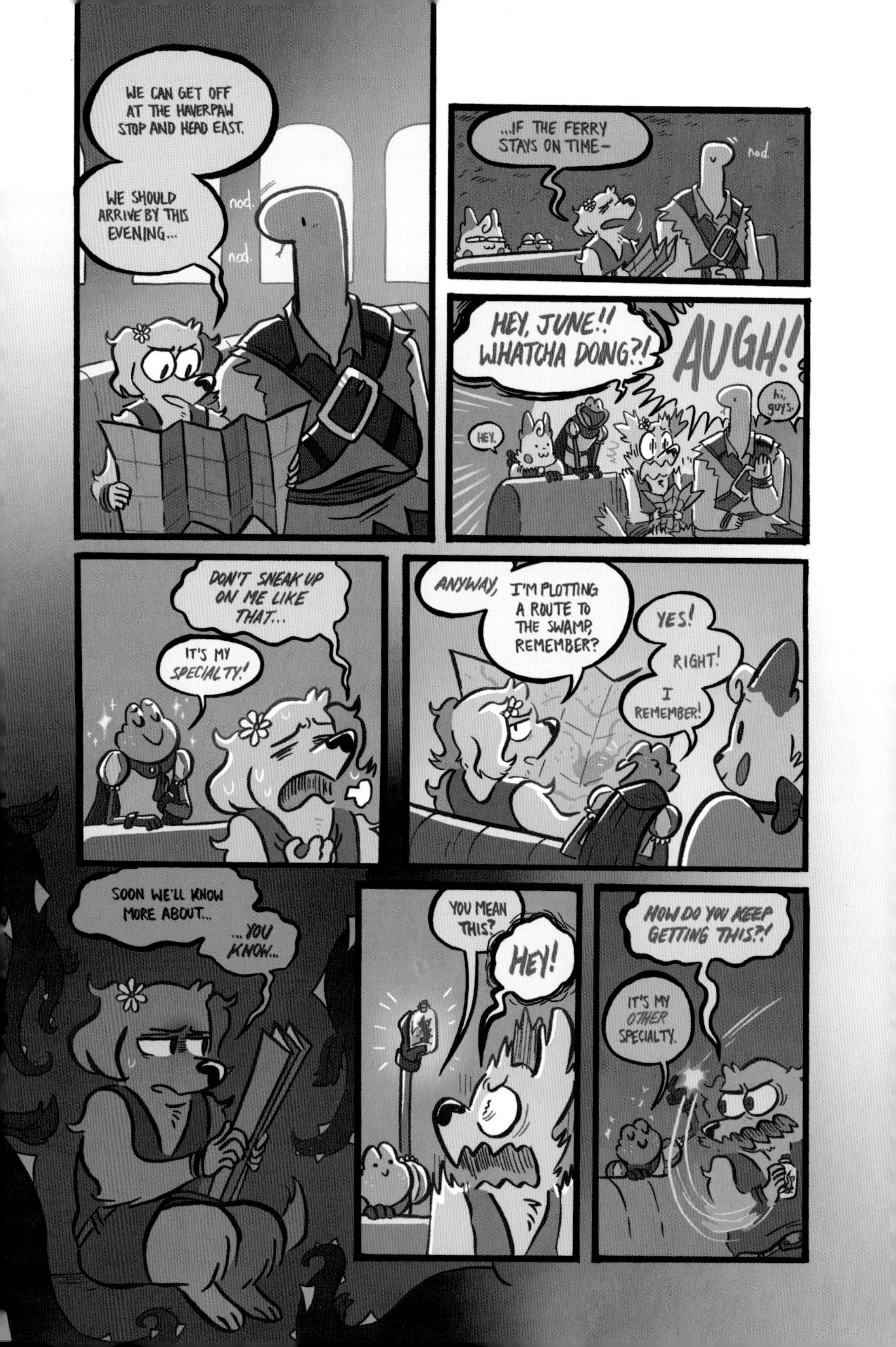
WE CAN GET OFF AT THE HAVERPAW STOP AND HEAD EAST.
WE SHOULD ARRIVE BY THIS EVENING...
nod.
nod.
...IF THE FERRY STAYS ON TIME-
nod.
HEY, JUNE!! WHATCHA DOING?!
AUGH!
HEY.
hi, guys.
DON'T SNEAK UP ON ME LIKE THAT...
IT'S MY SPECIALTY!
ANYWAY, I'M PLOTTING A ROUTE TO THE SWAMP, REMEMBER?
YES!
RIGHT!
I REMEMBER!
SOON WE'LL KNOW MORE ABOUT...
...YOU KNOW...
YOU MEAN THIS?
HEY!
HOW DO YOU KEEP GETTING THIS?!
IT'S MY OTHER SPECIALTY.

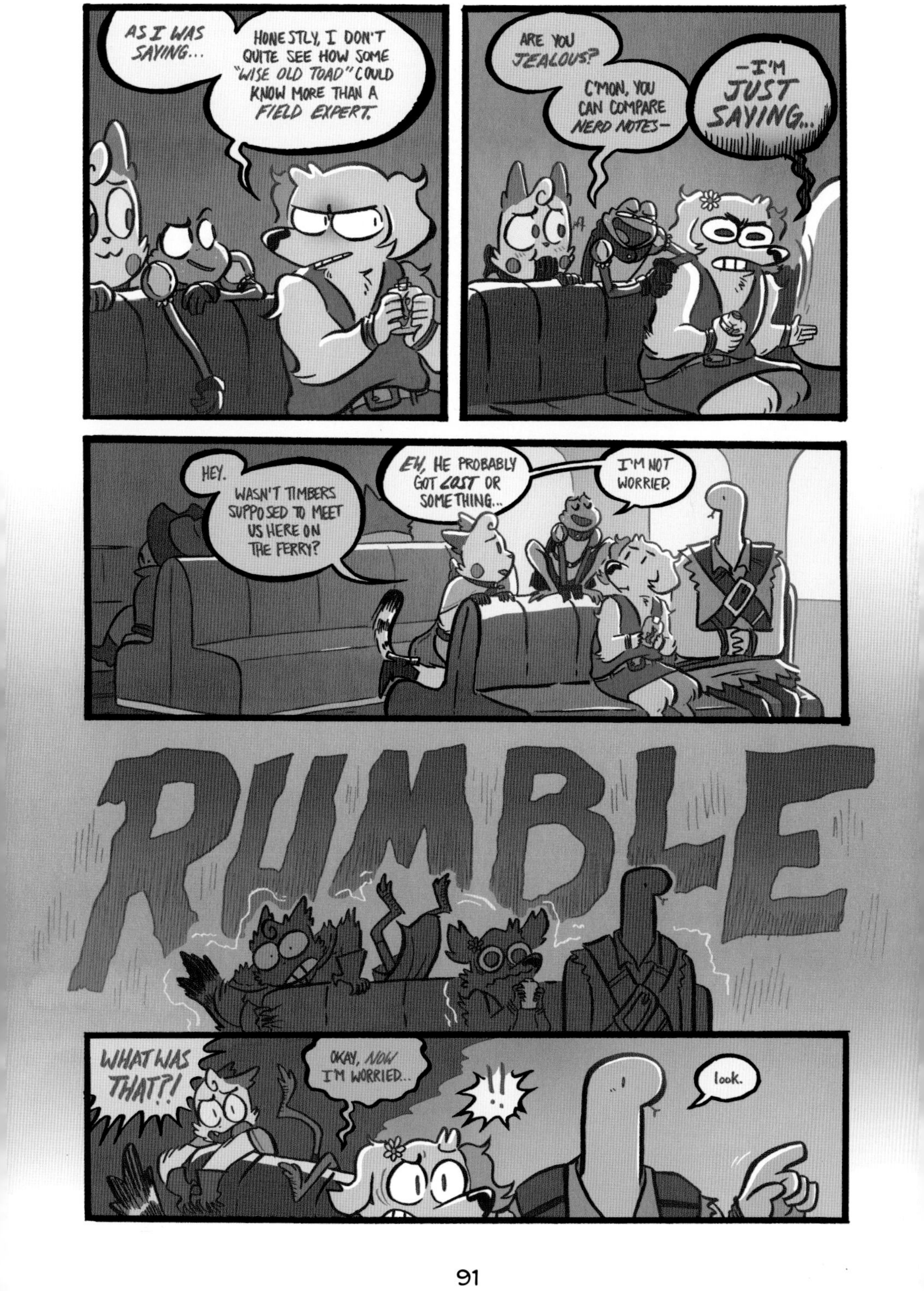
AS I WAS SAYING...
HONESTLY, I DON'T QUITE SEE HOW SOME "WISE OLD TOAD" COULD KNOW MORE THAN A FIELD EXPERT.
ARE YOU JEALOUS?
C'MON, YOU CAN COMPARE NERD NOTES–
–I'M JUST SAYING...
HEY.
WASN'T TIMBERS SUPPOSED TO MEET US HERE ON THE FERRY?
EH, HE PROBABLY GOT LOST OR SOMETHING...
I'M NOT WORRIED.
RUMBLE
WHAT WAS THAT?!
OKAY, NOW I'M WORRIED...
!!
look.

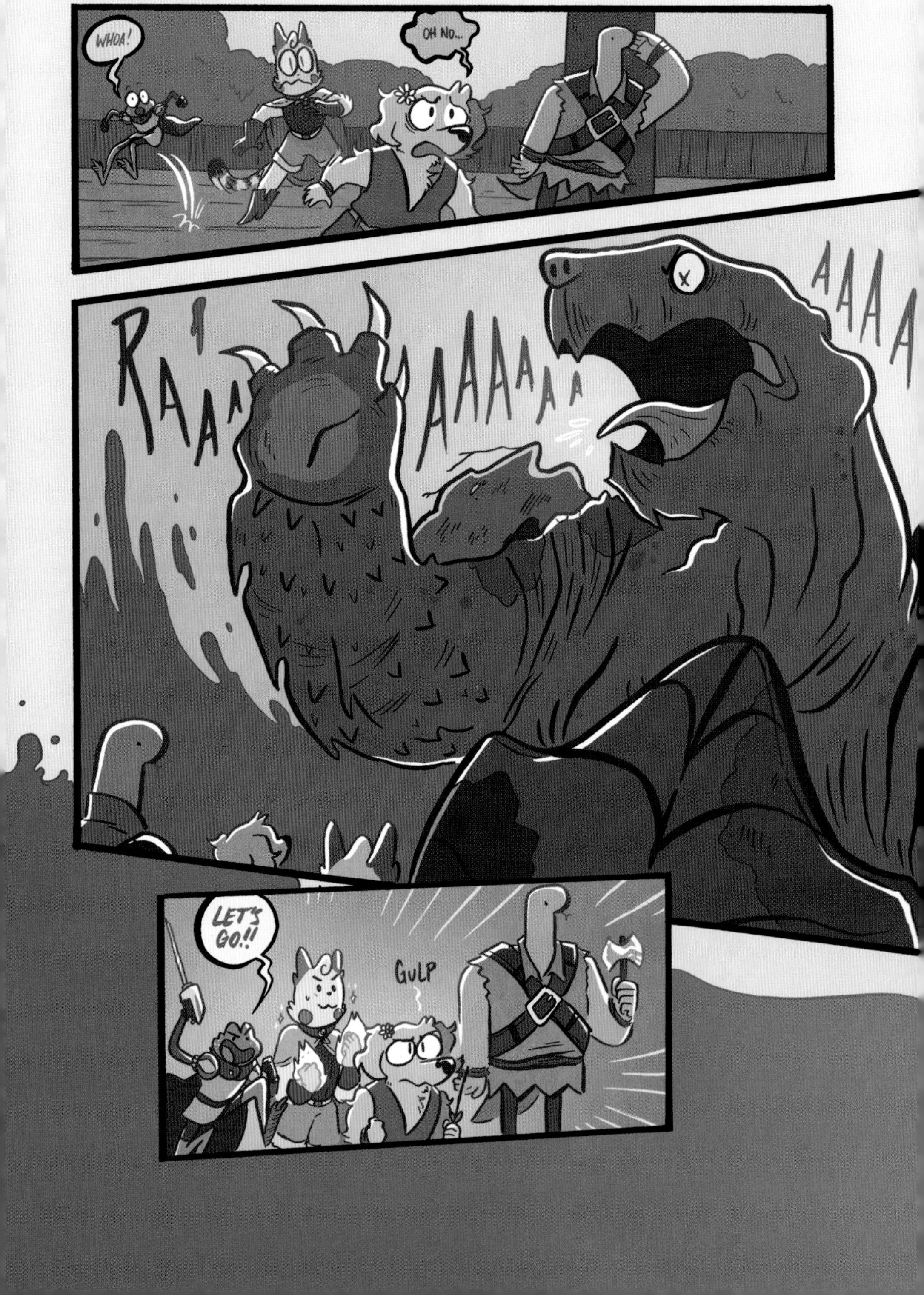
WHOA!
OH NO...
RAAAAAAAAAAA AAAA
LET'S GO!!
GULP

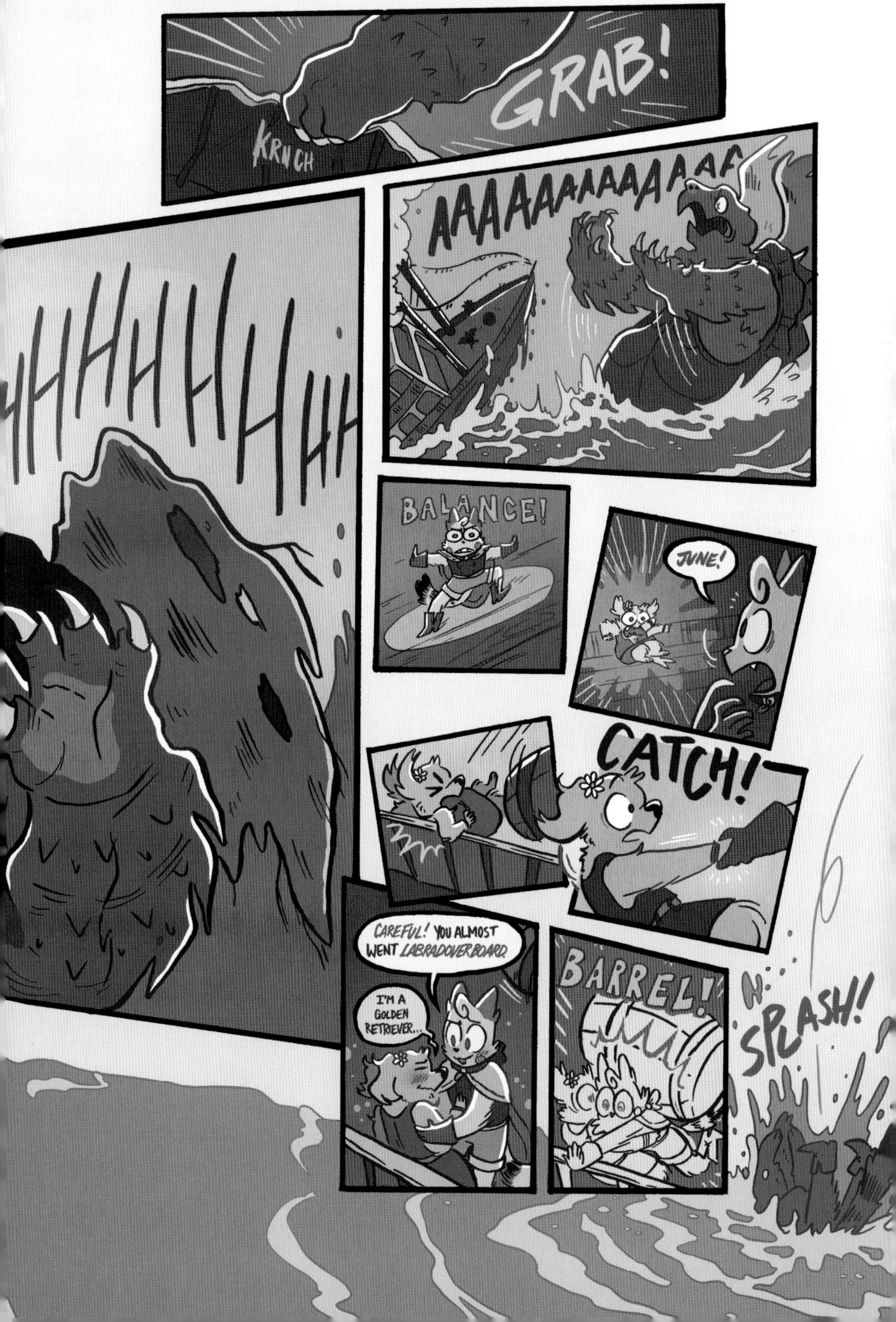
KRNCH
GRAB!
AAAAAAAAAAAAAF
HHHHHHHHHHH
BALANCE!
JUNE!
CATCH!
CAREFUL! YOU ALMOST WENT LABRADOVERBOARD.
I'M A GOLDEN RETRIEVER...
BARREL!
SPLASH!

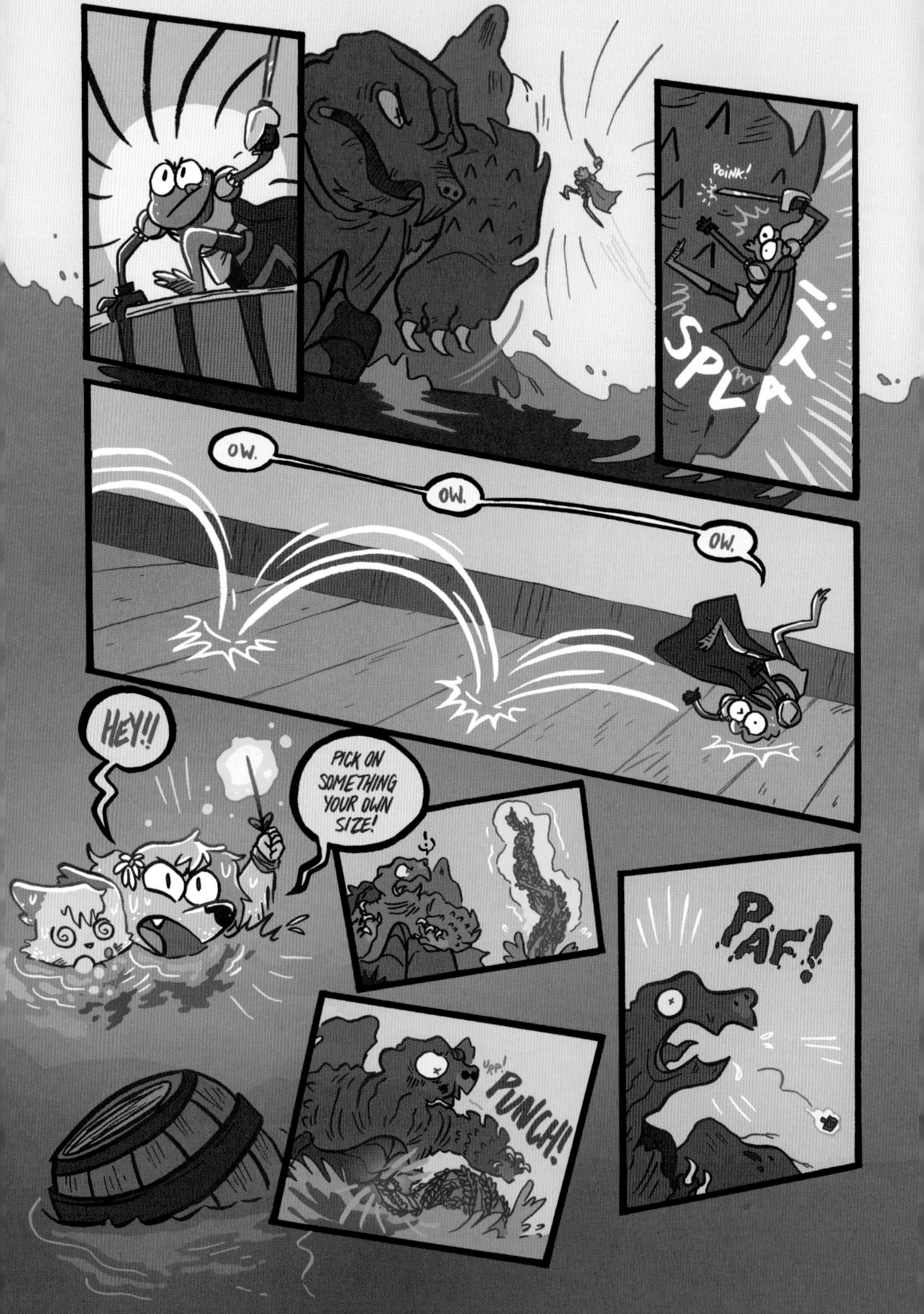
POINK!
SPLAT!!
OW.
OW.
OW.
HEY!!
PICK ON SOMETHING YOUR OWN SIZE!
PAF!!
URP!
PUNCH!

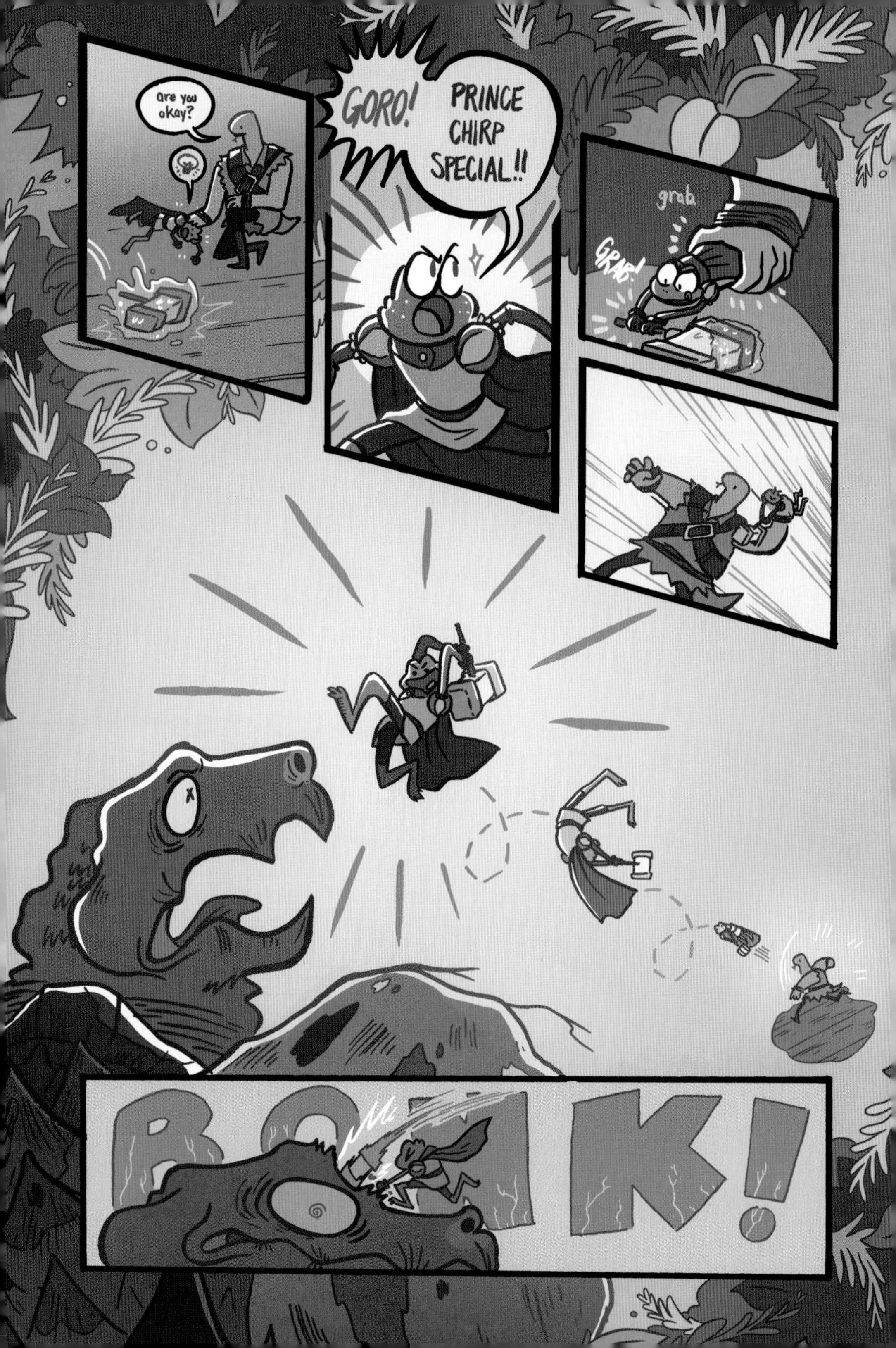
are you okay?
GORO!
PRINCE CHIRP SPECIAL!!
grab
GRAB!
BONK!

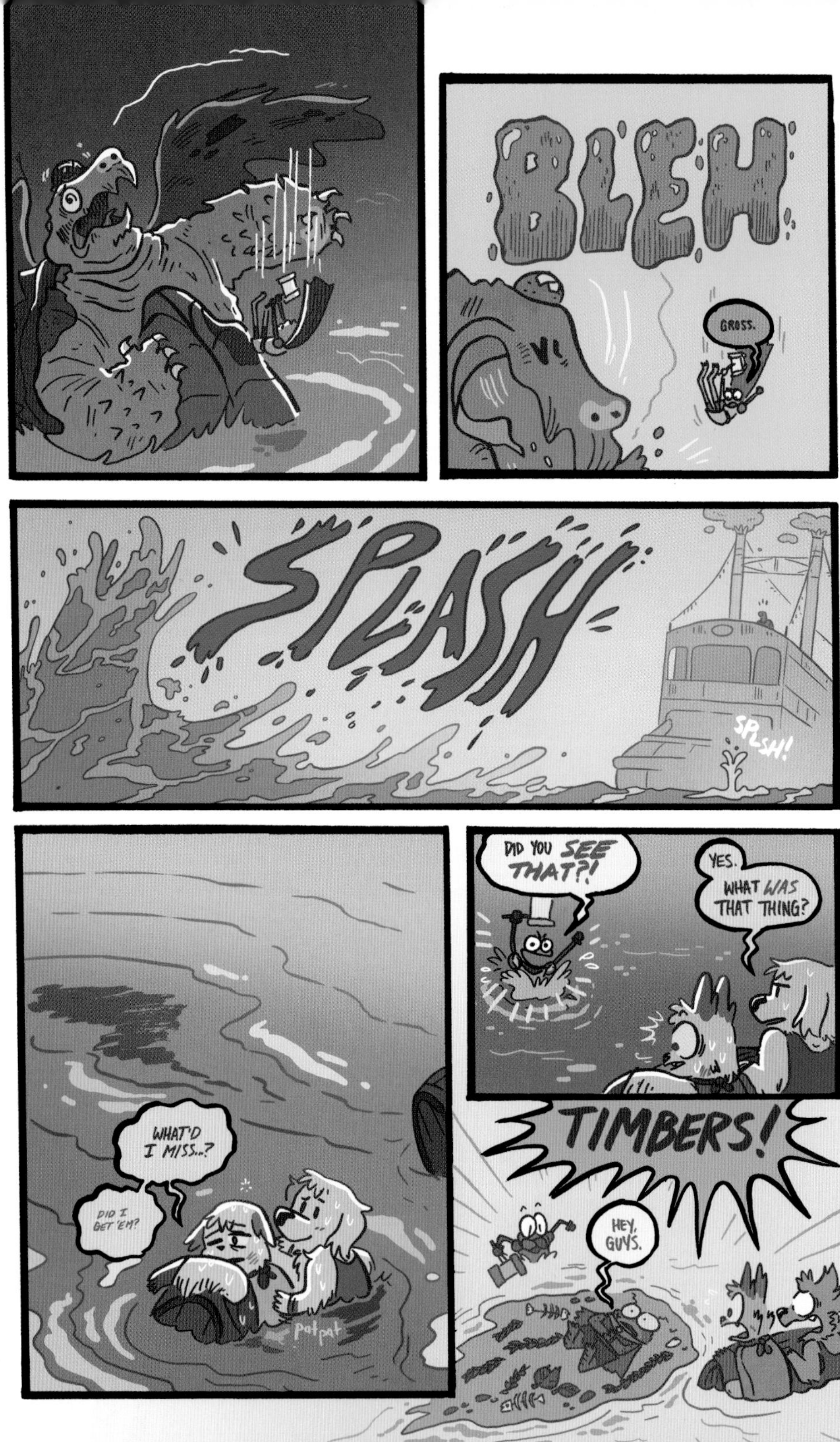
BLEH
GROSS.
SPLASH
SPLSH!
DID YOU SEE THAT?!
YES.
WHAT WAS THAT THING?
WHAT'D I MISS...?
DID I GET 'EM?
patpat
TIMBERS!
HEY, GUYS.

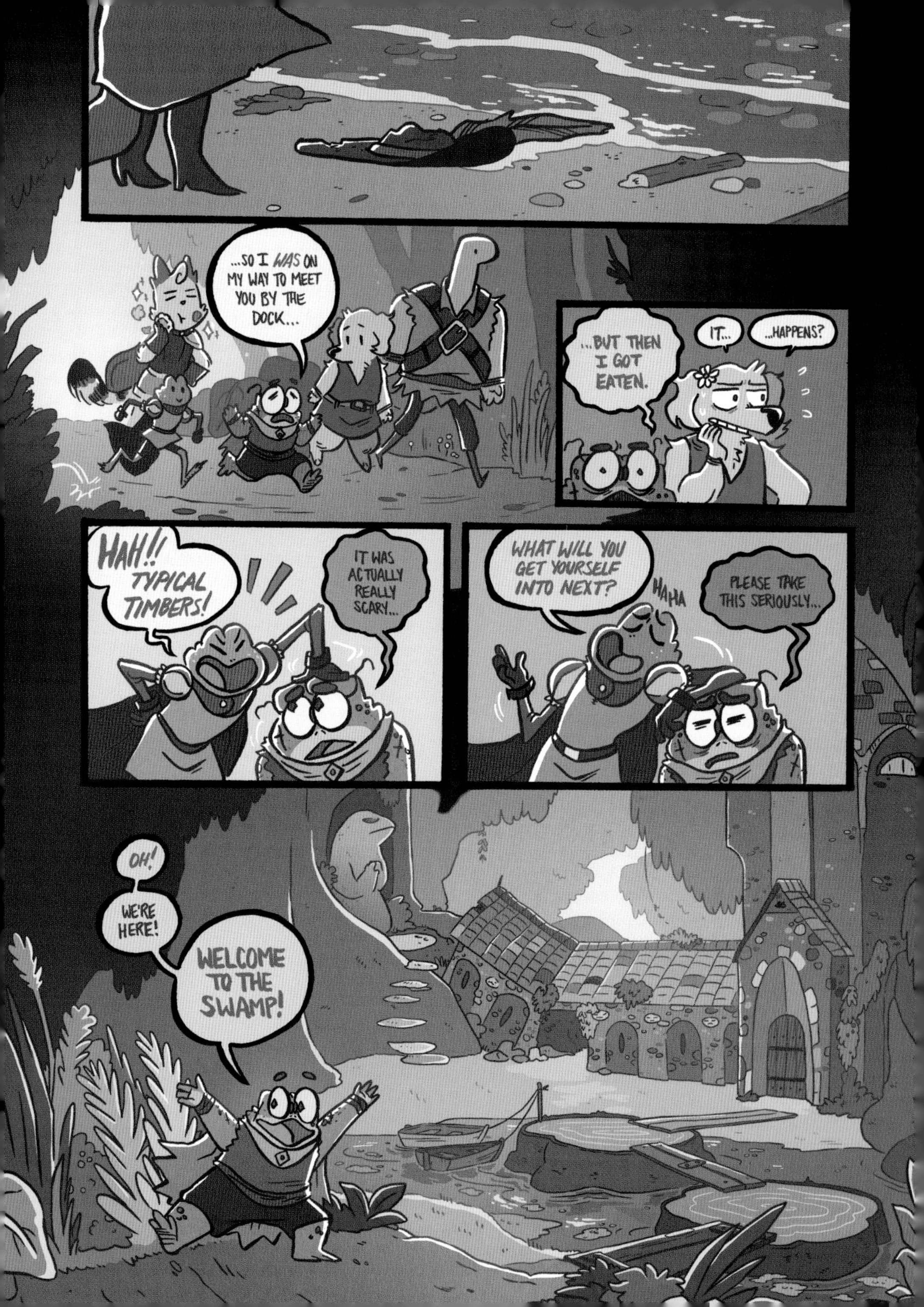

...SO I WAS ON MY WAY TO MEET YOU BY THE DOCK...
...BUT THEN I GOT EATEN.
IT...
...HAPPENS?
HAH!! TYPICAL TIMBERS!
IT WAS ACTUALLY REALLY SCARY...
WHAT WILL YOU GET YOURSELF INTO NEXT?
HAHA
PLEASE TAKE THIS SERIOUSLY...
OH!
WE'RE HERE!
WELCOME TO THE SWAMP!

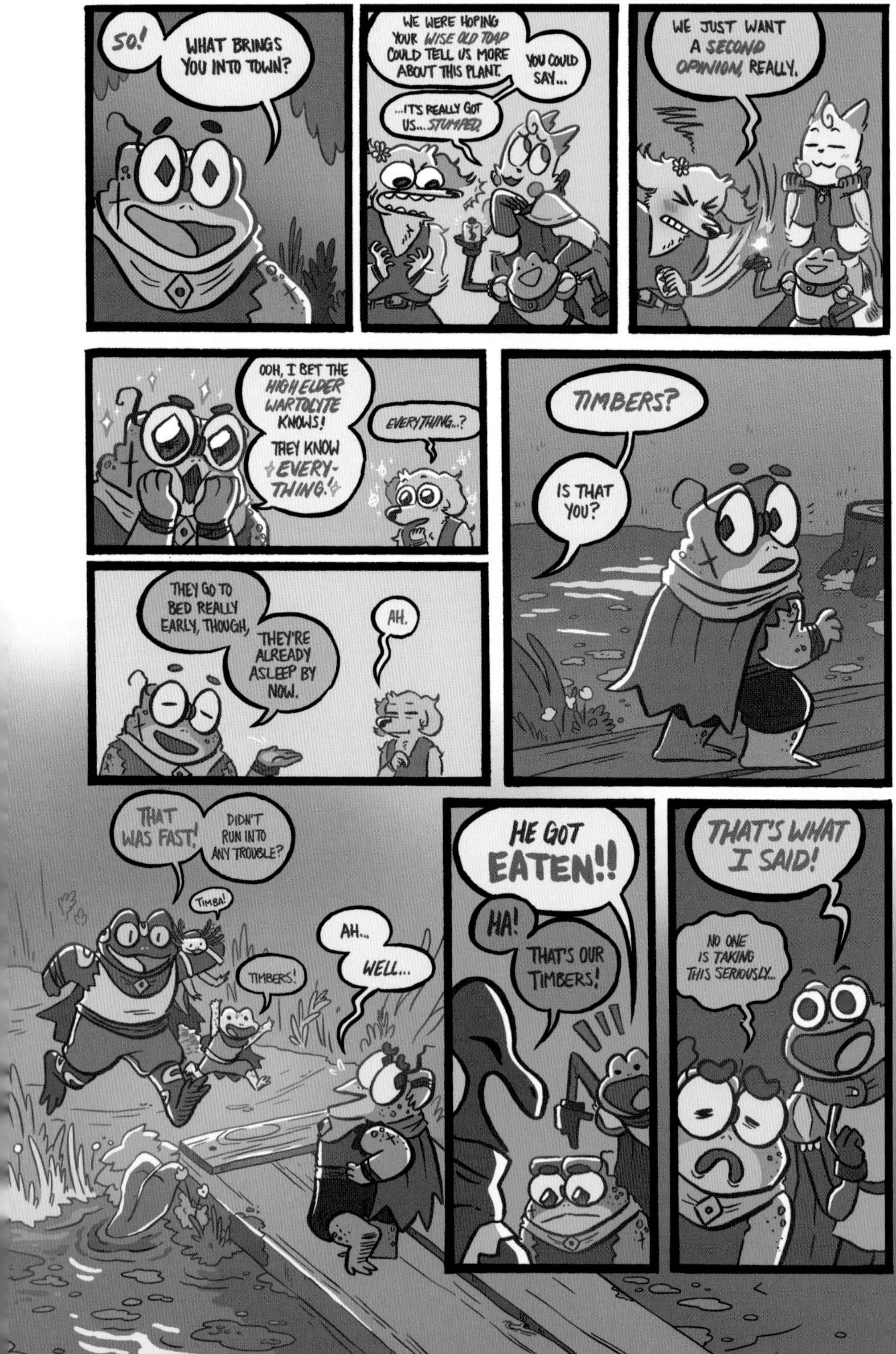
SO!
WHAT BRINGS YOU INTO TOWN?
WE WERE HOPING YOUR WISE OLD TOAD COULD TELL US MORE ABOUT THIS PLANT.
YOU COULD SAY...
...IT'S REALLY GOT US... STUMPED.
WE JUST WANT A SECOND OPINION, REALLY.
OOH, I BET THE HIGH ELDER WARTOLYTE KNOWS!
THEY KNOW EVERYTHING.
EVERYTHING...?
THEY GO TO BED REALLY EARLY, THOUGH.
THEY'RE ALREADY ASLEEP BY NOW.
AH.
TIMBERS?
IS THAT YOU?
THAT WAS FAST!
DIDN'T RUN INTO ANY TROUBLE?
TIMBA!
TIMBERS!
AH...
WELL...
HE GOT EATEN!!
HA!
THAT'S OUR TIMBERS!
THAT'S WHAT I SAID!
NO ONE IS TAKING THIS SERIOUSLY...

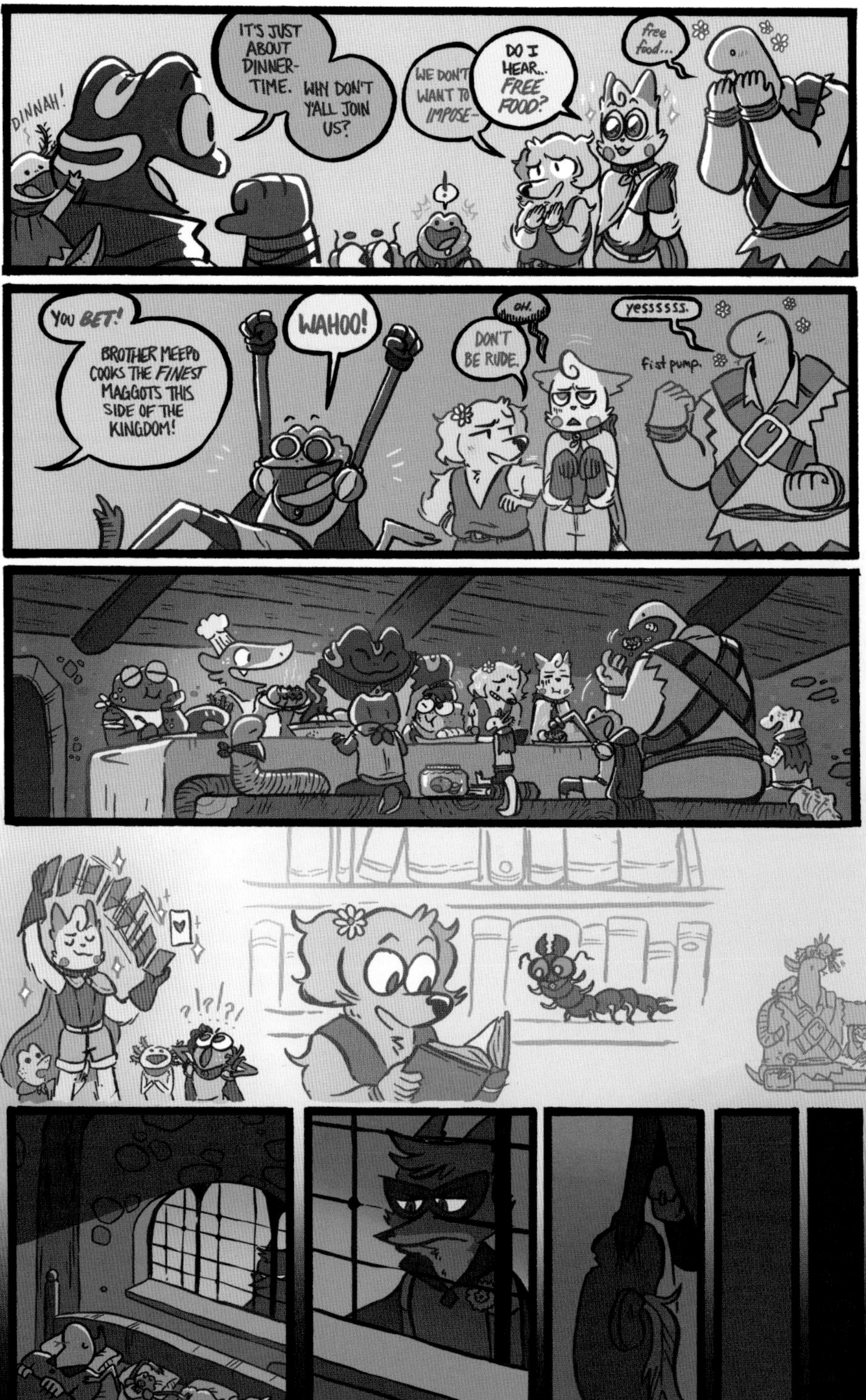
DINNAH!
IT'S JUST ABOUT DINNER-TIME.
WHY DON'T Y'ALL JOIN US?
WE DON'T WANT TO IMPOSE—
DO I HEAR.. FREE FOOD?
free food...
YOU BET!
BROTHER MEEPO COOKS THE FINEST MAGGOTS THIS SIDE OF THE KINGDOM!
WAHOO!
OH.
DON'T BE RUDE.
yessssss.
fist pump.
?!?/?!

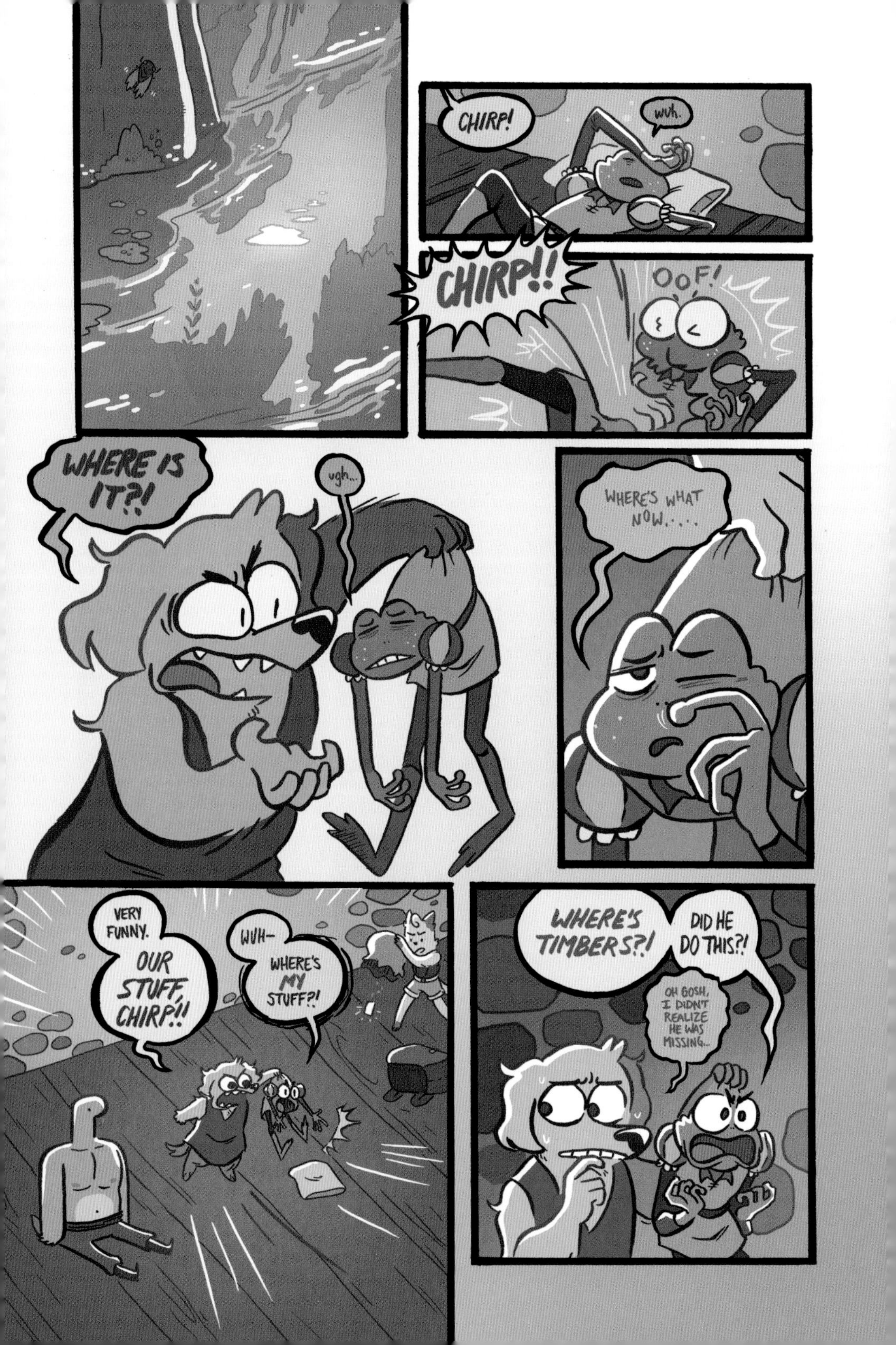
CHIRP!
wuh.
CHIRP!!
OOF!
WHERE IS IT?!
ugh...
WHERE'S WHAT NOW.....
VERY FUNNY. OUR STUFF, CHIRP!!
WUH- WHERE'S MY STUFF?!
WHERE'S TIMBERS?!
DID HE DO THIS?!
OH GOSH, I DIDN'T REALIZE HE WAS MISSING...

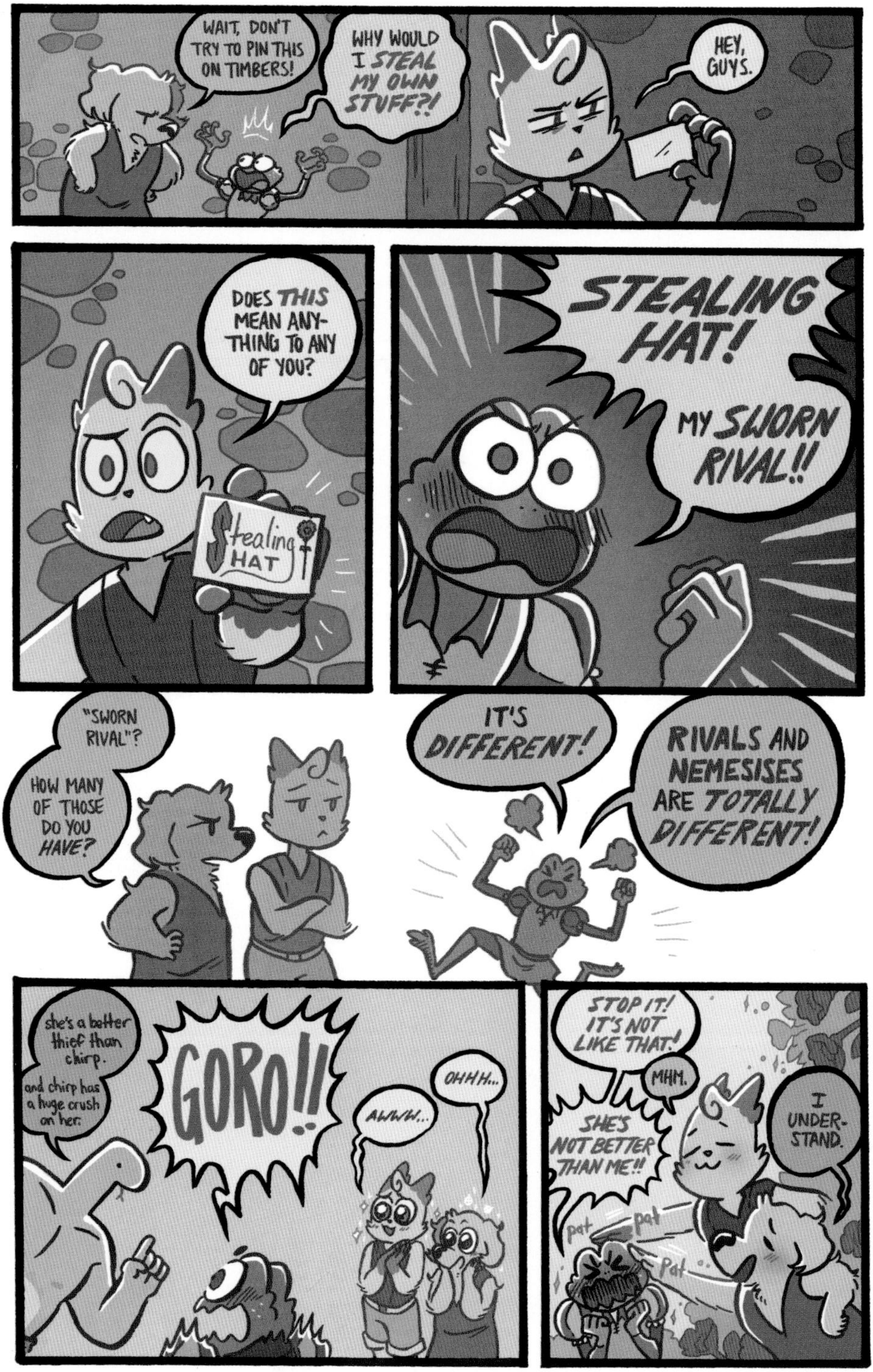
WAIT, DON'T TRY TO PIN THIS ON TIMBERS!
WHY WOULD I STEAL MY OWN STUFF?!
HEY, GUYS.
DOES THIS MEAN ANY-THING TO ANY OF YOU?
Stealing HAT
STEALING HAT!
MY SWORN RIVAL!!
"SWORN RIVAL"?
HOW MANY OF THOSE DO YOU HAVE?
IT'S DIFFERENT!
RIVALS AND NEMESISES ARE TOTALLY DIFFERENT!
she's a better thief than chirp.
and chirp has a huge crush on her.
GORO!!
AWWW...
OHHH...
STOP IT! IT'S NOT LIKE THAT!
MHM.
SHE'S NOT BETTER THAN ME!!
I UNDER-STAND.
pat pat pat

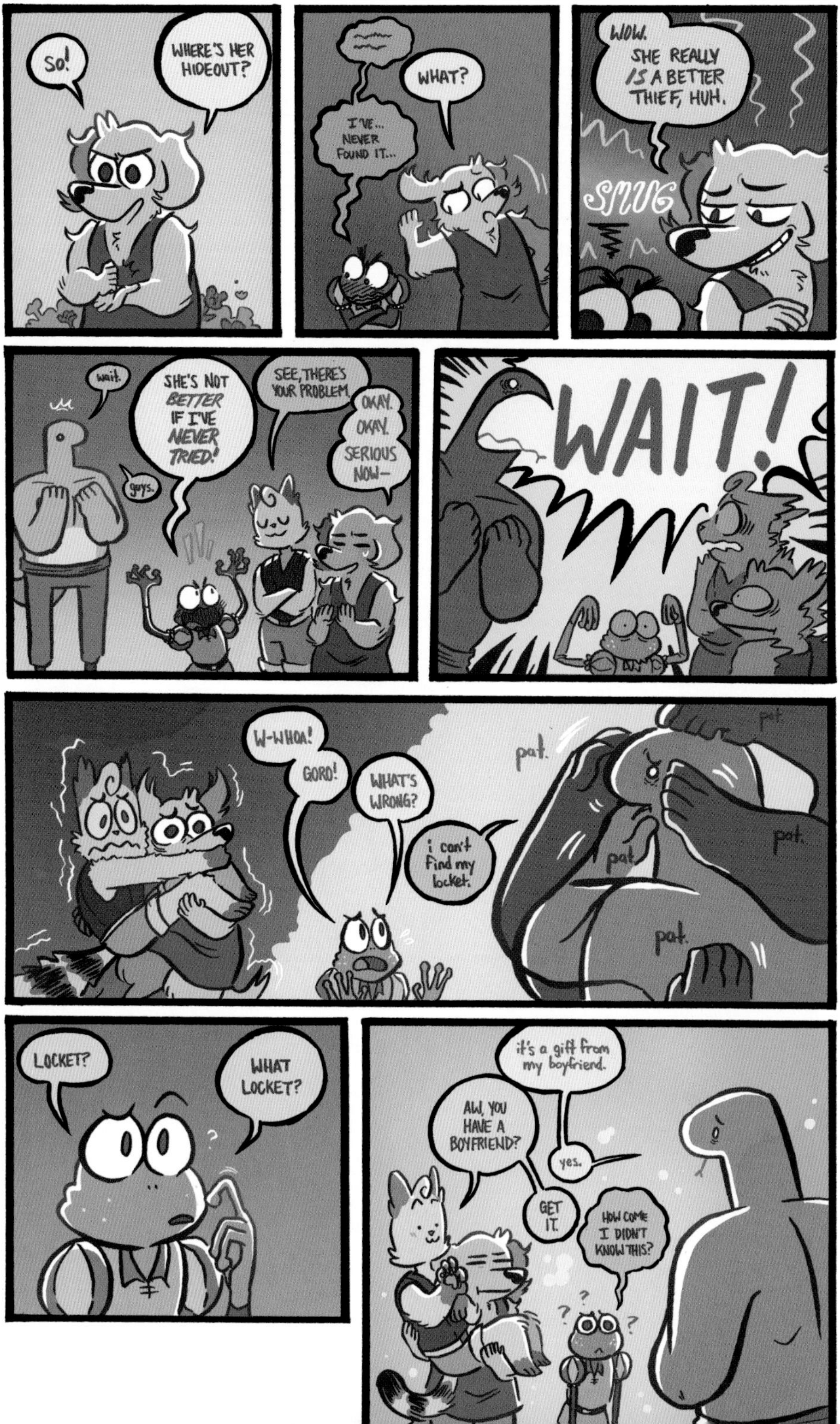

SO!
WHERE'S HER HIDEOUT?
~~~
WHAT?
I'VE... NEVER FOUND IT...
WOW. SHE REALLY IS A BETTER THIEF, HUH.
SMUG
wait.
SHE'S NOT BETTER IF I'VE NEVER TRIED!
guys.
SEE, THERE'S YOUR PROBLEM.
OKAY. OKAY. SERIOUS NOW—
WAIT!
W-WHOA!
GORO!
WHAT'S WRONG?
i can't find my locket.
pat.
pat.
pat.
pat.
pat.
LOCKET?
WHAT LOCKET?
it's a gift from my boyfriend.
AW, YOU HAVE A BOYFRIEND?
yes.
GET IT.
HOW COME I DIDN'T KNOW THIS?
~~~

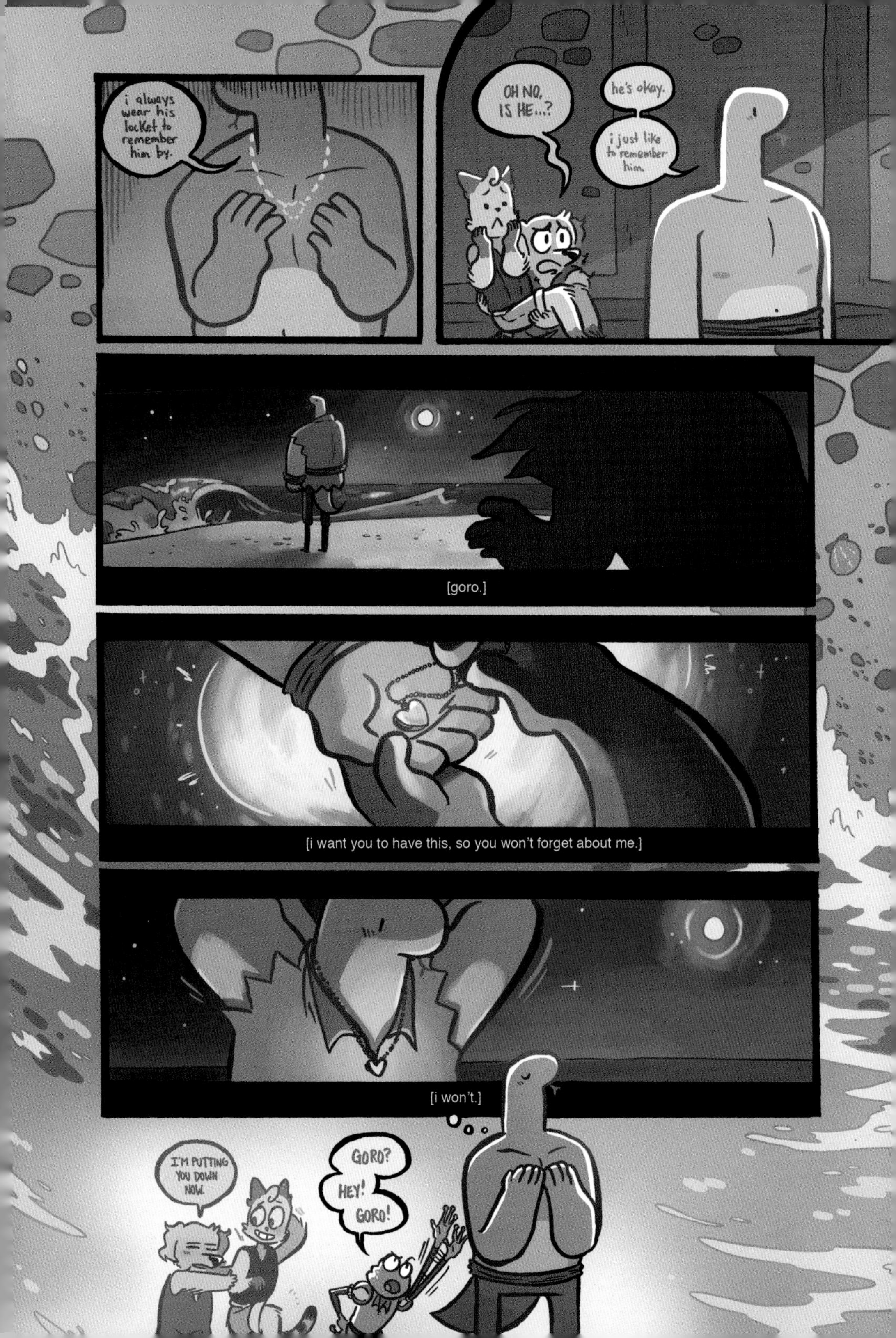

i always wear his locket to remember him by.
OH NO, IS HE...?
he's okay.
i just like to remember him.
[goro.]
[i want you to have this, so you won't forget about me.]
[i won't.]
I'M PUTTING YOU DOWN NOW.
GORO?
HEY! GORO!

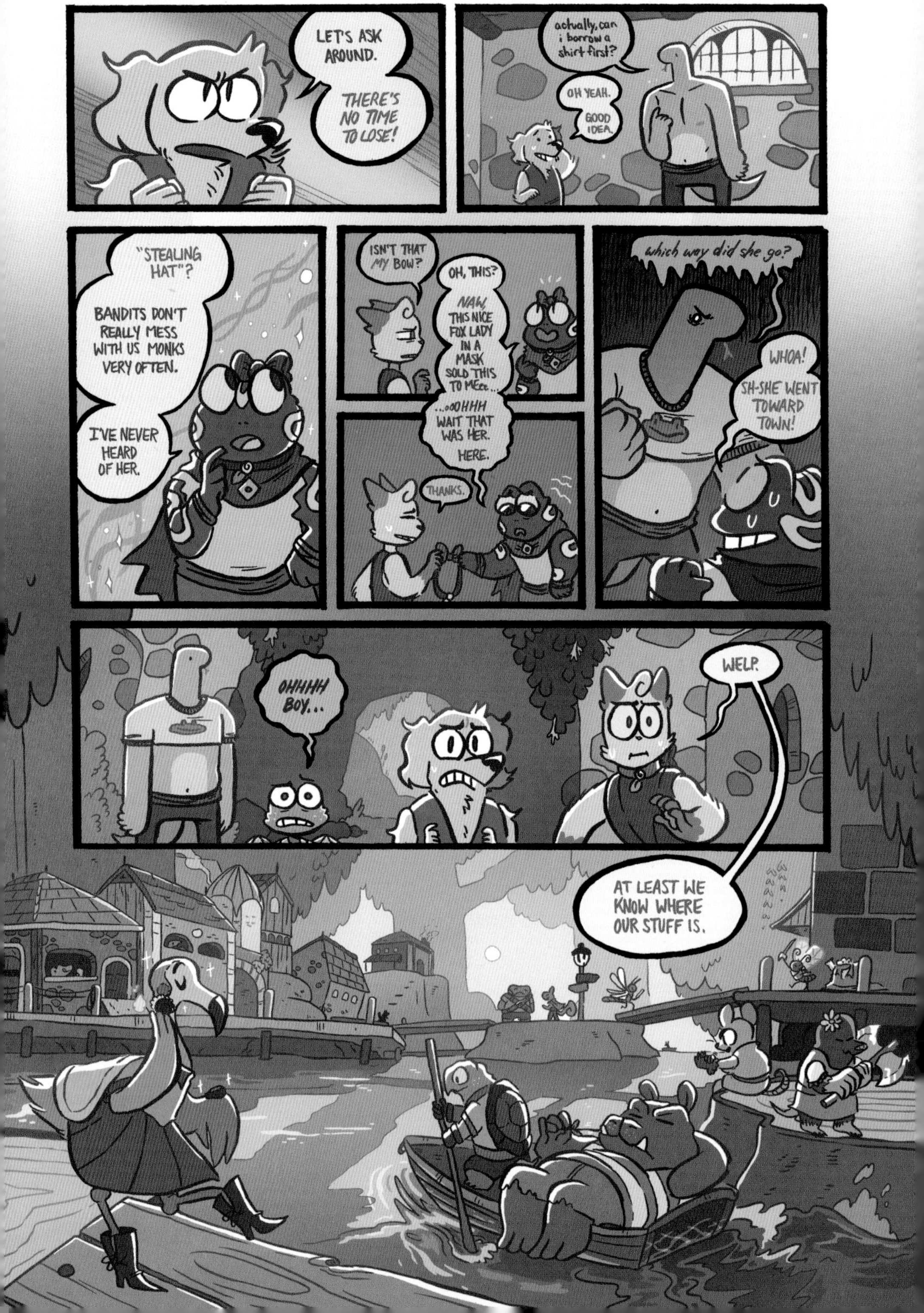

LET'S ASK AROUND.
THERE'S NO TIME TO LOSE!
actually, can i borrow a shirt first?
OH YEAH.
GOOD IDEA.
"STEALING HAT"?
BANDITS DON'T REALLY MESS WITH US MONKS VERY OFTEN.
I'VE NEVER HEARD OF HER.
ISN'T THAT MY BOW?
OH, THIS?
NAW, THIS NICE FOX LADY IN A MASK SOLD THIS TO ME...
...OOHHH WAIT THAT WAS HER.
HERE.
THANKS.
which way did she go?
WHOA!
SH-SHE WENT TOWARD TOWN!
OHHHH BOY...
WELP.
AT LEAST WE KNOW WHERE OUR STUFF IS.

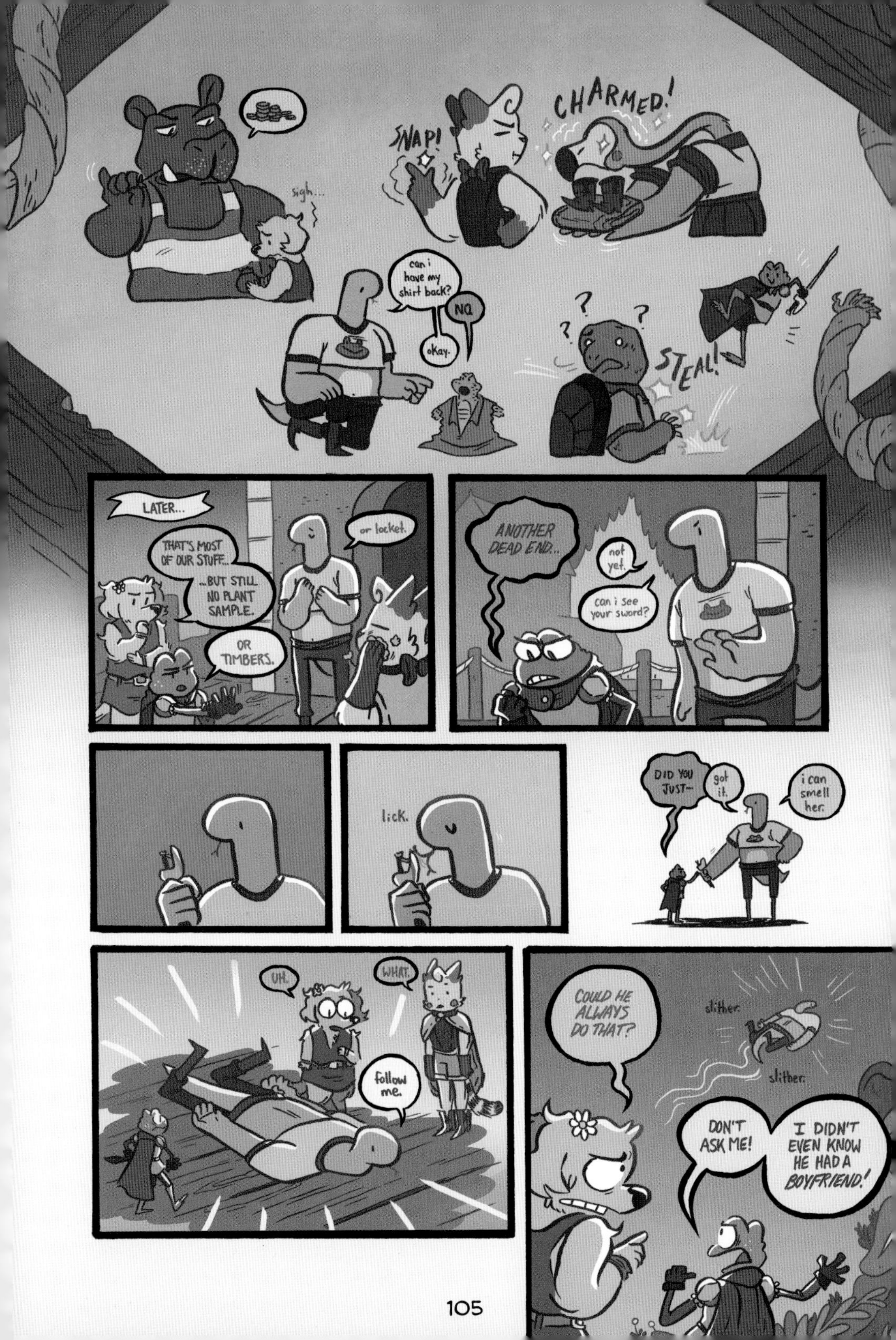
sigh...
SNAP!
CHARMED!
can i have my shirt back?
NO.
okay.
? ? ?
STEAL!
LATER...
THAT'S MOST OF OUR STUFF...
...BUT STILL NO PLANT SAMPLE.
or locket.
OR TIMBERS.
ANOTHER DEAD END...
not yet.
can i see your sword?
lick.
DID YOU JUST--
got it.
i can smell her.
UH.
WHAT.
follow me.
COULD HE ALWAYS DO THAT?
slither.
slither.
DON'T ASK ME!
I DIDN'T EVEN KNOW HE HAD A BOYFRIEND!

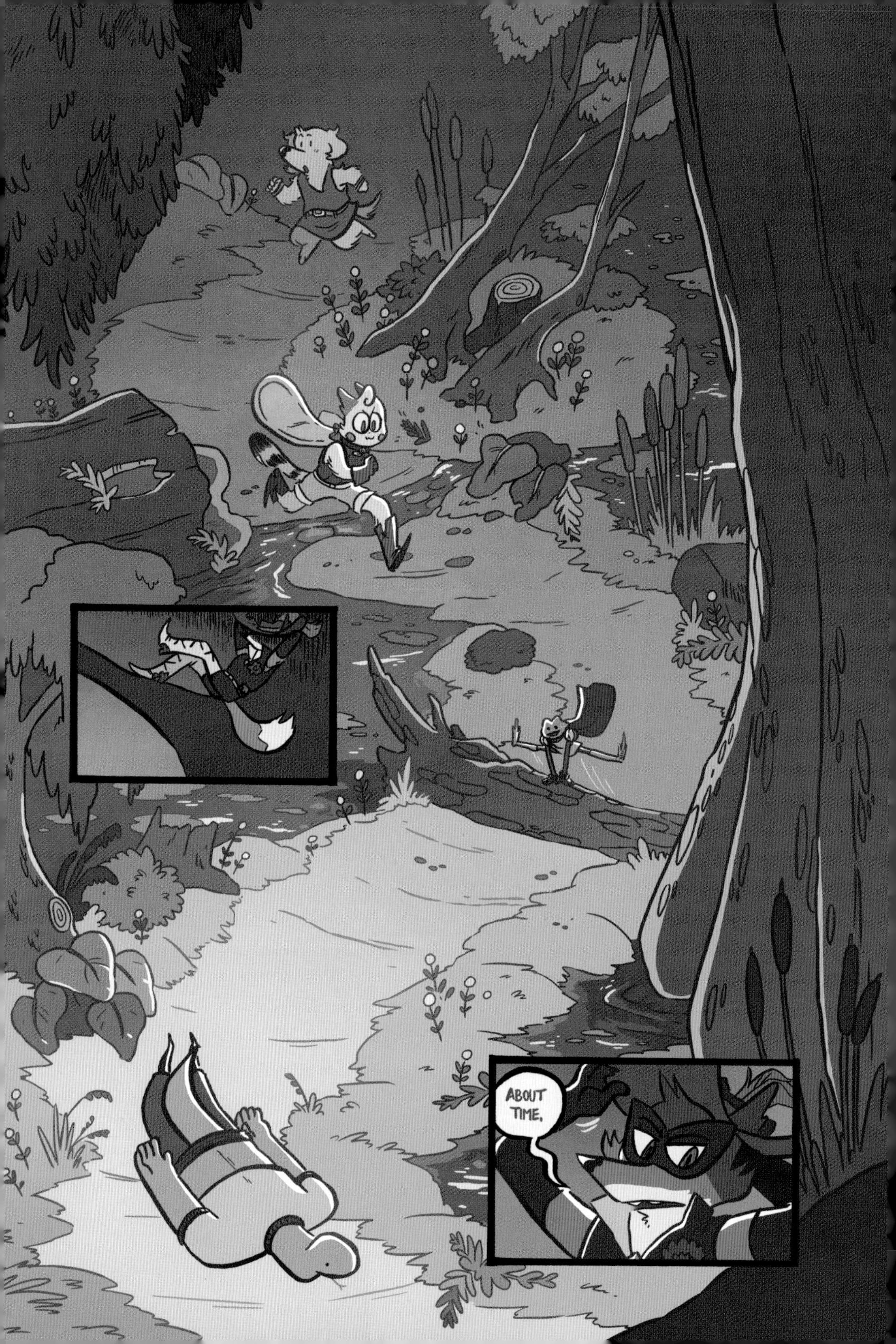
ABOUT TIME,

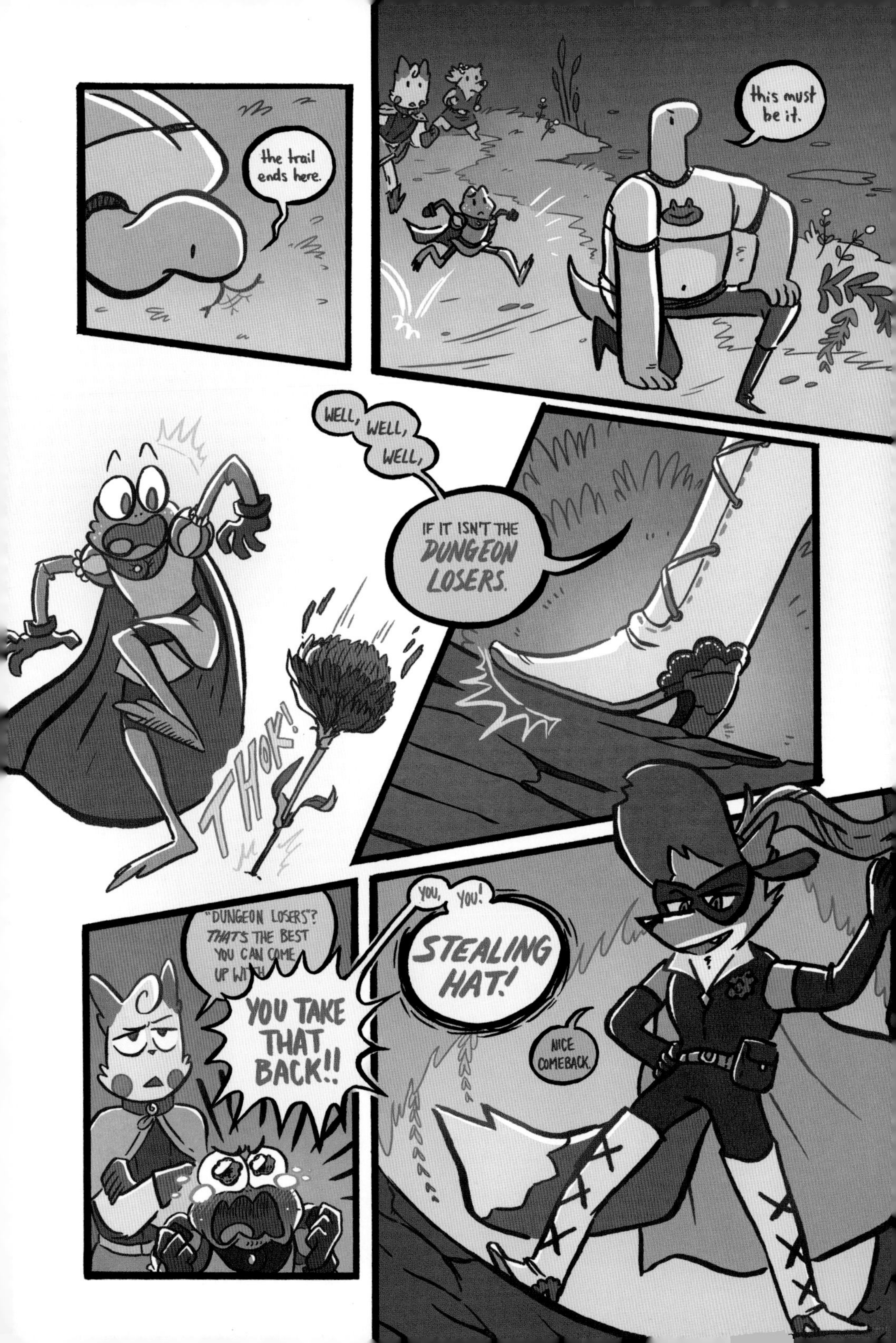
the trail ends here.
this must be it.
WELL, WELL, WELL,
IF IT ISN'T THE DUNGEON LOSERS.
THOK!
"DUNGEON LOSERS"? THAT'S THE BEST YOU CAN COME UP WI
YOU TAKE THAT BACK!!
YOU, YOU!
STEALING HAT!
NICE COMEBACK.

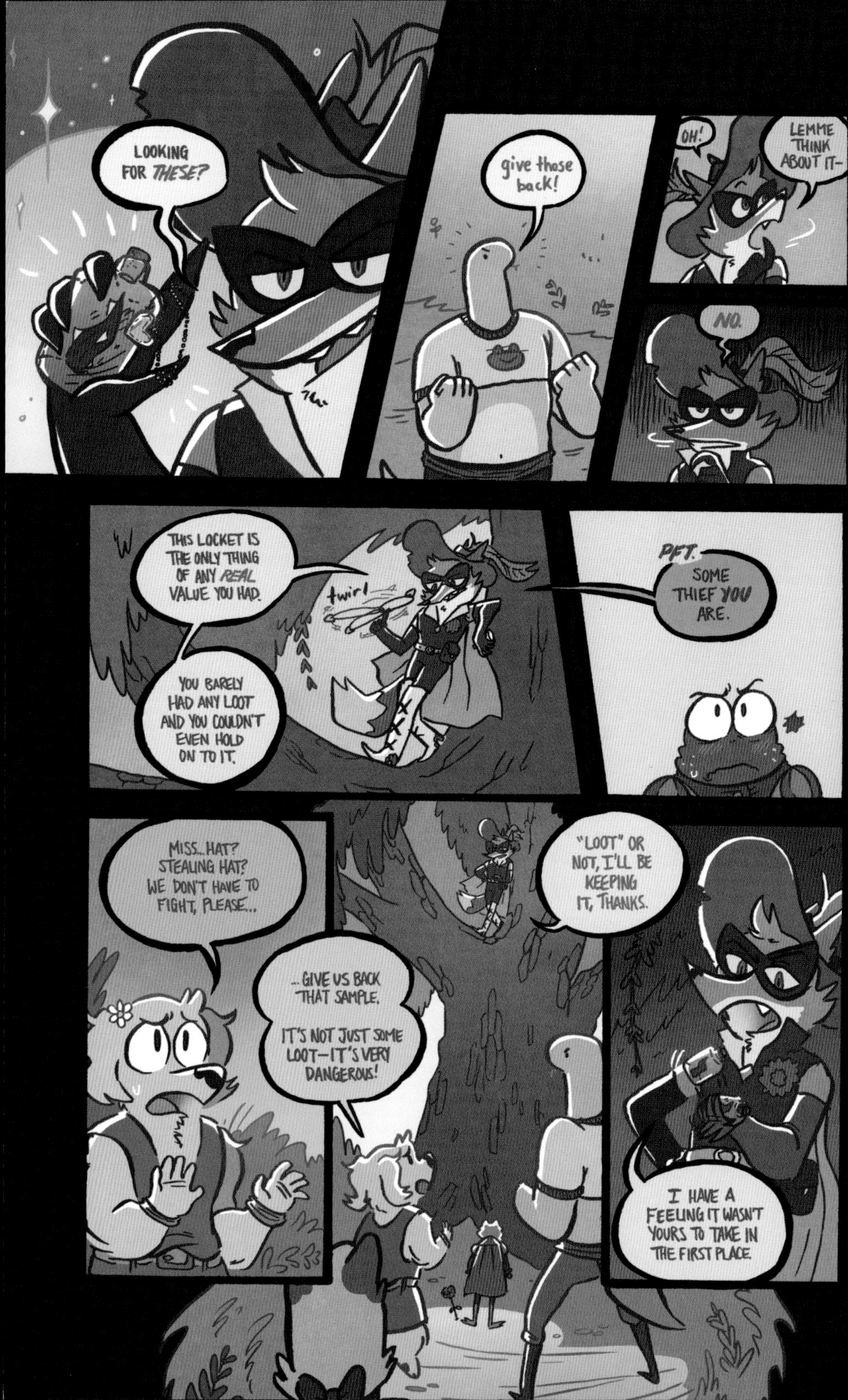
LOOKING FOR THESE?
give those back!
OH!
LEMME THINK ABOUT IT-
NO.
THIS LOCKET IS THE ONLY THING OF ANY REAL VALUE YOU HAD.
twirl
YOU BARELY HAD ANY LOOT AND YOU COULDN'T EVEN HOLD ON TO IT.
PFFT. SOME THIEF YOU ARE.
MISS...HAT? STEALING HAT? WE DON'T HAVE TO FIGHT, PLEASE...
...GIVE US BACK THAT SAMPLE.
IT'S NOT JUST SOME LOOT—IT'S VERY DANGEROUS!
"LOOT" OR NOT, I'LL BE KEEPING IT, THANKS.
I HAVE A FEELING IT WASN'T YOURS TO TAKE IN THE FIRST PLACE.

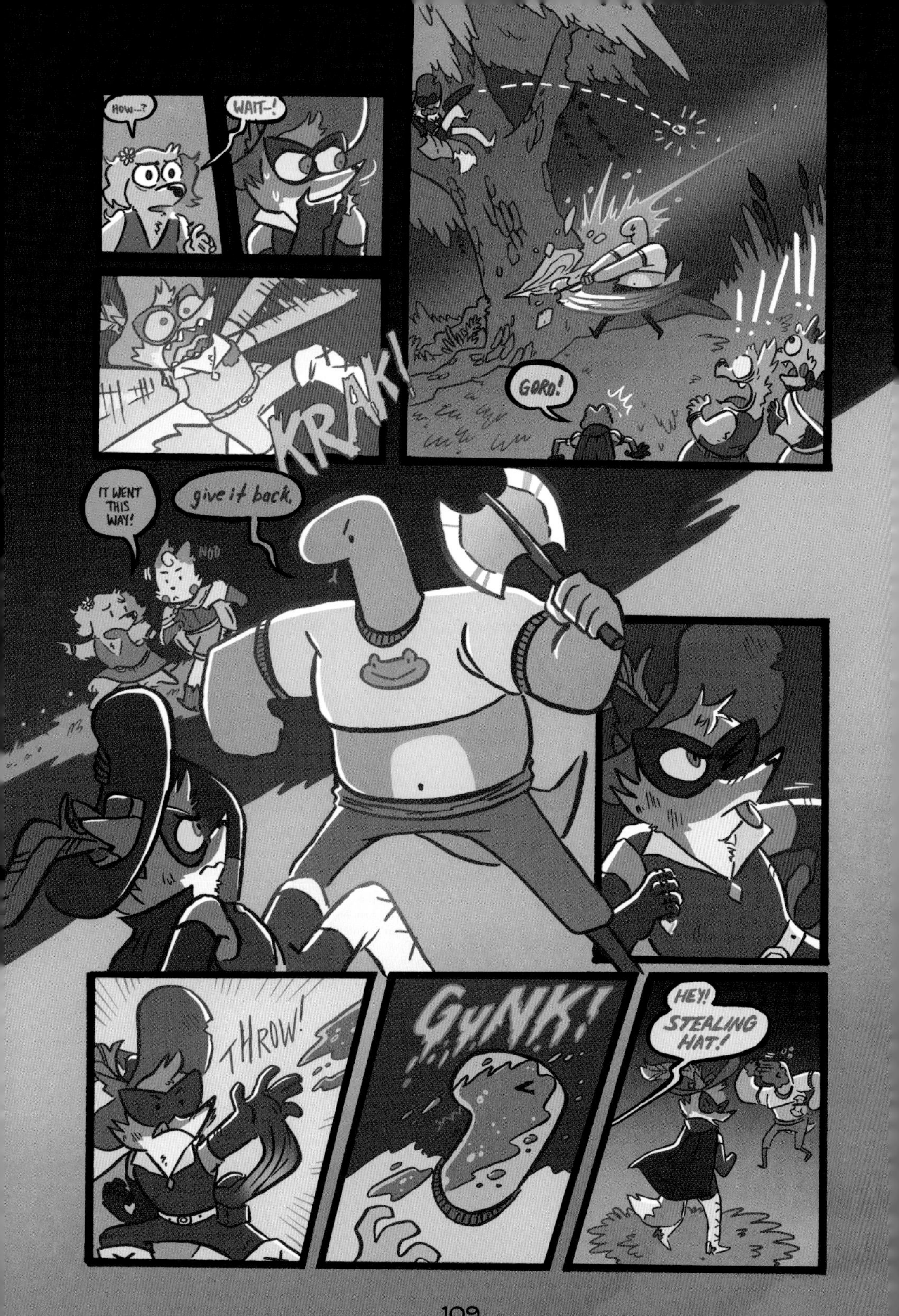
HOW...?
WAIT-!
KRAK!
GORO!
IT WENT THIS WAY!
NOD
give it back.
THROW!
GUNK!
HEY! STEALING HAT!

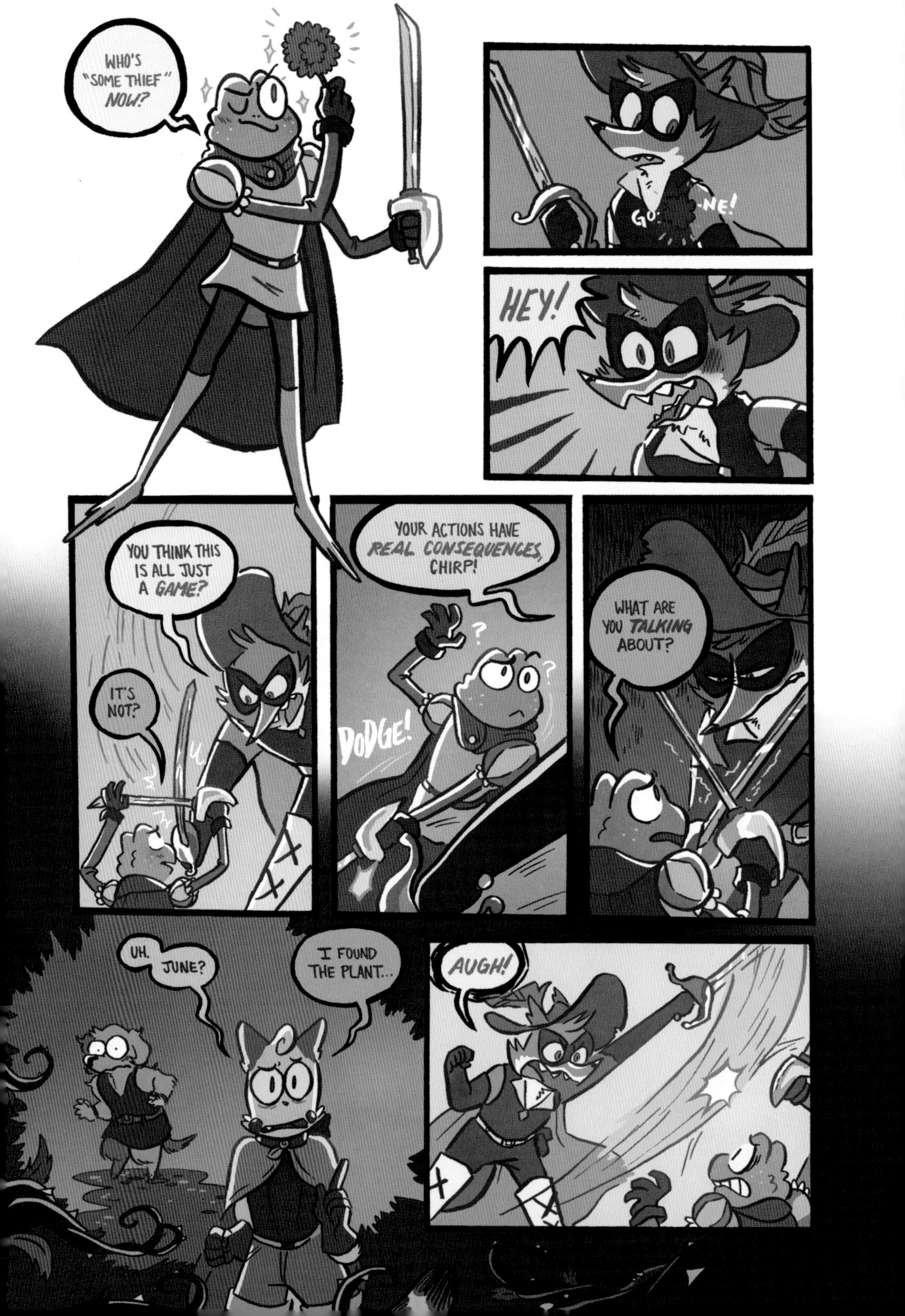
WHO'S "SOME THIEF" NOW?
GO- -NE!
HEY!
YOU THINK THIS IS ALL JUST A GAME?
IT'S NOT?
YOUR ACTIONS HAVE REAL CONSEQUENCES, CHIRP!
? ?
DODGE!
WHAT ARE YOU TALKING ABOUT?
UH. JUNE?
I FOUND THE PLANT...
AUGH!

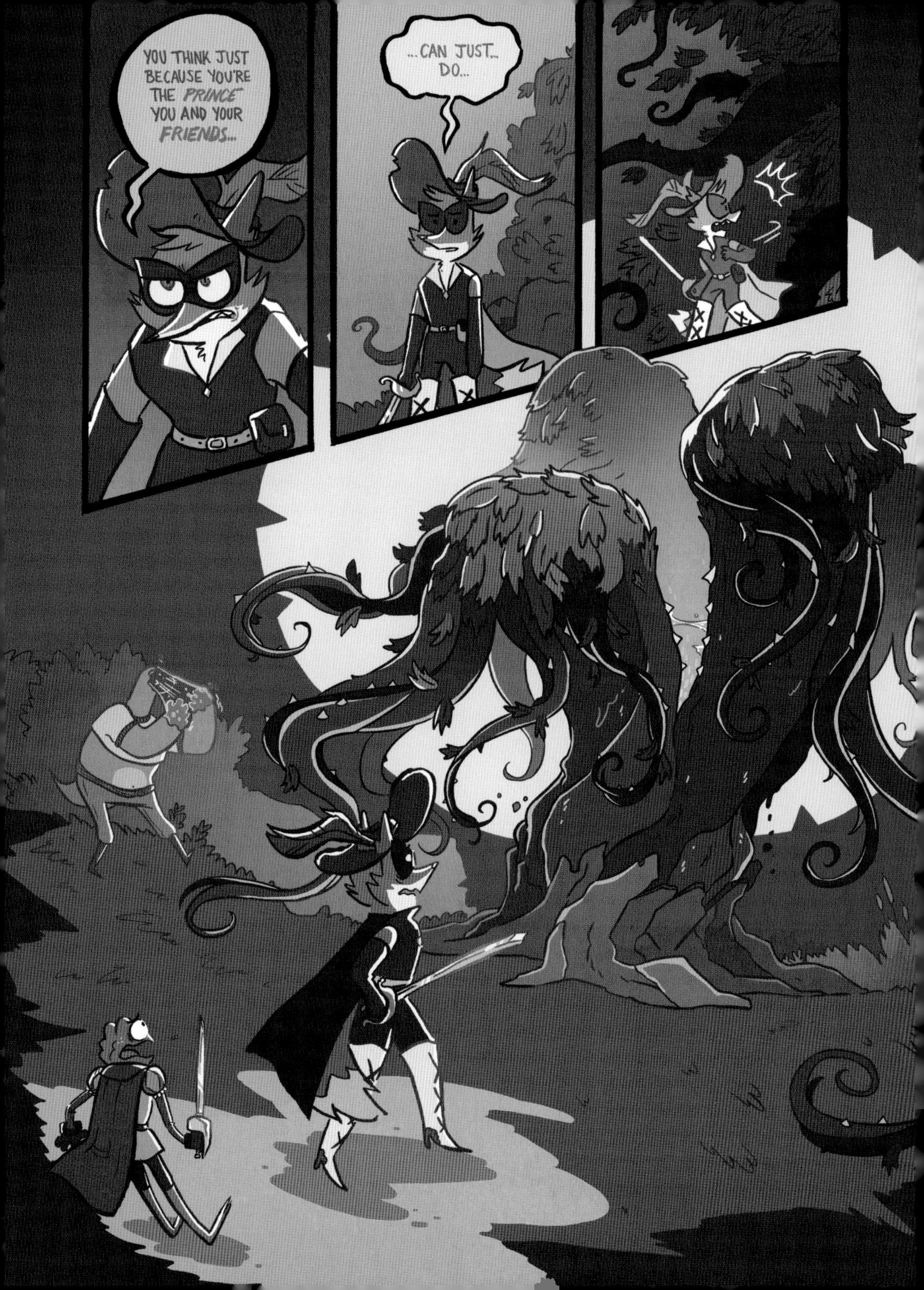

YOU THINK JUST BECAUSE YOU'RE THE PRINCE YOU AND YOUR FRIENDS...
...CAN JUST... DO...

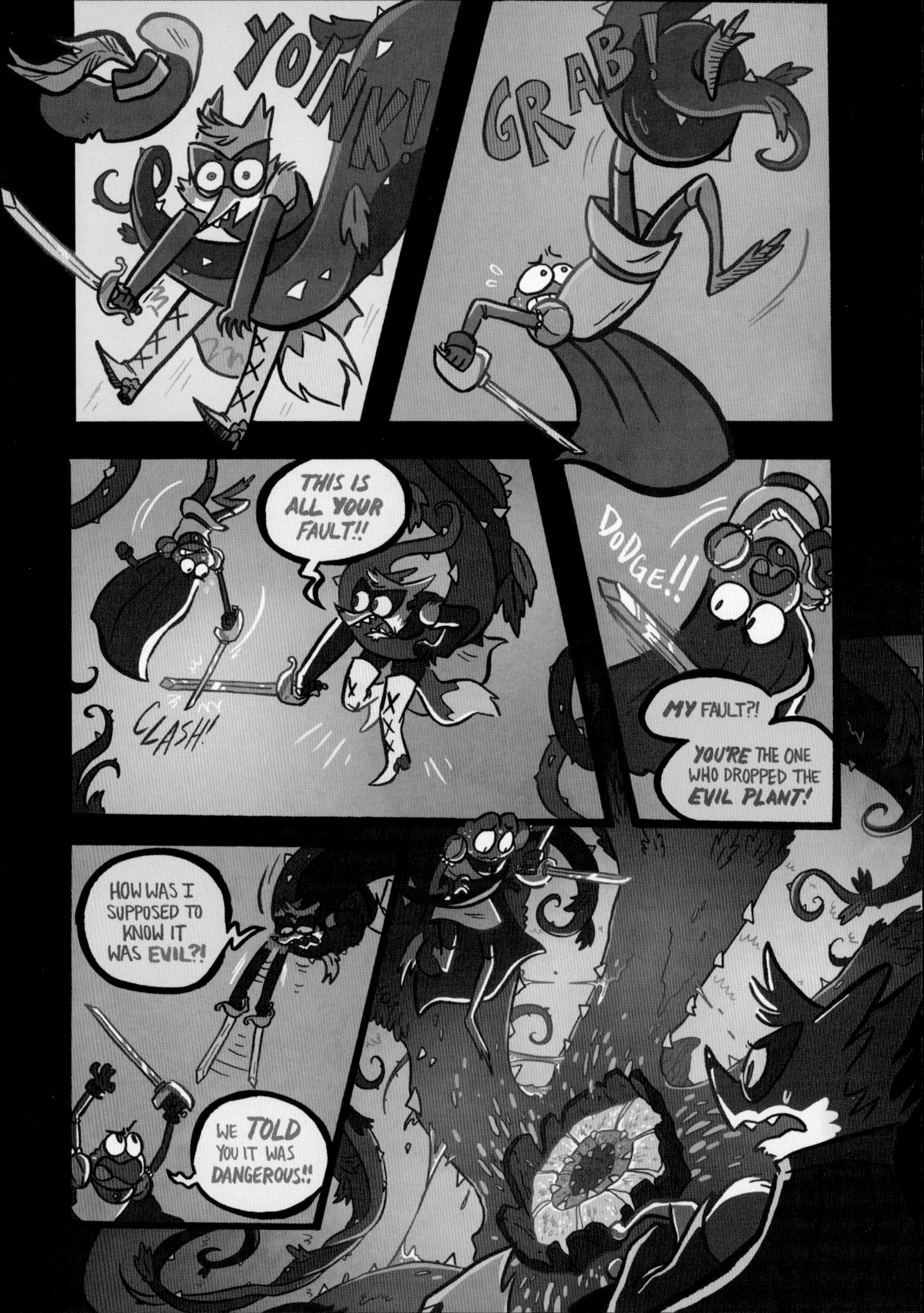
YOINK!
GRAB!
THIS IS ALL YOUR FAULT!!
CLASH!
DODGE!!
MY FAULT?!
YOU'RE THE ONE WHO DROPPED THE EVIL PLANT!
HOW WAS I SUPPOSED TO KNOW IT WAS EVIL?!
WE TOLD YOU IT WAS DANGEROUS!!

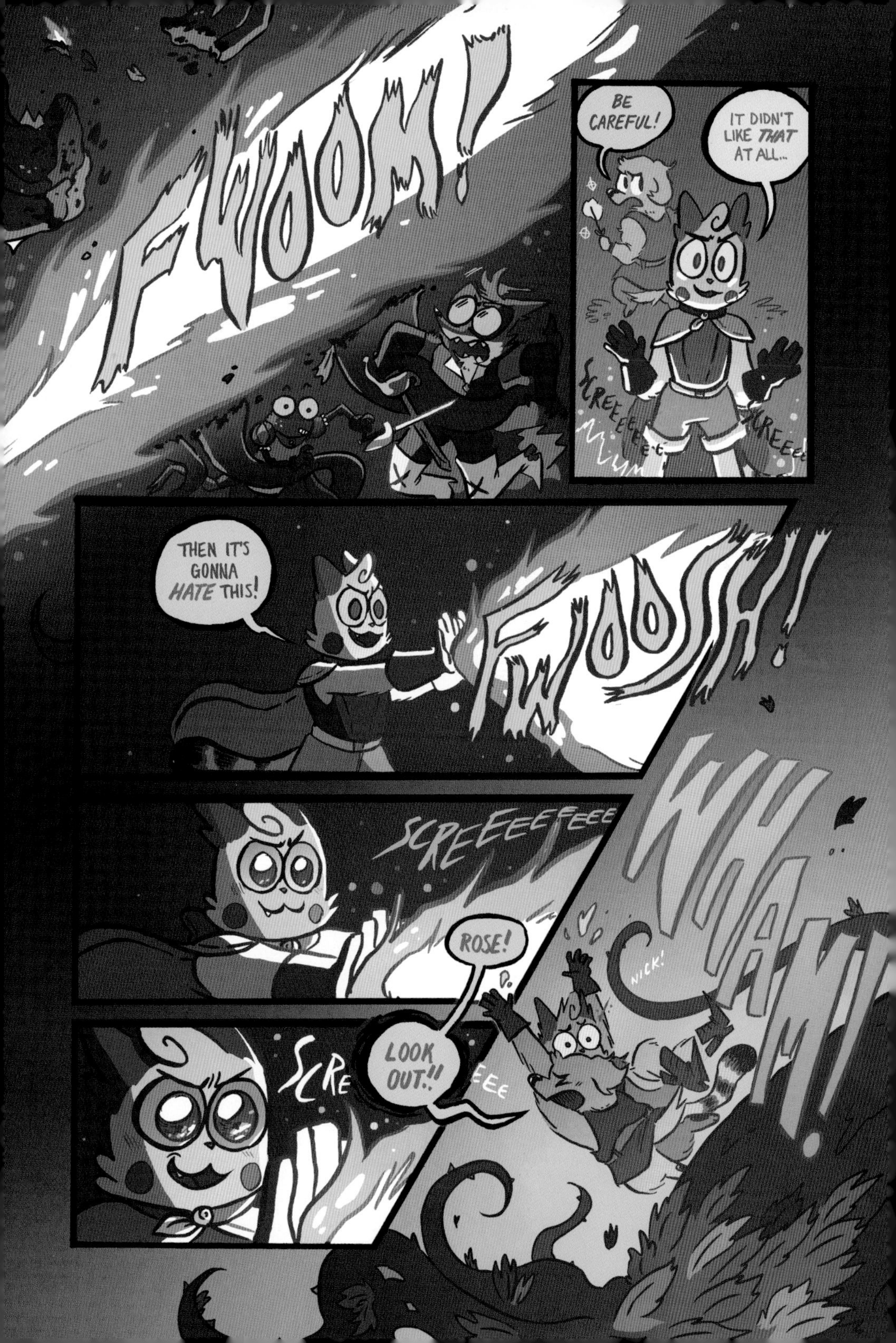
FWOOM!
BE CAREFUL!
IT DIDN'T LIKE THAT AT ALL...
SCREEEEEEEE
SCREEEEE
THEN IT'S GONNA HATE THIS!
FWOOSH!
SCREEEEEEEEEE
ROSE!
LOOK OUT!!
SCRE EEE
NICK!
WHAM!

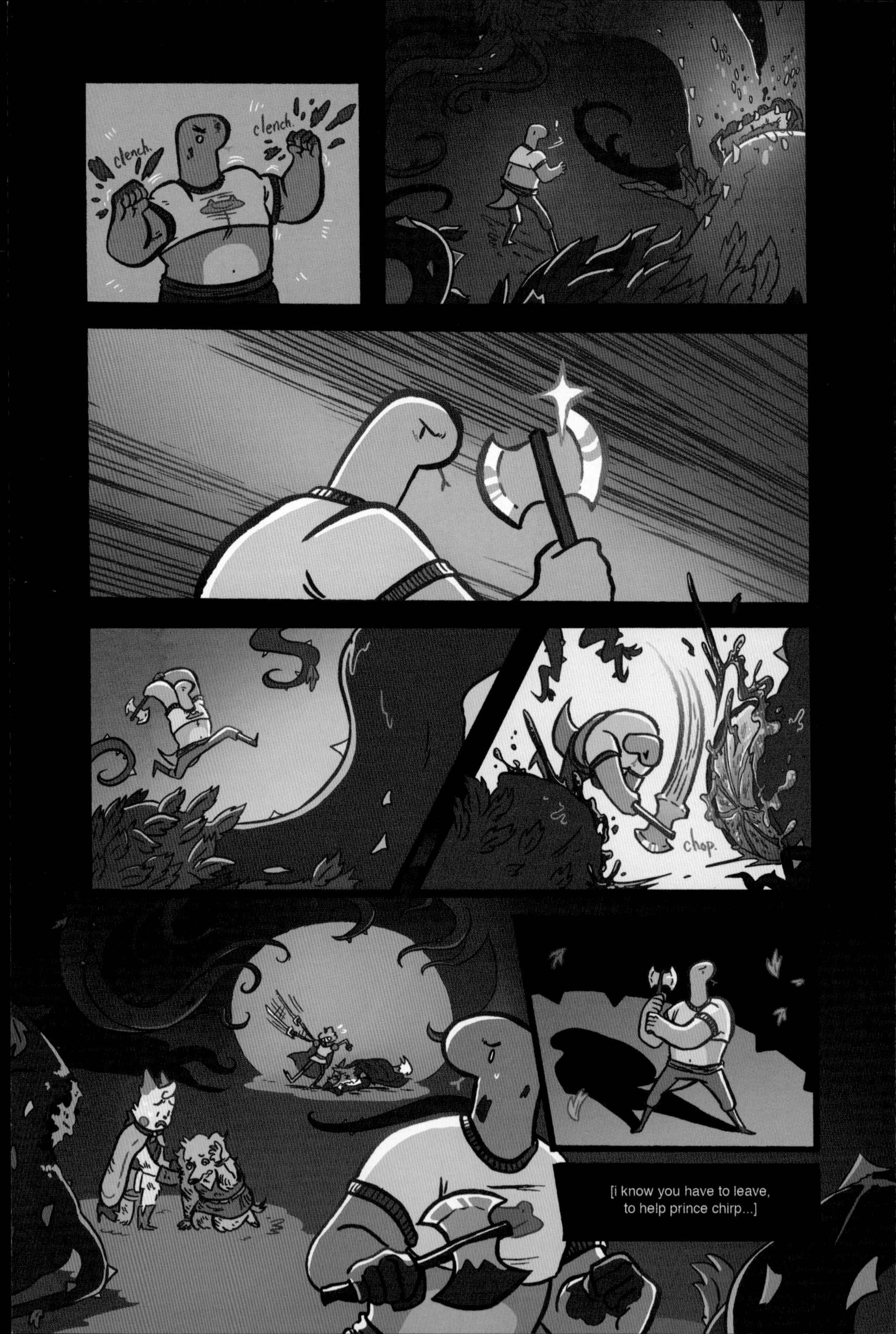
clench.
clench.
chop.
[i know you have to leave,
to help prince chirp...]

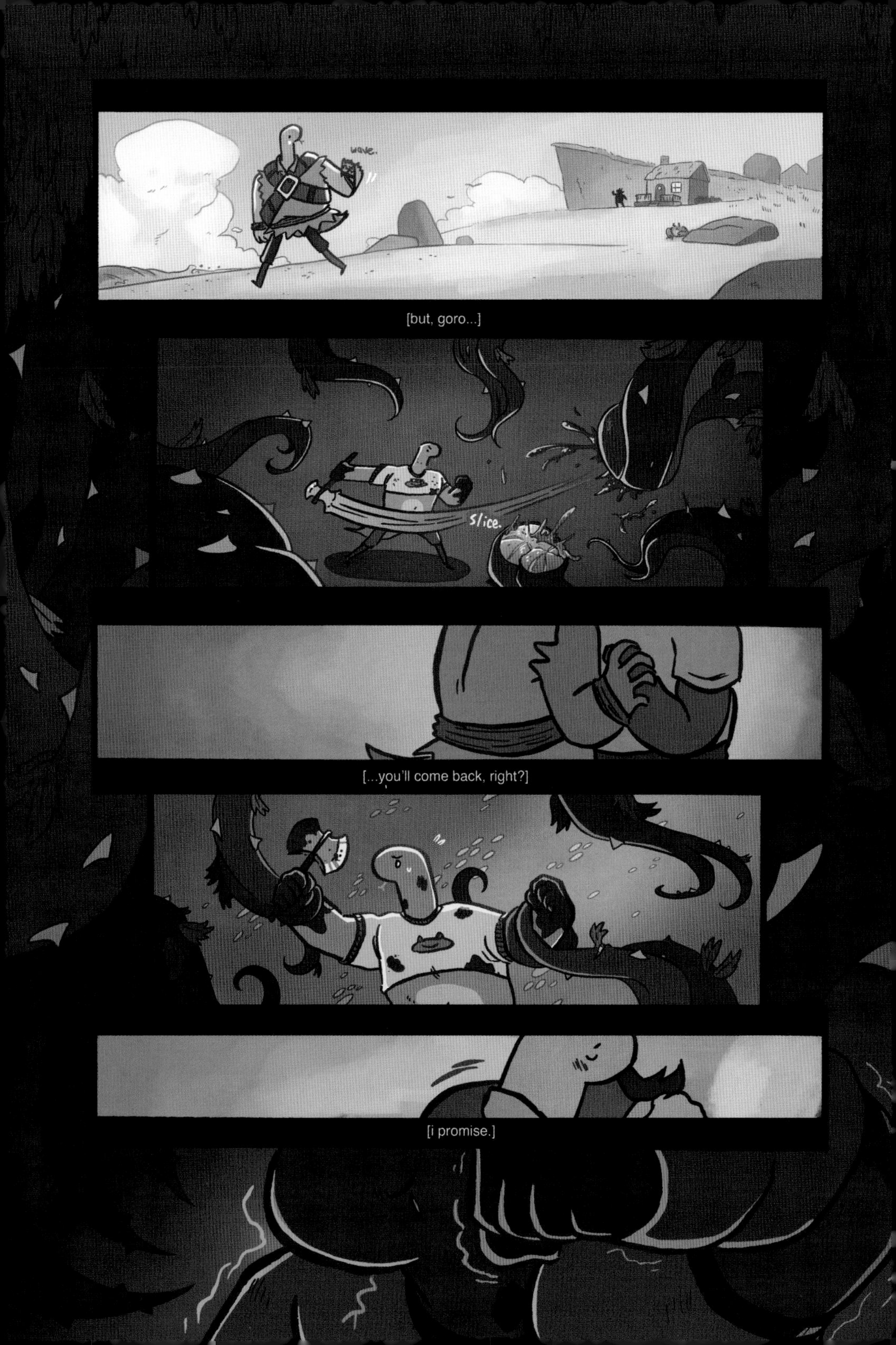
wave.
[but, goro...]
slice.
[...you'll come back, right?]
[i promise.]

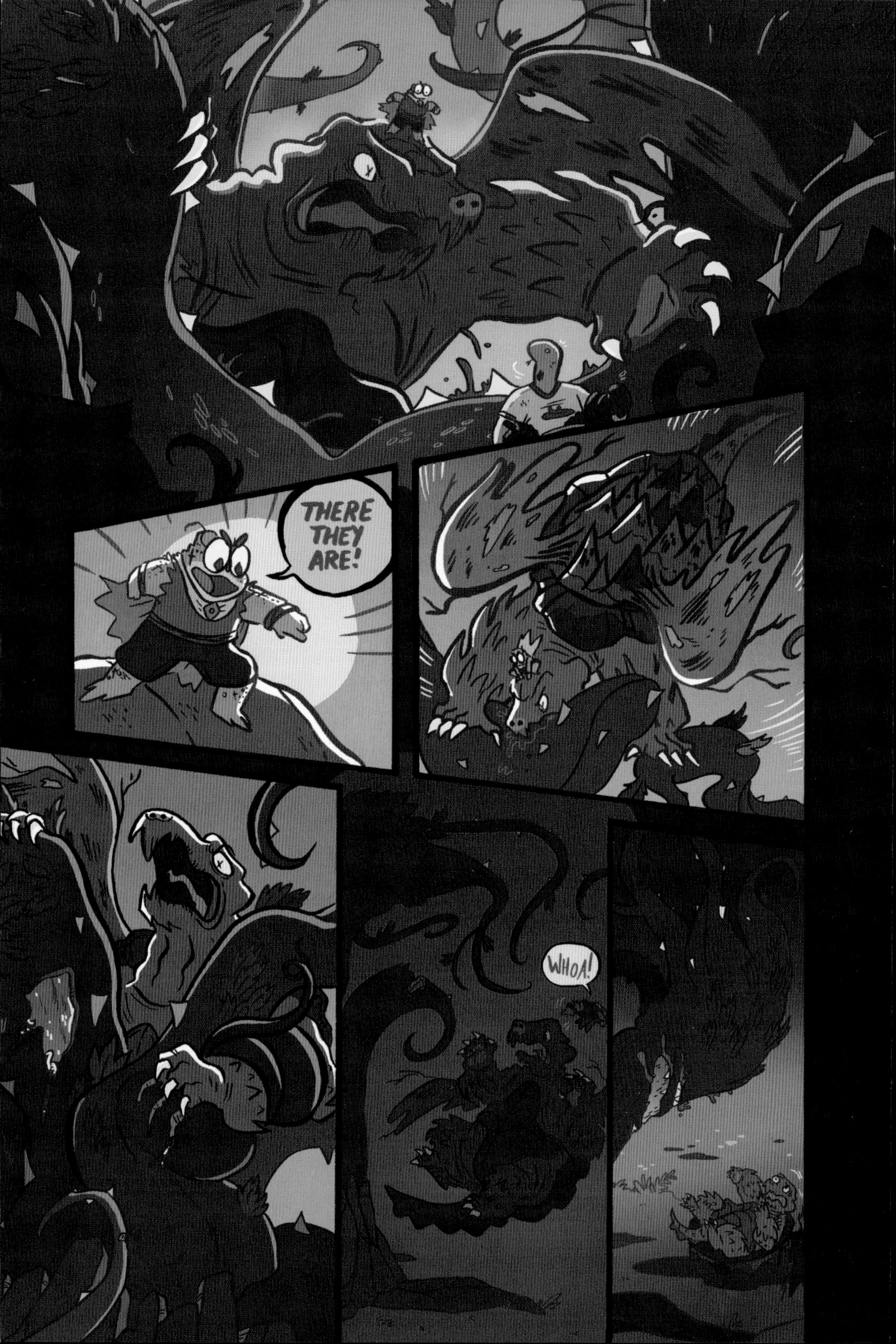
THERE THEY ARE!
WHOA!

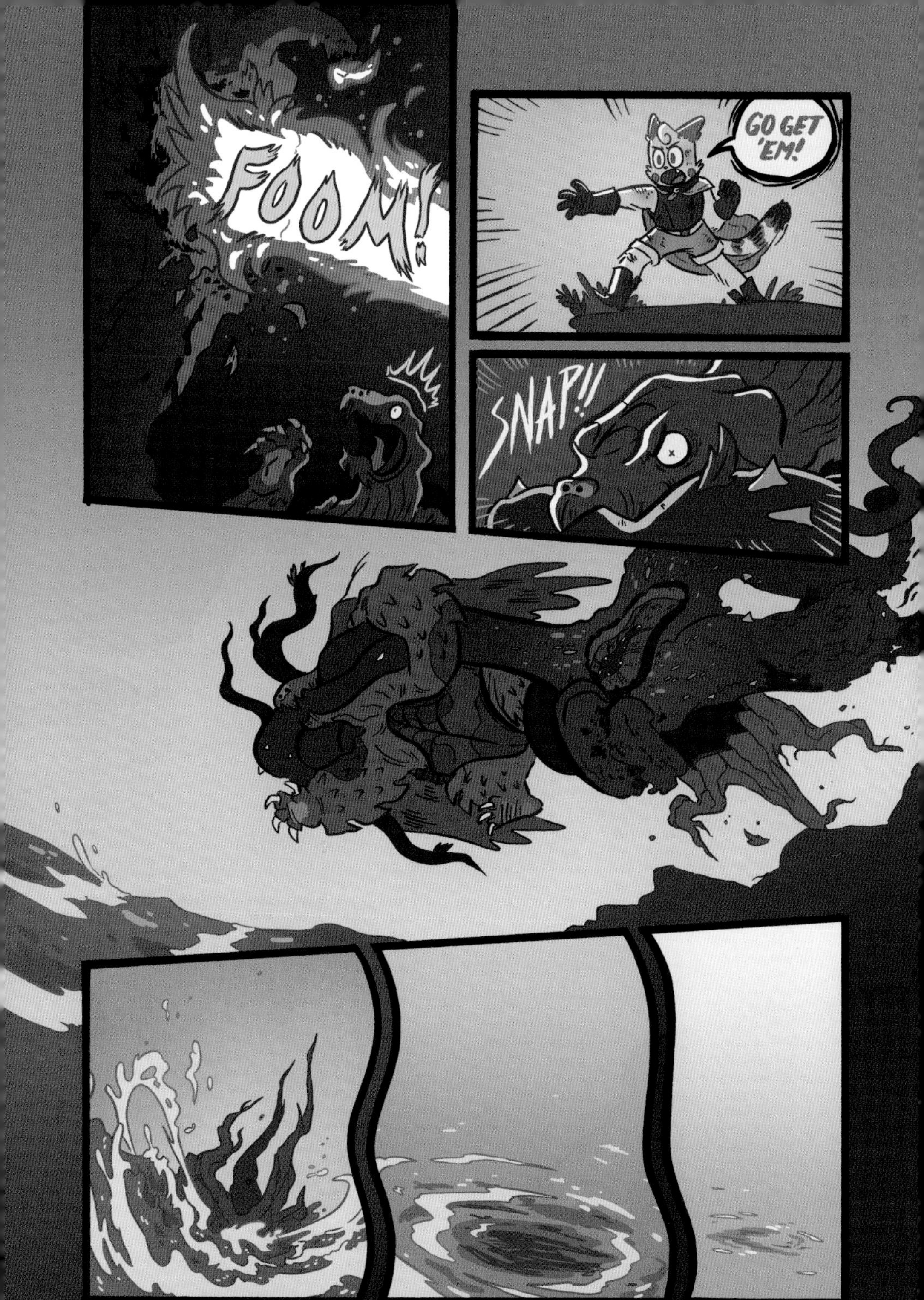
FOOM!
GO GET 'EM!
SNAP!!

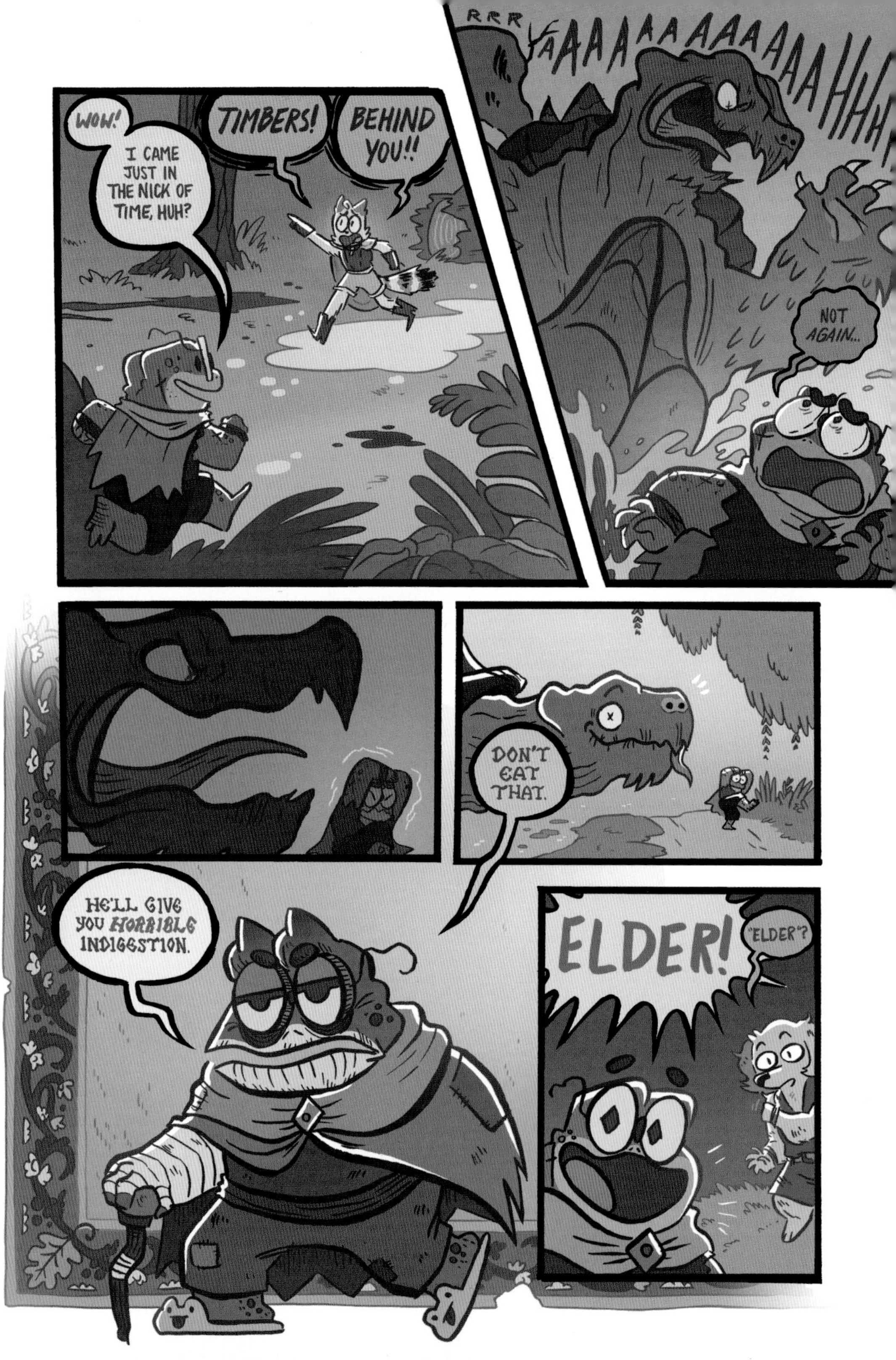
WOW!
I CAME JUST IN THE NICK OF TIME, HUH?
TIMBERS!
BEHIND YOU!!
RRRYAAAAAAAAAAAAAHHHH
NOT AGAIN...
DON'T EAT THAT.
HE'LL GIVE YOU HORRIBLE INDIGESTION.
ELDER!
"ELDER"?

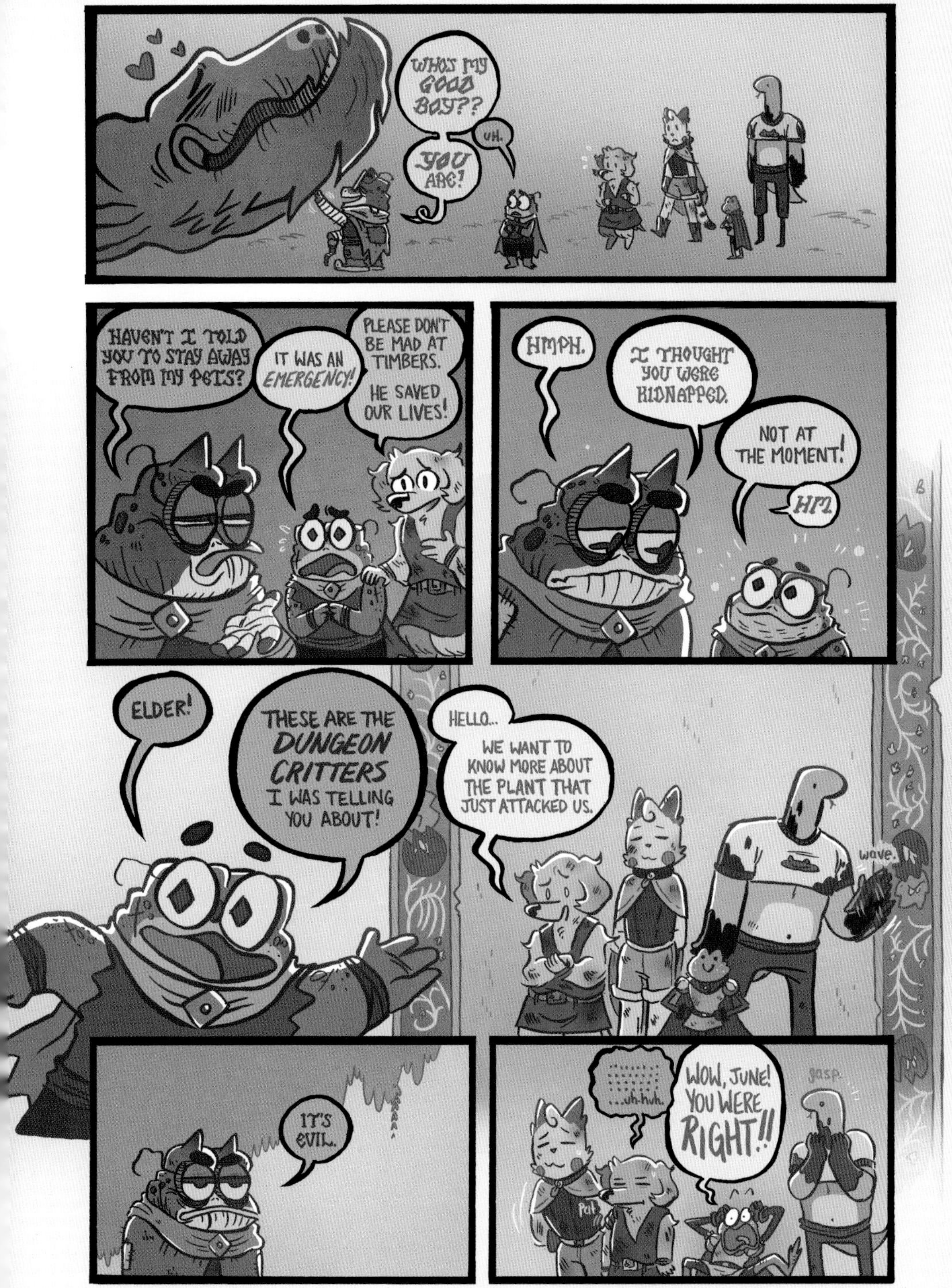

WHO'S MY GOOD BOY??
UH.
YOU ARE!
HAVEN'T I TOLD YOU TO STAY AWAY FROM MY PETS?
IT WAS AN EMERGENCY!
PLEASE DON'T BE MAD AT TIMBERS.
HE SAVED OUR LIVES!
HMPH.
I THOUGHT YOU WERE KIDNAPPED.
NOT AT THE MOMENT!
HM.
ELDER!
THESE ARE THE DUNGEON CRITTERS I WAS TELLING YOU ABOUT!
HELLO...
WE WANT TO KNOW MORE ABOUT THE PLANT THAT JUST ATTACKED US.
wave.
IT'S EVIL.
...uh-huh.
Pat
WOW, JUNE! YOU WERE RIGHT!!
gasp.

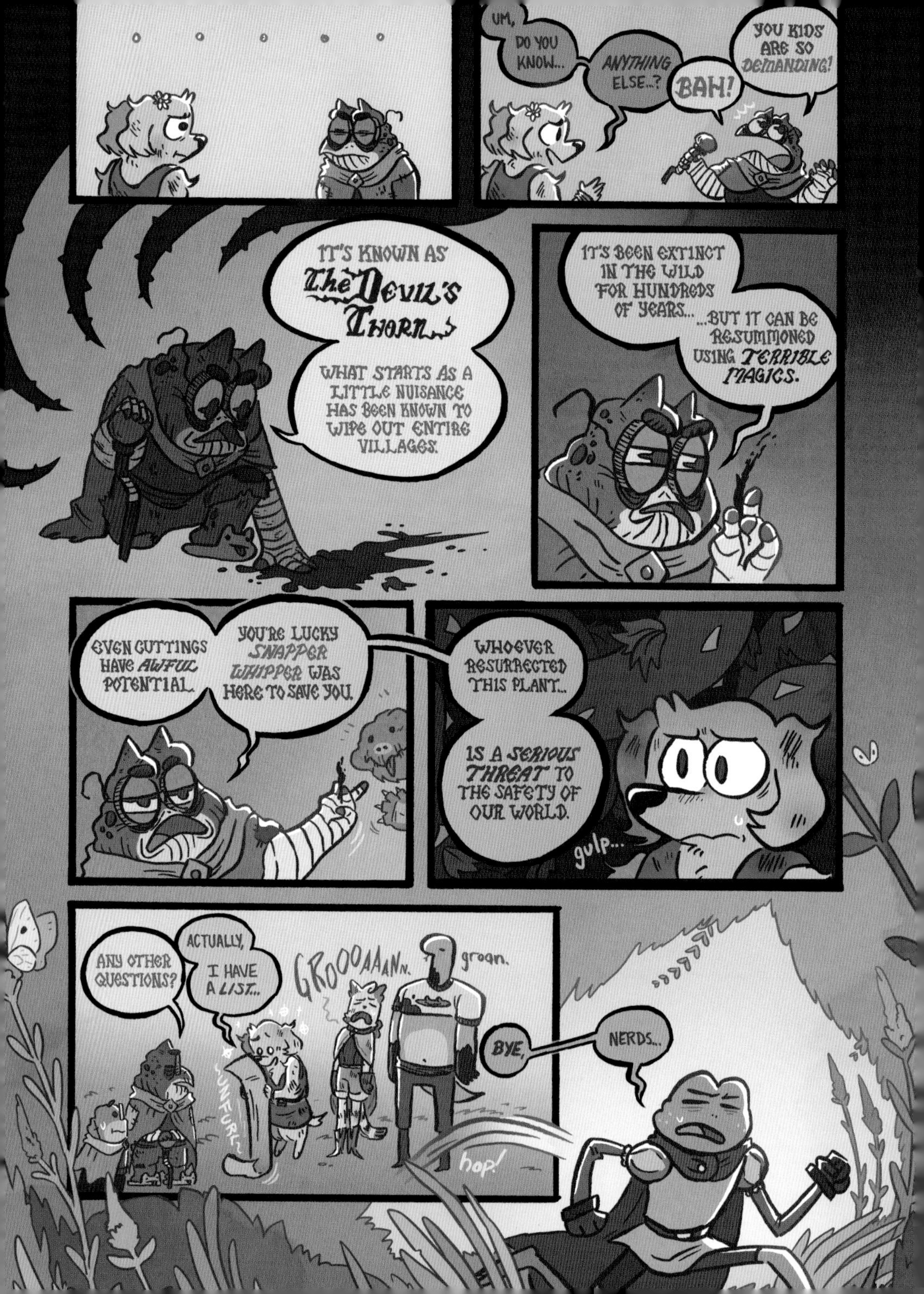
. . . . .
UM,
DO YOU KNOW...
ANYTHING ELSE...?
BAH!
YOU KIDS ARE SO DEMANDING!
IT'S KNOWN AS The Devil's Thorn...
WHAT STARTS AS A LITTLE NUISANCE HAS BEEN KNOWN TO WIPE OUT ENTIRE VILLAGES.
IT'S BEEN EXTINCT IN THE WILD FOR HUNDREDS OF YEARS...
...BUT IT CAN BE RESUMMONED USING TERRIBLE MAGICS.
EVEN CUTTINGS HAVE AWFUL POTENTIAL.
YOU'RE LUCKY SNAPPER WHIPPER WAS HERE TO SAVE YOU.
WHOEVER RESURRECTED THIS PLANT...
IS A SERIOUS THREAT TO THE SAFETY OF OUR WORLD.
gulp...
ANY OTHER QUESTIONS?
ACTUALLY,
I HAVE A LIST...
GROOOAAANN.
groan.
UNFURL
BYE,
NERDS...
hop!

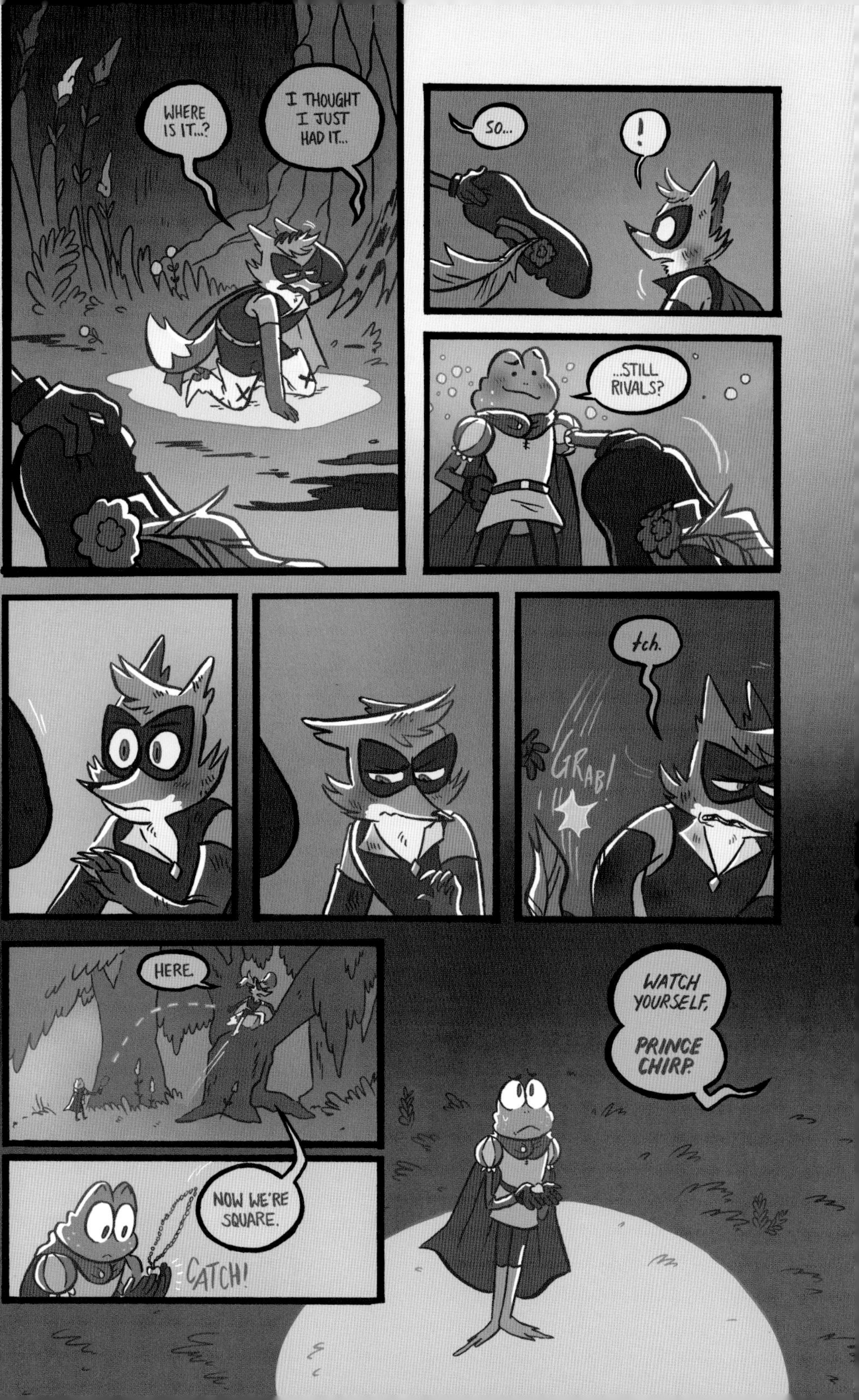

WHERE IS IT...?
I THOUGHT I JUST HAD IT...
SO...
!
...STILL RIVALS?
tch.
GRAB!
HERE.
NOW WE'RE SQUARE.
CATCH!
WATCH YOURSELF,
PRINCE CHIRP.

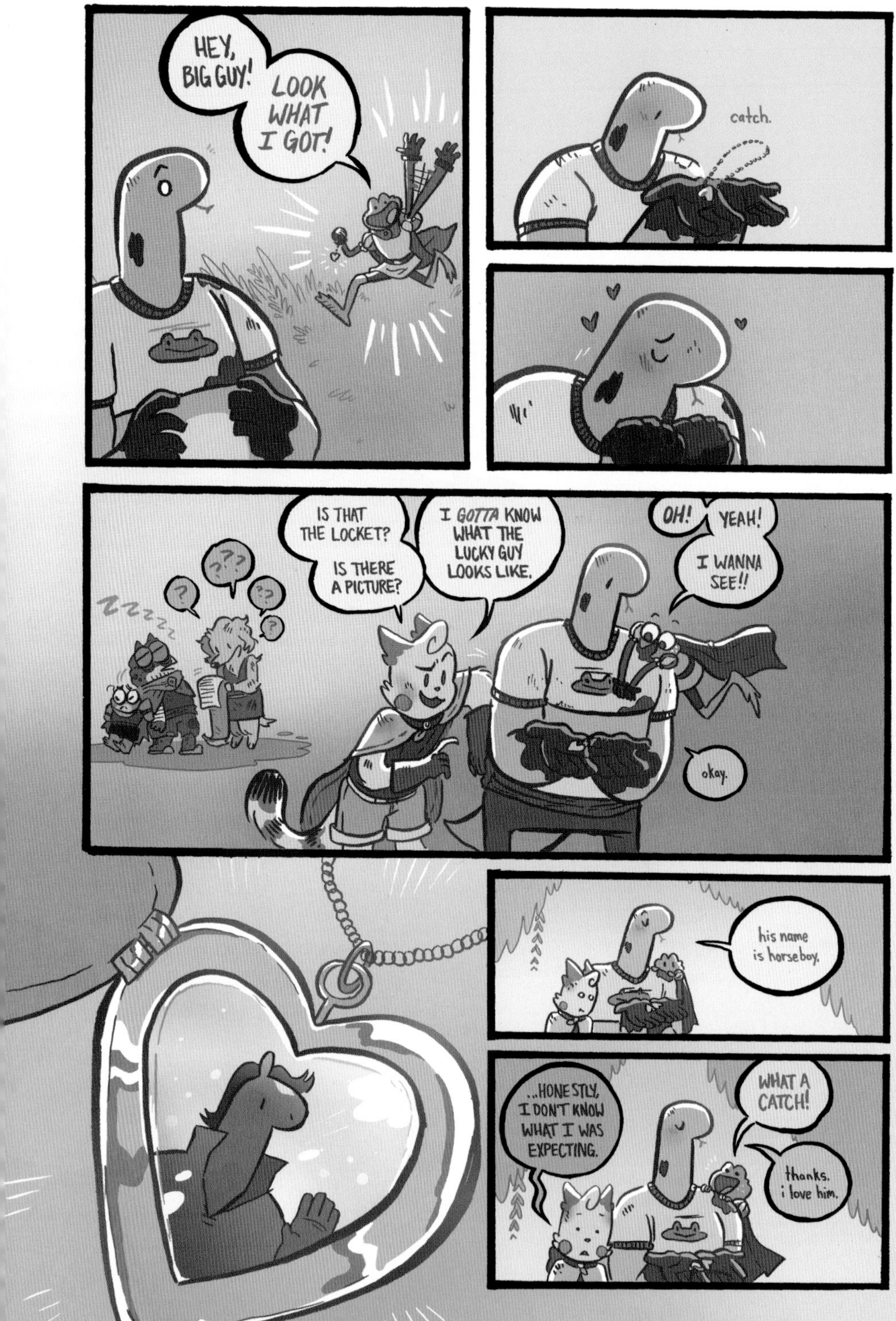
HEY, BIG GUY!
LOOK WHAT I GOT!
catch.
IS THAT THE LOCKET? IS THERE A PICTURE?
I GOTTA KNOW WHAT THE LUCKY GUY LOOKS LIKE.
OH!
YEAH! I WANNA SEE!!
okay.
his name is horseboy.
...HONESTLY, I DON'T KNOW WHAT I WAS EXPECTING.
WHAT A CATCH!
thanks. i love him.

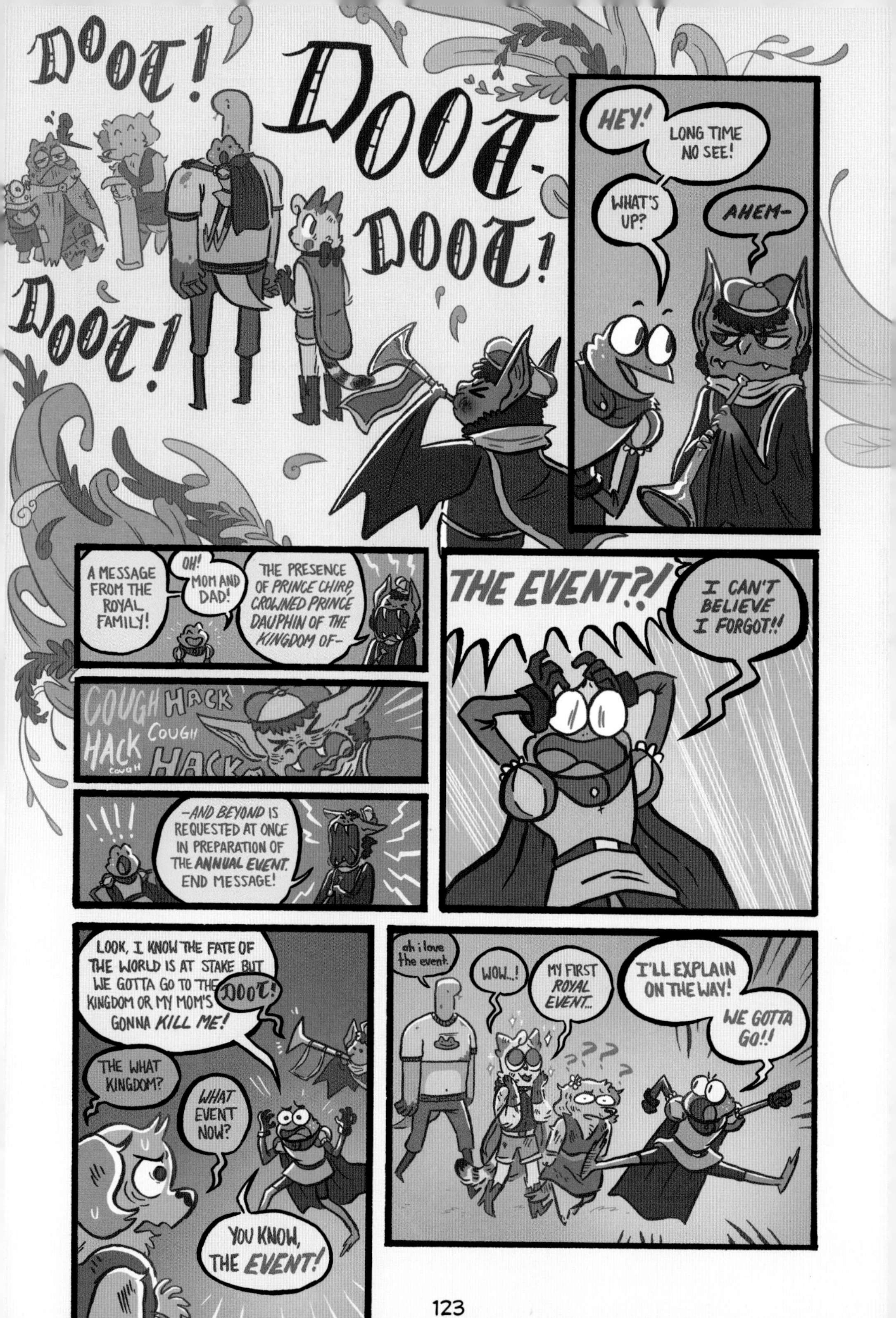
DOOT!
DOOT-
DOOT!
DOOT!
HEY!
LONG TIME NO SEE!
WHAT'S UP?
AHEM-
A MESSAGE FROM THE ROYAL FAMILY!
OH! MOM AND DAD!
THE PRESENCE OF PRINCE CHIRP, CROWNED PRINCE DAUPHIN OF THE KINGDOM OF-
COUGH HACK
HACK COUGH
HACK
COUGH
-AND BEYOND IS REQUESTED AT ONCE IN PREPARATION OF THE ANNUAL EVENT. END MESSAGE!
THE EVENT?!
I CAN'T BELIEVE I FORGOT!!
LOOK, I KNOW THE FATE OF THE WORLD IS AT STAKE BUT WE GOTTA GO TO THE KINGDOM OR MY MOM'S GONNA KILL ME!
DOOT!
THE WHAT KINGDOM?
WHAT EVENT NOW?
YOU KNOW, THE EVENT!
oh i love the event.
WOW...!
MY FIRST ROYAL EVENT...
I'LL EXPLAIN ON THE WAY!
WE GOTTA GO!!

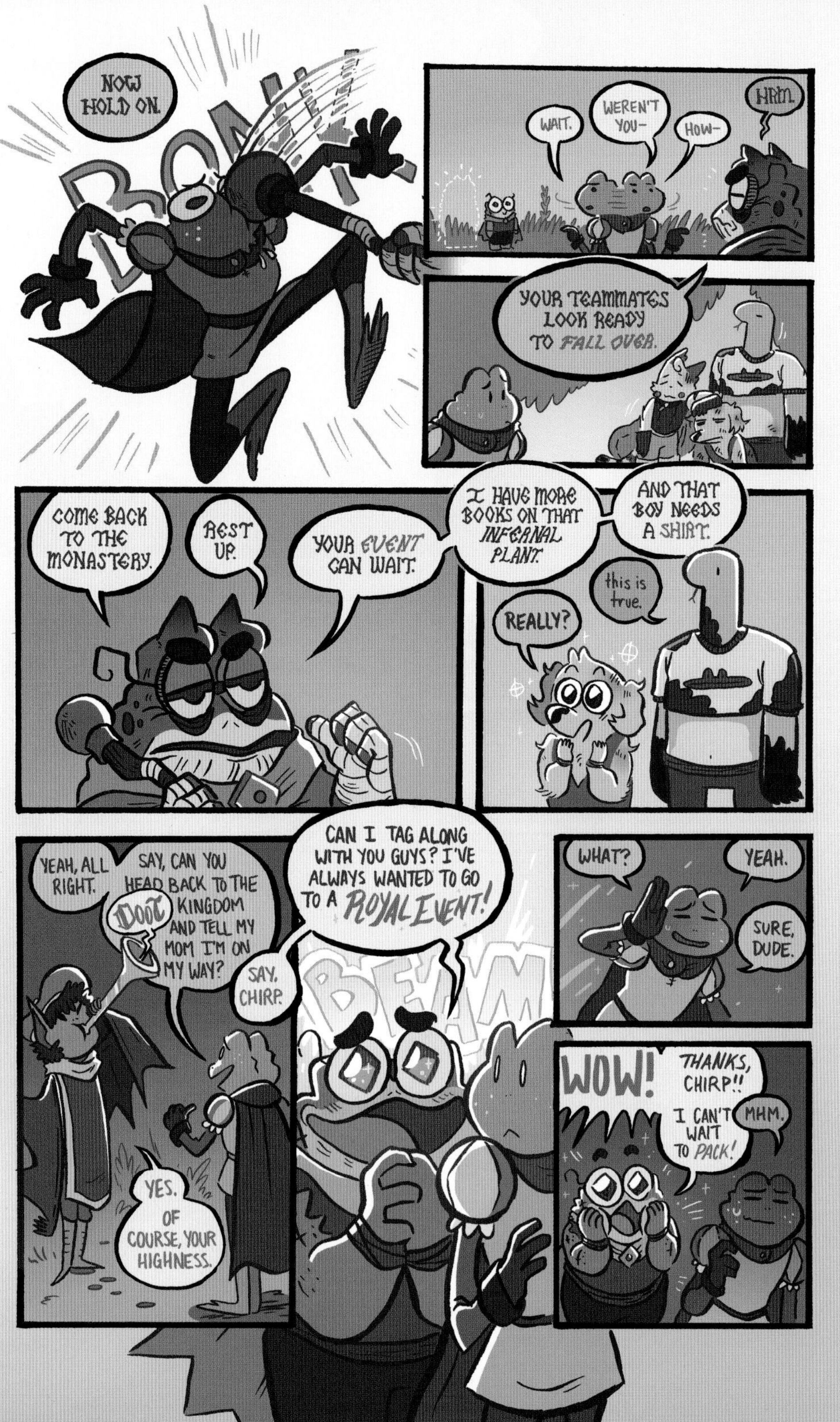
NOW HOLD ON.
BONK!
WAIT.
WEREN'T YOU-
HOW-
HRM.
YOUR TEAMMATES LOOK READY TO FALL OVER.
COME BACK TO THE MONASTERY.
REST UP.
YOUR EVENT CAN WAIT.
I HAVE MORE BOOKS ON THAT INFERNAL PLANT.
AND THAT BOY NEEDS A SHIRT.
this is true.
REALLY?
YEAH, ALL RIGHT.
SAY, CAN YOU HEAD BACK TO THE KINGDOM AND TELL MY MOM I'M ON MY WAY?
DOOT
SAY, CHIRP.
YES. OF COURSE, YOUR HIGHNESS.
CAN I TAG ALONG WITH YOU GUYS? I'VE ALWAYS WANTED TO GO TO A ROYAL EVENT!
BEAM
WHAT?
YEAH.
SURE, DUDE.
WOW!
THANKS, CHIRP!! I CAN'T WAIT TO PACK!
MHM.

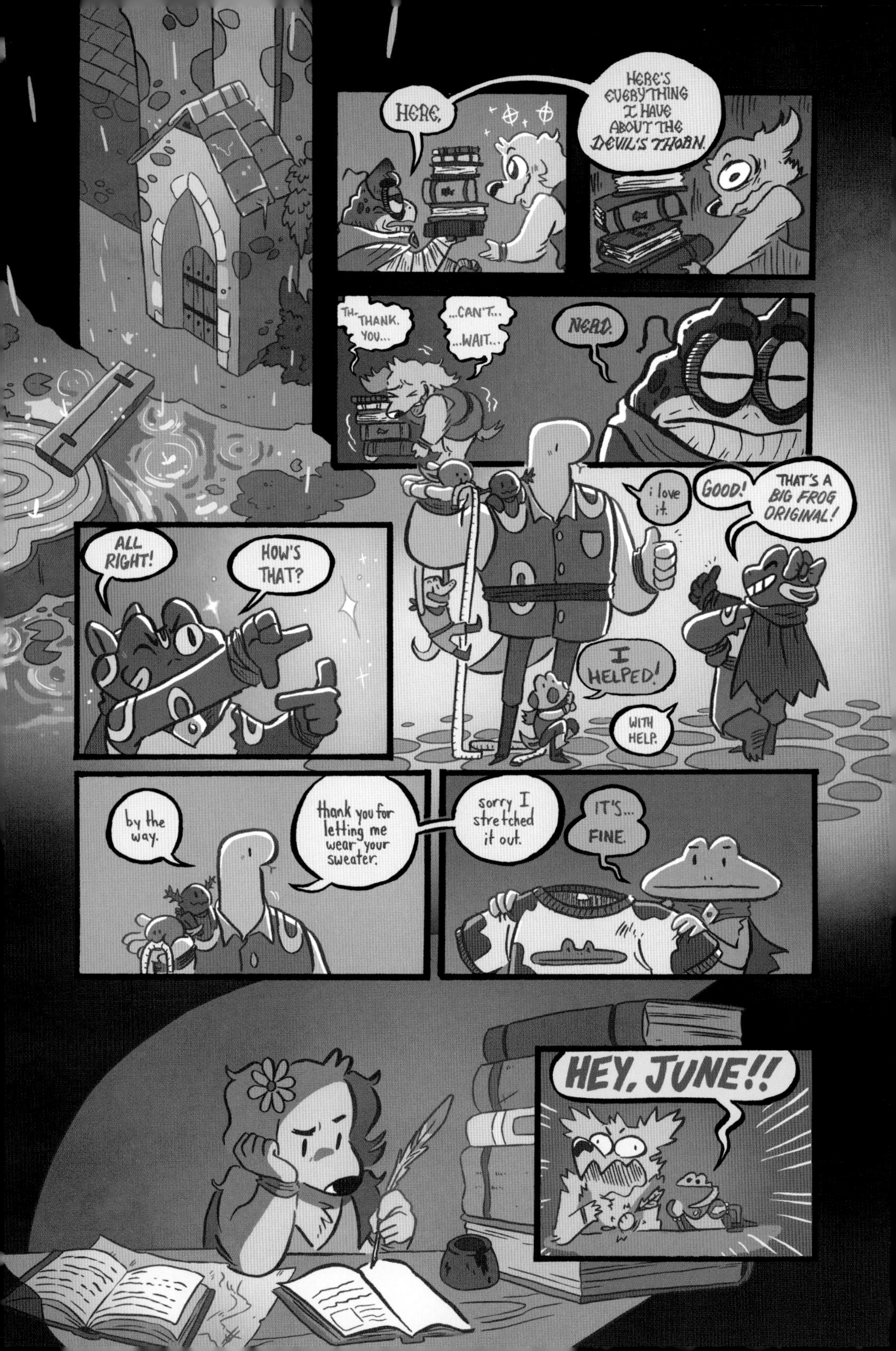
HERE.
HERE'S EVERYTHING I HAVE ABOUT THE DEVIL'S THORN.
TH-THANK. YOU...
...CAN'T... ...WAIT...
NERD.
ALL RIGHT!
HOW'S THAT?
i love it.
GOOD!
THAT'S A BIG FROG ORIGINAL!
I HELPED!
WITH HELP.
by the way.
thank you for letting me wear your sweater.
sorry I stretched it out.
IT'S... FINE.
HEY, JUNE!!

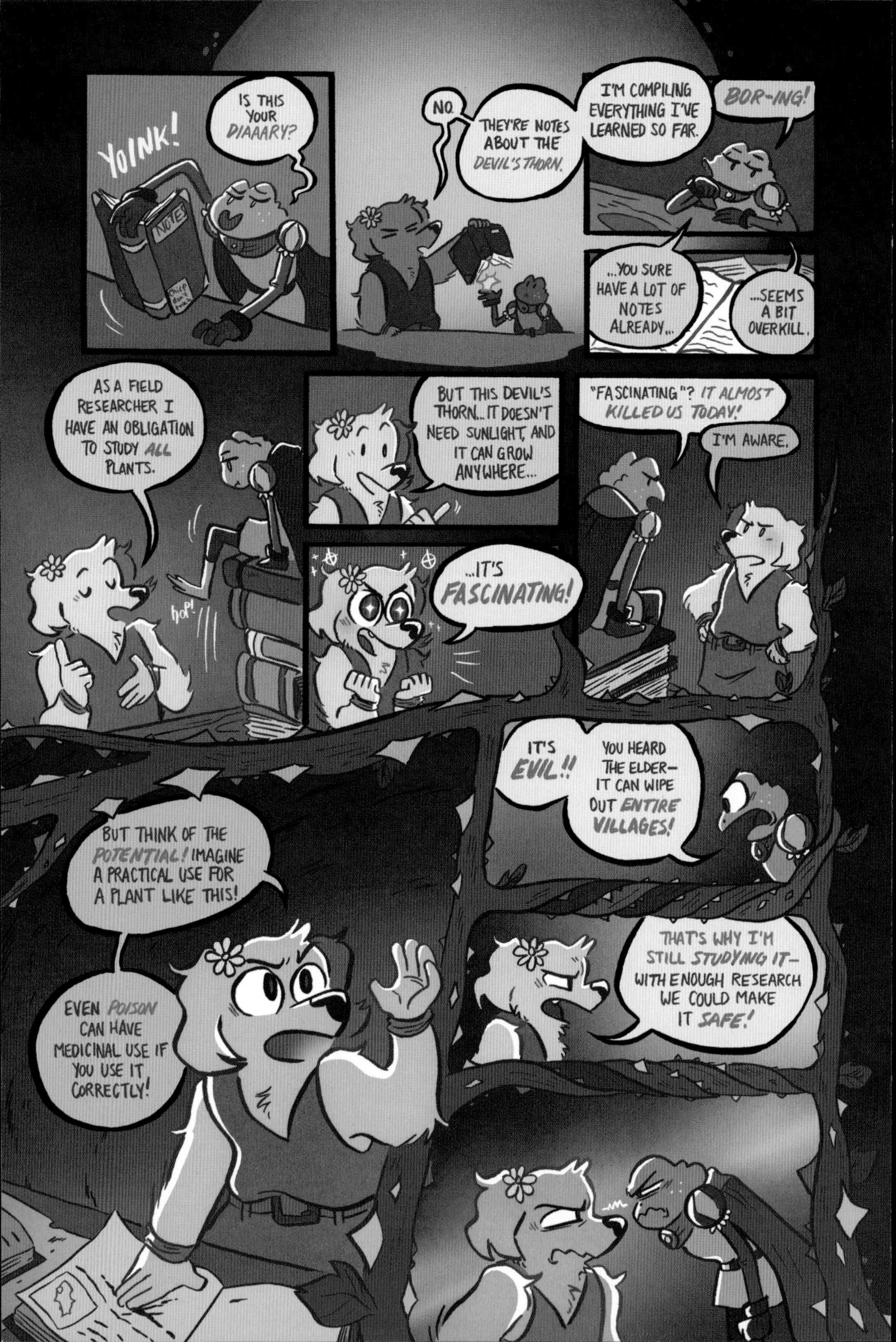
YOINK!
IS THIS YOUR DIAAARY?
NO.
THEY'RE NOTES ABOUT THE DEVIL'S THORN.
I'M COMPILING EVERYTHING I'VE LEARNED SO FAR.
BOR-ING!
...YOU SURE HAVE A LOT OF NOTES ALREADY...
...SEEMS A BIT OVERKILL.
AS A FIELD RESEARCHER I HAVE AN OBLIGATION TO STUDY ALL PLANTS.
HOP!
BUT THIS DEVIL'S THORN... IT DOESN'T NEED SUNLIGHT, AND IT CAN GROW ANYWHERE...
...IT'S FASCINATING!
"FASCINATING"? IT ALMOST KILLED US TODAY!
I'M AWARE.
IT'S EVIL!!
YOU HEARD THE ELDER— IT CAN WIPE OUT ENTIRE VILLAGES!
BUT THINK OF THE POTENTIAL! IMAGINE A PRACTICAL USE FOR A PLANT LIKE THIS!
EVEN POISON CAN HAVE MEDICINAL USE IF YOU USE IT CORRECTLY!
THAT'S WHY I'M STILL STUDYING IT— WITH ENOUGH RESEARCH WE COULD MAKE IT SAFE!

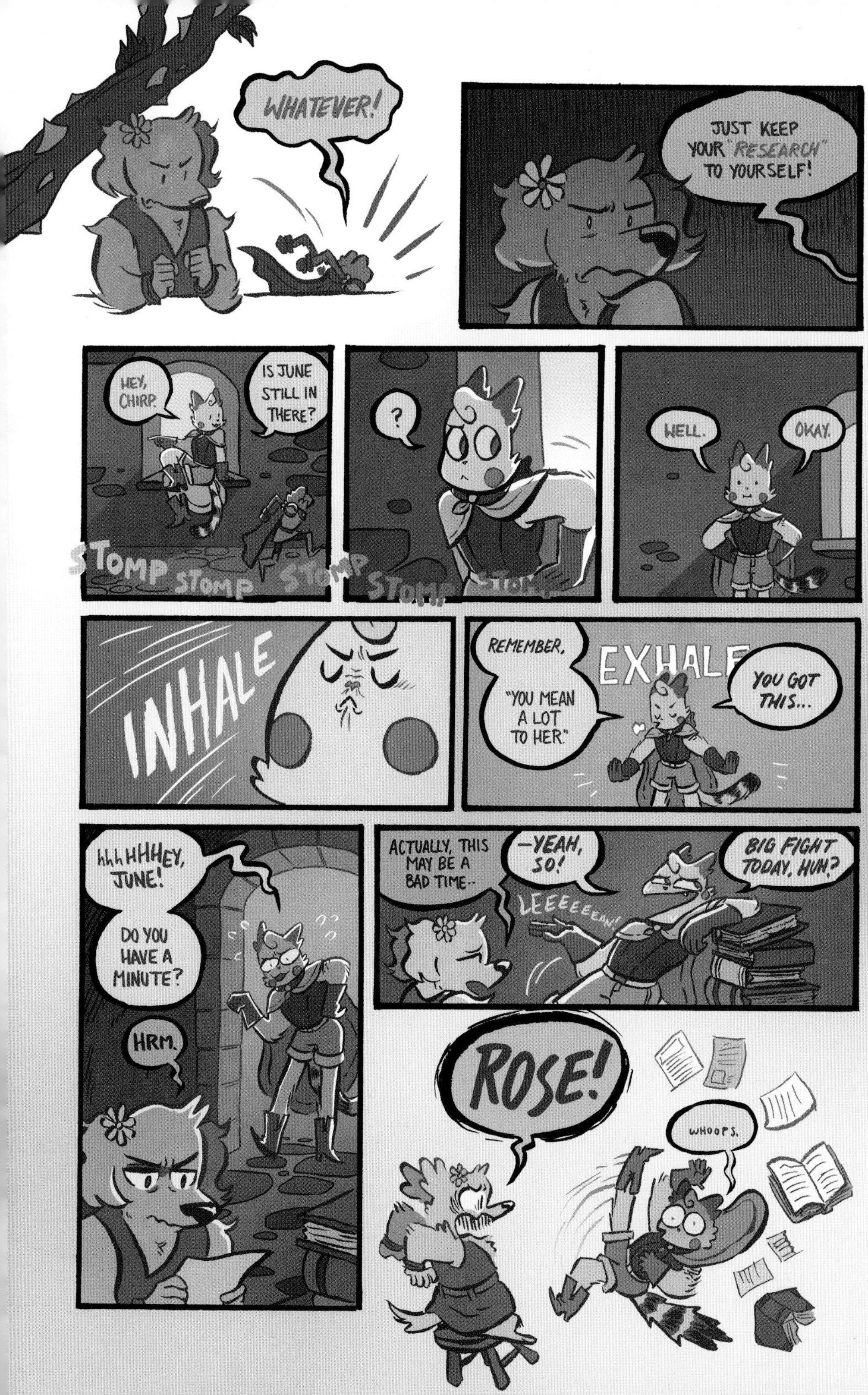
WHATEVER!
JUST KEEP YOUR "RESEARCH" TO YOURSELF!
HEY, CHIRP.
IS JUNE STILL IN THERE?
STOMP STOMP STOMP STOMP STOMP
?
WELL.
OKAY.
INHALE
REMEMBER,
"YOU MEAN A LOT TO HER."
EXHALE
YOU GOT THIS...
hhhHHHEY, JUNE!
DO YOU HAVE A MINUTE?
HRM.
ACTUALLY, THIS MAY BE A BAD TIME--
—YEAH, SO!
BIG FIGHT TODAY, HUH?
LEEEEEEAN!
ROSE!
WHOOPS.

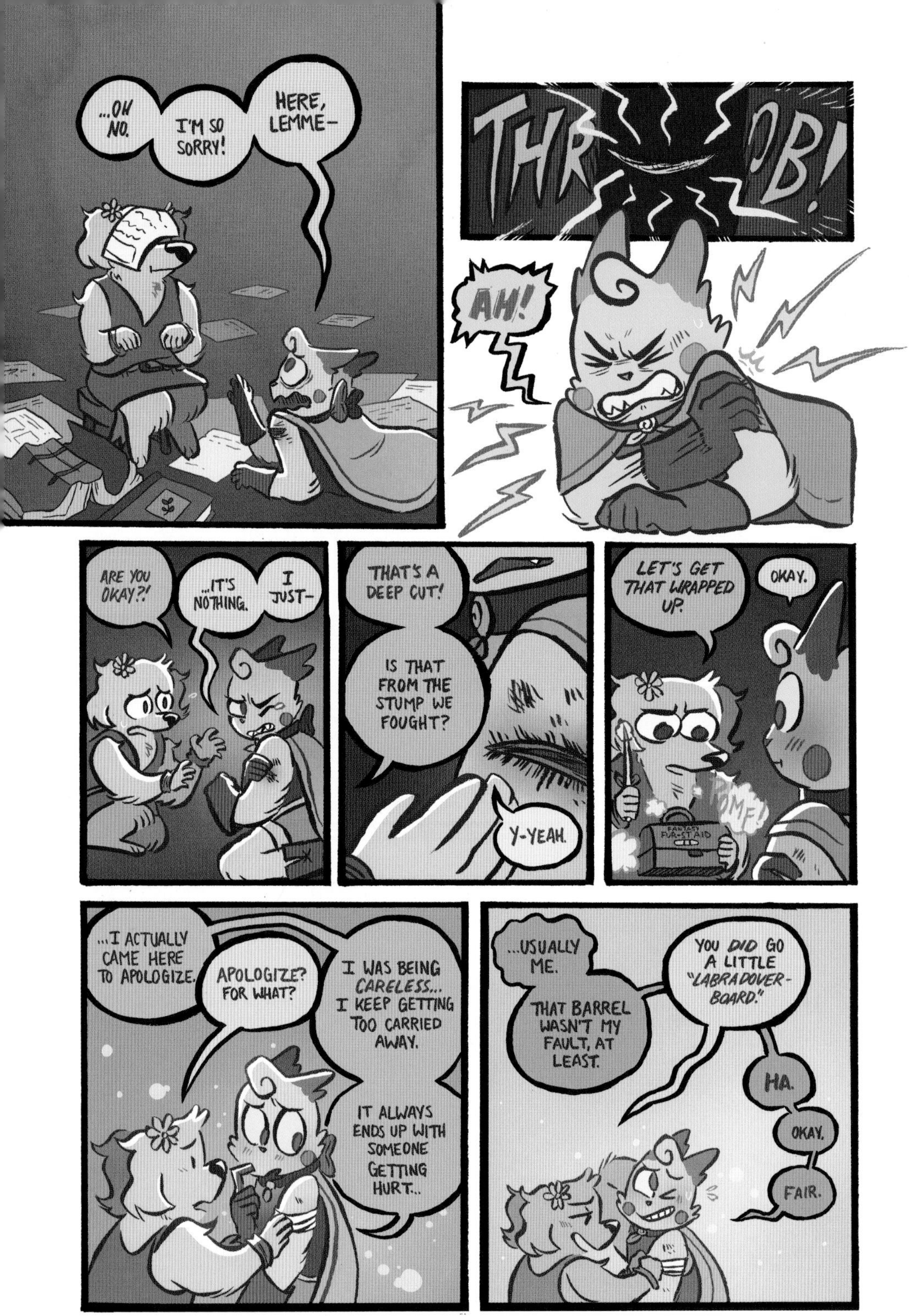
...OH NO.
I'M SO SORRY!
HERE, LEMME-
THR OB!
AH!
ARE YOU OKAY?!
...IT'S NOTHING.
I JUST-
THAT'S A DEEP CUT!
IS THAT FROM THE STUMP WE FOUGHT?
Y-YEAH.
LET'S GET THAT WRAPPED UP.
OKAY.
POMF!
FANTASY FUR-ST AID
...I ACTUALLY CAME HERE TO APOLOGIZE.
APOLOGIZE? FOR WHAT?
I WAS BEING CARELESS... I KEEP GETTING TOO CARRIED AWAY.
IT ALWAYS ENDS UP WITH SOMEONE GETTING HURT..
...USUALLY ME.
THAT BARREL WASN'T MY FAULT, AT LEAST.
YOU DID GO A LITTLE "LABRADOVER-BOARD."
HA.
OKAY.
FAIR.

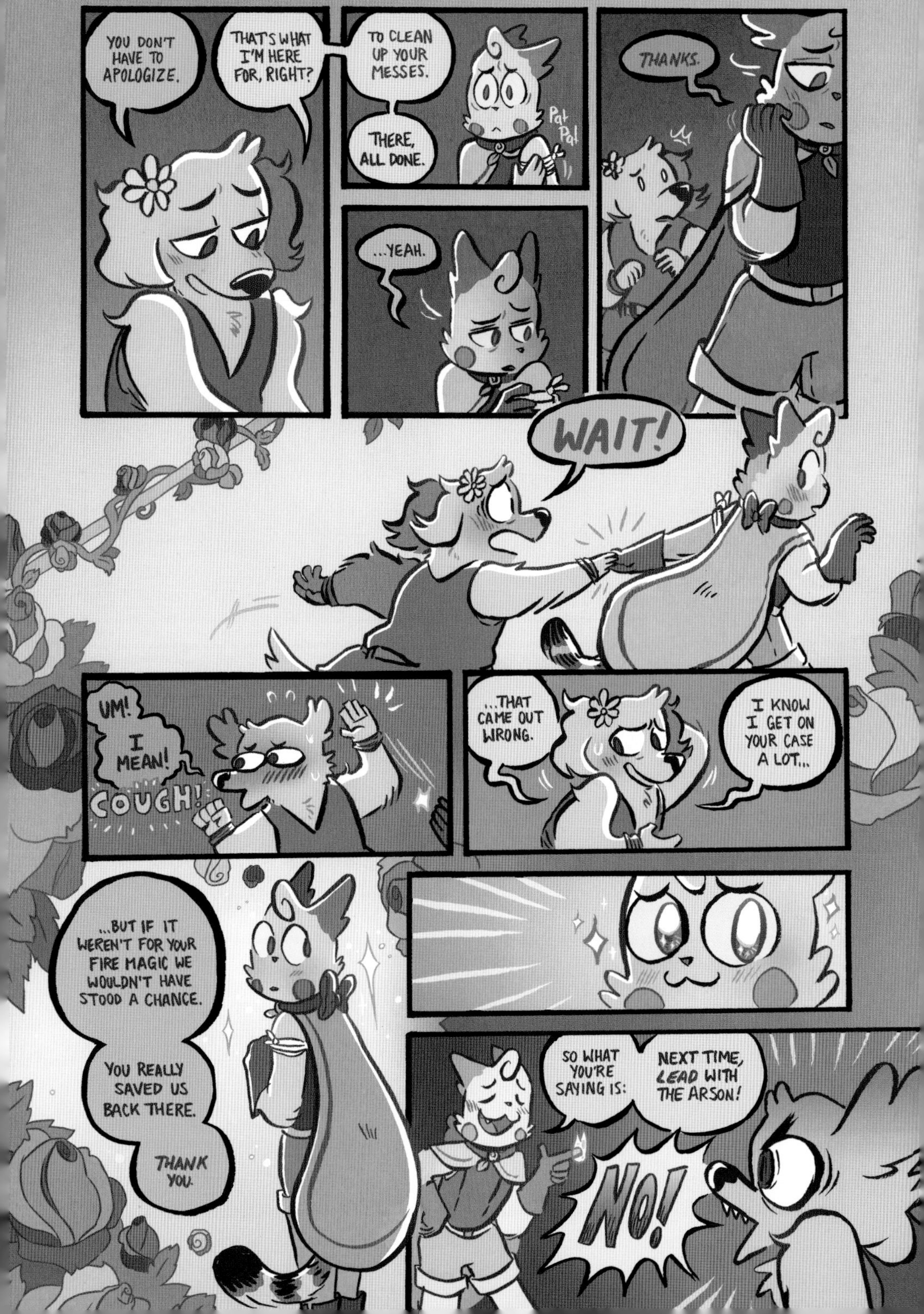
YOU DON'T HAVE TO APOLOGIZE.
THAT'S WHAT I'M HERE FOR, RIGHT?
TO CLEAN UP YOUR MESSES.
THERE, ALL DONE.
Pat Pat
...YEAH.
THANKS.
WAIT!
UM! I MEAN!
COUGH!
...THAT CAME OUT WRONG.
I KNOW I GET ON YOUR CASE A LOT...
...BUT IF IT WEREN'T FOR YOUR FIRE MAGIC WE WOULDN'T HAVE STOOD A CHANCE.
YOU REALLY SAVED US BACK THERE.
THANK YOU.
SO WHAT YOU'RE SAYING IS:
NEXT TIME, LEAD WITH THE ARSON!
NO!

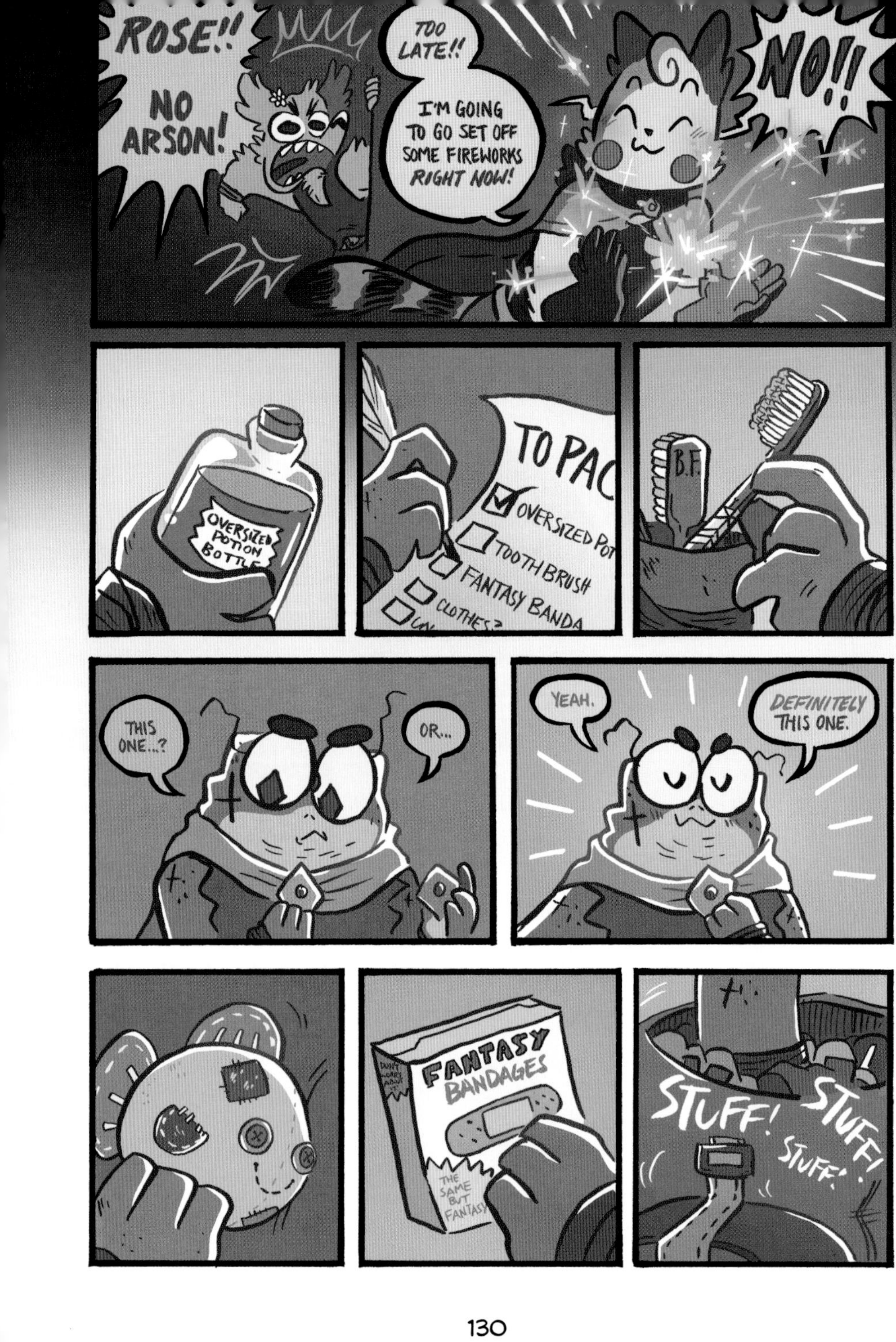
ROSE!!
NO ARSON!
TOO LATE!!
I'M GOING TO GO SET OFF SOME FIREWORKS RIGHT NOW!
NO!!
OVERSIZED POTION BOTTLE
TO PAC
OVERSIZED POT
TOOTH BRUSH
FANTASY BANDA
CLOTHES?
B.F.
THIS ONE...?
OR...
YEAH.
DEFINITELY THIS ONE.
FANTASY BANDAGES
THE SAME BUT FANTASY
STUFF! STUFF! STUFF!

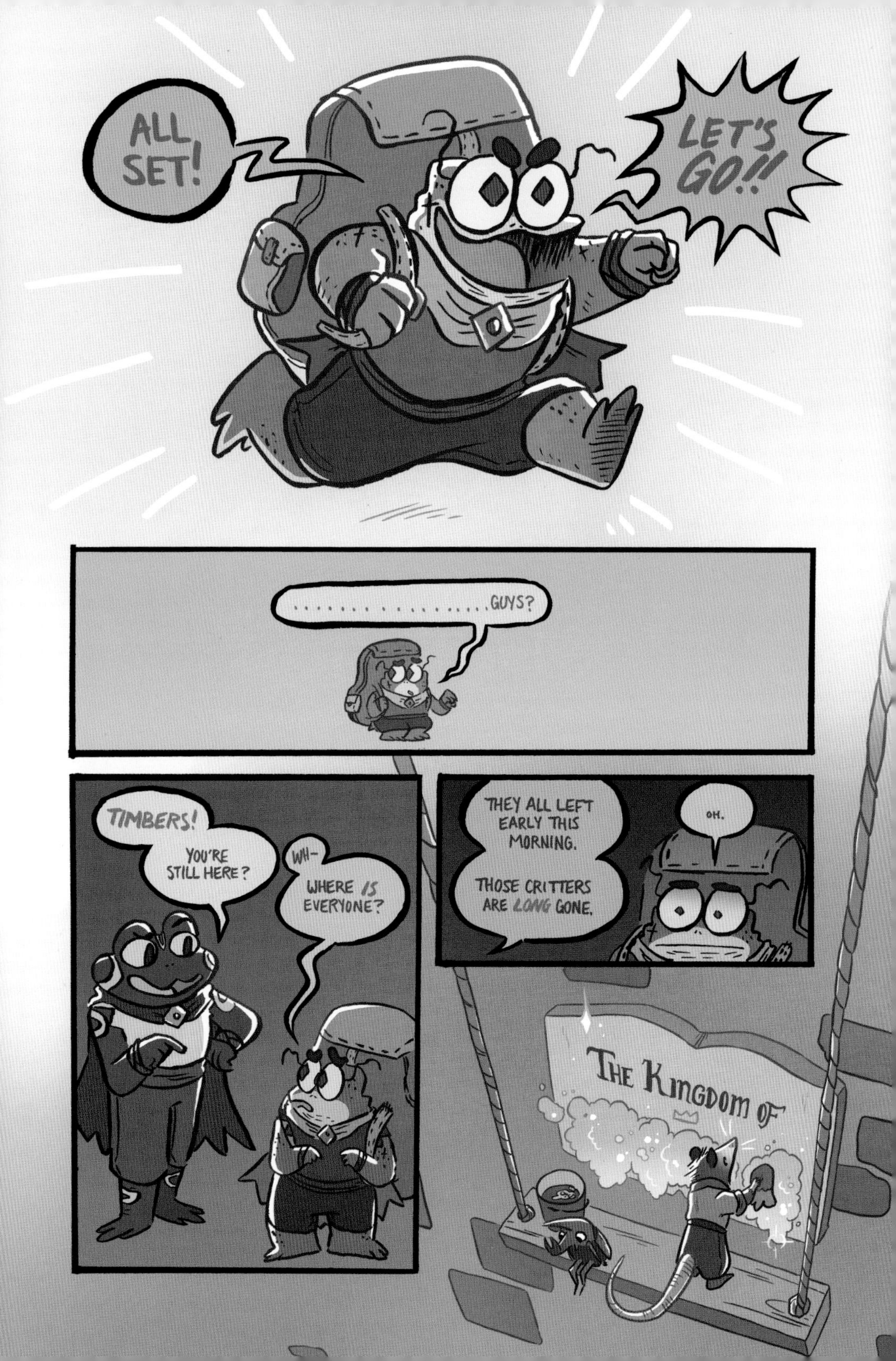
ALL SET!
LET'S GO!!
.......................GUYS?
TIMBERS!
YOU'RE STILL HERE?
WH-
WHERE IS EVERYONE?
THEY ALL LEFT EARLY THIS MORNING.
THOSE CRITTERS ARE LONG GONE.
OH.
THE KINGDOM OF

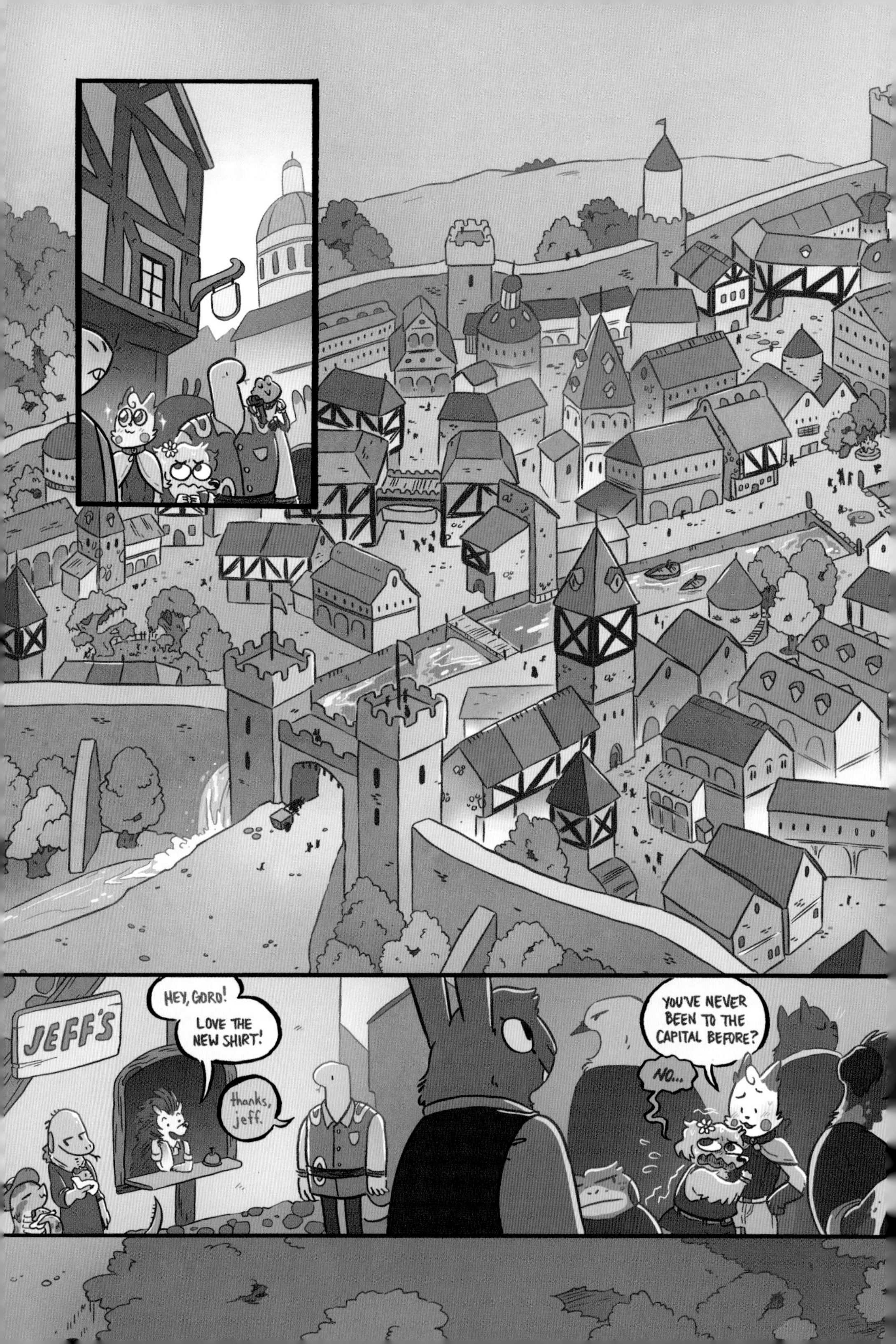
JEFF'S
HEY, GORO!
LOVE THE NEW SHIRT!
thanks, jeff.
YOU'VE NEVER BEEN TO THE CAPITAL BEFORE?
NO...

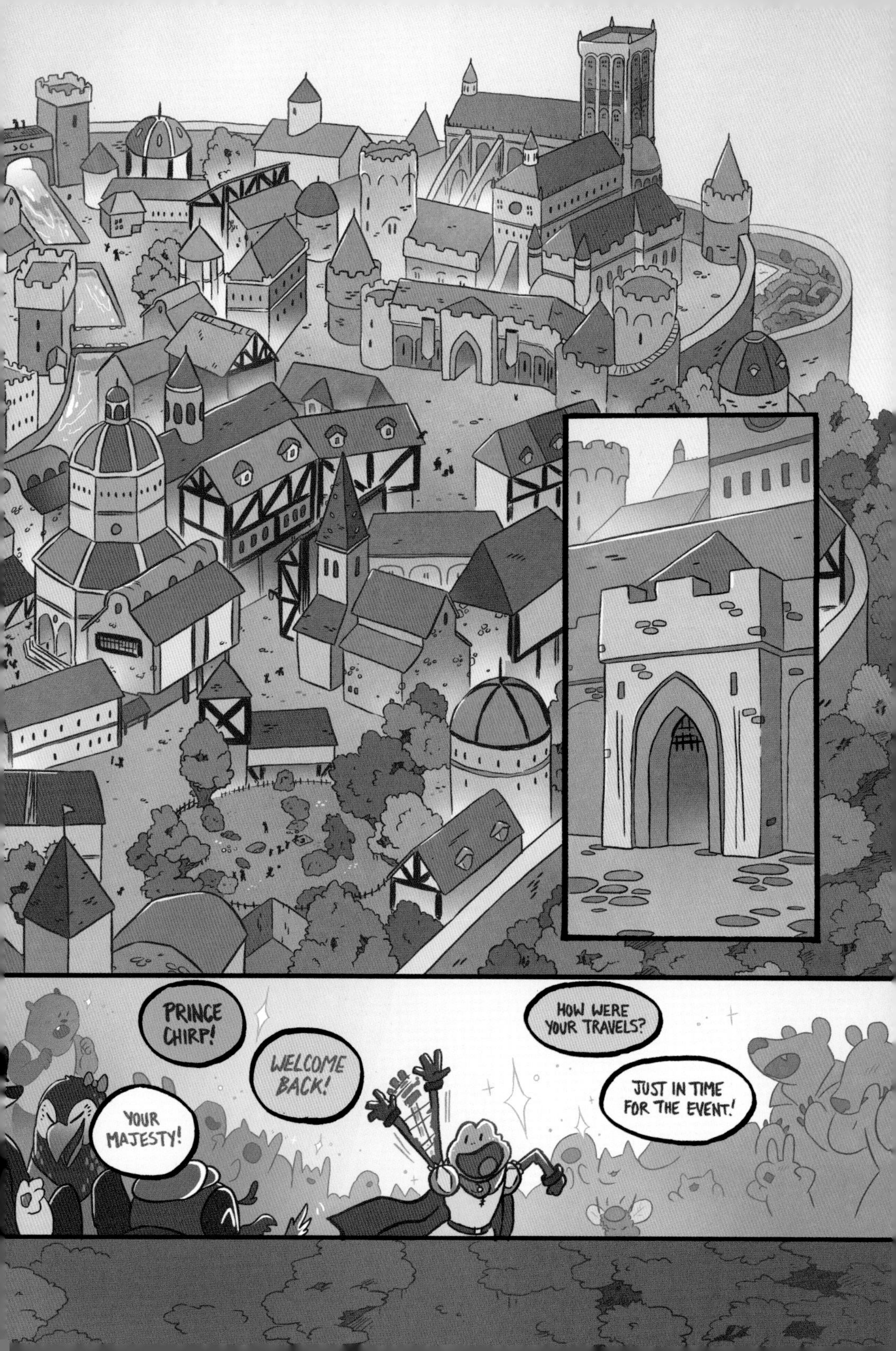
PRINCE CHIRP!
YOUR MAJESTY!
WELCOME BACK!
HOW WERE YOUR TRAVELS?
JUST IN TIME FOR THE EVENT!

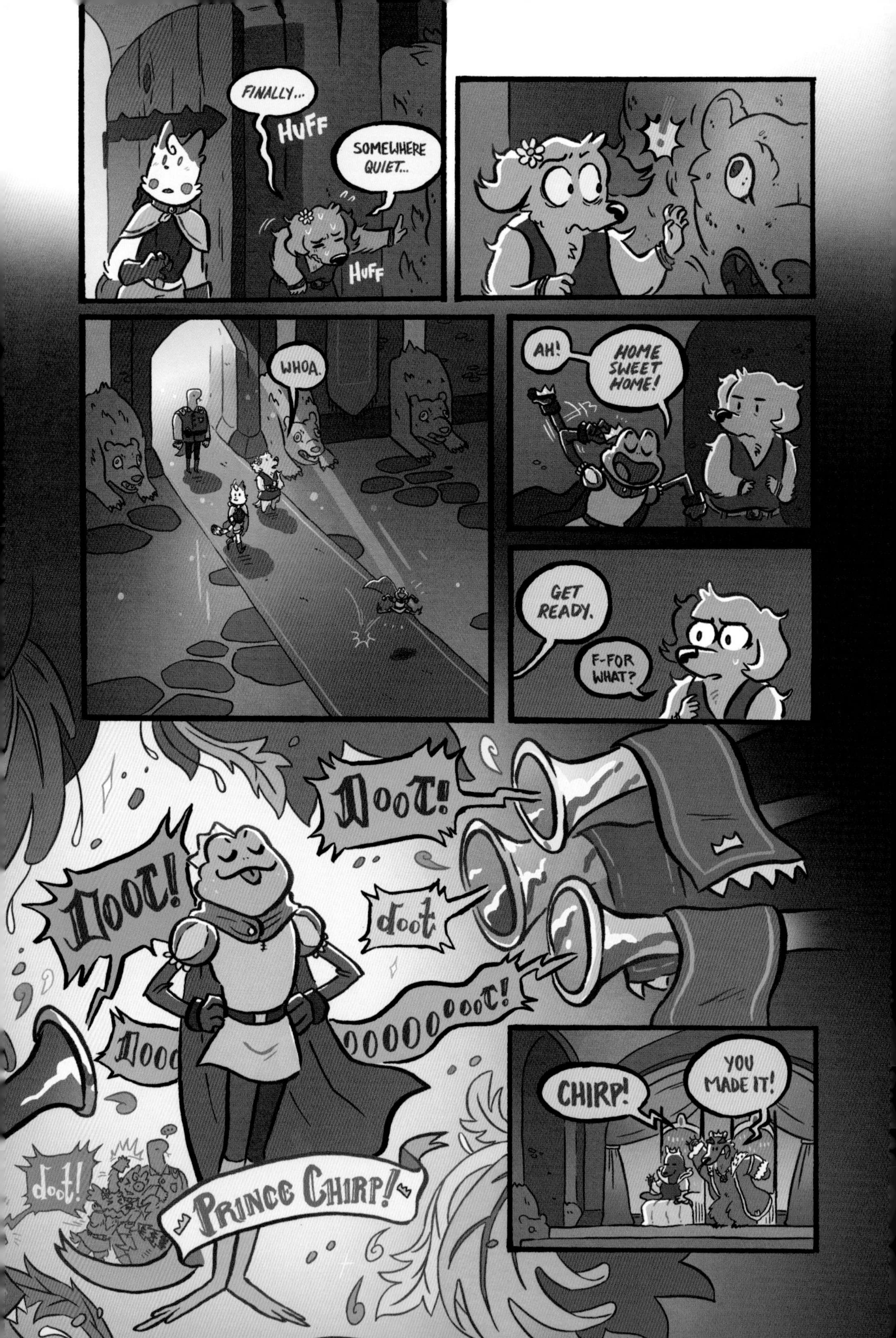
FINALLY...
HUFF
SOMEWHERE QUIET...
HUFF
WHOA.
AH!
HOME SWEET HOME!
GET READY.
F-FOR WHAT?
DOOT!
DOOT!
doot
DOOOOOOOOOOOOOT!
doot!
PRINCE CHIRP!
CHIRP!
YOU MADE IT!

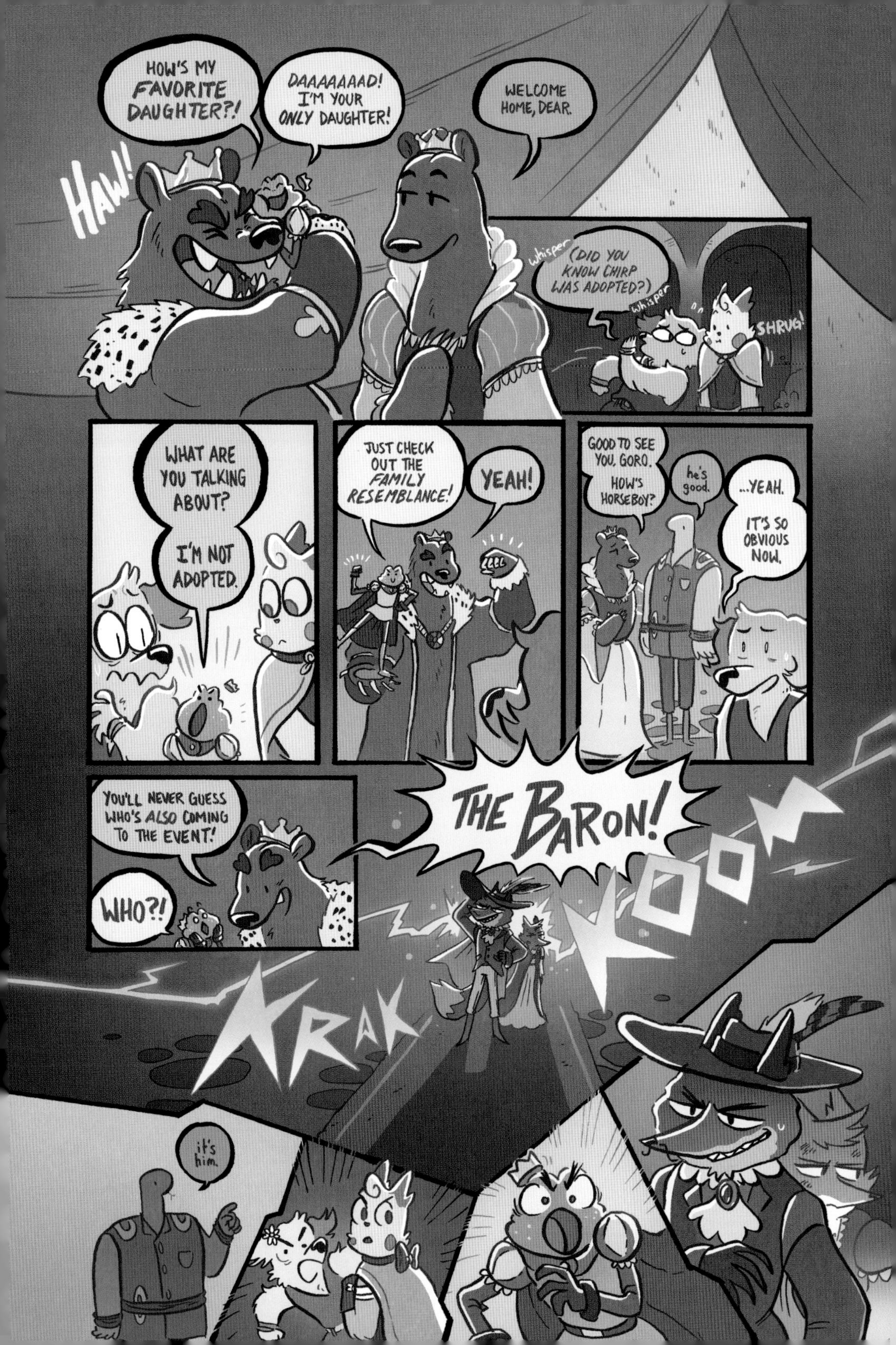

HOW'S MY FAVORITE DAUGHTER?!
DAAAAAAAD! I'M YOUR ONLY DAUGHTER!
HAW!
WELCOME HOME, DEAR.
whisper
(DID YOU KNOW CHIRP WAS ADOPTED?)
whisper
SHRUG!
WHAT ARE YOU TALKING ABOUT?
I'M NOT ADOPTED.
JUST CHECK OUT THE FAMILY RESEMBLANCE!
YEAH!
GOOD TO SEE YOU, GORO.
HOW'S HORSEBOY?
he's good.
...YEAH.
IT'S SO OBVIOUS NOW.
YOU'LL NEVER GUESS WHO'S ALSO COMING TO THE EVENT!
WHO?!
THE BARON!
KRAK
KOOOM
it's him.

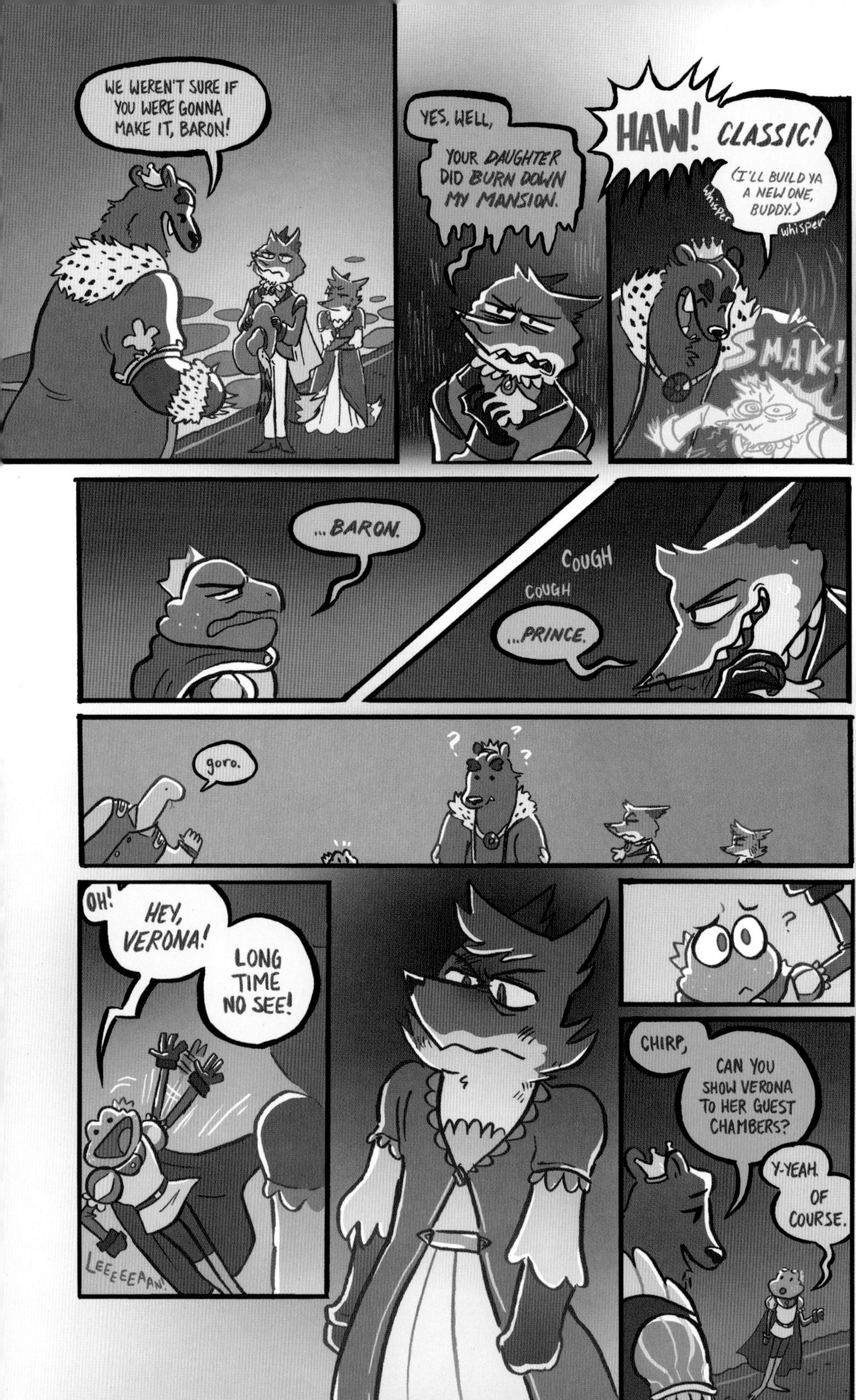
WE WEREN'T SURE IF YOU WERE GONNA MAKE IT, BARON!
YES, WELL,
YOUR DAUGHTER DID BURN DOWN MY MANSION.
HAW!
CLASSIC!
(I'LL BUILD YA A NEW ONE, BUDDY.)
whisper
whisper
SMAK!
...BARON.
COUGH
COUGH
...PRINCE.
goro.
OH!
HEY, VERONA!
LONG TIME NO SEE!
LEEEEEAAN!
CHIRP,
CAN YOU SHOW VERONA TO HER GUEST CHAMBERS?
Y-YEAH.
OF COURSE.

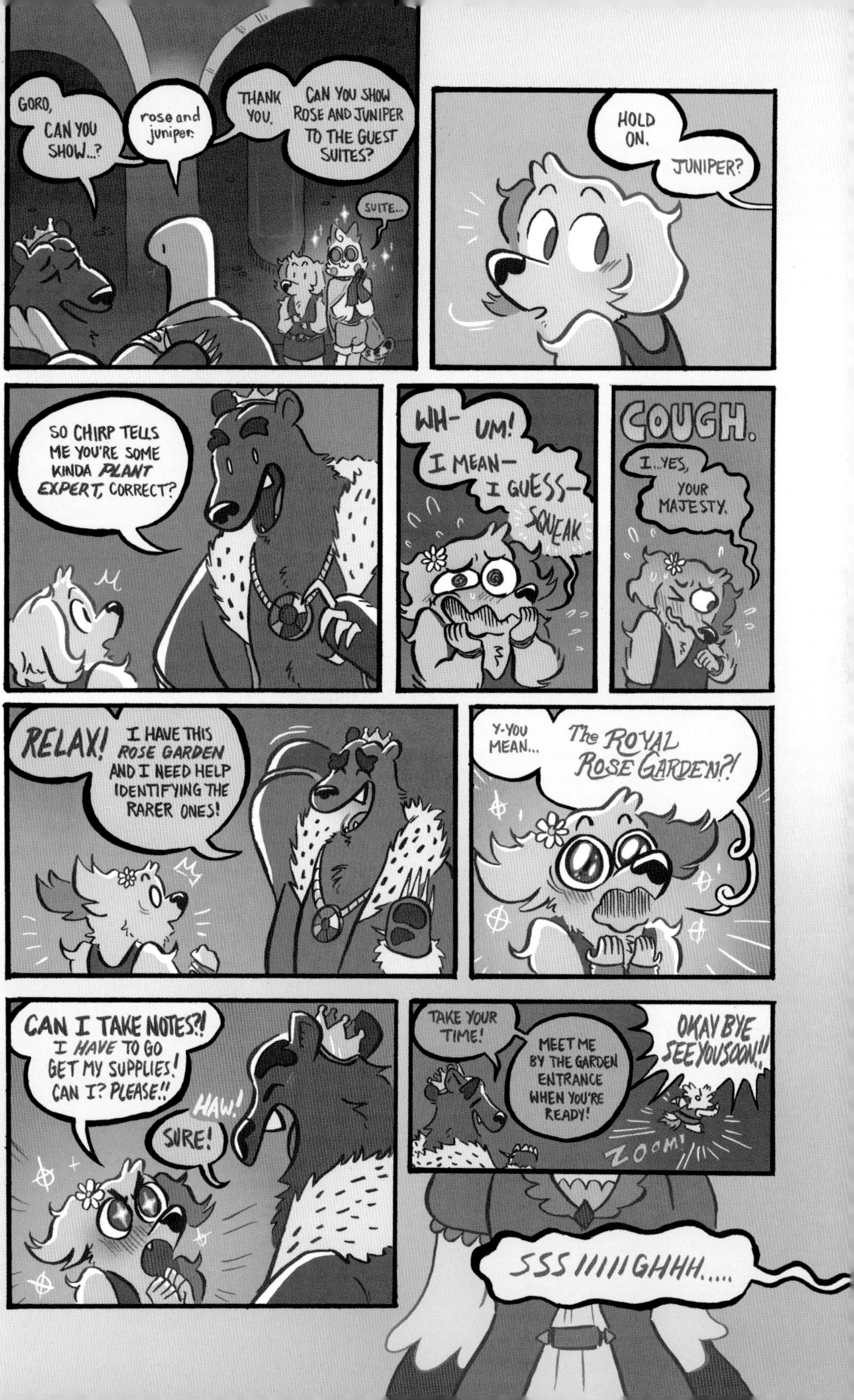
GORO, CAN YOU SHOW...?
rose and juniper.
THANK YOU.
CAN YOU SHOW ROSE AND JUNIPER TO THE GUEST SUITES?
SUITE...
HOLD ON. JUNIPER?
SO CHIRP TELLS ME YOU'RE SOME KINDA PLANT EXPERT, CORRECT?
WH- UM! I MEAN— I GUESS—
SQUEAK
COUGH.
I...YES, YOUR MAJESTY.
RELAX! I HAVE THIS ROSE GARDEN AND I NEED HELP IDENTIFYING THE RARER ONES!
Y-YOU MEAN...
The ROYAL ROSE GARDEN?!
CAN I TAKE NOTES?! I HAVE TO GO GET MY SUPPLIES! CAN I? PLEASE!!
HAW!
SURE!
TAKE YOUR TIME!
MEET ME BY THE GARDEN ENTRANCE WHEN YOU'RE READY!
OKAY BYE SEE YOU SOON!!
ZOOM!
SSSIIIIIGHHH.....

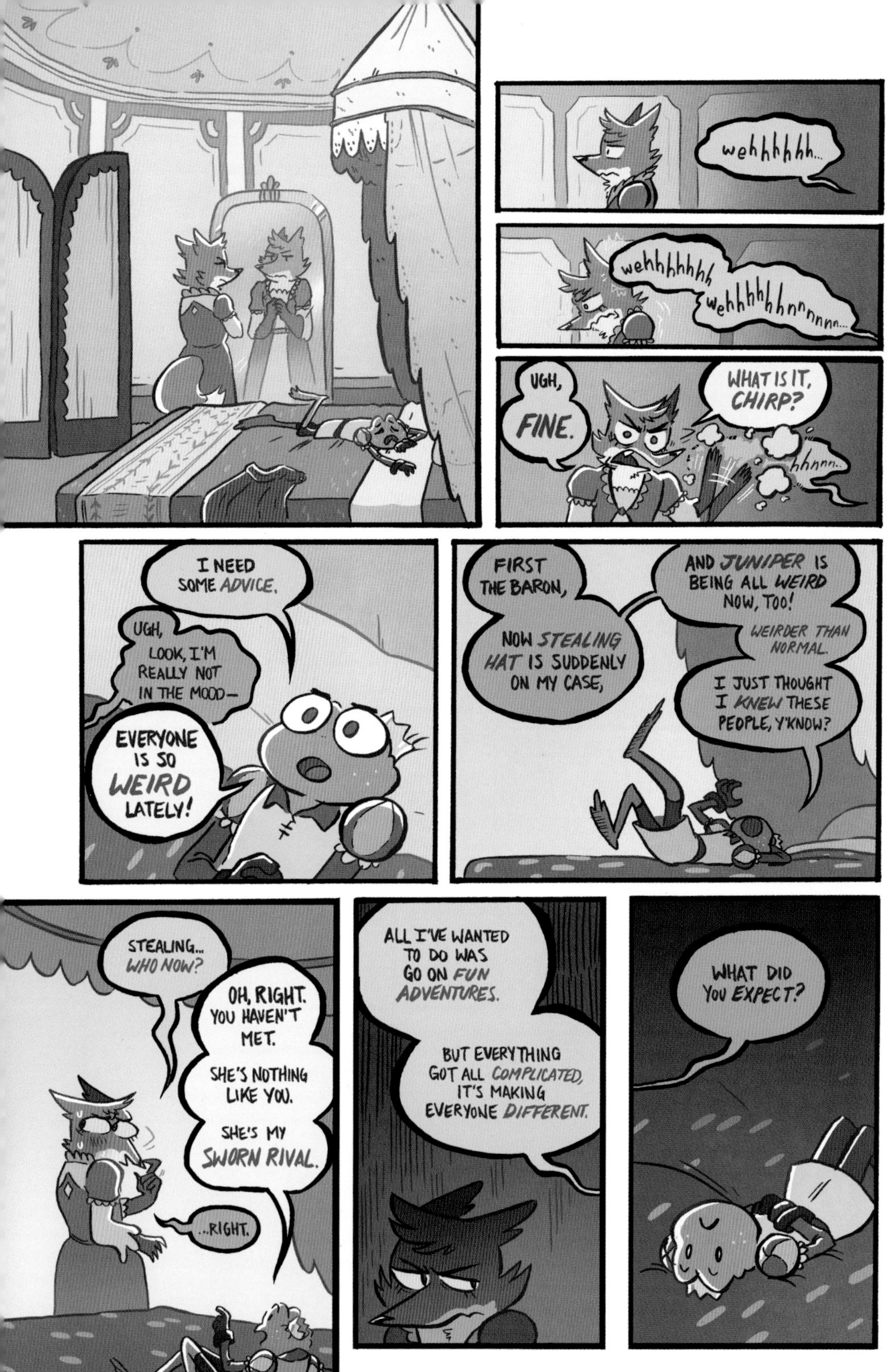
wehhhhhh...
wehhhhhhh
wehhhhhhnnnnnn...
UGH, FINE.
WHAT IS IT, CHIRP?
hhnnn...
I NEED SOME ADVICE.
UGH, LOOK, I'M REALLY NOT IN THE MOOD—
EVERYONE IS SO WEIRD LATELY!
FIRST THE BARON,
NOW STEALING HAT IS SUDDENLY ON MY CASE,
AND JUNIPER IS BEING ALL WEIRD NOW, TOO!
WEIRDER THAN NORMAL.
I JUST THOUGHT I KNEW THESE PEOPLE, Y'KNOW?
STEALING... WHO NOW?
OH, RIGHT. YOU HAVEN'T MET.
SHE'S NOTHING LIKE YOU.
SHE'S MY SWORN RIVAL.
...RIGHT.
ALL I'VE WANTED TO DO WAS GO ON FUN ADVENTURES.
BUT EVERYTHING GOT ALL COMPLICATED, IT'S MAKING EVERYONE DIFFERENT.
WHAT DID YOU EXPECT?

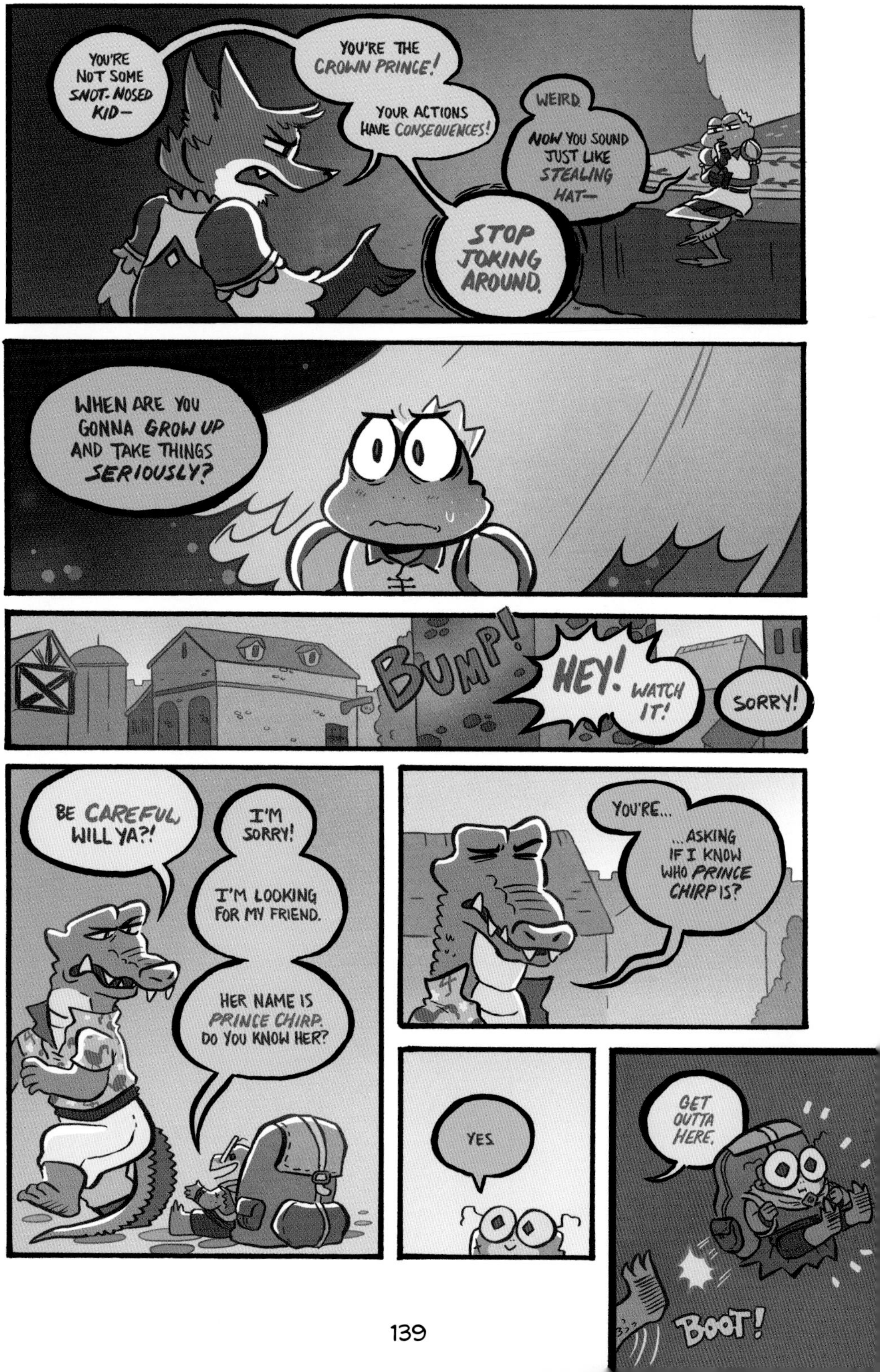
YOU'RE NOT SOME SNOT-NOSED KID—
YOU'RE THE CROWN PRINCE!
YOUR ACTIONS HAVE CONSEQUENCES!
WEIRD.
NOW YOU SOUND JUST LIKE STEALING HAT—
STOP JOKING AROUND.
WHEN ARE YOU GONNA GROW UP AND TAKE THINGS SERIOUSLY?
BUMP!
HEY! WATCH IT!
SORRY!
BE CAREFUL, WILL YA?!
I'M SORRY!
I'M LOOKING FOR MY FRIEND.
HER NAME IS PRINCE CHIRP. DO YOU KNOW HER?
YOU'RE...
...ASKING IF I KNOW WHO PRINCE CHIRP IS?
YES.
GET OUTTA HERE.
BOOT!

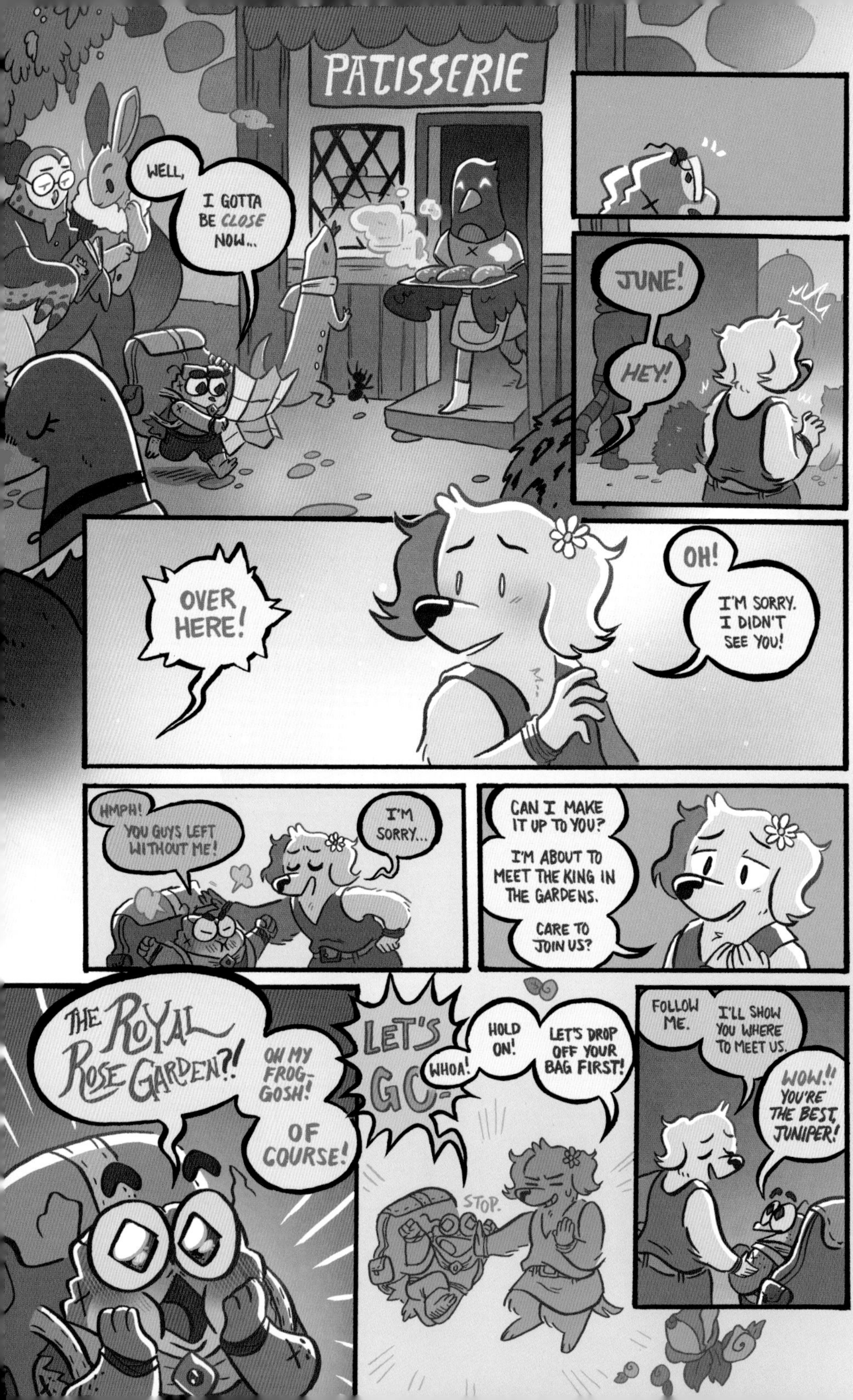
PATISSERIE
WELL,
I GOTTA BE CLOSE NOW...
JUNE!
HEY!
OVER HERE!
OH!
I'M SORRY. I DIDN'T SEE YOU!
HMPH!
YOU GUYS LEFT WITHOUT ME!
I'M SORRY...
CAN I MAKE IT UP TO YOU?
I'M ABOUT TO MEET THE KING IN THE GARDENS.
CARE TO JOIN US?
THE ROYAL ROSE GARDEN?!
OH MY FROG-GOSH!
OF COURSE!
LET'S GO-
WHOA!
HOLD ON!
LET'S DROP OFF YOUR BAG FIRST!
STOP.
FOLLOW ME.
I'LL SHOW YOU WHERE TO MEET US.
WOW!! YOU'RE THE BEST, JUNIPER!

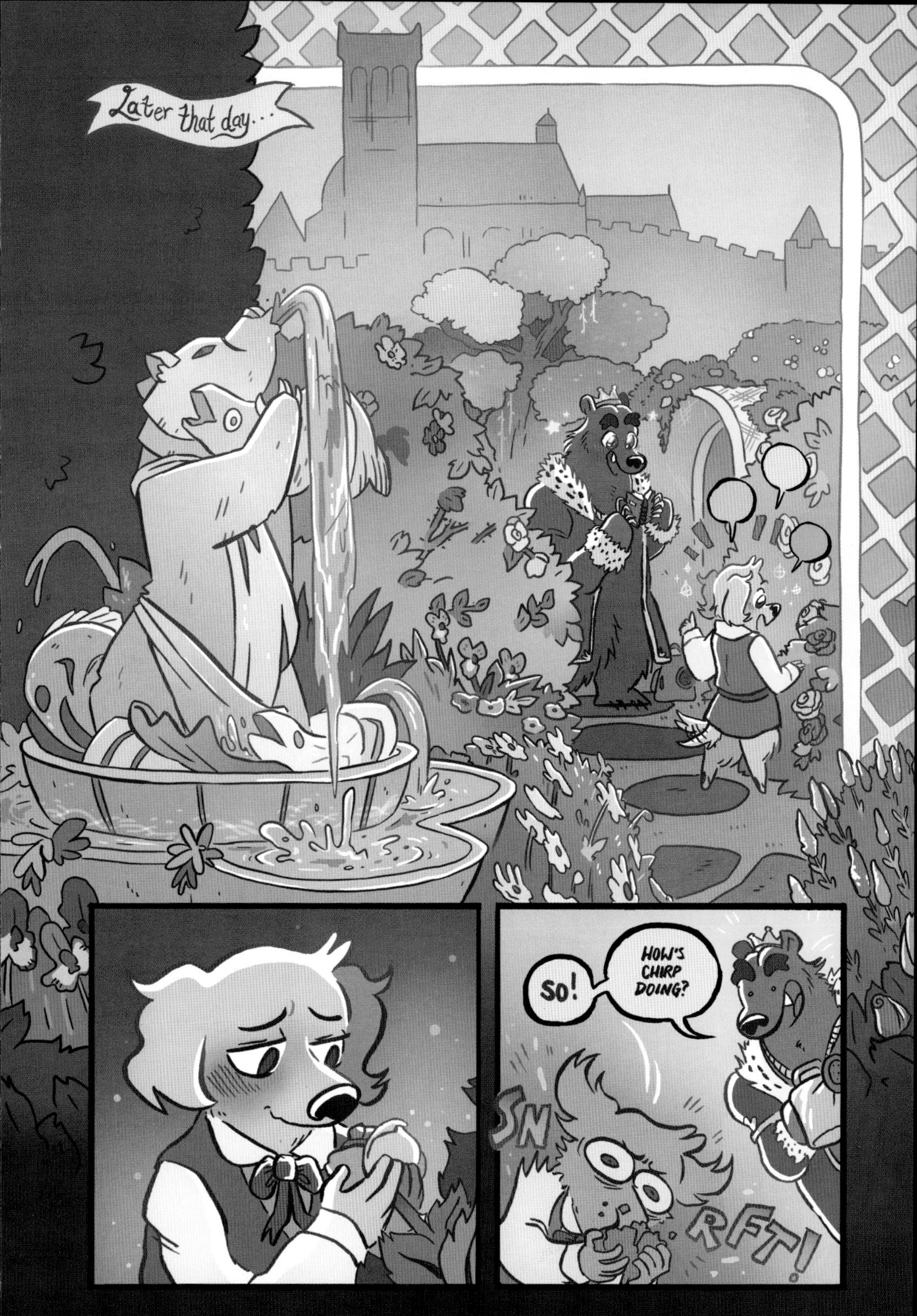
Later that day...
SO!
HOW'S CHIRP DOING?
SNORFT!

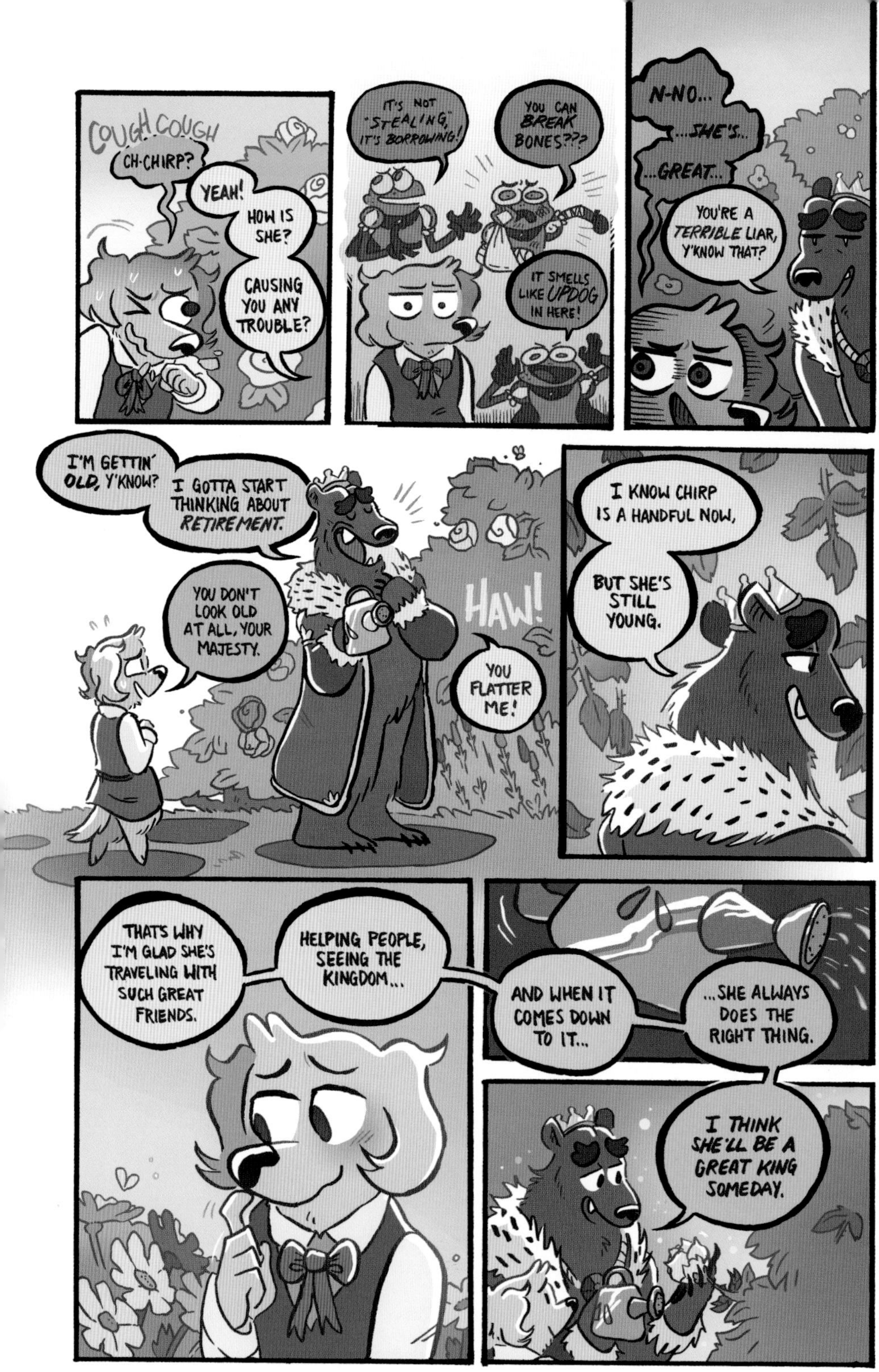
COUGH COUGH
CH-CHIRP?
YEAH!
HOW IS SHE?
CAUSING YOU ANY TROUBLE?
IT'S NOT "STEALING," IT'S BORROWING!
YOU CAN BREAK BONES???
IT SMELLS LIKE UPDOG IN HERE!
N-NO...
...SHE'S...
...GREAT...
YOU'RE A TERRIBLE LIAR, Y'KNOW THAT?
I'M GETTIN' OLD, Y'KNOW?
I GOTTA START THINKING ABOUT RETIREMENT.
YOU DON'T LOOK OLD AT ALL, YOUR MAJESTY.
HAW!
YOU FLATTER ME!
I KNOW CHIRP IS A HANDFUL NOW,
BUT SHE'S STILL YOUNG.
THAT'S WHY I'M GLAD SHE'S TRAVELING WITH SUCH GREAT FRIENDS.
HELPING PEOPLE, SEEING THE KINGDOM...
AND WHEN IT COMES DOWN TO IT...
...SHE ALWAYS DOES THE RIGHT THING.
I THINK SHE'LL BE A GREAT KING SOMEDAY.

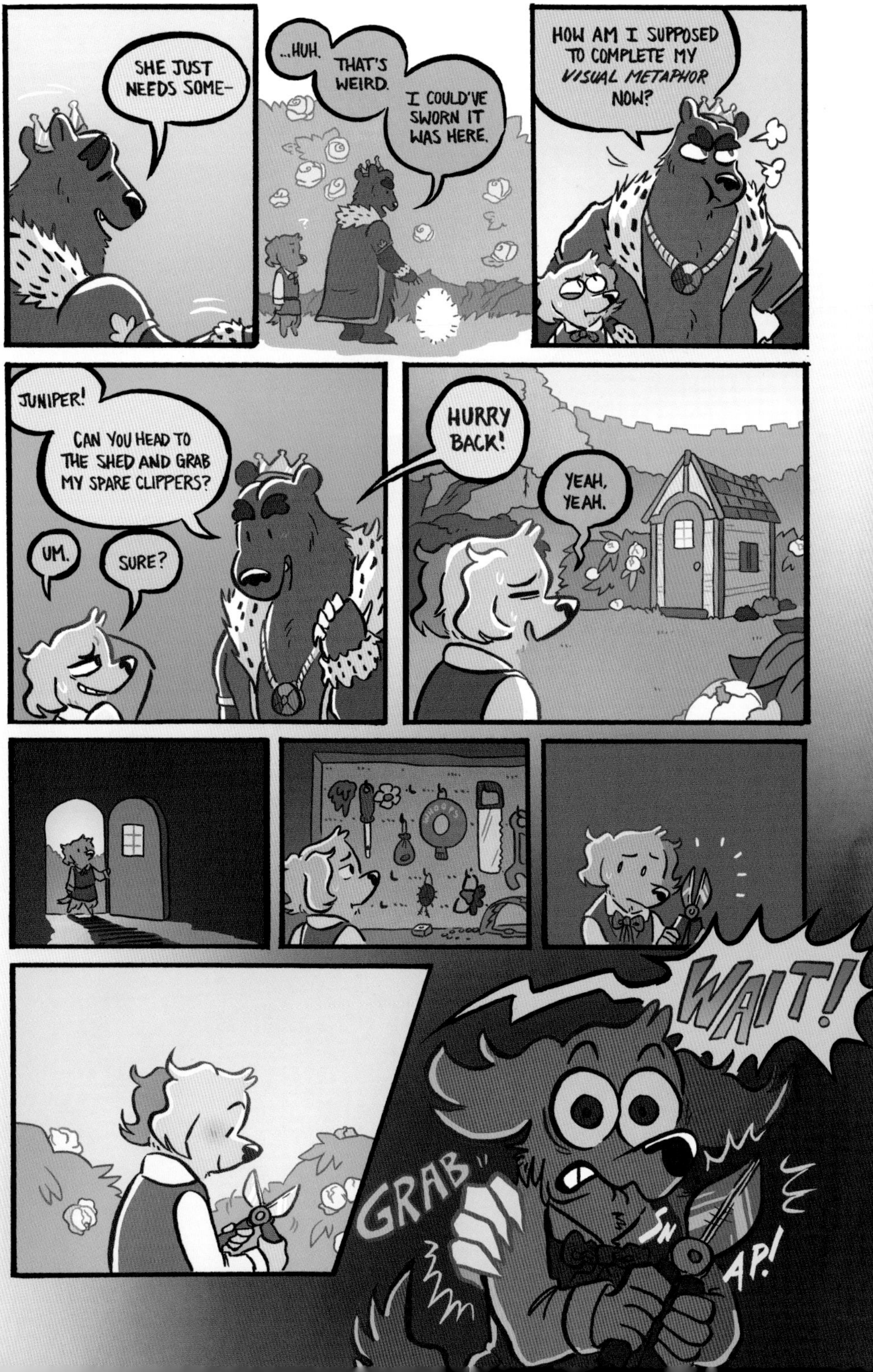
SHE JUST NEEDS SOME-
...HUH.
THAT'S WEIRD.
I COULD'VE SWORN IT WAS HERE.
HOW AM I SUPPOSED TO COMPLETE MY *VISUAL METAPHOR* NOW?
JUNIPER!
CAN YOU HEAD TO THE SHED AND GRAB MY SPARE CLIPPERS?
UM.
SURE?
HURRY BACK!
YEAH, YEAH.
WAIT!
GRAB
SNAP!

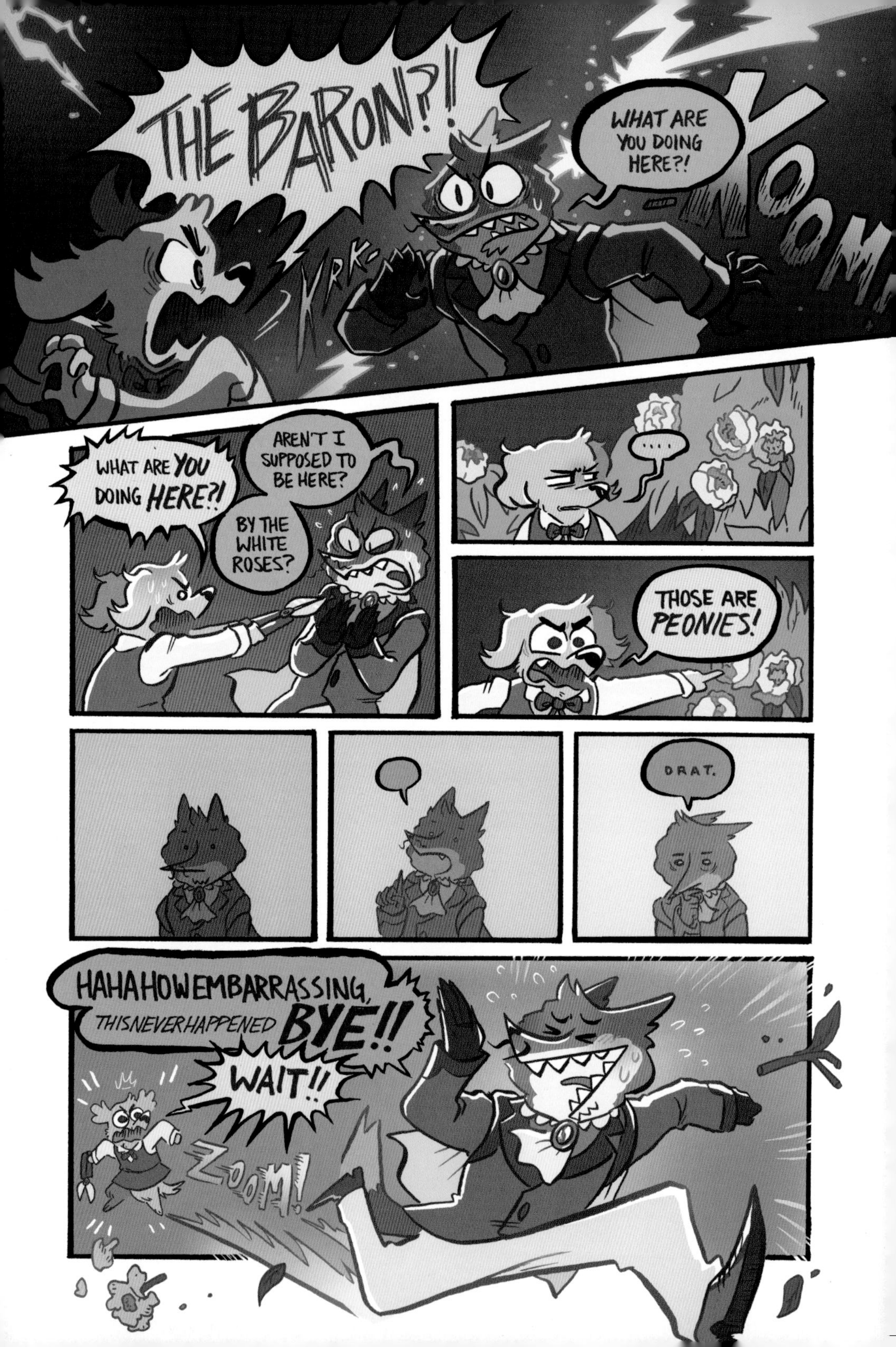
THE BARON?!
WHAT ARE YOU DOING HERE?!
VYOOM!
KRRK
WHAT ARE YOU DOING HERE?!
AREN'T I SUPPOSED TO BE HERE?
BY THE WHITE ROSES?
....
THOSE ARE PEONIES!
DRAT.
HAHAHOWEMBARRASSING, THISNEVERHAPPENED BYE!!
WAIT!!
ZOOM!

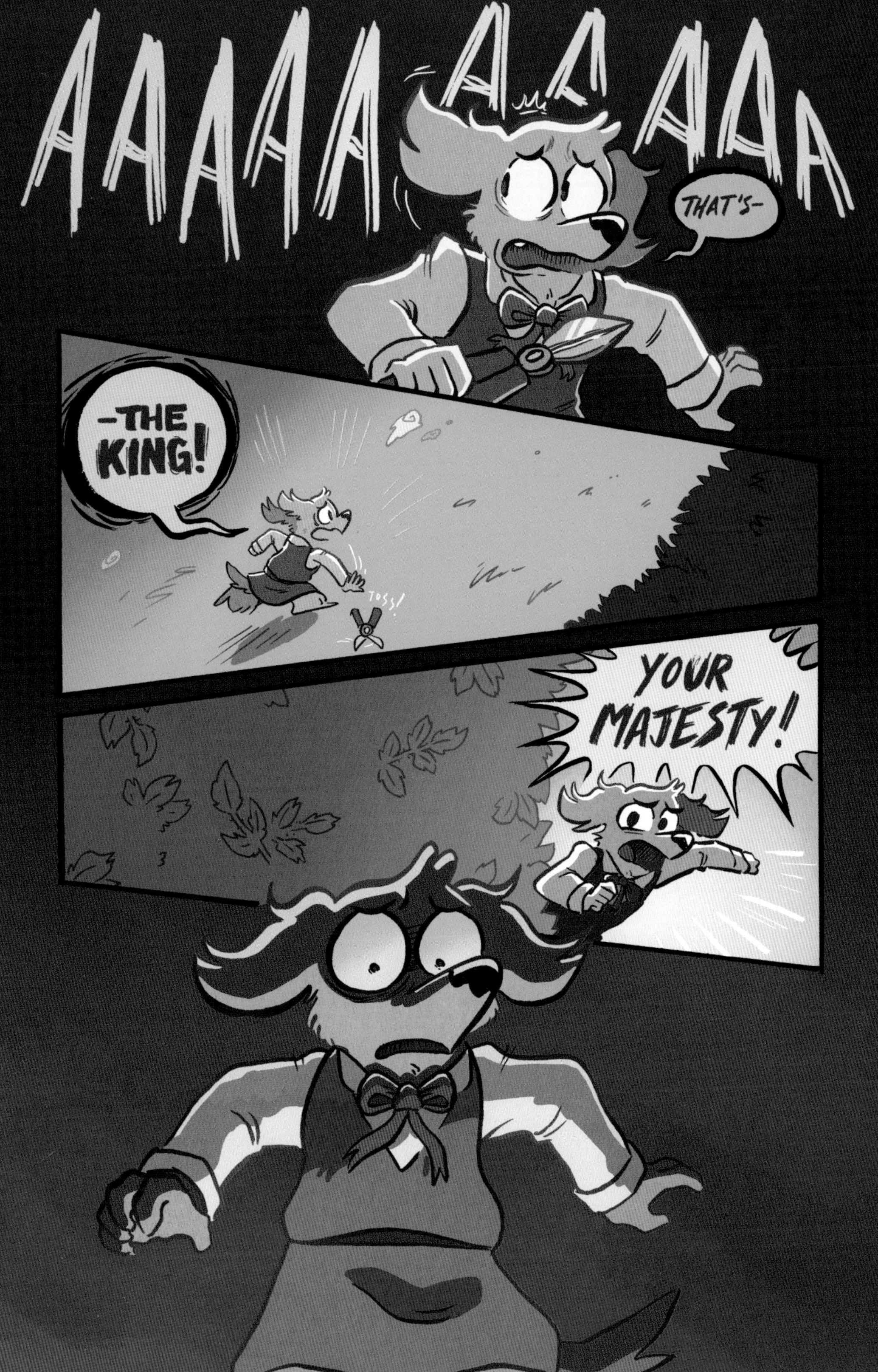
AAAAAAAAAA
THAT'S-
-THE KING!
TOSS!
YOUR MAJESTY!

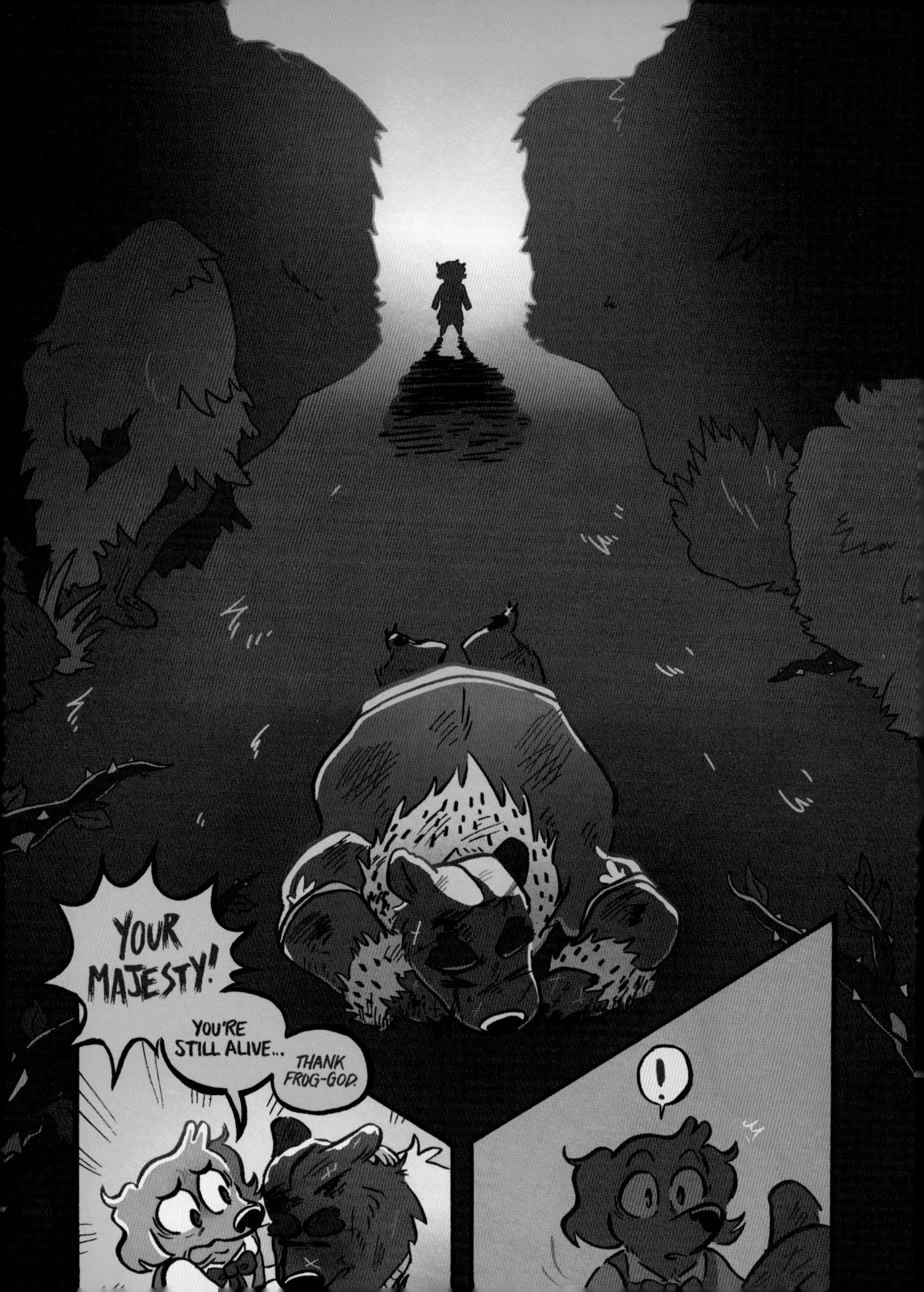
YOUR MAJESTY!
YOU'RE STILL ALIVE...
THANK FROG-GOD.
!

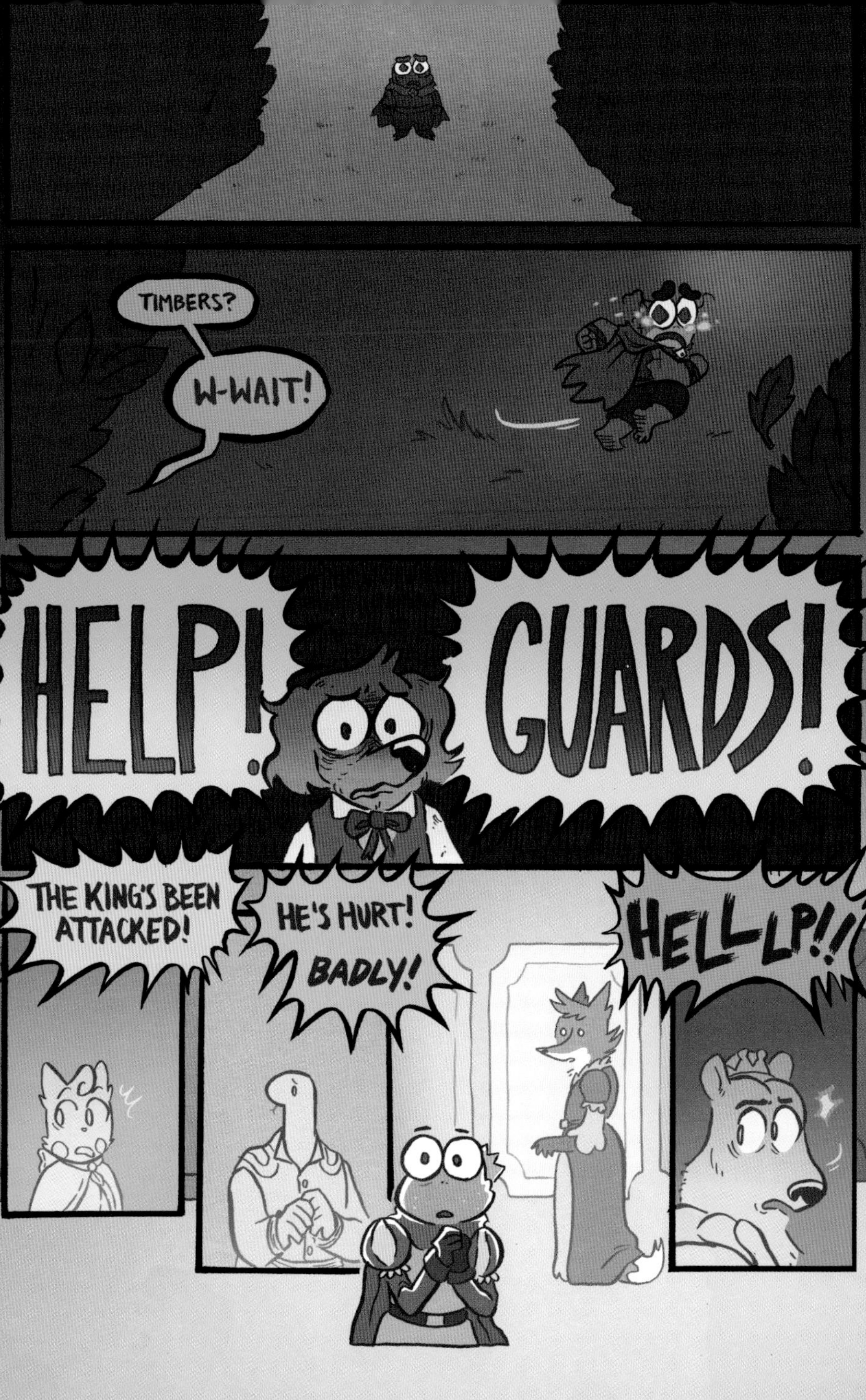
TIMBERS?
W-WAIT!
HELP! GUARDS!
THE KING'S BEEN ATTACKED!
HE'S HURT! BADLY!
HELLLP!!

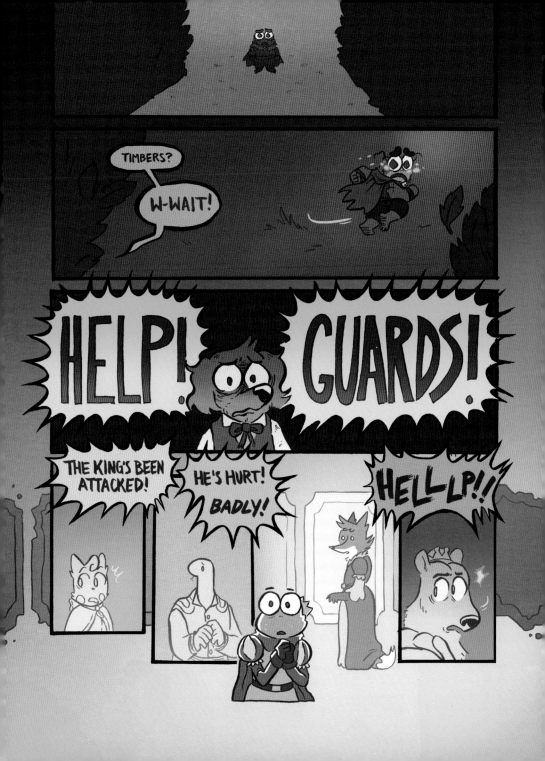

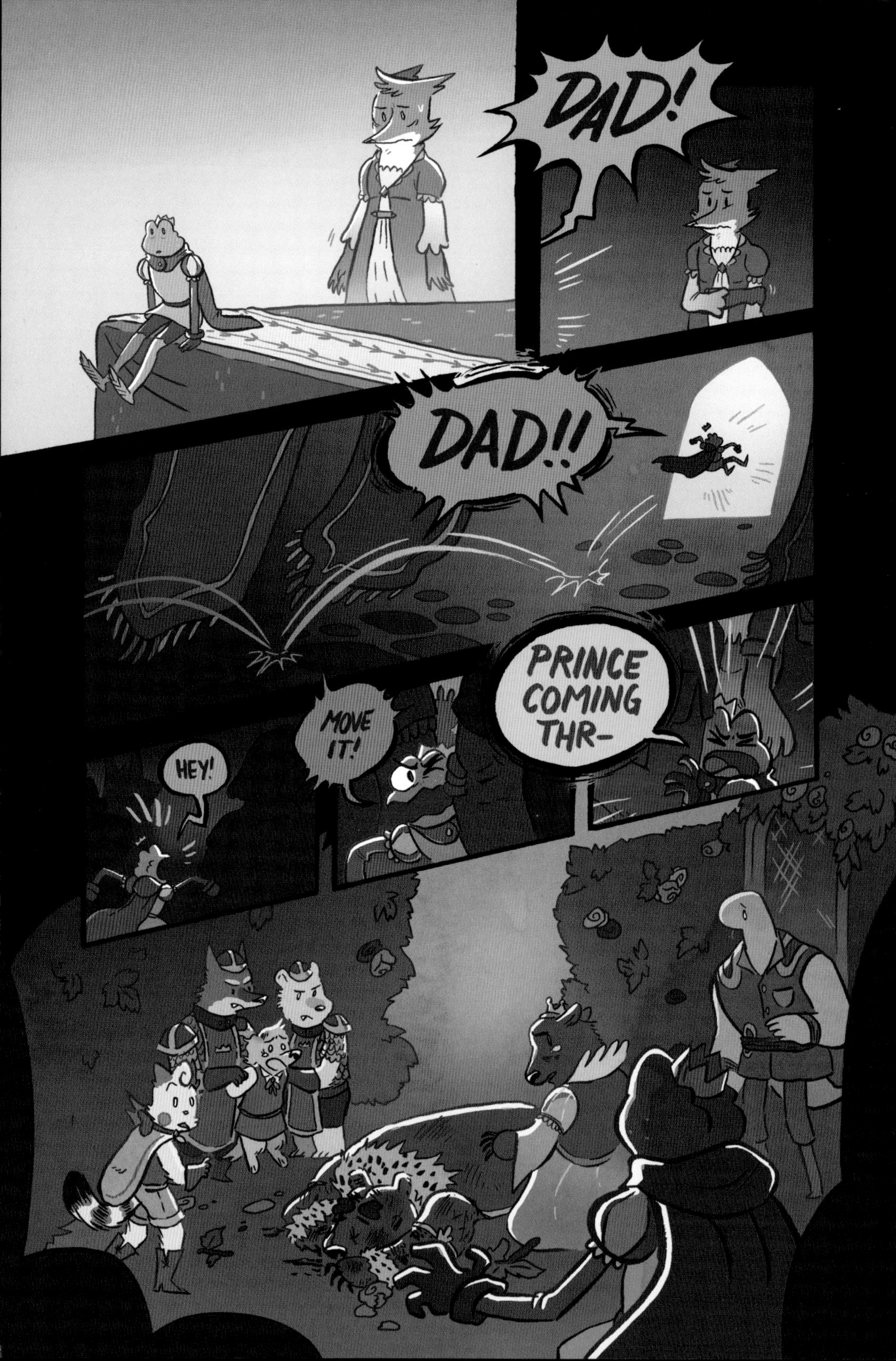
DAD!
DAD!!
HEY!
MOVE IT!
PRINCE COMING THR-

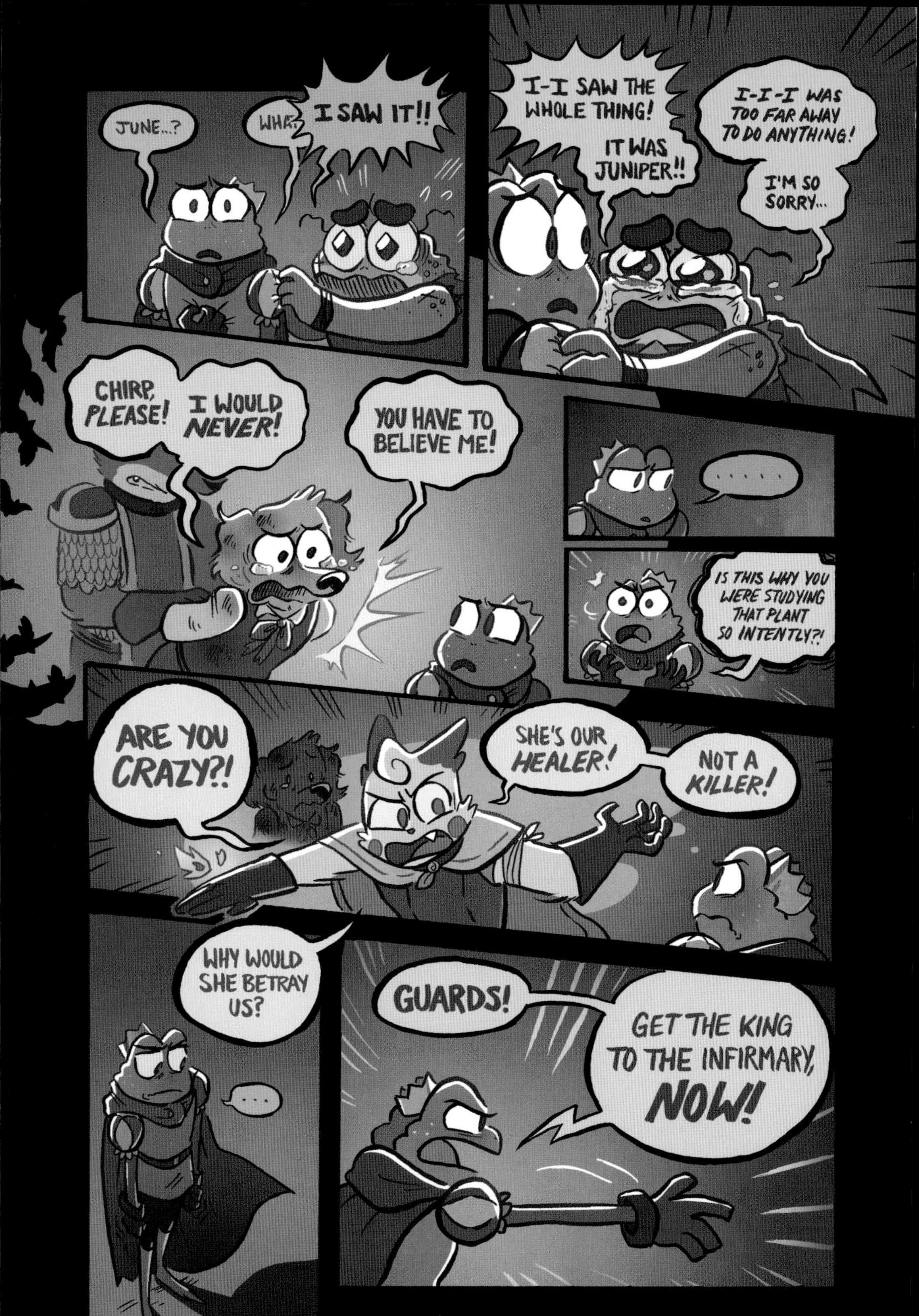
JUNE...?
WHA-
I SAW IT!!
I-I SAW THE WHOLE THING!
IT WAS JUNIPER!!
I-I-I WAS TOO FAR AWAY TO DO ANYTHING!
I'M SO SORRY...
CHIRP, PLEASE!
I WOULD NEVER!
YOU HAVE TO BELIEVE ME!
.....
IS THIS WHY YOU WERE STUDYING THAT PLANT SO INTENTLY?!
ARE YOU CRAZY?!
SHE'S OUR HEALER!
NOT A KILLER!
WHY WOULD SHE BETRAY US?
...
GUARDS!
GET THE KING TO THE INFIRMARY, NOW!

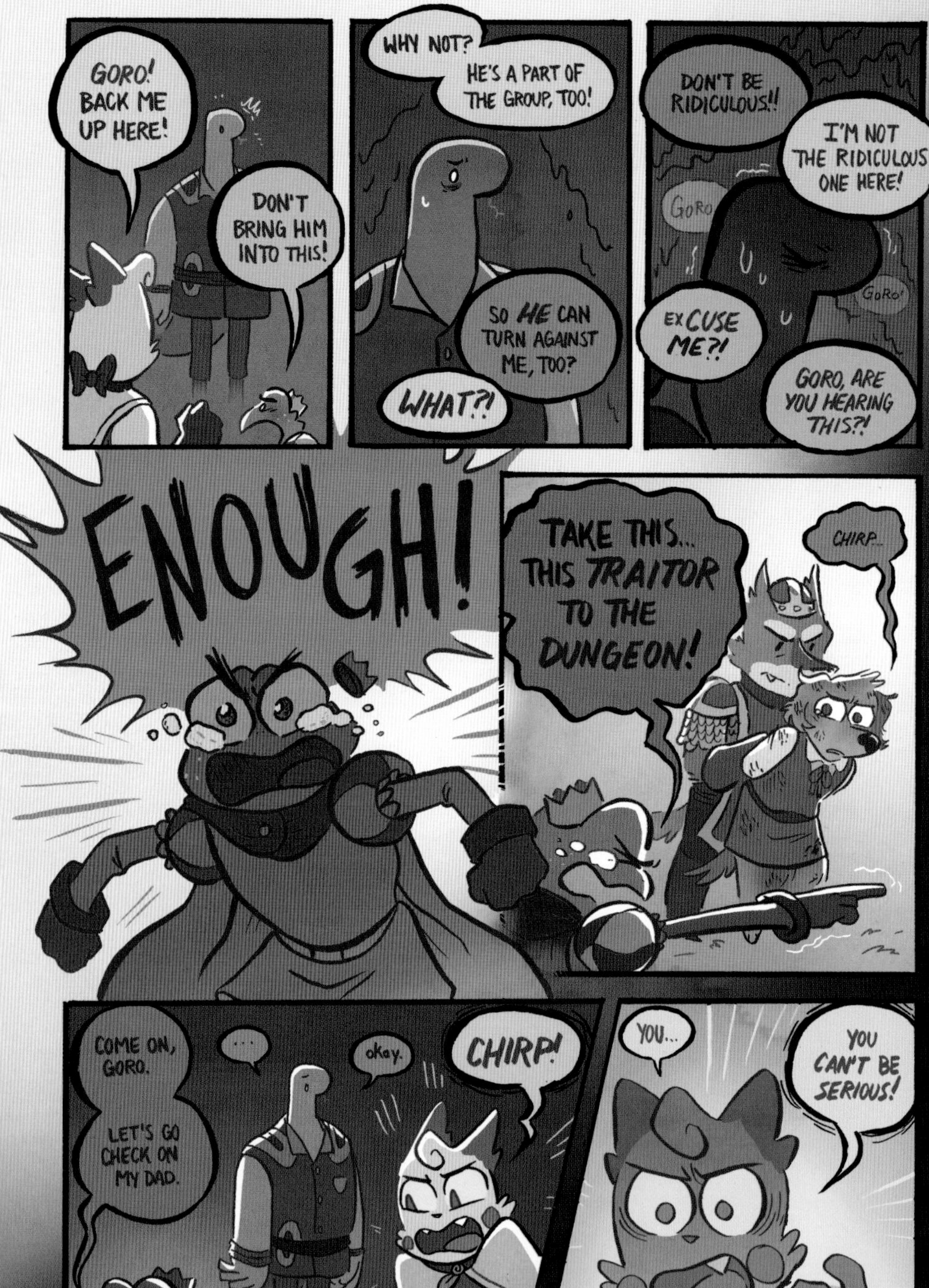
GORO! BACK ME UP HERE!
DON'T BRING HIM INTO THIS!
WHY NOT?
HE'S A PART OF THE GROUP, TOO!
SO HE CAN TURN AGAINST ME, TOO?
WHAT?!
DON'T BE RIDICULOUS!!
I'M NOT THE RIDICULOUS ONE HERE!
GORO
GORO!
EXCUSE ME?!
GORO, ARE YOU HEARING THIS?!
ENOUGH!
TAKE THIS... THIS TRAITOR TO THE DUNGEON!
CHIRP...
COME ON, GORO.
LET'S GO CHECK ON MY DAD.
...
okay.
CHIRP!
YOU...
YOU CAN'T BE SERIOUS!

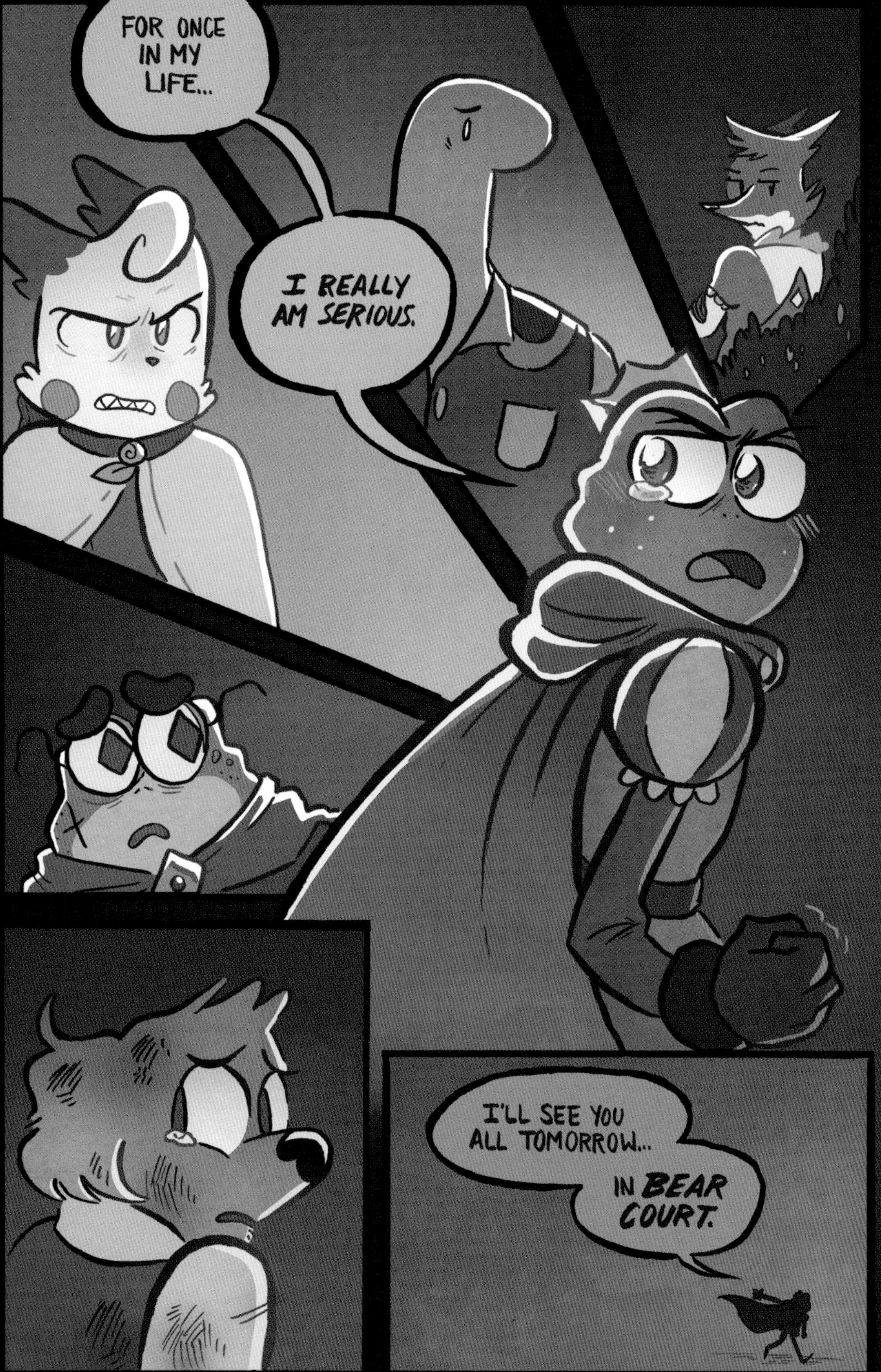
FOR ONCE IN MY LIFE...
I REALLY AM SERIOUS.
I'LL SEE YOU ALL TOMORROW...
IN BEAR COURT.

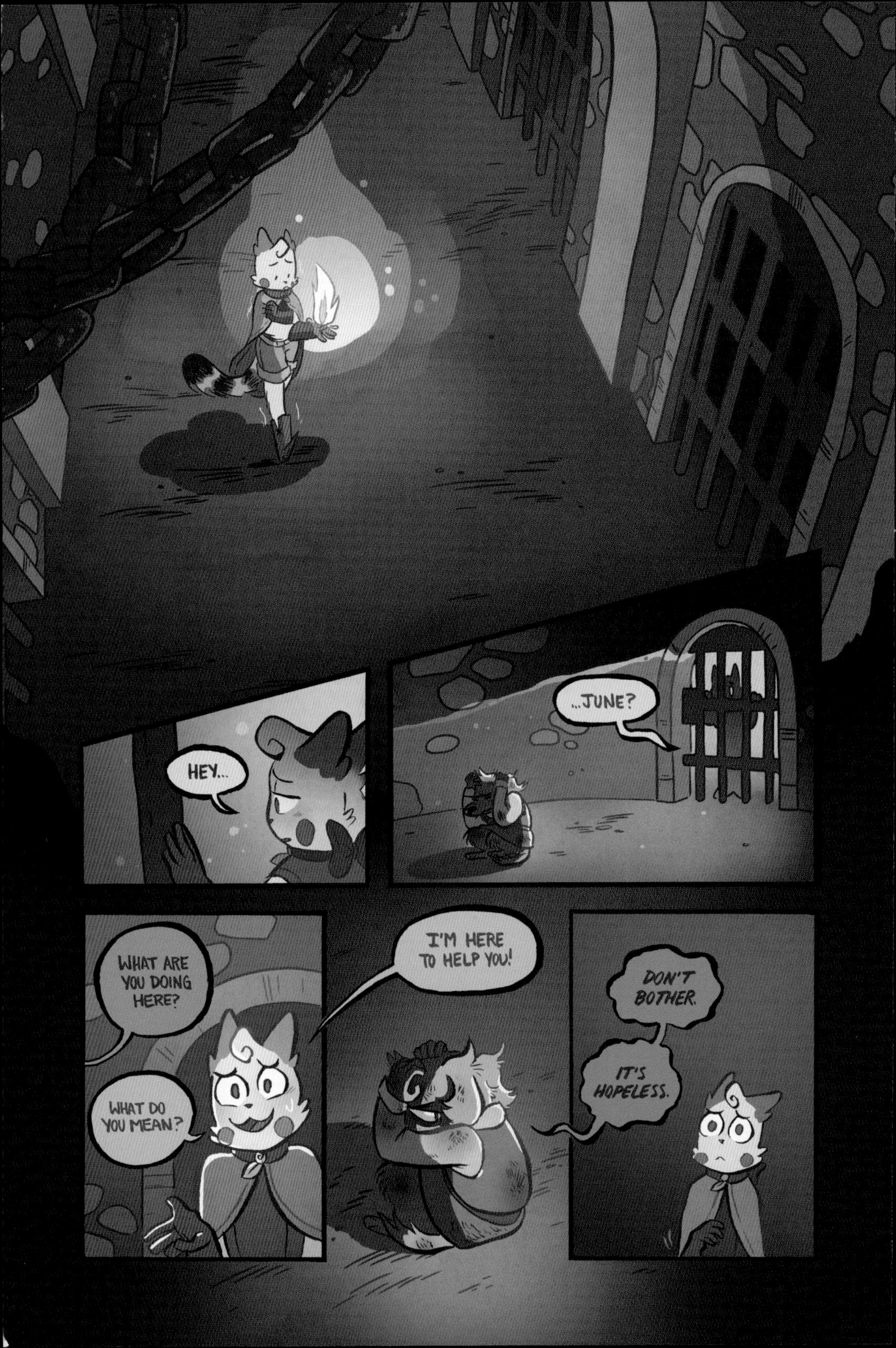
HEY...
...JUNE?
WHAT ARE YOU DOING HERE?
I'M HERE TO HELP YOU!
WHAT DO YOU MEAN?
DON'T BOTHER.
IT'S HOPELESS.

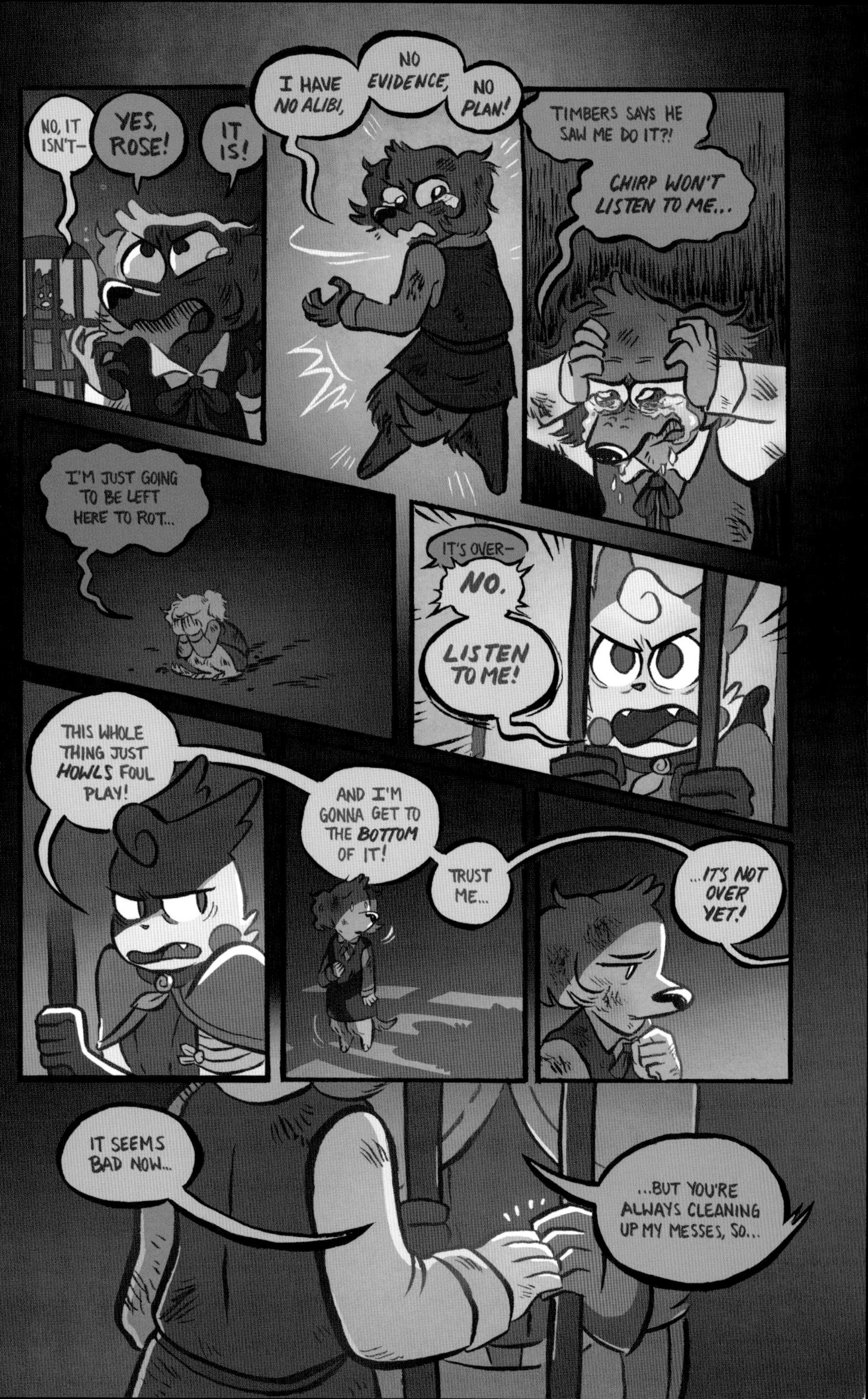
NO, IT ISN'T-
YES, ROSE!
IT IS!
I HAVE NO ALIBI,
NO EVIDENCE,
NO PLAN!
TIMBERS SAYS HE SAW ME DO IT?!
CHIRP WON'T LISTEN TO ME...
I'M JUST GOING TO BE LEFT HERE TO ROT...
IT'S OVER-
NO.
LISTEN TO ME!
THIS WHOLE THING JUST HOWLS FOUL PLAY!
AND I'M GONNA GET TO THE BOTTOM OF IT!
TRUST ME...
...IT'S NOT OVER YET!
IT SEEMS BAD NOW...
...BUT YOU'RE ALWAYS CLEANING UP MY MESSES, SO...

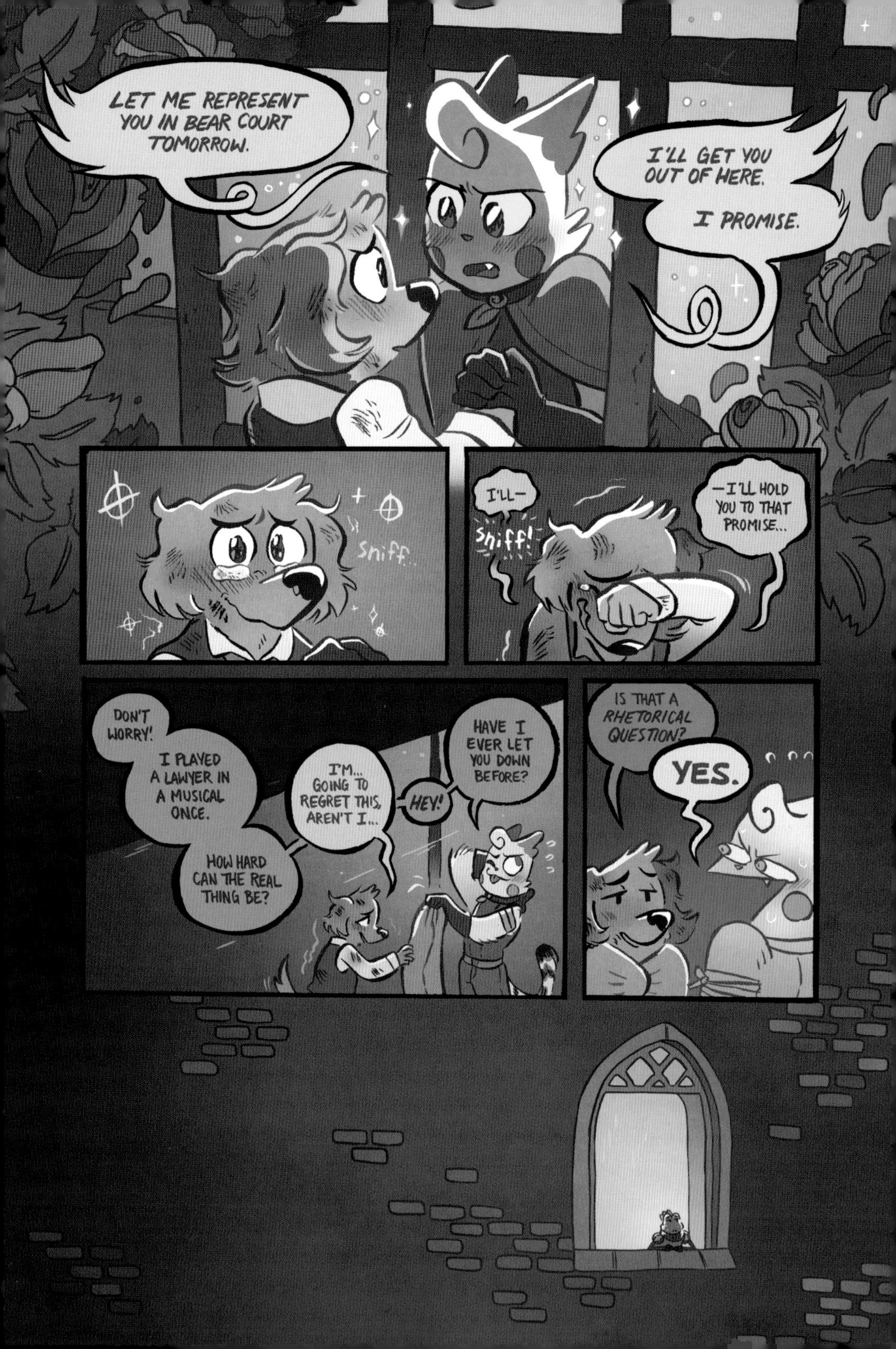
LET ME REPRESENT YOU IN BEAR COURT TOMORROW.
I'LL GET YOU OUT OF HERE.
I PROMISE.
SNIFF..
I'LL—
SNIFF!
—I'LL HOLD YOU TO THAT PROMISE...
DON'T WORRY!
I PLAYED A LAWYER IN A MUSICAL ONCE.
HOW HARD CAN THE REAL THING BE?
I'M... GOING TO REGRET THIS, AREN'T I...
HEY!
HAVE I EVER LET YOU DOWN BEFORE?
IS THAT A RHETORICAL QUESTION?
YES.

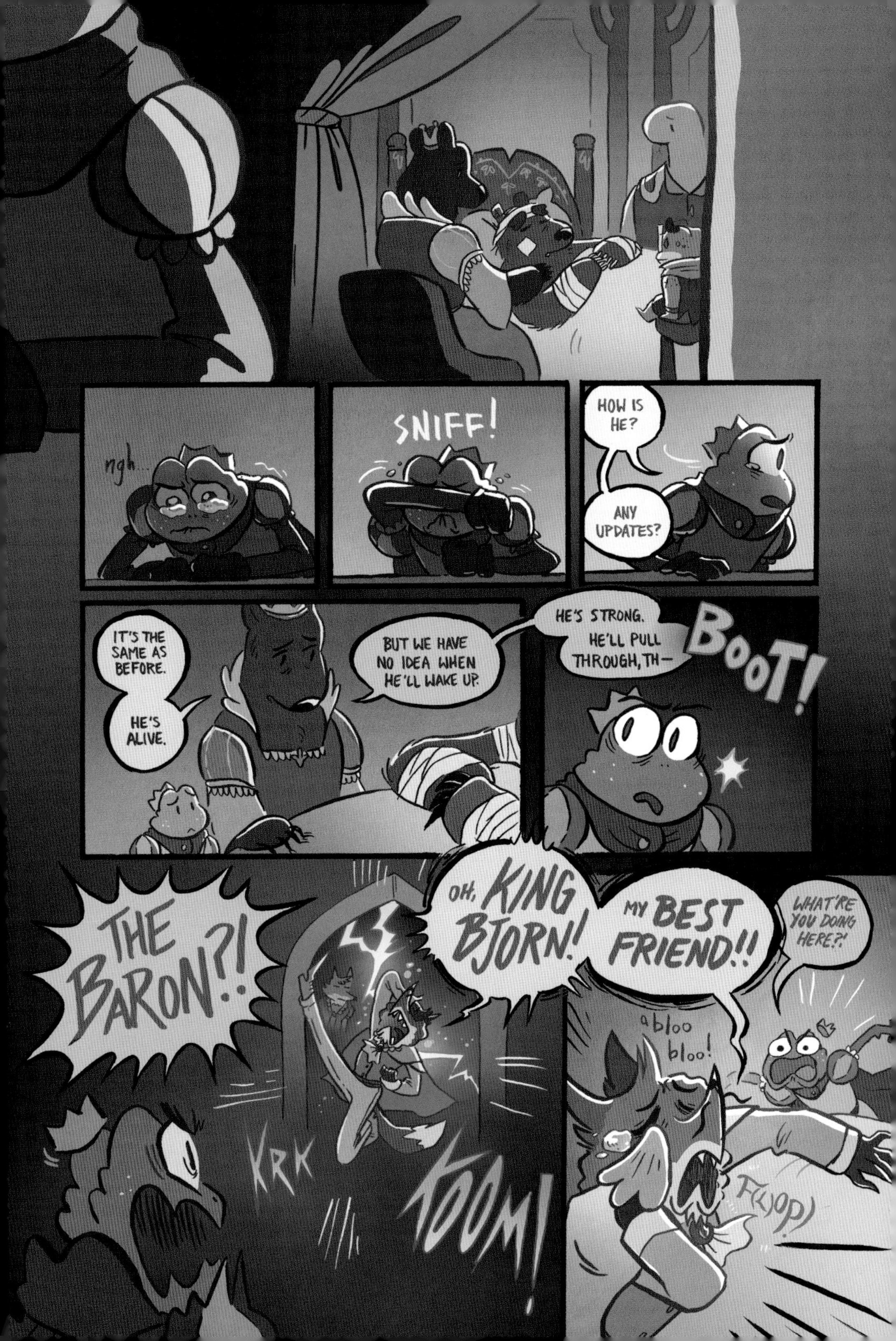
ngh...
SNIFF!
HOW IS HE?
ANY UPDATES?
IT'S THE SAME AS BEFORE.
HE'S ALIVE.
BUT WE HAVE NO IDEA WHEN HE'LL WAKE UP.
HE'S STRONG. HE'LL PULL THROUGH, TH—
BOOT!
THE BARON?!
KRK
KOOM!
OH, KING BJORN!
MY BEST FRIEND!!
WHAT'RE YOU DOING HERE?!
abloo bloo!
F(L)OP!

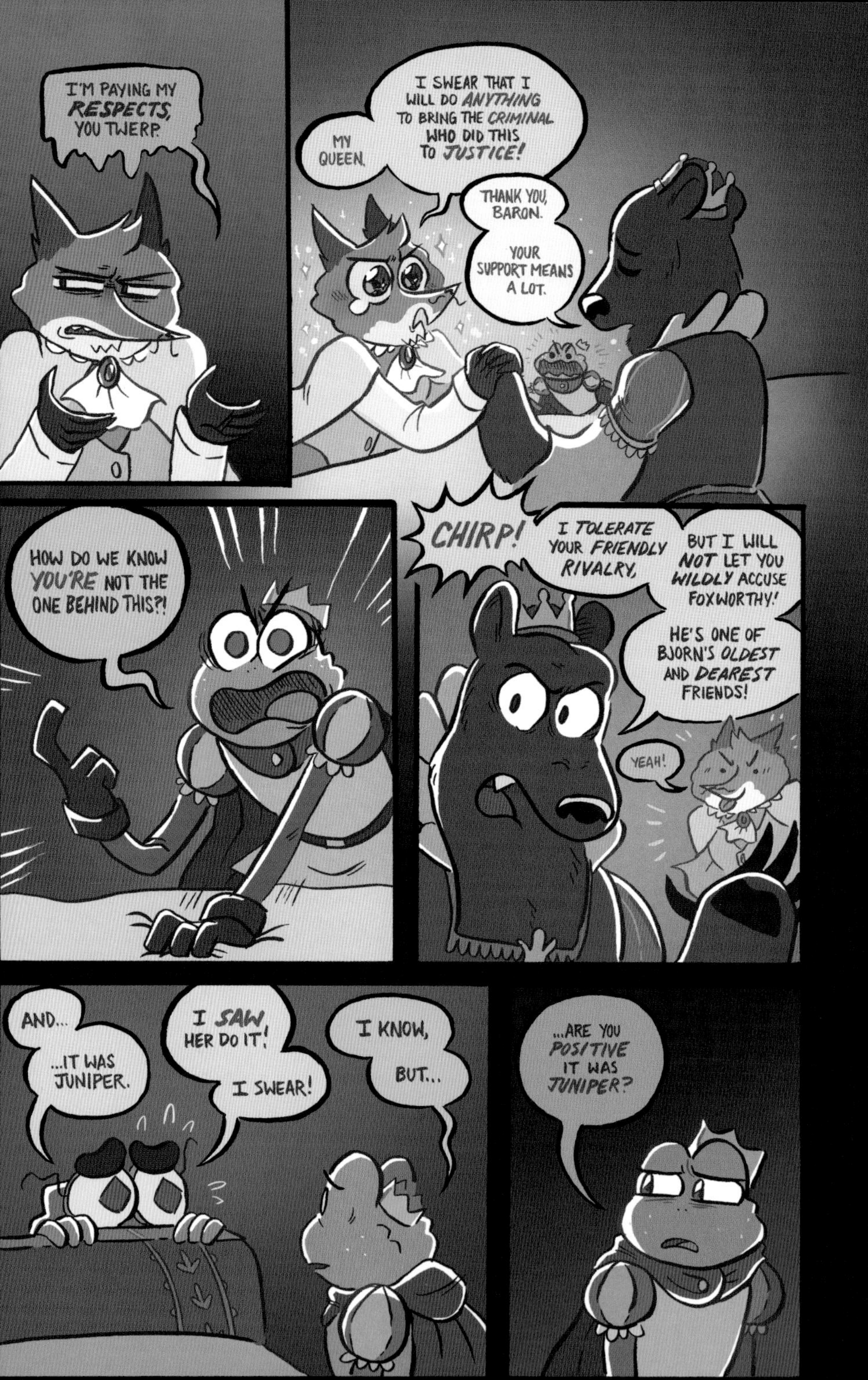

I'M PAYING MY RESPECTS, YOU TWERP.
MY QUEEN.
I SWEAR THAT I WILL DO ANYTHING TO BRING THE CRIMINAL WHO DID THIS TO JUSTICE!
THANK YOU, BARON.
YOUR SUPPORT MEANS A LOT.
HOW DO WE KNOW YOU'RE NOT THE ONE BEHIND THIS?!
CHIRP!
I TOLERATE YOUR FRIENDLY RIVALRY,
BUT I WILL NOT LET YOU WILDLY ACCUSE FOXWORTHY!
HE'S ONE OF BJORN'S OLDEST AND DEAREST FRIENDS!
YEAH!
AND...
...IT WAS JUNIPER.
I SAW HER DO IT!
I SWEAR!
I KNOW,
BUT...
...ARE YOU POSITIVE IT WAS JUNIPER?

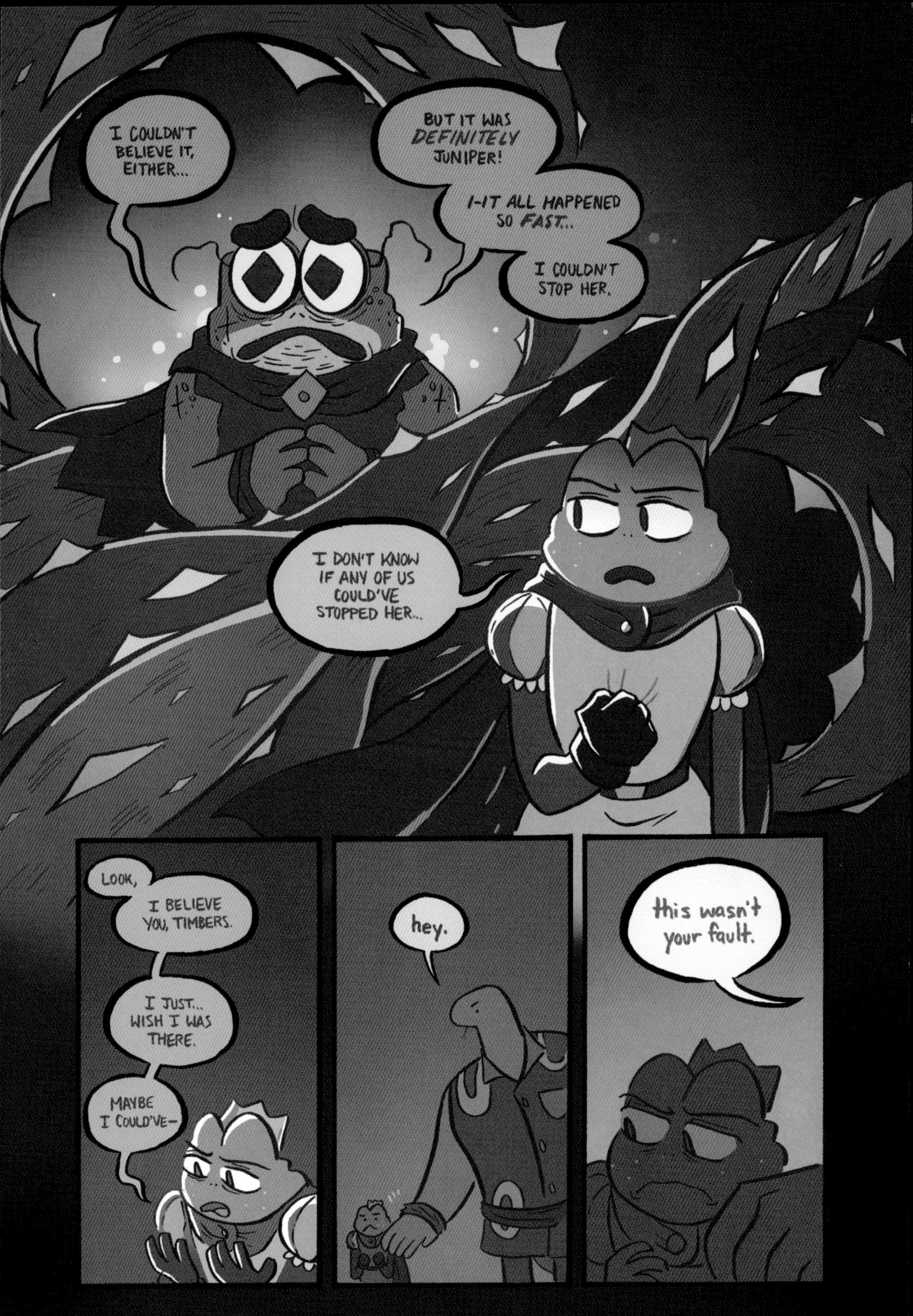
I COULDN'T BELIEVE IT, EITHER...
BUT IT WAS DEFINITELY JUNIPER!
I-IT ALL HAPPENED SO FAST...
I COULDN'T STOP HER.
I DON'T KNOW IF ANY OF US COULD'VE STOPPED HER...
LOOK,
I BELIEVE YOU, TIMBERS.
I JUST... WISH I WAS THERE.
MAYBE I COULD'VE—
hey.
this wasn't your fault.

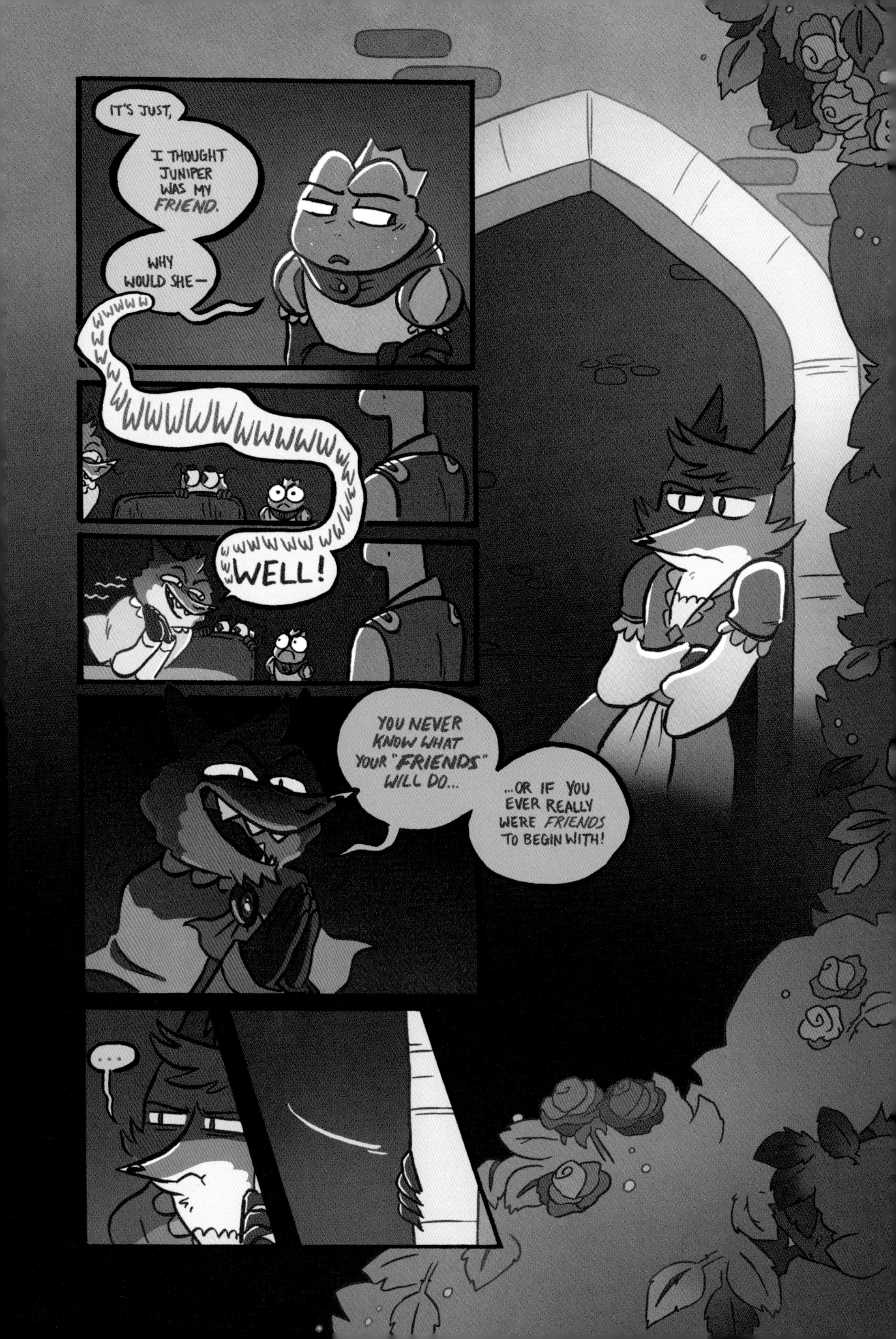
IT'S JUST,
I THOUGHT JUNIPER WAS MY FRIEND.
WHY WOULD SHE—
WWWWWWWWWWWWLWWWWWWWWWWWWWWWWWWWWWWWWWWWWWWWWWWWELL!
YOU NEVER KNOW WHAT YOUR "FRIENDS" WILL DO...
...OR IF YOU EVER REALLY WERE FRIENDS TO BEGIN WITH!
...

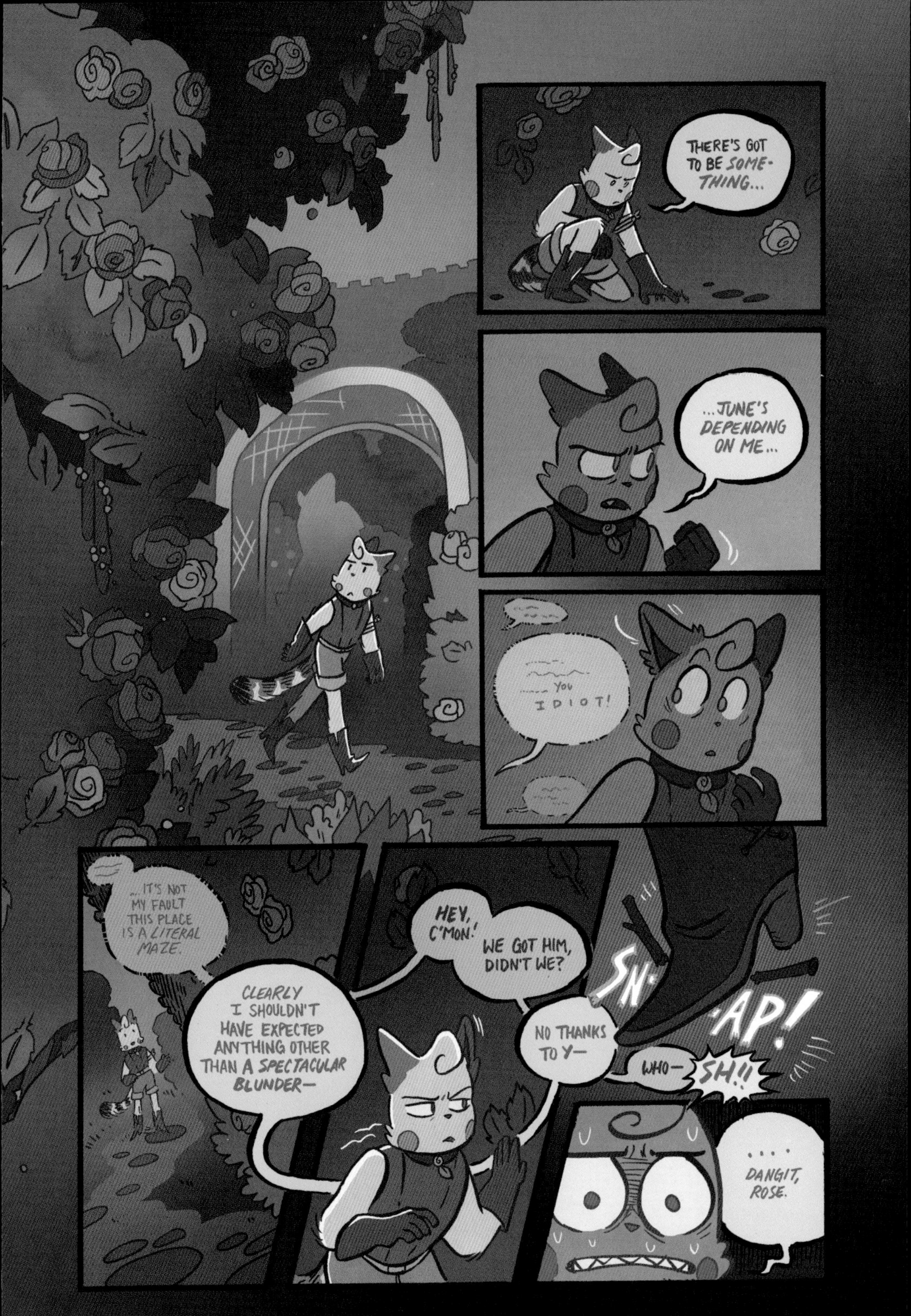
THERE'S GOT TO BE SOME-THING...
...JUNE'S DEPENDING ON ME...
YOU IDIOT!
...IT'S NOT MY FAULT THIS PLACE IS A LITERAL MAZE.
HEY, C'MON!
WE GOT HIM, DIDN'T WE?
CLEARLY I SHOULDN'T HAVE EXPECTED ANYTHING OTHER THAN A SPECTACULAR BLUNDER—
NO THANKS TO Y—
SNAP!
WHO-SH!!
.... DANGIT, ROSE.

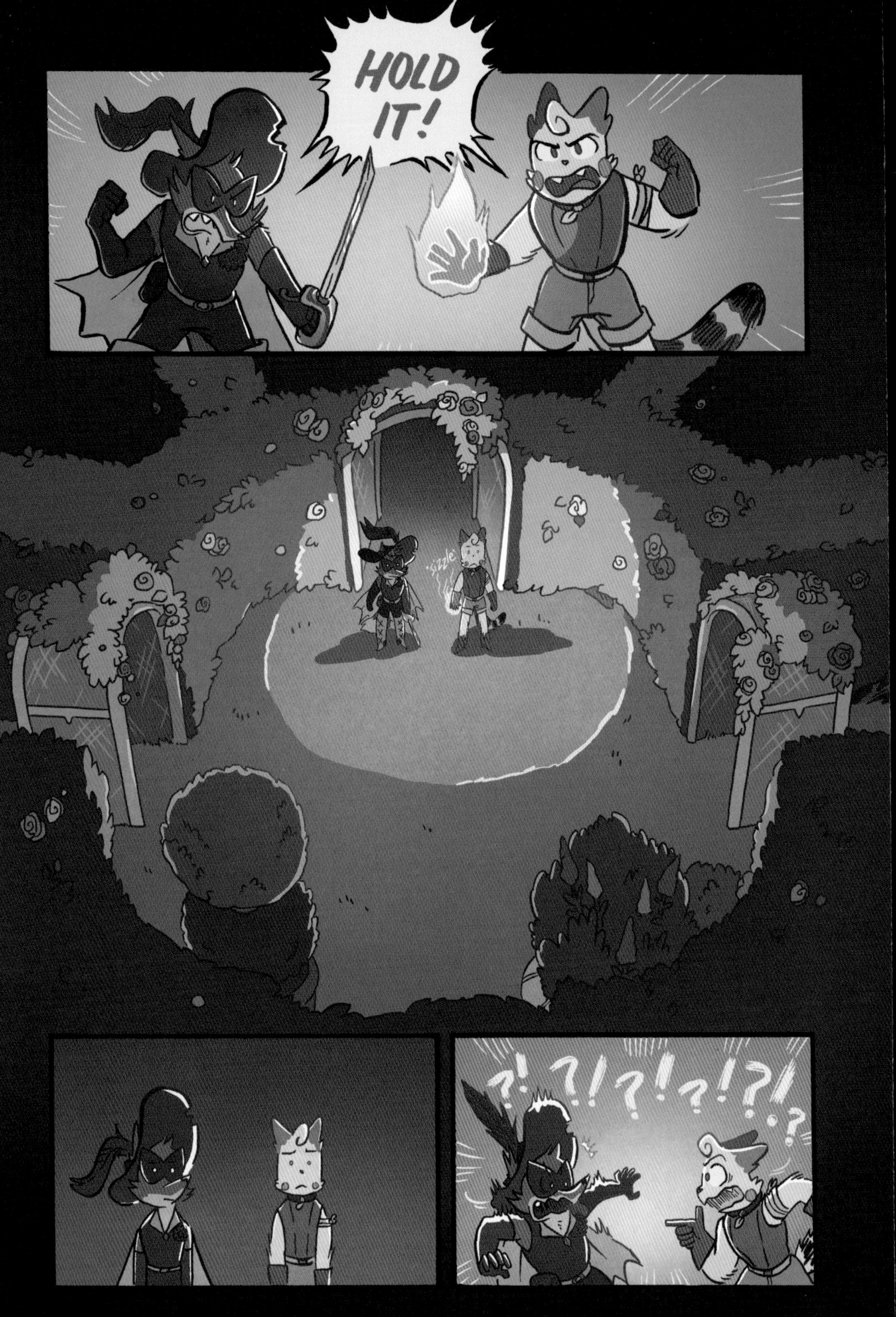
HOLD IT!
sizzle
?!?!?!?!?!?

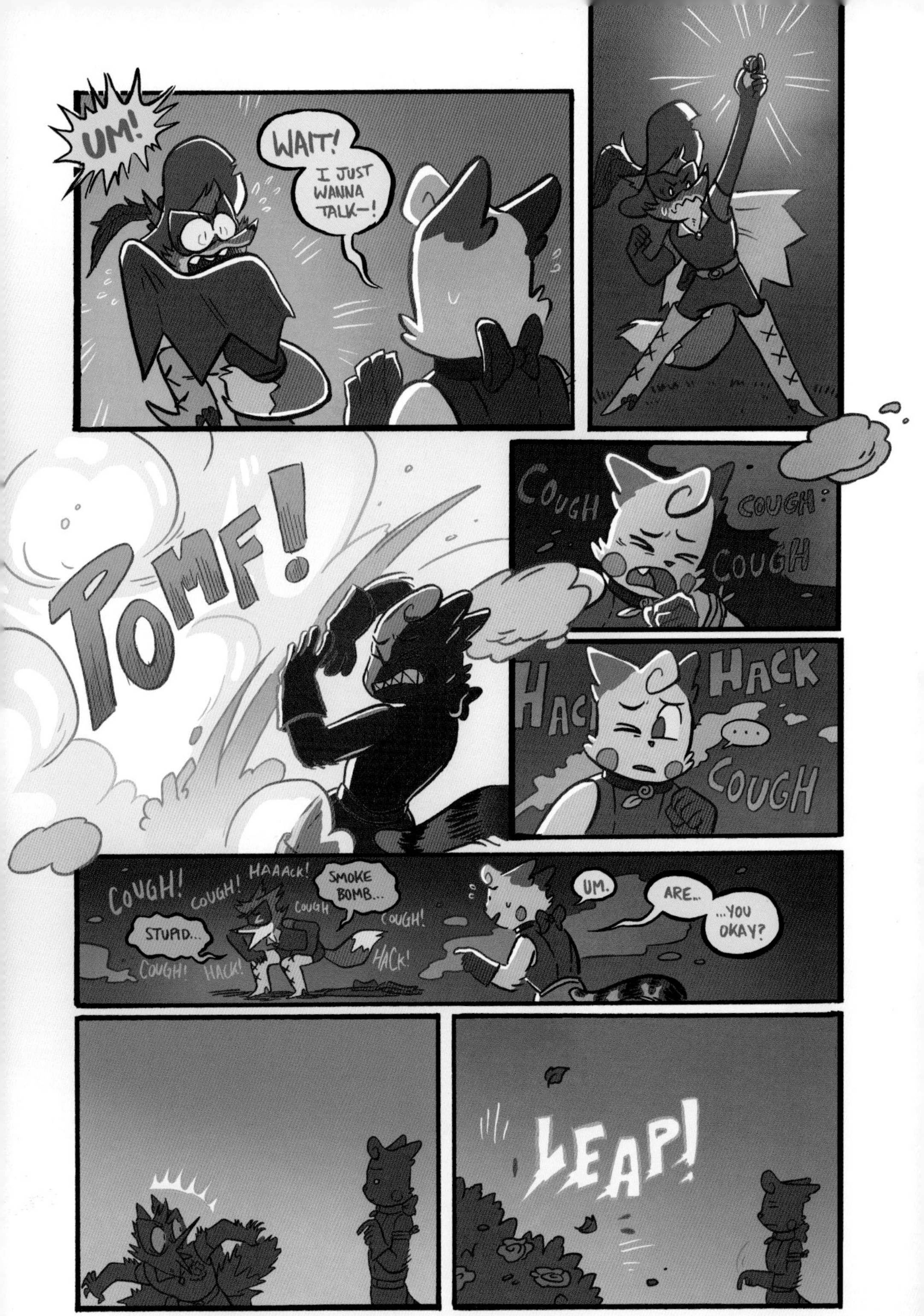
UM!
WAIT!
I JUST WANNA TALK—!
POMF!
COUGH
COUGH
COUGH
HACK
HACK
...
COUGH
COUGH!
COUGH!
HAAACK!
SMOKE BOMB...
COUGH
COUGH!
STUPID...
COUGH!
HACK!
HACK!
UM.
ARE...
...YOU OKAY?
LEAP!

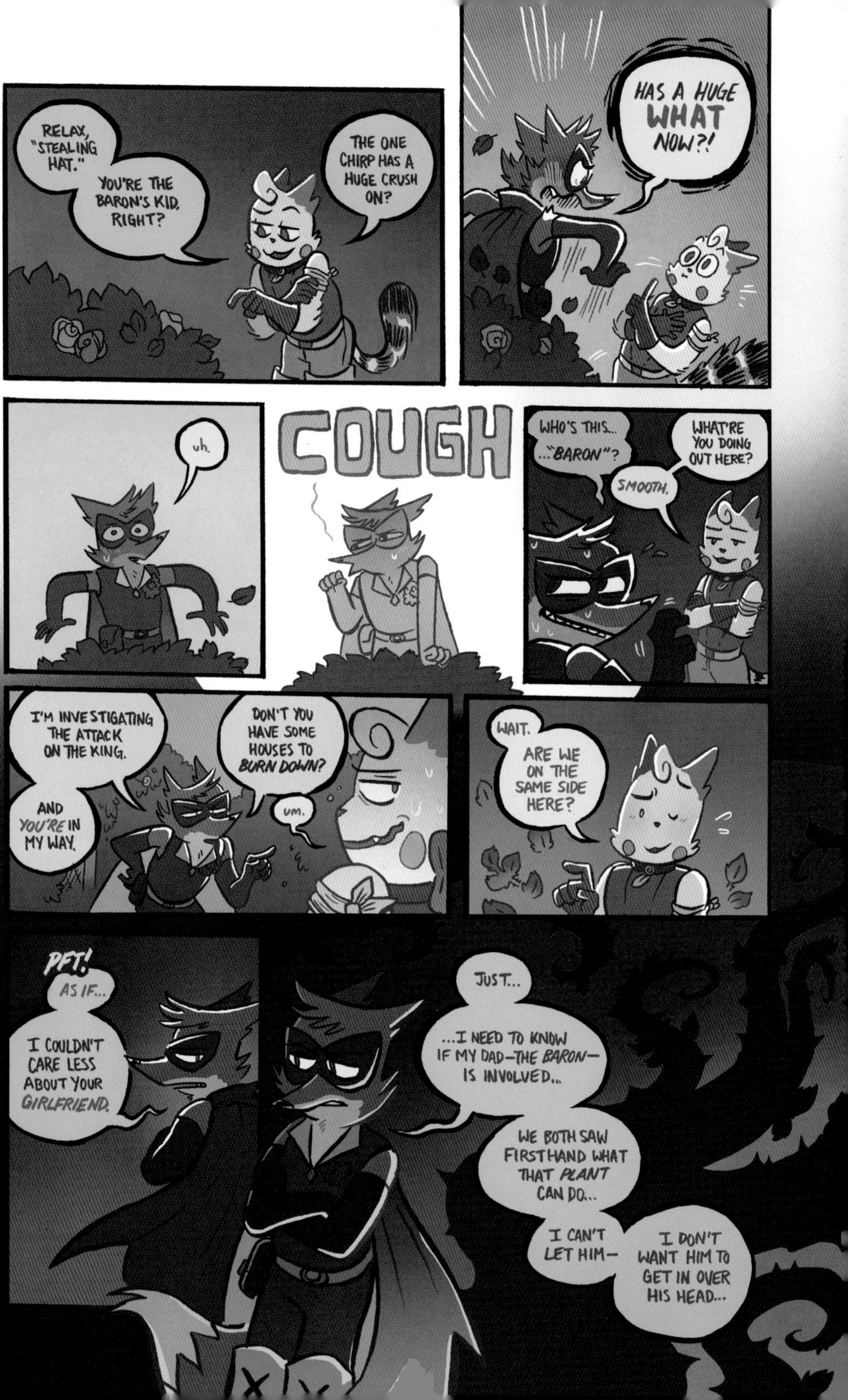

RELAX, "STEALING HAT."
YOU'RE THE BARON'S KID, RIGHT?
THE ONE CHIRP HAS A HUGE CRUSH ON?
HAS A HUGE WHAT NOW?!
uh.
COUGH
WHO'S THIS... ..."BARON"?
SMOOTH.
WHAT'RE YOU DOING OUT HERE?
I'M INVESTIGATING THE ATTACK ON THE KING.
AND YOU'RE IN MY WAY.
DON'T YOU HAVE SOME HOUSES TO BURN DOWN?
um.
WAIT.
ARE WE ON THE SAME SIDE HERE?
PFT!
AS IF...
I COULDN'T CARE LESS ABOUT YOUR GIRLFRIEND.
JUST...
...I NEED TO KNOW IF MY DAD—THE BARON—IS INVOLVED...
WE BOTH SAW FIRSTHAND WHAT THAT PLANT CAN DO...
I CAN'T LET HIM—
I DON'T WANT HIM TO GET IN OVER HIS HEAD...

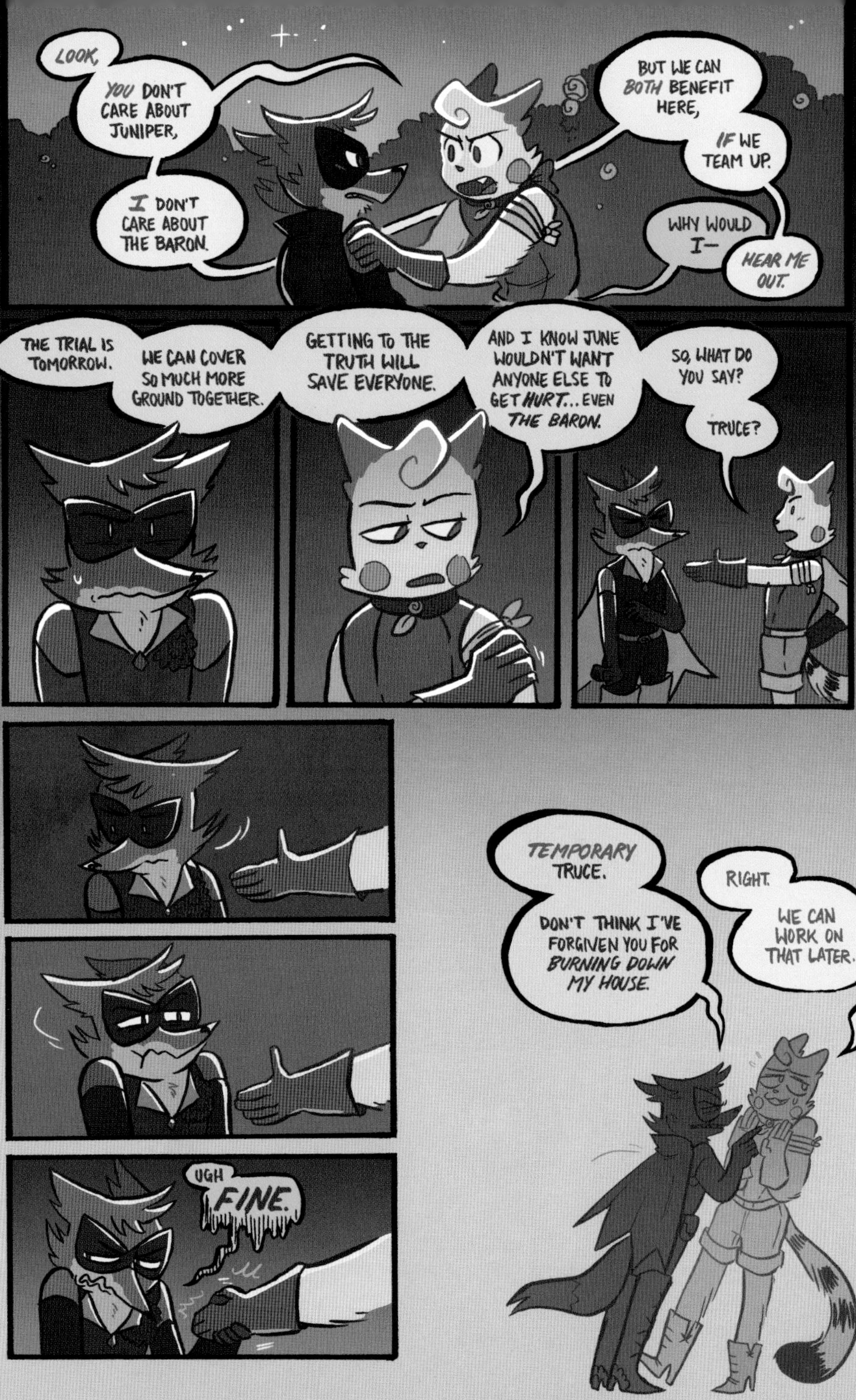
LOOK,
YOU DON'T CARE ABOUT JUNIPER,
I DON'T CARE ABOUT THE BARON.
BUT WE CAN BOTH BENEFIT HERE,
IF WE TEAM UP.
WHY WOULD I—
HEAR ME OUT.
THE TRIAL IS TOMORROW.
WE CAN COVER SO MUCH MORE GROUND TOGETHER.
GETTING TO THE TRUTH WILL SAVE EVERYONE.
AND I KNOW JUNE WOULDN'T WANT ANYONE ELSE TO GET HURT... EVEN THE BARON.
SO, WHAT DO YOU SAY?
TRUCE?
UGH
FINE.
TEMPORARY TRUCE.
DON'T THINK I'VE FORGIVEN YOU FOR BURNING DOWN MY HOUSE.
RIGHT.
WE CAN WORK ON THAT LATER...

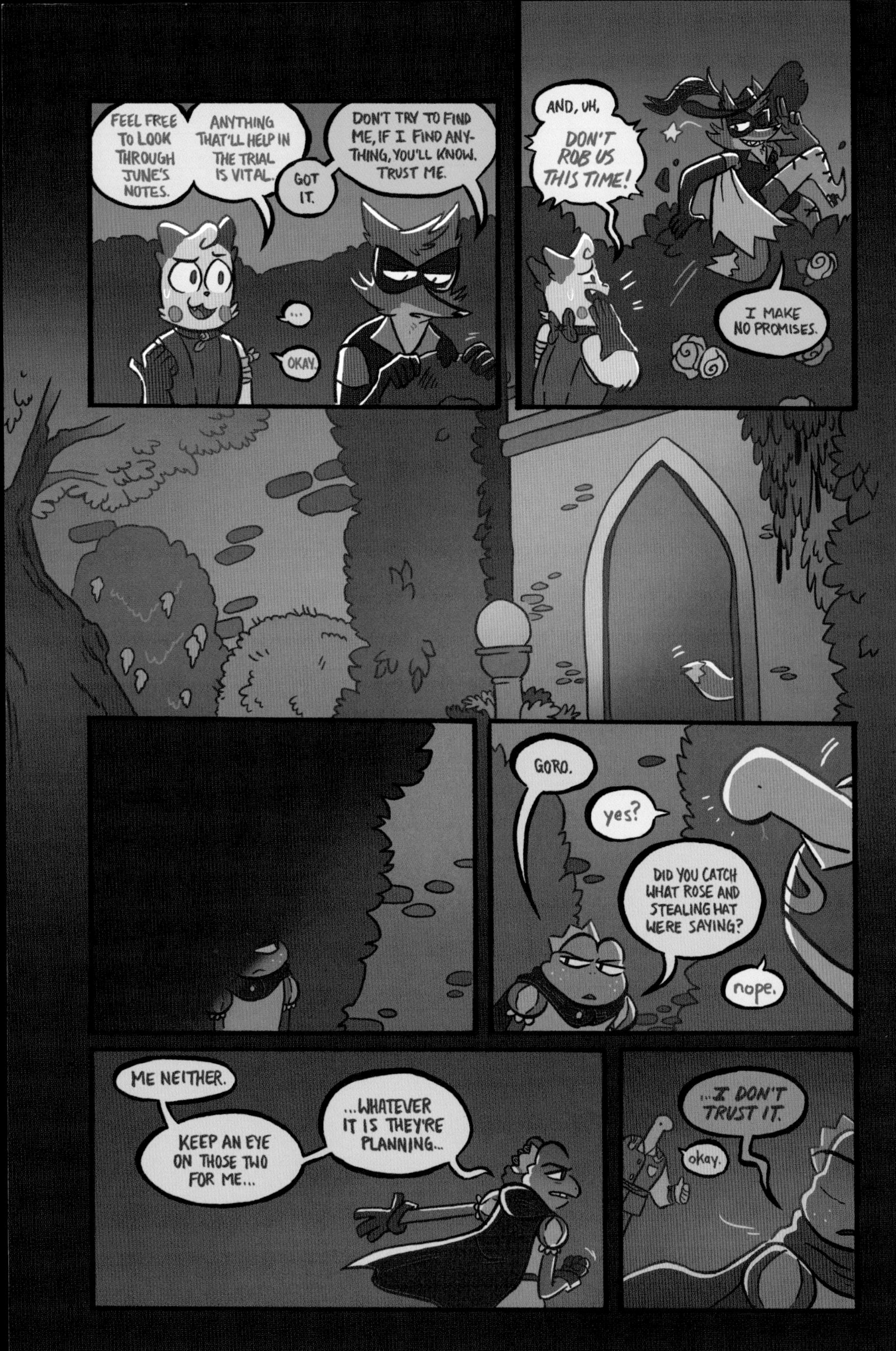
FEEL FREE TO LOOK THROUGH JUNE'S NOTES.
ANYTHING THAT'LL HELP IN THE TRIAL IS VITAL.
GOT IT.
DON'T TRY TO FIND ME, IF I FIND ANYTHING, YOU'LL KNOW. TRUST ME.
...
OKAY.
AND, UH,
DON'T ROB US THIS TIME!
I MAKE NO PROMISES.
GORO.
yes?
DID YOU CATCH WHAT ROSE AND STEALING HAT WERE SAYING?
nope.
ME NEITHER.
KEEP AN EYE ON THOSE TWO FOR ME...
...WHATEVER IT IS THEY'RE PLANNING...
...I DON'T TRUST IT.
okay.

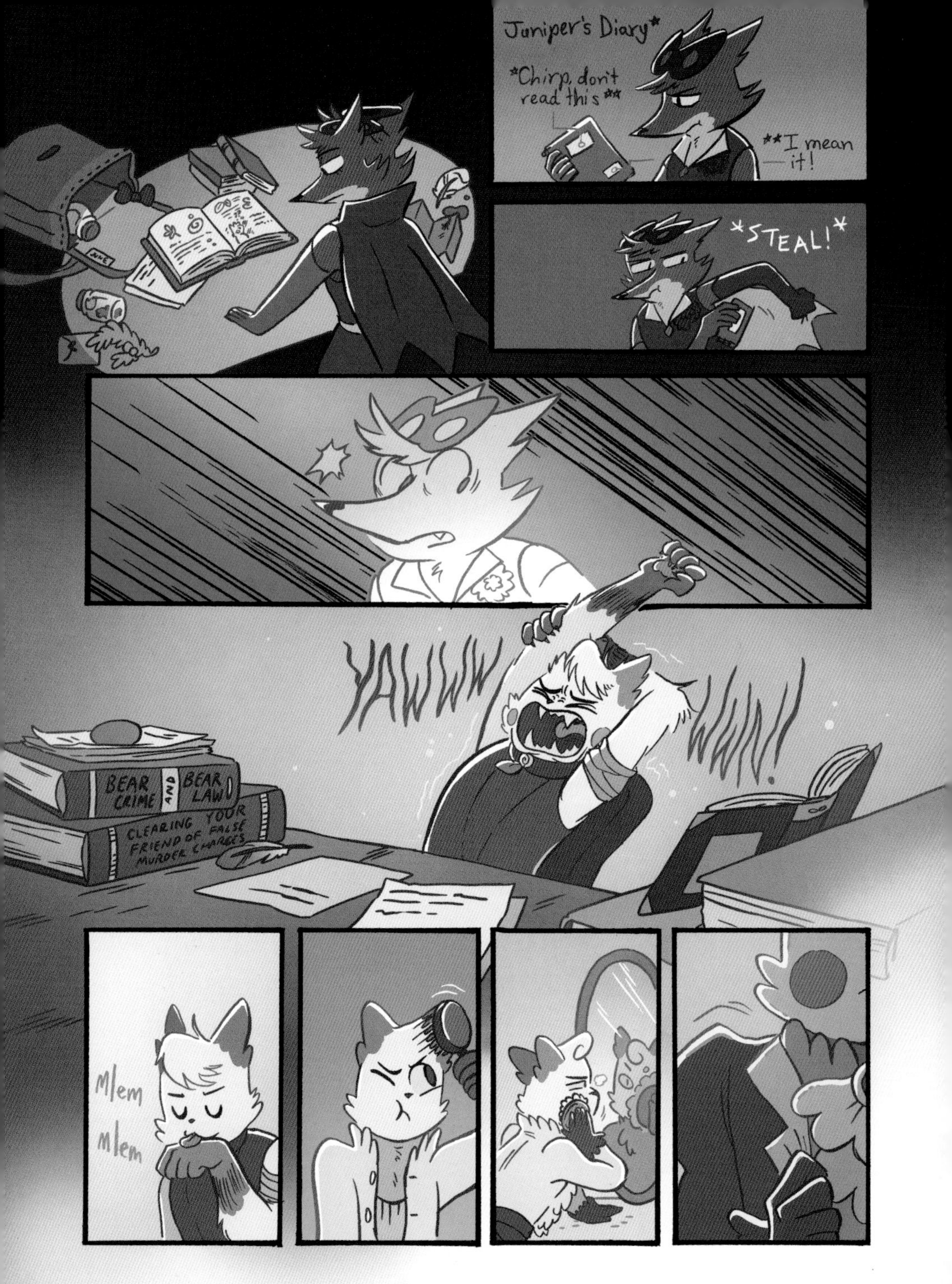

Juniper's Diary*
*Chirp, don't read this**
**I mean it!
STEAL!
YAWWW
WWN!
BEAR CRIME AND BEAR LAW
CLEARING YOUR FRIEND OF FALSE MURDER CHARGES
Mlem
mlem

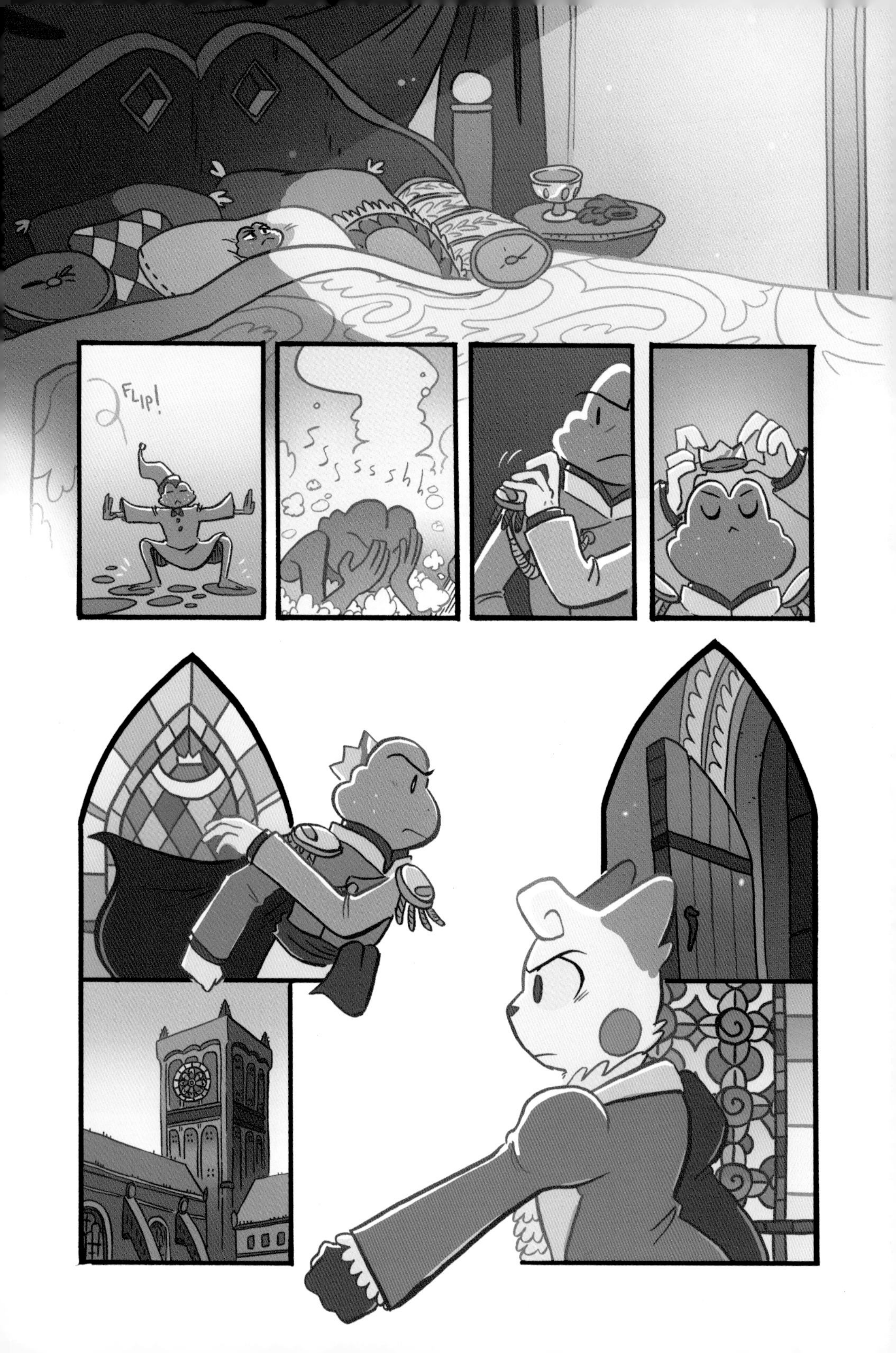
FLIP!
Ssssshh

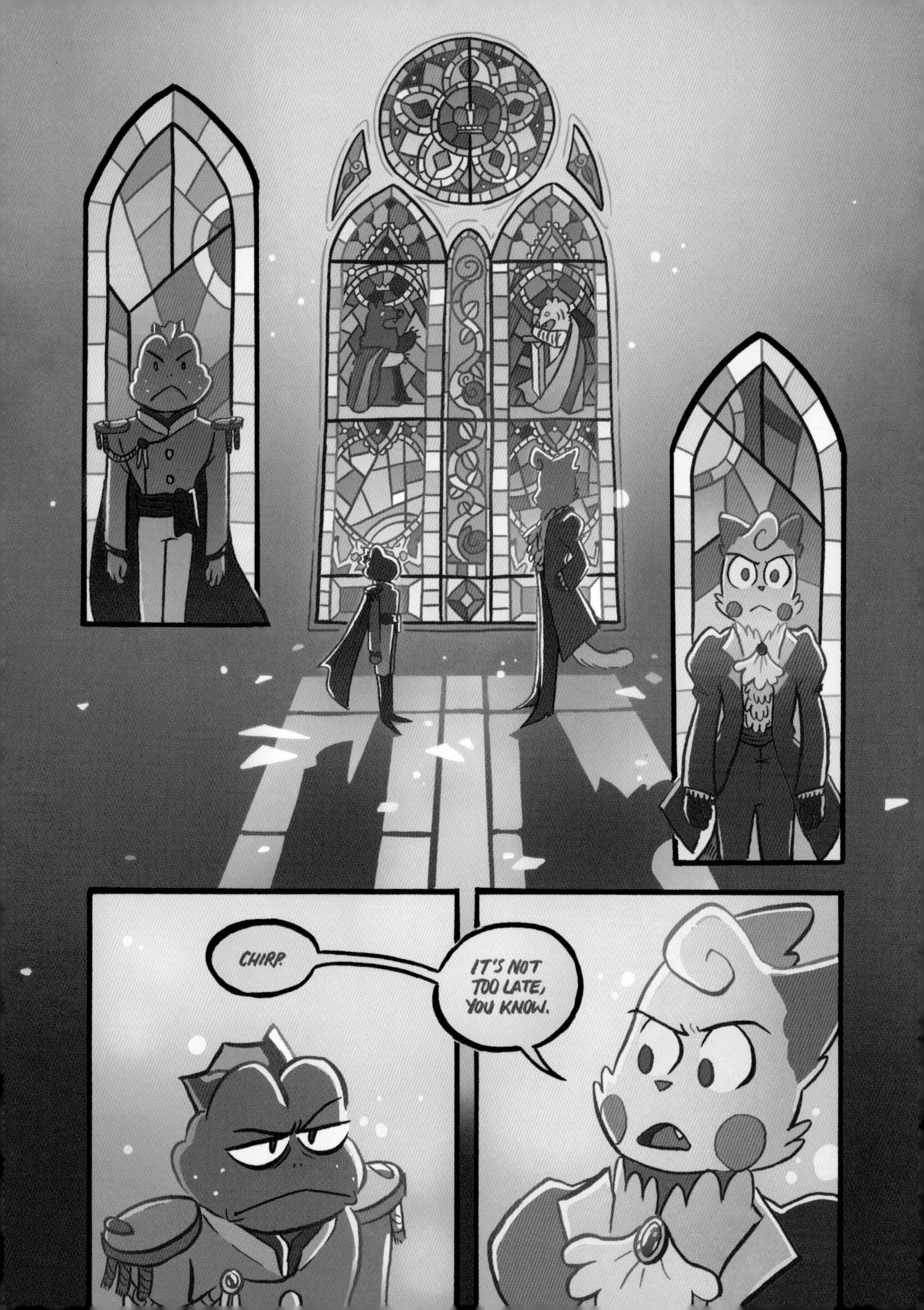
CHIRP.
IT'S NOT TOO LATE, YOU KNOW.

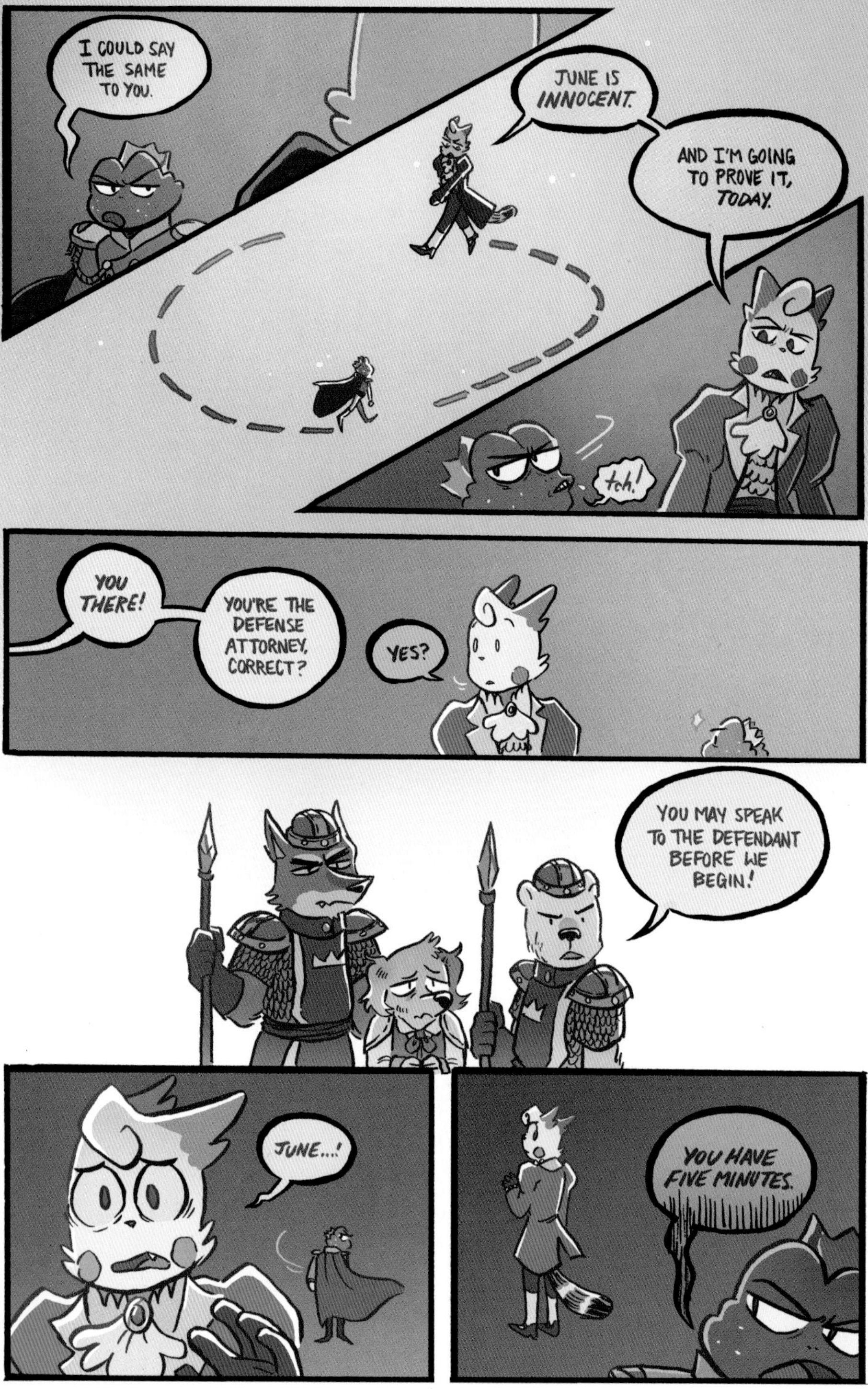
I COULD SAY THE SAME TO YOU.
JUNE IS INNOCENT.
AND I'M GOING TO PROVE IT, TODAY.
tch!
YOU THERE!
YOU'RE THE DEFENSE ATTORNEY, CORRECT?
YES?
YOU MAY SPEAK TO THE DEFENDANT BEFORE WE BEGIN!
JUNE...!
YOU HAVE FIVE MINUTES.

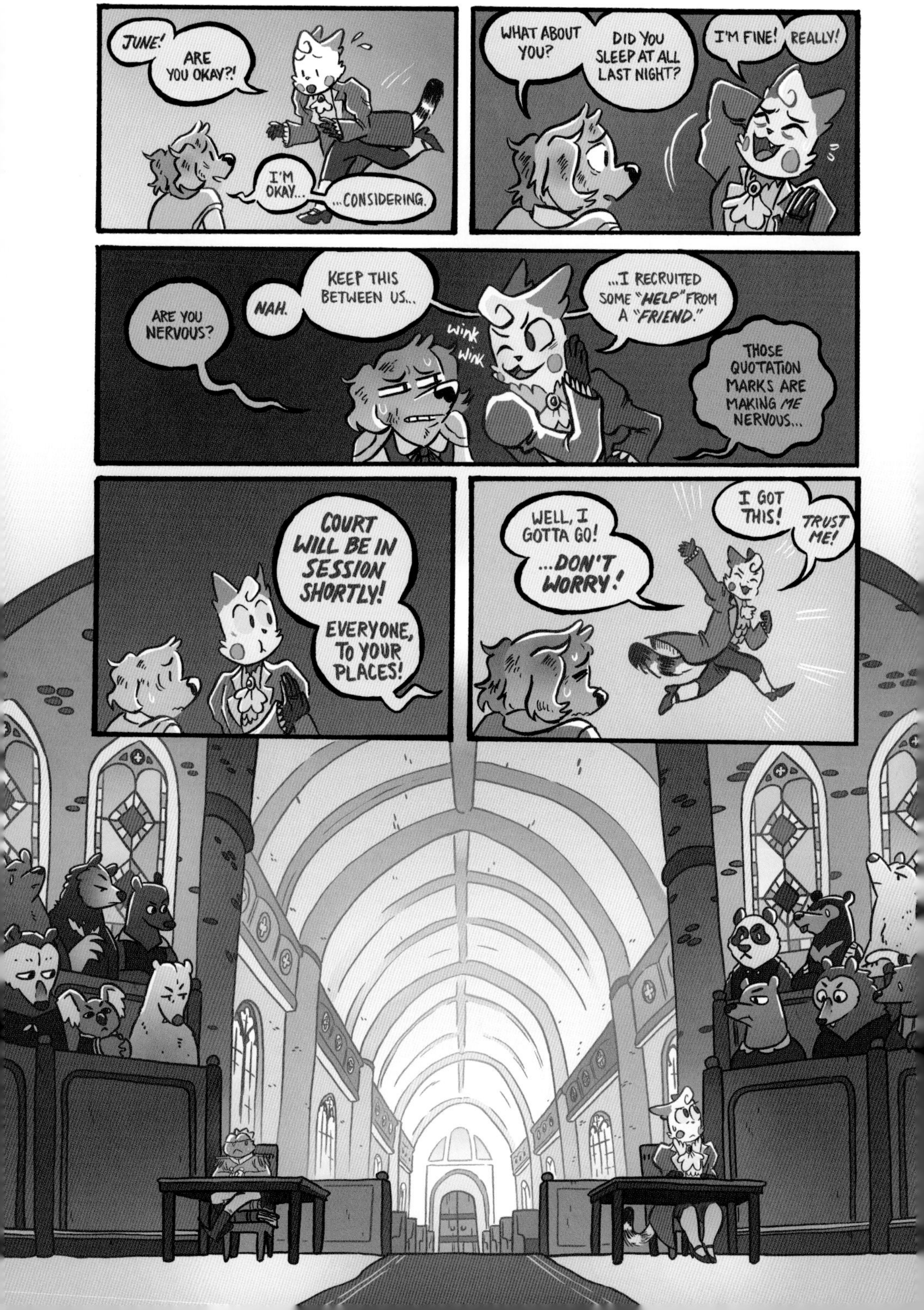

JUNE!
ARE YOU OKAY?!
I'M OKAY...
...CONSIDERING.
WHAT ABOUT YOU?
DID YOU SLEEP AT ALL LAST NIGHT?
I'M FINE!
REALLY!
ARE YOU NERVOUS?
NAH.
KEEP THIS BETWEEN US...
...I RECRUITED SOME "HELP" FROM A "FRIEND."
wink wink
THOSE QUOTATION MARKS ARE MAKING ME NERVOUS...
COURT WILL BE IN SESSION SHORTLY!
EVERYONE, TO YOUR PLACES!
WELL, I GOTTA GO!
...DON'T WORRY!
I GOT THIS!
TRUST ME!

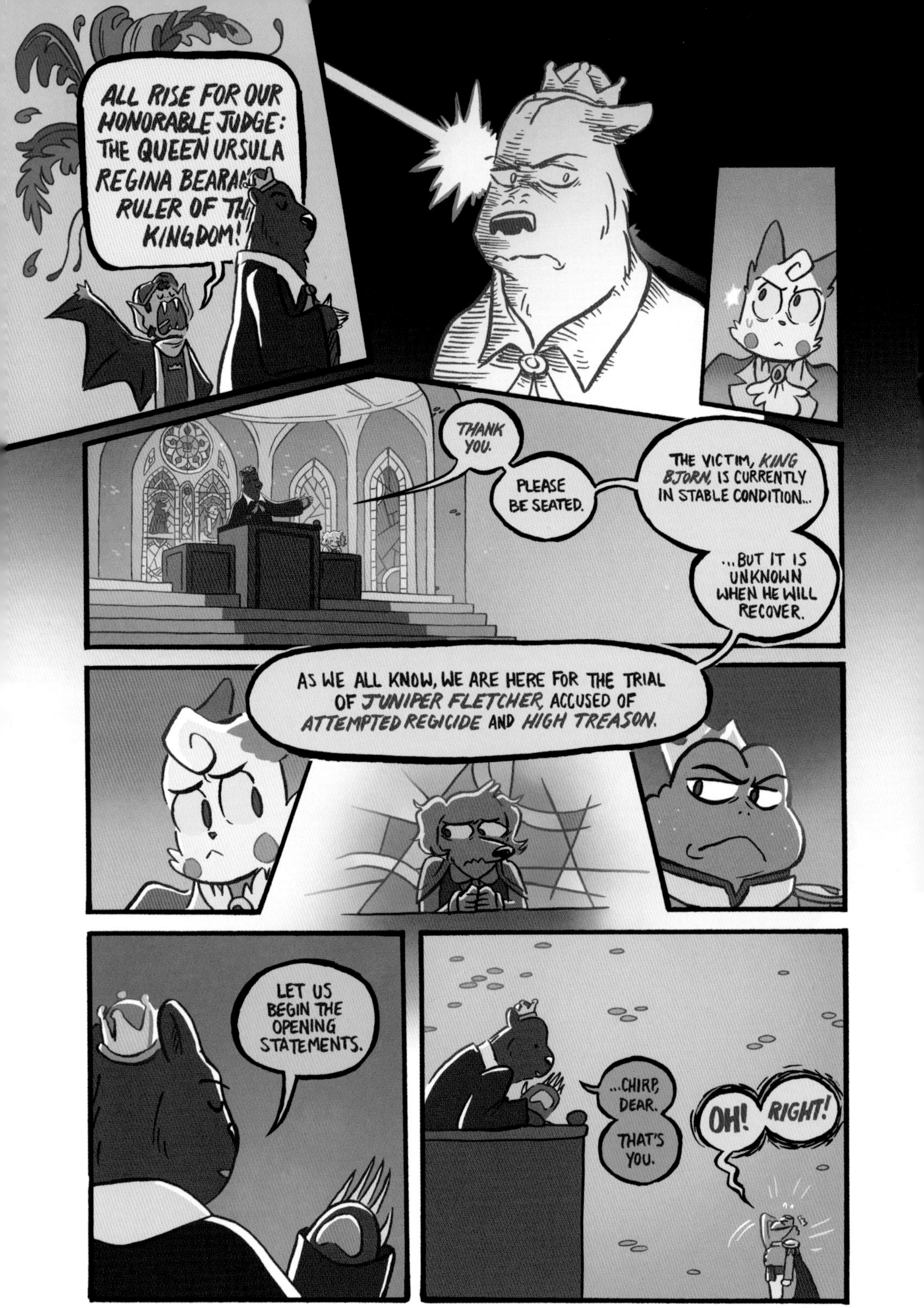
ALL RISE FOR OUR HONORABLE JUDGE: THE QUEEN URSULA REGINA BEARAN[?] RULER OF TH[?] KINGDOM!
THANK YOU.
PLEASE BE SEATED.
THE VICTIM, KING BJORN, IS CURRENTLY IN STABLE CONDITION...
...BUT IT IS UNKNOWN WHEN HE WILL RECOVER.
AS WE ALL KNOW, WE ARE HERE FOR THE TRIAL OF JUNIPER FLETCHER, ACCUSED OF ATTEMPTED REGICIDE AND HIGH TREASON.
LET US BEGIN THE OPENING STATEMENTS.
...CHIRP, DEAR.
THAT'S YOU.
OH! RIGHT!

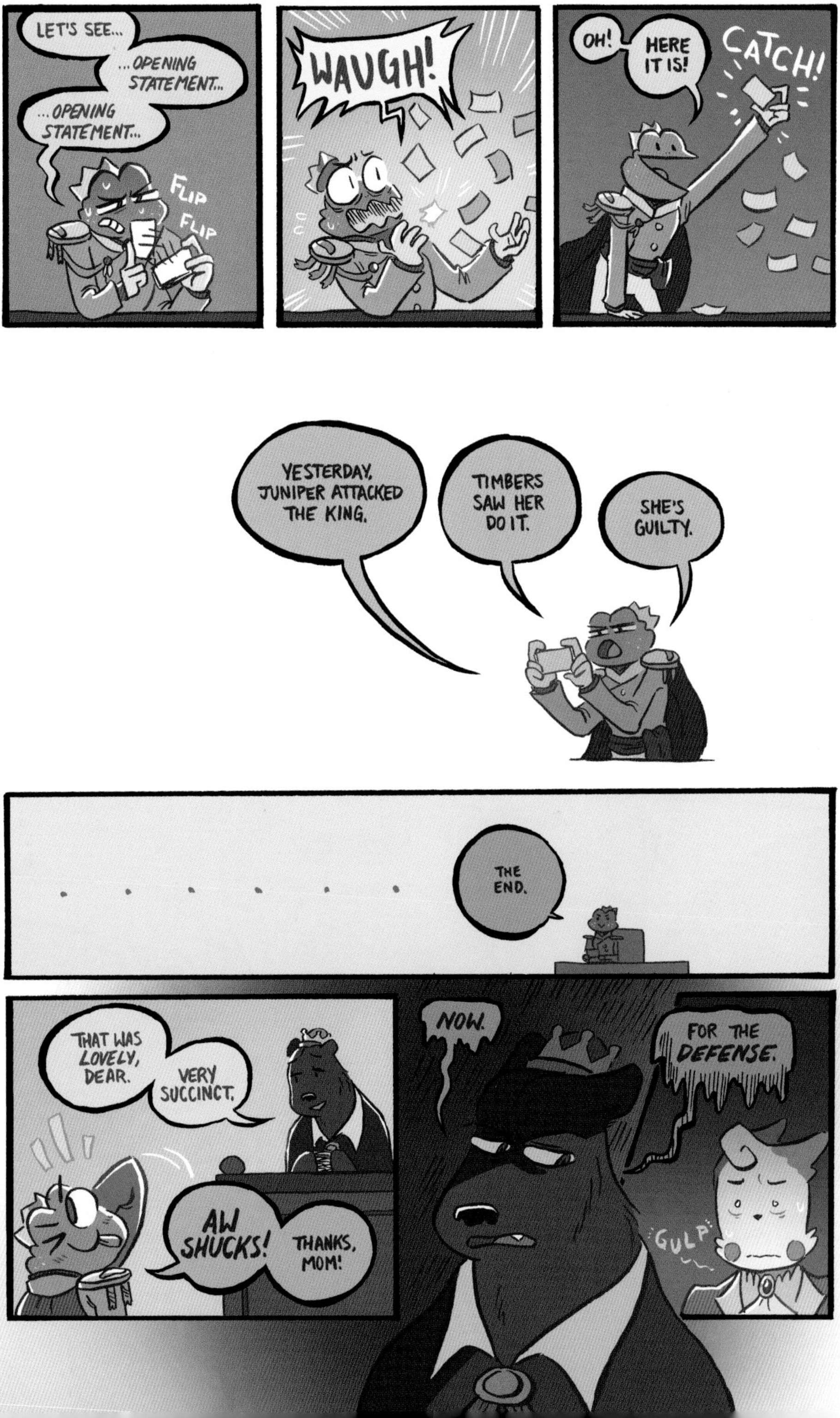
LET'S SEE...
...OPENING STATEMENT...
...OPENING STATEMENT...
FLIP
FLIP
WAUGH!
OH!
HERE IT IS!
CATCH!
YESTERDAY, JUNIPER ATTACKED THE KING.
TIMBERS SAW HER DO IT.
SHE'S GUILTY.
. . . . . .
THE END.
THAT WAS LOVELY, DEAR.
VERY SUCCINCT.
AW SHUCKS!
THANKS, MOM!
NOW.
FOR THE DEFENSE.
GULP

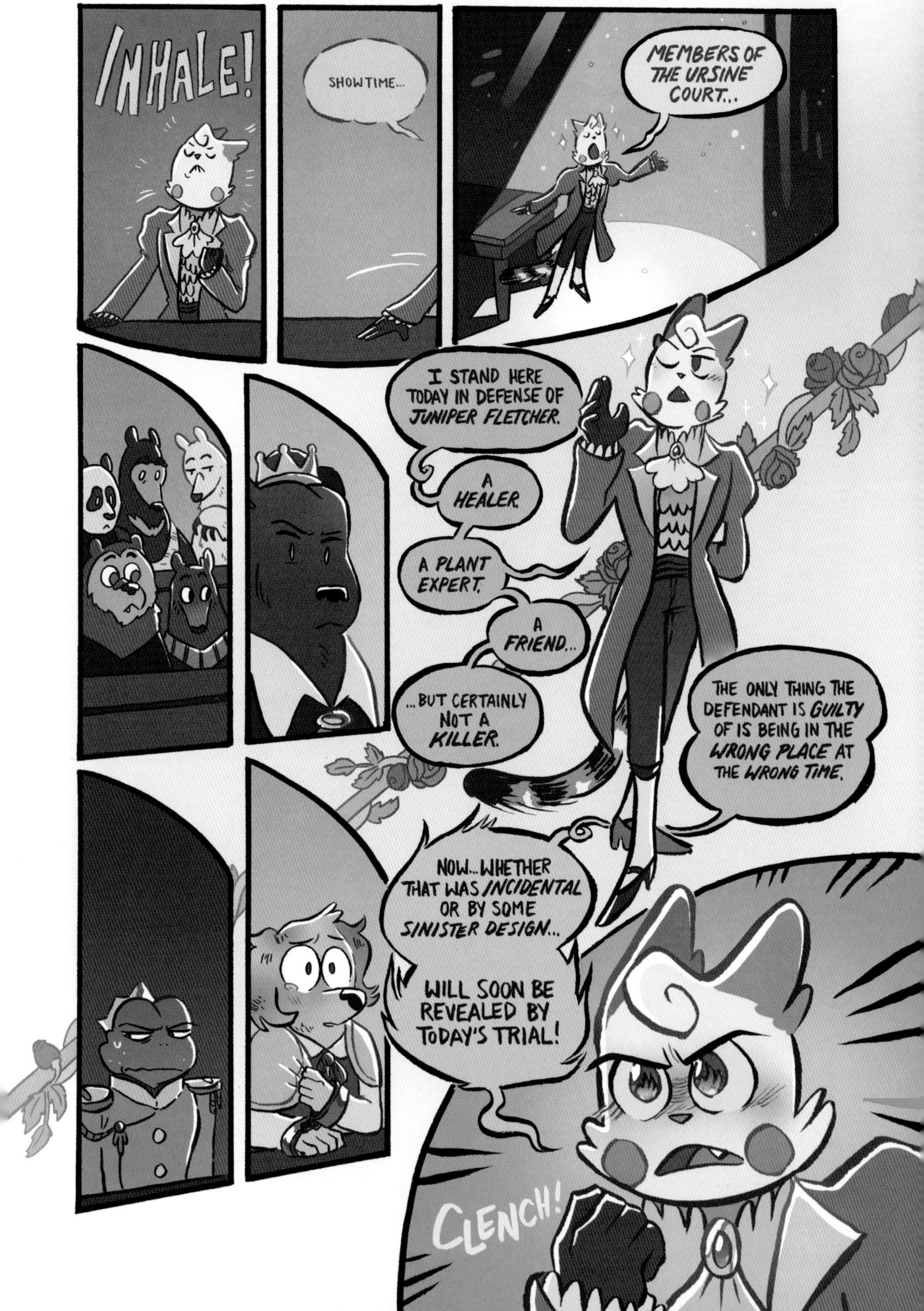
INHALE!
SHOWTIME...
MEMBERS OF THE URSINE COURT...
I STAND HERE TODAY IN DEFENSE OF JUNIPER FLETCHER.
A HEALER.
A PLANT EXPERT.
A FRIEND...
...BUT CERTAINLY NOT A KILLER.
THE ONLY THING THE DEFENDANT IS GUILTY OF IS BEING IN THE WRONG PLACE AT THE WRONG TIME.
NOW...WHETHER THAT WAS INCIDENTAL OR BY SOME SINISTER DESIGN...
WILL SOON BE REVEALED BY TODAY'S TRIAL!
CLENCH!

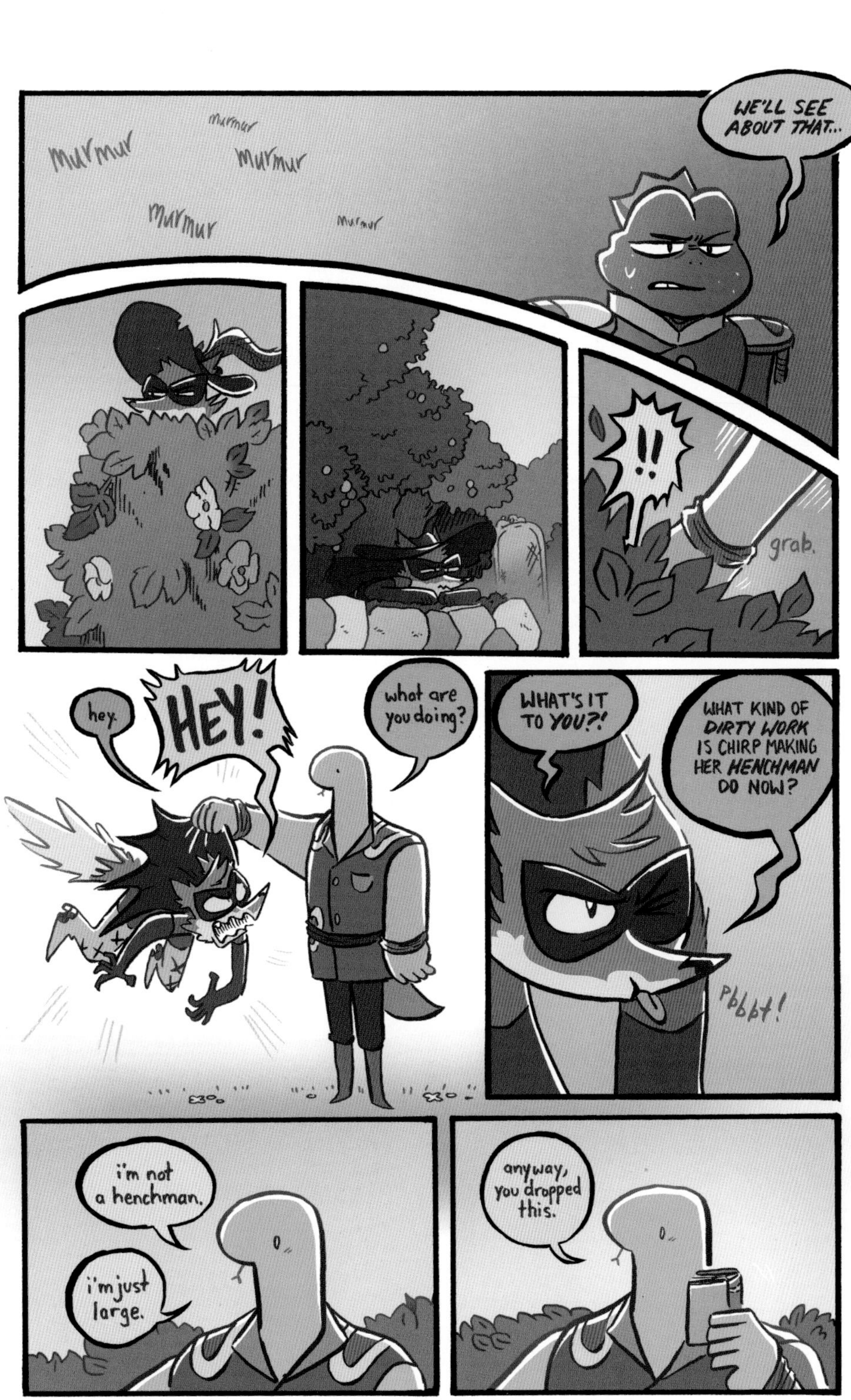
murmur
murmur
murmur
murmur
murmur
murmur
WE'LL SEE ABOUT THAT...
!!
grab.
hey.
HEY!
what are you doing?
WHAT'S IT TO YOU?!
WHAT KIND OF DIRTY WORK IS CHIRP MAKING HER HENCHMAN DO NOW?
Pbbbt!
i'm not a henchman.
i'm just large.
anyway, you dropped this.

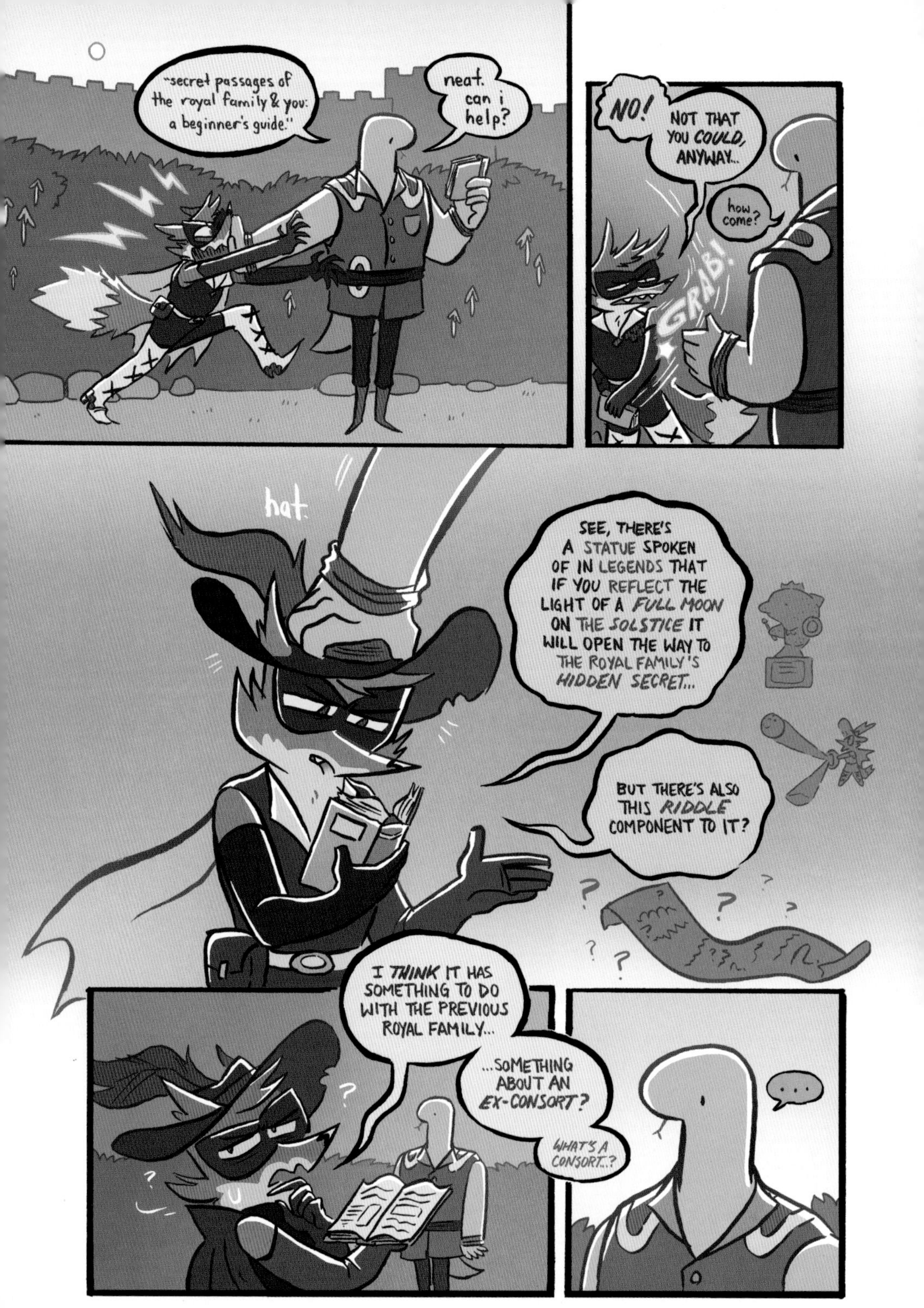

"secret passages of the royal family & you: a beginner's guide."
neat. can i help?
NO!
NOT THAT YOU COULD, ANYWAY...
how come?
GRAB!
hat.
SEE, THERE'S A STATUE SPOKEN OF IN LEGENDS THAT IF YOU REFLECT THE LIGHT OF A FULL MOON ON THE SOLSTICE IT WILL OPEN THE WAY TO THE ROYAL FAMILY'S HIDDEN SECRET...
BUT THERE'S ALSO THIS RIDDLE COMPONENT TO IT?
I THINK IT HAS SOMETHING TO DO WITH THE PREVIOUS ROYAL FAMILY...
...SOMETHING ABOUT AN EX-CONSORT?
WHAT'S A CONSORT...?
...

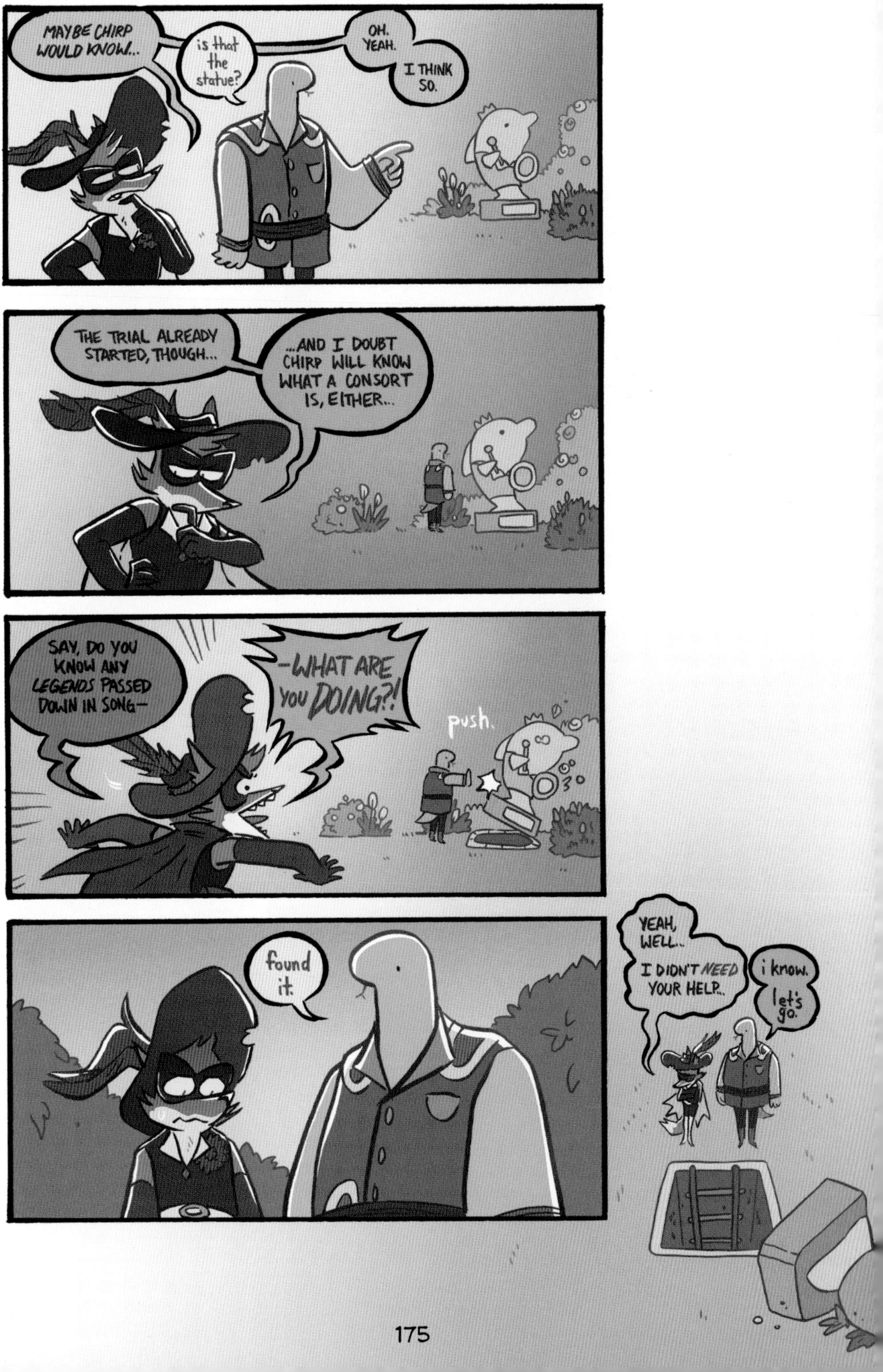
MAYBE CHIRP WOULD KNOW...
is that the statue?
OH. YEAH.
I THINK SO.
THE TRIAL ALREADY STARTED, THOUGH...
...AND I DOUBT CHIRP WILL KNOW WHAT A CONSORT IS, EITHER...
SAY, DO YOU KNOW ANY LEGENDS PASSED DOWN IN SONG—
—WHAT ARE YOU DOING?!
push.
found it.
YEAH, WELL...
I DIDN'T NEED YOUR HELP...
i know.
let's go.

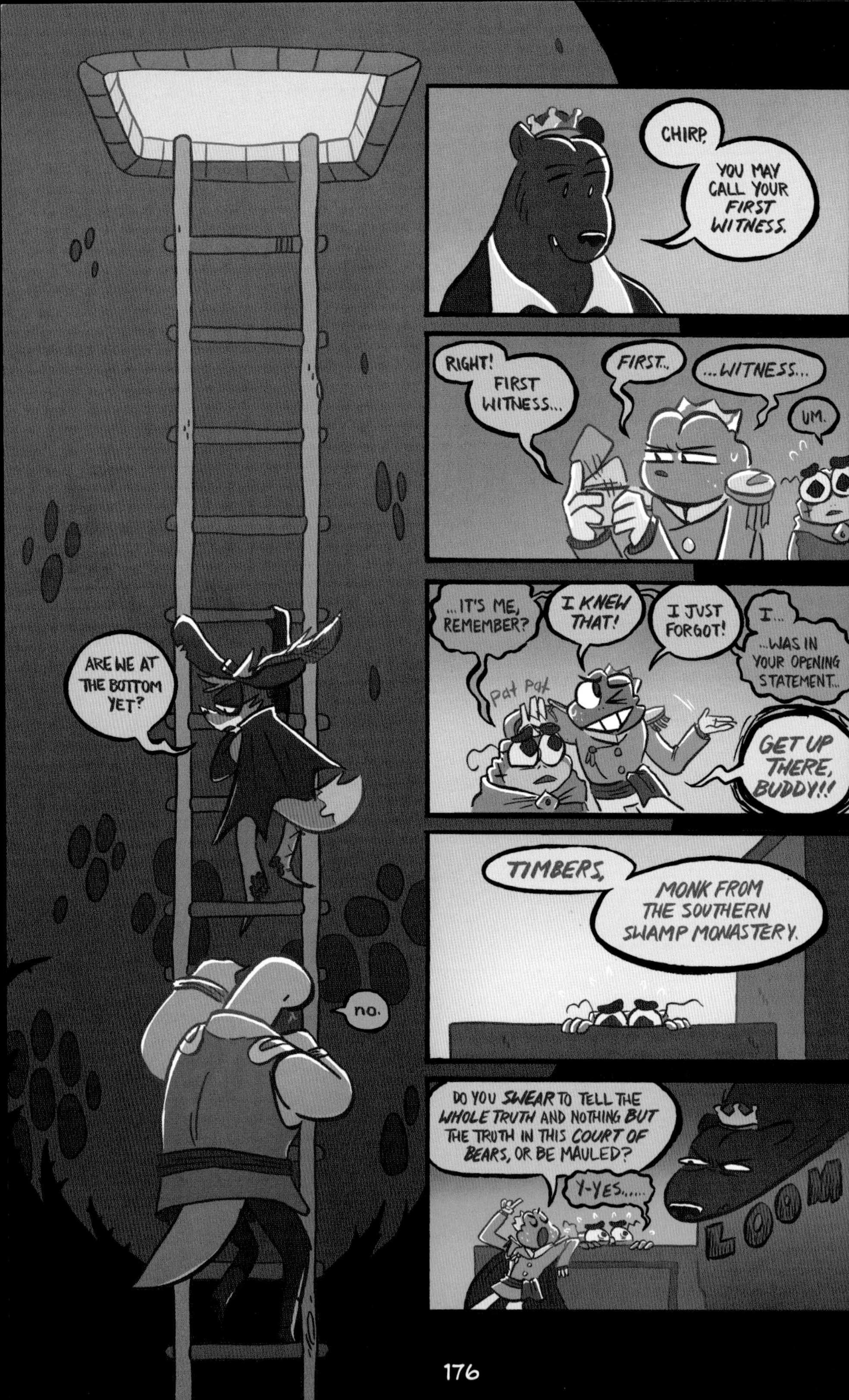
ARE WE AT THE BOTTOM YET?
no.
CHIRP,
YOU MAY CALL YOUR FIRST WITNESS.
RIGHT! FIRST WITNESS...
FIRST...
...WITNESS...
UM.
...IT'S ME, REMEMBER?
pat pat
I KNEW THAT!
I JUST FORGOT!
I... ...WAS IN YOUR OPENING STATEMENT...
GET UP THERE, BUDDY!!
TIMBERS,
MONK FROM THE SOUTHERN SWAMP MONASTERY.
DO YOU SWEAR TO TELL THE WHOLE TRUTH AND NOTHING BUT THE TRUTH IN THIS COURT OF BEARS, OR BE MAULED?
Y-YES......
LOOOM

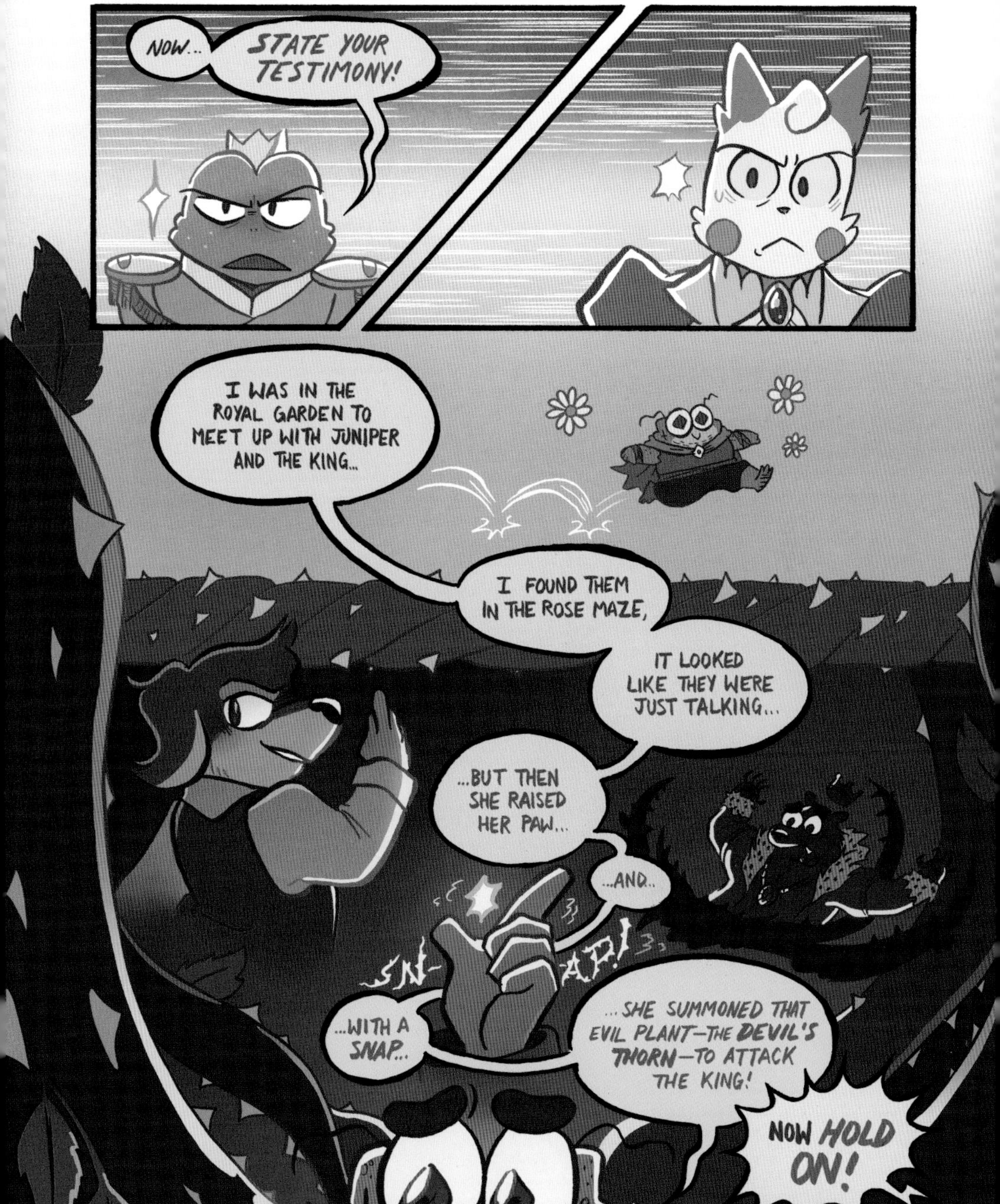
NOW...
STATE YOUR TESTIMONY!
I WAS IN THE ROYAL GARDEN TO MEET UP WITH JUNIPER AND THE KING...
I FOUND THEM IN THE ROSE MAZE,
IT LOOKED LIKE THEY WERE JUST TALKING...
...BUT THEN SHE RAISED HER PAW...
...AND...
SN-AP!
...WITH A SNAP...
...SHE SUMMONED THAT EVIL PLANT—THE DEVIL'S THORN—TO ATTACK THE KING!
NOW HOLD ON!

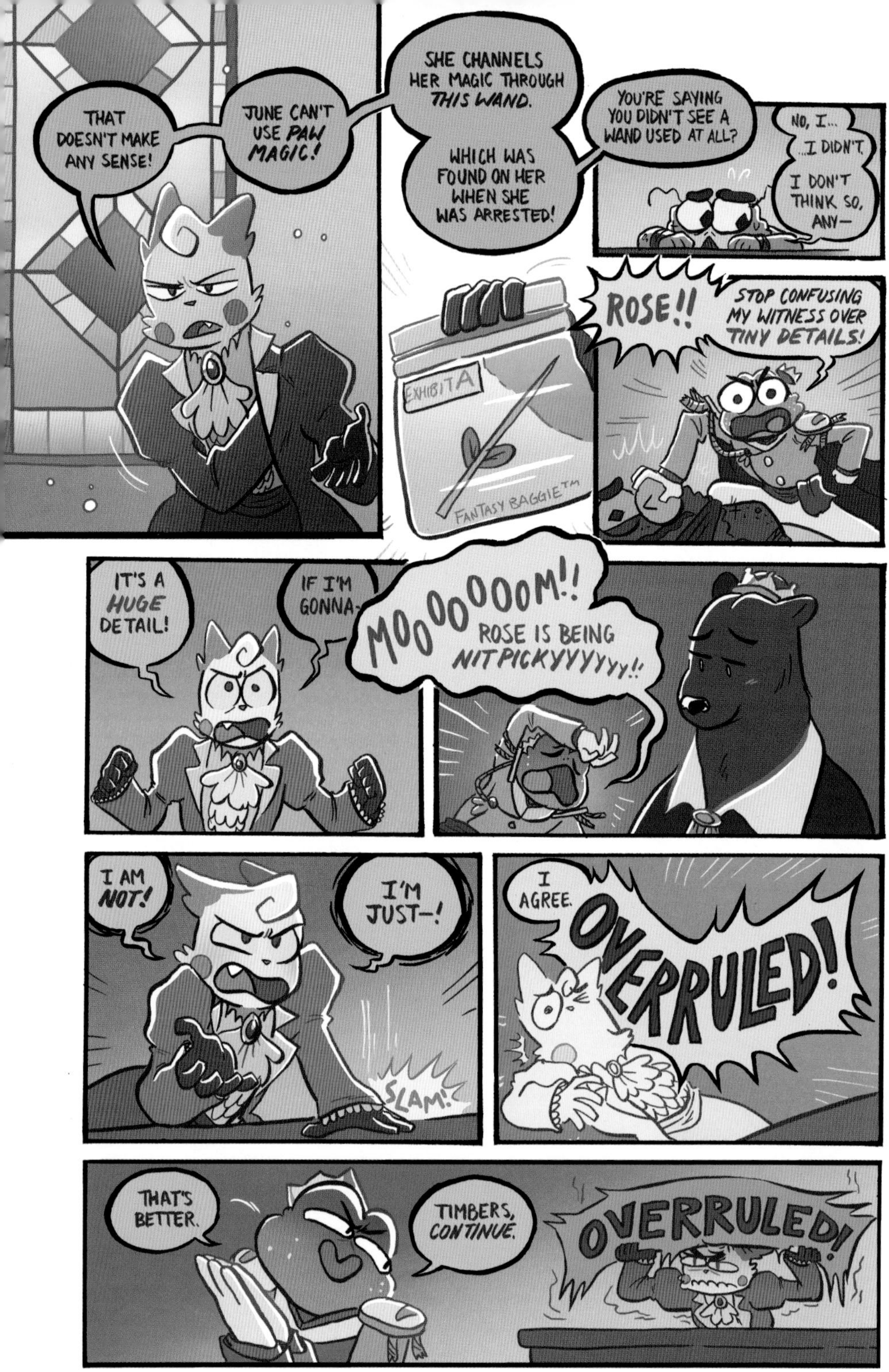

THAT DOESN'T MAKE ANY SENSE!
JUNE CAN'T USE PAW MAGIC!
SHE CHANNELS HER MAGIC THROUGH THIS WAND.
WHICH WAS FOUND ON HER WHEN SHE WAS ARRESTED!
YOU'RE SAYING YOU DIDN'T SEE A WAND USED AT ALL?
NO, I... ...I DIDN'T.
I DON'T THINK SO, ANY—
EXHIBIT A
FANTASY BAGGIE™
ROSE!!
STOP CONFUSING MY WITNESS OVER TINY DETAILS!
IT'S A HUGE DETAIL!
IF I'M GONNA—
MOOOOOOOM!!
ROSE IS BEING NITPICKYYYYYYY!!
I AM NOT!
I'M JUST—!
SLAM!
I AGREE.
OVERRULED!
THAT'S BETTER.
TIMBERS, CONTINUE.
OVERRULED!

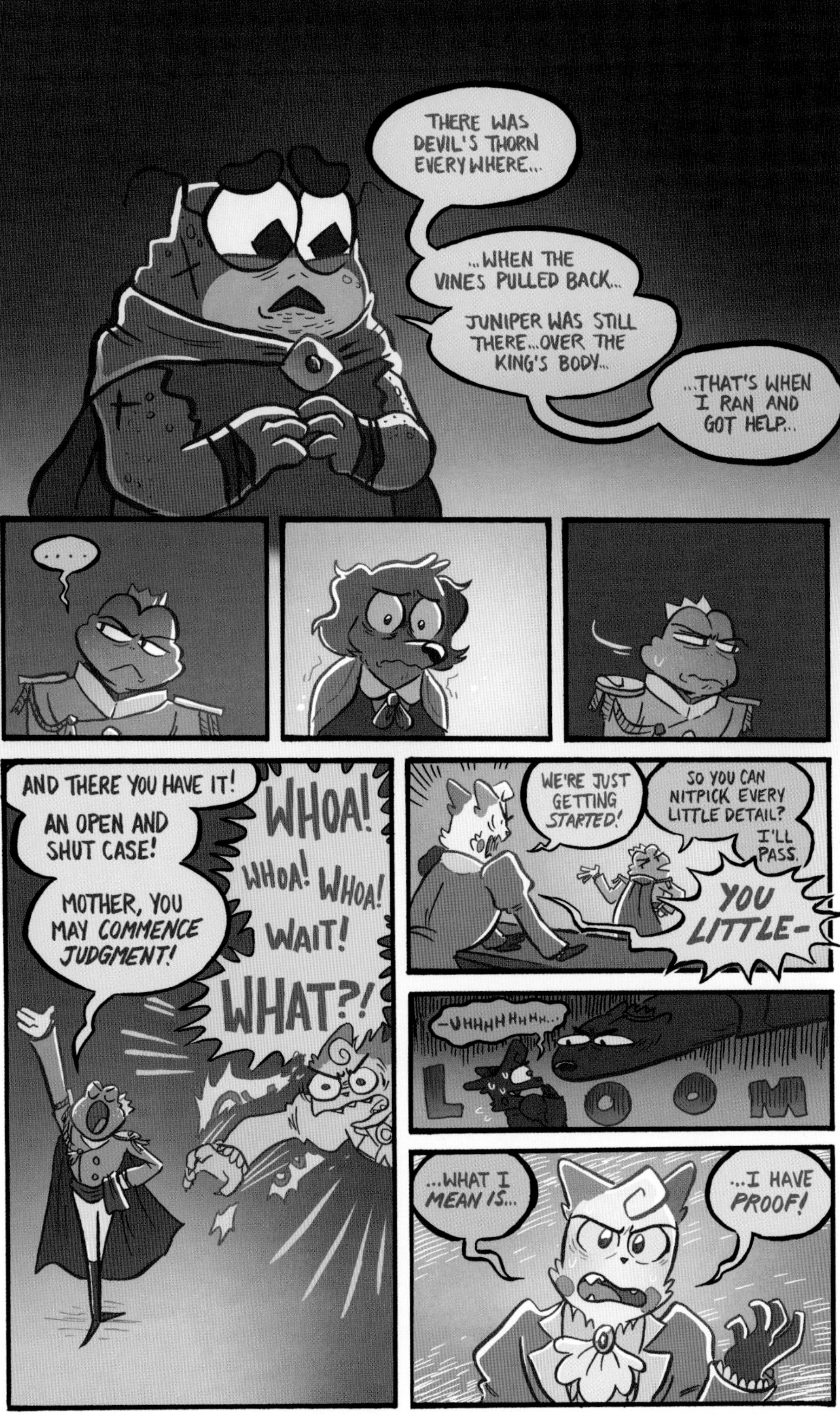
THERE WAS DEVIL'S THORN EVERYWHERE...
...WHEN THE VINES PULLED BACK...
JUNIPER WAS STILL THERE...OVER THE KING'S BODY...
...THAT'S WHEN I RAN AND GOT HELP...
. . . .
AND THERE YOU HAVE IT!
AN OPEN AND SHUT CASE!
MOTHER, YOU MAY COMMENCE JUDGMENT!
WHOA!
WHOA! WHOA!
WAIT!
WHAT?!
WE'RE JUST GETTING STARTED!
SO YOU CAN NITPICK EVERY LITTLE DETAIL?
I'LL PASS.
YOU LITTLE-
-UHHHHHHHH...
LOOOM
...WHAT I MEAN IS...
...I HAVE PROOF!

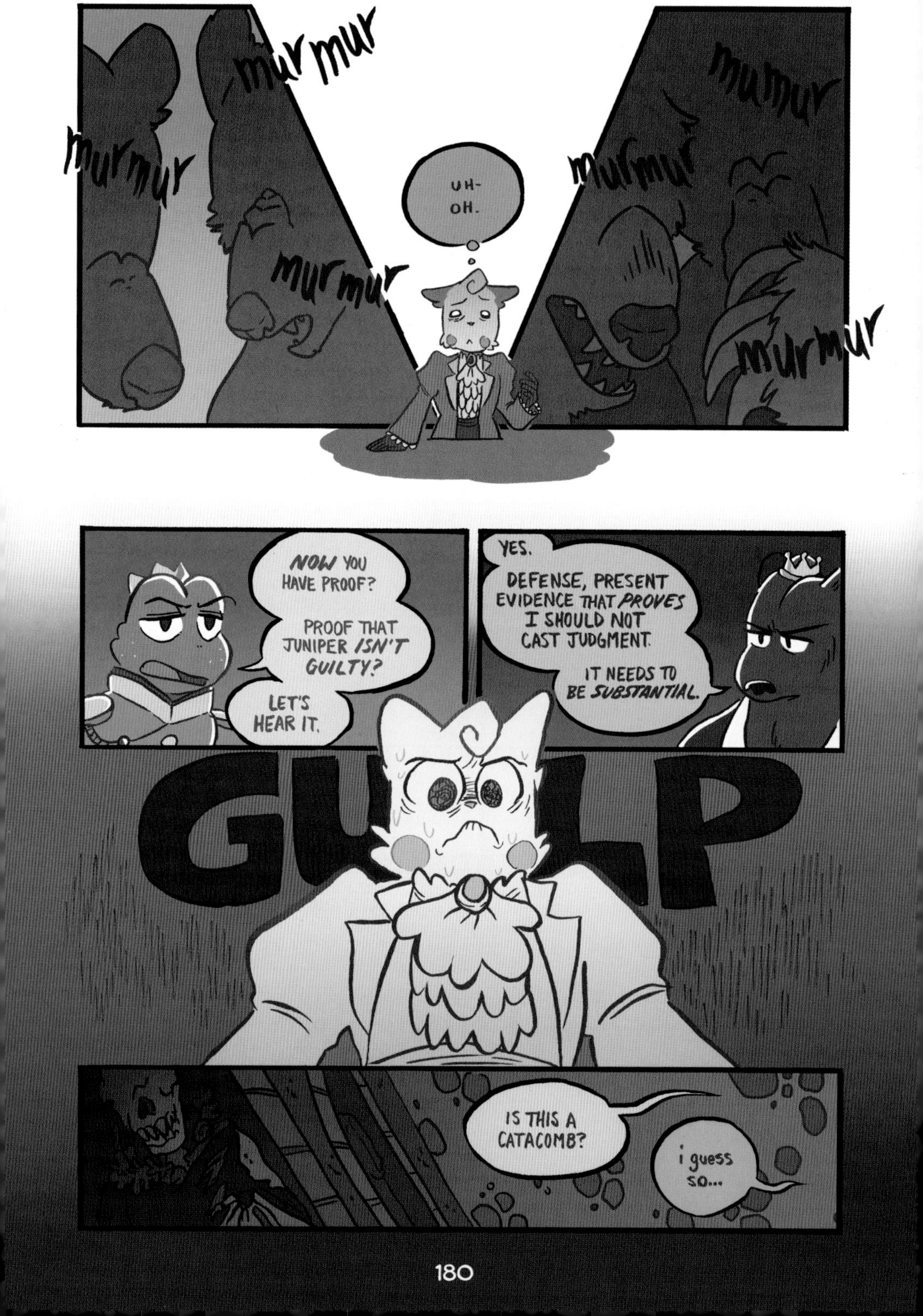
murmur
murmur
murmur
mumur
murmur
murmur
UH-OH.
NOW YOU HAVE PROOF?
PROOF THAT JUNIPER ISN'T GUILTY?
LET'S HEAR IT.
YES.
DEFENSE, PRESENT EVIDENCE THAT PROVES I SHOULD NOT CAST JUDGMENT.
IT NEEDS TO BE SUBSTANTIAL.
GULP
IS THIS A CATACOMB?
i guess so...

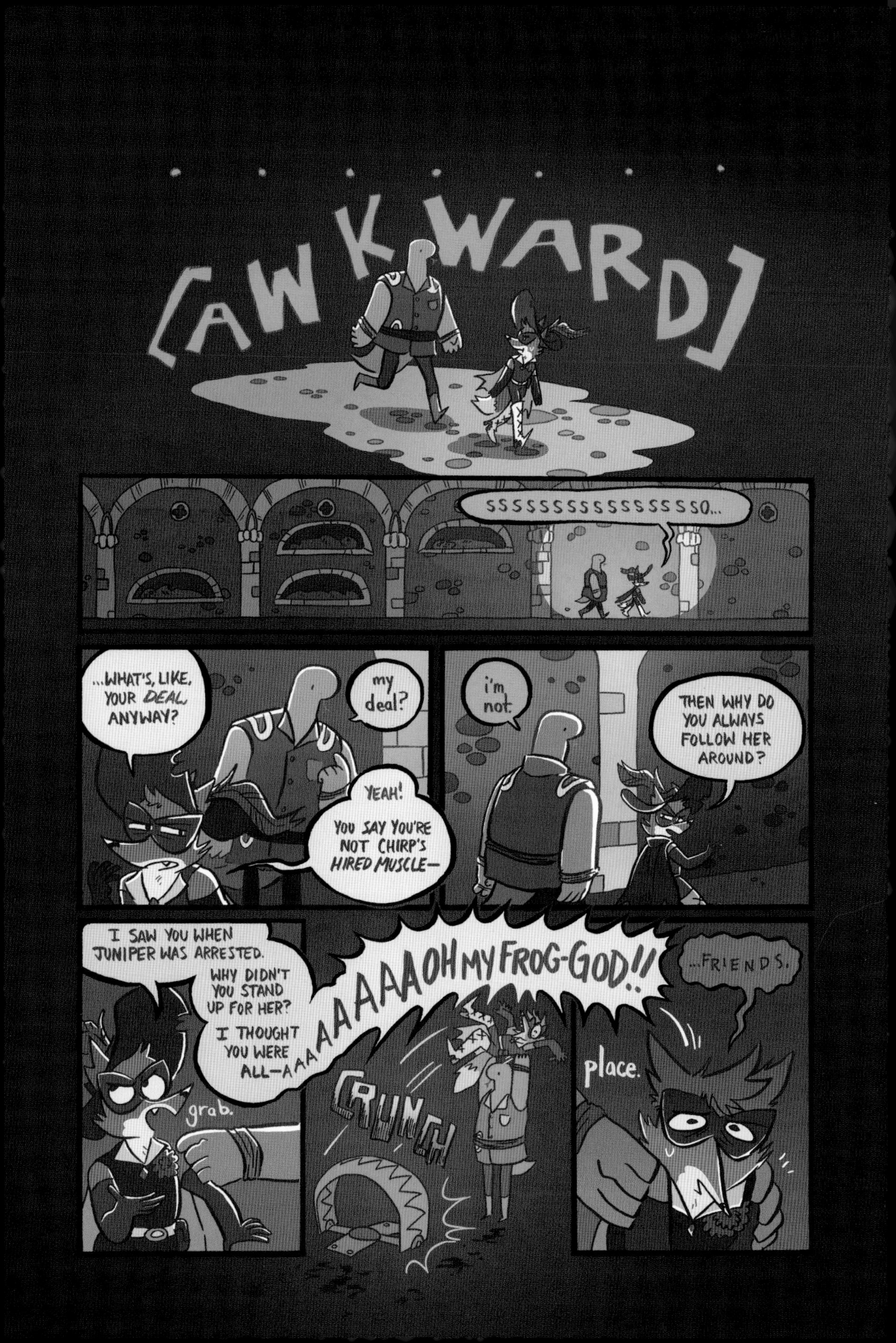
. . . .
[AWKWARD]
SSSSSSSSSSSSSSSSO...
...WHAT'S, LIKE, YOUR DEAL, ANYWAY?
my deal?
YEAH!
YOU SAY YOU'RE NOT CHIRP'S HIRED MUSCLE—
i'm not.
THEN WHY DO YOU ALWAYS FOLLOW HER AROUND?
I SAW YOU WHEN JUNIPER WAS ARRESTED.
WHY DIDN'T YOU STAND UP FOR HER?
I THOUGHT YOU WERE ALL—AAAAAAAAAOH MY FROG-GOD!!..
grab.
CRUNCH
...FRIENDS.
place.

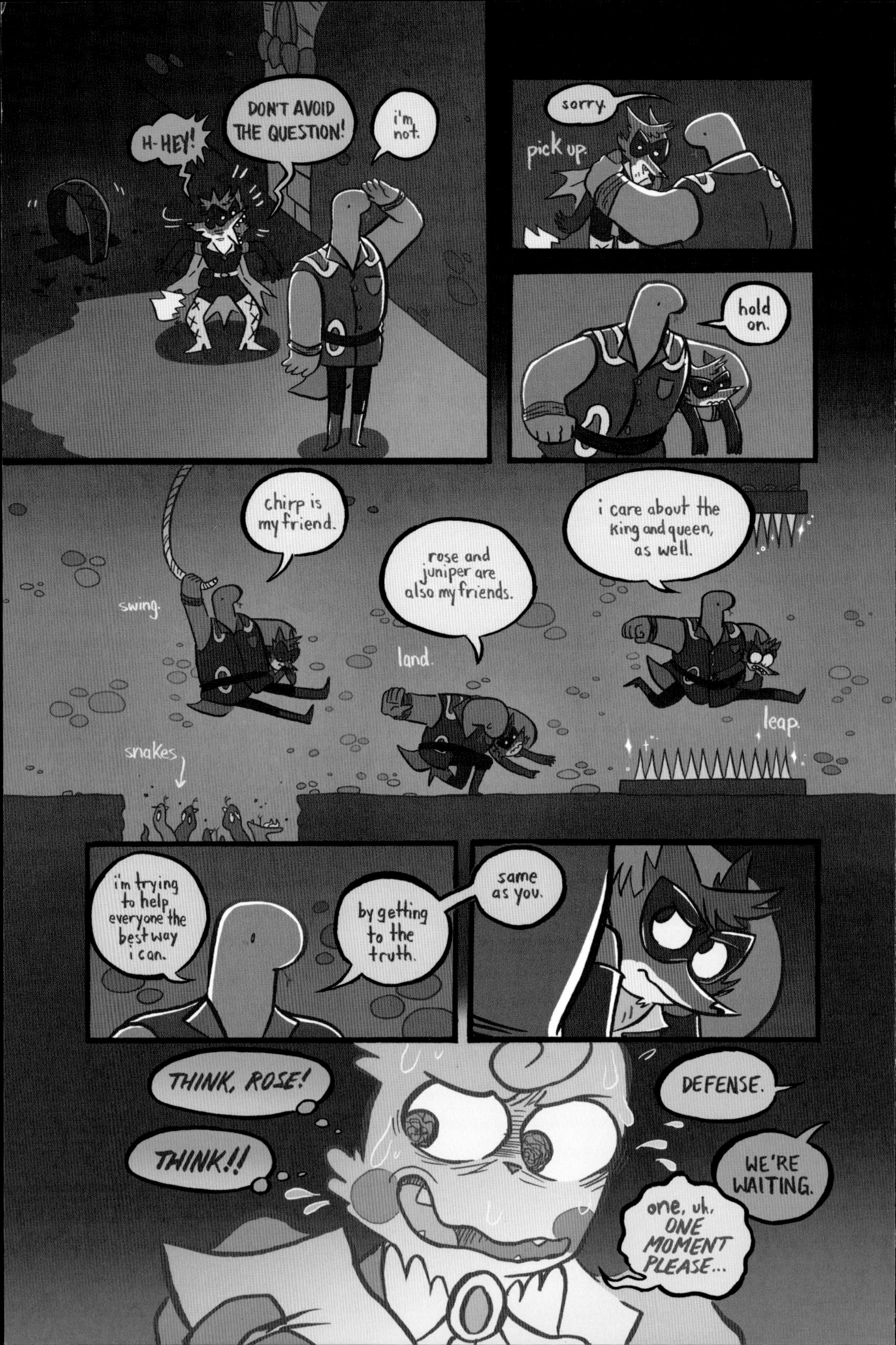
H-HEY!
DON'T AVOID THE QUESTION!
i'm not.
sorry.
pick up.
hold on.
chirp is my friend.
swing.
rose and juniper are also my friends.
land.
i care about the king and queen, as well.
leap.
snakes
i'm trying to help everyone the best way i can.
by getting to the truth.
same as you.
THINK, ROSE!
THINK!!
DEFENSE.
WE'RE WAITING.
one, uh, ONE MOMENT PLEASE...

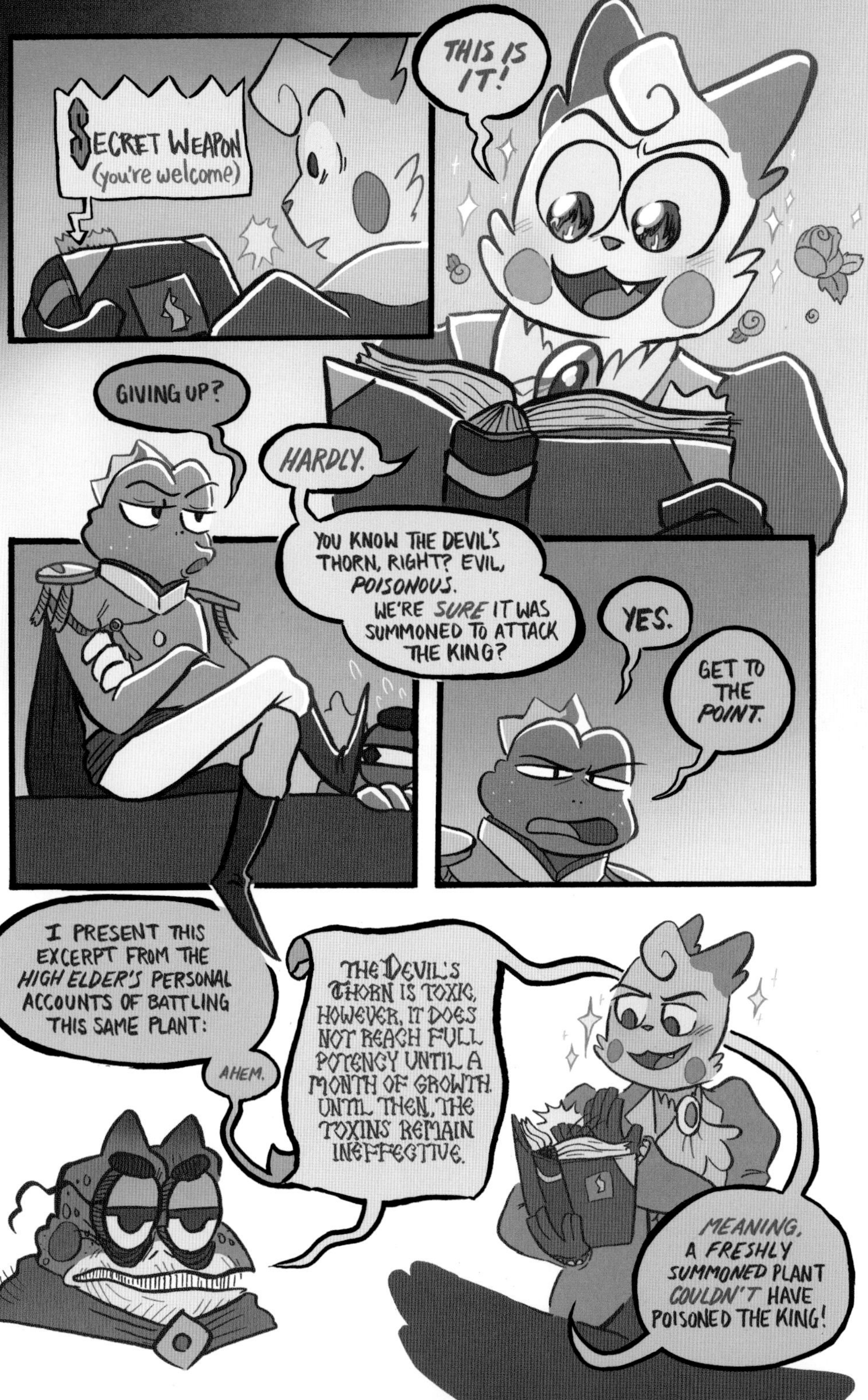
SECRET WEAPON (you're welcome)
THIS IS IT!
GIVING UP?
HARDLY.
YOU KNOW THE DEVIL'S THORN, RIGHT? EVIL, POISONOUS. WE'RE SURE IT WAS SUMMONED TO ATTACK THE KING?
YES.
GET TO THE POINT.
I PRESENT THIS EXCERPT FROM THE HIGH ELDER'S PERSONAL ACCOUNTS OF BATTLING THIS SAME PLANT:
AHEM.
THE DEVIL'S THORN IS TOXIC. HOWEVER, IT DOES NOT REACH FULL POTENCY UNTIL A MONTH OF GROWTH. UNTIL THEN, THE TOXINS REMAIN INEFFECTIVE.
MEANING, A FRESHLY SUMMONED PLANT COULDN'T HAVE POISONED THE KING!

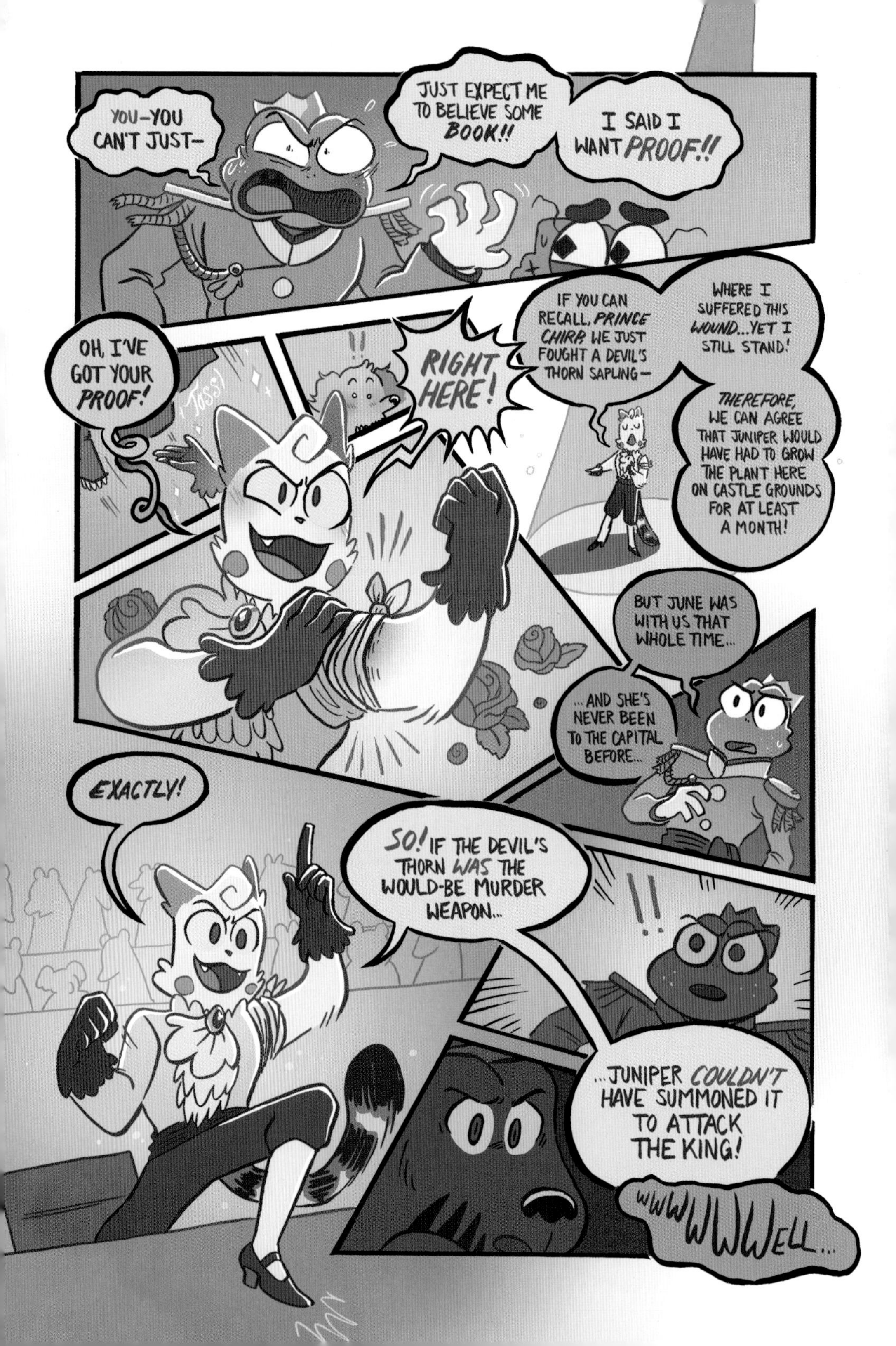
YOU—YOU CAN'T JUST—
JUST EXPECT ME TO BELIEVE SOME BOOK!!
I SAID I WANT PROOF!!
OH, I'VE GOT YOUR PROOF!
TOSS!
!!
RIGHT HERE!
IF YOU CAN RECALL, PRINCE CHIRP, WE JUST FOUGHT A DEVIL'S THORN SAPLING—
WHERE I SUFFERED THIS WOUND... YET I STILL STAND!
THEREFORE, WE CAN AGREE THAT JUNIPER WOULD HAVE HAD TO GROW THE PLANT HERE ON CASTLE GROUNDS FOR AT LEAST A MONTH!
BUT JUNE WAS WITH US THAT WHOLE TIME...
...AND SHE'S NEVER BEEN TO THE CAPITAL BEFORE...
EXACTLY!
SO! IF THE DEVIL'S THORN WAS THE WOULD-BE MURDER WEAPON...
!!
...JUNIPER COULDN'T HAVE SUMMONED IT TO ATTACK THE KING!
WWWWWWELL...

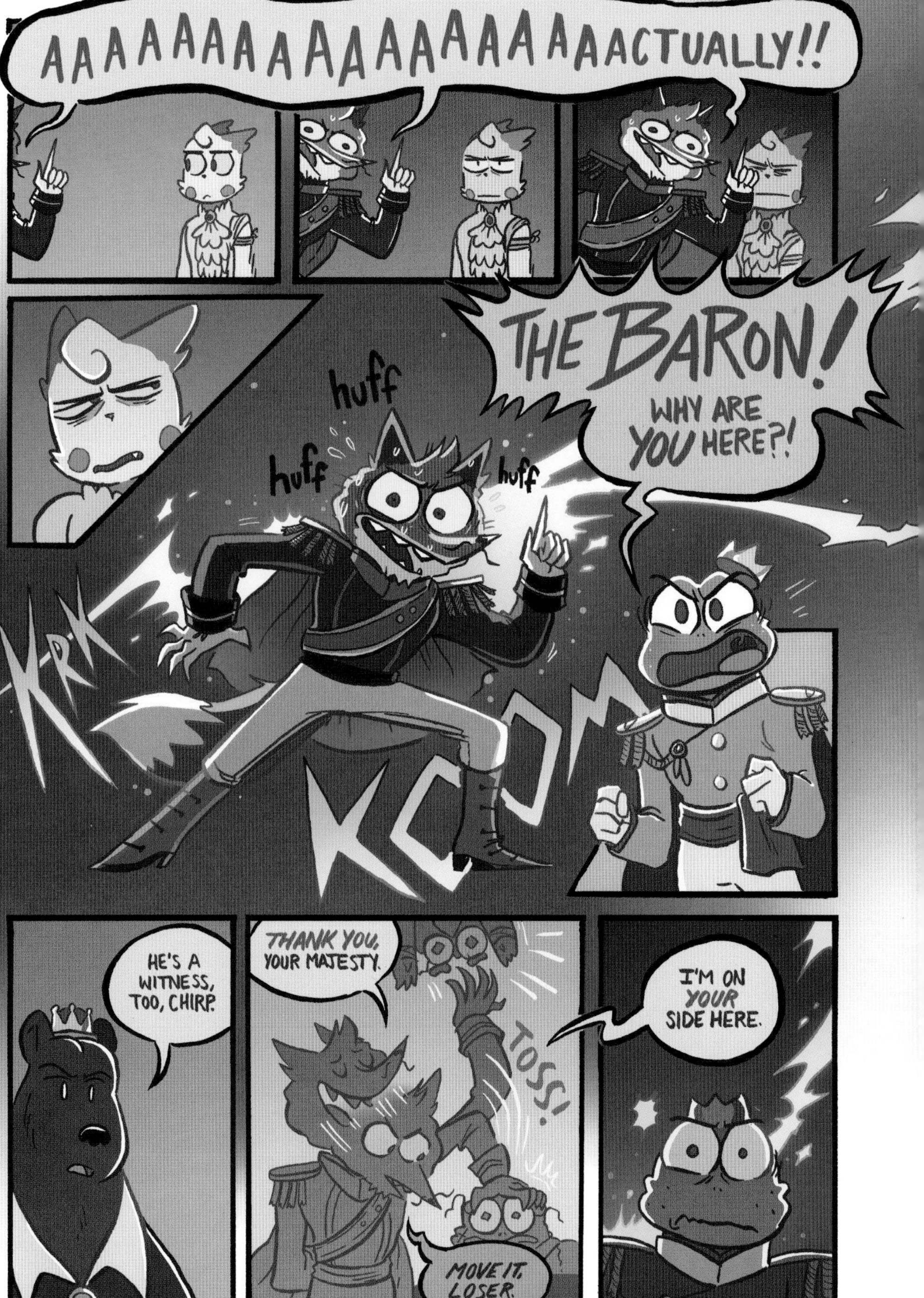
AAAAAAAAAAAAAAAACTUALLY!!
THE BARON!
WHY ARE YOU HERE?!
huff
huff
huff
KRK
KCOOM
HE'S A WITNESS, TOO, CHIRP.
THANK YOU, YOUR MAJESTY.
TOSS!
MOVE IT, LOSER.
I'M ON YOUR SIDE HERE.

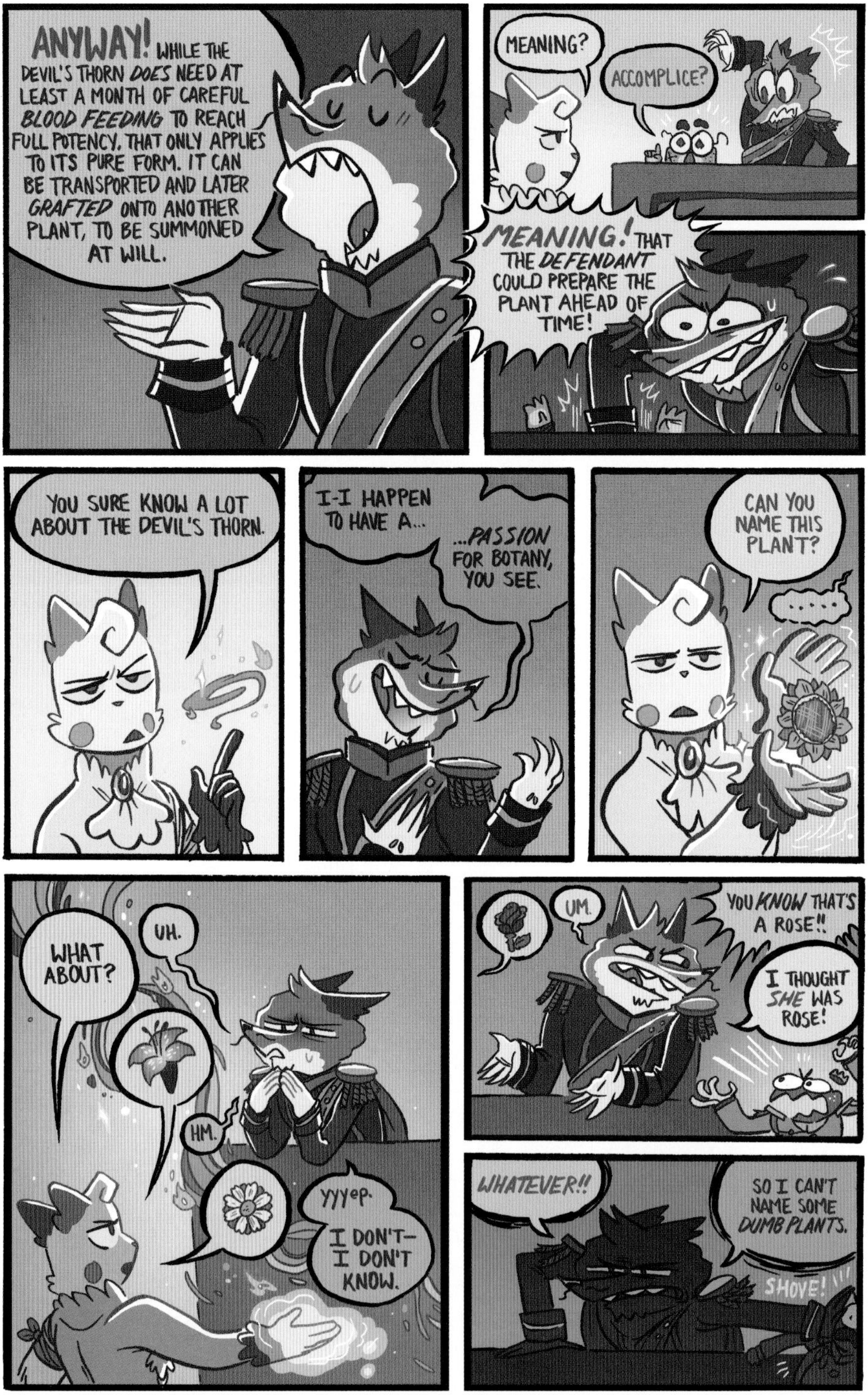
ANYWAY! WHILE THE DEVIL'S THORN DOES NEED AT LEAST A MONTH OF CAREFUL BLOOD FEEDING TO REACH FULL POTENCY, THAT ONLY APPLIES TO ITS PURE FORM. IT CAN BE TRANSPORTED AND LATER GRAFTED ONTO ANOTHER PLANT, TO BE SUMMONED AT WILL.
MEANING?
ACCOMPLICE?
MEANING! THAT THE DEFENDANT COULD PREPARE THE PLANT AHEAD OF TIME!
YOU SURE KNOW A LOT ABOUT THE DEVIL'S THORN.
I-I HAPPEN TO HAVE A...
...PASSION FOR BOTANY, YOU SEE.
CAN YOU NAME THIS PLANT?
.....
WHAT ABOUT?
UH.
HM.
yyyep.
I DON'T- I DON'T KNOW.
UM.
YOU KNOW THAT'S A ROSE!!
I THOUGHT SHE WAS ROSE!
WHATEVER!!
SO I CAN'T NAME SOME DUMB PLANTS.
SHOVE!

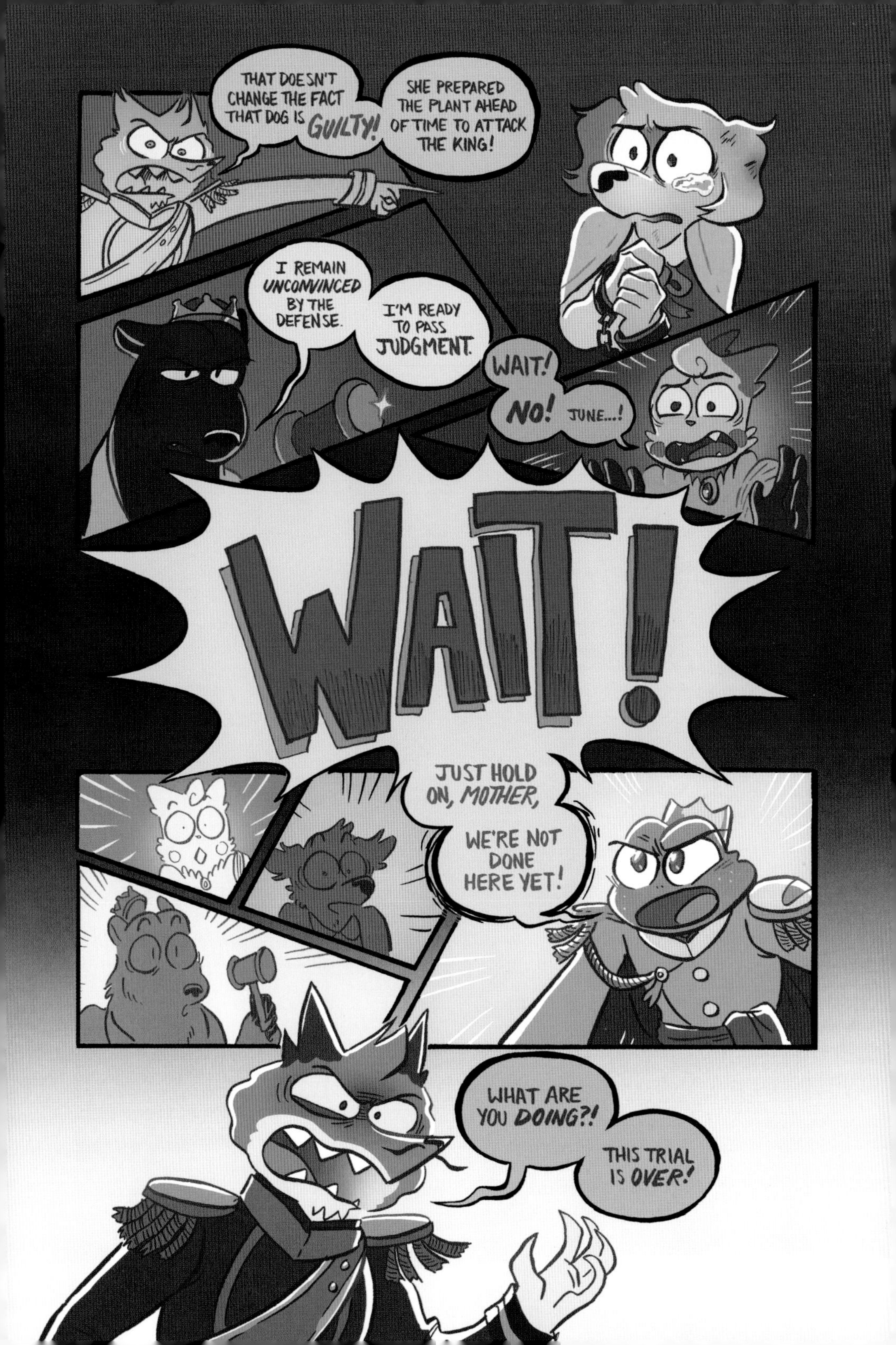
THAT DOESN'T CHANGE THE FACT THAT DOG IS GUILTY!
SHE PREPARED THE PLANT AHEAD OF TIME TO ATTACK THE KING!
I REMAIN UNCONVINCED BY THE DEFENSE.
I'M READY TO PASS JUDGMENT.
WAIT!
NO!
JUNE...!
WAIT!
JUST HOLD ON, MOTHER,
WE'RE NOT DONE HERE YET!
WHAT ARE YOU DOING?!
THIS TRIAL IS OVER!

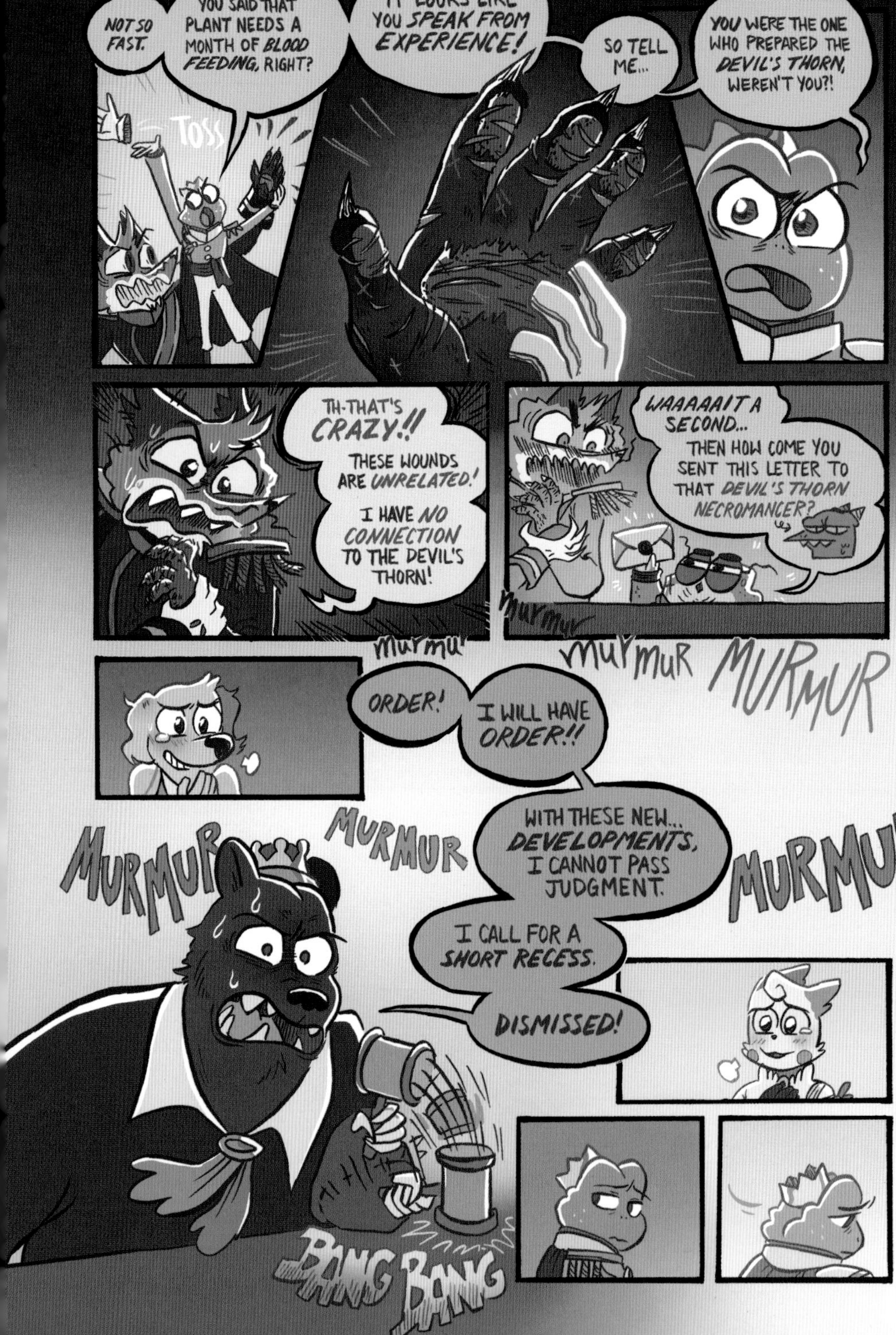
NOT SO FAST.
YOU SAID THAT PLANT NEEDS A MONTH OF BLOOD FEEDING, RIGHT?
TOSS
IT LOOKS LIKE YOU SPEAK FROM EXPERIENCE!
SO TELL ME...
YOU WERE THE ONE WHO PREPARED THE DEVIL'S THORN, WEREN'T YOU?!
TH-THAT'S CRAZY!!
THESE WOUNDS ARE UNRELATED!
I HAVE NO CONNECTION TO THE DEVIL'S THORN!
WAAAAAIT A SECOND...
THEN HOW COME YOU SENT THIS LETTER TO THAT DEVIL'S THORN NECROMANCER?
MURMUR
MURMUR
MURMUR
MURMUR
ORDER!
I WILL HAVE ORDER!!
MURMUR
MURMUR
WITH THESE NEW... DEVELOPMENTS, I CANNOT PASS JUDGMENT.
MURMUR
I CALL FOR A SHORT RECESS.
DISMISSED!
BANG BANG

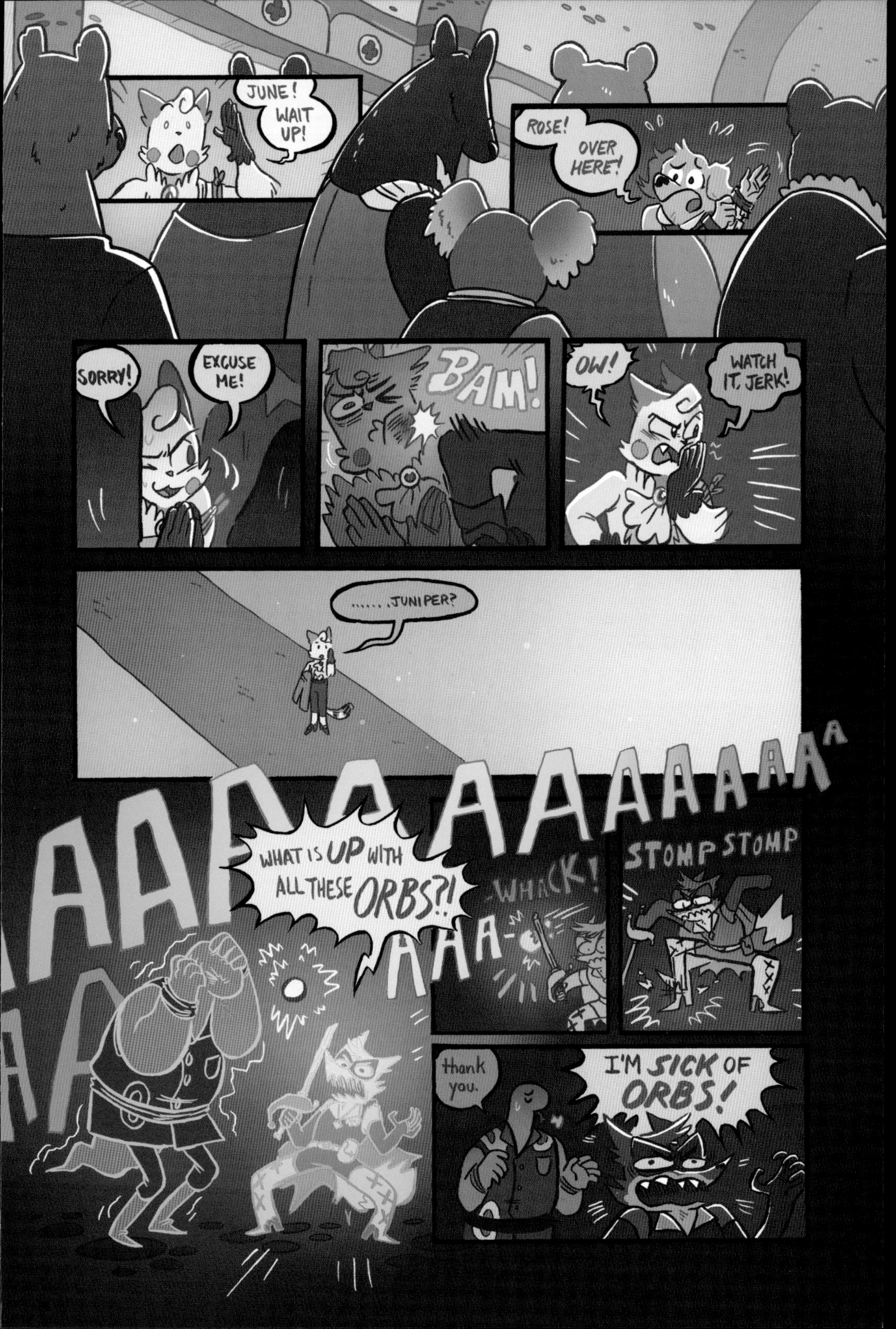
JUNE! WAIT UP!
ROSE! OVER HERE!
SORRY!
EXCUSE ME!
BAM!
OW!
WATCH IT, JERK!
.......JUNIPER?
AAAAAAAAAAAAAAA
WHAT IS UP WITH ALL THESE ORBS?!
WHACK!
AAA-
STOMP STOMP
thank you.
I'M SICK OF ORBS!

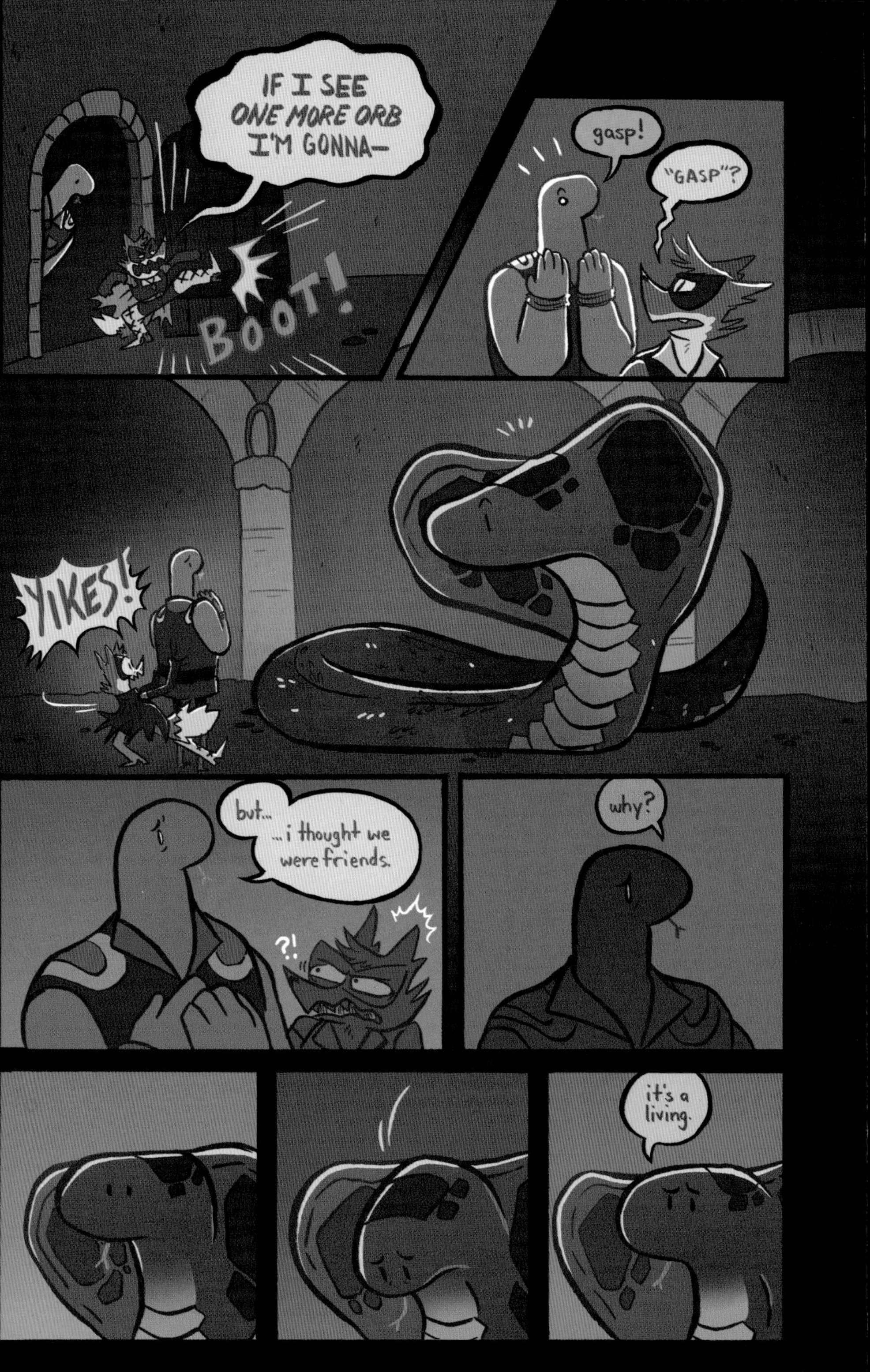

IF I SEE ONE MORE ORB I'M GONNA—
BOOT!
gasp!
"GASP"?
YIKES!
but... ...i thought we were friends.
?!
why?
it's a living.

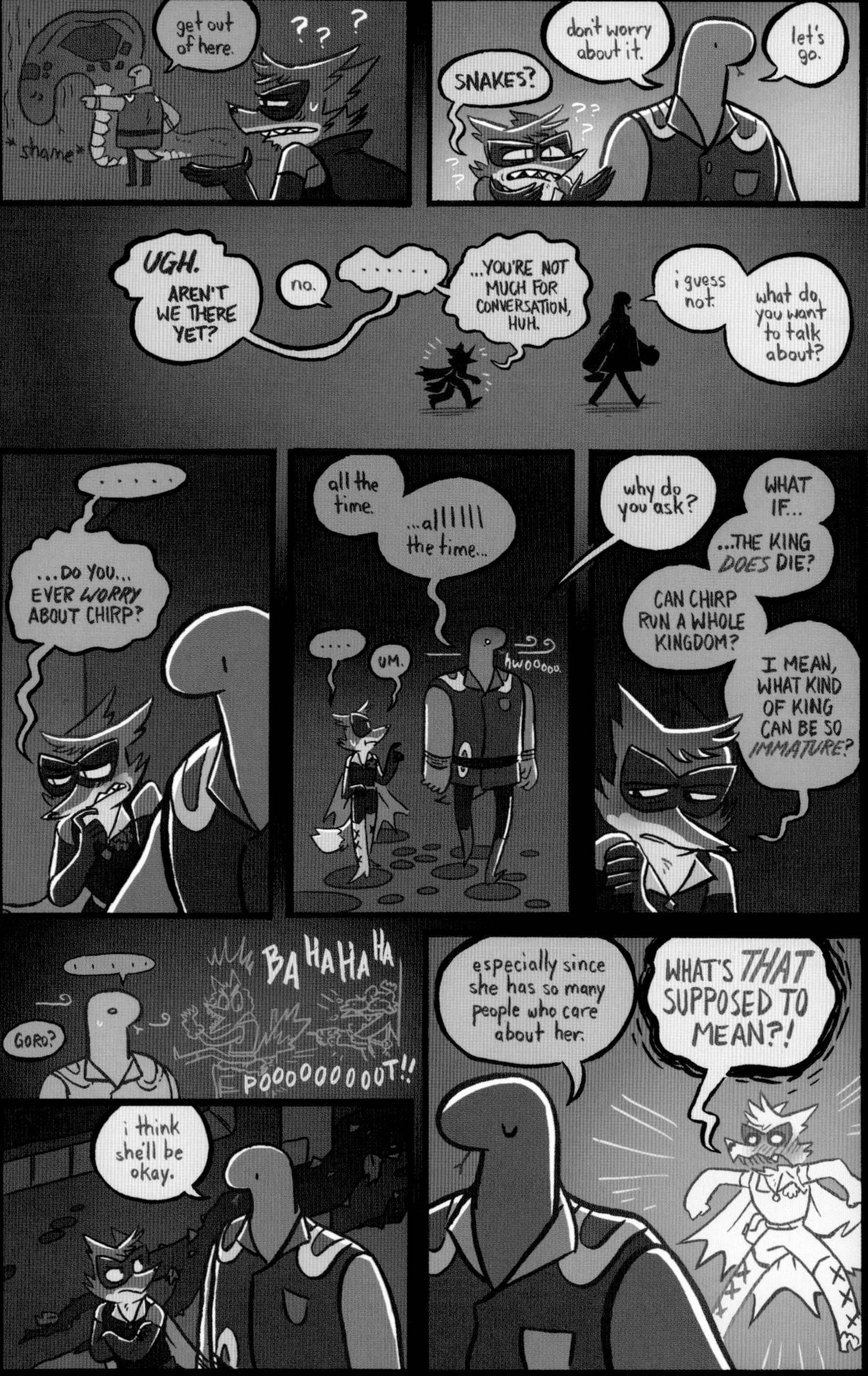
get out of here.
shame
? ? ?
SNAKES?
don't worry about it.
let's go.
UGH. AREN'T WE THERE YET?
no.
......
...YOU'RE NOT MUCH FOR CONVERSATION, HUH.
i guess not.
what do you want to talk about?
.....
...DO YOU... EVER WORRY ABOUT CHIRP?
all the time.
...allllll the time...
....
UM.
hwooooo.
why do you ask?
WHAT IF...
...THE KING DOES DIE?
CAN CHIRP RUN A WHOLE KINGDOM?
I MEAN, WHAT KIND OF KING CAN BE SO IMMATURE?
.....
GORO?
BAHAHAHA
POOOOOOOOOUT!!
i think she'll be okay.
especially since she has so many people who care about her.
WHAT'S THAT SUPPOSED TO MEAN?!

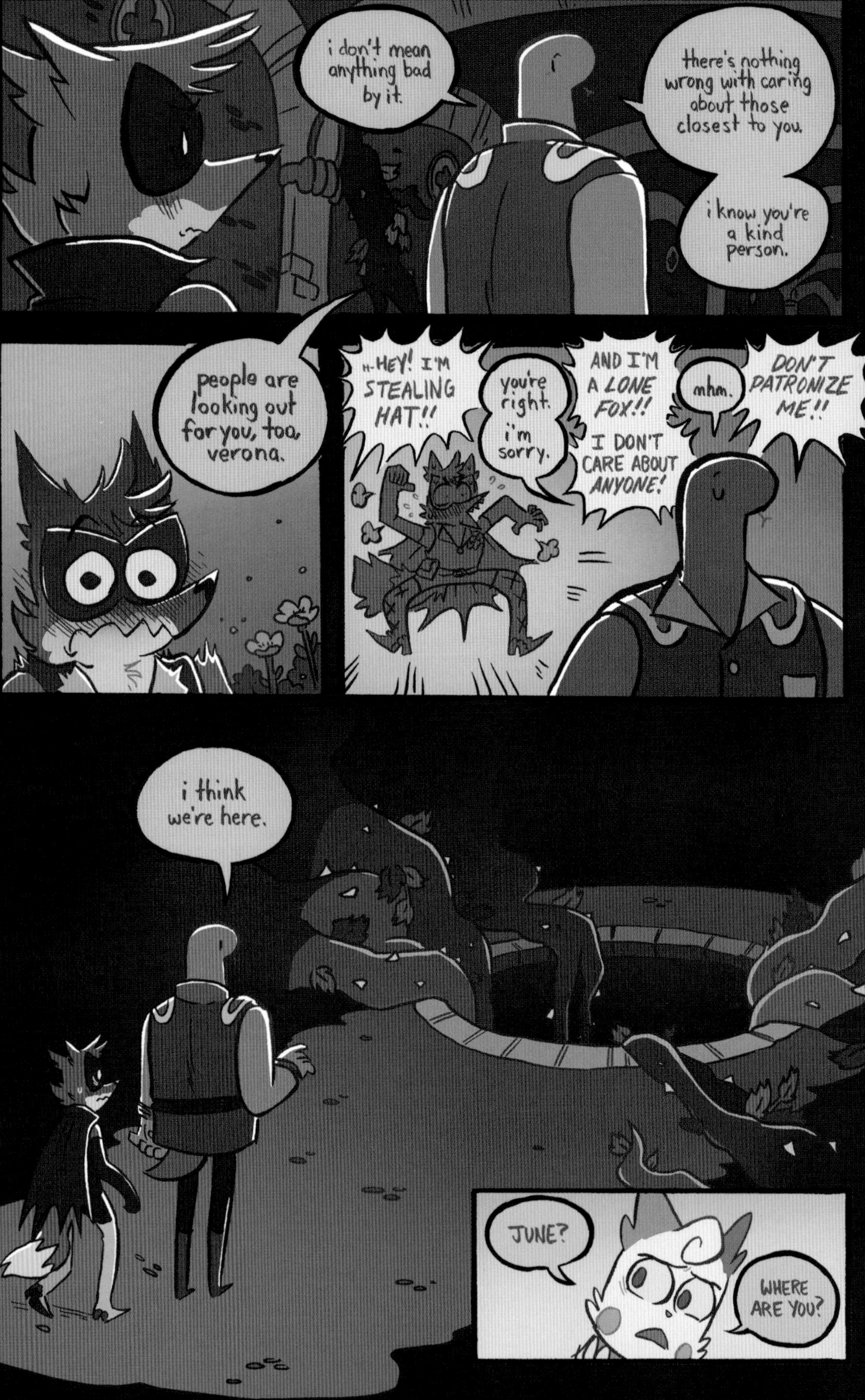

i don't mean anything bad by it.
there's nothing wrong with caring about those closest to you.
i know you're a kind person.
people are looking out for you, too, verona.
H-HEY! I'M STEALING HAT!!
you're right.
i'm sorry.
AND I'M A LONE FOX!!
I DON'T CARE ABOUT ANYONE!
mhm.
DON'T PATRONIZE ME!!
i think we're here.
JUNE?
WHERE ARE YOU?

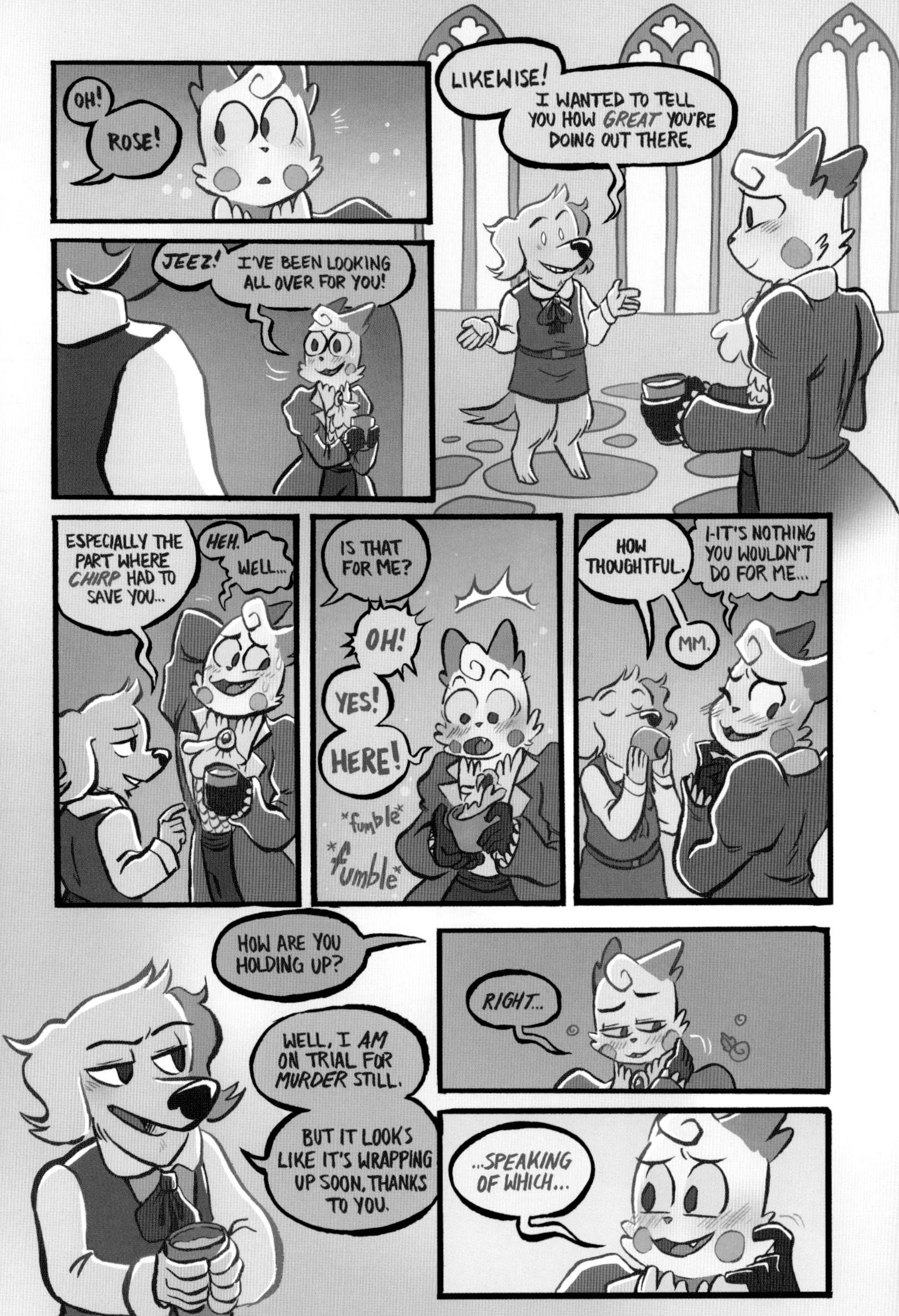
OH!
ROSE!
LIKEWISE!
I WANTED TO TELL YOU HOW GREAT YOU'RE DOING OUT THERE.
JEEZ!
I'VE BEEN LOOKING ALL OVER FOR YOU!
ESPECIALLY THE PART WHERE CHIRP HAD TO SAVE YOU...
HEH.
WELL...
IS THAT FOR ME?
OH!
YES!
HERE!
fumble
fumble
HOW THOUGHTFUL.
MM.
I-IT'S NOTHING YOU WOULDN'T DO FOR ME...
HOW ARE YOU HOLDING UP?
WELL, I AM ON TRIAL FOR MURDER STILL.
BUT IT LOOKS LIKE IT'S WRAPPING UP SOON, THANKS TO YOU.
RIGHT...
...SPEAKING OF WHICH...

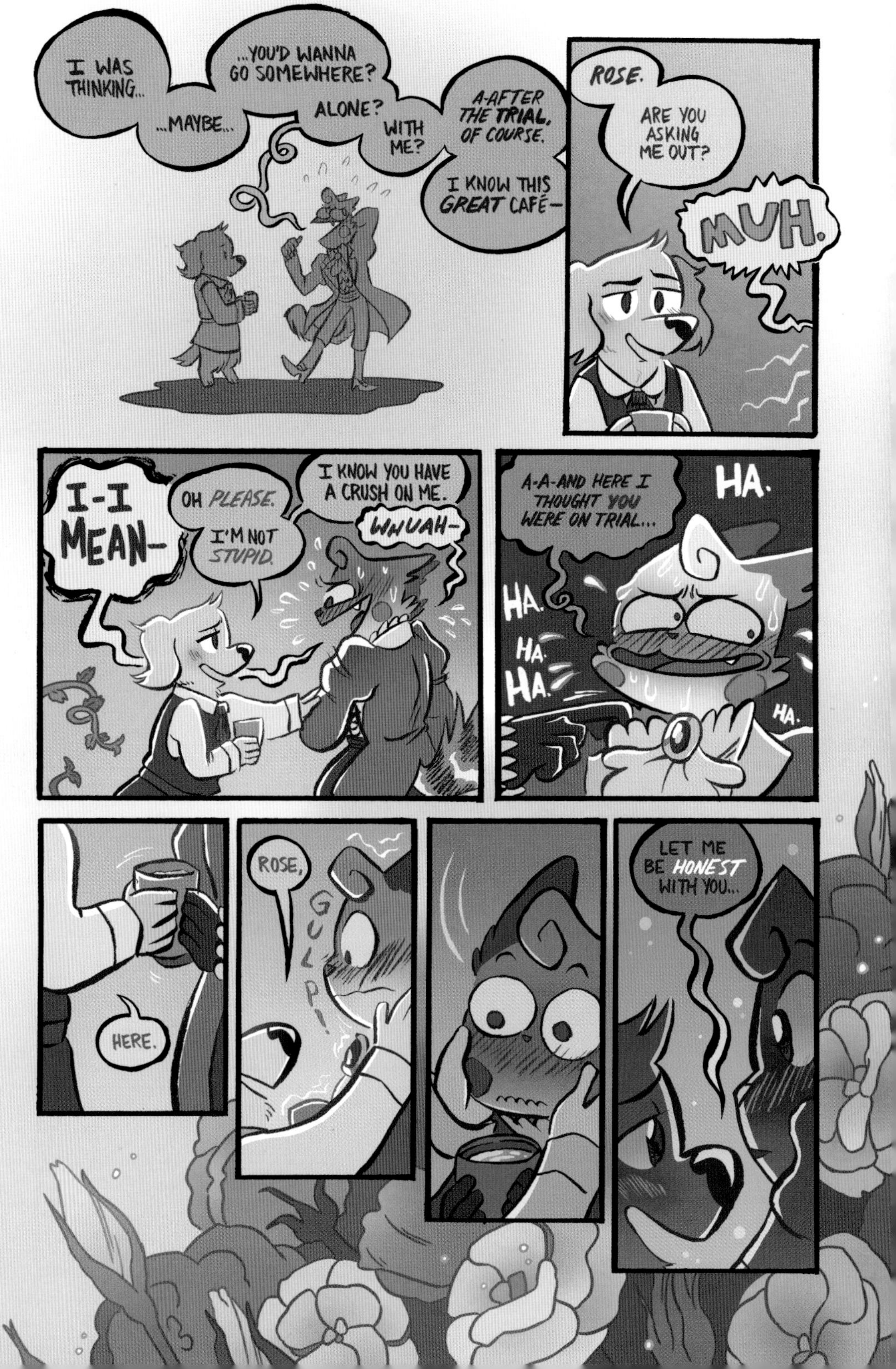
I WAS THINKING...
...MAYBE...
...YOU'D WANNA GO SOMEWHERE?
ALONE?
WITH ME?
A-AFTER THE TRIAL, OF COURSE.
I KNOW THIS GREAT CAFÉ—
ROSE.
ARE YOU ASKING ME OUT?
MUH.
I-I MEAN—
OH PLEASE.
I'M NOT STUPID.
I KNOW YOU HAVE A CRUSH ON ME.
WHUAH—
A-A-AND HERE I THOUGHT YOU WERE ON TRIAL...
HA.
HA.
HA.
HA.
HA.
HERE.
ROSE,
GULP!
LET ME BE HONEST WITH YOU...

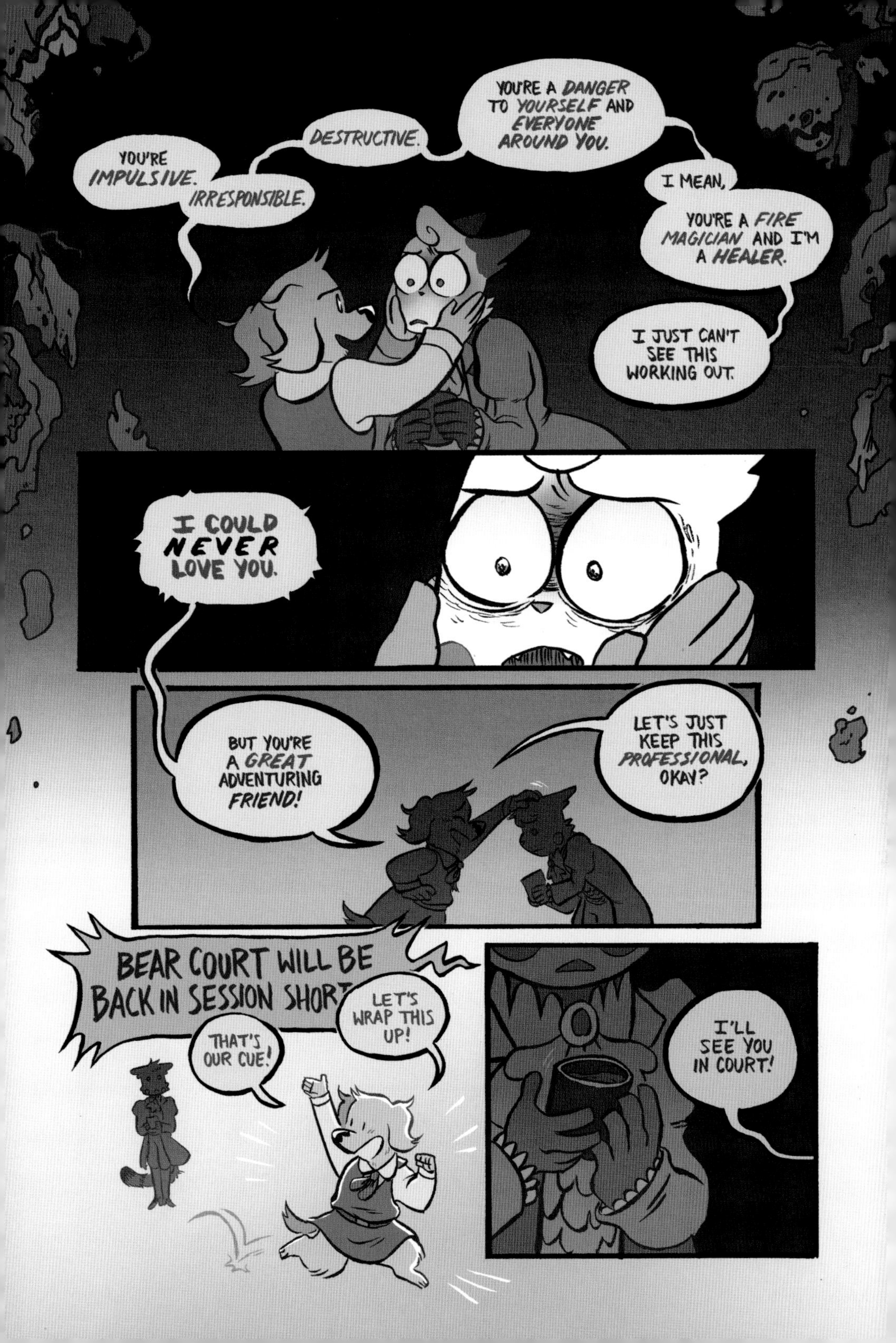
YOU'RE IMPULSIVE.
IRRESPONSIBLE.
DESTRUCTIVE.
YOU'RE A DANGER TO YOURSELF AND EVERYONE AROUND YOU.
I MEAN,
YOU'RE A FIRE MAGICIAN AND I'M A HEALER.
I JUST CAN'T SEE THIS WORKING OUT.
I COULD NEVER LOVE YOU.
BUT YOU'RE A GREAT ADVENTURING FRIEND!
LET'S JUST KEEP THIS PROFESSIONAL, OKAY?
BEAR COURT WILL BE BACK IN SESSION SHORT
THAT'S OUR CUE!
LET'S WRAP THIS UP!
I'LL SEE YOU IN COURT!

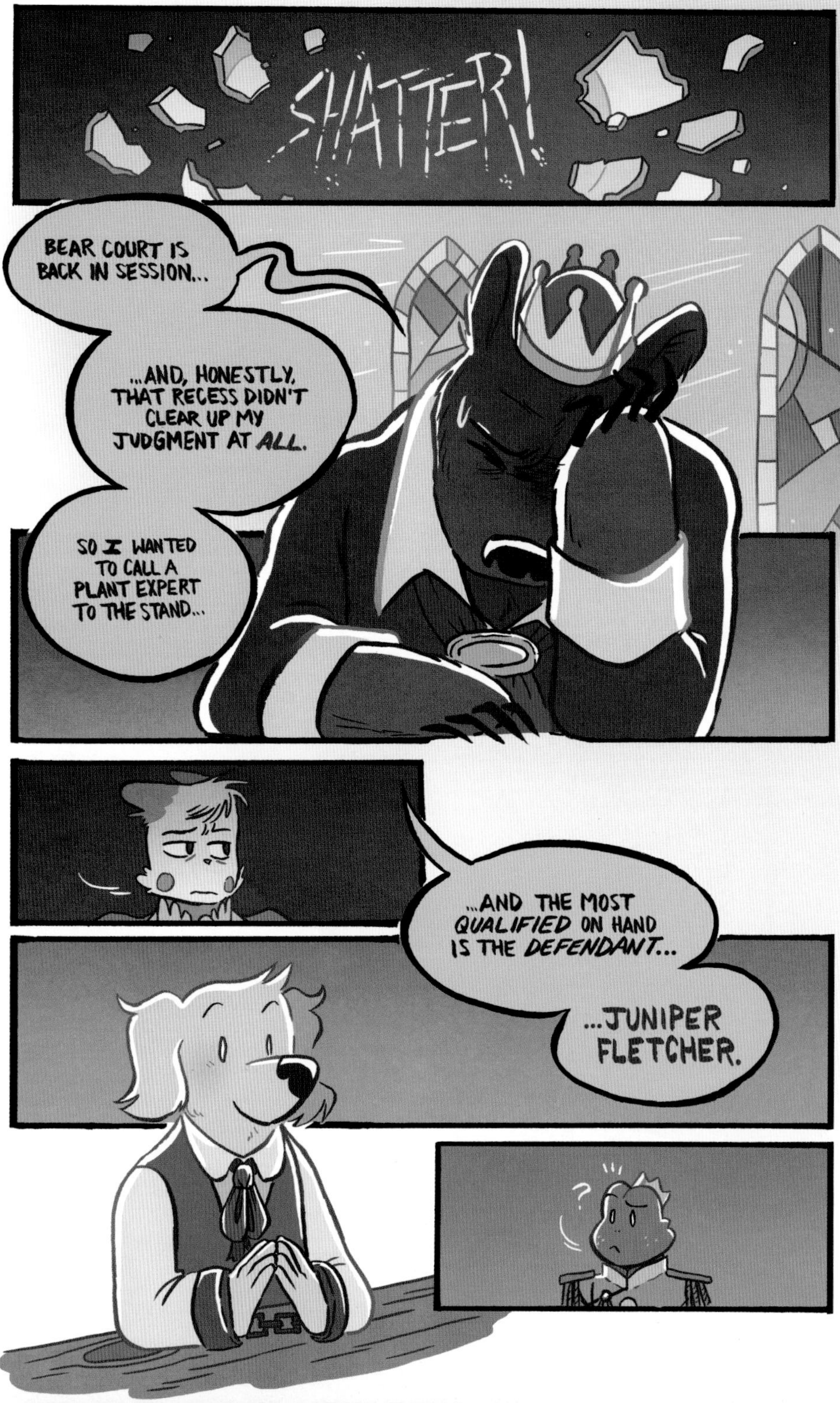
SHATTER!
BEAR COURT IS BACK IN SESSION...
...AND, HONESTLY, THAT RECESS DIDN'T CLEAR UP MY JUDGMENT AT ALL.
SO I WANTED TO CALL A PLANT EXPERT TO THE STAND...
...AND THE MOST QUALIFIED ON HAND IS THE DEFENDANT...
...JUNIPER FLETCHER.
?

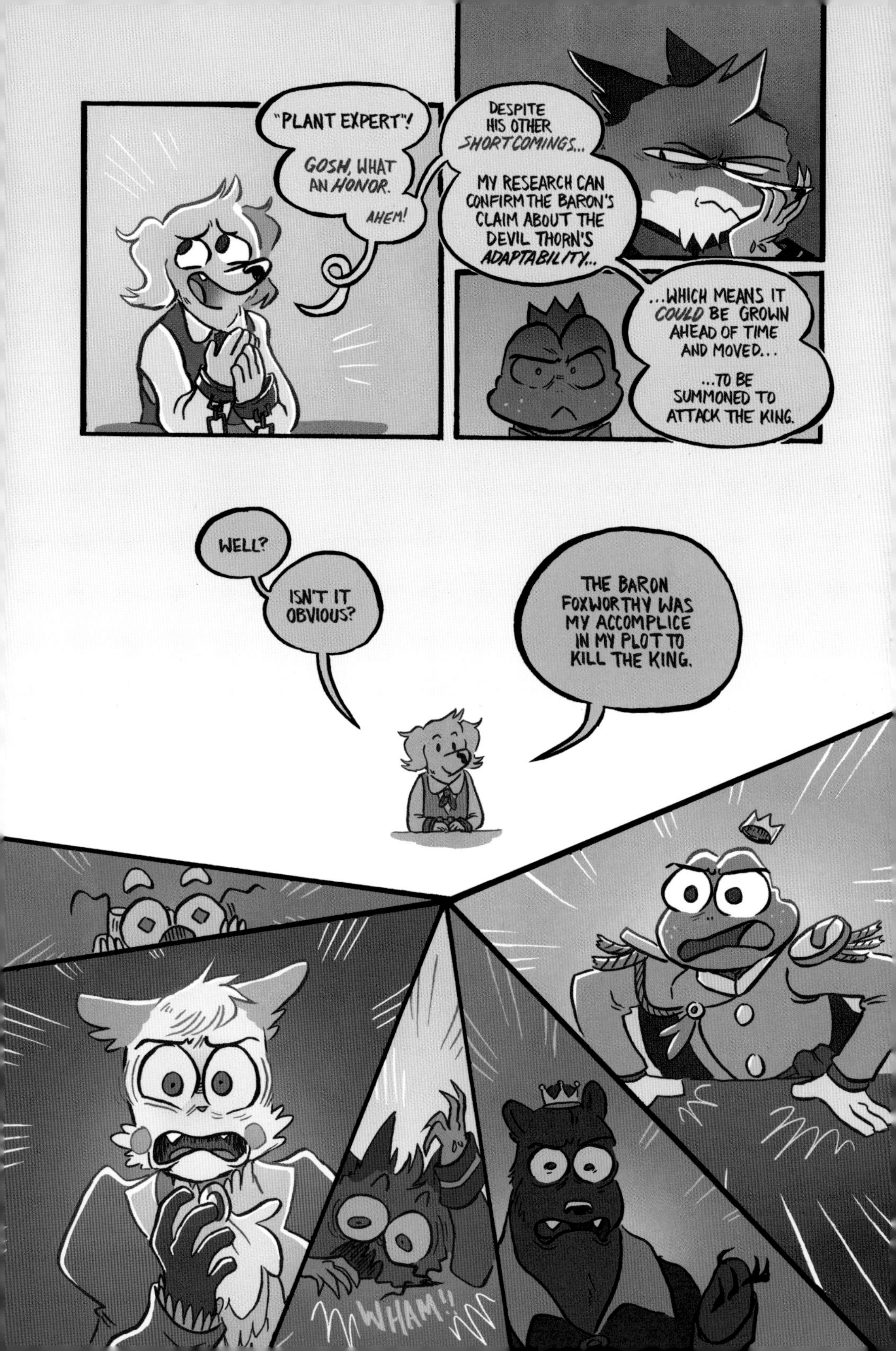
"PLANT EXPERT"!
GOSH, WHAT AN HONOR.
AHEM!
DESPITE HIS OTHER SHORTCOMINGS...
MY RESEARCH CAN CONFIRM THE BARON'S CLAIM ABOUT THE DEVIL THORN'S ADAPTABILITY...
...WHICH MEANS IT COULD BE GROWN AHEAD OF TIME AND MOVED...
...TO BE SUMMONED TO ATTACK THE KING.
WELL?
ISN'T IT OBVIOUS?
THE BARON FOXWORTHY WAS MY ACCOMPLICE IN MY PLOT TO KILL THE KING.
WHAM!!

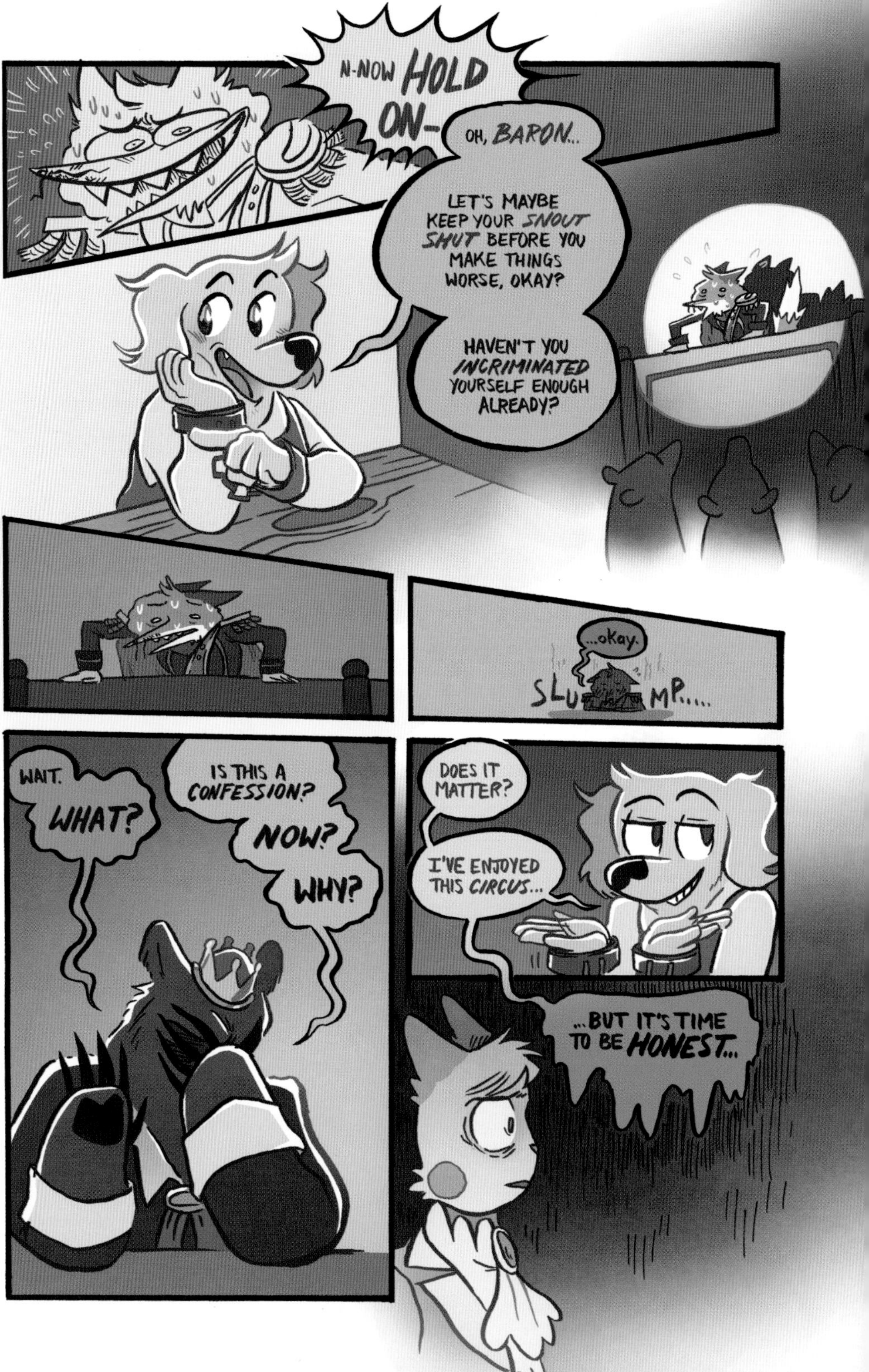
N-NOW HOLD ON-
OH, BARON...
LET'S MAYBE KEEP YOUR SNOUT SHUT BEFORE YOU MAKE THINGS WORSE, OKAY?
HAVEN'T YOU INCRIMINATED YOURSELF ENOUGH ALREADY?
...okay.
SLUMP.....
WAIT.
WHAT?
IS THIS A CONFESSION?
NOW?
WHY?
DOES IT MATTER?
I'VE ENJOYED THIS CIRCUS...
...BUT IT'S TIME TO BE HONEST...

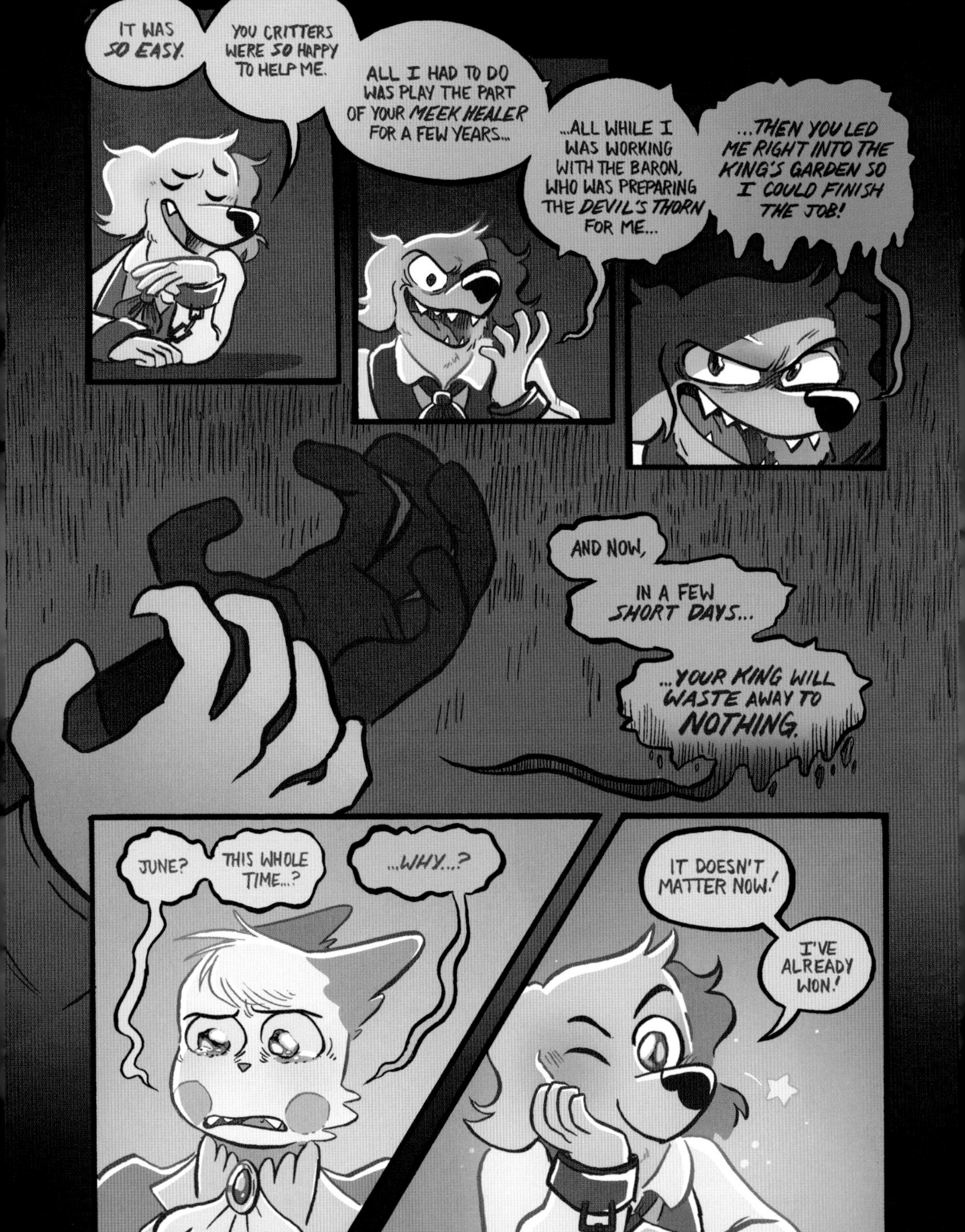
IT WAS SO EASY.
YOU CRITTERS WERE SO HAPPY TO HELP ME.
ALL I HAD TO DO WAS PLAY THE PART OF YOUR MEEK HEALER FOR A FEW YEARS...
...ALL WHILE I WAS WORKING WITH THE BARON, WHO WAS PREPARING THE DEVIL'S THORN FOR ME...
...THEN YOU LED ME RIGHT INTO THE KING'S GARDEN SO I COULD FINISH THE JOB!
AND NOW,
IN A FEW SHORT DAYS...
...YOUR KING WILL WASTE AWAY TO NOTHING.
JUNE?
THIS WHOLE TIME...?
...WHY...?
IT DOESN'T MATTER NOW!
I'VE ALREADY WON!

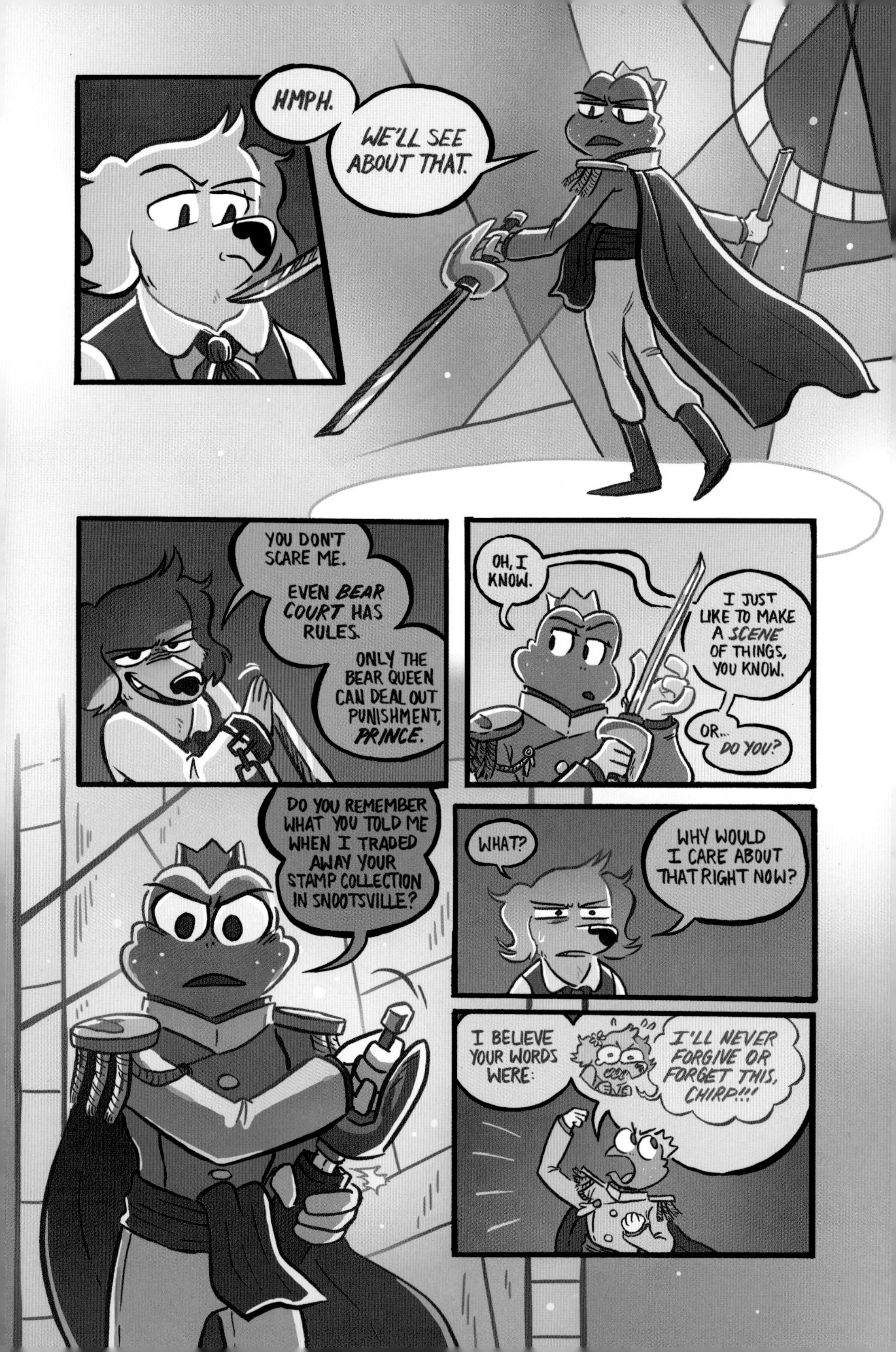

HMPH.
WE'LL SEE ABOUT THAT.
YOU DON'T SCARE ME.
EVEN *BEAR COURT* HAS RULES.
ONLY THE BEAR QUEEN CAN DEAL OUT PUNISHMENT, *PRINCE*.
OH, I KNOW.
I JUST LIKE TO MAKE A *SCENE* OF THINGS, YOU KNOW.
OR... *DO YOU?*
DO YOU REMEMBER WHAT YOU TOLD ME WHEN I TRADED AWAY YOUR STAMP COLLECTION IN SNOOTSVILLE?
WHAT?
WHY WOULD I CARE ABOUT THAT RIGHT NOW?
I BELIEVE YOUR WORDS WERE:
I'LL NEVER FORGIVE OR FORGET THIS, CHIRP!!!

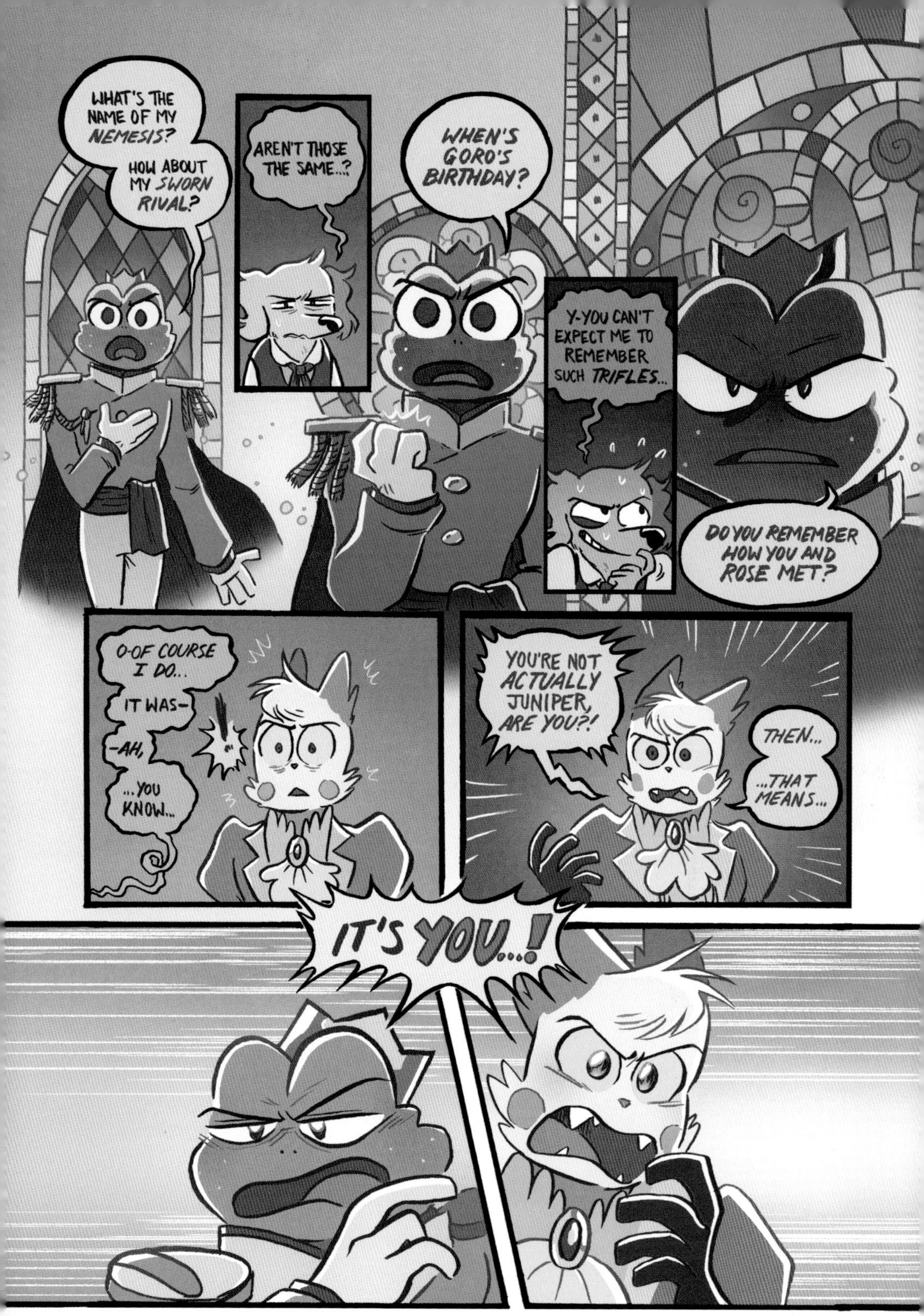
WHAT'S THE NAME OF MY NEMESIS?
HOW ABOUT MY SWORN RIVAL?
AREN'T THOSE THE SAME...?
WHEN'S GORO'S BIRTHDAY?
Y-YOU CAN'T EXPECT ME TO REMEMBER SUCH TRIFLES...
DO YOU REMEMBER HOW YOU AND ROSE MET?
O-OF COURSE I DO...
IT WAS-
-AH,
...YOU KNOW...
YOU'RE NOT ACTUALLY JUNIPER, ARE YOU?!
THEN...
...THAT MEANS...
IT'S YOU...!

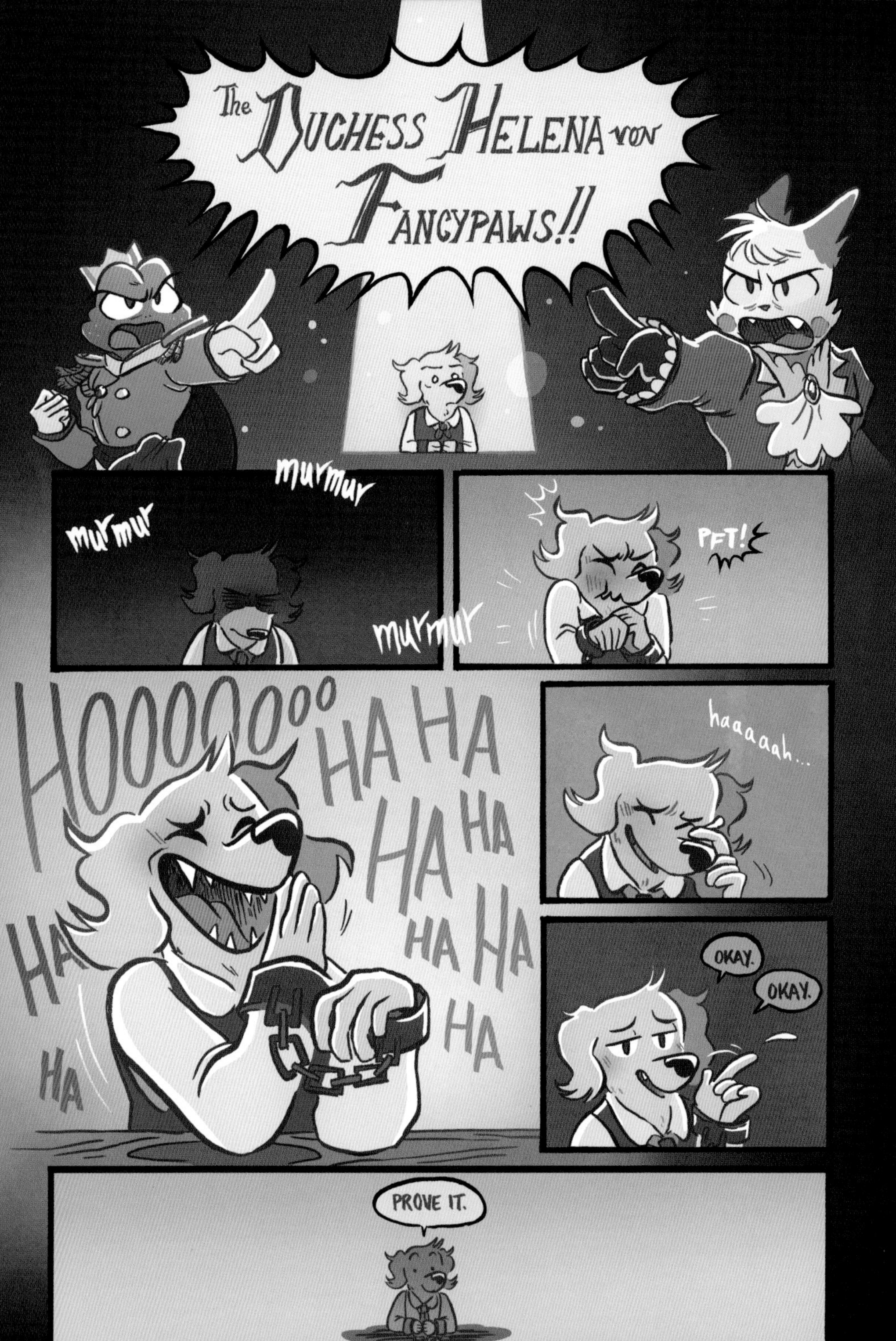
The Duchess Helena von Fancypaws!!
murmur
murmur
murmur
PFT!
HOOOOOoo HA HA HA HA HA HA HA HA HA HA
haaaaaah...
OKAY.
OKAY.
PROVE IT.

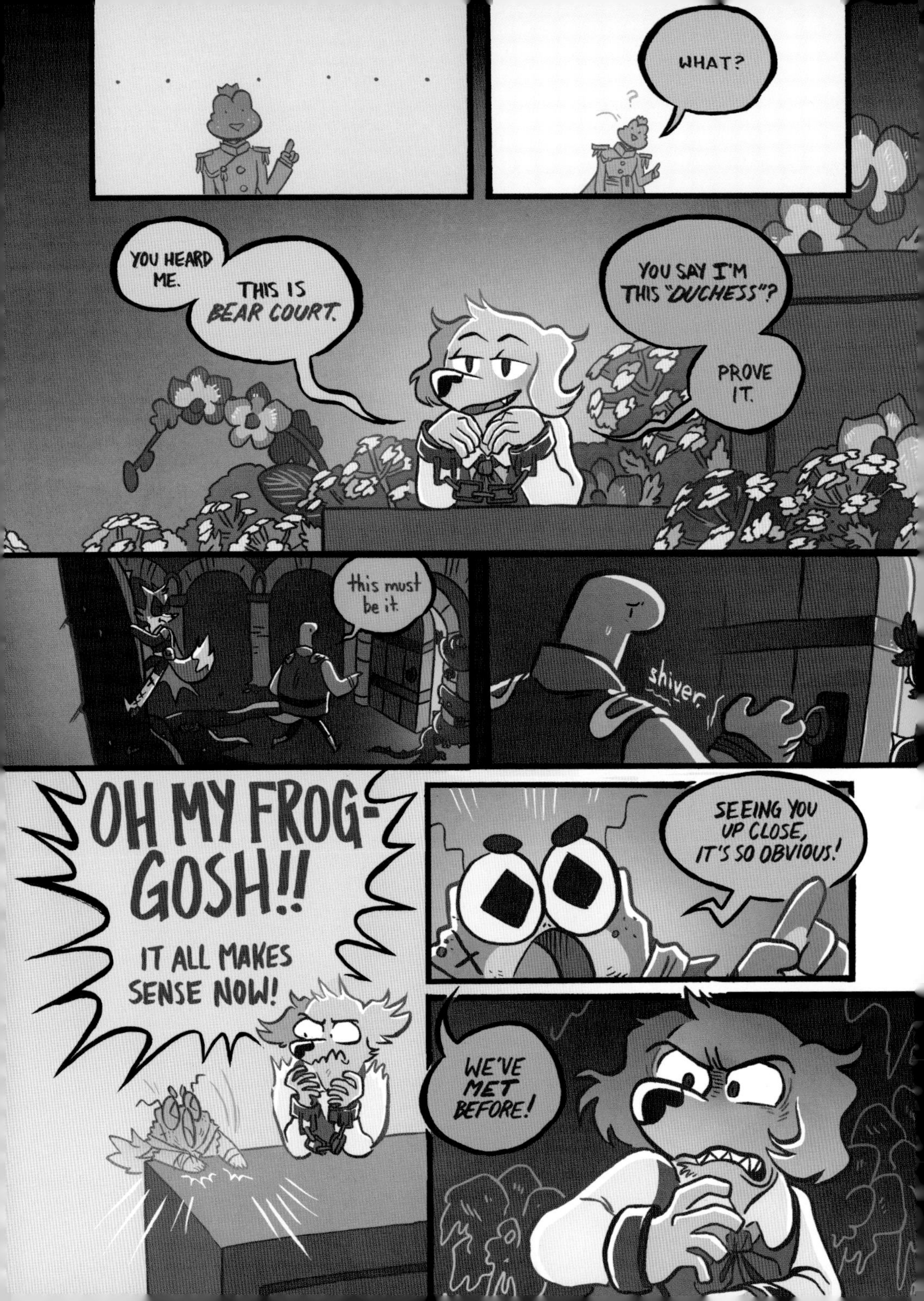
. . . .
WHAT?
YOU HEARD ME.
THIS IS BEAR COURT.
YOU SAY I'M THIS "DUCHESS"?
PROVE IT.
this must be it.
shiver
OH MY FROG-GOSH!!
IT ALL MAKES SENSE NOW!
SEEING YOU UP CLOSE, IT'S SO OBVIOUS!
WE'VE MET BEFORE!

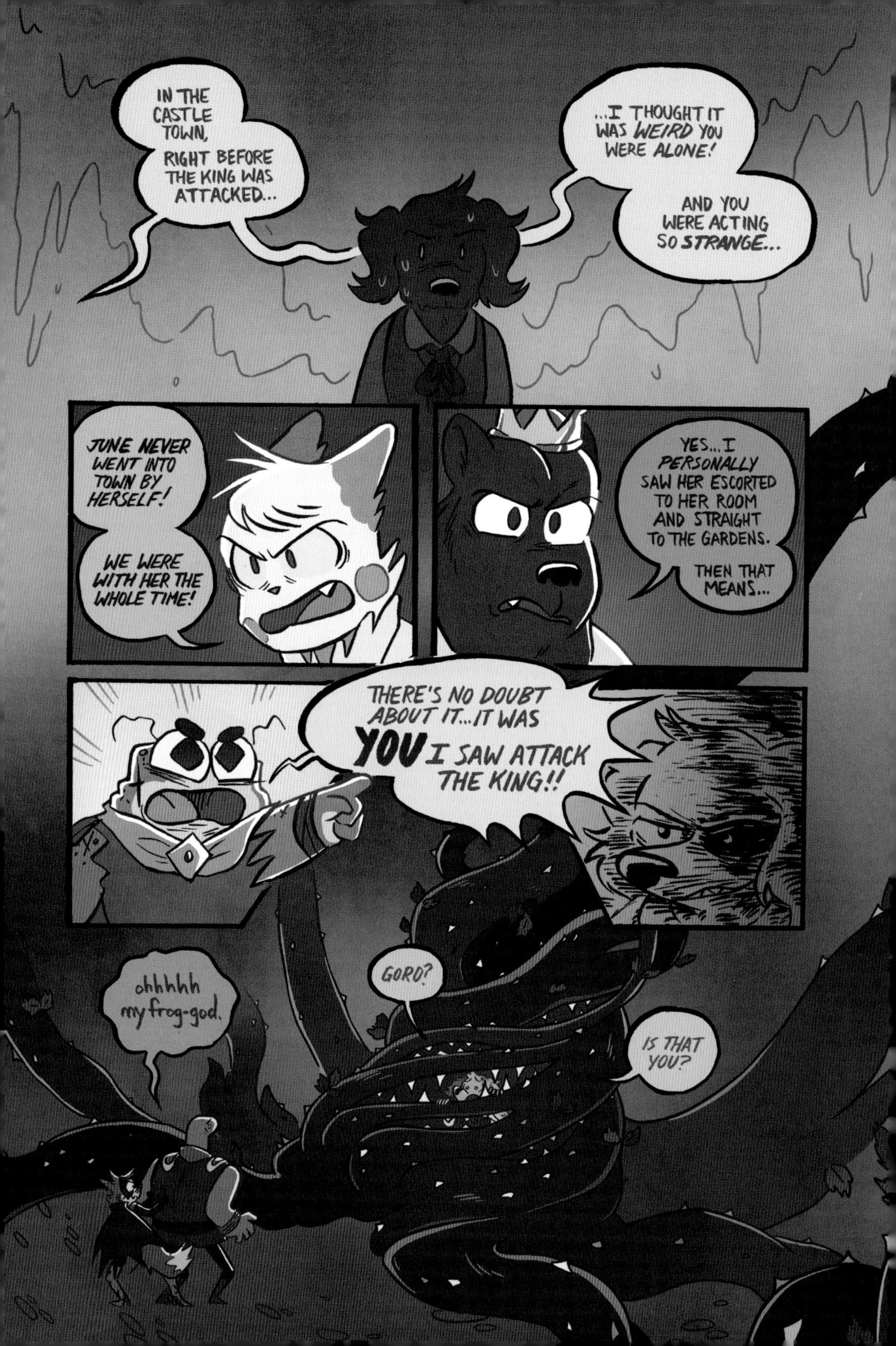
IN THE CASTLE TOWN, RIGHT BEFORE THE KING WAS ATTACKED...
...I THOUGHT IT WAS WEIRD YOU WERE ALONE! AND YOU WERE ACTING SO STRANGE...
JUNE NEVER WENT INTO TOWN BY HERSELF! WE WERE WITH HER THE WHOLE TIME!
YES...I PERSONALLY SAW HER ESCORTED TO HER ROOM AND STRAIGHT TO THE GARDENS. THEN THAT MEANS...
THERE'S NO DOUBT ABOUT IT...IT WAS YOU I SAW ATTACK THE KING!!
ohhhhh my frog-god.
GORO?
IS THAT YOU?

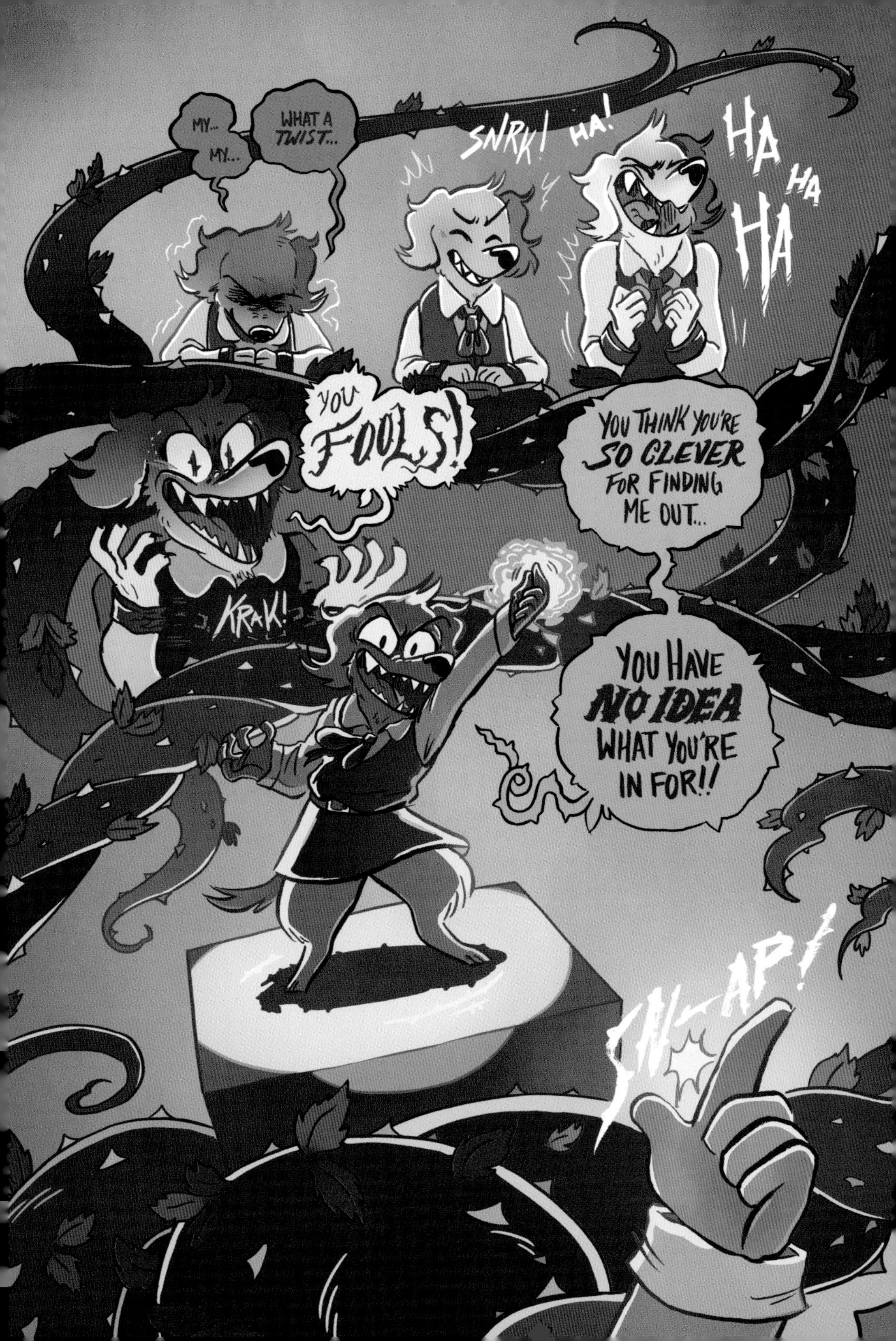
MY... MY...
WHAT A TWIST...
SNRK! HA!
HA HA HA
YOU FOOLS!
YOU THINK YOU'RE SO CLEVER FOR FINDING ME OUT...
KRAK!
YOU HAVE NO IDEA WHAT YOU'RE IN FOR!!
SN-AP!

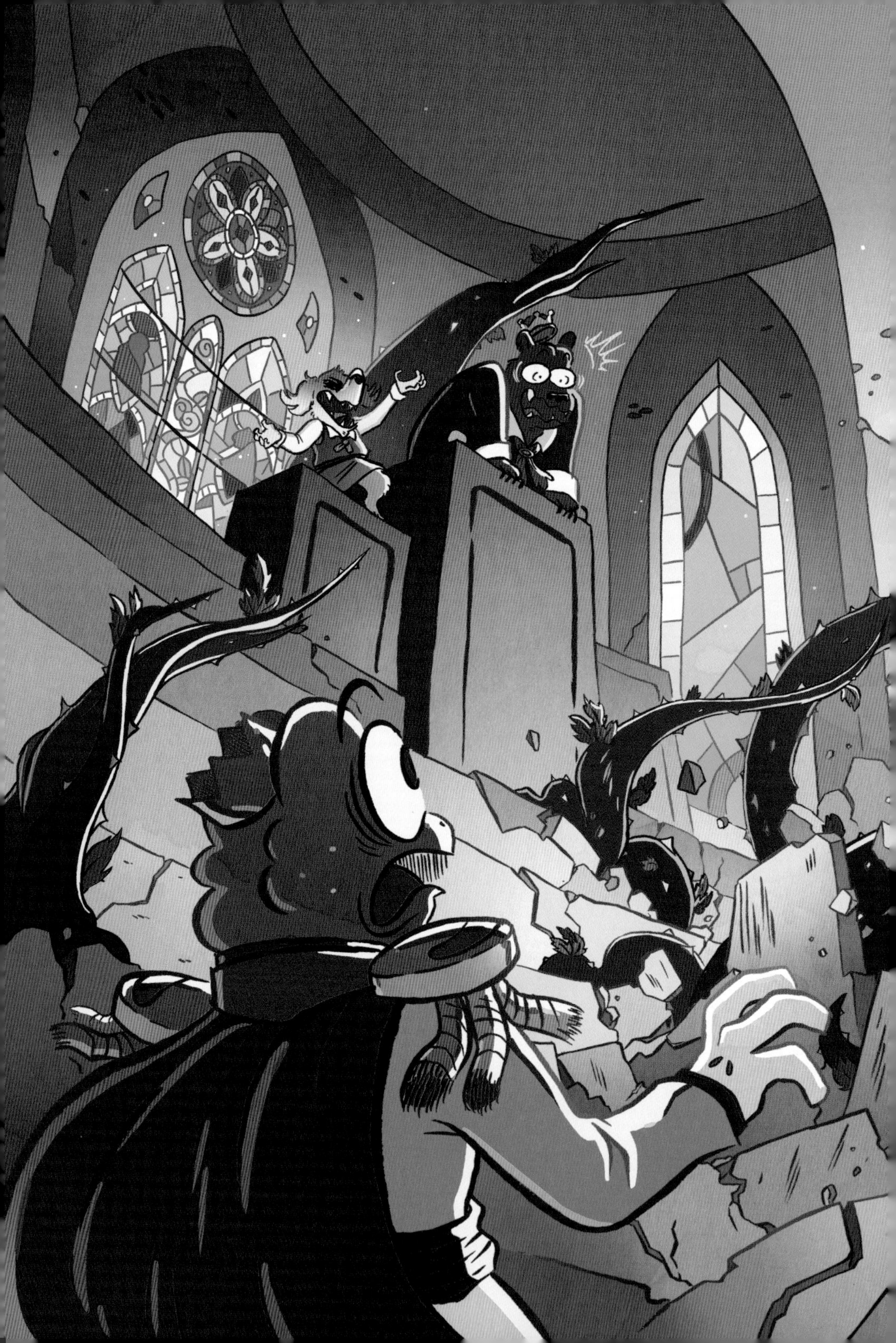

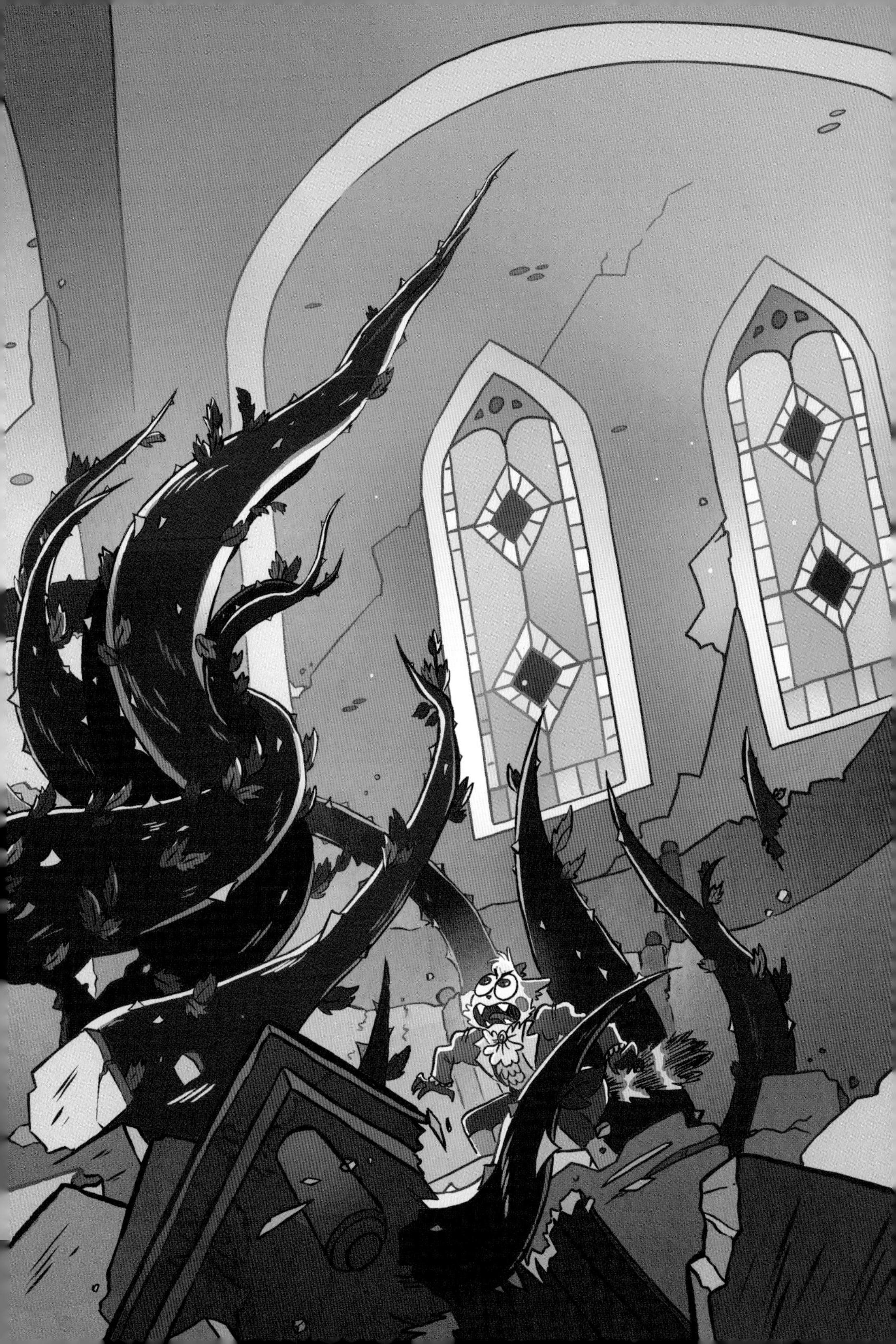

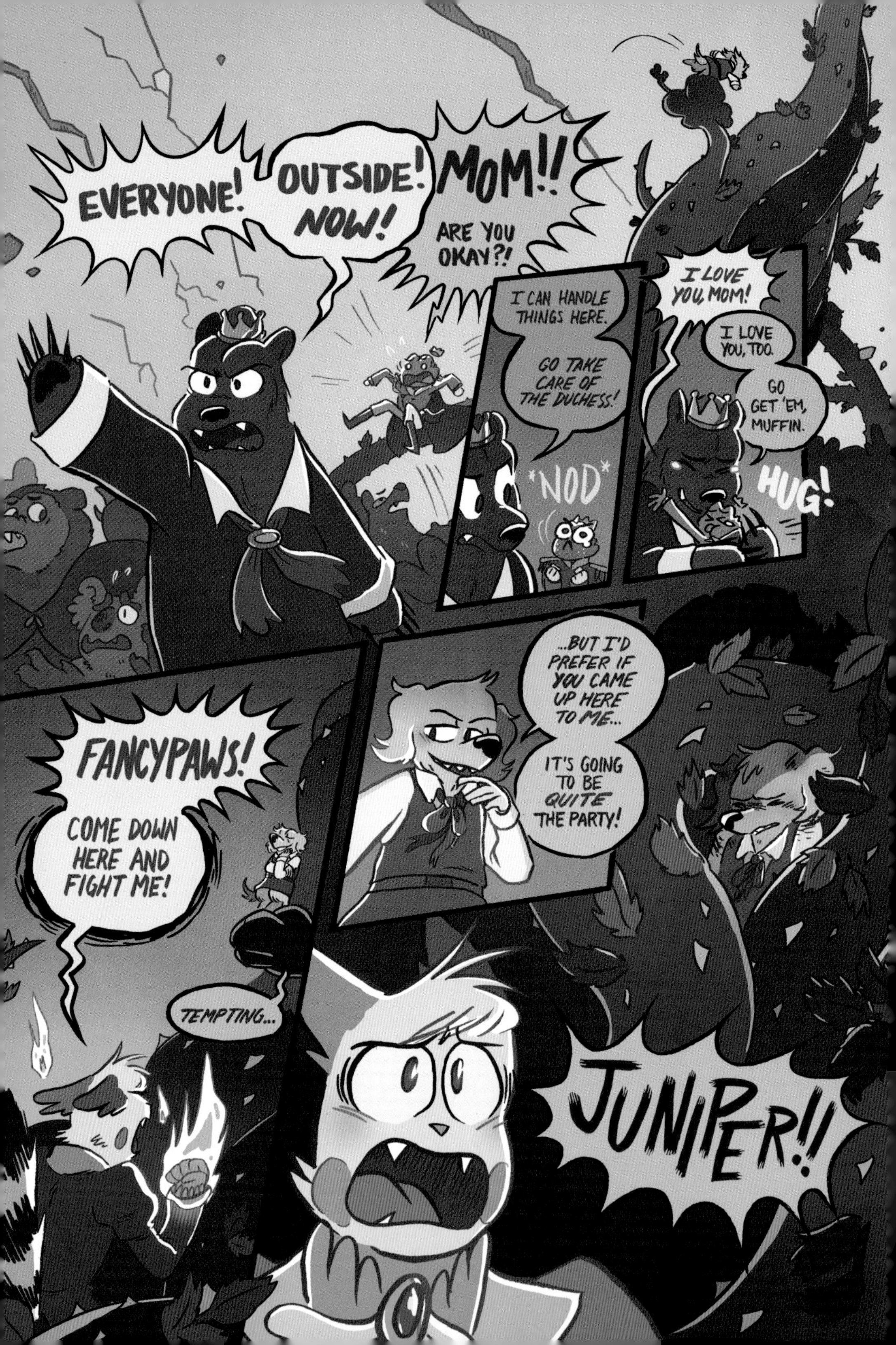
EVERYONE!
OUTSIDE! NOW!
MOM!!
ARE YOU OKAY?!
I CAN HANDLE THINGS HERE.
GO TAKE CARE OF THE DUCHESS!
NOD
I LOVE YOU, MOM!
I LOVE YOU, TOO.
GO GET 'EM, MUFFIN.
HUG!
FANCYPAWS!
COME DOWN HERE AND FIGHT ME!
...BUT I'D PREFER IF YOU CAME UP HERE TO ME...
IT'S GOING TO BE QUITE THE PARTY!
TEMPTING...
JUNIPER!!

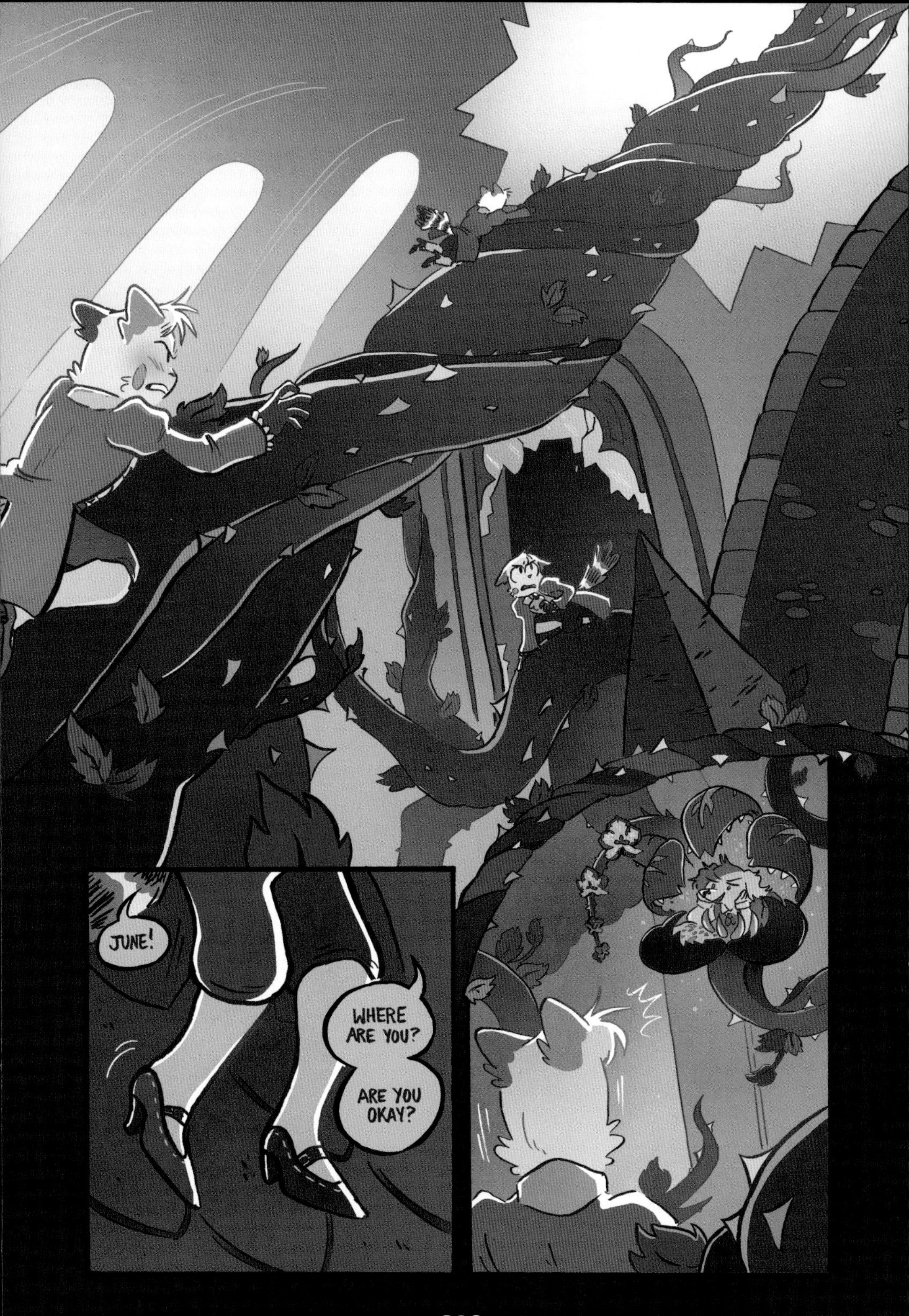
JUNE!
WHERE ARE YOU?
ARE YOU OKAY?

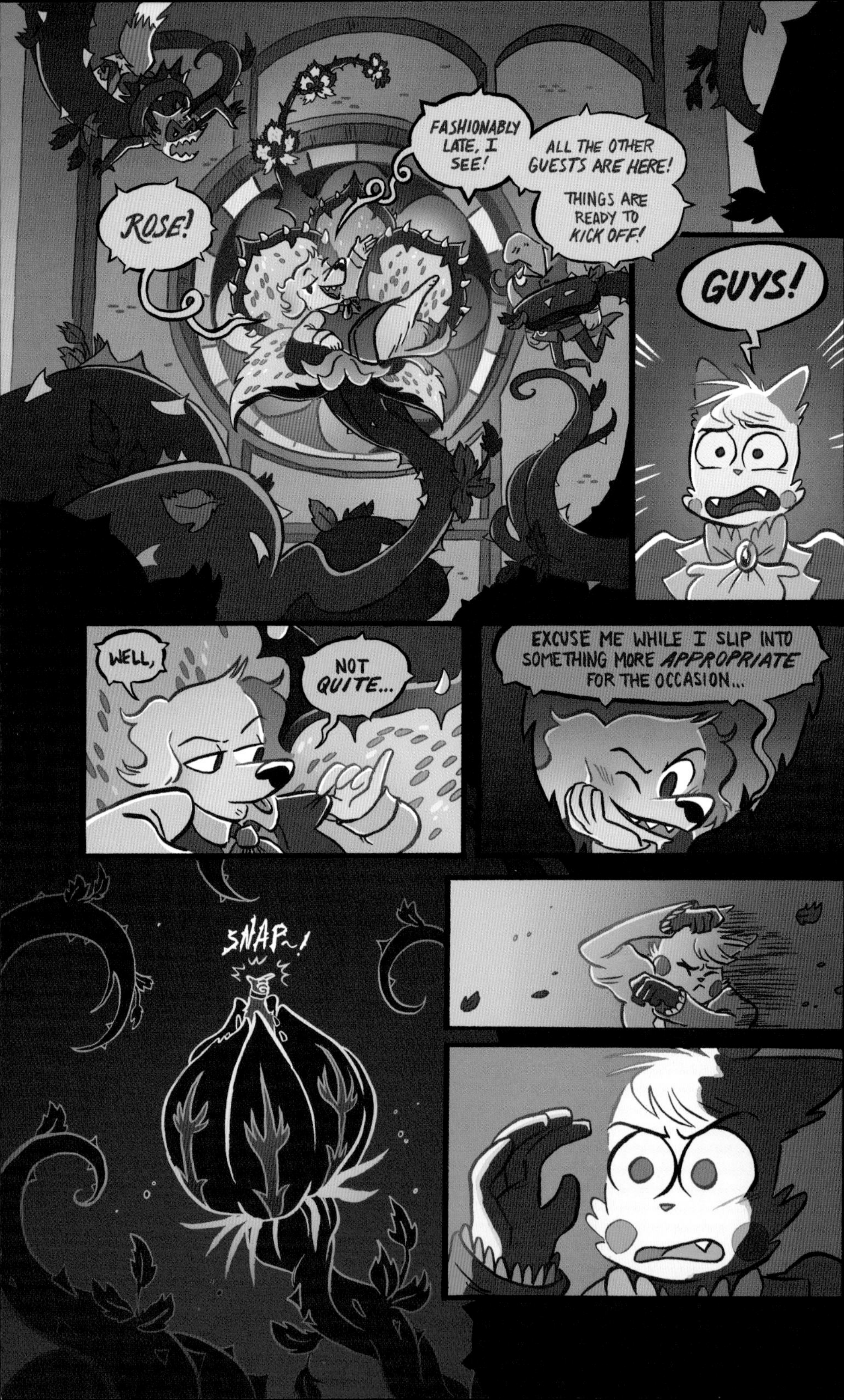
ROSE!
FASHIONABLY LATE, I SEE!
ALL THE OTHER GUESTS ARE HERE!
THINGS ARE READY TO KICK OFF!
GUYS!
WELL,
NOT QUITE...
EXCUSE ME WHILE I SLIP INTO SOMETHING MORE APPROPRIATE FOR THE OCCASION...
SNAP~!

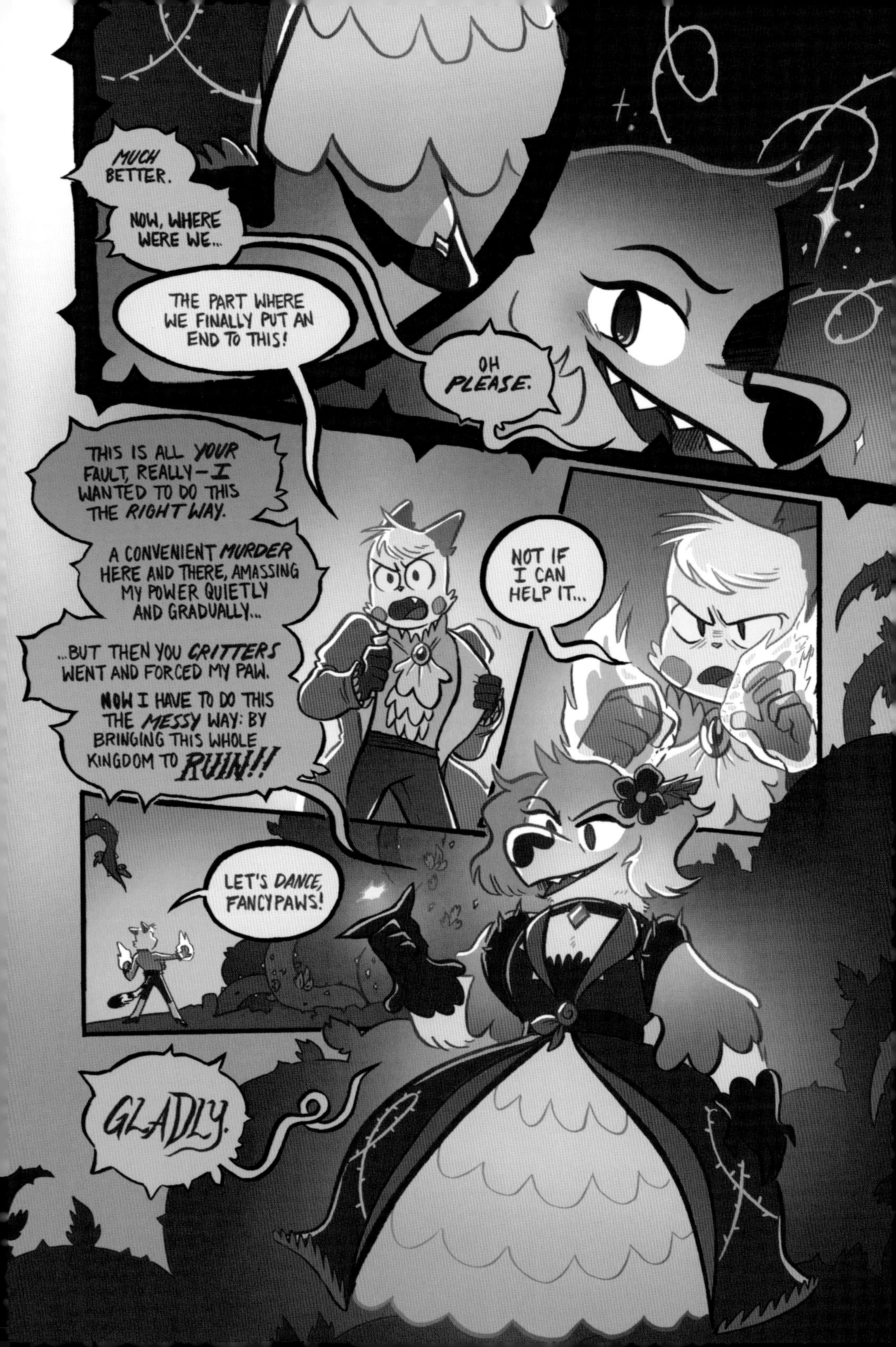
MUCH BETTER.
NOW, WHERE WERE WE...
THE PART WHERE WE FINALLY PUT AN END TO THIS!
OH PLEASE.
THIS IS ALL YOUR FAULT, REALLY—I WANTED TO DO THIS THE RIGHT WAY.
A CONVENIENT MURDER HERE AND THERE, AMASSING MY POWER QUIETLY AND GRADUALLY...
...BUT THEN YOU CRITTERS WENT AND FORCED MY PAW.
NOW I HAVE TO DO THIS THE MESSY WAY: BY BRINGING THIS WHOLE KINGDOM TO RUIN!!
NOT IF I CAN HELP IT...
LET'S DANCE, FANCYPAWS!
GLADLY.

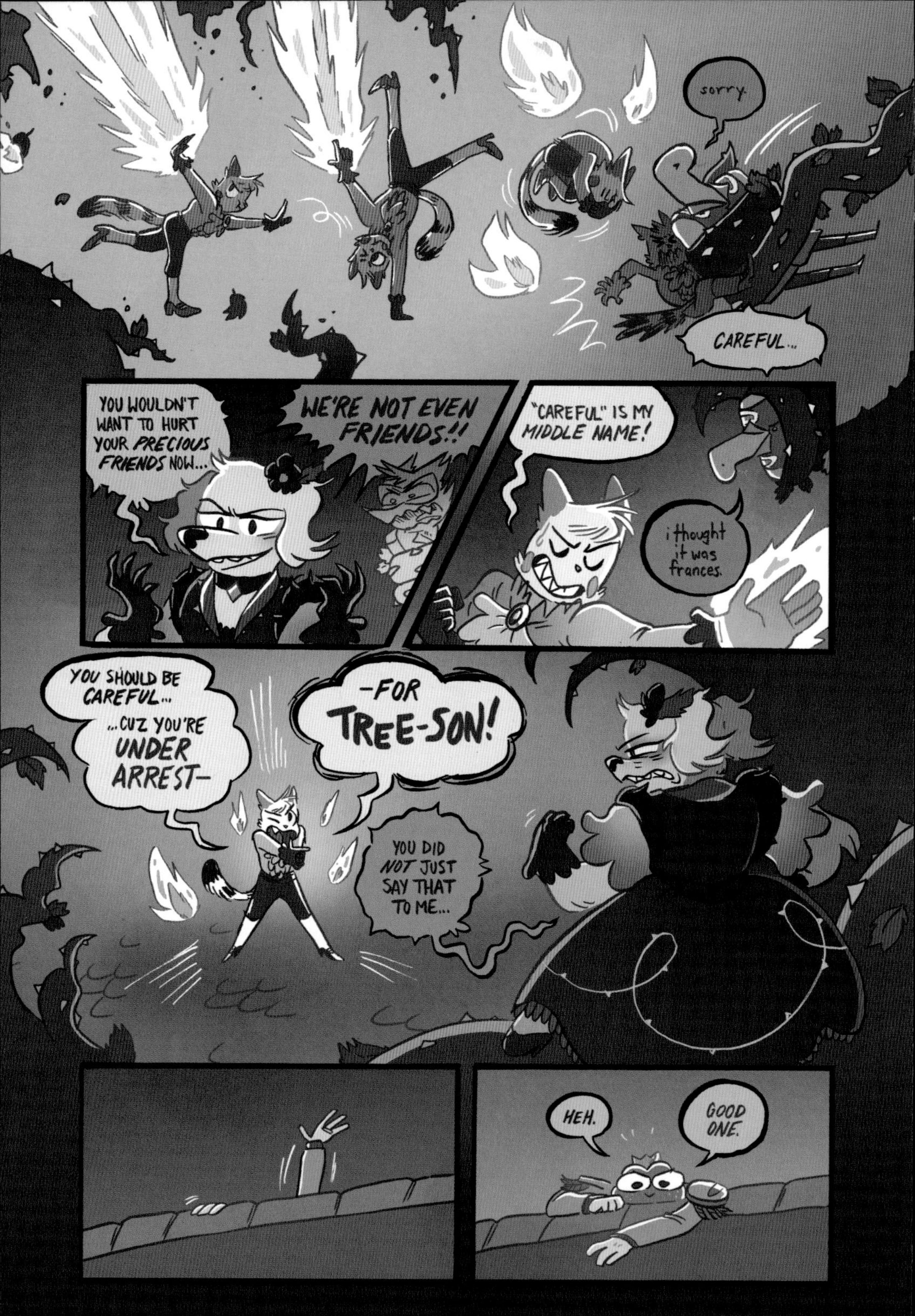
sorry.
CAREFUL...
YOU WOULDN'T WANT TO HURT YOUR PRECIOUS FRIENDS NOW...
WE'RE NOT EVEN FRIENDS!!
"CAREFUL" IS MY MIDDLE NAME!
i thought it was frances.
YOU SHOULD BE CAREFUL...
...CUZ YOU'RE UNDER ARREST-
-FOR TREE-SON!
YOU DID NOT JUST SAY THAT TO ME...
HEH.
GOOD ONE.

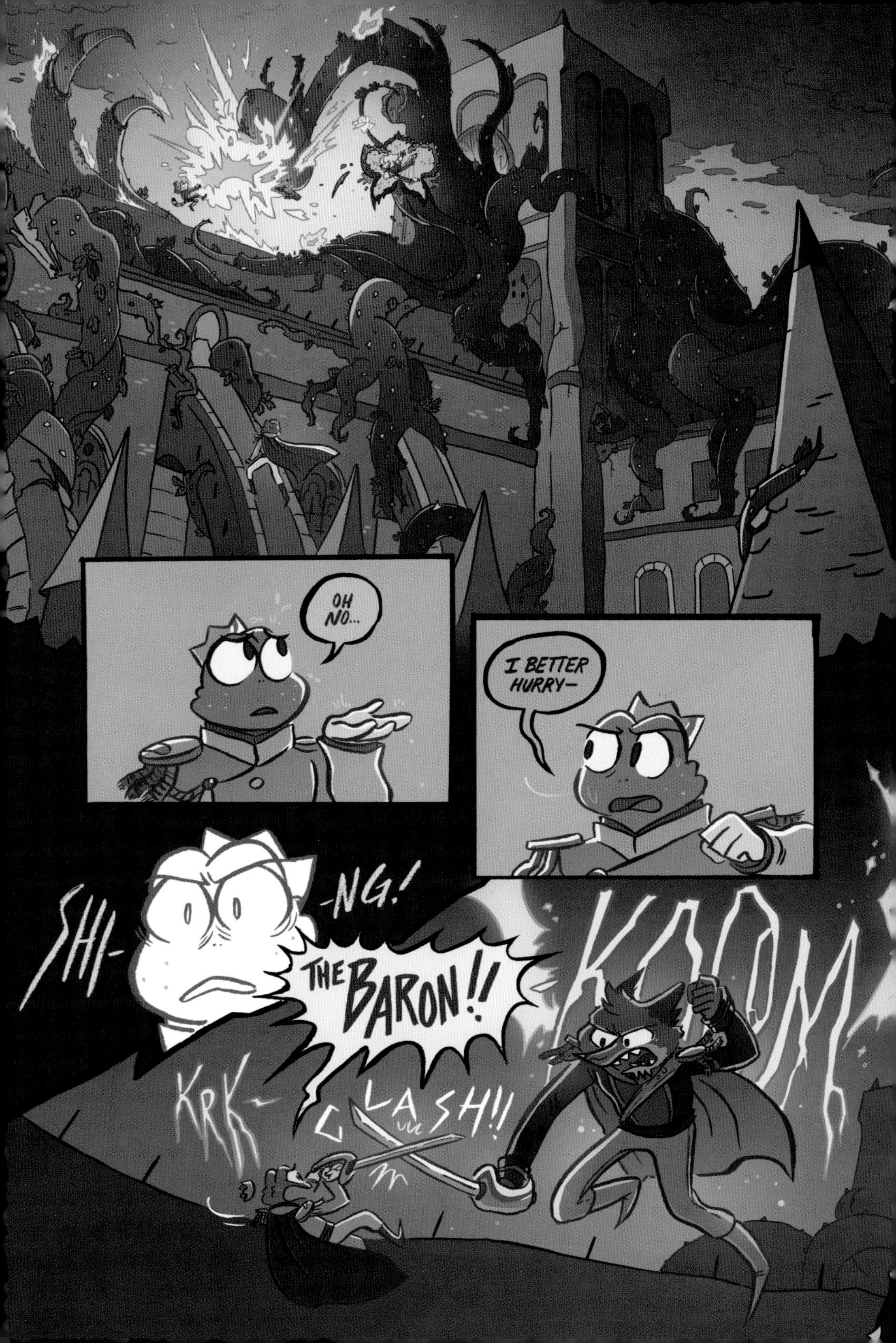
OH NO...
I BETTER HURRY—
SHI-
-NG!
THE BARON!!
KAOOM
KRK-
CLASH!!

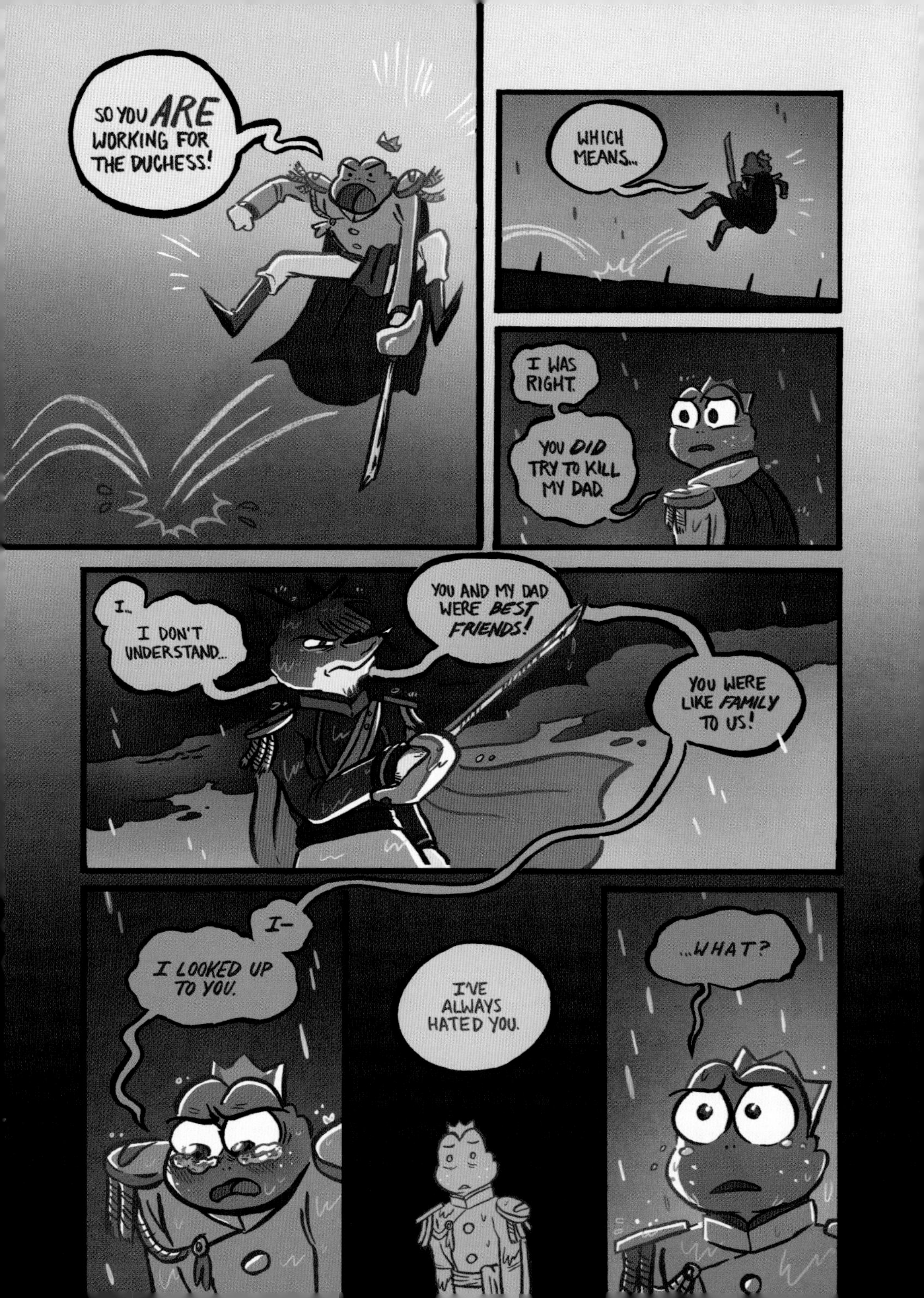
SO YOU ARE WORKING FOR THE DUCHESS!
WHICH MEANS...
I WAS RIGHT.
YOU DID TRY TO KILL MY DAD.
I...
I DON'T UNDERSTAND...
YOU AND MY DAD WERE BEST FRIENDS!
YOU WERE LIKE FAMILY TO US!
I–
I LOOKED UP TO YOU.
I'VE ALWAYS HATED YOU.
...WHAT?

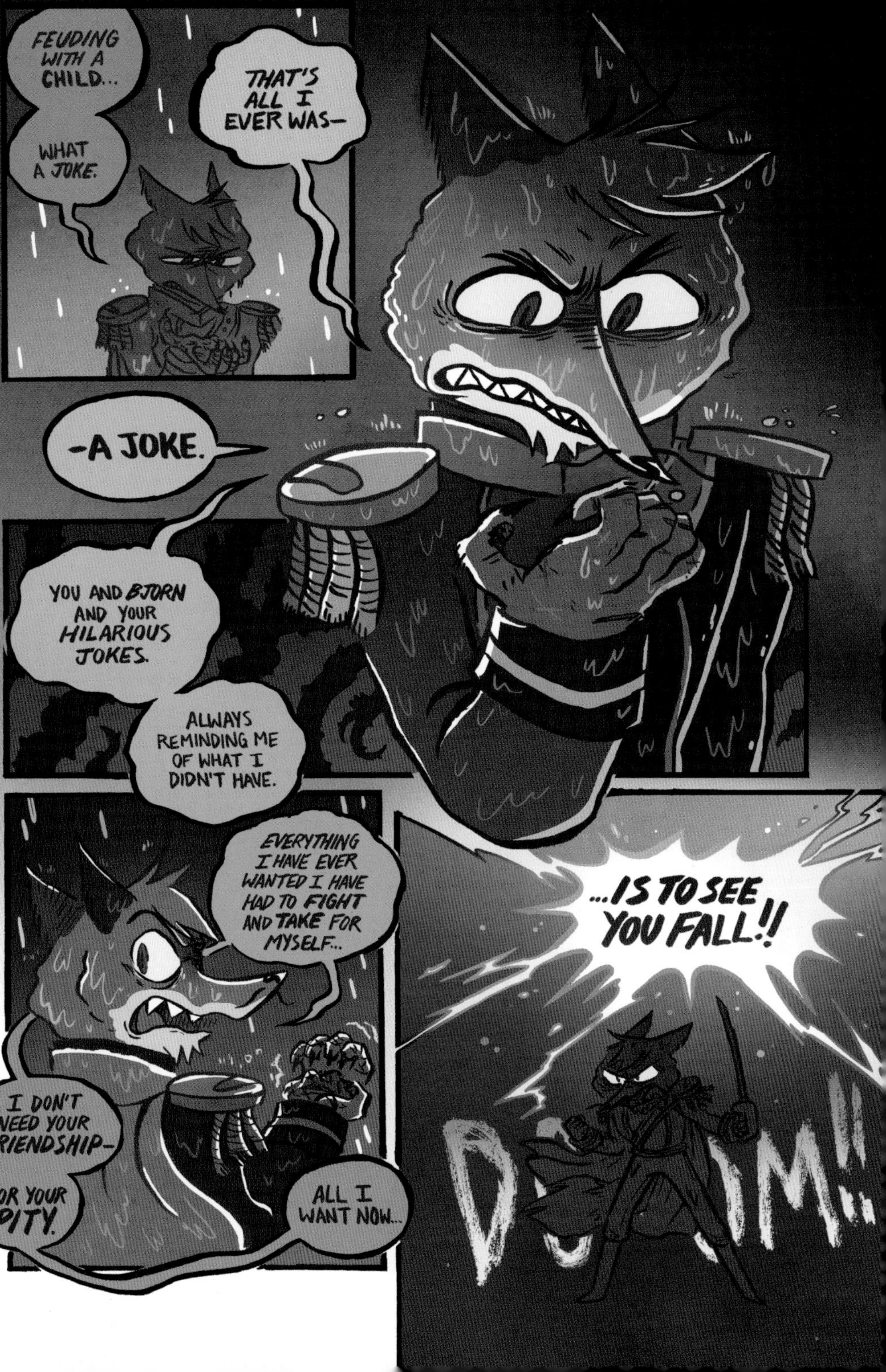
FEUDING WITH A CHILD...
WHAT A JOKE.
THAT'S ALL I EVER WAS—
-A JOKE.
YOU AND BJORN AND YOUR HILARIOUS JOKES.
ALWAYS REMINDING ME OF WHAT I DIDN'T HAVE.
EVERYTHING I HAVE EVER WANTED I HAVE HAD TO FIGHT AND TAKE FOR MYSELF...
I DON'T NEED YOUR FRIENDSHIP—
—OR YOUR PITY.
ALL I WANT NOW...
...IS TO SEE YOU FALL!!

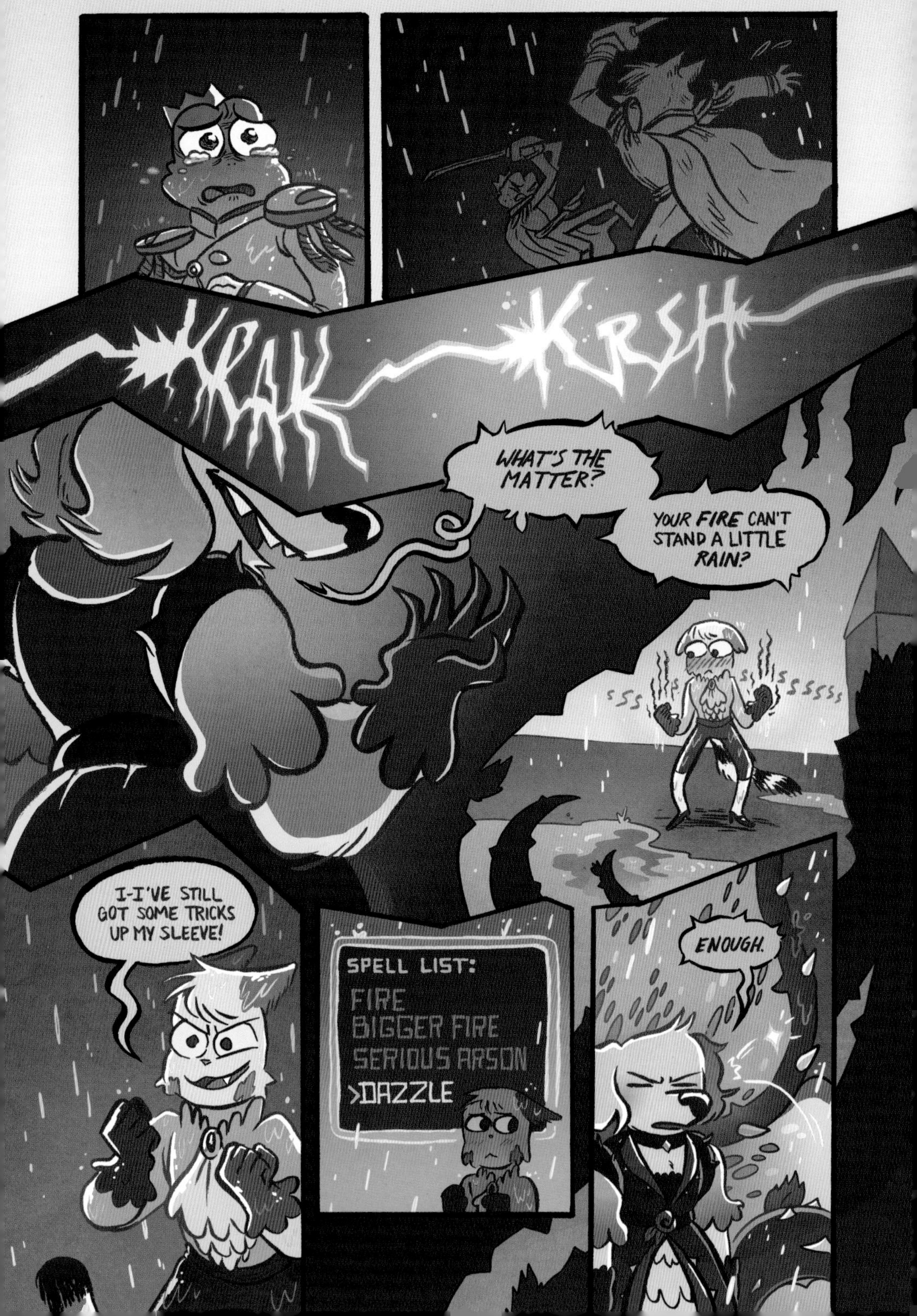
KRAK
KRSH
WHAT'S THE MATTER?
YOUR FIRE CAN'T STAND A LITTLE RAIN?
SSS
SSSSSS
I-I'VE STILL GOT SOME TRICKS UP MY SLEEVE!
SPELL LIST:
FIRE
BIGGER FIRE
SERIOUS ARSON
>DAZZLE
ENOUGH.

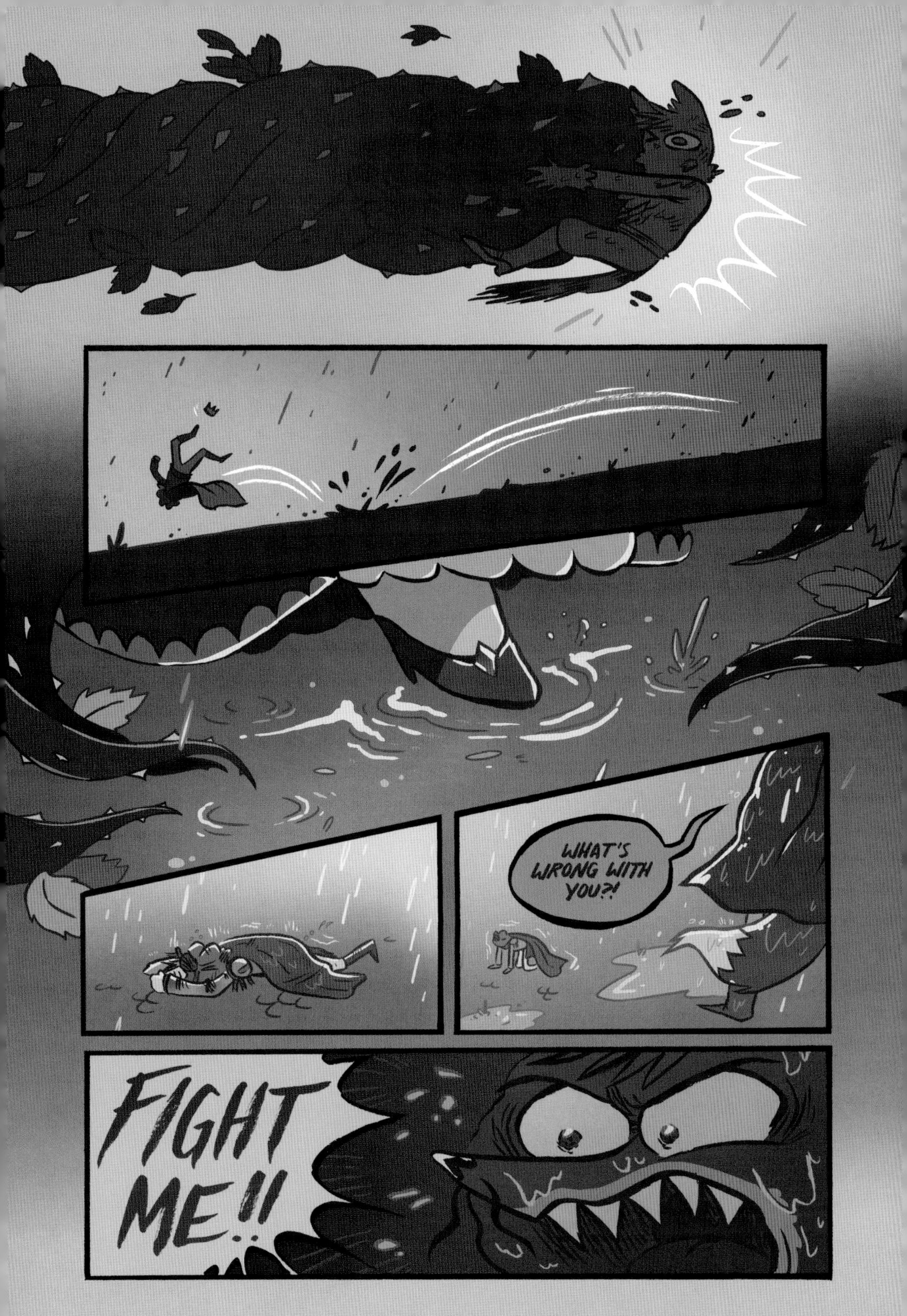
WHAT'S WRONG WITH YOU?!
FIGHT ME!!

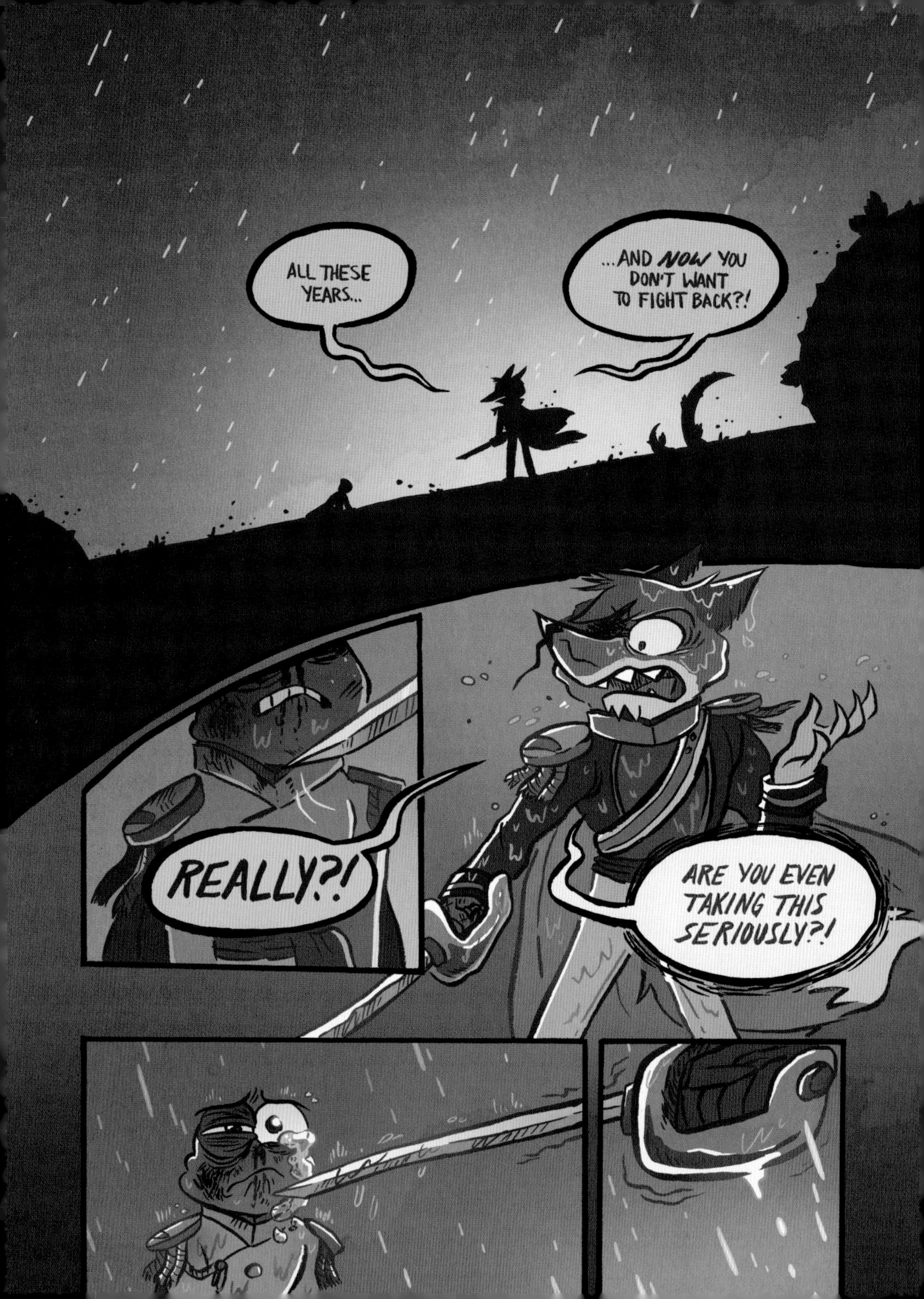
ALL THESE YEARS...
...AND NOW YOU DON'T WANT TO FIGHT BACK?!
REALLY?!
ARE YOU EVEN TAKING THIS SERIOUSLY?!

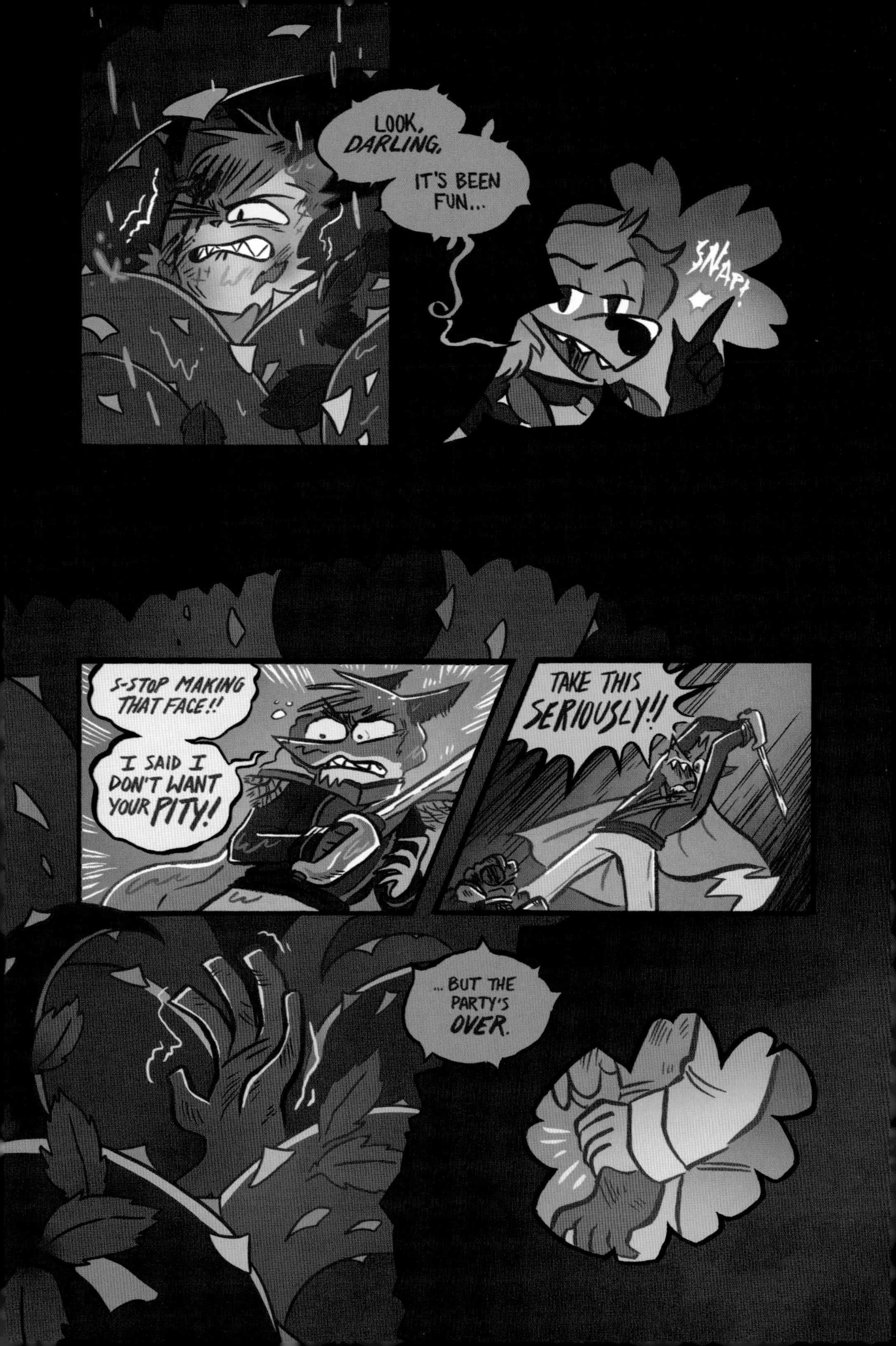
LOOK, DARLING,
IT'S BEEN FUN...
SNAP!
S-STOP MAKING THAT FACE!!
I SAID I DON'T WANT YOUR PITY!
TAKE THIS SERIOUSLY!!
...BUT THE PARTY'S OVER.

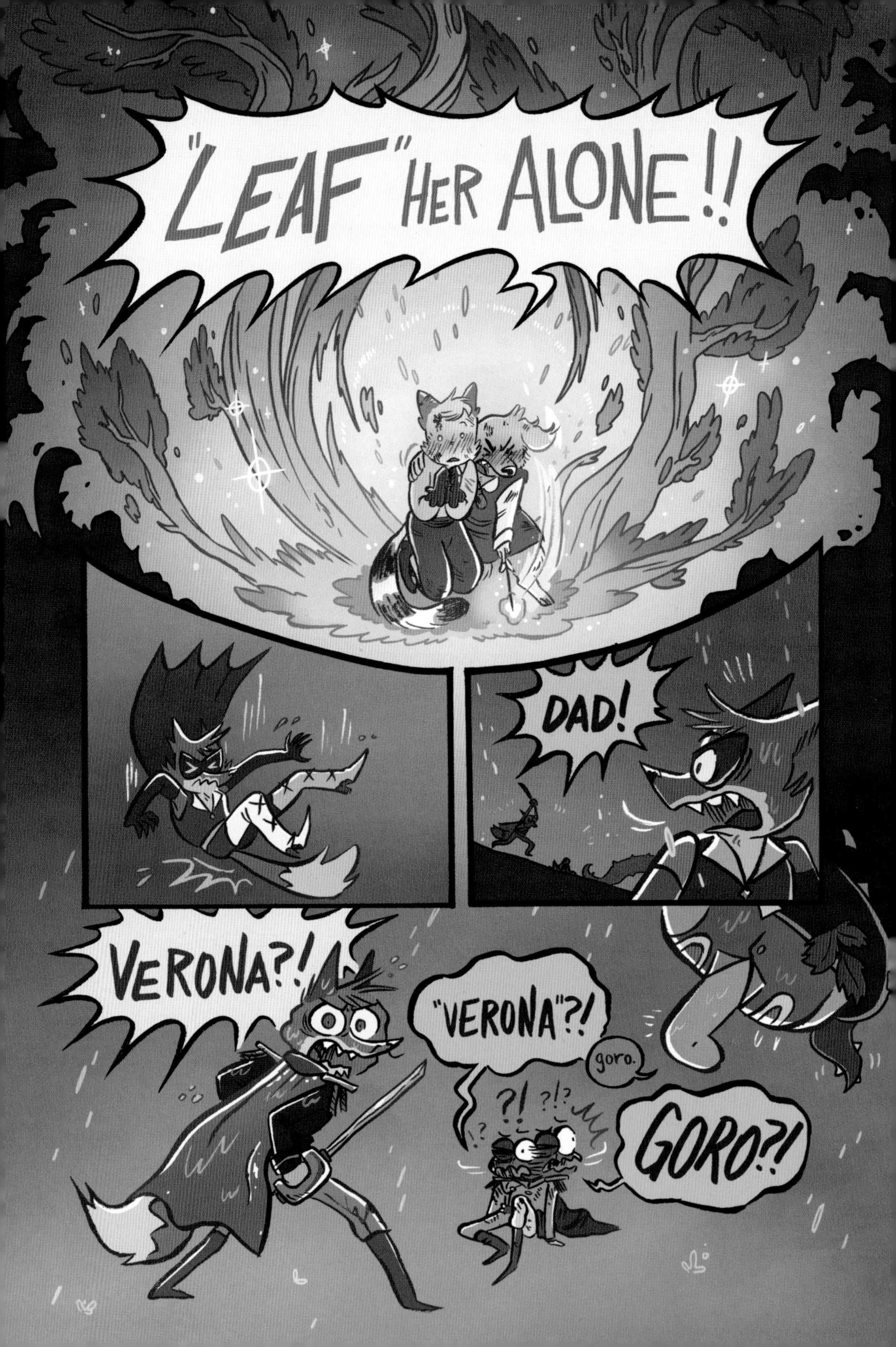
"LEAF" HER ALONE!!
DAD!
VERONA?!
"VERONA"?!
goro.
?! ?!?
GORO?!

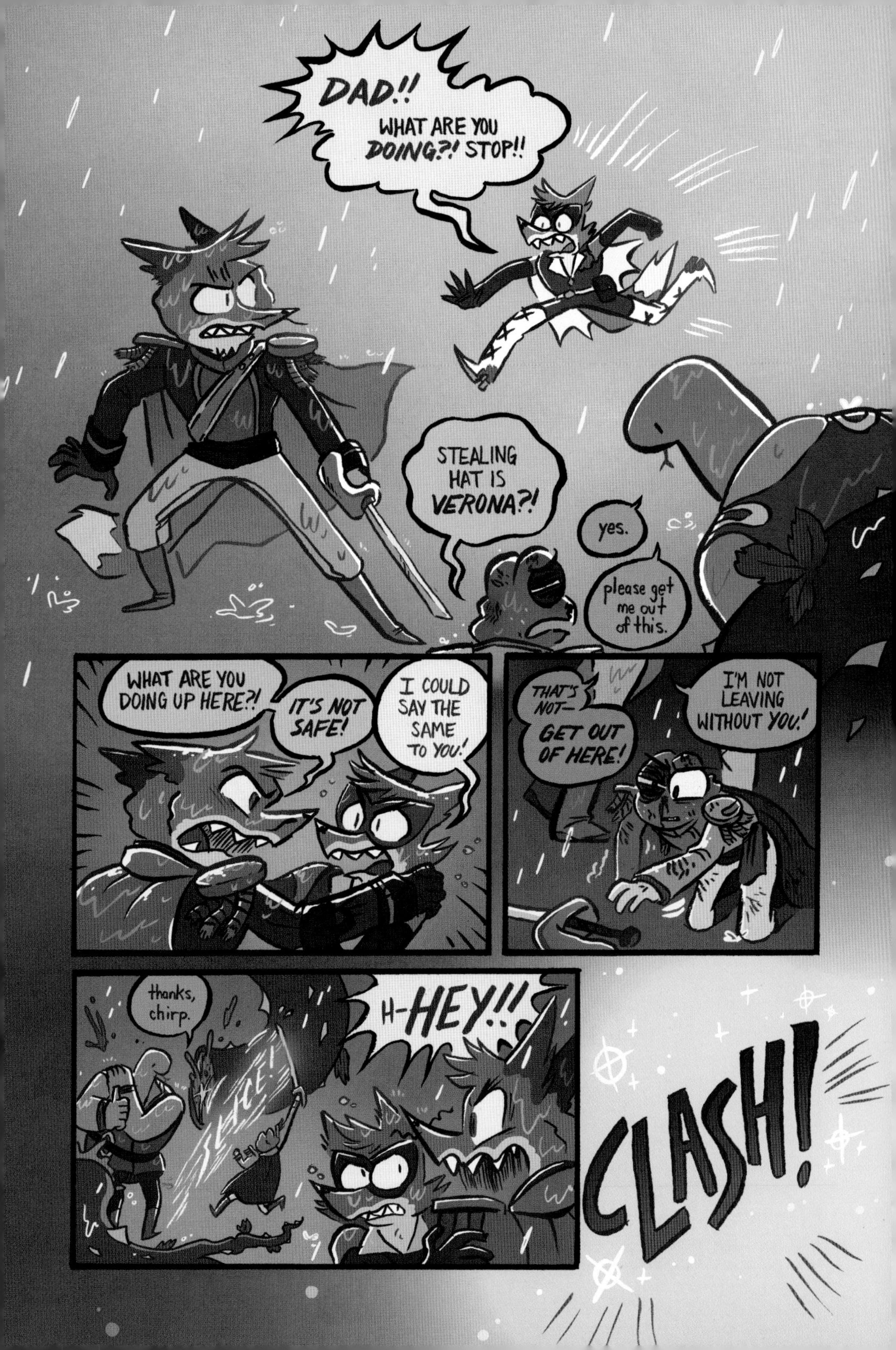
DAD!! WHAT ARE YOU DOING?! STOP!!
STEALING HAT IS VERONA?!
yes.
please get me out of this.
WHAT ARE YOU DOING UP HERE?!
IT'S NOT SAFE!
I COULD SAY THE SAME TO YOU!
THAT'S NOT—
GET OUT OF HERE!
I'M NOT LEAVING WITHOUT YOU!
thanks, chirp.
H-HEY!!
SLICE!
CLASH!

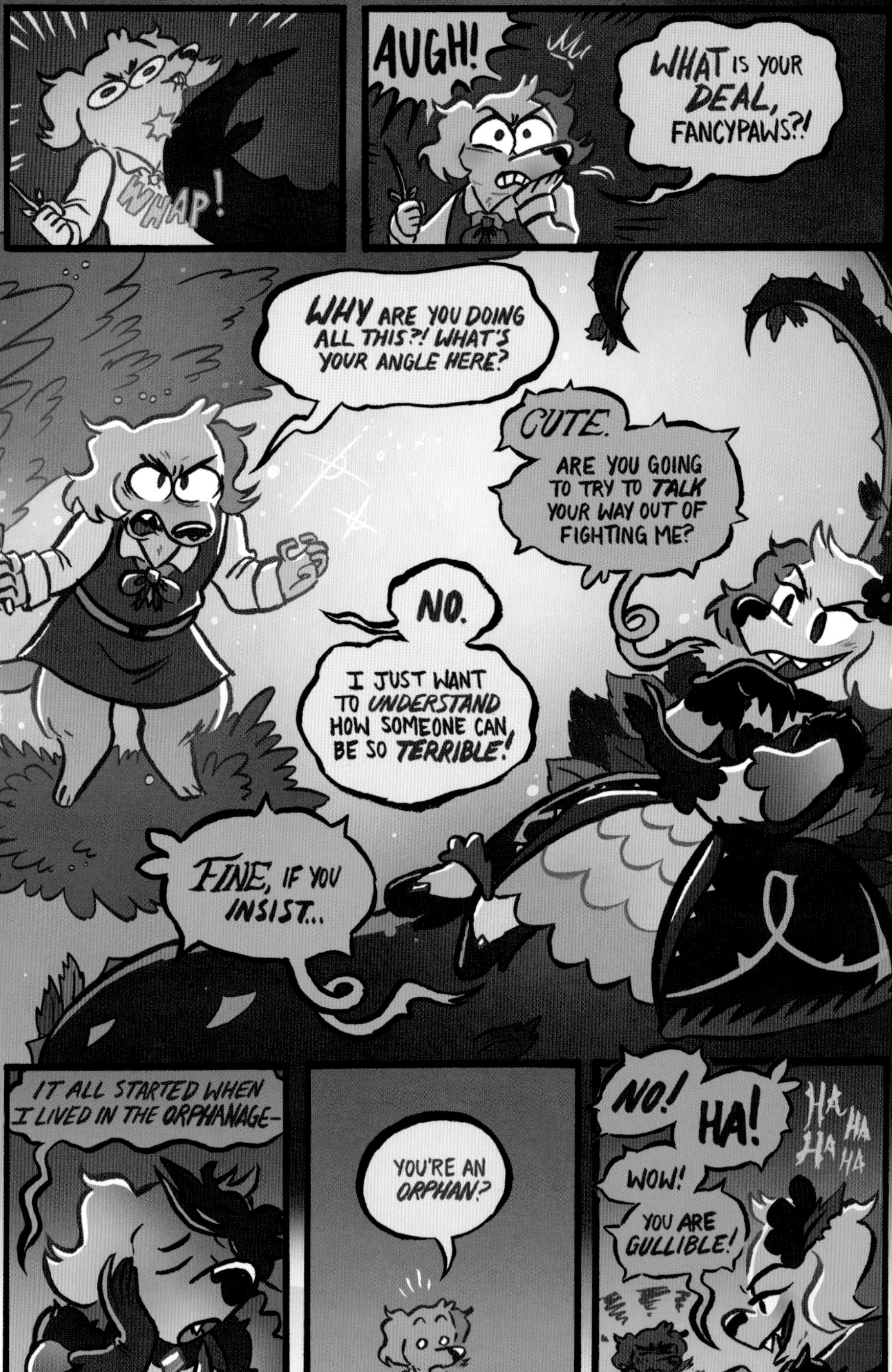

WHAP!
AUGH!
WHAT IS YOUR DEAL, FANCYPAWS?!
WHY ARE YOU DOING ALL THIS?! WHAT'S YOUR ANGLE HERE?
CUTE.
ARE YOU GOING TO TRY TO TALK YOUR WAY OUT OF FIGHTING ME?
NO.
I JUST WANT TO UNDERSTAND HOW SOMEONE CAN BE SO TERRIBLE!
FINE, IF YOU INSIST...
IT ALL STARTED WHEN I LIVED IN THE ORPHANAGE—
YOU'RE AN ORPHAN?
NO! HA!
HA HA HA HA
WOW!
YOU ARE GULLIBLE!

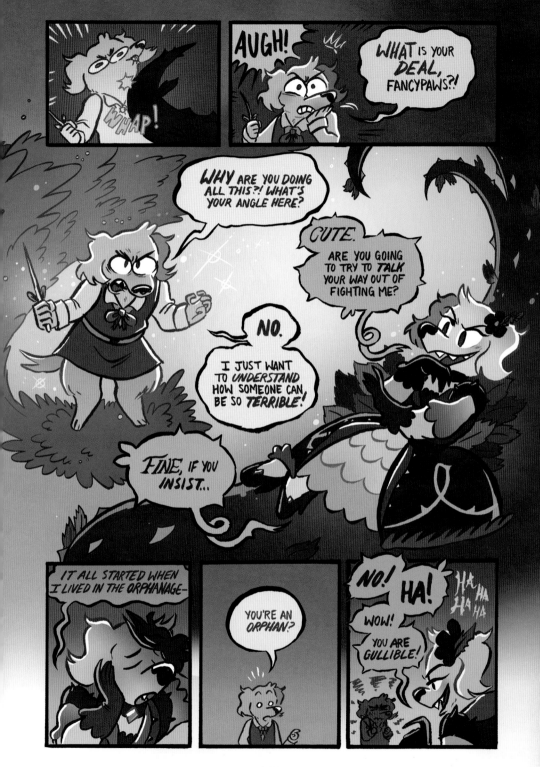

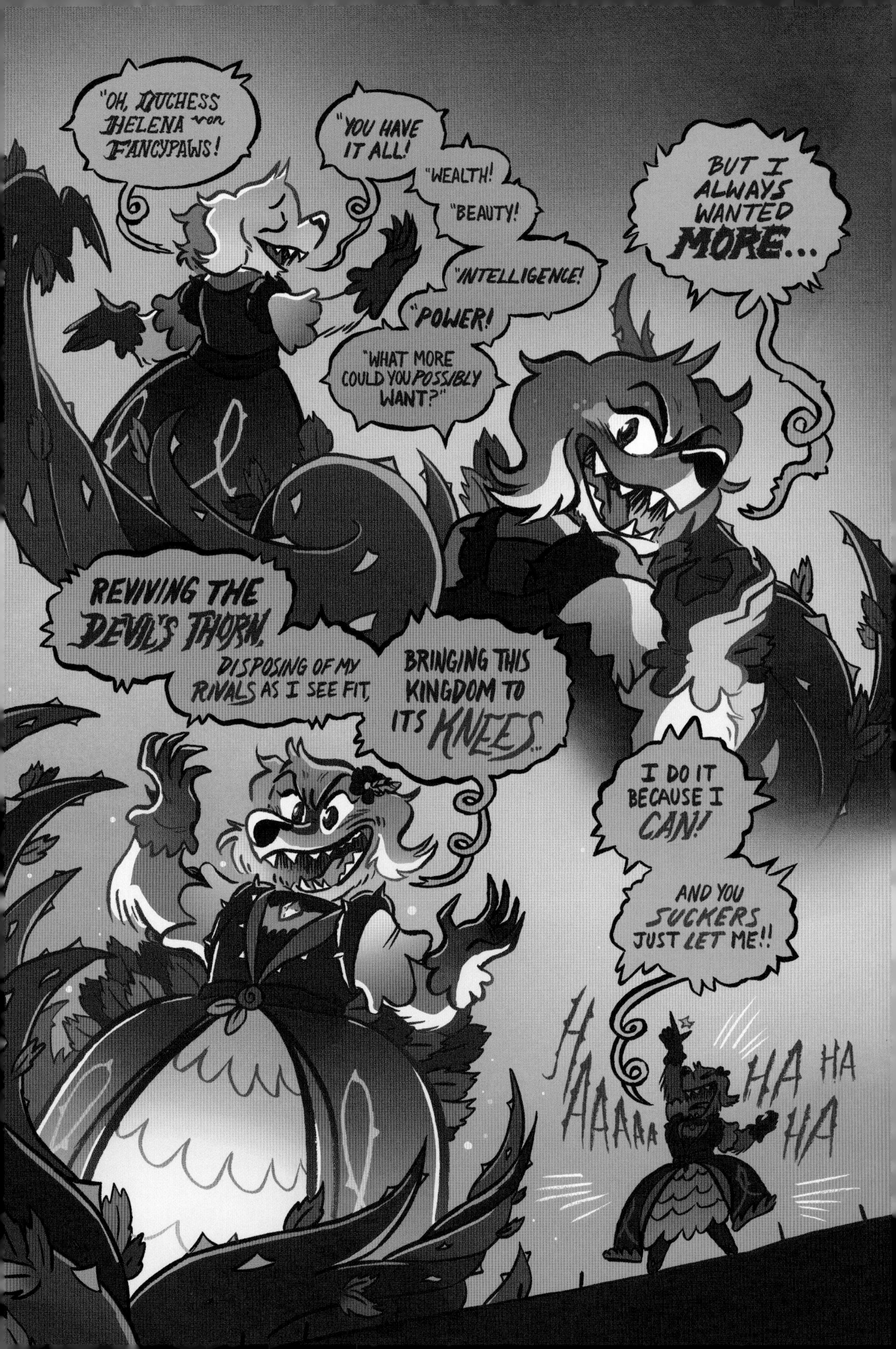
"OH, DUCHESS HELENA von FANCYPAWS!
"YOU HAVE IT ALL!
"WEALTH!
"BEAUTY!
"INTELLIGENCE!
"POWER!
"WHAT MORE COULD YOU POSSIBLY WANT?"
BUT I ALWAYS WANTED MORE...
REVIVING THE DEVIL'S THORN,
DISPOSING OF MY RIVALS AS I SEE FIT,
BRINGING THIS KINGDOM TO ITS KNEES...
I DO IT BECAUSE I CAN!
AND YOU SUCKERS JUST LET ME!!
HA HAAAA HA HA HA HA

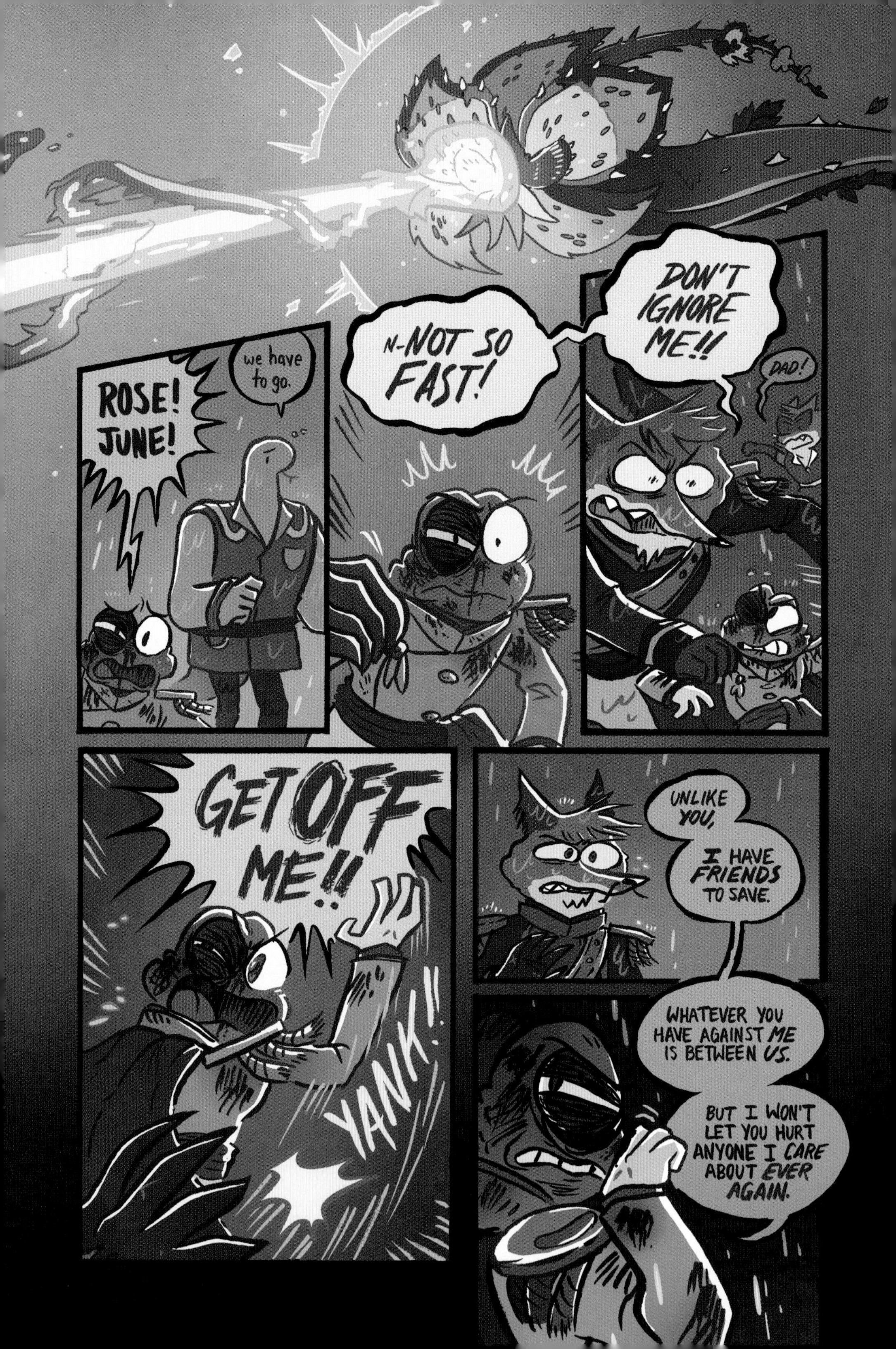
ROSE! JUNE!
we have to go.
N-NOT SO FAST!
DON'T IGNORE ME!!
DAD!
GET OFF ME!!
YANK!!
UNLIKE YOU,
I HAVE FRIENDS TO SAVE.
WHATEVER YOU HAVE AGAINST ME IS BETWEEN US.
BUT I WON'T LET YOU HURT ANYONE I CARE ABOUT EVER AGAIN.

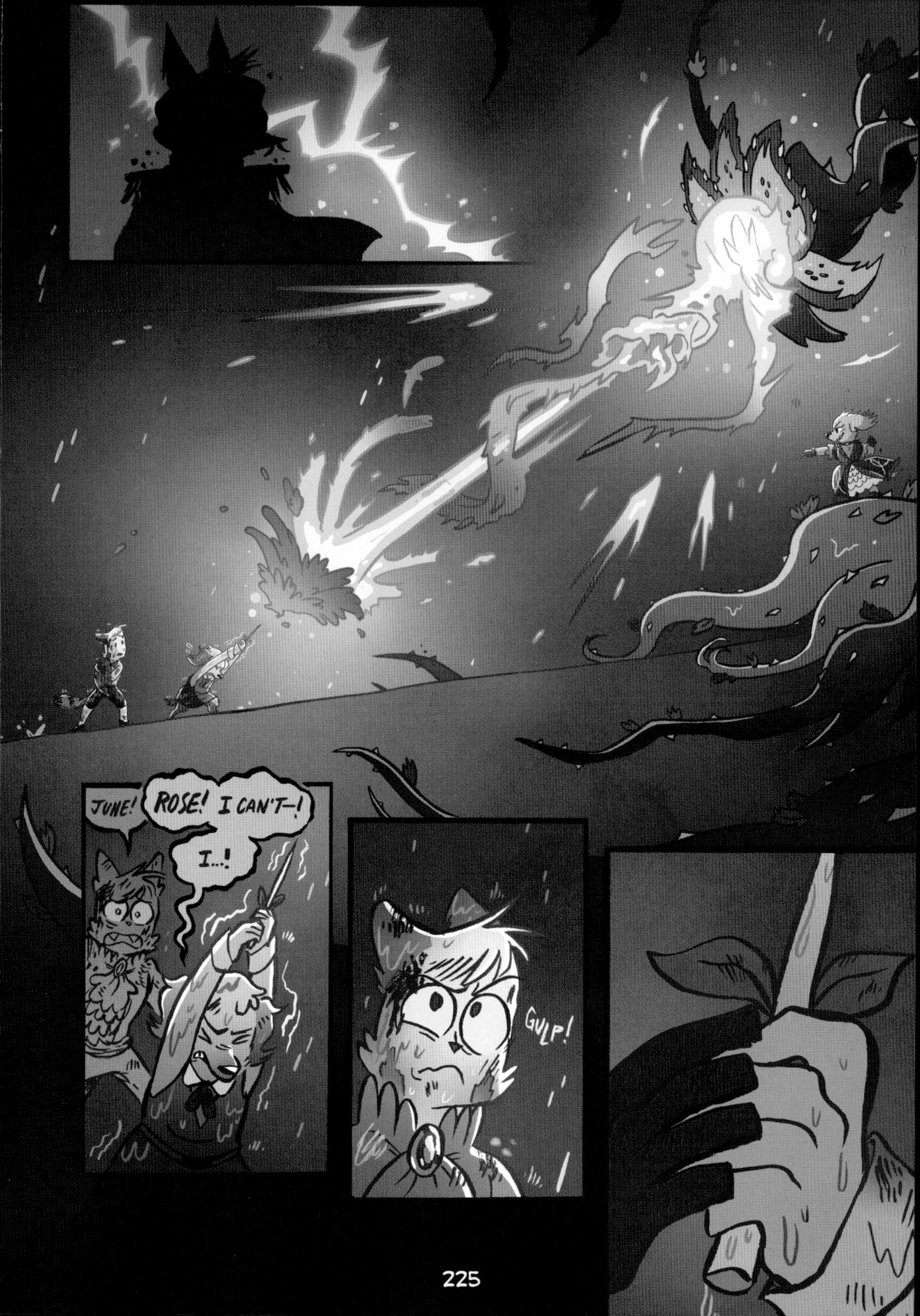
JUNE!
ROSE! I CAN'T—!
I...!
GULP!

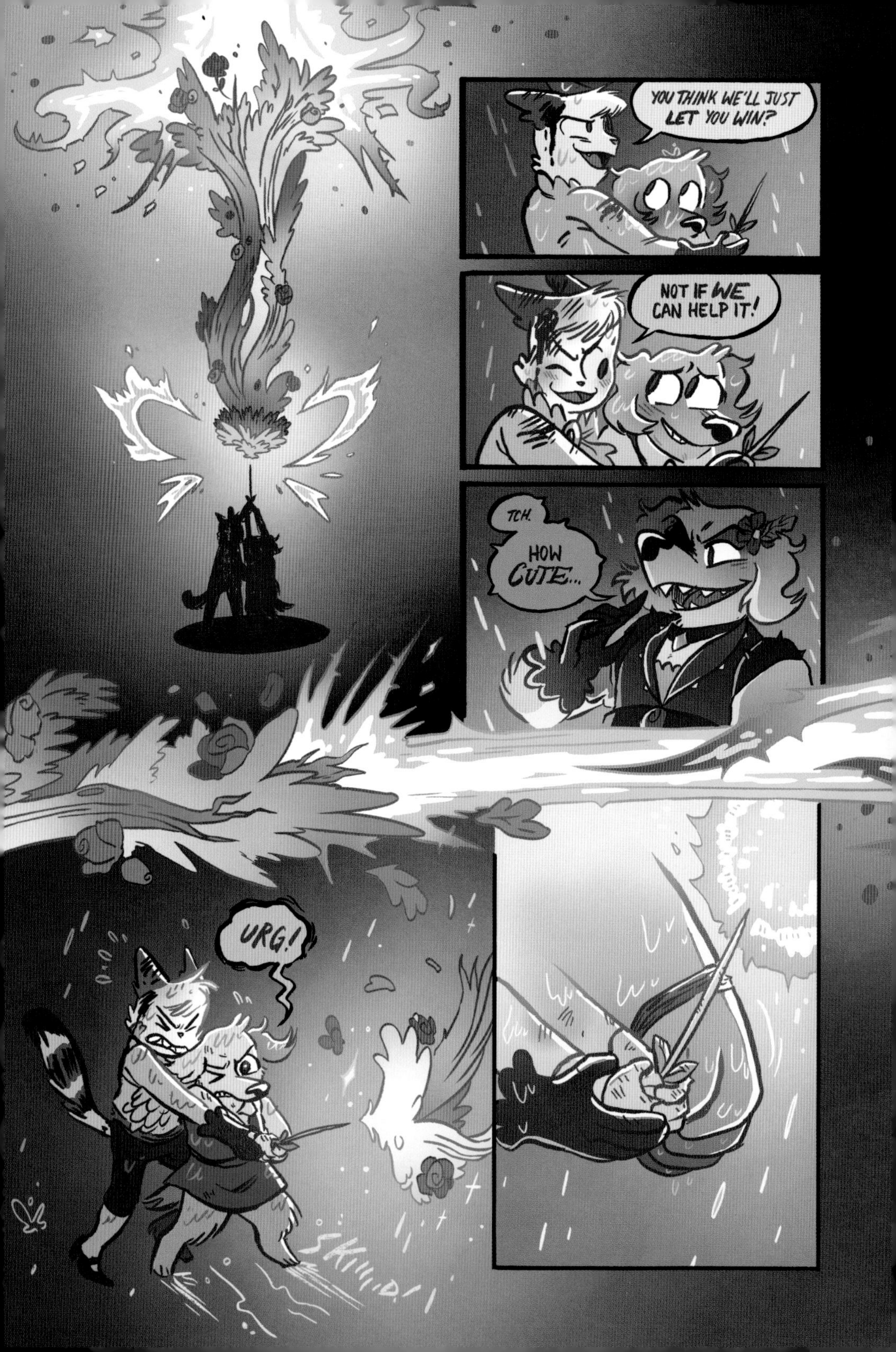
YOU THINK WE'LL JUST LET YOU WIN?
NOT IF WE CAN HELP IT!
TCH.
HOW CUTE...
URG!
SKIIIID!

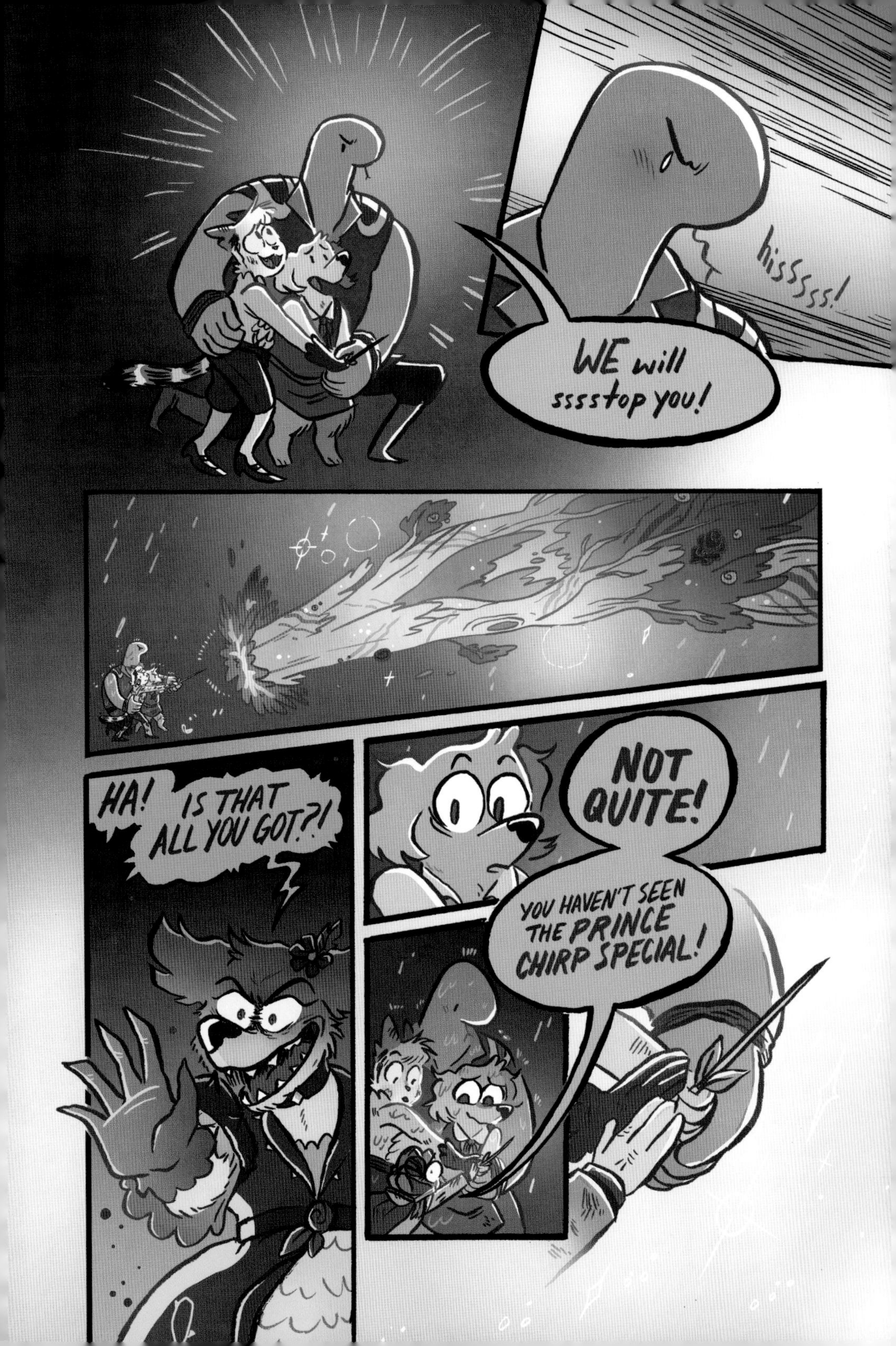
hisSsss!
WE will ssssstop you!
HA! IS THAT ALL YOU GOT?!
NOT QUITE!
YOU HAVEN'T SEEN THE PRINCE CHIRP SPECIAL!

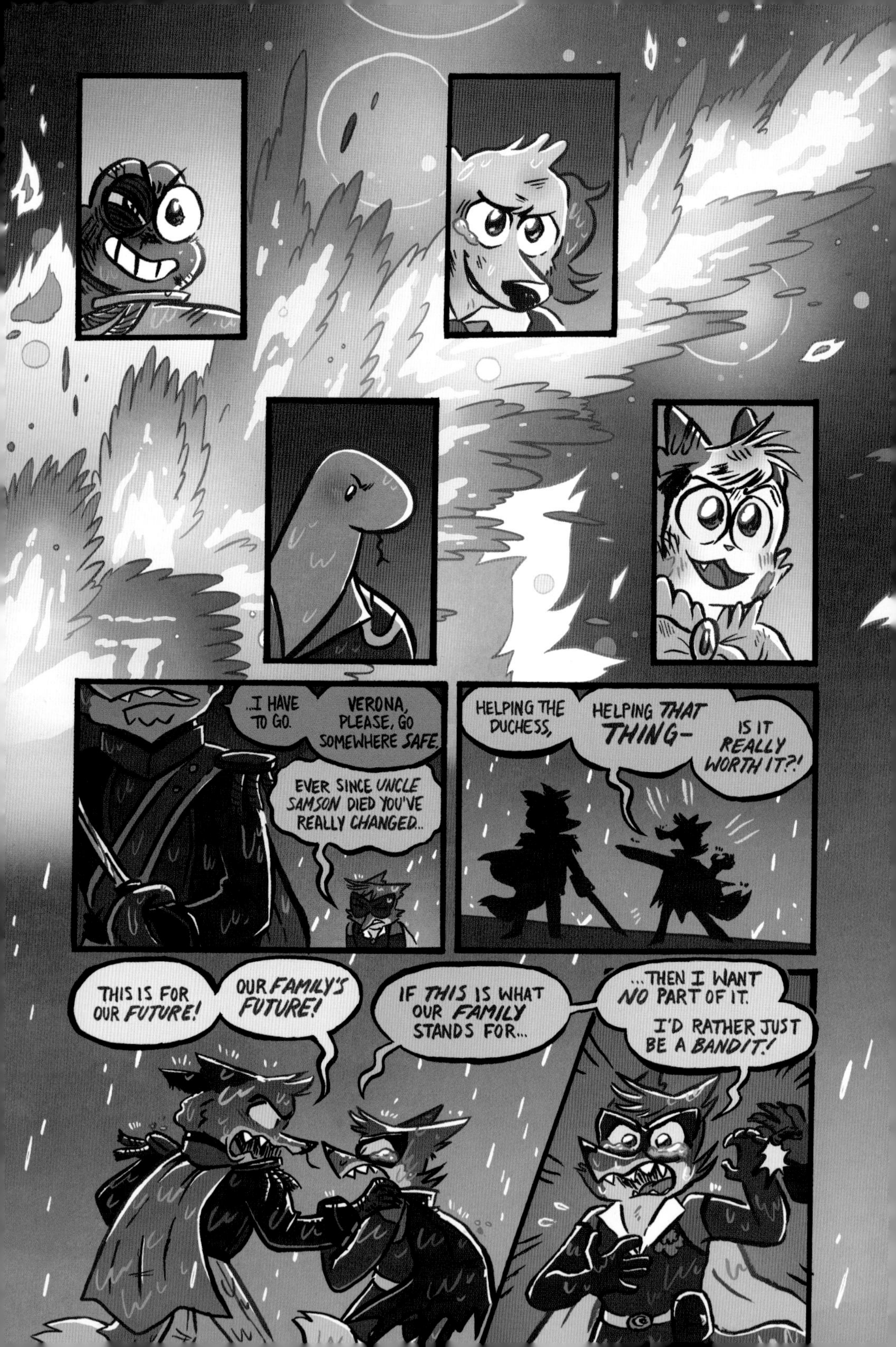
..I HAVE TO GO.
VERONA, PLEASE, GO SOMEWHERE SAFE.
EVER SINCE UNCLE SAMSON DIED YOU'VE REALLY CHANGED...
HELPING THE DUCHESS,
HELPING THAT THING-
IS IT REALLY WORTH IT?!
THIS IS FOR OUR FUTURE!
OUR FAMILY'S FUTURE!
IF THIS IS WHAT OUR FAMILY STANDS FOR...
...THEN I WANT NO PART OF IT.
I'D RATHER JUST BE A BANDIT!

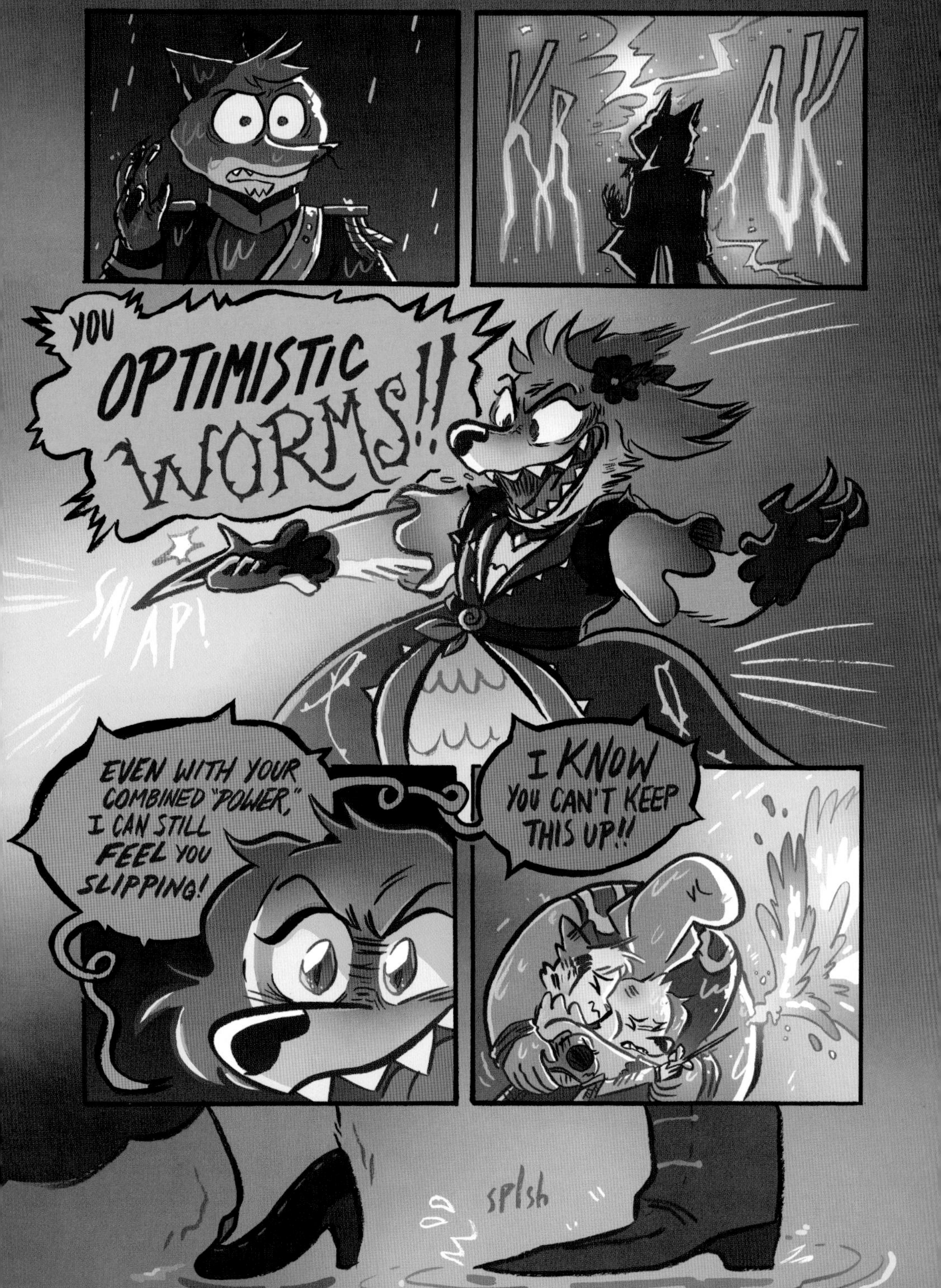
KRAK
YOU OPTIMISTIC WORMS!!
SNAP!
EVEN WITH YOUR COMBINED "POWER," I CAN STILL FEEL YOU SLIPPING!
I KNOW YOU CAN'T KEEP THIS UP!!
splsh

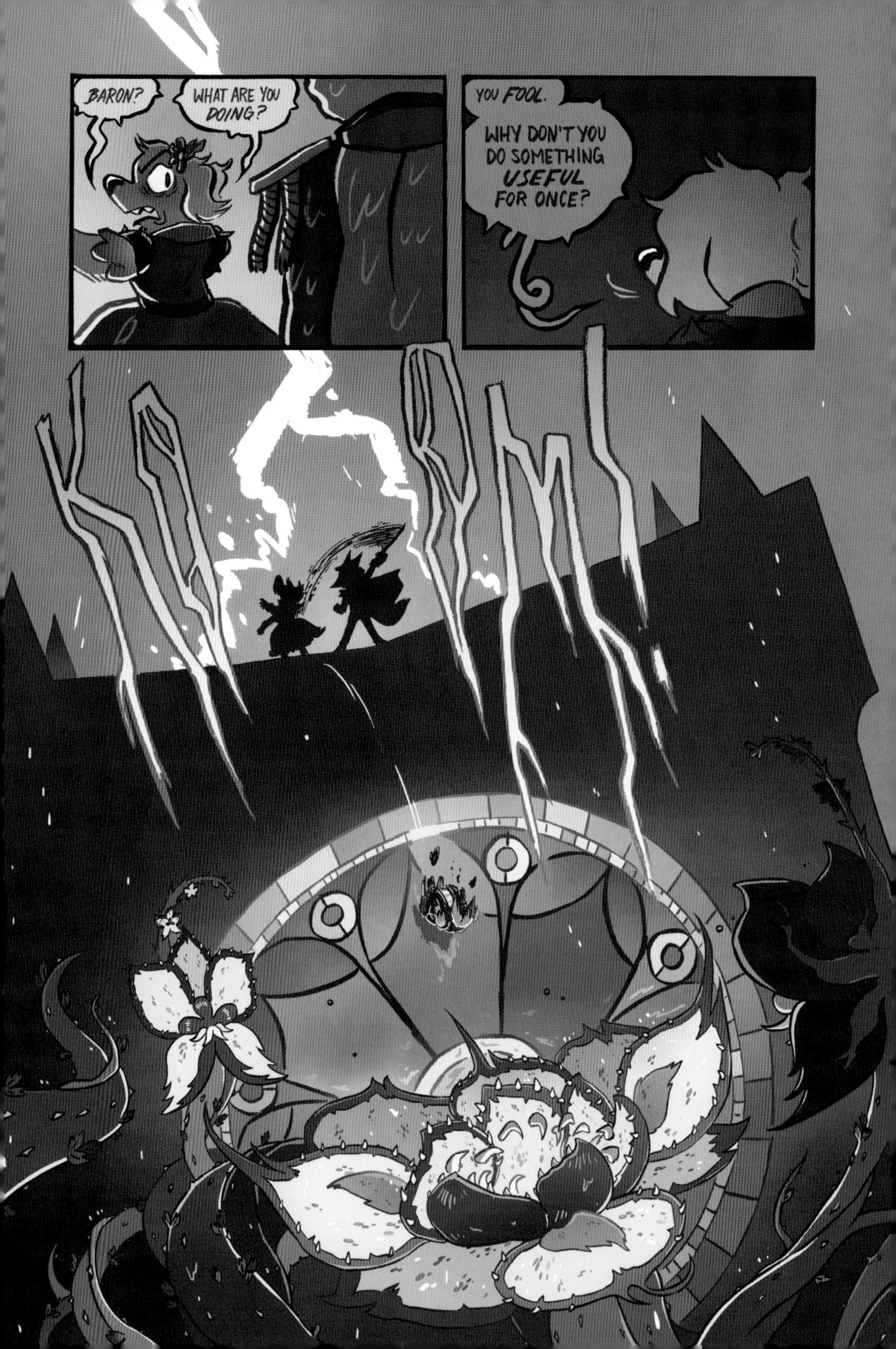

BARON?
WHAT ARE YOU DOING?
YOU FOOL.
WHY DON'T YOU DO SOMETHING USEFUL FOR ONCE?

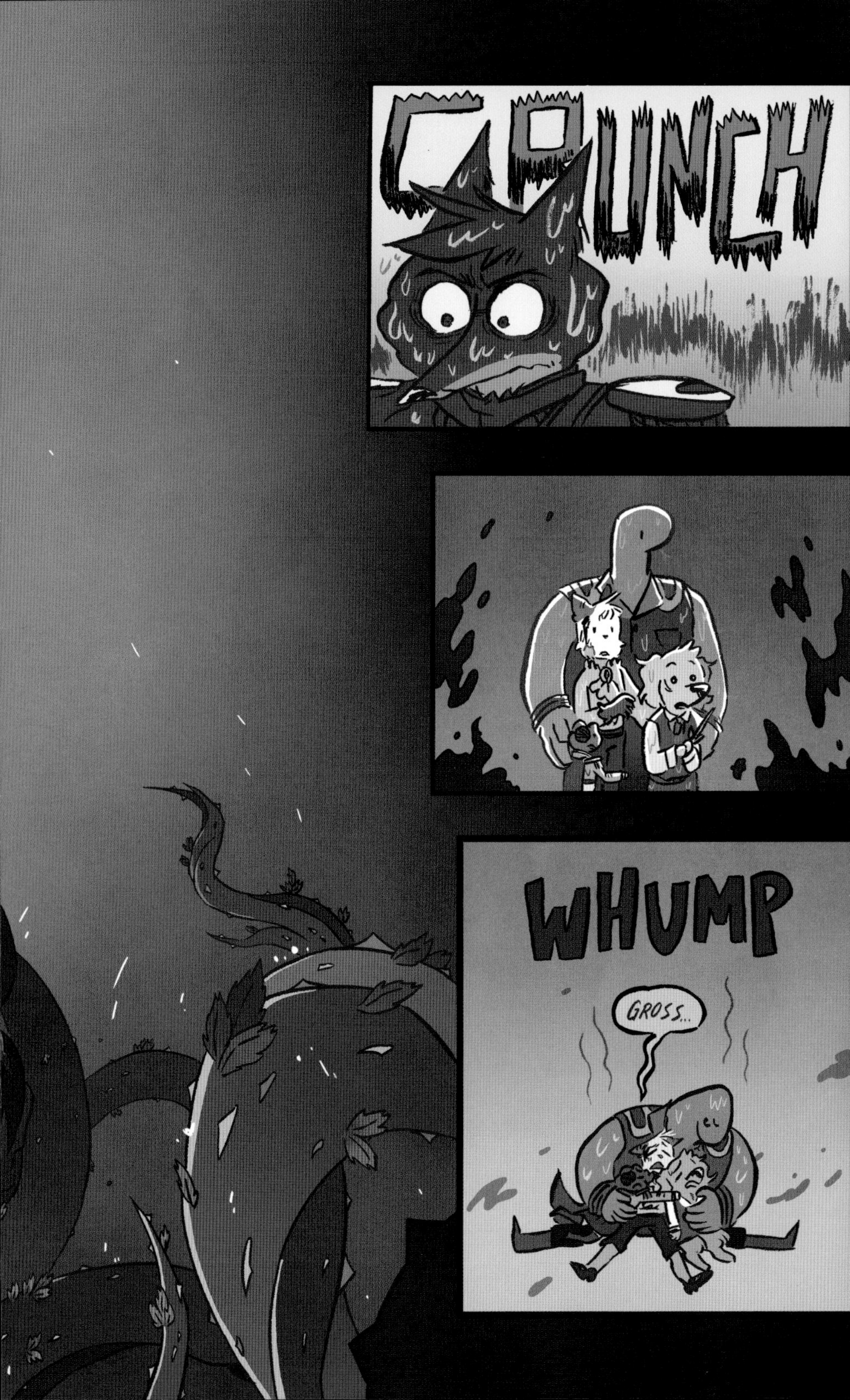
CRUNCH
WHUMP
GROSS...

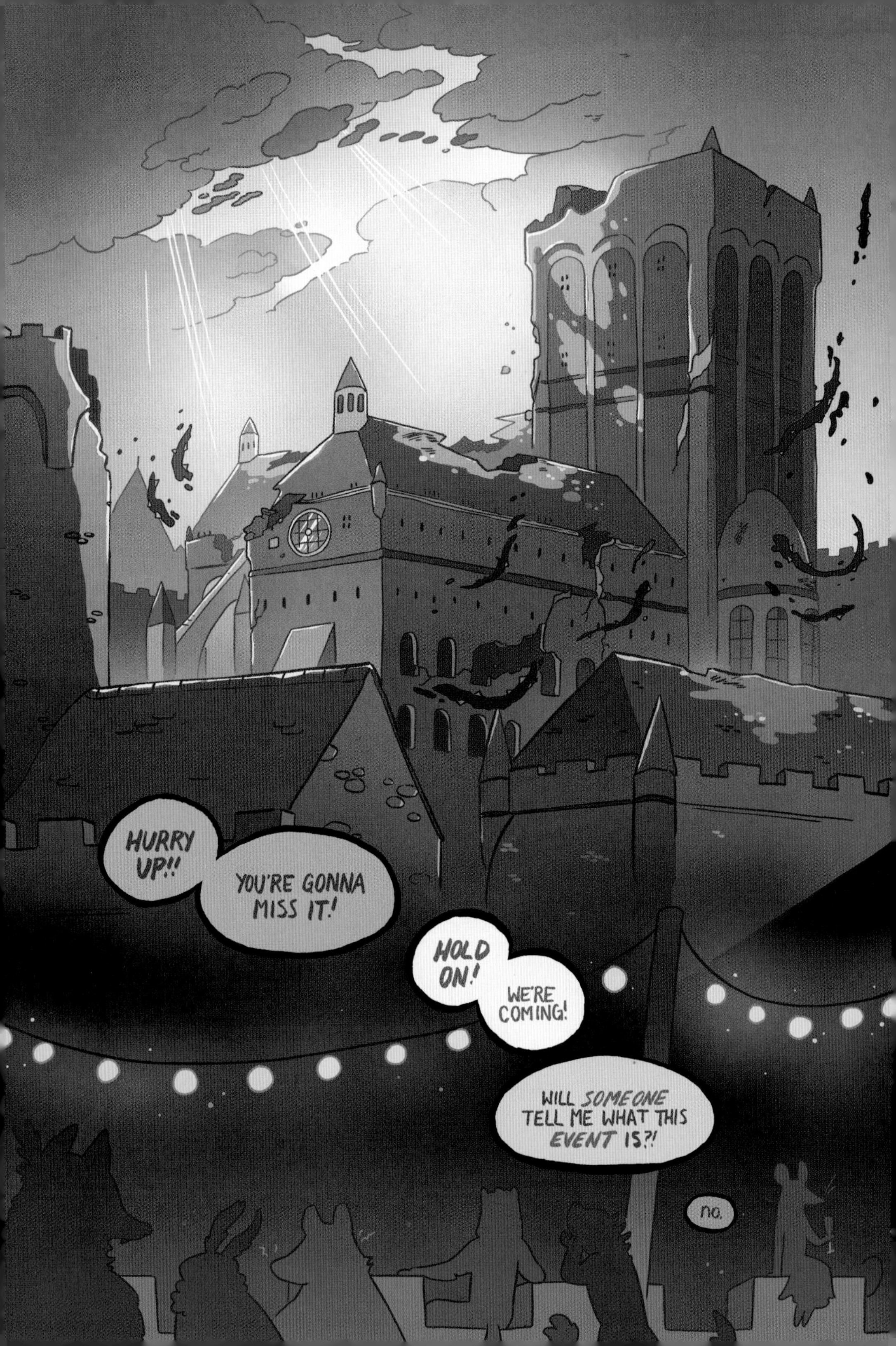
HURRY UP!!
YOU'RE GONNA MISS IT!
HOLD ON!
WE'RE COMING!
WILL SOMEONE TELL ME WHAT THIS EVENT IS?!
no.

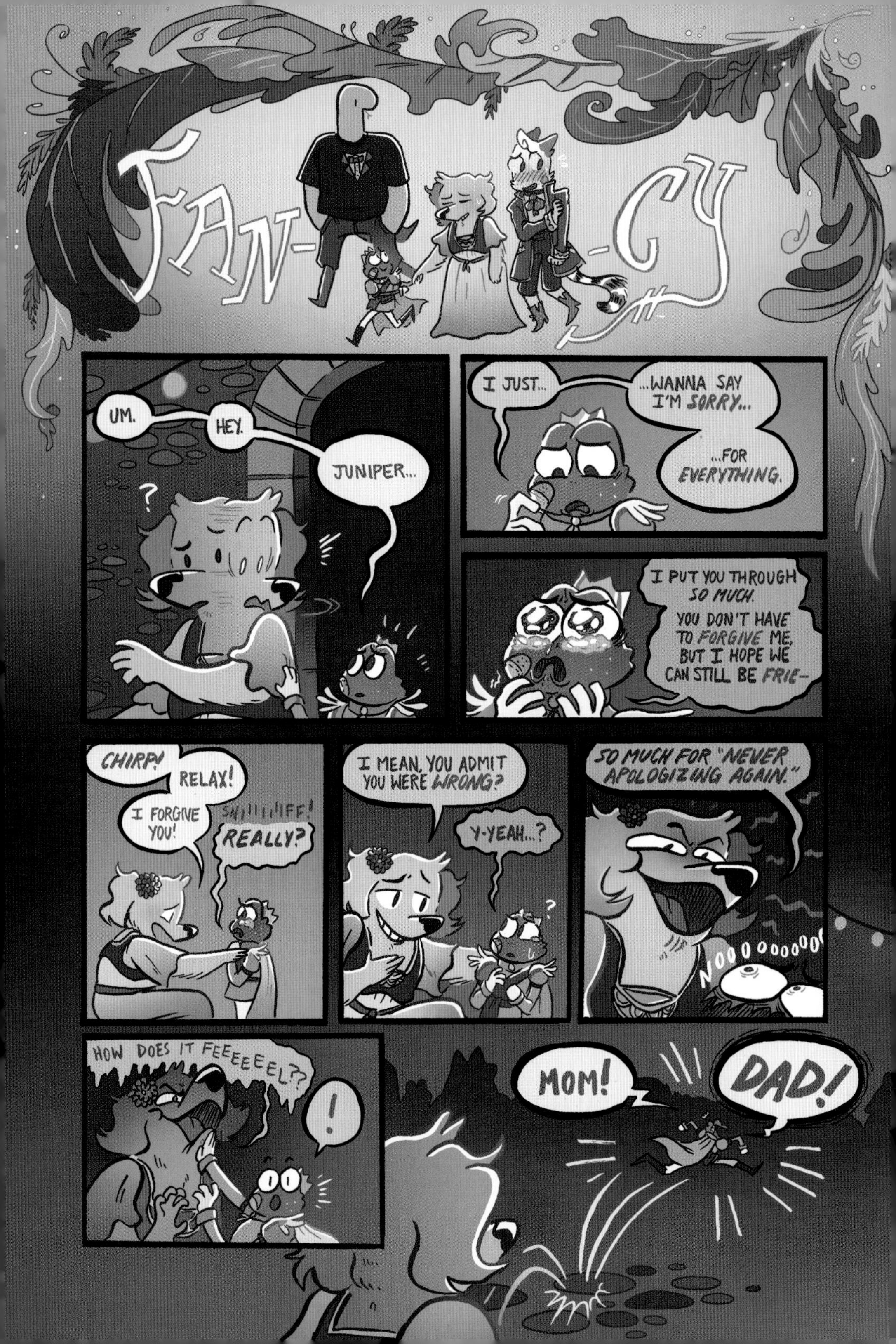
FAN-
-CY
UM.
HEY.
JUNIPER...
?
I JUST...
...WANNA SAY I'M SORRY...
...FOR EVERYTHING.
I PUT YOU THROUGH SO MUCH.
YOU DON'T HAVE TO FORGIVE ME, BUT I HOPE WE CAN STILL BE FRIE-
CHIRP!
RELAX!
I FORGIVE YOU!
SNIIIIIFF!
REALLY?
I MEAN, YOU ADMIT YOU WERE WRONG?
Y-YEAH...?
?
SO MUCH FOR "NEVER APOLOGIZING AGAIN."
NOOOOOOOOOO
HOW DOES IT FEEEEEEL??
!
MOM!
DAD!

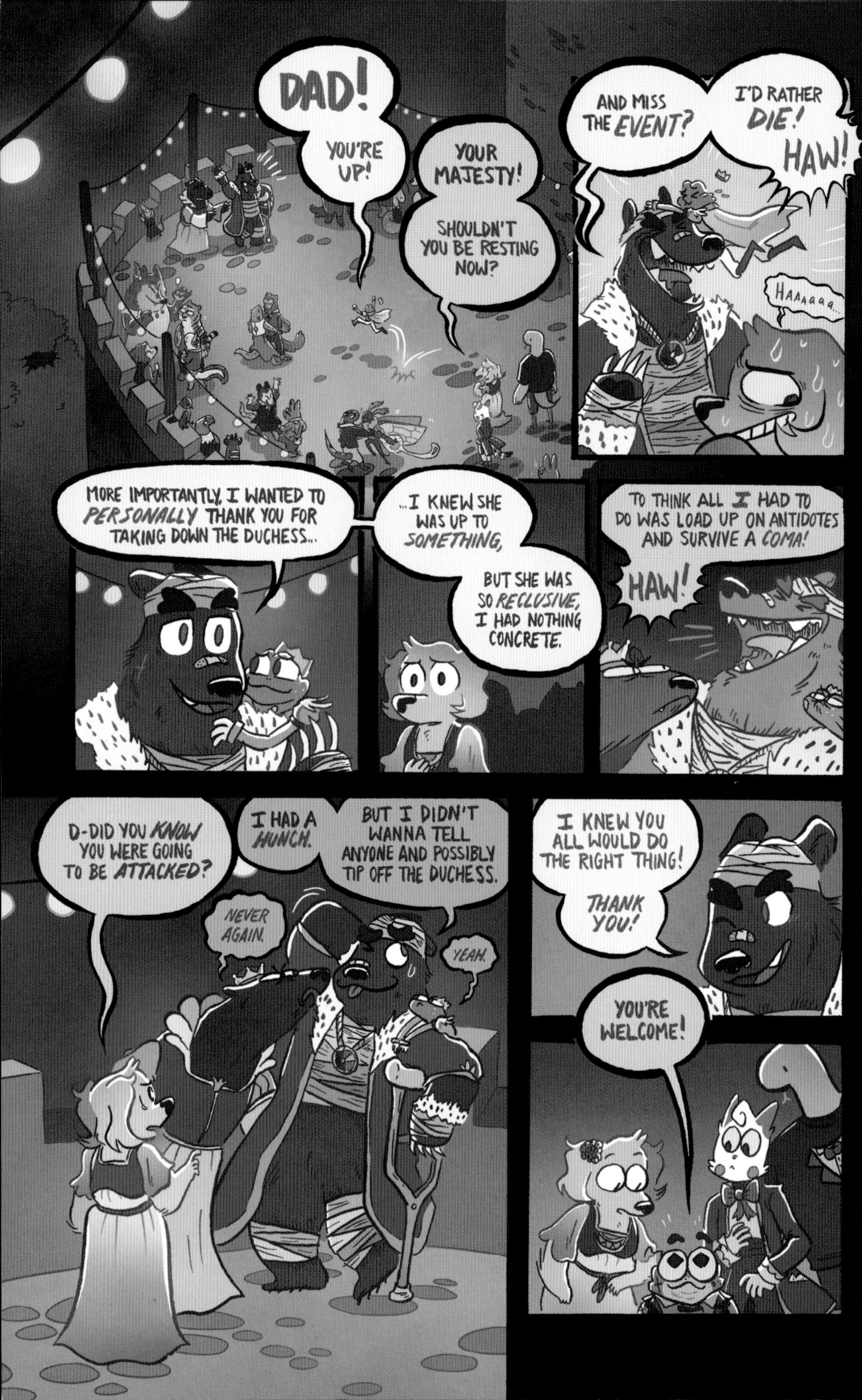
DAD!
YOU'RE UP!
YOUR MAJESTY!
SHOULDN'T YOU BE RESTING NOW?
AND MISS THE EVENT?
I'D RATHER DIE!
HAW!
Haaaaaa...
MORE IMPORTANTLY, I WANTED TO PERSONALLY THANK YOU FOR TAKING DOWN THE DUCHESS...
...I KNEW SHE WAS UP TO SOMETHING,
BUT SHE WAS SO RECLUSIVE, I HAD NOTHING CONCRETE.
TO THINK ALL I HAD TO DO WAS LOAD UP ON ANTIDOTES AND SURVIVE A COMA!
HAW!
D-DID YOU KNOW YOU WERE GOING TO BE ATTACKED?
I HAD A HUNCH.
BUT I DIDN'T WANNA TELL ANYONE AND POSSIBLY TIP OFF THE DUCHESS.
NEVER AGAIN.
YEAH.
I KNEW YOU ALL WOULD DO THE RIGHT THING!
THANK YOU!
YOU'RE WELCOME!

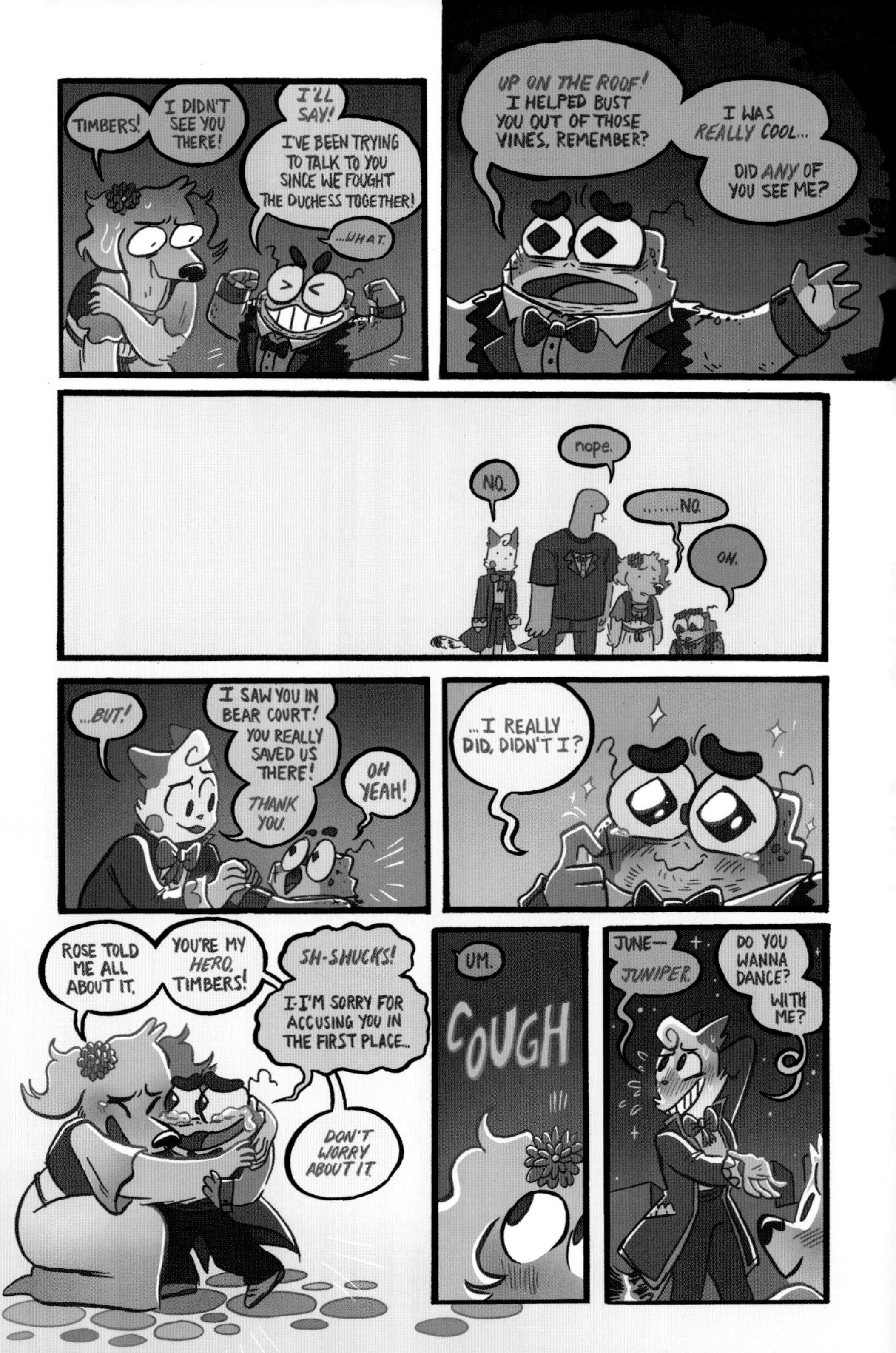
TIMBERS!
I DIDN'T SEE YOU THERE!
I'LL SAY!
I'VE BEEN TRYING TO TALK TO YOU SINCE WE FOUGHT THE DUCHESS TOGETHER!
...WHAT.
UP ON THE ROOF! I HELPED BUST YOU OUT OF THOSE VINES, REMEMBER?
I WAS REALLY COOL...
DID ANY OF YOU SEE ME?
NO.
nope.
.......NO.
OH.
...BUT!
I SAW YOU IN BEAR COURT! YOU REALLY SAVED US THERE!
THANK YOU.
OH YEAH!
...I REALLY DID, DIDN'T I?
ROSE TOLD ME ALL ABOUT IT.
YOU'RE MY HERO, TIMBERS!
SH-SHUCKS!
I-I'M SORRY FOR ACCUSING YOU IN THE FIRST PLACE...
DON'T WORRY ABOUT IT.
UM.
COUGH
JUNE—
JUNIPER.
DO YOU WANNA DANCE?
WITH ME?

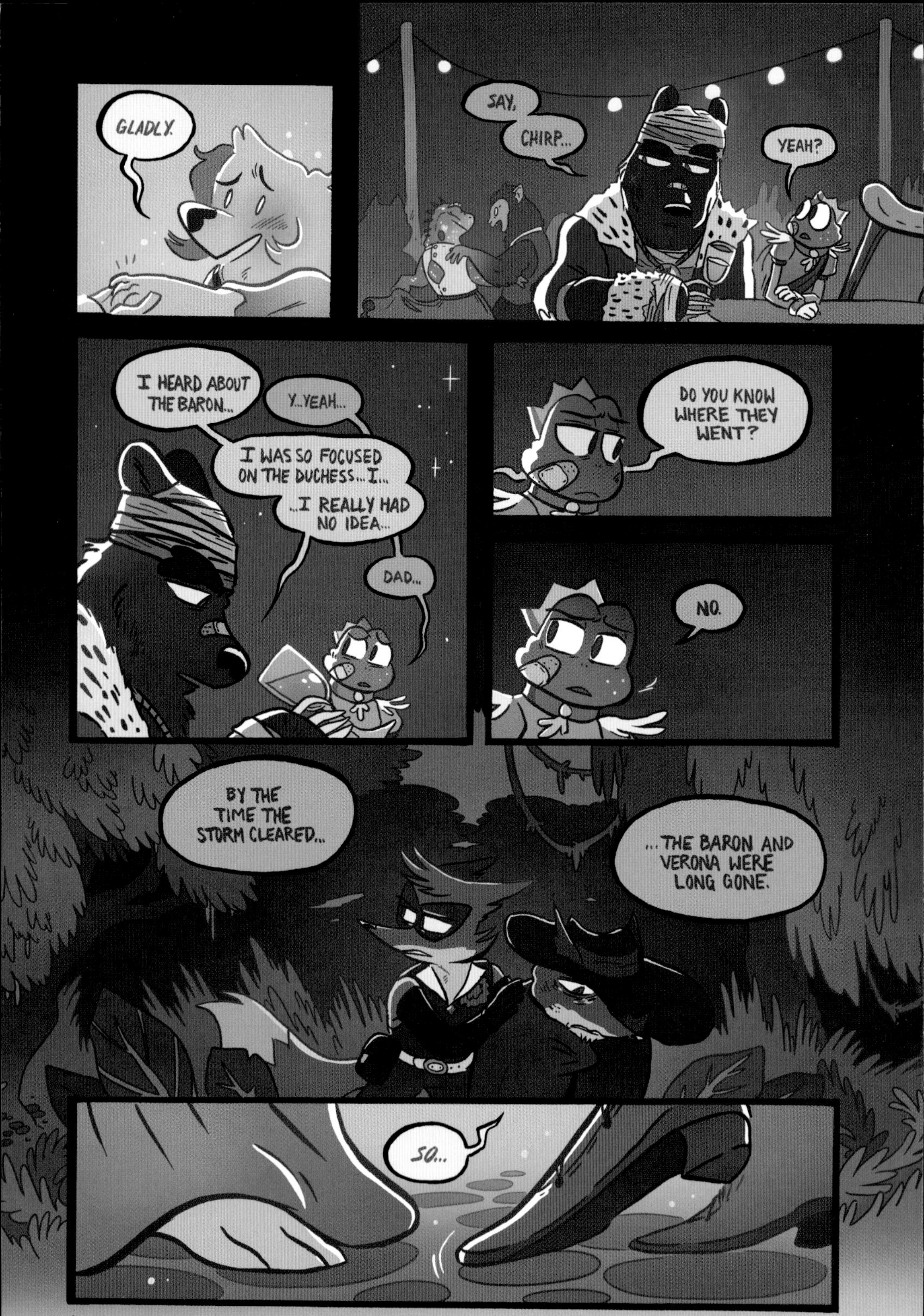
GLADLY.
SAY,
CHIRP...
YEAH?
I HEARD ABOUT THE BARON...
Y...YEAH...
I WAS SO FOCUSED ON THE DUCHESS... I...
...I REALLY HAD NO IDEA...
DAD...
DO YOU KNOW WHERE THEY WENT?
NO.
BY THE TIME THE STORM CLEARED...
...THE BARON AND VERONA WERE LONG GONE.
SO...

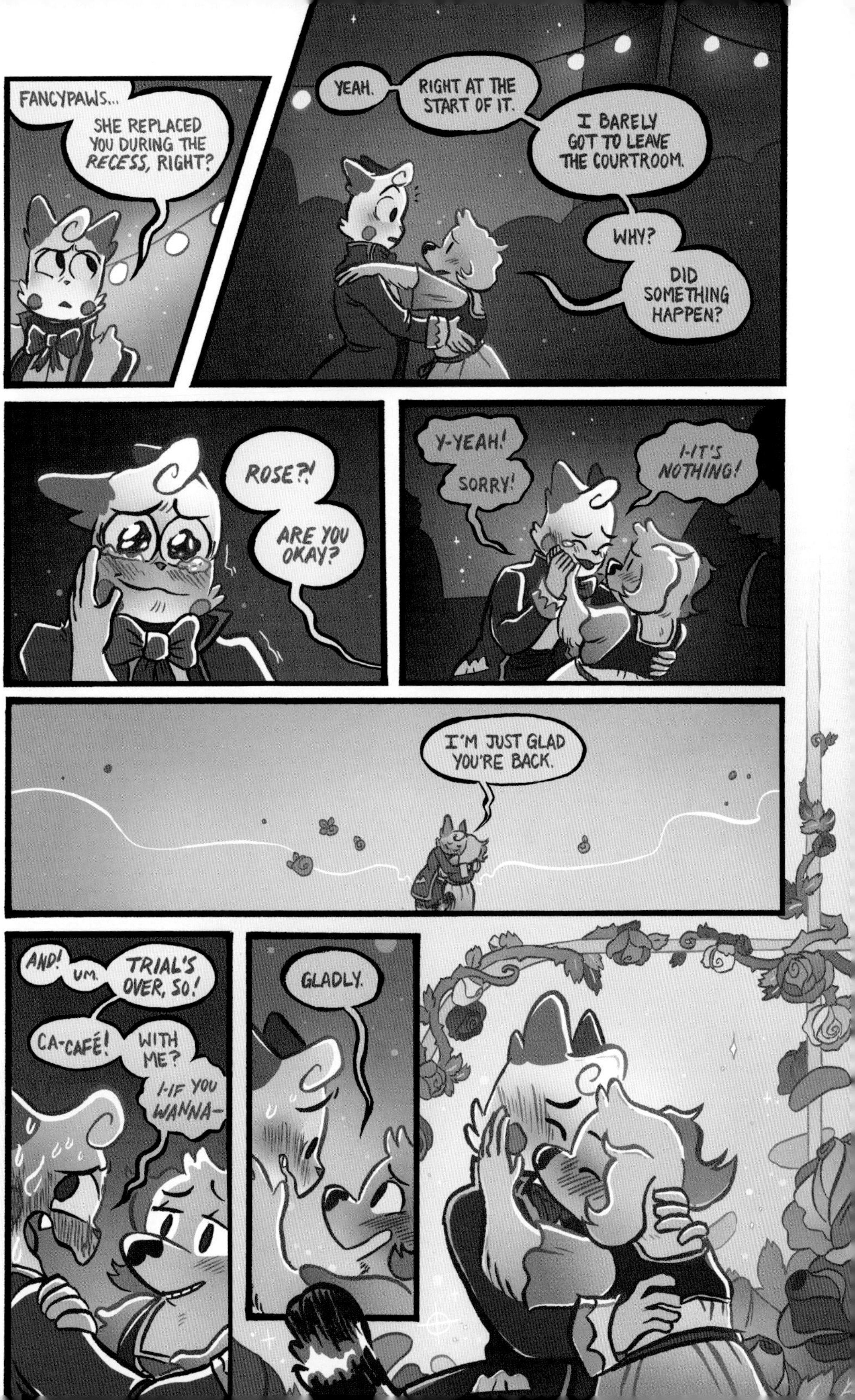
FANCYPAWS...
SHE REPLACED YOU DURING THE RECESS, RIGHT?
YEAH.
RIGHT AT THE START OF IT.
I BARELY GOT TO LEAVE THE COURTROOM.
WHY?
DID SOMETHING HAPPEN?
ROSE?!
ARE YOU OKAY?
Y-YEAH!
SORRY!
I-IT'S NOTHING!
I'M JUST GLAD YOU'RE BACK.
AND!
UM.
TRIAL'S OVER, SO!
CA-CAFÉ!
WITH ME?
I-IF YOU WANNA-
GLADLY.

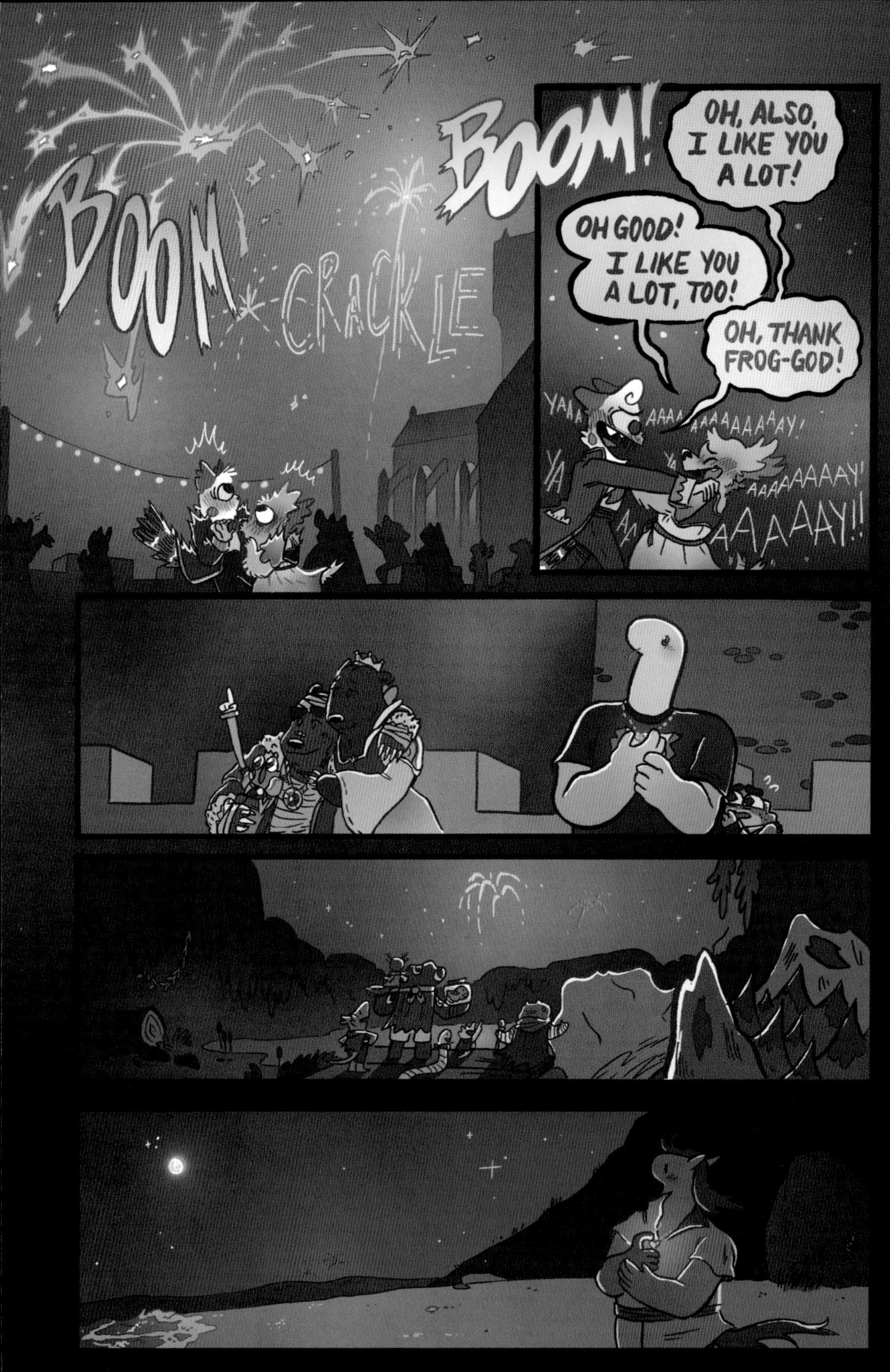
BOOM
CRACKLE
BOOM!
OH, ALSO, I LIKE YOU A LOT!
OH GOOD! I LIKE YOU A LOT, TOO!
OH, THANK FROG-GOD!
YAAAAAAAAAAAAAAY!
YAAAAAAAAY!
YAAAAAAAAAAY!!

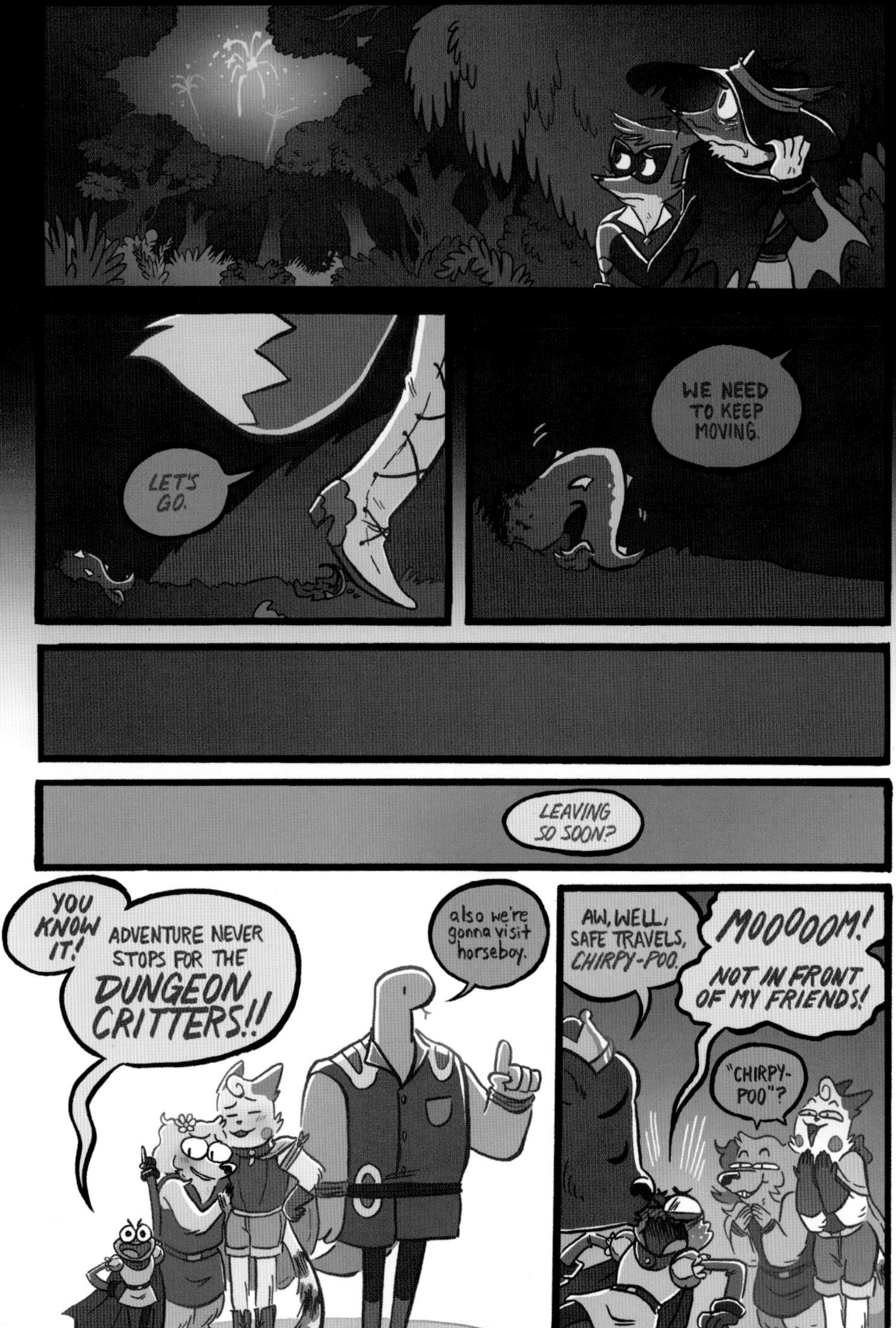
LET'S GO.
WE NEED TO KEEP MOVING.
LEAVING SO SOON?
YOU KNOW IT!
ADVENTURE NEVER STOPS FOR THE DUNGEON CRITTERS!!
also we're gonna visit horseboy.
AW, WELL, SAFE TRAVELS, CHIRPY-POO.
MOOOOOM! NOT IN FRONT OF MY FRIENDS!
"CHIRPY-POO"?

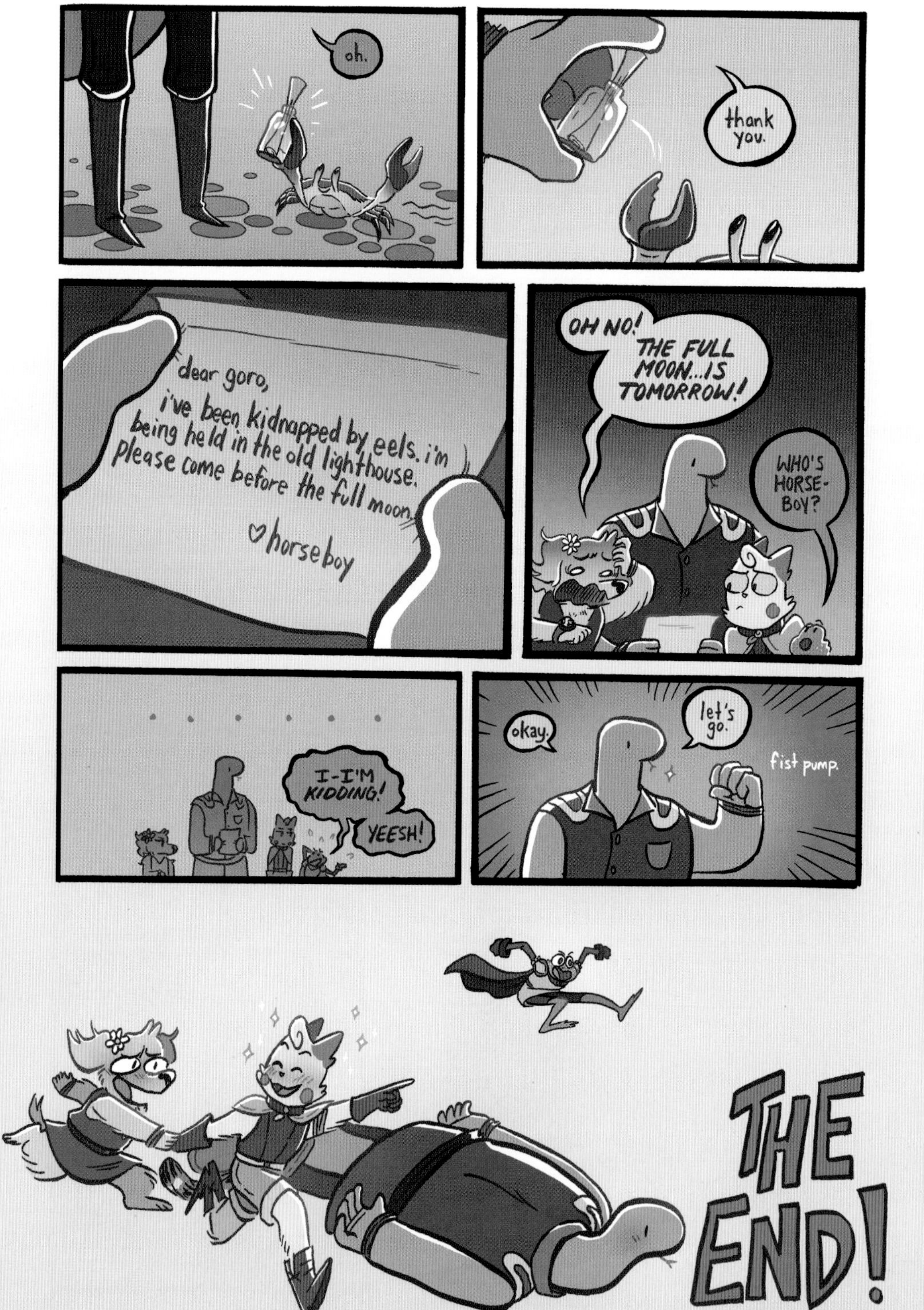
oh.
thank you.
dear goro,
i've been kidnapped by eels. i'm being held in the old lighthouse. please come before the full moon.
♡ horseboy
OH NO! THE FULL MOON...IS TOMORROW!
WHO'S HORSE-BOY?
I-I'M KIDDING!
YEESH!
okay.
let's go.
fist pump.
THE END!

Acknowledgments

A lot of people helped get this book made! Thank you to:

Everyone at First Second, but especially our editors Calista and Mariah,
Kirk, for the cover design, and Kiara and Gina
for answering our emails.

Our agent, Steven, and everyone at Curtis Brown for their expertise.

Our cartoonist peers for their constant support, community, friendship,
and advice, because we barely know what we're doing.

Elli, Sin, and Nate for teaching us how to play tabletop games
and sparking this adventure.

Tilly, my cat, who is so beautiful and also small and loves
to scream, for always being there for inspiration.

Last but not at all least, our families, without whom
none of this would be possible.

Thank you for reading our book!

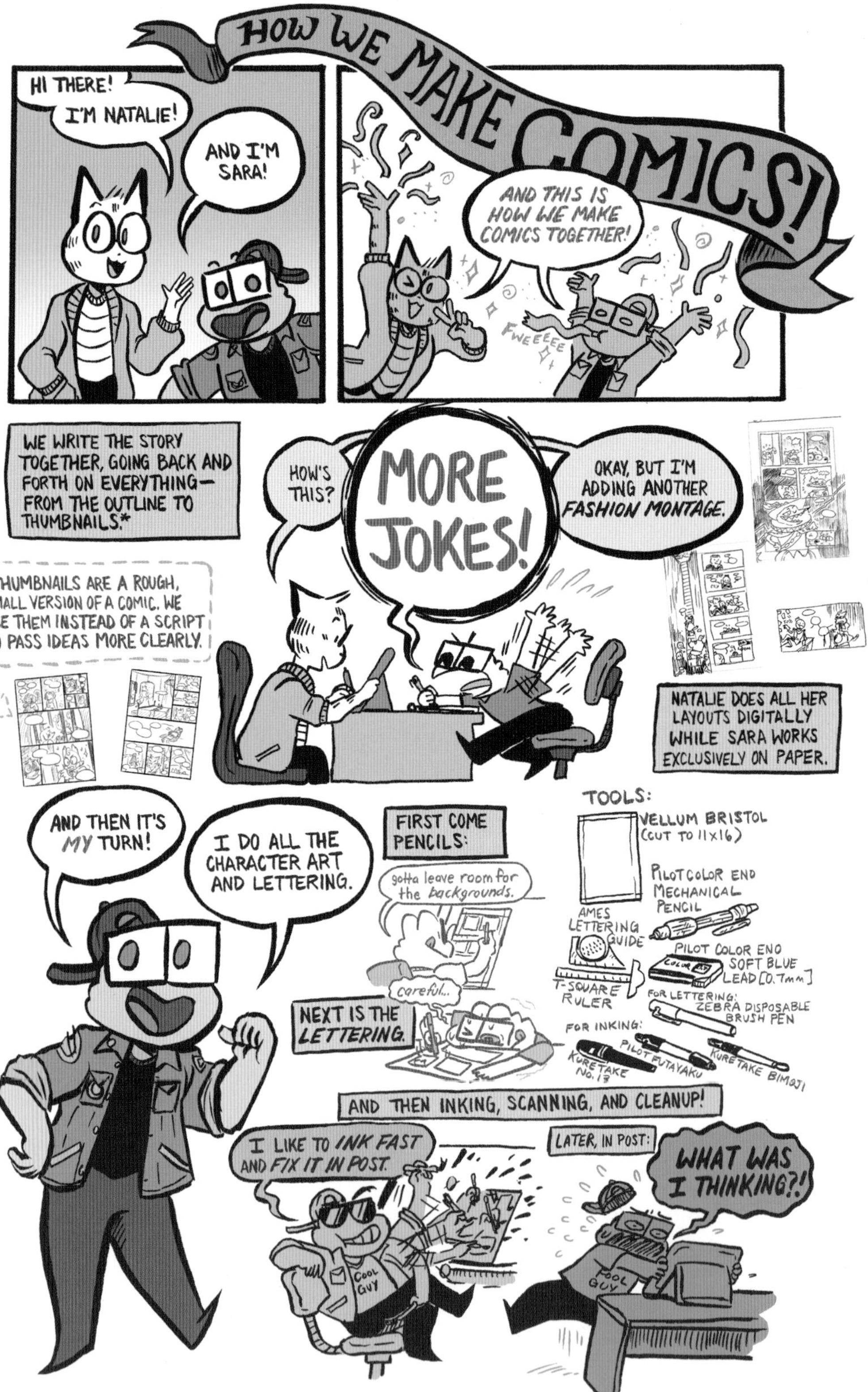
HOW WE MAKE COMICS!
HI THERE!
I'M NATALIE!
AND I'M SARA!
AND THIS IS HOW WE MAKE COMICS TOGETHER!
FWEEEEEE
WE WRITE THE STORY TOGETHER, GOING BACK AND FORTH ON EVERYTHING—FROM THE OUTLINE TO THUMBNAILS.*
HOW'S THIS?
MORE JOKES!
OKAY, BUT I'M ADDING ANOTHER FASHION MONTAGE.
*THUMBNAILS ARE A ROUGH, SMALL VERSION OF A COMIC. WE USE THEM INSTEAD OF A SCRIPT TO PASS IDEAS MORE CLEARLY.
NATALIE DOES ALL HER LAYOUTS DIGITALLY WHILE SARA WORKS EXCLUSIVELY ON PAPER.
AND THEN IT'S MY TURN!
I DO ALL THE CHARACTER ART AND LETTERING.
FIRST COME PENCILS:
gotta leave room for the backgrounds.
NEXT IS THE LETTERING.
careful...
TOOLS:
VELLUM BRISTOL (CUT TO 11x16)
PILOT COLOR ENO MECHANICAL PENCIL
AMES LETTERING GUIDE
PILOT COLOR ENO SOFT BLUE LEAD [0.7mm]
T-SQUARE RULER
FOR LETTERING: ZEBRA DISPOSABLE BRUSH PEN
FOR INKING:
KURETAKE NO. 13
PILOT FUTAYAKU
KURETAKE BIMOJI
AND THEN INKING, SCANNING, AND CLEANUP!
I LIKE TO INK FAST AND FIX IT IN POST.
COOL GUY
LATER, IN POST:
WHAT WAS I THINKING?!
FOOL GUY

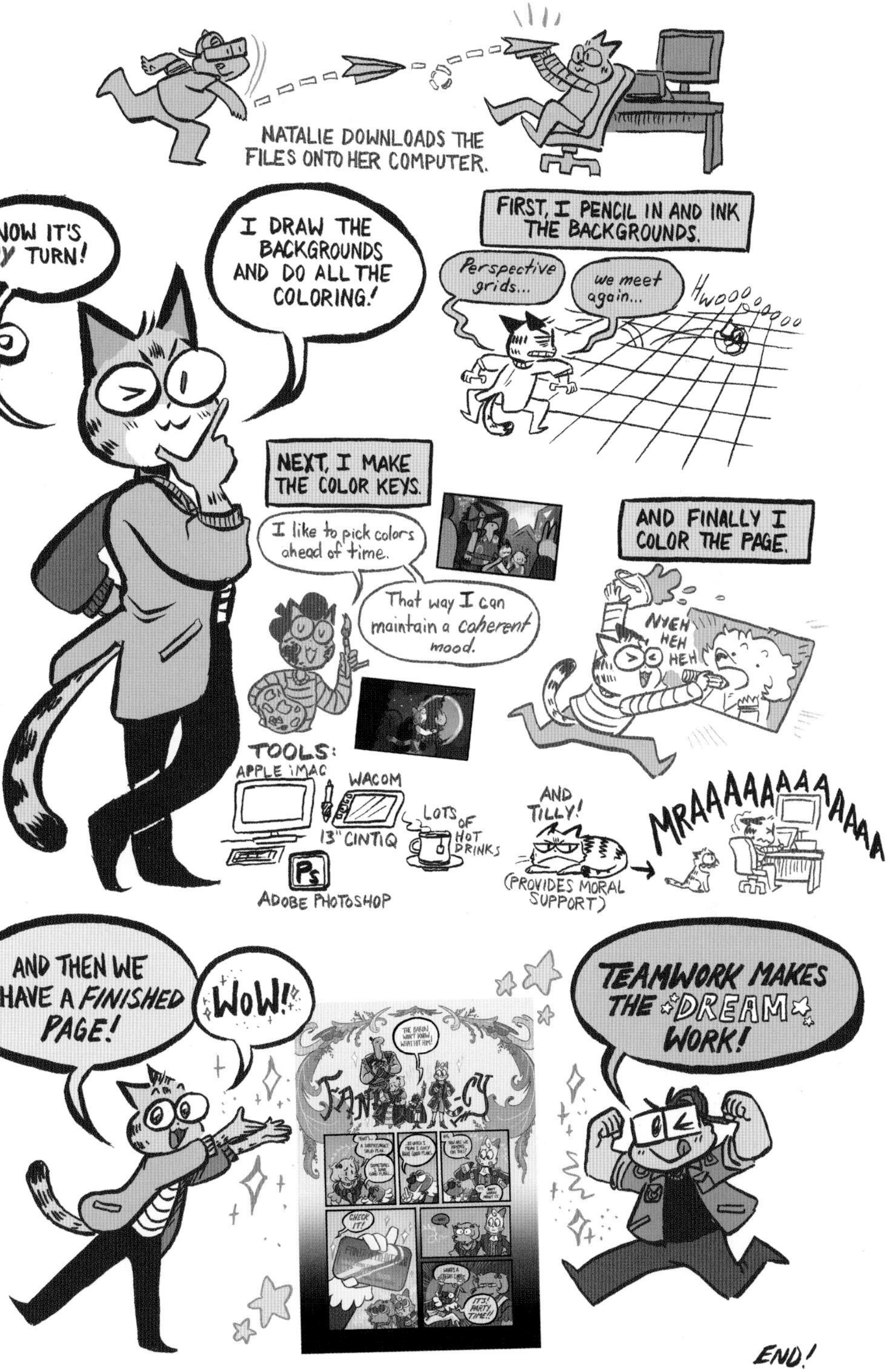

NATALIE DOWNLOADS THE FILES ONTO HER COMPUTER.
NOW IT'S MY TURN!
I DRAW THE BACKGROUNDS AND DO ALL THE COLORING!
FIRST, I PENCIL IN AND INK THE BACKGROUNDS.
Perspective grids...
we meet again...
HWOOOOOOOO
NEXT, I MAKE THE COLOR KEYS.
I like to pick colors ahead of time.
That way I can maintain a coherent mood.
AND FINALLY I COLOR THE PAGE.
NYEH HEH HEH
TOOLS:
APPLE iMAC
WACOM
13" CINTIQ
LOTS OF HOT DRINKS
ADOBE PHOTOSHOP
AND TILLY!
(PROVIDES MORAL SUPPORT)
MRAAAAAAAAAAAA
AND THEN WE HAVE A FINISHED PAGE!
WoW!
TEAMWORK MAKES THE DREAM WORK!
END!

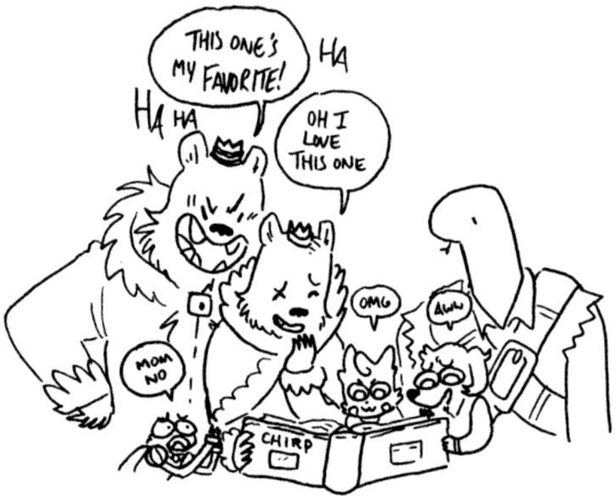
THIS ONE'S MY FAVORITE!
HA
HA HA
OH I LOVE THIS ONE
MOM NO
OMG
AWW
CHIRP

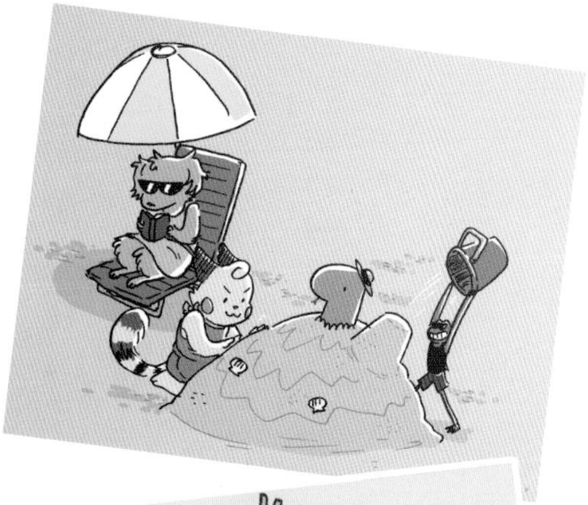

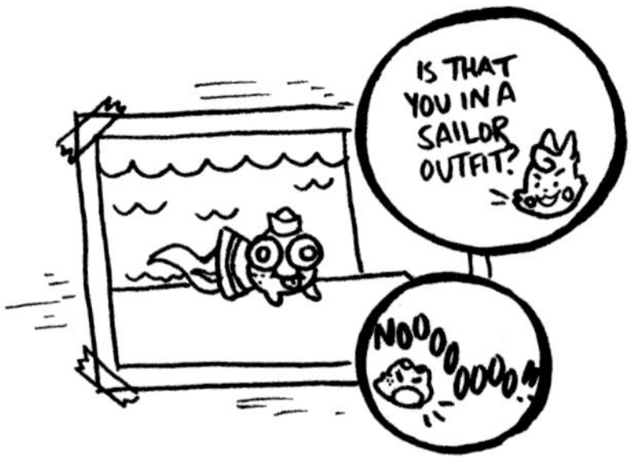
IS THAT YOU IN A SAILOR OUTFIT?
NOOOOOOOOO!!

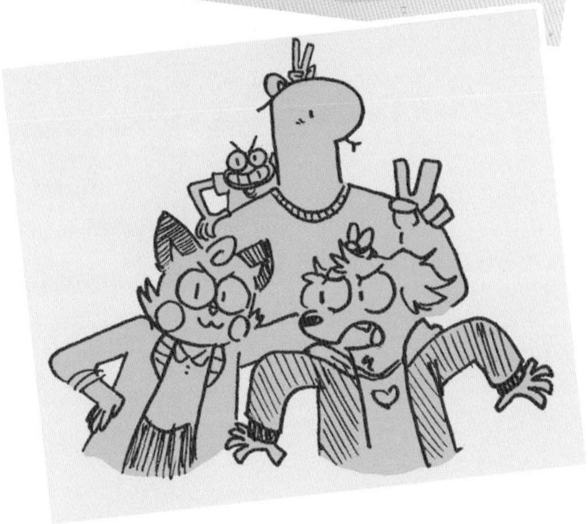

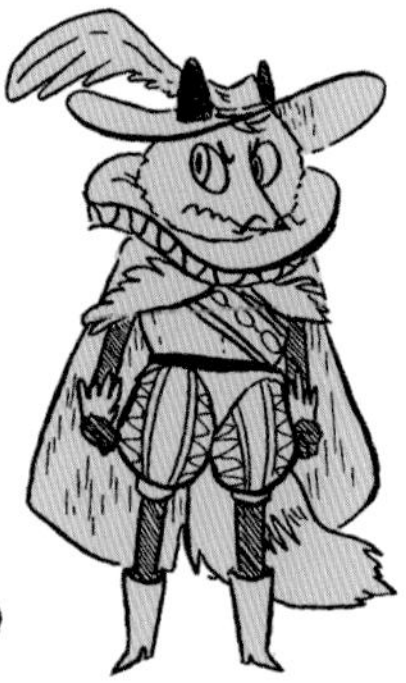

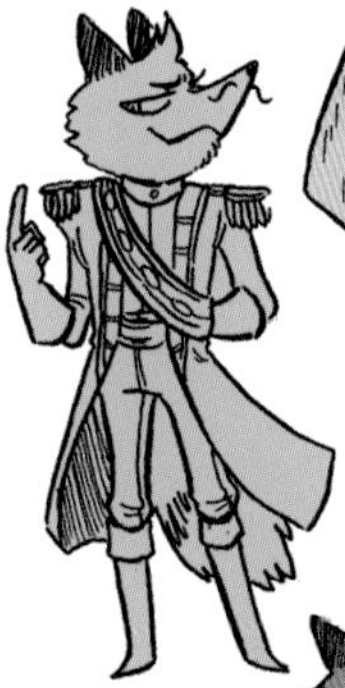

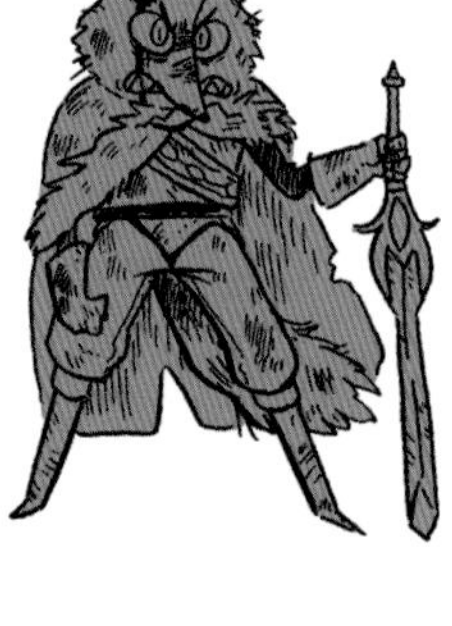

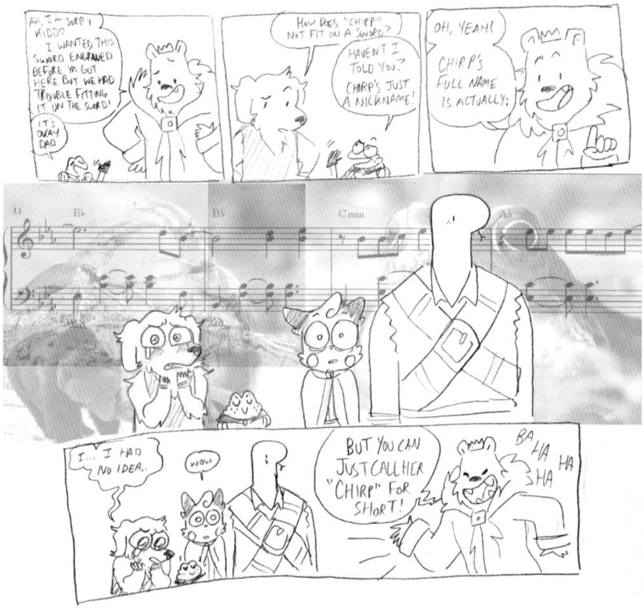
AH, I'M SORRY KIDDO. I WANTED THIS SWORD ENGRAVED BEFORE YA GOT HERE BUT WE HAD TROUBLE FITTING IT ON THE SWORD!
IT'S OKAY DAD
HOW DOES "CHIRP" NOT FIT ON A SWORD?
HAVEN'T I TOLD YOU? CHIRP'S JUST A NICKNAME!
OH, YEAH!
CHIRP'S FULL NAME IS ACTUALLY:
11
Eb
Bb
Cmin
Ab
I... I HAD NO IDEA..
WOW
BUT YOU CAN JUST CALL HER "CHIRP" FOR SHORT!
BA HA HA HA

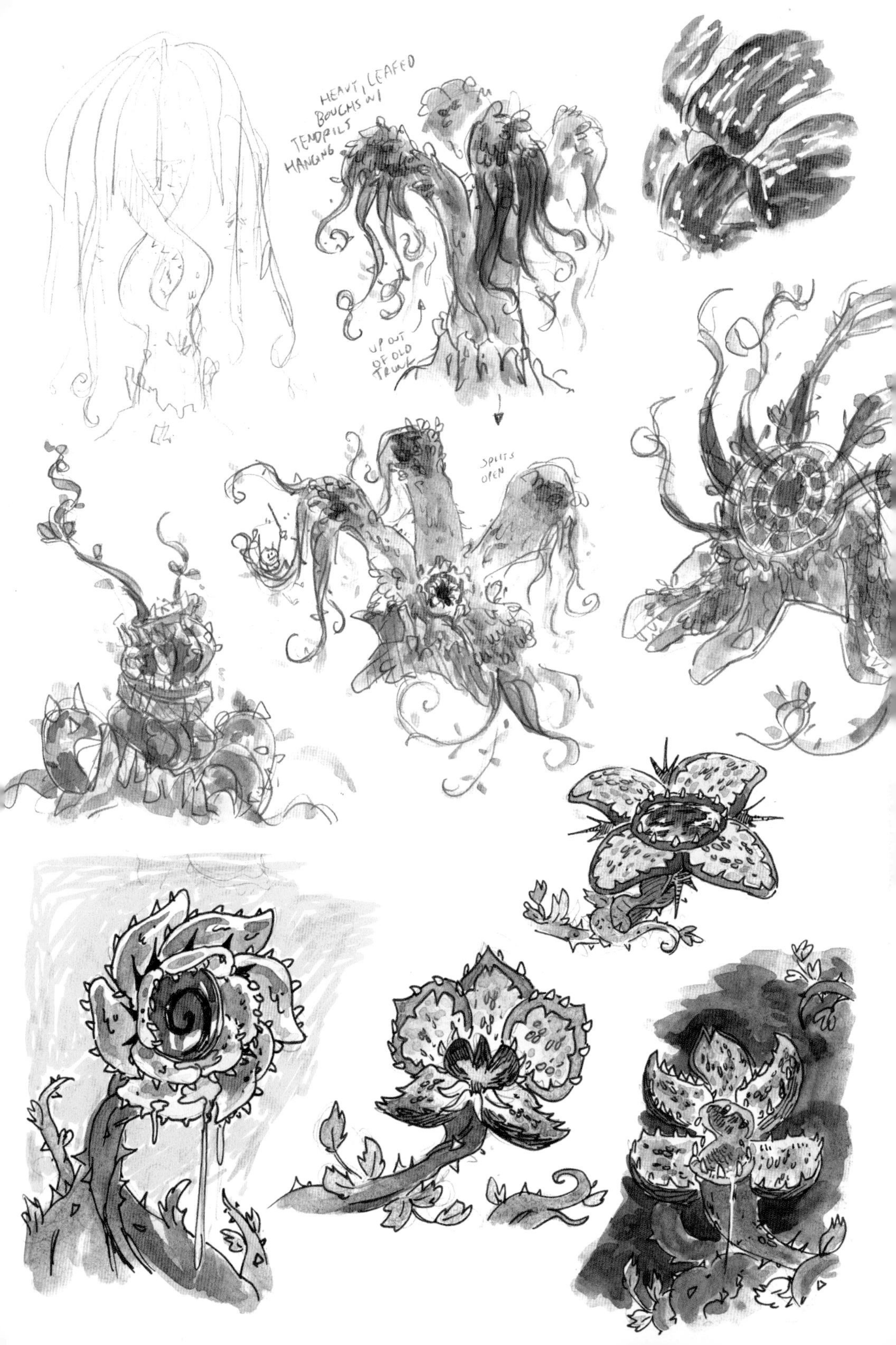
HEAVY, LEAFED BOUGHS W/ TENDRILS HANGING
UP OUT OF OLD TRUNK
SPLITS OPEN

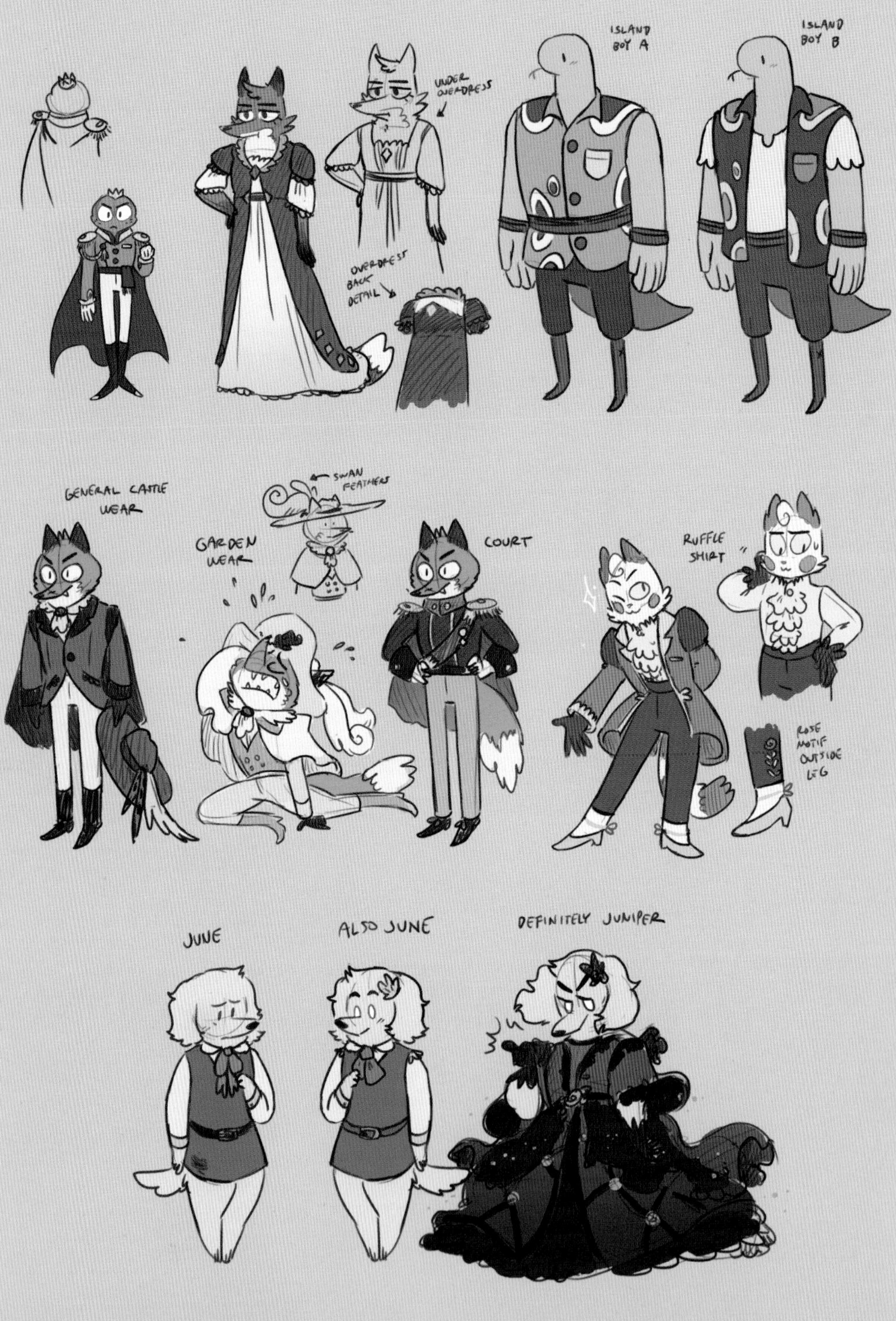

UNDER OVERDRESS
OVERDRESS BACK DETAIL
ISLAND BOY A
ISLAND BOY B
GENERAL CASTLE WEAR
SWAN FEATHERS
GARDEN WEAR
COURT
RUFFLE SHIRT
ROSE MOTIF OUTSIDE LEG
JUNE
ALSO JUNE
DEFINITELY JUNIPER

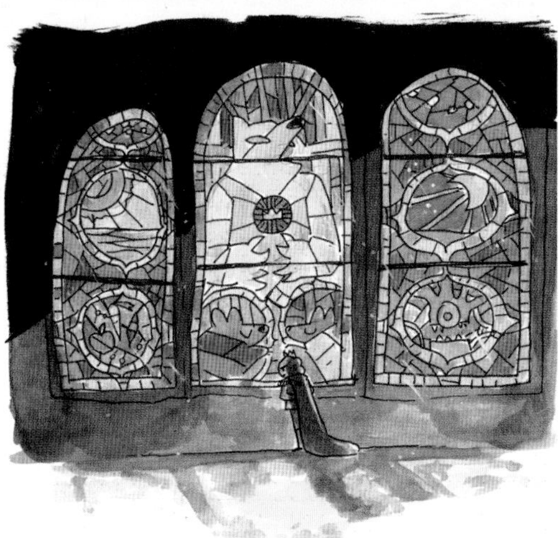

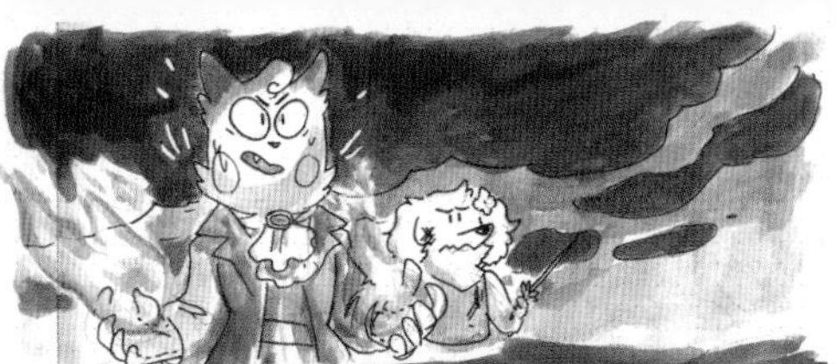

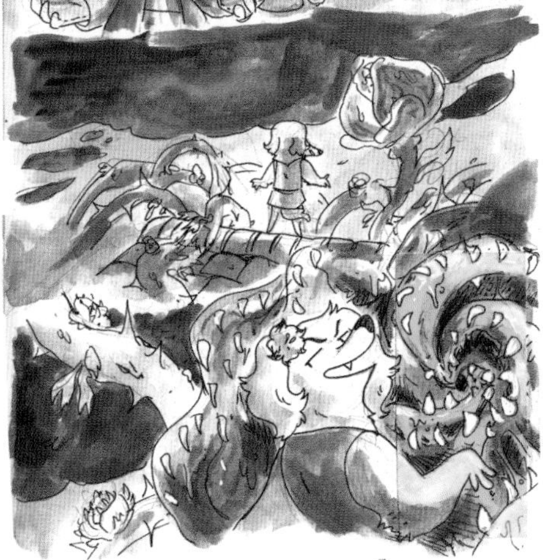

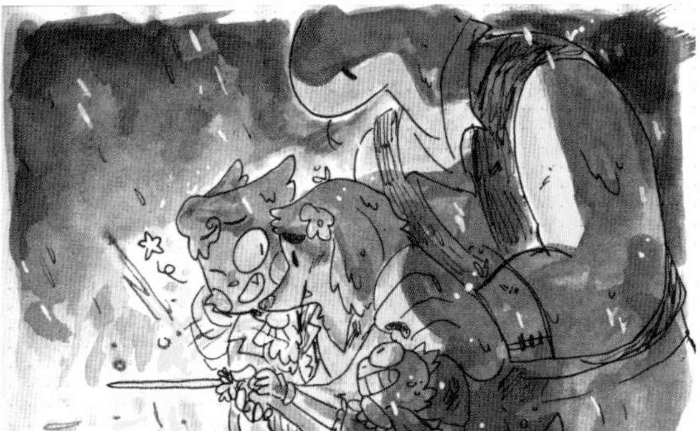

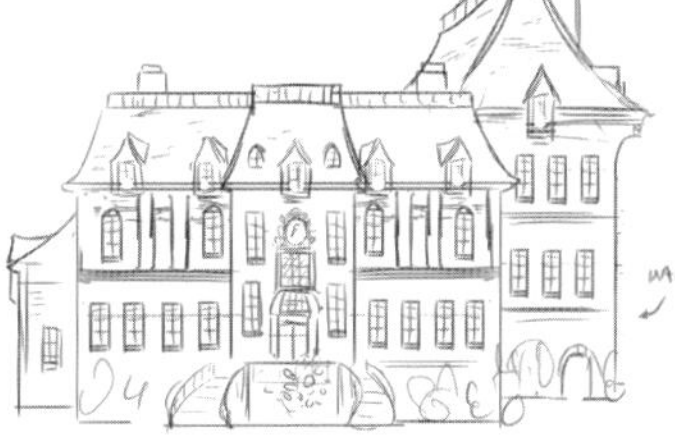
MANOR

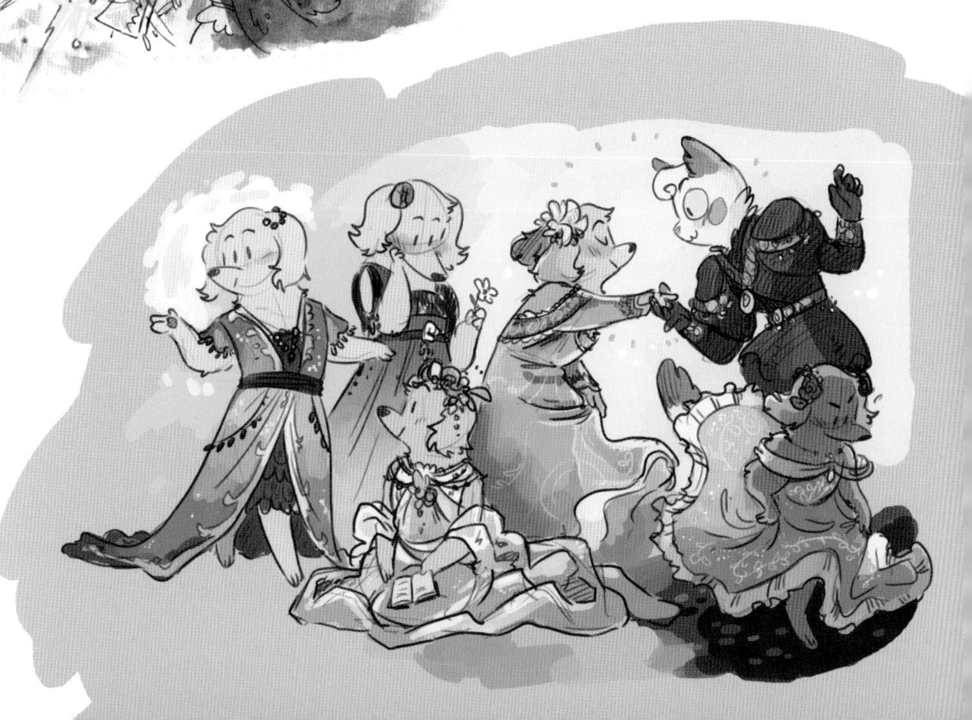

:01
First Second

Copyright © 2020 Natalie Riess and Sara Goetter

Published by First Second
First Second is an imprint of Roaring Brook Press,
a division of Holtzbrinck Publishing Holdings Limited Partnership
120 Broadway, New York, NY 10271

Don't miss your next favorite book from First Second!
For the latest updates go to firstsecondnewsletter.com and
sign up for our enewsletter.

Library of Congress Control Number: 2109947771

Paperback ISBN: 978-1-250-19547-0
Hardback ISBN: 978-1-250-19546-3

Our books may be purchased in bulk for promotional, educational, or business use.
Please contact your local bookseller or the Macmillan Corporate and Premium Sales Department at
(800) 221-7945 ext. 5442 or by email at MacmillanSpecialMarkets@macmillan.com.

First edition, 2020

Edited by Calista Brill and Mariah Huehner
Cover design by Kirk Benshoff
Interior design by Rob Steen and Molly Johanson
Printed in China by 1010 Printing International Limited,
North Point, Hong Kong

Character art was penciled with Pilot Eno light blue lead and inked with a combination of a
Kuretake Brush Pen, Pentel Futayaku Double-Sided Brush Pen, and Kuretake Bimoji Brush Pen.
Lettering was done with a Zebra Disposable Brush Pen. Corrections were done in Photoshop.

Paperback: 10 9 8 7 6 5 4 3 2 1
Hardcover: 10 9 8 7 6 5 4 3 2

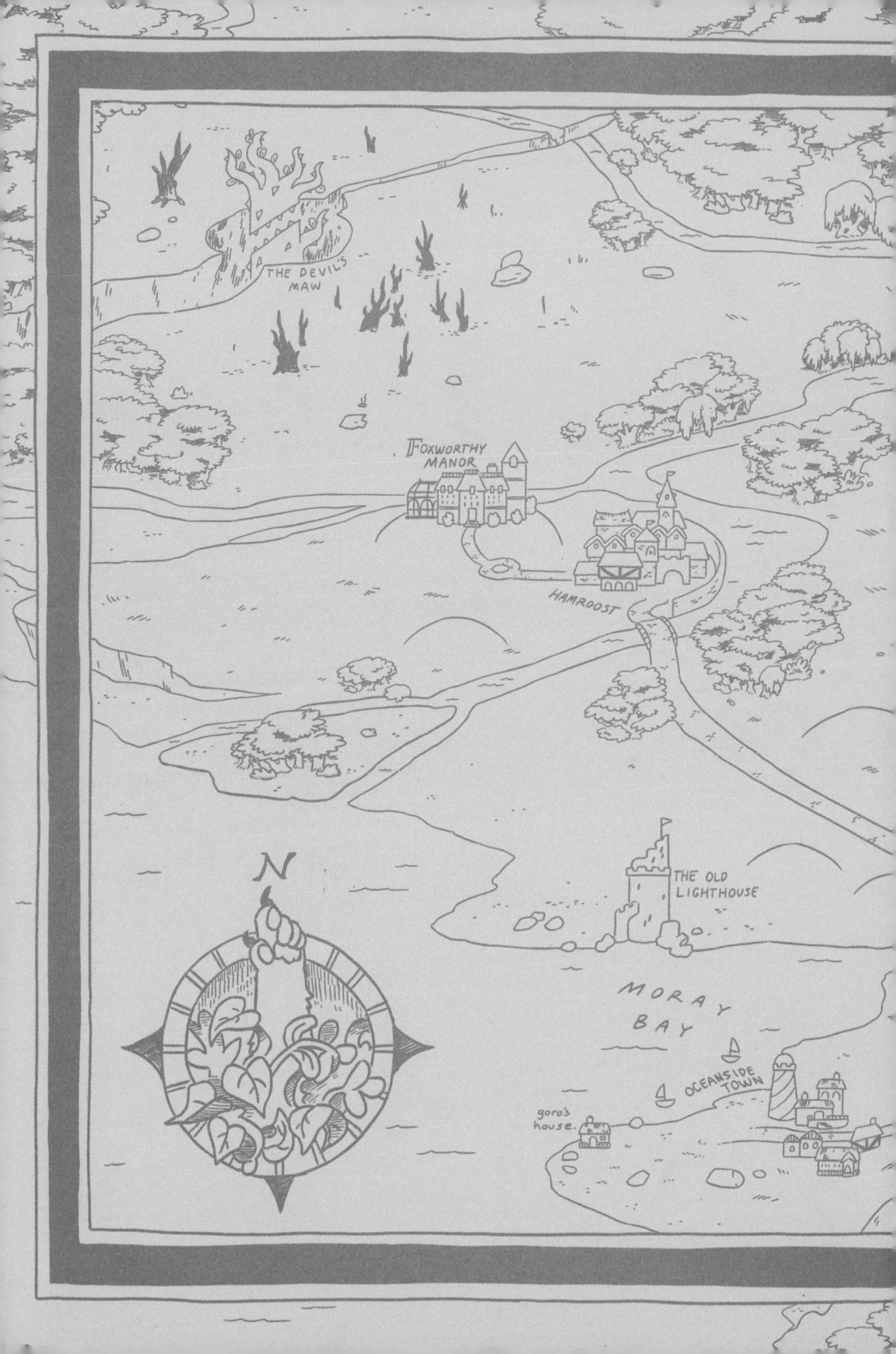

THE DEVIL'S MAW
FOXWORTHY MANOR
HAMROOST
N
THE OLD LIGHTHOUSE
MORAY BAY
OCEANSIDE TOWN
goro's house.